THE UNRAVELED TRILOGY

THE UNRAVELING OF *Raven*

Darkness INTO *Dawn*

Shattered Lies

THERESA SEDERHOLT

Other Books by Theresa Sederholt

The Unraveled Trilogy
The Unraveling of Raven
Darkness Into Dawn
Shattered Lies

Uniquely Mine

The Letter: Dear Michael

The Bench

THE UNRAVELING OF
Raven
THERESA SEDERHOLT

Chapter One

Raven

"RAVEN?" *KNOCK, KNOCK, KNOCK.* "Raven?" *Knock, knock, knock.* "Wake up, Raven! You've overslept for the second time this week!"

This can't be happening. "What the hell, Marco! How could that be?" *He can't be right.*

"Your alarm has been going off for the past forty minutes; it's now 6:30 a.m.."

Oh crap! School starts at 7:30 a.m.. "Why the hell didn't you wake me up sooner?" Why didn't I hear the alarm? Damn it all to hell! I jump out of bed, grab a quick shower, do a fast make-up job, and run out the door—smack into Manhattan rush hour traffic.

I'm trying to make some sort of normal look with my long, wavy black hair as I race to catch the train. Thank God I only have three stops to go! I make it to my usual Starbucks with little time to spare. I must look deranged. I'm bouncing from one foot to the other while the girl in the front of the line starts asking about calories in the muffins! *Really, lady?* If it looks or tastes good, spit it out, damn it! Finally my turn and the Barista already knows my order: large redeye with two pumps of sugar-free hazelnut, no cream, and a bottle of water. I don't need anyone's drama today. It's a big day for my second graders and I need to be there now.

I run out of the door, and crash into someone with a chest like a brick wall. My coffee lid pops off and douses both of us. I can feel the weight of his stare as I try to wipe the coffee off of his chest, and I feel like I'm being zapped with a stun gun.

"Oh my God, I'm so sorry."

He growls, "Lady, please, just stop. You're not helping matters any."

As I look up to protest, I'm hit with the deepest blue eyes I have ever seen.

At this point, I'm a flustered mess and all I can do is run away, leaving him with half the damage from the rough start of my morning. *What the hell was that anyway?* I have no time to dwell on it as class starts in five minutes. As I run to class, I toss Mick his bottle of water. "Nice catch, Mick."

I teach second grade at Weinstein Academy, a private school in midtown

Manhattan. It just so happens that today is "Bring a Parent To School Day." And not only did I oversleep, douse the most beautiful man and myself with coffee, I now get to meet said parents with a wet shirt. Luckily, Jackie, my best friend and co-worker, has a spare shirt I can borrow. However, with her being smaller on top than me, I now look like a hooch woman!

Jaxson

WHAT THE FUCK WAS that? Or, more to the point, *who the fuck was that?* I'm left standing outside Starbucks with a wet shirt, courtesy of a beautiful woman, and I didn't even get her name! Her delicate fingers, trying to wipe off the coffee, didn't help. I was instantly hard and all I could do was stare at her in disbelief. She had the most beautiful violet eyes. Eyes that felt as though they could look into my soul. Then she ran away! I head inside and ask the Barista if he knows her name. He says he only knows her drink. He then informs me that she comes in every morning for her usual large coffee and a bottle of water for the homeless guy, Mick, across the street.

"She buys him water every morning?"

"Yeah, and when she's not running late, she buys him breakfast."

I order a breakfast sandwich, instead of my usual, and head out across the street. I walk up to the man and hand him the sandwich, "I figured you might be hungry since the girl that usually buys you breakfast was running late."

He looks at me apprehensively. "Thanks, she's a sweetheart."

I need to know more than that. "What do you know about her?"

He gets really quiet, but I wait. "What's it to you?"

I can tell I'm not going to get much past him. "Well, I could stand here and feed you a line of bullshit."

"Yeah, you could, but that doesn't mean I would tell you anything about her."

Well, at least he's honest. "Look, mate, she ran into me this morning, as you can tell by my shirt. I just want to know who she is."

Great, now he's looking me up and down. "By the looks of you, you can afford to buy another shirt so, again, what's it to you, who she is?"

I offer him my hand. "My name is Jax. She is beautiful and I want to know more."

He just looks at me. "Well, Jax, my name is Mick, and yeah, she is beautiful, but more so on the inside. Not very many people will even give me the time of day, let alone buy me breakfast. I'm back from the war and things just aren't right sometimes; she just gets it. She doesn't judge me. What she gives me is more valuable than money—her time. She just gets it. If you want to know more about her, come back tomorrow, she's here every day. That's all you'll get from me, Jax."

He's done talking and I know when not to push my luck. "Okay, Mick. Thanks."

As I head up to my office, I'm even more intrigued. I change my shirt into one of the spares I keep here. Sitting at my desk, overlooking the city, I'm aware that I have all the money I will ever need and yet I'm bored. I own *Raiders Inc.*, a multibillion-dollar company. I raid companies that are in trouble, either because the owners are stupid or greedy. There are only so many companies you can raid before it just gets old. Nothing holds my interest anymore—not work or parties—nothing. At least, not until this morning. I have to find that girl. Her eyes were a beautiful violet color, eyes that looked right into my soul, and her hair was as dark as a raven.

Maybe I should have Max help me find her. Max is my best friend and the head of my security. I hired him away from the Queen, one drunken night, in a seedy, London pub. After the mess with Erica, I usually have Max run a check on anyone I go out with. I don't bring any women out in public, if I can avoid it. The paparazzi are ruthless whenever I step out with anyone. I will have to stalk that Starbucks until I find her.

I'm lost in my thoughts when my new assistant, Duke Jensen, rings to inform me that my sister, Isabella, has arrived. Great, just what I need, more family, reminding me that I'm thirty-three years old and not married. I don't see what the big deal is; I'm happy with my life. Yes, I'm bored, but putting myself out there again just isn't an option that I want to explore.

Bella comes storming into my office, "Jax, Michael got stuck at the airport in Atlanta and can't make it back in time, so you have to cover for him."

I throw my hands up, "Cover for him, Bella. Do you think I don't work for a living?" She has the nerve to think I do nothing!

"Come on, Jax, this is for your nephew. They're having a 'bring your parent to school' day, and Michael is stuck in Atlanta."

I'm not his parent. *What the hell would I do at his school?* "Well, last time I looked, Bella, you're his parent too." Oh boy, she's giving me the evil eye. This is not good—she's almost as bad as Mum.

"Don't be an arse, Jax, no young boy wants to bring his mum to school. Just go to the school and talk a little bit about whatever it is you do all day long. Tell them all the places you go and about all your toys; boys love that shit."

Hmm, let's just see what I can get out of her. "What do I get if I do this for you?" She'll guilt me, I know it.

"Jax, besides the fact that you're doing it for *your* nephew, I will run interference for you next time Mum wants to match you up with one of her friend's daughters."

Well it doesn't take me long to agree to that one, anything to get my mum off my back. "Okay, where and when? But don't forget—you owe me."

I HEAD OVER TO the school and sign in before they escort me to my nephew's classroom. I open the door, walk in, and am hit, square in the face, with those violet eyes. My nephew's teacher is the same beautiful girl that doused me with coffee this morning. I never had a teacher like her. I would have made sure to be held back, if I did. She keeps her eyes fixed on me as she walks towards me.

"Can I help you?" She extends her hand and, upon grasping it, I feel a jolt of electricity from her touch.

"I'm here for the 'Bring a Parent To School Day'. I'm Michael Vizzano's uncle, Jaxson Phillips. His dad is stuck in Atlanta."

She introduces herself as *Miss Raven Anderson*, and directs me to a table, in the back, with other parents. I apparently have to wait until its Michael's turn to introduce me. I don't do *waiting* very well. *Who am I kidding? I never wait for anyone or anything.*

I can't stop staring at her. I can see that's she's changed her shirt. She must have borrowed it because it's much smaller, accentuating her ample chest. Her skin is olive, but her eyes are the deepest violet I have ever seen, they are mesmerizing. Her hair looks *so* silky. How the fuck does my nephew get any work done? She keeps tugging on her ear, and I've no idea why, but it's making me crazy.

As I'm sitting here, thinking of all the ways I can shag her, my cock instantly hardens. Oh no, it's my turn—*fuck!* Michael goes to the front of the room and announces to the class that his Uncle Jax is here with him today. I go up front, doing my best to hide my raging hard-on, and begin to talk a little about the life of a corporate raider in a way, I think, they can best understand. When it's time for questions, of course the first one is, *do you have your own plane?* I don't understand what the big deal is, but when I tell them I do, they get excited. Michael stands up and announces, "My uncle has lots of toys because my mom said he raids companies."

Great! Now the other parents are looking at me like I'm a dick or an evil monster, putting people out of work and taking all their money. I look at the kids and tell them I'm not like that; I help companies that are in trouble. I don't think the parents are buying it. I glance over in Raven's direction. *Oh no, big trouble!* She's tugging on her ear, causing me to lose my train of thought. I need to focus on the kids and their questions instead of my wicked thoughts of what I could be doing . . . with her.

Class is finally over and I hang back to wait for Michael while Raven and I keep staring at each other. Between the constant tugging on her earlobe and the way she has those violets locked onto me, I swear the hair on the back of my neck is standing at attention. I can't take this anymore; it's not like me to be so nervous. I'm just going to lay the "Jax charm" on her. "Raven? Would you like to get a cup of coffee that we can drink rather than wear?"

She's looking at me like a deer in the headlights. "I'm sorry, but I have a couple of hours of work ahead of me, maybe another time, sir."

Sir? How fucking old does she think I am? Before I can say anything, she picks up her stuff and runs out the door. Why the fuck does this girl keep running away from me? Just like that—she's gone and I'm left with a raging hard-on, wondering what the fuck that was all about.

AS JUNIOR AND I head back to my office, I decide to pump him for information. Okay, I know I shouldn't, but I have to find out what he knows. "So, Junior, do you like your teacher?" That's a stupid question, even to my ears; what's not to like?

"She's pretty cool, and funny too." I can't ask him if she has a boyfriend. Okay, maybe there is a way I can. "Does she ever talk about her family?"

He shrugs his shoulders, "I don't know, why?"

Oh shit. Okay, what to say here? "I was just wondering, since all of the kids' parents got up to tell what they do and a little about their families, that's all." I don't think he's buying it but then he starts telling me something that his dog, Vito, did. "Junior, that dog only likes you. He's afraid of your grams, but everyone is terrified of her. By the way, if you tell Grams what I just said, you're in trouble."

He laughs at me. "Don't worry, Uncle Jax, your secret is safe with me. Vito knows when Grams is coming; he hides under my bed!"

I knew that dog was smart. "He's very intelligent, that's why your dad got him for you."

We get back to the office to find Bella waiting for us. "Did everything go okay?"

What the fuck did she think I was going to do? "Of course, what did you think . . . I was going to steal all their possessions and run away? Oh, and why the fuck did you tell Junior that I *raid companies?* Do you know what that made me look like?"

"Jax, what do you do for a living?"

I just stare at her. "I would have explained it a little differently for Junior." I have to watch what I say here, Bella and I can read each other like an open book.

"Hey, we never sugar-coat anything in this family so why start now? And why are you so ruffled?"

I growl, "I'm not ruffled for Christ's sake. I just don't want my nephew thinking I'm a prick."

She's glaring at me. "Oh no, Jax, no, don't you dare!"

Fuck it all, I'm so busted. "Dare what, sis?" The evil eye is back!

"You met his teacher, Miss Raven. I can see it all over your face!"

I can't look at her without laughing. "If you must know, I met her for the first time at Starbucks this morning, so technically, I already know her." She shoots me a look like she's going to strangle me.

"This is why you're good at what you do. You could split hairs with a bald man!"

I need to get her out of here before she sees how interested I am in Junior's teacher. "I have work to do. Glad I could help you today, but don't forget your promise to run interference for me with Mum."

Junior looks up from his homework. "Uncle Jax. Why does Mum have to run interference for you with Grams?" I just laugh, now Bella will have to deal with the questions.

"Junior, I'll let your mum explain it to you on the way home." I hug Junior as I push Bella out the door. "Bye, sis."

Chapter Two

Raven

"MARCO, ARE YOU HOME?" It figures, when I need my crazy-ass room-mate the most, he's not around. Why did I say no and run away? *Probably because when he looked at me, I felt it down to my frigging toes—that's why.* I could never get involved with someone like him, he's way too intense. Plus, I would never date one of my student's parents or even his uncle. Besides, love stories are for other people. My life is anything but normal.

I decide to make some tea while I wait for Marco to come home. Finally, he comes through the door, and of course, he is complaining about something. "Marco, can we go out and celebrate the weekend?" He takes one look at me and I can tell he knows something is up.

"Okay, baby girl, what happened? And why are you wearing a shirt that's way too small for your boobs?"

He won't believe this one. "Well, after running late this morning, I was in Starbucks and got my coffee which I ended up not only spilling on myself, but on the most beautiful man I have ever seen. His hair was as dark as coal. It looked so silky and wavy, but his eyes are *so* blue and when our eyes locked, I swear he looked right into my soul."

His eyes light up; Marco loves a juicy story. "Oh, do tell, baby girl."

I curl up on the sofa, "Oh, trust me, Marco, this gets better. Today was 'Bring a Parent To School Day' and one of the kids' fathers couldn't make it, so his uncle came instead. Guess who it was?"

He looks at me with his mouth wide open. "Oh no, Starbucks guy?"

I reach over and lift his chin off the ground. "Yep, Starbucks guy! Apparently, he is some corporate raider, who tried to downplay what he does, so that he didn't seem like a total dick. He asked me to go for coffee that we can 'drink rather than wear.'"

Marco curls up next to me. "That was clever. So what did you do?" I don't know why he's asking when he already knows exactly what I did.

"What do you think I did? I freaked out and told him I have too much work to do; maybe another time." Here it comes; he is going to ride my ass for running.

"You ran again. Why, baby girl? You have to let go of the past and test the waters. You need to trust yourself again."

I shake my head, "Not with this guy, he's too much of everything. He's too intense, too beautiful, and way-the-hell out of my league. Oh, who the fuck am I kidding? I don't even have a league."

He takes my hand. "Raven, you are a beautiful girl with a heart of gold, you just need to open it again. Who is this uncle and what's the name of the company he runs?"

I don't know why he cares what company this guy runs. "The only thing I know, is the company is called *Raiders Inc.*, apparently, he owns it. I've never heard of it, but then again, I was too nervous to even think," I admit. Marco looks lost in his thoughts and then, he suddenly throws his hands in the air and orders me to change into something fun. Just like that, the conversation is done.

He informs me that he was able to get reservations in *Locanda Verde* for the *Trufflepalooza*. It is three different courses, each course uses white truffles as the base. The food is very rich and people wait all year for this event. Robert DeNiro owns the restaurant and it is always booked. But Marco has a friend that works there, so he gets us in.

It's a beautiful, fall evening, so I decide to wear a deep violet, sheath dress that matches my eyes with black high-heeled boots. Let's face it, a girl can never be too tall and these boots make my legs look really good. My hair is behaving tonight, so I leave it loose in waves down my back.

We arrive and are seated at a long table with many other diners around us. The music is soft in the background which means we don't have to shout to be heard. The food is like a dream. Three different chefs are showcasing the white truffle. Each course has a different wine to enhance the flavors of the foods that are presented to us. By the time the coffee comes, I'm stuffed and a little tipsy. Marco has made friends with the other diners around us and he is exchanging numbers with a good-looking man across the table. I wish I could be more like Marco. He is so carefree and open; he has everyone at the table laughing and relaxed. I excuse myself as I head to the ladies room, feeling a little tipsy and a bit shaky on my feet. I start to head back to the table, when I turn the corner and come face to face with those deep blue eyes from this morning. *Oh no!* I don't want to get too close or I know what will happen. He puts his hands on my arms and our eyes lock. My nerve endings are on fire. I feel like I'm being zapped again!

"Well, hello again, Miss Raven. I thought you had hours of work, or were you just trying to avoid me?" His voice is deep and smooth, like the most delicious chocolate in the world. He has a slight British accent that I didn't notice before; I was flustered and unable to even think straight.

"Excuse me, if you must know, I'm here with a friend for the Trufflepalooza." As I look into his eyes, there it is—the look that curls my frigging toes. *What the hell is that?* I feel a jolt right between my legs. I'm fixed on those deep blue eyes, onyx silky hair, and only God knows what's under those clothes!

"Can I buy you a drink, Miss Raven?"

I shake my head, "I'm sorry but, like I said, I'm with someone. Maybe another time." I rush back to Marco who, of course, has the whole table in laughter. As I settle back into my chair, Marco leans in to me, placing his arm around my shoulder. "You okay, baby girl? You look flustered, at best."

I lean into him, "I'm fine, just getting a little tired from today."

Jaxson

DAMN! SHE'S RUNNING AGAIN. What the fuck is up with this girl that, every time she sees me, she's running? Well, not this time, sweetheart. I look to see where she went and find her sitting at a window table with a group of people. There is a guy with his arm around the back of her chair—*I don't think so!* As I walk up to her table, I see her tugging that fucking ear again and I want to lick it and drag my teeth over it. Just the thought is making me fucking hard! I step up to her table, reach down, taking her hand in mine, and I kiss the back of her wrist. "Raven, please introduce me to your friend." *Yeah, sweet cheeks, you're not getting rid of me that easy.* She looks at me then back to her friend, but she won't be pulling a runner tonight—that's for sure.

Raven

WHEN I LOOK TO Marco for some help, he is practically drooling. *A lot of good he is.* There is very little that has ever rendered Marco speechless, until now. "Jaxson, this is my roommate, Marco Green."

Maybe he'll think Marco and I are a couple and leave me alone. Yeah, right, I don't think this man would care if the Pope told him to back off. Marco looks very flustered, but then he snaps out of it and invites Jax to join us. I swear I want to pick up my fork and stab Marco with it! Before I realize what is going on, Marco informs me that the table we are at is for singles only, the bill is paid, and he is leaving with one of the guys.

"Don't worry, Marco. I'll make sure she gets home safely." With a wink and a kiss, Marco is gone and I'm left with Mr. Toe Curler! "So, Raven, please tell me all about yourself."

My stomach is in knots. "There's not much to tell, at least, what I would share with a total stranger."

He cocks his head to the side and smirks at me. "Oh, I think you have plenty to tell. Let's start out simple, how long have you been teaching?"

At least it's a subject that's easy for me to talk about. "I have been teaching for three years. I really love it especially when I see the moment they get *it*. That's when I love my job the most." His eyes are locked on mine.

"When do you not love your job?"

My eyes fill instantly with tears, and I fight to hold them back. "I don't like to see the children abused. I will fight for them no matter what," I say quietly. He strokes his chin, and I find it sexy as hell.

"You're in one of the top private schools, in a great neighborhood. You must not see too much abuse."

Why do people think that just because people have money, there is no abuse? "Just because someone has money doesn't mean they're not abused. Abuse comes in many forms, not just physical." Time to turn the tables on this guy. "What about you, Jax? Why do you do what you do?"

Jaxson

SHE COCKS HER HEAD to the side, clearly waiting for me to answer. She starts tugging that ear again. Why does it make my fucking cock hard when she does that? "Contrary to what you may think, I'm not the typical corporate raider."

"Okay, enlighten me. What kind of corporate raider are you?"

Alright, time to grace her with some of the "Jaxson charm" here. "That's just it, I don't just raid companies, break them apart, and sell them off in pieces to the highest bidder. I first look at small companies that are struggling and see if they have a marketable product or idea. From there, I either back them with the funding they need to get over the 'hump' or buy them from the owner who has no clue how to run a business. If it's a viable business, I'll revamp it and get it running. If I can't, then I sell the assets off while trying to place the workers in other companies that I own. Most people that go into business have a great idea but they don't have a solid business plan. I invest in agriculture, technology, and clean energy. People will always have to eat, travel, and use technology."

"You're right. That's not what I was thinking. What made you go into this type of business?" she restructures her question.

I usually play things pretty close to the vest, but for some reason, I find her so easy to talk to. "I grew up very poor and watched my mother work for a big box company that didn't care about its employees. She worked sixty hours a week and then went to work at night, cleaning offices just to keep a roof over our heads and food on the table. I never want to live that way again, and if I can help other families in the process, then I will." I can tell I'm getting to her, she seems to relax and take an interest.

"What about your father, Jax? Is he still alive?"

I scoff, "My father walked out on us when I was five years old and he never looked back. It's always been my mum and my sister; that's all the family I've ever needed." I adjust in my seat. She's tugging that fucking ear! I don't know how long I can last before I lean over and take it between my teeth, slowly grazing down it. Oh fuck, I'm hard—*again!*

"Jax, I notice you have a slight accent. Where are you from?"

I reach up, and pull her hand away from her ear, trying to maintain my concentration. "I was born in Wales. We lived there until I was thirteen, and sometimes my accent is heavier than others." I run circles with my thumb in the palm of her hand.

"When does it get heavier?"

Raven

HE LAUGHS LIGHTLY, "WHEN I have too much drink or when I'm intimate." Then he hits me with that killer smirk. "What about you? Where is your family?"

I tighten up before I bring my eyes back up to his. "It's just Marco and me. My mom died when I was fifteen. After that, I left home and never looked back. Marco has been the only family I have ever needed."

I can see him processing what I'm saying. "What does Marco do for a living?"

I smile, always happy to brag about Marco. "He's a graphic artist and in great demand. He has an eye for details."

"Why did you leave home at such a young age?"

Just at that point, the server comes over to inform us that the restaurant is getting ready to close, which saves me from answering his questions. I can't believe how fast the time went, neither of us realizing the restaurant was empty. As we head out the door, his driver is waiting at the curb. "Jax, I can get myself home; I do it all the time."

"Not tonight, sweetheart, I promised Marco I would see you home safely, and I always keep my promises. Your address, please?"

WE PULL UP TO my building and my stomach starts to turn into knots. Then he does something I never would have expected; he looks over to me, pulls my hand from my ear, and kisses it. He didn't move in for the kill, he didn't even ask to come up. He just kissed my hand, then the inside of my wrist. "Goodnight, I had a wonderful evening, Raven." The driver opens the door and walks me into the building, where the doorman is waiting. And then he leaves.

Jaxson

"MAX, TAKE ME HOME, please." Maxwell has been my driver and best friend for eight years now. I think even *he* was surprised by my actions tonight—I know I was. At least, he has the grace not to call me on it. She makes me feel very different; she peaks my interest and leaves me wanting more. I have never felt that before. Most women throw themselves at me. All they see is money and good looks which, thanks to my mum, I have never been lacking in that department. When Raven looked at me, I felt her passion. That's something I've never experienced before. I want more of her; I need more of her. I decide, in this moment, that I *will have* more of her.

Chapter Three

Raven

I GET UPSTAIRS, UNDRESS, and decide on a cup of tea to settle my nerves. Marco comes flying through the door with the guy from the restaurant. "Sorry, baby girl, I thought you would be out for the night, especially the way Mr. Tall, Dark, and Beautiful was staring at you."

I look at him in confusion. "Well, you're mistaken." I inform him, before focusing my attention on his guest. "Hi, I'm Raven Anderson, Marco's roommate."

"Oh, sorry. Raven, this is Sam. He owns a few hair salons in the village." Marco offers.

I shake his hand. "Nice to meet you. You can have the living room. I have papers to grade. Have fun." *I know he wants all the dirt.*

"Wait, what happened to Jax?" How do I tell him that I'm more confused than ever?

"We talked for hours. He took me home and kissed my hand. That's it, then, he left."

He is gaping at me, "Oh."

I gather my tea and head to my room. "Yeah, *oh*." I walk away, completely flustered.

SLEEP BARELY CAME FOR me and before I know it, Marco is banging on my door. "You better have a damn good reason for waking me up so early on a Saturday?" I call out. I'm going to smack him.

"Um, Raven. You need to come out here, like now!"

What the hell is his problem? As I open my door, I'm hit with the smell of flowers, coffee, and fresh pastry. I swear the best smell in the world is coffee and pastry together. If it were a perfume, I would wear it. I look at Marco as he watches some strange man set the table for us. The man hands me an envelope, turns, and leaves. Okay, this is very strange.

"I'm busting, baby girl, what does it say?"

I pull out a beautiful hand written note:

> *I hope I invaded your dreams like you invaded mine. I look forward to having breakfast with you, but for now, this will have to do.*
>
> *~ Jax*

Marco looks over at me. "Well, it seems our Jax is very deep, and he has great taste when it comes to breakfast. Let's eat, I'm starved!"

The pastry is like butter melting on my lips, and the coffee is exactly how I like it. We are enjoying the wonderful breakfast when we hear a phone start to ring. It's not Marco's or mine. We look around and find a phone in a box with the flowers. "Hello?" *Oh my God, really?*

"Good morning, Raven. How is your breakfast?"

This man is so over the top. "Jax, the breakfast is wonderful, but why the phone?"

He laughs, "I never got your phone number last night and I wanted to talk to you, it just seemed like a great idea. A phone just for me."

I can't tell if he's serious or snarky. "Do you really think I will carry two phones just so you can have your own phone?" I ask as I take a closer look at the flowers. "These flowers are very unusual, what kind are they?"

"Yes, they are very unusual. They're from Germany and they're called *Abracadabra Roses*—they reminded me of you. They're different from the everyday rose. And to answer your question, yes, I do think you should carry a phone just for me. I'm calling to ask you to accompany me to a charity event this evening. It's being held at Chelsea Pier." He is so confident.

Do I want to continue this? "What type of event is it?"

He sounds very passionate as he tells me about the charity event. "It's part of a children's charity that my company sponsors, and I would be honored if you went with me."

The charity is for children, how could I ever say no? "Okay, what time should I meet you there?"

"Raven, I would never have you meet me there. I will pick you up at eight."

I feel like a teenager again. "Okay, Jax, I'll see you at eight." I hang up and I'm sure I have a stupid look on my face.

"Marco, get your ass dressed, we have a lot to do from now until tonight!"

WE HIT BLOOMINGDALES FIRST, to find something to wear. I need something that will render him speechless. I like to wear plum and I find just the right cocktail dress. The back has a cut-out, covered in plum lace and it has a low-cut front. It has a drop waist and it is very well fitted to my curves. It falls below my knees and has a slit up the back. It's a combination of sexy, yet subtle. I find peep-toe stilettos in black patent leather with a matching bag to complete the ensemble. Next, it's off to the spa for a mani pedi, waxing, and a deep conditioning treatment on my hair. I'm a little nervous. Oh, who the hell am I kidding? I'm scared to death! Marco invites Sam over to help with my hair and makeup. He pulls one side of my hair up and secures it with a beautiful clip. I feel like a teenager going on a first date.

At exactly 8 p.m., my doorman rings to let me know Jax has arrived. Marco opens the door and I am stunned. *He's more beautiful than I remembered!* This is a good thing because if I had remembered, I would have been even more nervous and I probably would not have agreed to go. He's wearing a black tux and a black shirt with a deep violet bow tie—the same color as my eyes. He looks at me and there it is again, my frigging toes are curling and there is a buzzing in my ears.

"Raven, you look amazing, more beautiful than I remembered."

AS WE DRIVE TO Chelsea Pier, I ask him about the charity that he is sponsoring, anything to get my mind off of the buzzing in my ears. "It's to help the families of children with brain tumors."

"Why this charity?"

I see that passion again in his eyes. "My company sponsors many different charities; I believe in giving back to society. Sometimes, it is through a charity and sometimes, it's something random such as, sponsoring a garden in Harlem. If we want change, then we need to do something to bring about that change. Just talking about it does nothing."

I wonder why I never heard of his company. "I agree. However, I've never heard of your company or the charitable works that it sponsors."

He laughs, "Good, I like it like that. I don't need a feather in my cap or recognition on what I do. I do it, expecting nothing, that's what makes it the most rewarding. By the way, I have to warn you the press will be here. They will be hounding me for pictures, which means they will also hound you. I'm sorry."

He looks so sad. "I think I can handle it. How bad could it be? A few pictures doesn't seem like a big deal."

He stares at me and I wish I knew what he was thinking. I wonder why he suddenly looks so lost and sad. "Jax, are you okay?" Before he can answer, we pull up. Holy crap, there are flashes everywhere! I thought this was a small event; there are thousands of people! We get out of the car to head in and are immediately caught up in the frenzy. Flashes are popping in my face as I'm introduced to the *who's who* of New York. By the time we sit down at our table, my face hurts from smiling so much.

"Jax, is this what you go through every time you go somewhere?"

He grimaces. "Unfortunately, yes, but if it means I can get more money for the cause, then I am willing to do it. I usually don't attend these events with anyone, so I'm sure the wolves will be circling soon. Again, I'm sorry."

I try to put him at ease. "Don't worry, I think I can handle them. Let's face it, I handle a classroom filled with second graders every day!" Glancing around, I notice his driver is never really out of sight; he's always within reaching distance of Jax.

Dinner was a typical banquet affair, but instead of dancing, they rolled out gambling tables. "I thought there would be dancing at an event like this."

He smiles. "No. I found, if we offer gambling with all the proceeds going to the charity, more money is donated than just writing a check."

I never really thought of it that way. "How much money can you expect to take in tonight?"

I can see the wheels in his head spinning. "The charity will probably take in three million dollars, after expenses. That will help many families, not just with the initial surgery, but also, with the aftercare. Caring for someone who has had brain surgery takes a lot of time and money. Most of these families are living pay check to pay check." *Wow, this man is nothing like I thought he would be.*

"Let's gamble a little and see if you're my lucky charm, sweetheart."

We walk up to the blackjack table and Jax hands me some chips to play with. "I don't gamble and I don't want to lose your money."

He smirks. "You're not losing my money, you're donating it. Besides, it's easy. Just try to get to twenty-one without going over."

I try a few hands, but it doesn't hold my interest; it seems too much like work. What I do find interesting is the roulette table. There are many different ways to bet, and it's all up to the wheel. Turns out, I'm better at it than I thought. After an hour of gambling, I decide to cash in my winnings. I hand the cashier my chips and she gives me a check for $100,000.00. "Excuse me, but there is some kind of mistake here. This is too much money."

Jax laughs and informs me I was playing with $10,000 dollar chips! I'm glad I didn't know, otherwise, I wouldn't have bet anything. I sign the check and put it in the donation box. I see Jax watching me with a very strange look, but he says nothing.

As we head back to the limo, Jax stops and takes me in his arms, he pulls my chin up, and stares into my eyes. There it is—my toes are doing that curl thing again! "Raven, I had a wonderful evening, and I don't want it to end, will you come home with me?"

"OKAY," I WHISPER. I can't believe I just said okay without a single thought. Even though I'm nervous, I feel so safe with him, which is something I never have experienced before.

WE PULL UP TO a building across from Central Park. As he steps out of the car, he takes my hand and informs me that he lives here. We walk through the lobby and get on his private elevator. We enter the penthouse and I'm struck with the most incredible view of the park. "You live here by yourself?"

He looks at me like I'm nuts. "I have a housekeeper, but other than that, yes, just me."

Taking in everything surrounding me, I'm stunned. "This place is huge! Do you ever get lost in here?"

He strokes his chin and gifts me with that crooked smirk. "Let me give you a quick tour. There is a guest room, office, gym, and then there is a rooftop garden area with a hot tub."

I can't believe he lives here. "Jax, this place is amazing and the views are spectacular. Does your place take up the entire floor?"

He shakes his head. "No, there is another penthouse that mirrors mine. My driver, Max, lives in the other one."

Oh. My. God. His driver lives in a penthouse! "Wait, your driver lives in a penthouse?"

He laughs. "Max is much more than just my driver. He does my security and he's my best friend. He has to be—I trust him with my life and the lives of my family." He smiles at me. "Come, sit down, Raven, I want to know more about you.

"You're so beautiful and not just tonight. When you stumbled into my world, you threw it off kilter." He leans in slowly, his soft lips brushing against mine. The sparks are flying to all my nerve endings and then, I look into his eyes—yep, there's that toe thing again.

He's tender, yet firm; our tongues doing a slow dance. He runs his cheek against mine and the scruff of his beard softly grazes my cheek. "Raven, please tell me you feel that too… that I'm not imagining it."

I hum, "Yes, Jax, just what *it* is, I have no clue."

He slowly puts little flutter kisses up and down my neck, and then, he reaches in and nibbles on my ear lobe. *Oh sweet, Jesus!* His teeth gently pull on my ear. Oh my God, his lips are so soft. He swipes his tongue over my bottom lip and I shiver. He takes my hand and kisses the inside of my wrist. Damn, when he does that, it's like a jolt between my legs. *How could that one spot be so damn sensitive?* This man is way out of my league! He's rich, beautiful, and, I'm sure, a player; he seems used to getting what he wants—when he wants it. I need to stop this before I get to the point of no return. "Jax, I need to go."

His jaw is tight, and he's fisting his hands. He seems shocked I need to leave. "You want to leave now? Is something wrong? Did I offend you?"

I'm trying not to let the tears fall, "It's not you, Jax, I just…I really need to go."

He locks his eyes on mine. "Okay, let me ring Max." As he gets up to leave, I can see the confusion on his face.

Heck, even I'm confused "Jax, I can take a cab, it's no big deal."

Okay, now, he looks pissed off. "Sweetheart, there is no way I would dream of you ever taking a cab home, and if I offended you in any way, I'm truly sorry." He leads me to the elevator.

I can't lose it here. I take a deep breath, "It's not you, Jax," I whisper as we head down the elevator in silence. I really don't know what to say to him. When we get downstairs, Max is waiting for us. We get right into the car and take off.

The ride to my place is long and quiet. I need to stop this now before it goes too far. We pull up and I jump out so fast, it only gives him time to watch me. "I'm sorry, Jax." And with that, I'm gone.

Jaxson

AS WE DRIVE AWAY from Raven's place, Max glances at me in the rearview mirror. "Jax, you okay?"

I stare out the window. "Fuck if I know? This girl keeps running away from me."

"Do you want me to run a check on her?" he asks. Usually, I would have Max run a check, but for some reason, I want to find out about her like a normal guy would.

"No, Max, not just yet. I'm not ready for that." I'm not ready to go home yet, either. "Please drive around the park for a while, mate, I need some time to think. I just don't get why this girl keeps running away from me. I never have this problem." Max glances in the rear view mirror at me again, "Spit it out, Max, I see the fucking bloody looks you're giving. I know you have something to say."

He's laughs. "Well, Jax, you can be a tad intimidating, don't you think?"

If he weren't my best friend, I would probably wipe that smirk off of his face right now. "You know, Max, eight years and you're still cheeky as hell. I'm trying not to bulldoze her, but it's very hard." He laughs at me again. I'm glad my love life, or lack thereof, is amusing to him.

"Jax, you operate at a hundred miles an hour and that can be too much for most people."

I hate when he's right. "That's just it, Max, she's not 'most people', she's different."

He looks at me like he's had some great revelation. "Well, Jax, maybe that is the answer."

What the fuck? Is he Dr. Phil now? "Oh bloody hell, Max! What the fuck are you trying to say?" He doesn't usually give advice on relationships so this should be interesting.

"She is different. So your usual bulldozer approach to life will not work on her. Slow it down, mate, and see how she reacts."

The rest of the ride is in silence. Damn if I know how to slow down.

Raven

WHEN I GET UPSTAIRS, Marco is waiting for me. "How was the ball, princess?" I burst into tears and throw myself on the couch.

"Oh no, baby girl, what happened?"

I let the tears fall. "It's me, I'm such a mess. He was so perfect. We had a wonderful night, then he took me back to his place and I felt like putty in his arms."

Marco pulls me into his arms as I wipe my tears on his shirt. "So, why the tears? Did you panic and run again?" he asks. I nod. I can't even say the words out loud, because then it makes it real. "Honey, give him a chance, just tell him you need to go slow. He's probably never had anyone say no. I mean, look at him. Have you googled him yet?"

I've never googled a date, why would I start now? "No, why would I do that?"

He's growling at me now! *What is it with the men in my life and all their growling?* "In today's world, you almost have to. Do you know anything about him other than what he's told you?" he asks. I shake my head. "Okay, now you're making me worried. You're usually more level- headed than this. Raven, What the fuck is going on in your head?"

Marco grabs the iPad and googles 'Jaxson Phillips.' It doesn't take long. *Holy crap there are thousands of hits!* There are tons of articles about his company; some good and some not so good. A lot of hits are about the different charities he is involved with. But what is most surprising is when I pull up images for him, he's always alone. If he is such a player, why are there no images of him with a girl? Could I have possibly been so wrong about him? Maybe my impression of him was way off base, and he's not a player. Marco clicks on a link—oh my word, it's from tonight . . . and—it's me! *Is that why he kept apologizing?*

Marco looks over to me and then starts reading, "Who is the mystery woman that was seen with New York's most eligible bachelor, Jaxson James Phillips, tonight at Chelsea Pier? Could this mean he's finally off the market?"

"I don't want to know anymore, please shut it down."

He shuts it off. "I think you need to talk to him. He can't read your mind, and the way he was looking at you, I don't think he wants this to end."

I can't listen to this anymore. "I've had enough, I'm going to bed. Do not wake me up early." I head to my room, leaving Marco to himself.

As I get into bed, I replay the night's events. I think about how hard it must be to always have people, watching your every move. Always having to filter what you say would be a big problem for me. It always amazes me how people get so wrapped up in the lives of celebrities. I have a lot to do to manage my own life, let alone wonder what some celebrity is doing or with whom they are doing it. As I try to fall asleep, all I see are the bluest eyes and how sad they looked tonight.

Chapter Four

Raven

IT'S SUNDAY MORNING, I just want to snuggle in bed for a while, but I hear music playing. The music stops and starts again. *Where is that coming from?* I look at the dresser and see the phone that Jax sent, lighting up and I realize the music is coming from there. "Hello?" I can't believe he's calling, especially after last night.

"Good morning, did you sleep well?"

How could he even think that I would sleep well after last night? "Not really, how about you?"

He sighs. "No, I think we need to talk. Can we go for breakfast, Raven?"

This guy just doesn't give up. "Even after I ran, you still want to see me?"

"Yes, I need to understand why you did, and what I can do to stop you from constantly running away from me. You're giving me a complex, sweetheart."

Maybe I'm a challenge for him? "That's a tall order, Jax."

He laughs. "I believe I'm up for the challenge. Can you be ready in an hour? It's a beautiful fall day, and I would like to enjoy it with you."

How could I say no to that? "Okay, Jax."

I HEAD OUTSIDE, AND there's Jax. He's wearing worn jeans, a button down Oxford shirt, with a polo tied around his neck. He has on aviators and is leaning against the most beautiful sports car I have ever seen. He tells me it's a *1957 Jaguar XK-SS*; a replica of Steve McQueen's car. It just takes my breath away. "I hope that look is for me and not just the car."

I can't help but laugh. "I guess you'll never know." I allow him to open the door for me and I get in. Within a minute, he's in the driver's seat and we're off.

We pull up to a little café on the East Side that I have never been to. We enter the quaint café and Jax orders our coffee and pastries. We then grab a table by the window, so we can be alone.

"Raven, I thought we were having a good time last night getting to know each other, but then you ran…again."

He doesn't demand an answer, but I know he is not leaving without one. "Jax, I'm a simple, second grade teacher. I have no worldly experience, and quite honestly, my sexual experience has been very little and very bad. You make me feel things I've never felt before and that scares me." There, I said it as honestly as I could. I'm sure he'll be taking me home now.

"First, sweetheart, let me say, there is nothing simple about you. You don't get to choose what I can or can't handle, only I do. If I didn't want to be with you, then I wouldn't. I feel things with you I've never felt before and I like it; I want more. You said 'your sexual experience is very little and was very bad', is that something you feel you can share with me? I can't fix something if I don't know what it is."

What do I say? "I need time, Jax, I barely know you."

He seems content with my answer. "If time is what you need, then you've got it. I'm not prepared to walk away so don't expect me to," he states. I cock my head, trying to figure him out. His eyes seem to hone in on me tugging my ear (a nervous habit of mine). "Did you expect me to walk away?" he continues.

I laugh, "Quite frankly, Jax, yes. I mean, you can have your pick of anyone."

He smirks again. "Raven, maybe I finally found *my someone*, but how would I know if you keep running?"

I lock eyes with him. "Oh."

"Yeah, *oh*," he whispers.

WE HEAD TO THE car and Jax informs me that we are going apple picking. I've never done that before and I'm excited to try something new, so . . . off we go. It's such a beautiful day. He puts on some music and it's one of my favorite bands, Snow Patrol.

"We seem to have similar taste in music. Jax, I'm going to ask you some questions, for every one that you answer, I will let you ask me a question."

His eyes light up. "So let me get this straight, Raven. I can ask you any question and you'll answer it?"

I laugh, "Nice try, Jax." I'll start with an easy one. "What's your favorite movie?"

He strokes his chin and it's sexy as hell. "Alright, but, Raven, no laughing."

Oh boy, that's going to be hard. "Okay, fess up, Jax, favorite movie?"

He's got a serious look on his face. "If you tell another living soul, I will deny it . . . *When Harry Met Sally*."

"Oh."

He seems surprised. "That's it, just *oh*?"

Not at all what I thought he would say. "Well, it wasn't what I was expecting, that's for sure. Why is that your favorite movie?"

He seems lost in thought. "It's the struggle of friendship and how important it is to a relationship."

Hmm. "I never thought of it that way."

He cocks his head. "What's your favorite movie?"

I know he's going to laugh. "Don't laugh."

"You didn't laugh at mine, sweetheart, why would I laugh at yours?"

Here goes nothing. "Okay, *Die Hard*." He looks over at me and gets hysterical.

"Really, Jax? You promised not to laugh."

"I'm sorry, but clearly you have to see the irony that my favorite is a 'chick flick' and yours is a 'macho dick flick'." Well, when he put it like that, I guess I can see the humor in it.

"Why is *Die Hard* your favorite movie?"

I can't believe this is not everyone's favorite movie. "Well, it's the story of survival, how one man relies on himself to save so many. He is simple, but very brave, and let's face it—the good guy wins."

I think he gets it. "Okay, sweetheart, enough on movies, what's your favorite food?"

This one is easy. "I love pizza, really good pizza, not the kind that comes frozen in a box."

I look over to him and he's thinking. I can tell when he is deep in thought, he strokes his chin. "I would have to say mine is sushi. Not only does it taste wonderful, the presentation is like a piece of art that is made just for me." He pats his chest. Wow, I never thought of it as art but I guess it could be. "iPhone or Droid?"

Another easy one. "I'm an Apple girl, they work great and they keep it simple. You?"

He's like a little boy talking about his toys. "I like Droid phones. They have better apps, but Apple computers, so I guess both."

*J*axson

SHE IS SITTING THERE, seemingly deep in thought, tugging at that fucking ear. I need to keep this conversation going so she doesn't try and pull a runner. But if she keeps doing *that*, I'm going to get crazy hard. "What other types of music do you like?"

She laughs and I love the sound of it. "If you listened to what's on my iPod you would probably be in shock. I like to sing so I have a lot of stuff I can sing along with, but only when no one is around!"

"I would love to hear you sing, and I think you would sound beautiful." I smile.

Raven

NO ONE HAS HEARD me sing except Marco, when he came home early one day. "Ha, I'm tone deaf, so only when I'm home cleaning or driving alone." I bet he has an extensive music collection. "What type of music do you listen to, Jax?"

"I really like many different types; it just depends on my mood and where I am at that moment. My top band is Snow Patrol, most people are aware of their famous songs, 'Chasing Cars' and 'Run' however, I like a lot of their older stuff; it's the lyrics that grab you. They are the ultimate story tellers.

"Okay, Raven, we're here, out you go, sweetheart. We'll take turns climbing up the ladder to pick the apples. Why are you looking at me like I have three heads?"

I freeze. "I'm afraid of heights. No way can I climb up a ladder!"

He's thinking while stroking his chin; it's such a turn on when he does that. "Raven, you can't let fear rule you or fear wins. Why are you afraid?"

I won't even stand on a chair. "What if I fall?"

He takes on a more serious look. "Do you trust me?"

I don't even have to think about that one. "Yes, Jax, totally."

He smiles, "Okay then, up you go."

I grab the ladder, "*Wait!*"

He shakes his head. "No wait, up you go, sweetheart, I've got you. I'll always have your back." He holds the ladder as I slowly climb, maintaining a white-knuckle grip the whole way. "Hold on with one hand and use the other one to pick the apple."

Oh crap, if he wants me to let go, he is out of his fucking mind! "Jax, I'm scared." Before the words are completely out of my mouth he's on the ladder behind me. His body blankets mine; he covers my hand with one of his. He takes my other hand and stretches it up to pick an apple.

"I will always have your back, sweetheart," he whispers deep and low in my ear.

After completely filling our bag, we head back to the car. "What are you going to do with all these apples?"

He cocks his head and gives me that look that shoots to my toes. "Oh, Raven, not me. We are going to make an apple pie, of course."

The look on my face must be priceless because he is laughing so hard, he has tears rolling down his cheeks. "Jax, I don't cook and I wouldn't have a clue how to make a pie!"

He tilts his head and hits me with that killer smirk. "Yeah, I kind of figured that by the look of fear on your face. I think it was worse than the look when you found out you had to climb up a ladder. Not to worry, I don't know either, but I did get a book and we can do this together."

I really think he's nuts, but I'm having fun for the first time in a long time so I go along with it. As we get in the car, I notice Max standing by another car. "Isn't that Max?"

He doesn't even bother to look. "Yes, he goes everywhere with me."

He has a bodyguard that lives in a penthouse and follows him everywhere? What am I getting myself into? "Why does he go everywhere with you?"

Jaxson

I DON'T WANT TO scare her into pulling another runner on me. "Max is in charge of security, he is usually with me at all times. When he can't be with me, then he has someone else shadow."

She locks her eyes with mine and there it is—that charge. "Why do you need so much security?"

I pull her hand away from her ear before I lose it completely. "Unfortunately, when someone has money and does what I do for a living, it makes them a target. Max can be a tad overprotective at times, but he keeps us safe."

Raven

WE GET BACK TO his ivory tower in the sky and he gets out a book . . . something about pie baking for dummies. It's not as hard as I thought, and we actually put together something that resembles an apple pie. He puts it in the oven to bake and soon the house begins to smell wonderful. "Would you like a glass of wine?" he asks casually. He seems so sure of himself, so comfortable in his own skin.

"Yes, please."

As he gets the wine, he puts on some music. He tells me that the music is David Garrett, who lives six months in New York and six months in London. And that he plays the violin like it is part of him. He hands me a glass of wine that I never heard of, "Michael's dad and my sister own a vineyard in Italy. This is one of the wines they produce," he explains.

I take a sip and I'm surprised. "Wow, it's very good. I never knew that's what Michael's parents did for a living. Is it hard for them, living here with their business in Italy?"

He just shrugs. "No, they spend the summers in Italy and the school year here; they make it work." He puts his glass down. "Raven, I'm going to jump right in here . . . you said your sexual experiences were very few and very bad, why?" he asks, completely out of the blue. I look up at him and my eyes are filled with tears, Marco is in my head yelling at me to tell him. "I would never judge you, Raven, we all have a past."

I study his face, he's so beautiful and looks so sincere right now, "Jax, that's just it, it's my past."

He pulls my hand away from my ear. "But it's not if it's affecting your future."

The timer rings and I thank all that's holy for the interruption.

THE PIE SMELLS WONDERFUL and looks like something out of a magazine, I take a picture with my phone and Jax laughs.

"Would I be correct in guessing it has something to do with why you left home at such a young age?" Great, we're back on this subject again. He's not going to stop until I tell him.

"Yes, I was fifteen when my mom died from cancer. My dad and I were never close, but after she died, he started drinking very heavily. I guess it was his way of coping. His drinking brought out some nasty things. One night, he came into my room and he tried to rape me. After that, I left."

"Don't stop now, sweetheart. Nothing you can say is going to scare me away."

Okay, wow that is not what I was expecting, so I continue. "I had no one to turn to for help. I have no other family. I found myself volunteering at a shelter and that is where I met Marco. His parents disowned him when he told them he was gay. We took care of each other, never relying on anyone but ourselves. I graduated high school without the school knowing I was homeless. I earned scholarships and worked hard to put myself through college."

He keeps his focus on me, intently listening, "So where does this bad sexual experience come into play?"

I sigh heavily, "I met someone and tried to have a sexual relationship with him but . . . he was only concerned about himself. It was always about his pleasure and his needs. He became physically abusive, and after a night in the ER, Marco convinced me to get a restraining order." There… I put it all out there, and now it's time to make my exit with as much grace and dignity as I can muster up.

As I attempt to leave, he takes my hand, his eyes on mine. "Where do you think you're going?"

"I don't want you to feel like I'm a charity case, and I definitely don't want you to pity me."

He growls. "You know, Raven, I really wish you would stop deciding for me what I can and can't handle. I just said you're not going to scare me away and I meant that. I'm not going anywhere. Not because of charity or pity, I'm with you because I want to be, and for no other reason. Now, I think it's time for pie." Just like that, he's finished. He doesn't dwell on stuff; he deals with it and then puts it away.

"I am very impressed with our pie making ability, and, Jax, I have to say you make the best coffee ever."

He gives me that beautiful smile. "Thank you. My sister, Bella, taught me well, she believes coffee is God's nectar."

He leans in and kisses me quickly and softly. He looks into my eyes, like he's searching for permission. I lean up and kiss him, stroking his velvet tongue. The taste of him mixed with apple pie and coffee is surreal.

He pulls away first, "Stay with me tonight," he whispers.

Part of me wants to stay and part of me wants to run. "I have school tomorrow."

He kisses me softly again, "I promise to get you to class on time."

I shake my head, "I'm not ready to spend the night. I need... time. I'm sorry."

He rests his forehead on mine, "Don't ever be sorry for being honest with me. Let me take you home."

MARCO IS WAITING FOR me as soon as I walk in the door. "Well, baby girl, how was your date?"

"I really like him, but there is so much unknown with him. He is a very private person, considering he's always in the public eye.

Marco furrows his brows, seemingly concerned. "How much have you told him?"

I run over the conversation in my head. "I told him about the ex and the restraining order that is in place, but that's it."

He hugs me. "Maybe it's time to tell him the truth . . . the whole truth?"

I look at him, "I'm going to bed. I have work tomorrow. Love you." I leave him lost in his thoughts as I head to my room for the night.

MY SLEEP IS VERY restless so I decide to get up super early and go for a run. I live in Gramercy Park, one of the only private parks in Manhattan. I like running here. It's two miles with great trails and it's safe. I do a total of six miles, then head back home. Running helps clear my head and today it made me realize that I need to steer clear of Jax. He is just too much for me and I know I'm going to get hurt.

I get ready for school and head to Starbucks. Jax is there waiting with my coffee. "Wow, this is nice, can I expect this every day?"

He looks at me with that crooked smirk. "If you want to have breakfast together every day I can arrange it, sweetheart."

"Oh." I have to laugh because he would.

There's that smirk. "Yeah, *oh*."

On that note, I have to leave. I thank him and tell him that I need to run, school starts soon. He hands me a bottle of water and a breakfast sandwich. "What's this for?"

He kisses me softly. "Mick. I know you usually buy him breakfast, and I didn't want him to miss a meal because of me."

Does this guy know everything I do? "How do you know about Mick?"

He smirks, "When you doused me with your coffee, I had to find out who you were, so I asked around and all roads led me to Mick. He's an interesting bloke, that's for sure."

I start to walk. "He just needs someone to listen, that's the least I can do, and give him a meal. I have to run, have a good day, Jax." I look back at him and he's stroking his chin. Hmm . . . I wonder what he's thinking.

Jaxson

AS I HEAD TOWARDS my office, all I can think about is Raven and her constant need to run from me! My mind drifts to every second spent with her, and that fucking tugging on her ear thing; why does that make me instantly hard? Maybe I should have Max run a check on her? As I approach my building, I see Max and he's pacing—that's never a good sign. When I get closer, I can tell he's really pissed off. His hands are flying and he's yelling into the phone. "Max, is there a problem?"

He has fire in his eyes. "You want to know if there is a fucking problem! How about my bloody boss, whom I'm en-trusted to keep safe, wandering off, repetitively, without letting his detail know or giving proper *fucking* notice?!"

I know I have to take Max seriously, but sometimes, he is over the top. "Okay, Max, you need to calm down. I'm not in any danger and I just needed some time to think."

He looks at me like he's going to blow a gasket. "*Think*? You needed to think? Jax, I have guarded the Royal family, I have led Special Forces for the United Kingdom, and have avoided death on many occasions, but you, my friend, will be the one to put me in an early fucking grave! I understand she is frustrating you—fuck, she's even frustrating me, but don't—and I mean, *don't* ever leave your fucking detail again!"

"Okay, just calm down. I need you to look into something for me. There is a homeless man near the Starbucks that Raven checks in on his name is Mick. I want you to find out what his story is and then see what we can do to help him out."

"What's this about, Jax?" he asks with a bit of irritation mixed with the confusion painted on his face.

"Raven buys him breakfast every morning. I spoke to him and he is a war veteran who is most likely suffering from PTSD. It's simple; I want to know what I can do for him."

"Jax, nothing with you is ever simple."

Rather than argue, I decide to head up to my office. I sit behind my desk, looking out at the New York skyline and the only thing I really see are those violet eyes and a beautiful girl tugging on her fucking ear. And I'm instantly hard, *again*! Fuck, I have a meeting in ten minutes. I can't head in there with a raging hard-on. I grab the phone and call my assistant. "Duke, call everyone and change the meeting to my office." At least it's a temporary fix. I will need to come up with something more permanent later, so I'm not walking around with a constant hard-on.

Maxwell

I DON'T KNOW WHAT Jax thinks he can do for this bloke, but I head toward his office with the info he wanted. "Duke? Is Jax in his office?"

He nearly jumps out of his chair. "Yes, Mr. Fleming, he is just finishing up a meeting."

What is this guy's problem? "Okay, I'll wait." I step into the shadows, just watching; it's what I do best. I must make this kid nervous because he always seems so flustered when I'm around. Maybe its new job jitters? Managers are coming out of Jax's office so I head on in.

"I got that information you asked for on Mick." At least this wasn't too much trouble.

"Wow, that was quick."

I laugh, "Yeah, well, most of it is public knowledge, and I wasn't sure how far back you wanted to go since I don't know what the fuck you're looking for."

He strokes his chin, which is a sure sign that Jax's wheels are turning. "Just the basic stuff, for now."

I sit across from him. "Okay, Jax, he is an Air Force veteran who did six tours in Iraq. He was awarded the *Medal of Honor* when his jet was shot down. He saved his crew one-by-one while suffering two broken legs, all while keeping the enemy at bay. He's been diagnosed with PTSD and before you ask, he doesn't get any additional funding. The problem is, funding is low, so it is distributed based on need. He is on the cusp, so he is not seen as a priority. Jax, what are you thinking?"

He paces. "I'm thinking that his situation is wrong. This man fought for his country and this is the way they take care of him?!"

I don't know when Jax finds the time to think about this when so much else is happening around him? "Jax, there are thousands of *Mick's* out there. There is a good organization, *The Wounded Warrior Project*. Let me reach out to them and see what we can do."

He nods, "Okay, but sooner rather than later, mate."

Now comes the hard question, which I'm sure will get my blood boiling. "How are things with Raven?"

He shakes his head. "Just as confusing as ever, Max." He stares out the window, seemingly deep in thought so I decide not to push any further and leave.

Raven

SCHOOL IS UNEVENTFUL WHICH is just fine by me. Jackie and I decide to go out for a few drinks and an early dinner. Jackie is beautiful; her father is Swedish and her mom is Asian. She is very tall and her complexion is light like her dad's, but she has her mom's almond-shape eyes that are almost golden. She is very lean; she runs marathons. And she attracts men like a magnet. We enjoy trying different mom and pop restaurants, so we do this every week.

"Okay, Raven, you have to tell me about Michael's uncle. Don't even think of denying it; I saw the way he was looking at you, so spill." I tell her everything, including my tendencies to keep running from him.

"Are you afraid of him, is that why you keep running?"

I shake my head. "Absolutely not, if anything, I feel very safe with him. I think I keep running because he is so intense and he is everything I'm not."

She rolls her eyes and huffs. "You're kidding, right? I mean, you're beautiful, smart, and I know if you wanted to, you could run circles around him."

I hug her. "I love you, Jackie, but I think you're nuts. With him, I feel very insecure; he's so beautiful and ridiculously rich. I could never be in the same league as some of the people he must run with. What about you? Didn't you have a date last night?"

She throws her hands up in disgust. "Yes, and it was terrible. I mean, one dinner and he thinks I should put out. I know I'm old fashioned in a lot of ways, but I just want someone that does it for me. I want to be someone's end all."

I feel bad for her; she is so sweet but also very smart. Men see her and think she is submissive, which is totally off base. "You're a great girl and you deserve only the best. There is no crime in holding out for it as long as you see it when it's right in front of your eyes. Enough about men. Let's hit some stores, I need retail therapy."

A couple of hours later and I'm back home with at least ten shopping bags! There is nothing better than some good scores, during retail therapy. Marco's not home yet, but the doorman informs me I had a visitor that didn't leave his name. I check my phone and see I have six missed calls, all from Jax. I also have a text message and a voice mail.

I check the text first:

Please answer your phone.

Then, the voicemail:

"I don't understand why you're ignoring me, and why you keep running away. What is it going to take to get you to trust me?"

I trust him, I just don't trust myself. I decide to shut it off and go to sleep. My head hits that pillow and I'm out for the count.

Chapter Five

Raven

MORNING COMES WITH MARCO, banging on my door again. The banging can only mean one thing—I must have slept through the alarm. "How bad is it, Marco?"

"Raven, its 6:30 a.m.!" he yells. *Oh fuck!* This man has me way too preoccupied and now he is making me late again.

"Marco, why does this keep happening to me?" I ask as I jump out of bed and frantically move about my room to get ready.

"Life gets in the way of living, baby girl, you know that." I push him out the door as I race into the shower.

Finally pulling it all together, I hurry out the door to get my morning coffee. Just as I have myself convinced that I should forget about Jax, I run into Starbucks and see him standing there with my coffee. "God, you're wonderful, thank you so much."

His eyes are dark and he's glaring at me. "Are you ever going to answer my calls?"

As I look up at him, I realize, he's really pissed. "I'm sorry, I just need time."

He leans in and kisses me softly on the forehead, "Well, sweetheart, time's up. I'm picking you up after school."

Before I can even answer, he's gone.

I CAN'T FOCUS ON anything today. I thank, all that's holy, Jackie is in my room, helping me. She sends the kids out to recess which gives us a twenty minute break. "Raven, what's going on with you today? You're not yourself."

I know Jackie will understand. "I've been trying to ignore, Jax. I told him I need time, but then I ran into him at Starbucks this morning. He informed me that *time is up* and he's picking me up after school today."

She gives me a big hug. Oh, how I love the fact that I get to work with my best friend. "Go with your gut and get out of your own head; that's half the battle."

The kids all start running back in and before I know it, school is over. I peek out the window of my classroom and see that Jax is waiting at the curb. *God, he's beautiful.* Will I ever get past that? Who am I kidding?—I don't want to. I gather my things and make my way to his car.

"Hi, Jax."

He pulls me up against him and brushes his lips upon mine. *Sweet Jesus, they are soft!* He tastes like vanilla and spice. It's a good thing he is holding me close to him, otherwise I would be in a puddle at his feet right now. He opens the car door, guides me in, and then tosses my stuff in the back.

"Where are we going?" I ask. He's driving like a man on a mission!

"My place. We are going to sit down and talk about why you feel the need to run away from me and ignore my calls."

"Oh."

He pulls my hand away from my ear. "Yeah, *oh.*"

WE REACH THE IVORY tower in the sky, in record time. He says nothing the entire ride, but I can tell he is deep in thought because he is stroking his chin again. We step into the elevator as the doors close and my heart begins to flutter. I'm flushed almost to the point of fainting. He looks over at me, his eyes cutting into my core.

"Lucky for you my mum raised a gentleman, otherwise I would throw you up against that wall and fuck your brains out until you tell me everything. I sense there is more to you and your life that you are not sharing."

I can't believe he just said that! The doors open and my chin is still on the ground. In one quick motion, he turns around, scoops me up, and carries me into the living room. He gently puts me on top of the bar, pours himself a scotch and then smirks at me. "Do you need anything?

"Water, please," my voice comes out in nothing but a squeak. He hands me my glass, then takes off his jacket, and loosens his tie.

He pulls my hand away from my ear, "Times up, woman. Talk. Why the fuck do you keep running away from me?"

I take a steadying breath. "Jax, this is a hell of a way to have a conversation, don't you think?"

He pulls me towards him, landing his rock hard body up against mine. His long, hard cock is hitting me right at my core, and I whimper. He leans in and starts putting feather light kisses on my lips, my cheeks, down my neck, and up to my ear where he starts to nibble on the lobe… *oh sweet, Jesus, I can't think!* How could I even form a sentence? Let alone talk. "I'll say it again." He puts a smirk on his beautiful face… "Please tell me why you're running…is that better?"

Time for a mental pep talk, Raven. Take a deep breath. "When you're this close to me, I can't think. Hell, I can barely form a complete sentence," I confess.

He throws his hands up. "So, then why the fuck do you run?"

I'm almost embarrassed. I can't even raise my eyes to him. "Because I can very easily lose myself in you. You're too much, too intense. I'm a simple girl, and my sex life was very little and very bad."

He lifts my chin so our eyes meet. "Look. At. Me," he demands. I look into his eyes and there it is, that look that cuts clear into my soul. "Raven, did you ever stop to think that maybe I don't want someone with a vast sexual past. Maybe I don't want someone that is like everyone else, so fake and materialistic. Maybe, just maybe, I'm looking for someone who is sweet and kind, a person who cares about someone other than herself. You can't decide for me what I want and what I can handle. I can do that on my own."

I have a white-knuckle grip on the bar. "There's a lot about me you don't know."

He takes a deep breath, staring into my eyes. "Then you need to let me in, otherwise how will I ever know?"

"Okay," I whisper. Was that my voice? Oh boy, what did I just agree to and why did I agree so quickly? It's okay, this will be fine… don't panic.

He reaches in and softly kisses my lips. "Do you trust me?"

I nod, "Jax, that was never a question. I do." He lifts me off the bar and carries me to his bedroom; it's bigger than my whole apartment. He places me gently on the bed and removes my shoes. He is crouched between my legs, staring up at me with his amazing baby blues. He takes my hand and kisses my wrist. His lips linger there and chills run up my spine.

"I want to discover every inch of you, there will be no rushing and no running. Just you and me, in the here and now." He works his lips up and down my arms, kissing each of my fingertips. My breathing begins to get heavier as his tongue runs up the inside of each finger. He places a kiss in the palm of my hand never once averting his eyes away from mine. He lifts my sweater off and starts kissing my neck. When he reaches my ear he stops, "When you tug on this ear, it makes me crazy. I can't see straight. I just want to nibble it and lick it," he whispers.

Now I understand why he's always pulling my hand from my ear. "Oh," is all I can manage as a response.

"Yeah, *oh*," he barely whispers.

Before I know it, he's working that tongue down my chest. He rubs my nipples through my bra and they become instantly hard. He kisses and nibbles at each one of them, taking his time, driving me insane. Oh my God, he can just hang out here doing this forever and I will be very happy. Just as I finish that thought, he starts working his way down my body. He unbuttons my jeans and slowly pulls them off. "Raven, do you know how beautiful you are?"

I shake my head slowly, he has rendered me speechless. He stands up and removes his shirt and I think I'm going to hyperventilate. He has a frigging *V!* I want to run my tongue up and down his chest, but it seems, he has other plans. He lifts my foot and pulls my ankle to his lips. He peppers light kisses all the way up my leg, working his way up to the inside of my thigh. When he reaches the top, he stops and picks up the other foot to start the process all over again. He kisses his way up my tummy and in an instant has my bra above my head and my breasts are exposed to him. He begins slowly licking and nibbling my nipples; first one, and then the other. The more turned on he is getting, the heavier his accent is getting which is really hot. In a flash he has my panties off and he is heading south!

"Jax, I never..." but before I can say anymore, he is between my legs, kissing, licking, and nibbling. Lord, I don't know what he is doing, but my whole body is tingling, its magical and all for me. The entire time, his eyes are watching me; becoming darker, hooded, and I can tell we are far from done. He puts one finger inside me and starts to slowly work in and out of my body. On each outward stroke, he gathers my wetness and brings it up to circle my clitoris before repeating the whole tortuous process. My body is quivering and there is a buzzing in my ears. I really think my head is going to explode. My skin is flushed. I am at the peak of what is going to be an epic orgasm when Jax just stops.

"Sorry, baby, you're so wet and tight. I need to be buried deep in you when you come." Jax removes his pants and I get my first look at him totally naked and I think I'm going to pass out. He sees the look of fear on my face. "Don't worry, I'll go very slowly."

He's huge! He puts on a condom; I'm thankful that he has his wits, because I sure don't. I feel him at my opening, but he only works in a little bit before he stops and closes his eyes for a moment. When he opens them, his eyes find mine. "I want to work every inch in very slowly so you feel it all. There is only one chance for a first and I want our first to be spectacular." Propped on his knees, he brings my legs around his waist. He clasps both of my hands in his, above my head. He works himself in and out, stretching me, and going deeper with each move. When he is finally all the way in, he stops. I don't understand why but then I see the look on his face and can tell he is fighting to control the tidal wave that is coming. His eyes are closed and his head is tilted all the way back; his beauty and chiseled face mesmerizes me. He leans down and kisses me. When he starts to move again, it's slowly as if to ensure I feel every inch of him, gliding rhythmically in and out of my body.

He changes our position and tilts me so that he is hitting the tip of my cervix, and then starts to increase the speed of his thrusts. *Oh, God!* I start to whimper as my body begins to climb, I never knew that sex could be this amazing. "Don't come, Raven; hold it. I want us together when we fall."

He can't be serious? "I'm trying, Jax, but I'm losing it!" I cry. He stops. Why is he stopping again?! "Oh, sweet Jesus, and all that is holy, please don't stop!"

He's growling again and it's so fucking hot! "Slow, baby, real slow. I want this to last." He's buried deep within me, rocking up and down, then side to side; he circles right, then left. He leans down, devoting all of his attention to my nipples again. He pulls my nipple between his teeth and I scream as he concentrates on first one, then the other. He pulls out really slow and I think he's going to go back in really slow but all of a sudden, he slams into me! Stars, rockets . . . you name it and I see it. I'm yelling and I don't even feel like it's me!

"Jax, are you there yet?"

"Yes, for the love of God, *yes!*" His voice is low and his accent really heavy. "Raven, look into my eyes *now!*" he yells. Our eyes lock and, for a split second, I see him . . . I mean really see him, and I feel like I can't breathe.

"Oh *fuck!*" we both scream. A heat rushes over my whole body and I can feel him twitching inside of me. My body is trembling. He's looming over me; both of us breathing hard, just trying to get some oxygen into our lungs. He starts kissing me, long and slow, and all I can do is hum. He ditches the condom and continues kissing my lips so softly. I curl into him and finally find a calm within me that I never had before.

His eyes are darker and so intense. "You're beautiful, sweetheart."

He starts kissing his way down my chest and my body is buzzing. He runs his tongue around my belly button really slowly as he nibbles his way down my body and parts my legs. His tongue is soft, yet firm. And all too quickly, he has me worked into a ball of nerves. "You want to come again, sweetheart?"

I nod, "Oh God, yes." He stops again. Now I'm fucking growling!

"Hold on, baby, I want more, too. I'll always want more with you."

He puts on another condom and, this time, he gets us both there a little quicker. We roll into another orgasm together and I'm totally spent. I just lie here sprawled across Jax. He pulls the comforter over us, "Sleep now, my beautiful girl," he whispers.

I drift off, dreaming of the beautiful man whose arms I'm wrapped up in.

I'M WARM . . . ALMOST TOO warm. My eyes flutter open and I realize where I am. My head is on Jax's chest and my arm and leg are wrapped around him. I try to undo myself without waking him, but apparently, he's already awake and I notice him staring at me.

"Um, hi."

He graces me with a crooked smile and his blues are twinkling. "Um, hi yourself, sweetheart."

I jump up, "What time is it?"

He doesn't move. "It's early yet, no worries. Just let me enjoy this for a little bit." He pulls me back down so I'm on top of him; his morning erection wedged between us, hitting me in just the right spot.

"Jax, I need to get back to my place and get ready for work."

He sighs, "I know, but I need you more… cut me a little slack here. I just woke up from a wonderful evening with the most beautiful girl curled up next to me. Right now my cock needs to be buried in her." His hand slides down my body. I should be offended by some of the things he says, when we're intimate, but with the hint of the British accent, it has the opposite effect. His dirty talk makes me totally wet and ready for him. He leans over and grabs a condom from the bedside table, slipping it on quickly. He lifts me up and then impales me on to his cock. "Take the lead, baby, I know you can; just let loose and feel me buried, balls deep inside you."

I start to move slowly up and down, clenching my core muscles as I go. I knew Pilates classes would pay off. He holds my hips and I lean back, allowing him to go even deeper. He leans up as I arch my chest and he flicks my nipples with his tongue. First, the right, then the left, and back again. That's all it takes, I'm at the top of the cliff, ready to fall. "Are you ready, baby?" he asks as he pulls me back towards him.

"I'm there," I whimper.

"Open your eyes and look at me!"

Oh God, there it is! "*Now!*" We fall off the cliff; it's an amazing feeling. I crash into him and just hold on, waiting for the quivering to stop. There is something so deep and intimate at the way he demands my eyes on his when we come together.

"Jax, why do you demand my eyes?"

His eyes find mine again and it's so intense. "When you're at the top of the cliff and ready to fall, it's at that point there, in a split second, that I can see all the way into your soul. And I know you're real and all mine. Now, let's shower before you have to go." He carries me into a huge bathroom and places me on the vanity while he gets everything ready for our shower. He has the most amazing shower! It has four heads, hitting us from every direction, and at the top is a huge round disk that water falls from; like a giant cloud in the sky.

He begins to worship every inch of my body while paying special attention to my nipples, then he drops to his knees. *Sweet Jesus!* He lifts my leg and places my foot on his shoulder, burying his face, he starts kissing, licking, nibbling . . . one finger in, then two. His thumb swipes over me and that's all she wrote—I'm done. I pull his hair, riding the wave. I feel his finger start moving my moisture from front to back, and I panic. "Jax, I've never had anal sex. I don't know if I can."

He doesn't stop. "Relax, baby, not today… just a little fun." Working his finger in the back, his tongue plays up front while his other hand reaches up to play with my nipples. I scream, my knees buckle, he has me totally spent. He looks up at me, his eyes twinkling, "I could watch you come undone all day; it's such a beautiful sight."

I feel like I'm floating on a cloud, I only pray that I don't come crashing back to earth, anytime soon.

JAX GETS ME BACK to my place in record time; Manhattan traffic seems to be very afraid of his driving. He waits for me to change and get my stuff for work. I know Marco wants to ask a million questions but since Jax is here, he has to control himself.

"Baby girl don't forget we have a class tonight. Are we meeting there or will you come back here first?"

That's my reminder to grab my gym bag, "We'll meet there."

"What kind of class do you have?" Jax inquires.

I smile at him because I know what he's going to be thinking. "Marco and I do Pilates classes twice a week." I explain. He raises one eyebrow and I try not to laugh. I know I'm going to give my instructor an extra thank you tonight.

I'VE NEVER SEEN ANYONE handle New York traffic like Jax does, it's like they are moving out of the way for him. We pull up to my school, and he helps gather all my stuff for me. We get out of the car and Jax turns me to face him. "When can I see you again?"

I don't want to be one of those weak girls, waiting on his every whim. "I'm not sure, let's see what our schedules look like."

He grabs me and pulls my hand from my ear. "I told you what that does to me," he says, before he gives me a very deep and sensual kiss. "Telling me *you're not sure*, is not a good answer. While you're looking at your schedule, just think of what is waiting for you," he says with a painstakingly beautiful smile. He gets back in the car and takes off.

I get all my stuff settled in my classroom—still flustered. I jump when the phone in the room rings. When I answer it, it's Sheryl from the office, informing there is a delivery for me that I need to come and pick up. I thank her, hang up and head to the office. I get to the office and there is a coffee just the way I like it and a box with a huge piece of the apple pie in it, and a note:

> Raven,
> You didn't have breakfast and I wanted you to be thinking about me, and all I will do to you when I see you again.
>
>   Your Jax xo

Sheryl starts to laugh. "What are you laughing about?" I can tell she is happy for me.

"Honey, in the three years you've worked here, I've never seen you look so happy."

All I can say is, "Oh." but I know I have a ridiculous smile. I go back to my room, enjoying my breakfast. He signed it *Your Jax* . . . could he really be mine? I need to stop this daydreaming before it gets me into trouble.

MY DAY FLIES BY, which is good because I can barely concentrate on the work. When I get to the gym, Marco is already warming up.

"Okay, girl, I want all the dirt, I can't believe you didn't call me and let me know you were spending the night with him. Didn't you think I would worry?"

Shit, I forgot. "Oh." I think he's pissed off.

"Yeah, well, that seems to be your answer for everything lately."

First he wants me to go for it, and now he's getting mad? "I'm sorry. You're right, I should have told you, but it just happened so fast."

He laughs, "Well, I hope not!" he says with a knowing smirk.

"Very funny, wiseass. The sex was mind blowing and . . . I enjoyed it! I can't believe it."

He hugs me. "I tried to tell you that but you never listen to me, baby girl."

My feelings are all over the place. "Well, he wants more. Just what that means, I have no idea. I don't want to rush this and screw it all up. For the first time, in too long, I am actually happy and comfortable—and that scares the hell out of me!"

We start our warm up. "Just take it at a pace that works for you and if he really cares, he will understand. How much did you tell him about your past anyway?"

Tears instantly fill my eyes and I fight to hold them back. "I told him almost everything; I didn't give him too many details about my ex. He doesn't need to know that he beat me, to within an inch of my life. I don't want pity."

He wipes away a tear, "You know if someone digs, they will find the police reports?"

"If it comes up, I'll deal with it, but for now, I just want to experience normal." *Who am I kidding? I don't think normal is in my dictionary.*

"Raven, have you told him about the adoption yet?" He changes the subject slightly. I glance at Marco and I can tell something is bugging him, but I'm guessing he's not ready to share.

"No, maybe in time, but for now, I want to keep it simple," I reply. He shakes his head. He's obviously disappointed in my answer, but he doesn't keep pushing. I start to ask what's bothering him but class starts, so I drop it.

CLASS WAS BRUTAL BUT good. It was just what I needed to give my mind a break for a few hours.

"Want to grab a pizza? Or do you have plans with Jax?" Marco sounds like he is almost pleading.

"Pizza sounds great. I'll meet you out front."

When I step outside, Marco is yelling at someone. It looks like he is getting ready to slam him to the ground, but I distract him. "What the hell is going on?" The guy rushes off but not before getting a picture of me.

"Baby girl, that guy was a reporter and he is looking for a story about the girl that Jaxson Phillips is 'nailing.'"

What the fuck? "You're kidding, right?"

He's shaking his head as we start making our way down the street, "Afraid not, dear, the hounds have been released and they are circling for blood."

On the way, we stop and pick up a bottle of red wine and Ray's pizza—my kind of comfort food. We are a block away from home when Jax's phone rings. "Hello? I can't believe you have me carrying a second phone, why?"

He laughs, "Why not, sweetheart? I like knowing it's just for me. I don't share, Raven. *Ever.*"

I need to tell him what happened and I don't think he is going to be happy. "Jax, listen, a reporter was waiting outside the gym for me tonight, asking questions. Marco handled it, but the guy took my picture." Oh no, he's really quiet.

"I'm so sorry, they must have figured out who you were from Saturday night. Is Marco with you now?"

I sigh, "Yes, we're walking home now."

"*Walking*? You're walking home?" he yells, "Put Marco on the phone *now!*"

Wow, he sounds pissed. "Marco, Jax wants to talk to you." I hand him my spare phone and Marco cocks his head, giving me a curious look when he takes the phone.

"Hey, Jax, what's up?" Marco holds the phone away from his ear.

"Marco, what exactly did the reporter say?" Jax asks loud enough for me to hear. Marco tells him what the reporter said. "Okay, I'll handle the press, but why are you walking home instead of taking a cab?"

Marco looks at me for help but I put my hands up and just keep walking. "Jax, we do this every week and Raven is safe with me. Can I say the same thing about you?"

Why does Marco have to poke a burning fire? "Don't be an arse, Marco. I would never, knowingly put her in danger."

I can tell neither one is happy. "Hold on, Jax, I'll give you back to Raven." Marco hands me the phone back.

"When can I see you?" Just like that, he is done with that part of the conversation and moving on to the next.

"Saturday, if that works for you." He doesn't say anything and I look at the phone thinking maybe the call dropped, but then I hear him take a deep breath.

"I'm not waiting a whole week. How about Wednesday?"

Before I can even give him an answer he declares, "Wednesday. Dinner. I'll pick you up at seven."

I squeak out, "Okay." And with that, he hangs up! Truth is, I didn't want to wait till the weekend but I didn't want to seem like I was needy and desperate. I don't know who I think I'm kidding, when it comes to Jax—*I am needy and desperate.*

"So, I take it you're seeing him again? Even though you're going to be in the spotlight."

I want to see him; he is working his way under my skin. "I'll have to tell him the rest of the story. I feel like I don't have a choice, and it has to be sooner rather than later. Do you have a problem with Jax? You seem upset tonight."

He shakes his head. "I just worry about you, baby girl, that's all." By the time we reach home, both of us are lost in our own thoughts; our appetites are gone and we just head off to bed.

I TRY TO SLEEP, but I keep seeing those beautiful eyes and then they are being pulled away from me. I end up tossing and turning all night, finally giving up now, at 3:30 a.m., I start grading papers, instead. Morning comes, and I'm dragging ass. I head to my favorite Starbucks and Jax is sitting in the corner, smiling at me with his twinkling baby blues and I'm done. Good thing they already know my order, because the man renders me speechless. He gets up and pulls my chair out for me. "Good morning, sweetheart."

I wave to Max. I'm getting used to having him always around. "Morning, Jax, can I expect to see you here every morning?"

He smirks. "Well, I am typically at this exact spot every morning but I usually come here a little later. Now that I know you come here every day, around this time, to answer your question, yes."

I have to laugh at him. "Well, I would love to sit with you all day but I have to get to work. Have a great day."

I get up to leave and he walks me to the door, he pulls me into his arms and he brushes his lips over mine. "I will, now that I have seen you." He gives me a toe-curling kiss before sending me off to work. God, he is so sweet and beautiful. My stomach knots, waiting for the other shoe to drop, but hoping it doesn't.

I see Mick on my way to school and give him his breakfast. "Raven, can I walk with you for a little bit?"

I can tell something is bothering him. "Of course, Mick, everything okay?"

He's apprehensive. "Your friend, Jax, brings me breakfast when you can't. He asked me about you."

I have to laugh, "Did he? He's a good guy, Mick. How are the nightmares, any better?"

He shrugs, "Some days are better than others, what about you?"

I squeeze his hand. "Some days better than others for me too, Mick."

The bell rings and I hug Mick before running into school. I get settled in my room when Jackie comes in, looking a little flustered. "Hey, girl, is there a problem?" Her eyes are wide which is unusual; not much rattles Jackie.

"I'm not sure. I had playground detail this morning and I just felt like I was being watched. I know it's crazy, given the quality of security we have here, but I just felt like something was off."

Wow, not what I was expecting. "Did you let the front office know?"

She shakes her head. "Do you think I should? I mean, nothing happened, it was just a feeling."

I give her a reassuring hug. "I would just give them a heads up." The bell rings and starts off our day.

"Okay, but the kids are all coming in now. I'll talk to them at lunch time."

Jaxson

I JUST GET SETTLED in my office, when Duke rings to tell me that Michael Sr. is on his way.

Michael Sr. comes barreling into the door, "Hey, Jax, thanks for covering for me at school last week."

"I was more than happy to, mate." I grin.

"Oh, don't tell me you met Miss Raven?"

I laugh, "Yep, and we have been seeing each other outside of school. I took her to the charity event Saturday night."

He smiles, shaking his head at me. Suddenly, he lets out a big sigh and gets a somber look on his face, "Well, we have bigger problems. There is a reason I was not here, Jax, I only told Bella I was stuck in Atlanta."

"What the fuck is going on, Michael?" I already don't like the sound of this and I don't even know what *this* is.

He heads over to the bar and grabs a bottle of water. "A threat came through."

All right, not a big shock, that's for sure. "We get them all the time, what makes this one different?"

He takes a steadying breath. "They sent this." He gives me photos and they are of Junior and Bella at school. The next one is my mum and Junior at school.

"They came with a note. I gave a copy to the FBI and Interpol."

I'm trying to keep it together. "What did the note say?"

"*We can get to them at any time.*"

What the Fuck?! "Did you notify the school?"

He starts pacing. "Yeah, and I put an extra guard at the school."

The school already has good security, Max made sure of that. "What did the FBI and Interpol say?" Not that I expect them to do anything.

"They are looking into it, but I'm not holding my breath. Usually, when something like this happens, they don't do anything until something actually happens."

I'm just staring at the photos. "Did you tell Bella and Mum?"

He looks at me like I should know the answer. "No, I was waiting to tell you first, it's just… something is off."

I take a deep breath. "What do you mean by '*off*'?"

"Well, you're the high profile guy, not me!" he yells. "I'm a winemaker who runs a successful winery in Italy. I have no enemies, so why target my son and my wife?"

I pick up the phone and call Max. He needs to be informed about what is going on since he handles security for my whole family. I barely get off the phone with, Max, before he's running through the door. After turning everything over to Max, I remember something Raven mentioned. Max and Michael are studying the note and the pictures.

"You know, guys, Saturday night I took Raven to the charity function at Chelsea Pier and there were a lot of paparazzi. Then the other night, Raven said one of them showed up at the gym but her roommate, Marco, handled it. I'm just wondering if any of this could be connected."

Michael huffs, "You draw attention no matter where you go, so I would think anyone with you would get some attention, as well."

Max starts his usual pacing. "I would still like to talk to Raven and Marco, just to be on the safe side."

I pick up the phone to call the school. "Okay, I will give her a heads up that you're coming."

Max takes a deep breath and I know what's coming. "I also want to pull a background report on Raven and Marco, just as a precaution. I know you told me to wait but I think your waiting time is up."

"All right, Max, I know you're going to do what you have to do. Keep me posted."

Chapter Six

Raven

JACKIE COMES BACK AFTER lunch recess with a message from the front office for me. "Did you tell them about this morning?" I ask.

She seems calmer. "Yes. They said that Michael's father ordered some private security, and that's probably what was going on. What's the message about?"

I open it, "Apparently, Jax's security detail has some questions for me and he just wanted to give me a heads up. I need to let Marco know, too. I went on a date with him to a charity function Saturday night. The press had a field day with it. One of them followed Marco and me to the gym last night."

I know she understands about this kind of high profile stuff—she grew up with it. "Wow, that sucks. I know what it's like living in a fish bowl."

I fold the note up and give her my attention again. "I know, I can't begin to understand what that must feel like. Always having to watch everything I say and do, especially since my brain to mouth filter is on the fritz half the time!"

THE DAY IS FINALLY over and I find Max waiting outside for me. "Miss Raven, I will give you a ride home and we can talk along the way, if that's okay with you?"

I smile at him, "Sure, Max, but you can just call me Raven." I inform him as he opens the car door for me to get in.

He laughs at me. "I'm a gentleman and old habits die hard, Miss Raven." He closes the door after me and within a minute, he's made his way around to get into the driver's seat. "The man that approached you outside the gym, what did he look like?" he begins his inquisition as we pull away from the curb.

I have to think, it all happened so fast. "He was average, everything about him was average: height, weight, and looks. "

"Okay, how old do you think he was?"

I close my eyes to try and picture the guy, "He was maybe in his thirties."

As I glance at Max in the rear-view mirror, I can see such intensity in his eyes. He's focusing on every detail. "What exactly did he say to you?"

I see real concern on his face and I wonder what this is really about. "He didn't, he was having words with Marco when I stepped outside the gym. He saw me, snapped my picture, and then left without another word."

Before I know it we arrive at my apartment, and head upstairs. We find Marco isn't home yet. "Marco should be home soon, if you want to wait for him."

Max just nods. "You have a nice home."

I look around and smile. "Thank you. Would you like a cup of tea?"

He busies himself, looking at all my window and door locks, seemingly inspecting the security quality. "Sure," he replies.

I fix tea and then start to pull out my work. "Would you mind if I grade papers while you wait? A teacher's work is never really done."

He laughs, "That's no problem, Miss Raven. Would you like some help grading them?"

I will take help anytime when it comes to grading papers. "That would be great."

As we sit there, I study Max; I find him very interesting. He has a very heavy, British accent, where Jax's accent is only heavy when he's drinking or having sex. Max is shorter of the two, he keeps his hair short, and he always seems to have a five o'clock shadow with hints of grey in it.

"How long have you worked for Jax?"

He is very focused on the papers but glances up at me. "I've been employed by Jax for eight years."

I know Jax is thirty-three. "How old are you?" He gives me his attention again and I realize he has very light, pale-blue eyes.

He laughs, "Probably older than you think." And with that, the conversation was over.

After about an hour, all the papers are done and Marco comes strolling in. "Oh, hey, baby girl, didn't know you had company."

"Marco, this is Max, he does security for Jax and he has some questions for you about the reporter the other night." I inform him after introducing.

As they shake hands, I can see each one, eyeing the other up, not saying anything.

"Hi, Marco, I need to know what he said to you?"

Marco takes a deep breath. "He asked if I knew Raven and I asked what it was to him, he said *'I can get to them at any time.'* Then Raven stepped out, he snapped her picture, and ran away."

Max is pacing, he seems to do that a lot. "Did you notice if he had any identifying marks, such as: tattoos, scars, or maybe an accent?"

Marco shakes his head. "No, nothing. He was just creepy… should we be worried?"

"Jax takes security very seriously, I'm sure he will talk to Miss Raven about this later," he replies, walking back over to us. He shakes Marco's hand, turns, and wishes us a good evening before heading out the door.

Marco greets me with a giant smile. "Well, that was interesting to come home to, and . . . what a hunk of a security guy."

I roll my eyes, "I swear you have sex on the brain all the frigging time!"

He cocks an eyebrow at me. "Hey, the guy is very built, very good-looking… kind of Daniel Craig like, and he has a frigging accent! Of course I have sex on the brain!"

Marco is right, Max could very easily pass for Daniel Craig, maybe it's the whole security and James Bond thing. "Marco, all I did was go on a date. Now I'm being hounded by the press and have extra security at my school!"

"So Jax put extra security at the school?" He glances up from flipping through the mail on the table.

I gather up all my papers, "Yeah, just a couple of dates and now this!"

"Yeah, dates, with the most eligible bachelor in the world, who is also on Forbes billionaire list for the *4th year* in a row, I might add. You don't get like that and not make some enemies along the way, you know."

I glance at my watch, "Marco, if we leave now, we can still make it to our kickboxing class."

"Okay, but then we are going for drinks," he demands. I nod in agreement and we grab our gear, then head out.

CLASS WAS BRUTAL TONIGHT but I really needed to get out some frustration and the bag is the best place for that. After we shower and change at the gym, we find a little Cuban bar that has wonderful tapas and are seated in a nice quiet booth, toward the back.

"So how do you feel about Jax?" Marco asks.

I have to laugh. "Well, just start off with a bang, why don't you? I really like him, Marco, a lot, but I feel like I'm out of my league with him. He's just so much, that's really the only way I can explain him and it scares me. I know

I'm going to get hurt, I'm going to fall hard—*oh fuck*, who am I kidding? I've already fallen hard and I don't want it to end."

He rubs my hand. "Baby girl, you need to trust yourself; you're a good person who has a lot to offer someone, so don't sell yourself short."

"You have to say that because you're my best friend."

He hugs me. "No, I'm saying that because it's the truth."

I study his face and I know what he's going to say, but I have to ask.

"You think I should tell him about the adoption . . . why?"

He takes a sip of his wine and waits before he answers my question. Almost like he is I processing his thoughts. "Raven, he needs to know. And if he is a keeper, you'll know . . . when he doesn't run."

"Maybe I'm the one who needs to be running, with all the threats and the spotlight."

He shakes his head. "No, baby girl, maybe it's finally time you *stop* running." We head back to the apartment in silence. I don't know, maybe I can be the more that Jax is looking for. We get upstairs and I head into my room to get ready for bed. As I brush my teeth I glance at my tiny shower. I would love to be in that shower in Jax's Ivory Tower. That shower was kick ass and so was the man I was in it with. I'm exhausted and head straight to bed.

I STROLL UP TO Starbucks and there he is, just like clockwork. "You don't have to meet me here every morning."

He brushes my lips with his then leans in and grates his teeth along my earlobe. "You're right—I don't have to, but I want to and I only do what I want, not what anyone else thinks I should."

"Oh," I whisper.

He grazes his teeth up my jaw to my ear, "Yeah, *oh*." He gives me a slow, sensual kiss, and then he's done. And just like that, I'm speechless. "Don't forget our date tonight, sweetheart." Forget the date? I'm still trying to pick my scrambled brains up off the ground!

"I won't forget, and thanks for the coffee and for Mick's breakfast. He may not say it but he appreciates it." He gives me that crooked smirk and then he's off with Max, not too far behind him.

I cross the street and give Mick his breakfast. "Thank you, Raven."

"Mick, walk with me to school." As we walk I ask him, "What can I do to help you move forward?" I know he is a good guy who has been to hell and back. He deserves a hand, and it's the least I can do. He's quiet, and I know this is hard for him. "Mick, let's sit for a bit, I'm early." We sit on the bench outside the school.

Mick's eyes wander, seemingly taking the surroundings in. "Raven, why is there more security at the school?"

Wow, nothing gets by him. "There have been some threats to Michael, and Jax wants to make sure he is safe," I answer.

After a few minutes of silence, "You, just being here and listening to me, are all the help I can handle right now. I will keep an eye on the school grounds, too—just to make sure."

I hug him. "Mick, you're a wonderful guy and someday, you'll realize it. I have to go in, the bell is going to ring. Have a great day." I look back over my shoulder and see that he stays put on the bench, watching the grounds and the kids running into the building.

When I get inside, I find two dozen of the Abracadabra Roses; they are so unusual and I can't help but stare at them. I pull out the card:

> *You render me speechless.*
> *Looking at you takes my breath away.*
>
> *Your Jax xo*

Well, I could say the same about him, too, that's for sure. I bring them to the classroom and the smell fills the room.

"Wow, Raven, they are so beautiful; very different." Jackie gapes at them.

I smile. "I know. Oh, Jackie, I'm really falling hard for this guy."

She smiles at me while smelling the roses. "Just approach the relationship with an open mind and an open heart." What did I ever do to have such great friends? Jackie, Marco, and even Mick are always worrying about me.

"You're such a great friend, Jackie." I hug her quickly before turning my attention to my students walking in.

THE DAY WENT BY smoothly and I rush to finish my after-class work. I decide to surprise Jax at Raiders, Inc. As I head to his building, I realize I know so little about this man. I walk in and ask the guard, "What floor is Jaxson Phillips' office?"

"Is he expecting you?"

I look up at him. "No, it was going to be a surprise."

He raises one eyebrow, looking at me like I'm a nut—who knows how many other women have tried getting into his office? "Mr. Phillips does not do surprises." I give him my ID and he rings Max. "Sir, I have a Miss Raven Anderson here, she says she is trying to surprise Mr. Phillips. Yes, of course, sir." I don't know what Max tells him but he immediately gives me a visitor pass and escorts me to the bank of elevators.

"What floor, sir?"

He holds the door for me. "I've been instructed to escort you up, Miss Anderson, top floor." When we get to the top, I thank him. He nods and the elevator doors close behind him.

I look around, taking in my surroundings and notice everything is glass. Everywhere I look, there is a view to die for; how does this man get any work done? There is a bevy of beautiful women at the reception area and they are all staring at me. I think this was a bad idea. I feel very inadequate, in comparison to them. Just as I decide to bail, a man walks up to me and introduces himself as Duke Jenson, Jax's assistant. "Hello, Miss Anderson, Mr. Fleming has instructed me to escort you to Mr. Phillips' office." He has a familiarity about him, but then I see Jax and I lose all reason.

"Hey, sweetheart, this is a nice surprise. What brings you here?"

I look at this man and I'm amazed; he is so beautiful. "I finished work early and I thought I would surprise you. It looks like you're busy."

He opens his arms for me. "I am never too busy for my beautiful girl." He pulls me close to him and I give him one of those toe-curling kisses that he always gives me. I'm sure all eyes are on us now.

"Wow, what did I do to deserve that?"

I stare into those deep, blue eyes and I could just melt right here. "Well, honestly, you rendered me speechless this morning with a wonderful cup of coffee and a kiss that blew me away. Then I get to school and there are two dozen of those beautiful roses, waiting for me. I thought I would brighten your day like you do mine."

We walk into his office and I'm blown away, I still don't know how he can get anything done with that view! I turn back around towards the door and lock it. He watches me, totally speechless. "Jax, tell your assistant to hold all your calls."

He walks to his desk and pushes a button on his phone, "Duke, I do not want to be disturbed for the next hour."

I pull him into one of the club chairs and he stares at me, intently. "I have decided I want to have my way with you. Please sit back and let me have a little fun."

He has the most beautiful smile on his face and his baby blues are twinkling. I flash him an eager and sultry smile. I get down on my knees, between his legs and keep my eyes locked on his. I brush my hand up his cock to undo his belt and he sucks in a breath. *He's really hard.* I find my prize and slowly work the head of his velvet cock. He has a white-knuckle grip on the chair— *oh, yeah, I've got him.* I run my fingertips up and down his V. He closes his eyes and tries to steady his breath. "Eyes on me, Jax."

His eye's lock onto mine; violet to blues. I want him to watch so he will always remember this moment. Slowly I dip my head down, licking the tip of his beautiful cock and never taking my eyes from his. My hair is loose and draped over to one side. His lips part and his tongue starts to slowly stroke them while I swirl my tongue around his massive cock head. I lick the vein all the way to the base and back up again. He just watches me, not saying anything. His breathing speeds up. I swirl around the top again, then I put my lips around his cock and go all the way down. I relax my gag reflex to take him even further and that's when he lets out a strangled moan. *Oh yeah, he's coming undone.* He has both hands wrapped around my head. I'm sure he's trying not to pound into me but once my hand finds the underside of his sac, he loses all control. His grip tightens as I go deeper. When I reach the head of his cock, I bare my teeth. Just like that he comes endlessly and I swallow every drop. He finally pulls me off of him and drags me up onto his lap. Even after what I have just done, he kisses me.

"You're so beautiful. This was a great way to release stress." He runs his thumbs up and down both my cheeks.

"Well, I know there is so much going on and you're worried about Michael, so I just wanted to lighten your day."

He looks at me, smiling like a Cheshire cat. "I think I can get the rest of my work done now, or I can call it a day and take you home. I could make love to you day and night but it still wouldn't be enough." He gifts me with his beautiful smile.

"I would love that, but I have to run now. I have a class at the gym."

He gives me a look like a wounded puppy. "What class?"

I'm going to see him tonight so I can't give in, even though I want to.

"I go to the gym two days a week for Pilates and two days a week for kick boxing. One day a week I try different things. This week its Krav Maga."

He leans in and kisses me softly. "Okay, I'll bring Epson salts tonight," he laughs. We both fix our attire before he walks me to the elevators. All eyes are on us, but he's only looking at me.

JAX IS AT MY place at exactly seven, that's good, because I'm starving. "I brought all the stuff to cook in tonight."

I panic, "That's nice, except I don't cook, so I have no pots, pans, or anything."

He laughs hysterically at me. I'm so glad that I'm his source of amusement. "Yeah, I figured that, so I came prepared." He wasn't joking. Max walks in, just then, with half of Bloomingdales' kitchen department! He gives me the Epson salts and shoos me to the tub for a much needed soak. Wow, I really needed this—every part of my body feels bruised. I put some music on, close my eyes, and relax. I recently put some new music on my iPod, everything from Ellie Goulding to Florence + The Machine. I close my eyes and sing along. After a nice long soak, I put on my robe and head to the living room. He pours me a glass of wine, and I sit back and watch the man work. "Sweetheart, I must tell you, I love your singing!"

Oh crap! I must have been singing loud enough for him to hear! "You weren't supposed to be listening, and stop smirking at me. A real gentleman would never smirk at a woman's singing."

He comes around the counter and pulls me into his arms. He pulls my ponytail back so I'm looking into his eyes; violet to blues. "Sweetheart, I could listen to your singing all day long." He reaches down and gently kisses my lips, nibbling and swiping his tongue across them. He searches my eyes and I want him right now! He lifts me up and I wrap my legs around his waist. He's hard as stone and I can't help but whimper. Just as he's about to lift me onto the counter, Marco comes flying through the door and I swear his chin hits the ground. I can't help but laugh at him. Jax lifts me into the chair and whispers, "We'll finish this later, sweetheart."

"Don't worry, Marco. I'm making enough for you to eat, too."

Marco grabs a glass of wine and sits next to me. "Have you guys thought about what you're going to say to Michael?"

Jax puts his wine glass down and cocks his head. "What do you mean, mate?"

He eyes us both. "You're dating his teacher, which is every boy's fantasy. You need to tell him something."

I look at them both, "I never thought about it."

"Babe, it's every guy's wet dream to have a teacher, that looks like you and then—"

"—Enough!" I silence him before he can continue. I can't have that visual stuck in my head!" They both have that faraway look. *Oh, my God, what the hell are they thinking?*

"Don't worry, Raven, I'll talk to my sister and see how she wants to handle it."

We all begin to eat and the food is fantastic: chicken franchisee, roasted new potatoes, and a salad. Marco grins at Jax and declares his new found love for him. It probably has to do with the cooking.

"Marco, were you born in New York?"

He shakes his head. "No, I was born and raised in Washington, D.C. What about you, I hear a slight accent."

Jax smiles. "I was born in Wales and lived there until I was thirteen. Which is when we moved to New York.Where were you born, Raven?" Jax asks me before taking another sip of wine.

Oh shit, I'm not ready for this conversation. I glance at Marco, hoping he can help me. "Raven and I grew up together in D.C.," he pipes up. *Okay.* I let out the breath I was holding. If Jax noticed my panic, I'm not sure. A nice espresso and pastry for desert, and I'm officially stuffed.

Marco excuses himself, leaving us alone. We get up from the table, not worrying about the dishes, and head into the living room to snuggle up on the couch. No stress; just us.

"Why did your family move to the States?" I ask as his thumb traces circles on my arm.

"There were more opportunities here, and the people didn't judge my mum for being a single parent."

I know I should tell him and this would be a good time, but I'm not ready.

"What made you and Marco decide on New York instead of D.C.?"

I've rehearsed this answer so many times that after a while, I started to believe it myself. "We both liked the East Coast and city life. It just seemed logical that New York should be home for us. After college, I applied for a job here, and Marco followed. Jackie came about three months later. Jackie and I were roommates in college."

Jax's phone rings and he excuses himself to get it. He looks at me as he's speaking to someone. "Okay, I'm on my way."

"I had a wonderful time, but I have to go. I'm sorry. Something came up. Can we get together Friday?"

I shake my head, "I can on Saturday. Friday night, Jackie and I are going out." I don't always want to be available, but who am I kidding? I am. He starts stroking his chin, a sure sign he's deep in thought.

"If that's my only option, then okay." He leans in and gently kisses my lips, slow and softly. I moan and he's all over me, our tongues doing a sexual dance, his hands are roaming my body. We pull apart and I want more, so much more. "I'll leave you with that. Since, you're busy on Friday, we'll have to continue this on Saturday." Just like that, he's out the door.

Jaxson

"MAX, WE NEED TO get to my sister's house right away. Michael called, he got another threat that he says we need to see," I order before I'm barely in the car.

"Jax, when the hell did this happen?" he asks, speeding off as soon as he starts the engine up.

"Just now, I think."

Michael is already outside when we pull up to his house. "This must be serious if you're outside, waiting for me."

The look on his face is not good. "Look, Jax, first, I had to tell your sister since she got the envelope before I could intercept it."

Michael hands it to me. Inside is a picture of Raven taken outside her gym with a note that says, *"No one is out of my reach, ever."*

Max grabs the envelope, reading it before he shifts his eyes to Michael. "How was this delivered to Bella?"

Michael opens the door, "I'll let you ask her yourself, come in."

Bella is sitting in the living room, staring into space. Max puts the envelope down in front of her, "Bella, how was this delivered?" he asks.

Her eyes snap back into focus and she stares at the picture. "Max, I never heard anything, but Vito was barking. I went out to see why, and it was at the front door. I never saw anything. Why wasn't I told about the other threats? Why was I not aware that my brother is dating my son's teacher? Why does everyone feel it's okay to keep me in the fucking dark?!"

My sister is really pissed off and I'm not sure if it's at me, Michael, or both of us. "Bella, where is Junior?"

Michael steps up, "He's fine, Jax. He's upstairs watching *Doctor Who.*"

Bella turns to me. "Jax, what about Mum and Raven? Are they aware?"

I shake my head, "No, we weren't sure if the threats were real, and it all happened very quickly."

She glares at me, "Why did you take Raven to the charity function on Saturday? It's so high profile. You never do that."

No matter what I do, I'm always fucked. "I didn't find out about the threats until Tuesday. I try to keep my personal life private, but with all the latest acquisitions, it seems the public wants to know my every move. Bella, if I go out, you yell at me. If I don't, you yell at me!"

Max grabs my arm. "Jax, did you know Raven was adopted?"

Well, that floored me. "No, but apparently you do. What else do you know?"

"Not much. Her adoption records are marked as classified, which is really strange. She did have an abusive boyfriend. He beat her pretty badly before she was able to get a restraining order against him."

I feel like I'm in a bloody pinball game that just keeps tilting. "Jax, I take it by the look on your face that you didn't know any of this?"

I take a steadying breath. "She mentioned an ex, but not to that extent. Tonight, at dinner, we talked about where we were born and grew up. I told her we were originally from Wales. Marco said he was from D.C. When I asked Raven, Marco said they grew up together. However, Raven told me that she met Marco while volunteering at a shelter. She said his parents threw him out when he told them he was gay. She told me her mum died when she was fifteen and she left home right after that."

I didn't think I needed to share with everyone why she left home—after all, it was her story to tell. "Max, do you think Raven could be the target in all of this, or is it me? Now that they have seen us in public together, does she have a target on her back?"

Max starts pacing. "My first thought would be that she is just collateral damage in this. However, the adoption thing is making my hair stand on end." I know when he paces, he's processing information, but right now, it's fucking driving me nuts. I thank God when he stops.

"Do you think we need to bring her in on what's happening? I'm sure if I ask her directly, she would tell me, at least, I'd like to think so."

"What do you know about her roommate Marco?" Michael furrows his brows at me.

"I ran a background check on him at the same time I ran one on Raven and he's clean. Very protective of Raven, though. However, he just showed up one day."

First, I find out my girl is adopted and it's classified, and now, I find out her roommate just showed up one day! What the fuck?! Michael and Bella are both staring at me, probably waiting for me to lose it. I get up and grab Max's arm. "What do you mean, he *just* showed up one day?"

"Look, Jax, I don't like this anymore than you do. It's seems like they didn't meet until she left home. He's older than she is, so they didn't go to school together or even grow up in the same neighborhood. He just suddenly appeared in her life one day."

Max finally stops pacing. "Jax, I think for now, we should put extra security on everyone, and we need to find out from Raven about the adoption. I just feel like it's a missing piece of the puzzle."

I need answers and I need to keep everyone safe. "All right, but I want to talk to her about it myself—alone."

Bella grabs my arm, "Jax, are you going to call and tell Mum what's going on?"

The last thing I want to deal with right now is my mum. "Not just yet, Bella, I'm not even sure myself what the fuck is going on!"

Chapter Seven

Jaxson

I GET TO THE office early after trying to catch Raven at Starbucks. She never showed up there this morning but after racing to her school, I discovered she went in early. At least—for now—she's safe. "Everything okay, sir?" Duke asks, pulling me out of my thoughts.

"You're early today." I snap. I'm pissed, but I don't want to take it out on my employees.

"Yes, I just have some paperwork to catch up on. Can you get my sister on the line, please?"

"She's already in your office, waiting for you."

Wow, I wonder if she is going to rip into me, yet again. I head into my office and prepare myself to deal with Bella. "Hey, you're here early."

She gets up and hugs me, "Cut the bullshit, Jax, you really like her a lot, don't you?"

Bella and I can read each other like an open book, so I can't bullshit her.

"Why wouldn't she tell me something so simple, like being adopted? Does she think I would think less of her?"

"No, Jax, I really don't think so. Anyone who knows you would know you're not that kind of person. That's why I think there is much more to the story than we know. Did you go talk to her this morning?"

I sit in one of the chairs, remembering Raven on her knees, and fuck, I'm hard again! "I tried to catch her for coffee but she was already in school."

Bella looks at her watch. "I was so preoccupied last night, I almost forgot parent teacher conferences are today and tomorrow."

Well, at least I know Raven's not running away from me for a change. "What time is your meeting with her?"

She gets up and heads toward the door. "In an hour, so I have to go. I know, don't say anything, but you better get to the bottom of this and quick, oh and call Mum, please."

I don't want to make that call but Bella leaves me no choice. She is right, Mum needs to hear it from *me* about what is going on. The problem is that, I have *no* idea what the fuck is going on! Bella gives me a final wave before heading out. I take a deep breath as I pick up the phone and dial Mum, knowing I'm going to get an earful. I'm surprised she hasn't just shown up here and taken me to task for putting extra guards on her without telling her. She must be pissed. She answers on the first ring, and usually, I can't even get her to answer the fucking phone!

"Hey, Mum, how are you?" I take a deep breath, and wait for the storm—my mother.

"Don't you give me that *how are you* stuff, I already know that something is not right. If you were here, I'd box your ears, lad."

I can never get anything past this woman. "Mum, you need to calm down. I put extra security on everyone because there've been some pictures and notes that I'm concerned about."

Wow, she's growling? This is a first. "Jaxson James Phillips, when did all of this happen and why am I just finding out now?"

When she uses my middle name, I know I'm in deep shit. "Now, Mum, remember your high blood pressure."

Probably not a good idea to mention that. "Don't even think of going there, son. There's no need for you to remind me about my blood pressure. Just tell me everything, from the beginning. Maybe if you'd done that already, we wouldn't have to worry about my pressure."

My mum and I are very close. I don't have a problem telling her everything I know about Raven or about the different pictures and threats. She's been very quiet since I've finished. "Mum, are you there?"

"Yes, son, I'm just surprised. First, that you have kept me in the dark about the threats—you usually tell me everything. And second, that you have finally met someone that holds your interest for more than five minutes and this is how I find out about her. Really? I understand your need to protect us; you've always felt like it was your duty to keep us safe. But you need to keep Isabella and me informed about what's going on. We're not helpless women."

I know they are capable of taking care of themselves, but it's not easy for me to give up that kind of control. I've watched over them my whole life. "I know, but it's just hard for me. I want to keep everyone safe. And after getting burned by Erica, I never thought I would be vulnerable again. I'm at such a loss with Raven. She makes me crazy mad and then crazy happy. She runs from me, *a lot*, and I don't understand why." Maybe she can shed some light on this, because I sure can't.

"I raised you and Isabella to be direct and honest. Have you asked her, point blank, why she runs?"

I laugh, "Of course, and she said I'm intense and too much. Mum, I don't think I'm like that."

Now it's my mum who's laughing. "Son, life is not rainbows, fields of flowers, and butterflies. Its compromise, and unfortunately, you're not very good at that. I think it is time I met my grandson's teacher."

Oh, crap. "Mum, can you just try and go easy on her? She has already pulled a runner more times then I like to admit to." I know that no matter how much I protest, she'll just do whatever she feels she should. We hang up, and I know, for sure now, that I'm so screwed.

Raven

MY NEXT PARENT IS Mrs. Vizzano, Michael Jr's mom. She is as beautiful as her brother. This is going to be awkward. "Hi, Mrs. Vizzano, please, have a seat."

"Please, call me Bella. I have to ask, have you figured out what you're going to tell Michael Jr about you and Jax?"

This family is amazing. Everyone is so open and direct with each other. "Well, I can see that you and Jax are very much alike; you both jump right in," I laugh.

"I'm not one to beat around the bush, and neither is Jax."

I'm embarrassed that I'm involved with a student's relative, but I have to deal with this. "I have never dated someone related to one of my students, so I'm at a loss. Do you have any suggestions?" I'm hoping she has some ideas.

"I spoke to my husband about it and he started saying something about every boy's wet dream. I just cut him off," she giggles.

"Yeah, Jax and my roommate, Marco, started in on that and I cut them off, too. Guess it's a guy thing. Bella, I will do whatever you think is best for, Michael."

"I think we should just tell him you and Jax are friends and leave it at that. Sometimes if you make more about it, then it becomes a problem," she suggests.

I like her; she doesn't pull any punches. "Okay, I agree with you. As far as school, Michael is doing great. He struggles a little with math, but my co-teacher, Jackie, has been working with a small group of boys on mental math. It seems to be helping." I show her some of Michael's papers.

"If you think he needs a tutor, let me know."

I love it when parents take an active role in their children's education. So many just think the work is done when the school bell rings. "He is a very sweet boy and pleasure to have in class. He's very respectful of others and tender hearted."

She smiles. "Thank you, his dad is away a lot so sometimes Jax has to step in to help. We are a very close-knit family."

I wonder how much influence Jax has had with Michael. "Well, it shows. He's a great little boy."

After Bella leaves, I only have one more conference and then I am done for the day.

I PACK UP AND head home. As I round the corner to my building, I see Jax leaning against the car. Damn, he's beautiful. I can't help myself; I just stop and take him in. He's wearing a fitted, charcoal-grey suit with a dark, violet shirt and a frigging bow tie!

"Hey," I reach up to kiss him, taking note of his stolid expression. "Are you okay?"

"We need to talk. Is Marco home?" His eyes burn through me.

I shake my head, "No, he won't be home for, at least, two hours. Come on up."

As we head upstairs, I can tell he's upset. We are barely in the door, and he spins me around. "Why are you hiding the fact that you're adopted?"

I almost laugh, thinking, yeah, he is just like Bella, but then it hits me— *he knows.* "How do you know? I never mentioned it." He probably had Max run a check on me!

"This showed up last night." He shows me the picture that was taken outside the gym, with a threat. "I had to have Max run a check on you. You need to understand, I am high profile and with that, comes a whole lot of shit. Why are your records sealed and marked classified? Raven, what are you hiding?"

Clearly, he is really pissed off. But I think I should be the one who's pissed off. He can't just invade my privacy like that. "Jax, please leave."

He glares at me. "What? You're just going to throw me out—without an explanation? You need to know that I put security on you and Marco, as well as my whole family. You're going to have to tell me *what the fuck* is going on!"

I understand that he is worried and upset, but this is private. "Jax, this is a very private matter for me and the only one who knows all the details is Marco. I don't know if telling you is the right thing to do. It may put you in more danger."

He searches my eyes for the answers, I think. "Just tell me. We will deal with it together. I have a lot of resources at my disposal." He doesn't move, and I realize he's not leaving until he knows everything. Maybe Marco is right. Maybe it's time to share this with him. If he is a keeper, he won't run for the hills.

"Okay, Jax. I was born in California. My mother was a heart surgeon and my father was an FBI agent. I was seven-years-old when I was kidnapped."

Jaxson

I FREEZE AT THE word *kidnapped.* I'm feeling dumbfounded, not believing what I'm hearing. I step closer towards her, still in disbelief. "Oh, sweetheart, please don't stop now, not when you're on a roll."

She sits down and takes a deep breath. "At first, the FBI thought I was kidnapped because of something that my father might have been working on, but as it turned out, it had to do with my mother. She was a top heart surgeon, who had just perfected some new technique, that could possibly save the life of a very bad person. That person was the head of a Chicago Mafia crime family. I was being held so that my mother would perform the surgery."

Raven

I LOOK UP AT Jax and he raises an eyebrow at me, so, I continue. "In the process of all this, my father and his partner, Joseph Adessi, were able to rescue me. During the rescue, my father was shot. He lingered for two weeks in ICU before he died. My mother performed the surgery but the man didn't make it. My mother felt she sent my father to his death, and she killed herself. I was left in the care of Joseph. He brought me to Washington D.C. to live with him. Joseph didn't feel like I was safe, and after speaking with the director of the FBI, they agreed that I was young enough to be adopted and have a total name change. I was a very scared seven-year-old. I stopped talking and turned inward, trusting no one. I was entered into the Witness Protection Program and sent to live in a private boarding school in England. Eventually, a very nice family adopted me. They put me into therapy, and I was able to put the past behind me and move forward. That was, until, my adopted mother died from breast cancer. Well, then you know the rest. Oh, and while we're at full disclosure, my father and mother had a lot of insurance, which Joseph invested for me, so I'm a very wealthy woman.

His face turns to stone. "So when you and Marco were supposedly living on the streets, you really weren't?"

I shake my head, "No. I used some of the money for a small apartment that Marco and I lived in until I went to college. Now if you're done, can you please leave?"

His eyes cut me to the core. "Oh no, sweetheart, I'm not going anywhere, and we are far from done here. How did you meet Marco? He is older than you, so I know it wasn't in high school."

I take some steady breaths. "I told you, I met Marco when I was volunteering at a shelter. I would go help out one day a week. It made me feel like I had some sort of family. He was also a volunteer there and we just clicked."

His eyes search mine. "Max ran a check on Marco and he has no past until he showed up with you one day."

Marco and I never talked about any of his past, we only look forward. "I told you, I met him at the shelter. Prior to that, I don't know what he was doing. I just know he was always there for me."

He takes my hand. "What's your real name?"

Another deep breath and I'll be done. "My real name is Cara Josephina Giaconna. I have not said that out loud in twenty years." I get up and head toward the door. "Now, I think you should leave."

He's not budging. "I told you, sweetheart, I'm not going anywhere. I still have questions. Why do you think I should leave? Why didn't you tell me any of this sooner? How much does the school know about your past?"

I turn to him, "I want you to leave because my brain is on overload right now. I didn't tell you sooner because I really didn't know you, and I didn't think I would see you again after the first time I ran. The school knows nothing. My past is buried very deeply. I did nothing wrong but be born to parents who wanted to help right the wrongs in the world. I've suffered enough, now will you leave?"

He follows me to the door, takes a hold of my hand, but he's not moving. "Raven, I told you, you don't get to decide what I can and can't handle. I'm capable of that all on my own. How do you know there isn't a money trail?"

Another question. I just want this to be over. "Because Joseph made sure that nothing could ever be linked back to me."

He runs his hands through his hair, and strokes his chin. His wheels are definitely turning! "How do you know that Joseph can be trusted?"

I put my hand on his shoulder and look into his eyes. "Well, I have to trust someone, and my father trusted him with my life. He's now the Director of the FBI."

"That doesn't mean he can be trusted. Does he know what your adopted father tried to do to you? What about your ex-boyfriend beating you up, does he know about that?"

I shake my head. "No, I didn't turn to him. I felt he did enough and I needed to stand on my own two feet."

He paces and starts at his chin again. "There have been threats to my mum, sister, nephew, and now, you. Do you think this has to do with your past?"

I throw my hands up, "Jax, I honestly don't know. I don't think so. I mean, after all this time, why now? What has changed?"

I watch him fist his hands. His jaw begins to tick. I can tell he's losing any calm he had. "Raven, being in the spotlight with me could be what has changed. If I would have known, I would have never put you in that position, but I guess it's too late for that now!"

He reaches for the doorknob and I know he's pissed off, but then he turns to me. "I need time to process all this and then figure out our next step. In the meantime, I've put guards on everyone; I'm not taking any chances." He pulls me close to him and I just melt; he smells wonderfully of vanilla and spice.

"I'm not running for the hills, so you're just going to have to get use to me being here, and you're not running. either. Done! I need open, honest communication—at all times. If you're scared, tell me, but *no more fucking running*!"

Just as he leans in to kiss me, the door flies open and Marco comes barrelling in. "Why do you have one of your people following me?"

Marco looks as if he's ready to bust a gut. "Calm down, have a seat, and let me fill you in. Marco, I told Jax everything."

He is looking back and forth from Jax to me like a Ping-Pong ball. "Oh."

"I received another threat. It was attached to the picture of Raven, outside the gym, the other night. I'm not taking any chances, so I added extra security, until we can get to the bottom of this."

Marco's eyes grow wide. Maybe he's shocked, that I told Jax everything. "Do you think it has anything to do with Raven's parents?"

Jax shrugs. "I honestly don't know. I've made my share of enemies in my business. Nothing would surprise me, but I'm not about to take any chances." He pulls me close.

Marco gets up. "I'll give you both some space."

Jax shakes his head, "It's okay, Marco, I need to get going. I want to talk to Max and see if he's found out anything new." He leans down and gives me a long, soft kiss. "I will see you for coffee, in the morning." It was not a request, it was an order. He leans in and rubs his nose up the side of my neck, kissing along it with little flutters. He takes my hand and kisses my wrist, and I feel a jolt right down to my toes. I'm lost. He turns and leaves me a jumbled mess.

Marco gets up, pulls out the brandy, and pours us each a drink. He hands me a glass, "This is just fucked up on so many levels," he spits, looking as if he's about ready to blow a gasket.

"Raven can you say something? Because right now, I want to scream!"

Like I don't? I want to bury my head in the sand! "Don't you think I want to scream, too? But what good would it do? I can't change what has happened. If I could, I would go back twenty years to that awful day. Maybe I just need to walk away while my heart is still intact and before someone gets hurt."

He snorts at me, "That's bullshit. If you want this man, then fight for him. If you want a safe and happy life, then fight for it, but don't fucking sit there and do nothing."

I hate it when he's right. I'm just tired, really tired of all the bullshit. "Marco, do you think Jax and I have a chance at making this work?"

He hugs me. "Baby girl, if you want him bad enough, then yes. The ball is in your court."

I give him a hug. "I love you, but I'm just too tired right now—both mentally and physically—to deal with another thing." I cross my arms, rubbing them up and down. "Listen, I'm going to bed; I've got a lot to think about."

"That you do, baby girl." He puts his glass in the sink then wraps his arms around me for a hug. "Hopefully, you'll have everything figured out in the morning. Goodnight." And with that, he kisses the top of my head and sends me off.

AS MUCH AS SLEEP was hard coming last night, my exhausted body finally took over only to be greeted by morning too quickly. I head out the door to meet Jax at Starbucks. I'm happy to see him waiting with my coffee. Every time I see him, I am rendered speechless. He is just so beautiful, yet he doesn't flash it. He's wearing a black suit, black shirt, and a deep violet bow tie. I can't help but stare. My eyes keep traveling up and down his muscular body. He spots me and then gifts me with that crooked smile and his twinkling blue eyes; I'm done.

He walks up to me, "Are you enjoying the view?"

I reach up and adjust his tie. "Well, you already know the answer to that question. I have to say, I'm really surprised you wear bowties."

He hands me my coffee and smiles. "Well, if it's good for the *Doctor*, then who am I to argue?"

I have no clue what he's talking about. "Sorry, Jax, you lost me. What doctor?"

He actually has a look of disbelief on his face. "Raven, please don't tell me you've never heard of *Doctor Who*? Because this could be a big problem for us."

"Sorry, Jax, I've never heard of *Doctor Who*."

He's really very shocked. "Okay, Raven, I'm going to have to educate you. We need to have a *Doctor Who* marathon."

It must be some sort of television show, but I hardly watch any television. "Whatever you say, Jax. On another note, have you learned anything new since last night?"

His grip tightens on me at the mention of the threats. "Max has been in touch with Joseph. Apparently, when Max started looking into your past it sent a red flag for Joseph. Add to that, Michael contacting the FBI and Interpol when the first threats came in, and I can assure you, Joseph is very aware of the situation now." He sighs. "I'm going to sit down with the local FBI field agents and run through my business to see if something shakes loose. In the meantime, just be smart and don't take any chances." He leans in for a kiss, and I can't help but feel sad—my past might be responsible for all his trouble. "I'll pick you up this afternoon, after school."

I don't want him to worry about me. "Jax, you don't have to pick me up. I'll be fine. Just focus on getting to the bottom of this."

Oh holy hell, he's growling again! "Just, please, do what I tell you without any running away. I couldn't handle it if something happened to you, so just humor me, okay?"

I kiss him softly, "Okay, whatever."

The smirk is back. "Thank you."

MAX SHOWS UP TO take me to school. "Max, do you think I need protecting, or is Jax just over reacting?" I inquire as we stroll down the street. I see the stress on this man, and it worries me.

"Miss Raven, it can't hurt to be careful," he offers. This can't possibly be because of my parents. That was twenty years ago.

I decide to ask him anyway, "Do you think this is happening because of my parents?"

He's, seemingly, lost in his thoughts. "I honestly don't know, but what I do know is, Jax won't stop until he has all the answers."

As we walk together, I decide to try to pump him for some information about Jax. "How did you and Jax meet?"

He just smiles at me—which is not something I'm used to seeing from this man. "That, Miss Raven, is a tale for another day." Just like that, he's done.

JAX GETS STUCK AT work so he sends Max to pick me up. I let him know that Jackie and I are going shopping and then for drinks. Before we do this, I have to lose Max. It's ridiculous that he is following me around the city.

I call Jax and get his assistant, Duke. "Sorry, Miss Anderson, but he's in a meeting. Can I give him a message?" *He never puts me through to Jax.*

"Just tell him I'll meet him later at home." Before I can say any more, he thanks me and hangs up.

Losing Max is not as easy as I thought, but the sales lady lets us slip, out back, after we changed into our new outfits for clubbing. Jackie grabs my arm gently, "Why are we doing this?"

"Really, Jackie, I just want to go out for a few drinks and have fun. I don't need or want a bodyguard following me around town. Jax might be high profile, but I'm just a second grade teacher. Besides, I told Jax we were going out, and sending his bodyguard with us is like having a babysitter!"

"Raven, I wouldn't mind him following me," she admits.

I give her a once-over. Yep, there it is; *the look.* I can't believe I didn't notice this before. "Oh really, you like Max?"

She's blushing! "Well he's rugged, extremely handsome, and very *James Bond* looking, so what's not to like?"

I have to laugh. Everyone thinks Max is Bond. "Marco thinks he looks like Daniel Craig."

She gasps, "Oh, please tell me Marco's not after him, I would just die."

I can't believe she's really interested in him. "No, I don't think Max is gay, but I can ask Jax."

"*No*, I would die of embarrassment," she squeals, putting her hand to her chest.

I can't help but laugh. "Come on, girl, let's have fun."

We head down to the Village and find a really cute club with some of the most interesting people. I can just sit and watch people all night long, especially in the Village. Oh, the sights! I'm such a lightweight drinker, but Jackie has me drinking something called a *Bushwhacker.* It is heaven: Kahlua, rum, coconut milk, and ice, blended together, in a frozen cup. The entire inside of the cup is drizzled with chocolate syrup. The syrup is drizzled on top, as well, for the final touch. I'm officially a goner; I'm finally relaxed. It's been a long and stressful week.

The DJ starts playing fun dance music. I take my long hair out of its clip and hit the dance floor to Lady Gaga singing, "Do What U Want". He goes right in to Katy Perry's "Part of Me", and some random guy starts dancing with us. Before I realize what's happening, I feel hands on my hips and Jackie's face looks like she just got a jolt from a stun gun.

I'm not turning around—I know exactly who I'll find. *Damn it, how the fuck did he find us?* The DJ puts on The Police's" Every Breath You Take". I can't help but laugh—the frigging stalker song—how appropriate. I turn around and there it is . . . that toe-curling look. Jax pulls me close and sings in my ear. It's raspy and such a turn-on. He leans down to kiss me, "You're drunk."

I get lost in those blues, "Maybe, a little bit." He gives me that crooked smile and I melt. We are swaying to the music and I can feel his rock hard cock, hitting my core. Sweet Jesus, what this man does to me.

I look over to Jackie and Max is holding her up. Oh, she likes him. Interesting.

"Sweetheart, why did you ditch Max?" I know he's trying not to bull-doze me.

"I just wanted to go out with Jackie and have fun. Life with you is so much more." He looks confused. Maybe he just doesn't get it. Nothing is simple anymore.

"I'm confused. What do you mean, *so much more?*"

I don't want to hurt him. He's looking at me with such tenderness. "It's intense. You're intense. I'm only twenty-seven, and life has had more downs than ups. And you're so beautiful. Do you know that?" I can't believe I just said that.

"You're drunk, I'm taking you home."

He nods to Max and just like that, we're leaving. Apparently, Jackie's not allowed to stay, either. When we get outside, Max doesn't say anything. Jax has a word with Max and before I know it, Max is taking Jackie home. She looks very happy about it.

"Jax, I'm going back to my place tonight." Not that I want to, but I can't possibly let him win all the time.

"Do you really think you're going to win this argument?"

I throw my hands on my hips. "I'll have you know, I took a Krav Maga class and I take kickboxing classes too, remember?" I have no idea why he is laughing so hard that I can defend myself. Well, I can sort of defend my-self. He reaches for me. I make an attempt to swat him away but he is on me in a second—and he has me in the fireman carry. "Jax, everyone can see my panties!"

He's still laughing at me. "Only I can, and I know what's under them."

I try to wiggle free and he smacks my butt. "Keep it up and I'll do it again."

Now I'm growling like he does! "You wouldn't." Who am I kidding? He would in a heartbeat and I know it.

"Oh, do you want to try me?" He places me in his car, runs around to get in on the driver's side, starts it up and drives like a crazy man (which is hard to do in Manhattan). Before I know it, we're in his ivory tower in the sky. I'm too tired and too drunk to argue anymore. I drift off to sleep, smelling vanilla and spice.

Chapter Eight
Maxwell

I SWEAR THIS WOMAN frustrates me. I don't know how Jax is dealing with her. I'm used to order and routine. I have to be like that for the safety of my charges. I can't believe that Raven and Jackie ditched me! What the bloody hell were they thinking?

Thank God Jax is a crazy fucker and installed a tracker app on the phone he gave Raven. I thought Jax was going to rip my head off when I called to tell him what they did. I hack into the phone and find out where they ditched me. I call Jax and we both arrive at the club within minutes of each other and head in. Both girls are pissed and barely able to stand. Some random guy is on the dance floor with them, until Jax and I step in—this guy seems to know that he needs to slink back to wherever the fuck he came from.

I'm trying to guide Jackie off the floor but she's not having any of it. I decide to pull her into my arms and just sway to the music. Fuck, she smells fantastic, and I'm instantly hard! Finally, the music starts to change and Jax gives me the nod. Just like that, we are out the door.

"Jax is going to take Miss Raven home. I will be escorting you." I didn't give her much of a choice. As I put her in the car, I can't help but notice how long and lean her legs are—beautiful. We pull up to her flat. The first thing I notice is that security in the building is really good. At least that's something positive.

"Thank you, Max, for making sure I got home okay." I take her hand and guide her past the doorman.

"Excuse me, Miss Jackie, apparently you don't understand. I'm your security until I can make other arrangements."

She looks at me all wide eyed. "You mean you're coming upstairs?"

I nod, "Yes, I can assure you, I will be the perfect gentlemen."

She looks surprised. "Why?"

I guide her into the elevator. "Why will I be a perfect gentleman?" I'm playing with her, but I couldn't help having a little fun.

"No, Max, why are you coming upstairs?"

As the doors close, I look at her. *She really is beautiful.* "We will talk upstairs."

"But…" she starts to protest.

I swiftly pull her towards me, "No buts and no choice. Done. Especially after the stunt you and Miss Raven pulled earlier."

She opens the door and disarms the alarm. "Please wait here while I do a quick sweep of the flat." I know I'm over cautious, but I have my reasons.

"Don't you think you're being ridiculous?"

I glare at her. "Humor me. After all, it's the least you can do after ditching me earlier."

She has the nerve to smirk at me! "Whatever, Max, just make it quick."

After I give the "all clear," she comes in and locks up. I'm impressed she has an alarm and actually uses it—so many people don't.

"I'm going to change, make yourself at home."

I walk around the flat, taking in all the windows and making sure they're secure—just a habit. When I turn around, she's standing in the kitchen, wearing flimsy shorts and a short little top. *Oh bloody hell, I'm fucked!*

"Tea?"

She must think I'm an idiot. I can't take my eyes off of her legs! "Excuse me?"

I'm sure she knows what she is doing and just smiles. "I said, would you like a cup of tea?"

I'm trying to keep my eyes off of her legs or it could be game over. "Yes, please."

I sit down and she starts to question me. I'm having a hard time concentrating.

"Max, are you okay?"

I grit my teeth. "Yes, sorry, I just have a lot on my dish right now."

She smirks. "Plate."

I keep reminding myself to focus. "Excuse me?"

She cocks her head to the side, and her beautiful blonde hair cascades around her face.

"You have a lot on your plate. Sometimes the words are the same but different meanings."

I nod. "Plate … got it."

As she passes me my tea, she's back to questioning me. "Can you please fill me in on why I am in need of security?"

I try to play everything close to the vest. I'm not ready to tell her anything. "Well, it seems Miss Raven has some security issues that could be a problem, so better safe than sorry."

Her tongue rolls over her lips; fuck it all to hell I'm as hard as stone! "Well, Max, here's the thing, I am an educated woman and I know when someone is trying to bullshit me. You're in way deep here. Let's start again, except this time with the truth."

"Well, Miss Jackie, I don't know how much I'm at liberty to tell you, I don't want to put you in any danger."

She sips her tea and stares at me. "Max, did you do a background check on me?"

I shake my head. "Honestly, no. I didn't see any reason to. I'm not a bad guy. I'm just trying to keep everyone safe."

She puts her tea down, "My mother is from Japan and my father is from Switzerland. My father helped negotiate relations between Switzerland and Japan. He is a prominent businessman. I am very used to security and threats. I live in New York because it allows me some anonymity. As you can tell, I'm in a very secure building. However, if you feel I might need some additional protection, I won't question you on it."

She has rendered me speechless. She gets up, goes to the closet, and comes back with a pillow and a blanket. "The couch is pretty comfortable. If you need anything else, let me know." She turns and goes into her room, closing the door behind her. I can't imagine I will get much sleep tonight. I'm left with a raging hard-on and a cold cup of tea!

Jackie

I CAN'T BELIEVE SOME gorgeous man is asleep in my living room. If my parents knew, they would freak out. Shit, I'm freaking out. What the fuck did Raven get into that she needs this level of security? I try to get some sleep, but all I can think about is Max on my couch. I decide to read for a while. As I finally drift off to sleep, I realize, I don't even know his full name!

AS THE DAY DAWNS, I get out of bed and throw on my running gear before heading out to the kitchen. "Where are you going?" Max asks when he glances over at me from the coffee maker.

I need to work off frustration, and I'm training, but he doesn't need to know everything. "I like to start my day with a run, usually alone."

His jaw ticks. I can tell he's trying to control his temper. "Well, Miss Jackie, if you insist on running, then running it is, but we need to stop by my place to pick up my gear."

This is ridiculous. "Really, Max, you don't have to come with me." He glares at me, and I realize . . . it's fruitless to argue. "Okay, Max, let's go."

When we get to his place, I look around in shock. "You live here?"

He smiles and seems proud of where he lives. "Yes, there are two flats on the floor—I have one and Jax has the other. It makes it quite convenient since I head up Jax's detail."

The place is beautiful, but sadly, it doesn't look like a home. "Do you entertain much?" I ask him and see such sadness pass over his face that I just want to give him a hug.

"The only people that have ever been in here are Jax, his family, and now, you." He averts his eyes from me after the last bit. "I'll be right back," he adds then walks down the hall to his room, I bet.

He changes quickly and re-joins me. I am finally getting an up close and personal look at him. I realize he is very well built; his muscles are very well defined. He is so handsome. I have no clue how old he is but I know he is older than Jax.

"How far do you usually run? I like long distance running, so I hope that won't be a problem for you."

Maxwell

DOES SHE THINK I'M too old to keep up with her? "Not at all, Miss Jackie, whatever you decide, I promise not to hold you back."

As we enter the park, she does a few quick stretches, which I'm sure are for my benefit. Oh fuck, she's stretching out those legs. *When the fuck did I become a leg-man?*

"Any time you're ready, Miss Jackie."

Jackie

OH REALLY, WELL HE should know that I usually run marathons, and I've been in training for the NYC marathon, next weekend. We start to run and I keep the pace light. I don't want to kill the guy, especially since I don't know how old he is. He seems to be keeping up, maintaining a steady pace right behind me. When we finally finish, I stop on the grass and do my usual stretching so my muscles recover quickly. I glance over at Max and notice he's wincing. "Max, are you okay?"

He grimaces. "I'll be fine, just a sore muscle." Some men can be so stubborn.

"Max, in all fairness, I've been training for the New York City Marathon. Maybe this was too much for a man your age." I can't help but giggle. "Lie flat on the grass and let me help you."

He puts his hand up. "Don't worry, Miss Jackie, I'll be fine." I just want to smack him. He is so bull-headed!

"I can't have my bodyguard hobbling around all day. Sit now, mister."

Maxwell

I DO AS SHE says and sit on the grass. Watching her, I can't believe she's real. She takes off my trainers and massages my foot. Oh my God, I can't do this; I'm getting hard! She moves her hands up my calf to my thigh, pushing her whole body into the massage. I've got to stop this now! "Okay, thank you, Miss Jackie, I think I'm good now." I think she's doing this on purpose. I quickly put my trainers on. I take her hand and we head back across to my flat. I need a shower and I have to check in with Jax.

Jackie

"I'LL JUST JUMP IN for a quick shower. You can make yourself at home."

I walk along floor to ceiling windows, taking in the beautiful views. I grab a bottle of water and begin to wonder around the rest of his home. Everything is very neat, nothing out of place. He must like scotch, he has a very well stocked bar. As I go in search of the restroom, I pass by a home office. I head further down the hall, past an open door. When I glance over I can see his silhouette in the mirror. He has a towel wrapped around his waist, and his body is wet from his shower. Sweet Jesus, he's got the most beautiful body I have ever seen. I can't take my eyes off of him. Just when he begins to remove his towel, he catches me ogling. I'm sure I've just turned a million shades of red. I'm about to turn around and give him his privacy, but he gives me a huge smile, turns his back to me, and drops his towel. *Holy fuck, what the...* He has the most beautifully sculptured ass I have ever seen! I'm still stunned when he enters the room. He walks up to me, leans in, and puts his hand at the base of my neck. He pulls me close, reaches in, and gently kisses me. The whole time, his eyes are open, searching mine, almost like he's asking for permission but knows the answer.

"I have wanted to do that since last night," he growls. "Jax left me a message that they will not be available till tomorrow. Do you want to go back to your place to shower?"

I'm still flustered. "Um sure."

I PRACTICALLY RUN INTO the shower when we arrive at my place. I don't know what is going on with me. He is older than I am but I have no idea how old—shit! I don't even know his full name! I put on leggings and a sweatshirt and head out to the living room. "Wow, where did the breakfast come from?"

He's busy dishing it all up for us. "I made a few calls. Sit before it gets cold."

He keeps his eyes on me as we eat in silence. "Miss Jackie, what's the matter? You seem upset about something. Was it the kiss? Did I offend you?"

Crap, I'm blushing again; I can feel the heat rising to my cheeks. "I wasn't offended, just surprised. You slept in my apartment, I saw you naked, you kissed me, and I don't even know your full name."

He puts his coffee down. "Maxwell Fleming."

"Excuse me?"

He takes my hand. "My name is Maxwell Fleming."

I take a deep breath. "Okay. Maxwell Fleming, can I ask you some questions?"

He nods. "You can, and I will answer them as best and as honestly as I can."

I have so many. Where should I start? "How old are you? Where were you born? How did you meet Jax? And are you an only child?"

He laughs, "Whoa, one at a time, babe. I'm thirty-eight years old. I was born in Scotland, but went to live with my grams in London when my mum died. I have no siblings that I'm aware of. I don't remember much about my biological father, so I can't really know for sure. I met Jax eight years ago, in a bar, in London. I'm not married, and I don't do relationships. Now what about you?"

Everything he said, and yet what sticks is his comment on relationships. *So what are we doing here?*

"I'm twenty-five. I finished my degree at the age of twenty-two and I got my teaching job right out of college. I graduated from high school when I was sixteen. Raven is my closest friend. We were roommates in college and we've been teaching together for three years. I've never had a long-term relationship and I've yet to meet anyone that would make me want to have one.

I'm very close to my parents. I have a brother who is older than I am, he lives in Japan. I speak Japanese, French, Italian, German, Romansch, and English. I like running, but you know that already. I will be running the NYC marathon next week. I have been skiing since before I could walk. I don't eat meat, but I do eat fish. I love very strong coffee, and I can't live without chocolate."

He looks at me. "Wow, no meat?"

I laugh. "After all that, and all you can say is, '*Wow, no meat?*'"

He hits me with a killer smile. "What would you like to do for the rest of the day?"

Just like that, he's done. I hope Raven is having better luck getting through to Jax than I am with Mr. Maxwell Fleming . . .

Chapter Nine

Raven

I'M HAVING THE MOST wonderful dream. The air is filled with vanilla spice and I feel warm kisses all over my body. There is soft music playing and I feel like I'm floating on a cloud. I wake up in a haze, slowly opening my eyes only to be hit with the sparkling blues I've come to love. *Oh my God, did I just think the "L" word? Fuck . . .*

"Good morning, my defiant one, how are you feeling?"

I need to focus. "My brain feels like someone is playing ping pong. Why didn't you take me back to my place?"

"I didn't want you to be alone just in case you felt sick or you felt the need to pull a runner," snarky Jax replies. Oh, he's pissed. I start to get up to leave but he grabs me and throws me onto the bed, straddling me. "You're not going anywhere, sweetheart, so just forget it."

He's crazy. "Jax, you can't keep me here!"

He growls. "Wanna bet? I think it's time for a little chat about your defiance in having security!" With that, he takes both my hands and holds them above my head and slowly kisses them. Leaning his chest right over my face, I get a blast of vanilla and spice. I lean up and lick his nipples; first one, then the other. *Two can play at this game.* Oh, he tastes so wonderful.

"Why did you sneak away from Max last night?"

I'm trying to focus on him, but he's not making it easy. "I just wanted to go out with Jackie and have fun."

He locks his eyes onto mine, and what I see scares me—he's really worried. "Well, you do realize that, if *you're* the target, then you just put a big bullseye on Jackie's back?"

My heart drops, "No, I didn't think about that because I don't think this is about me. None of this started until I met you!"

He kisses me, trying to calm my fear for Jackie, I think. "Well, either way, I can't be sure, so I've also put a guard on Jackie. Max is with her now, and he will keep her safe. Now, back to what I was doing." With that, he is back, kissing my arms and neck.

He works his way down my body. My brain is buzzing. I'm not sure if it's from him or those bushwhacker drinks. Before I know it, he has me spread open and he's nibbling, sucking, and licking me front to back. *I think I'm going to pass out.* He flips me over and starts massaging me at the top of my head, then my neck, and down my back. He follows his path with kisses. It's so soft and peaceful. I feel him everywhere. He lifts my hips and slams into me. "Oh my God!" I scream.

He leans over me and growls, "No, sweetheart, that would be me, not God. Now you're not going to ditch your security detail, are you?" He pulls back, waiting for my answer but before I can give him one, he slams in again! He pulls back out of me slowly. "Let's talk security. Are you going to ditch them?"

I know I shouldn't get him riled up, but I can't help myself. "Why do I need to have a monitor?"

He smacks my ass and slams into me again. "Sorry, wrong answer, sweetheart."

If he does that one more time, I'm going to come and he knows it. He pulls out, bends down, and kisses my ass—slow, deliberate kisses. "Now are you going to ditch your security detail again?"

He licks right up my spine. Oh, sweet Jesus, now back down again, his finger following the path of his tongue and just like that, anal play is back. He works his finger into me really slowly. Oh God, it's going to hurt. I tense up.

"I would never hurt you Raven, you're so wet for me," he tries to reassure me probably picking up on my body language. He pulls out and starts working himself into my rear. All I feel is pressure and my panic, rising. I never thought I would want to try this.

"Jax, it's going to hurt," I finally voice my fear.

He trails kisses up and down my spine. "Sweetheart, I would never hurt you, I promise. You're so wet. I'll go slow, just relax and breathe. Do you trust me?"

"Yes," I don't hesitate. I know he wouldn't hurt me.

He pushes forward very slowly. "Push back and let me in," he says soothingly. As I push back, he pushes forward. There's a lot of pressure. "I'm almost in, baby, little bit more." He pushes a little more until he's all the way in. It's such a full feeling. "Oh God, Raven, you're so fucking tight, you feel so warm and tight around my cock. He stops and I know he is trying to control himself. I feel him squeezing the base of his cock to stop his impending orgasm. He hooks his arms under mine and pulls me into a sitting position on his lap. With one hand, he reaches around my body and goes back and forth from one nipple to the other. His free hand goes right to work on my clitoris. He starts to move, slowly at first, but then he starts to really pick up speed. The feeling is amazing. I never thought it could feel this unbelievable.

"Jax, I'm there, are you?"

He nibbles on my ear, "Come for me, baby," and with that, we both let go—screaming our release. We both collapse and he drapes over me. He pulls out and flips me over. He ditches the condom before setting his eyes back on me. He seems worried and stressed. I feel really bad, like I brought this on. "Are you going to ditch your security detail again?"

I search his eyes. "Jax, why is this so important to you?"

His gaze becomes intense. "I need to know your safe. I can't think and I can't work while I'm worried about you. Having security takes away a little bit of the worry."

I fight the tears back, I don't want to hurt him. "Okay, if it's that important to you, I won't ditch my detail."

He gifts me with that crooked smile and twinkling blues. "You have made me so happy." He nuzzles into my neck, stroking his fingers up and down my arm.

"Jax, how can you possibly be able to go again?"

He laughs, "Sweetheart, it's you. This is what you do to me. My cock always wants to be buried in you. It's a happy place for him." He slowly works his cock in and out. He pulls out again, but then he slams into me and my mind loses all reason. This man has moves that render me speechless. He presses his lips to all different parts of my body—parts that I never knew could be so sensitive. "You're quivering, baby. I love it when you quiver. I can feel you clenching my cock. It's beautiful. You're beautiful."

Oh God he's doing that swivel with his hips while he's buried so fucking deep! My hands fist his hair, "Jax! Oh! My! God!" I scream to all that's holy.

He laughs, "That would be me again, sweetheart. Oh fuck, Raven, I'm there. Please do that clench thing again!"

We both scream our release, barely catching our breath. I'm speechless, exhausted, and totally satisfied. "You are so beautiful, please don't run away." It's barely a whisper but I hear him. I wrap myself around him and drift off to sleep.

AFTER THE PROMISED *DOCTOR Who* marathon, we've been spending the entire weekend in bed, which is fine by me. He brings a tray in with coffee and pastry—*heaven!* "I need to ask you something. Are you on birth control?"

After almost choking on my coffee, I look at him and find him stroking his chin. "Why are you asking me now? You've been using condoms, so what's the problem?"

"I want nothing between us. I want you—one hundred percent. And I hate those cock blockers. I had my yearly physical, and I have a clean bill of health. I can give you a copy."

I made my ex wear a condom all the time, which was what fueled the beating he gave me. I trust Jax. "I've been on the pill for years to keep me regulated. I have a clean bill, also. We have to be tested at the beginning of every school year, and since I have not had sex in almost two years…"

He is on me, kissing me, doing a dance with his tongue that makes me instantly wet for him. He locks his eyes on mine, "Are we good?" he asks. I nod, but he doesn't continue. "I need to hear the words, baby."

"Yes, Jax, we're good. I trust you," I whisper.

The words barely leave my mouth and keeping his blues to my violets, he slowly enters me. The feeling is unreal. He is so hard and pulsing. When he is all the way in, he stops and closes his eyes. "Do you feel that? We can never be closer than we are, right at this minute. We are one body, one heart, and one soul."

I melt at the words. He says so much during sex, but my mind becomes a jumbled mess. He opens his eyes and starts to move real slowly. The feeling is unbelievable. When it comes to sex with this man, I am so out of my league. "Jax, I can't hold it much longer, please tell me you're close." I'm trying to hold on, but it's so hard.

"Go, sweetheart, I'm right behind you."

And with that, I fall, locking my eyes back onto his, holding onto him as if my life depended upon it—it probably does. He lets out a yell and floods me with his warmth. He stills, but his cock is still throbbing.

"I don't think I will ever get enough of you. You're like a book that I never want to put down." I'm not sure if I was meant to hear his words.

I'm curled up in Jax's arms as he runs his fingers up and down my spine. "Jax, this has been a great weekend."

He stops, "Why do I hear a "but" coming?"

I really don't want him to worry, but I have to think about my kids, too. "Well, tomorrow when I go to school, do you think the security can stay outside? I'm in a high security school and I don't think anyone would try anything. I really don't want the kids to be afraid that there are guards in the room. I know most of them are probably used to it, but still… Besides, can you picture Max in one of those little chairs in the back of the room?"

He laughs at the thought, "Okay, but no ditching Max. I need to know that you and Junior are safe." He traces circles on my arm. That was easier than I thought it was going to be.

"What would you like to do today?" he asks.

I need to get a run in. "Well, it's nice out, do you want to go for a run?" I can't believe we are having this conversation and he is still buried so deep within me.

"Whatever you want to do is fine with me."

WE HEAD DOWN TO Central Park and it's beautiful outside. Even though it's fall, it's still a little warm. We do the entire park. It's long, but it feels good to just run with no thoughts and no purpose.

"I really didn't think you were into running, but you're good." He smiles.

I have always loved running. "Thanks. I got into college on a track scholarship and I just kept it up. I try to run two times a week. It really depends on what workout classes I have planned. I never miss Pilates."

He gives me that smirk. "Well, you know I'm happy about that. Tell me about Pilates, I've never taken a class."

"It's all based on a technique developed by Joe Pilates. I like using a machine called *The Reformer*. The key is, the core muscles are always engaged. Picture Yoga with resistance."

He is stroking his chin, deep in thought. "I will have to put one of those machines in the gym so you can teach me."

I'm sure that's not the only reason he wants one!

WE HEAD OFF TO that wonderful shower. I swear, I really can't get enough of it. Jax washes my body like he's studying every inch, and then he washes my hair. The feeling of having my head massaged under that massive showerhead is unreal.

Jax steps in front of me and begins slowly kissing me. "You're so beautiful, sweetheart. I want to hold you forever." He lifts me up. "Wrap your legs around my waist and hold on tight." He rears back and slams into me, but then he stops.

"Why are you stopping?" His eyes are closed and his head is tilted all the way back. "Are you okay?"

He hums, "Yeah. Do you feel that? Just hold on tight and don't move." He looks down at me, and we lock eyes. He swipes his tongue across my lips, but he's still not moving. "Do you feel how deep I am? I don't have to move—I'm pulsing inside you, and you're clenching my cock." He throws his head back again, "Oh, Raven, fuck! What you do to me!" he yells, coming apart within me, and the thought that I have that much power, sends me over the edge to my own release. We slide down the wall, neither one of us saying a word. We finish cleaning up, when we start to come back to life. Both of us silent, lost in our own thoughts.

WE HEAD BACK TO my place for my stuff. Marco is there and he doesn't seem happy. "Hey, what's up? You look upset."

He's really pissed off, slamming stuff, and glaring at Jax. "Well, you could say that. My roommate doesn't come home for almost two days, doesn't return my calls or text messages, and I couldn't *fucking* find her!"

I didn't think he would be this upset. "Oh."

He steps towards me. "So help me, baby girl. If you say *oh* one more time, I just might throw you over my knee and…"

Jax jumps up. "Hold on, Marco." Jax is standing toe-to-toe with Marco.

"No, Jax, *you* hold on. Do you know how worried I was? There has been so much shit going on between guards and stalkers, and then she disappears without a trace. Put yourself in my shoes."

I step between them both. "I'm sorry, Marco. I shut my phone off, I will leave you Jax's number too so you can call him. I will also try to be more considerate." I touch his arm. He seems to calm down. Jax and I decide to hang around for a while and catch up.

"ARE YOU STAYING HERE tonight?" Marco questions, giving his bones a stretch.

"No, I'm staying at Jax's ivory tower in the sky."

Okay, crap! My brain-to-mouth filter is not working today. I watch as Jax takes on a perturbed expression and Marco laughs out loud. And with that, we head back to Jax's. When we get in the elevator, he comes towards me real slow, like a predator. "Ivory tower, eh?"

He grabs my hand, bringing it up to his lips and kisses my wrist. *Damn! Why does that get to me?* He pulls my hand away from my ear with a growl—I don't even realize I do it. When the doors open, he guides me inside, still kissing me. He turns on the fireplace and then slowly starts to undress me. Before he can have his way, I'm on my knees, working his cock out of his jeans. He's hard, and I slip my lips around the head. He's like silk on my tongue, leaving a trail of his arousal behind. "Take it deep, sweetheart. All the way." He holds my head, pushing himself in deeper. If I thought I was in control, boy, was I mistaken. He is totally in control now. I work my way around his sac, flutter kisses, and lick all the way around and back up again. I'm back on his cock, and he holds the base to stop from coming. He starts moving again and I bare my teeth slightly, causing him to lose it. He slams all the way to the back of my throat, screaming and coming in a hot flood, and I swallow it all. He pulls out and he's still hard!

He lies down in front of the fire. My eyes glide down every inch of his magnificent body, "Jesus, you are so beautiful."

"Sweetheart, you have on way too many clothes." He tugs on my shirt. I slowly start to remove my clothes and he gives me that crooked smile and opens his arms. "Come here," he beckons. I crawl onto his lap and wrap my legs around his waist. "Ride me, sweetheart, make me come inside you."

That's it, I'm done! I impale myself on his hard cock. He plays with my nipples. I know I'm not going to last much longer, but then he stops and flips me over! He starts slamming me from behind, pulling me back against him.

"Why is it an ivory tower?" *Now he wants to talk about this?* He smacks my ass. "Tell me why?" I can't think, let alone answer him. "Tell me," he growls, and he smacks my ass again; right then left. It's not hard, just enough to buzz. If I die right now, this is a hell of a way to go. "Tell me, Raven," he demands, pulls out, and waits. He starts rubbing his cock up and down my ass, spreading my cheeks, and begins to push himself into my ass.

I know what's coming and I want it. I grit my teeth, "You're up in this glass tower all alone, like something out of a fairy tale." I'm panting like a crazy woman. "It's like your hiding from the real world!"

He smacks my ass again. "Push out for me and I'll give you what I know your craving!"

I push out and he breaks through that barrier. The fullness is overwhelming. This is so new for me, yet I crave the intensity. I can feel my skin flush as he pushes even deeper. I'm there, and I can't hold it any longer. We are both screaming and coming. It's so powerful, and then we collapse and I can hardly move a muscle. We lie in front of the fire, in silence, trying to steady our breath. He gets up and gets a blanket from the couch. He covers us, and pulls me close to him.

"Raven, I'm not hiding in an ivory tower. I'm just a private person. The press is always hounding me. If I were just a blue-collar worker, they wouldn't care. It's only because I have money that they think they need to know everything about my life."

I don't see the logic in hiding. "Maybe if you show them you could care less, they might not bother with you. They all want what they can't have; you make it a big deal, so it's a big deal to them."

He runs his fingers up and down my spine. "Normally, I would agree with you. However, because I'm a billionaire, that puts everyone around me at risk. I'm not prepared to go through that, again."

My eyes fly up to his. "Jax, what do you mean by, *again*?"

His fingers stop. "Sweetheart, what are you talking about?"

I lift my face to focus on his expression. "Jax, you just said, 'you're not prepared to go through that again'. Go through *what*, again?" I push further. "Jax, your hiding stuff from me, makes me want to run."

He pulls me close to him, holding me really tight. "Okay, when I first started in this business, I realized I was good at it . . . really good. I can somehow anticipate the next move. I was dating someone and I believed her, when she said she loved me. What she loved was my money and the power that came with it. I started taking some business risks that could have destroyed everything I had built, if it wasn't done just right.

"During this time, the press was all over her and me because we were together. As it turns out, she was not in love with me. She was a corporate spy out to destroy me. I found out what she was up to and got her blackballed from the business she loved so much. Max and I got the press to agree to bury the story and all pictures of her and me together. I offered them an exclusive interview with access to *a day in the life of a corporate raider.*

"So, while you think I'm hiding in my ivory tower, I'm actually protecting the little bit of privacy I have left. People think that having money will give them freedom, but it's just the opposite. My money has put me in chains and the people around me at risk—a risk I'm not willing to take."

"Did you love her?" I whisper.

He pauses for a moment. "I thought I did. What I learned was, saying *I love you* is easy, but showing someone you love them is what matters. Those words are sometimes just words thrown out way too much. Raven, I'm not prepared to walk away from you, I need to keep you safe. If something happened to you, because of me, I couldn't take it."

I see so much in his eyes—so much pain and worry. I rest my head back down and snuggle into his chest. He resumes stroking my hair and my back with his fingers. He needs me and, at this moment, I let him have what he needs.

MORNING COMES TOO SOON and of course, Jax wants to drive me to school. "Make sure you don't lose Max, and keep your phone, so I can call you, please."

Now that I understand his fear, I will humor him. "No worries, Jax. I have two phones and Max. You have a great day. I'll call you on my break." I lean in and he gives me that toe-curling kiss. With that, he's gone.

FINDING IT HARD TO concentrate on anything but Jax all day, I'm about to call him, since it's break time. However, I stop when I hear a woman call my name. I turn to look at her and I know, in that instant, I am looking at Jax's mom. She has the same intense eyes, penetrating me. "Hi, I'm Raven, and you must be Mrs. Phillips?" She takes my hand and asks me to sit on a bench in the playground with her. "Are you here to see Michael?"

"No, dear. I'm actually here to meet with you. Please, call me An."

Why would she want to see me? "Oh."

Her smile is warm and inviting. "I understand, from my boy, that you and he are getting involved."

Okay, wow, I was not expecting that, but then again, this whole family just comes right out and says whatever they want. "Um, well, we have been seeing each other."

She picks up my hand. "My dear, sometimes in life, you have to just trust yourself and take that leap of faith. Fear should never define who we are. As Albert Einstein said, 'A person starts to live when they live outside themselves.'"

She takes my hand and she stands up. "I'll leave that thought with you and let you get back to work." Just like that, she's gone, and I'm left wondering, what the fuck that was all about.

I call Jax, as promised, but Duke tells me he's in a meeting. It's very strange that Duke never puts me through to Jax when I call. I'll talk to him about it tonight.

I'M TAKING JACKIE'S TURN as playground monitor today while she works one-on-one with a student. I actually enjoy being out here with the kids. Seeing them run and laugh without a care in the world, gives me faith. The bell rings, pulling me out of my thoughts. I get all the kids lined up and we start heading back in.

Within seconds, all hell breaks loose! Two men with guns come charging towards us. I'm looking for Max. I see him, trying to fight them to get to us, but they hit him with something and knock him out.

Then I see Mick running to help, but they hit him with their guns! I'm trying to push the kids through the door when they grab Michael out of the line. He is kicking and screaming as they are dragging him towards a van.

I reach him just as they are going to hit him, stepping in front of him. They hit me in the face and I'm dazed just long enough for them to grab Michael and me, shoving us into the back of the van. They toss my cell, but not both of them. Guns are pointed at us; Michael is crying. I try to put him behind me, protecting him from the kidnappers, but they duct tape our hands and feet and threaten to gag Michael to get him to shut up.

"Why are you doing this?"

He points his gun at my head. "Shut up or we'll gag you, too."

They all have on ski masks, preventing us from seeing their faces. But I recognize one of the voices as the one, from the other night, outside the gym. The ride is long, and there are no windows in the van. The sounds of the city seem to dissipate. I can feel thumping, almost like we are driving over a bridge. I think we're in New Jersey. I can hear a bay door go up. They open the doors and pull us out. We are in a warehouse; they were able to pull the van inside and out of sight.

"Michael, we need to work together and stay focused. Can you be really brave for me, please?"

He stops crying and looks at me. "Okay."

I need to be calm and focused. "We are going to sit back to back, and I'm going to try to untie you."

After a little bit, I'm able to untie him, and then he gets to work on me. "Michael, when they come in, we need to let them believe that we are still tied up."

He's trying so hard not to cry. "Miss Raven, I'm scared. What do they want?"

I see his fear, I need to help him. "I'm sure we'll find out, soon enough."

I try to use the spare phone to call Jax, but there is no signal. I leave it on.

Why is this happening to me again? I feel like I'm a little girl for a second, transported back in time. I need to keep it together for Michael. I know what he is feeling, and the fear is real. I can't let the fear win—not this time. Michael needs me, and I'm not that little girl anymore.

Jaxson

BELLA AND MICHAEL COME storming into my office. Bella is shaking and has a tear-stained face, and Michael looks grim.

"Jax, I just got this." She hands me a picture of Michael Jr. and Raven, being tossed into a van.

"Have they called yet?"

Michael looks at me. "Where the fuck was Max?" Just then, Max walks into my office, and he is visibly shaken. They beat him pretty good by the looks of his face.

Before I can tear into him, "They shot me with a tranquilizer, so they were able to grab them both. Raven tried to pull Michael away from them, so they grabbed her, too. There were, at least, four of them. Mick was outside the school, and he tried to stop them, too. Jax . . . they beat him pretty bad. They've taken him to the ER," he informs me.

Time seems to stand still before mayhem and madness erupts and then so much starts happening. My office door swings open and a very large man bounds in, announcing that he is Joseph Adessi, Director of the FBI.

He walks up to me. "So, you must be Jaxson James Phillips. "I've kept her safe for twenty years and it took you only two weeks to fuck it all up."

The scene unfolding before me is like something out of a Hollywood blockbuster. One of Joseph's men brings Marco in here. He looks pale and scared.

"Marco, I've been paying you all these years to keep her safe. First, it was the ex-boyfriend. We handled that, but didn't you learn anything from it?"

I jump up. "Marco works for you?"

Marco doesn't know whom to answer first, until Joseph bellows, "Marco, pay attention here! What the fuck happened? How could you let him anywhere near our girl?"

Marco looks scared—*he should be.* "I had no idea who he was until after the charity function, and by then, the photos were already out there."

Joseph gets in his face, "It's your fucking job to know who everyone is that she comes into contact with!" he yells.

Max steps in between the two of them. "I think it's time you filled in all the blanks, if we stand a chance of getting them both back alive."

Bella loses it. She tries to punch me before she hauls off and slaps Joseph across the face. Everyone freezes. Joseph turns to her, "Ma'am, I'm going to let that go because you're distraught over your child. Raise your hands to me again and you'll find yourself very alone, in a cold cell, for assaulting a federal agent." he warns. Michael grabs Bella before she hits him again. She starts a painful, wailing cry.

Joseph tells everyone but Michael, Bella, Max, and Marco to leave the room. "I have no choice but to tell you everything about my Cara. That's right. Her name is Cara Josephina Giaconna. She is my goddaughter and my name-sake. Cara's father, Antonio, was a very proud man. He was embarrassed by his family heritage and chose to join the Academy, turning his back on his Chicago Mafia crime family. He moved his wife to Los Angeles. That's where Cara was born."

"Antonio's wife, Gabriella, was a skilled heart surgeon. She was a rising star. She had the tiniest hands and the biggest heart. Gabriella was also doing cutting-edge research. She developed a new method to repair a part of the heart. Before her discovery, the patients could only wait for a transplant, but there was no guarantee that they would get one or that it would work. With this innovative method, she could give them a chance to extend their lives.

"When Cara was seven years old, she was kidnapped. At first, Antonio and I thought it had to do with some high-profile cases we were working on, but then Gabriella was kidnapped, as well. She was told that if she wanted her child returned safely, she had to perform the surgery she pioneered, on a very dangerous criminal. Of course, Gabriella agreed. In the process, Antonio and I were able to rescue Cara, but Antonio was shot. He hung on for two weeks, in the ICU. During that time, he made me Cara's godfather. He entrusted his family to me. He asked me to try to save Gabriella and protect them, at all cost. Gabriella performed the surgery, but the patient died—he was just too far gone, the years of the life he led, finally caught up to him. The patient's son held Gabriella a prisoner for two months. He beat and raped her. I was able to rescue her, but the damage was done. Gabriella was pregnant." He brings his gaze down to the floor, shaking his head before bringing his eyes back up with their sorrowful expression. "She didn't want the child, but her oath was to first, do no harm. She gave Cara to me and asked me to please raise her as my own. I didn't know what to do with her. I got her the therapy, she so desperately needed, to help her deal with the trauma. In the meantime, Gabriella gave birth to a healthy boy, but she couldn't look at him. Everyday she saw that boy, she was reminded of what she went through. She reached her breaking point and Gabriella hung herself. I thank God that I found her before Cara got home. I sent Cara to a private boarding school in England. I put the boy up for adoption, which went through, successfully, to a family in the Midwest."

There is more to this story than the version that Raven told me. "So why change Cara's name and put Marco on her?"

For the first time, I see fear register on Joseph's face. "The man who raped Gabriella was Antonio's brother, Vincent, and the patient was Antonio's father. They are the largest Mafia family in the Chicago area."

All I can do is stare at Joseph. It's as if he is talking another language. "Why target her now, if she even is the target? Joseph, by Max's account of what happened, it sounds like Michael Jr. was the target and Raven tried to stop the abduction, so they took her, too."

Marco stands up. "That would be something Raven would do, always trying to right the wrongs of the world."

"Damn it!" I yell at Max, "Do you remember anything else from the abduction?"

He begins to pace and I know, he's running over it again in his head. "They threw her phone out the back of the van."

"Oh shit, she has a second phone!" I jump up. Every head turns towards me. "I gave her a second phone that was only for me. She kept giving me a hard time about carrying two phones, but she promised she would. If they don't find the phone, we can locate her from the tracking app I put on it," I say, feeling hopeful. They all stare wide-eyed at me like I have issues. . "I know, I'm a little over the top, but I guess, right about now, everyone here is a little happy about that."

Joseph has me write the number down and he gives it to his assistant.

Max turns to Joseph, "Do you know where the half-brother is?"

Joseph's face turns pale. "When he was adopted, everything about the boy was turned over to the local office in Lansing, Michigan. I never saw him again. They are sending over everything they have on him. We didn't view him as a threat, and everything has been quiet, until two weeks ago, when Jax stepped into the picture."

Duke rings me. "I told you, no interruptions." He informs me that I have a delivery. *What the fuck?* I go out to his desk. "What's so important that you had to call me out here?"

He hands me an envelope. "I was opening the interoffice mail and this was in it."

I grab it from him. "Oh shit." I head back in my office and hand it to Joseph.

"Who took delivery of this?" he asks.

Michael jumps up. "Who cares? What do they want in exchange for my son?" "It was in interoffice mail which means; it could have been dropped off at any time, and handled by many different people. Max, we can pull security footage to see who has come in and out of the building."

Michael steps up. "What is it?" He looks and turns pale. It's a picture of Michael Jr. and Raven with a sticky attached:

"We have the boy and the teacher. The price just doubled, we will contact you soon."

The first thing Joseph does is put a tap on all my phones, as well as Michael and Bella's. We pull security footage from right after the abduction so Max can go through all of it. There is someone dropping off the envelope, but the person always keeps his head away from the cameras, so there's no way to tell if it's a man or a woman.

"Bella, where is Mum?" I ask her, suddenly feeling panicked. She stares through me like she's not really hearing me. *"Bella, where the fuck is Mum?"*

"I don't know," she whispers.

I ring my mum. She is not answering her phone. *Fuck.* "Max, call the detail that is on my mum and find out where the fuck she is and why she is not answering her phone!"

Bella rocks back and forth. She keeps repeating, "Jax, please get my baby back safe."

Max calls mum's detail. "The detail said your mum hasn't left the house since she got back from the school."

"Then, why the fuck isn't she answering the phone?! Why was she at the school?"

Max orders them to enter the house. "Jax, your mum is fine. She was in the shower. She is a little shaken up."

"Have her brought here. I don't want her alone right now. And find out if she saw anything when she went to the school today." I walk up to the bar in my office and pour myself three fingers of scotch before I have to deal with my mother.

"Joseph, how much do you think they're going to ask for?"

He shakes his head. "It's a lot more complicated."

"What the fuck do you mean; it's a lot more complicated? Isn't this about money? Wasn't Raven collateral damage?"

Joseph glares at me. "Well, let's see. First, they grab a billionaire's nephew. And at this point, I have to assume they know who Raven really is. Vincent, her uncle, is an animal and has made many enemies. The rival families will also come into play."

I pick up the phone and Joseph grabs it. "What the fuck do you think you're doing?"

I yank the phone away. "I am calling my banker and my broker to make sure I have enough liquid capital to pay whatever they ask for, if that's okay with you!"

He growls, "Okay, but don't do anything or talk to anyone without going through me first, Understood?"

Like I would really trust this guy. "Yes, understood," I humor him before ringing up the necessary people. When I finish getting things lined up, just in case, I decide to step outside of my office for a breather.

Duke is getting ready to leave for the day. "Sir, I'm leaving if that's okay, unless you need me to stay?"

I shoo him away. "It's fine, Duke. I'll see you in the morning."

Max steps out of my office. "What do you need that you don't want anyone to know?"

This is why Max is my best friend. "What did Mick say?"

I know he doesn't want to tell me something. "Just that Raven was trying to stop them from taking Junior, Raven stepped in front of him. They hit her in the face before they tossed both of them into the van. They beat Mick pretty good, but he did get a partial on the plate and a description of the van. Jax you've got to keep it together."

He knows how hard this is for me. "Yeah, for now."

Chapter Ten

Raven

WHEN THEY COME BACK, still concealed under ski masks, they take a picture of Michael and me. "We know you worked off the duct tape—you saved us the trouble," one of them says. Without another word, they turn and leave.

"Michael, look at me, please." I cradle his face in my palms. "When I was a little girl, about your age, I was kidnapped."

His eyes grow large. "What did you do, Miss Raven?"

I have to keep things positive for him. "Well, I was alone, so I had to trust myself and try to stay calm. I did what they asked, and eventually, my dad and uncle rescued me."

He smiles. "Do you think we will get rescued?"

I give myself a mental pep talk before I answer him. "I know that your dad and your Uncle Jax will move heaven and earth to find us." I don't doubt that they are trying; I just hope they find us in time, but I won't tell Michael that. I get up and start to explore our surroundings. There is a door to a bathroom with a toilet and sink. There are no windows. It is cold and when night comes it will get colder.

"Michael, we can get water from the bathroom sink. At least we can stay hydrated. Remember when we did the experiment with the flower in science? We colored the water, which made the flower change color"

He laughs. "Yeah, that was a cool trick."

Kids always think things they don't understand are tricks. "That wasn't a trick. It was to show you how everything the flower needed, it got from the water. We might not have any food right now, but we have water. That is what we need to survive."

He gets a huge smile on his face and I know he gets it. "Miss Raven, can I ask you something?"

"Of course."

He furrows his brows. "Do you ever do anything other than teach? I mean, you're always thinking about teaching stuff. Don't you just want to play video games or something?"

I burst out laughing, "Oh, Michael, thank you, I needed that."

He just shakes his head, smiling at me. "Miss Raven, are you going to marry Uncle Jax?"

I'm in total shock. "What would make you think that?"

He shuffles his feet. I can tell he's unsure of what to say. "My mom and dad were talking, and Mom said *'the handwriting is on the wall'* and then she was yelling at my dad… something about a dream. What did she mean by that? I would get into trouble if I wrote on the wall."

I really don't want to go into this with him but I need to be honest with him. "Okay, Michael, first, you shouldn't be listening to your parents when they're talking to each other and not to you. That's called eavesdropping. Secondly, I barely know your uncle; we're just friends."

I think it's time for a subject change, and quick. "Michael, do you have any pets?"

His face lights up. "Yeah, I have the coolest dog. His name is Vito. And he is a very big German shepherd. You would like him. He is very strong. Do you have any pets, Miss Raven?"

My mind goes back instantly to Winston. "Not now. I did when I was your age. I had a dog, too. His name was Winston, and anyone that came to my house would take one look at him and wait outside." I smile as I am telling him the story of the first time a boy tried to get close to me, "Winston walked up to the front door and that boy ran for the hills. He was a 235pound, chocolate-brown Newfoundland. When I walked him, people would cross the street. They thought he was a bear."

He pulls a kid's *Doctor Who* wallet out of his back pocket, opens it up, and shows me a picture of his dog. "This is Vito. When we get out of here, will you show me a picture of Winston?"

I hug him and give him the reassurance he needs that we will get out of here. "Sure. Why don't you go to the bathroom and wash up."

When Michael comes back in the room, he's back to his reticent behavior. I need to keep him distracted. "So, Michael, is your favorite television show, *Doctor Who*?"

His face takes on a serious expression again. "Miss Raven, it's okay if you're scared. I will protect you."

He is so precious, I just want to cry. "Thank you, Michael. We both need to stay strong together. So, back to television shows."

Sometimes, when I look at his face, I see the same facial expressions that Jax makes. "Well, isn't *Doctor Who* everyone's favorite television show?"

I start to laugh so hard I cry, which causes Michael to laugh along with me. Suddenly, one of the kidnappers comes in and videotapes us.

"Michael, do you watch *Doctor Who* with your Uncle Jax?"

He hits me with a huge smile. "Oh, all the time, Miss Raven. We wear bowties, eat PB and J's, and drink chocolate egg creams while we watch the show."

My heart is in my throat. This boy loves his uncle so much. "So, Michael, you could be a young *Doctor Who*."

There's that smile again. "Well, I guess when you put it like that, I could be!"

I pull him close to me, hopefully giving him the assurance he needs that we will be fine.

"Michael, now I know we will be fine because the *Doctor* is in the house."

Jaxson

MY MUM WALKS INTO the office, pale and crying. She runs right into my arms. Jesus, I can't take seeing her like this.

She pulls back a little, "Jaxson James Phillips, you get my grandson and future daughter-in-law back safe, right now!"

All heads turn to me. My mum has rendered me speechless. "Mum, what makes you think Raven will be your daughter-in-law? And what were you doing at the school today?"

Oh no, she's giving that look that will stop me in my tracks. "Well, if I waited for you or your sister to introduce me to Michael's teacher, I would still be waiting. I met the girl and I like her. She's genuine. You can always tell when someone is tender-hearted, and, my boy, she is. Now, do what you have to, but get my family back!"

Mum turns to Joseph, who is just staring at her, speechless. "Do you have a problem, sir?"

Joseph puts his glass down and walks up to my mum. "No, ma'am, I just wasn't expecting a ball of fire to come barrelling through the door."

Mum puts her hand out to Joseph, "I'm Anwen Phillips, and you are?"

He extends his hand. "I'm Joseph Adessi, Director of The FBI. Your name is very different; Welsh, if I'm not mistaken. I believe it means *very beautiful*."

Oh really, please tell me he's not hitting on my mum now! I'm about to say something but leave it to my mum to step up. "Mr. Director of the FBI, your knowledge of Welsh names is very impressive, however, that is not going to get my family back. So cut the crap and do your job," she bites. Joseph is speechless, and I'm pretty sure I have a stupid grin on my face.

My phone beeps. There is a short video of Raven and Michael, but there is no sound. I can see Michael laughing at something Raven is telling him. Leave it to my girl to find something to make him laugh at the worst possible time. Another text comes right after informing me that instructions will follow.

Joseph calls his tech guy in and gives him my phone. "There's a video on here. See if you can trace it through the cell towers. How are we doing with tracing the second phone?"

The tech informs us that the phone is indeed on, and they're trying to narrow down the location. All we can do now, is wait. Waiting is something I've never been good at.

Max decides he is going to Jackie's flat to see if there might be something she saw at the playground.

Maxwell

I PULL UP TO Jackie's building and I notice the doorman is helping another resident, so I wait.

"Please ring Miss Jackie Gerhard and let her know Maxwell Fleming is here."

The doorman informs me she's been expecting me, and I should go right up. When I get upstairs, I knock and the door fly's open. "Miss Jackie, are you crazy? You didn't even ask who was at the door!"

She looks so scared, and it rips me up inside to see it. "Oh, Max, you're the only one the doorman was instructed to let up."

I know I'm growling but I just can't help it. "I don't care. I have enough on my dish—I mean plate—right now!" I step inside and close the door. I turn around and she jumps into my arms. *Oh Fuck.*

"I'm sorry. Please, I'm scared. My best friend and the sweetest little boy were kidnapped right in front of me today." She's trembling and I pull her tighter to me.

"First, thank you for helping me today when they knocked me out. They used some sort of tranquilizer on me."

She runs her quivering fingers across my lips. "You should have let the paramedics look at you. They beat you up pretty good."

I shake my head. I need to keep it together, and right now—I just want to feel her touch all over. "I needed to get to Jax. Can you tell me what you saw prior to the kidnapping?" I hear the vulnerability in my voice, but I don't care to shake it. Holding her like this, feeling her breath in my face; it's giving me an achiness and a sense of urgency I haven't felt in a long time.

Her eyes instantly fill with tears. "Well, it was supposed to be me, not Raven."

She starts to rock back and forth, crying.

"Please explain. I'm confused. What do you mean; it was supposed to be you?" We sit on the couch and she takes a few calming breathes.

"We have a set schedule and this week was my turn to monitor the playground. I had a new student that I needed to do an assessment on, so Raven took my place. Oh Max, this is all my fault."

I pull her into my arms. "Hush, you don't know that. Did you notice anything this week that seemed odd or out of place?"

She looks up at me. "I did have a feeling like I was being watched, and I told Raven. She had me talk to the office about it but they said it was added security from Michael's dad."

I hold her tighter, not wanting to let her go. "Do you remember ever seeing the van before today?"

She shakes her head, "No, but I don't notice that kind of stuff. I'm too busy watching the children." She averts her eyes for a moment but brings them back. "They beat Mick up when he was trying to help. Do you know how he is?"

Gazing into her eyes, I see she genuinely cares about Mick. "He'll be okay. He was taken to the ER." I glide my hands up and down her arms to comfort her. "I'm sorry, Miss Jackie, but I need to get back to Raiders. I'm putting a guard on you, though. Do *not* ditch him. I'll call you later and update you. Lock the door and set the alarm, okay?" I pull her in for one final hug before getting up to head out. She follows me to the door and before I can walk out, she wraps me into another urgent hug, crushing me to her. I pull away and give her an encouraging nod. "I'll call, I promise." I reassure, and then leave.

I call Tony on my way back to Raiders. "Hey, Tony, how's the phone tracing coming along?"

"I should have it sooner, rather than later," he grumbles. I know he is working as fast as he can. "What did Jackie say?" I need to bounce this off of Tony before I let Jax know. Tony is my sounding board; he helps keep my thoughts clear.

"She said they have a set schedule and she was supposed to be on the playground, not Raven. That makes me think that Raven was never a target, but something has changed. Something is off and I can't put my finger on it."

He's quiet for a bit. "Do you think Jackie was the original target?" he finally asks.

I know where Tony is going with this. "I don't think she was, but I can't rule it out, either. Her father is a powerful man, but I know nothing about the brother. Maybe we need to pull a check on them." I rub the back of my neck to release some of the tension. "Just keep it between us right now." I wait for his agreement. "Any luck with the partial plate number?"

"The plate was reported stolen last week. This seems very well planned. If they knew who Raven was, then why do it this week when Jackie was on playground duty? Did they know about Jackie's dad? Maybe she and Michael where the original targets?" he rambles off his questions, barely a hint of breath taken between them. Even Tony is coming unhinged by all of this.

Fuck, this is so cocked up. "Just get that trace done. I'm almost to the office." And with that, I end the call.

Chapter Eleven

Duke

*F*UCK. *FUCK. FUCK.* WHAT the hell did I get myself into? She told me he would just pay up, and then we could go to one of the islands and never look back. I try calling her but she's not answering the fucking phone. This was supposed to be my one shot to get out of that hellhole in Michigan—permanently.

I can't go back home, but this is way more than I bargained for. *Why the hell does she not answer the phone?* Freezing my ass off, I decide to grab a coffee. Just as I step inside the coffee house, my phone rings. It's her—*finally!* "Where the fuck have you been?" She doesn't answer me right away. I actually look to see if she is still on the line.

"Relax, everything is going better than planned," she says, nonchalantly. *She's got to be kidding me.*

"Are you fucking nuts? They took the boy and the teacher. Why both?" I want to tell her to just fuck off and leave me out of this, but I'm in too deep now.

"Look, the boy was planned. I know Jax will pay up and pay big for his only nephew's safe return. The best part is, we now have a bonus—his girlfriend."

I get my coffee and sit down. "What makes you think he'll pay to get her back, too? He's only been with her for two weeks, and besides, she wasn't supposed to be out there this week. That's why we did it now." She's not answering me. "Hello, are you still there?"

"Where are you right now?" I close my eyes and tell her the location of the coffee house.

"Just wait there. I'm on my way. There is a lot you need to know." The phone goes dead; all I can do is wait. In the meantime, I try to calm down . Finally, she comes breezing through the door. Her long blonde hair and beautiful body renders me speechless. She sits next to me, stroking my arm. "Are you calm now? Can we talk?"

"Erica, you said this would be easy, this is anything but."

"Have you figured out who she is yet?"

"What are you fucking talking about, she is the teacher," I snap.

She laughs an almost sinister laugh. "Duke, guess again. She's not just the teacher. She is your half-sister."

I stare at her in total shock. "Erica, how long have you known?"

She leans in near my ear, "I found out two weeks ago," she whispers.

What the—is she fucking kidding me? "You've known for two weeks, and you're just telling me this now? How did you find out?"

She seems so proud of herself. "I have a friend at the Bureau, and when Jax hooked up with *the teacher*, red flags went up. He gave me a copy of her file."

Realization hits me. "Erica, is that why you pushed me to get the job as Jax's assistant?"

She's smiling like she's already won at this game of chess. "Duke, this works for both of us, don't you see? I get my revenge on Jax, and you get your revenge on a half-sister who took away your claim to any of your mother's money and your birth right within your Chicago Mafia family—".

"—Wait! What the *fuck* are you talking about?" I cut her off, unable to process the words that just flew out of her mouth. "Mafia family? Birthright? I don't know what you're talking about!"

"Duke, your adoption was arranged by the FBI. Your father is, Vincent Giaconna. He is the head of Chicago's largest crime family. That is your birthright Duke, that's what was taken from you.

"You have lived in near poverty when you didn't have to; never knowing your true family. As for me, because of Jax, I have been permanently banned from top businesses all over the world, and disowned by my family. It's time they both pay, and pay dearly." She hands me a file. "This is everything I could get on your sister."

"What's the next step? I mean, have you told anyone else who she really is?"

There's that sinister look again. "Not yet, but that doesn't mean that I don't have a plan in place to protect myself." I get her threat loud and clear. I'm seeing a side of Erica I didn't know existed. She gets up to leave, and then leans into my ear, "Just go to work tomorrow like you know nothing and I will be in touch." With that, she's gone, leaving me with the file.

I open it. It is filled with pictures of Raven and everything detailing what happened to our mother, including pictures of my father and grandfather. Reading everything, I realize I'm in way over my head here. It's not about a kidnapping anymore. It's about saving my own neck. This can of worms has been opened and there is no turning back. It's time to make a phone call and meet dear, old Dad.

Jaxson

MICHAEL TAKES BELLA AND Mum home, in case they try to contact him there. I decide to stay in my office. I can't go back to my house. Everything smells like her, and when I close my eyes, I see her everywhere. I don't understand how could she have become so embedded into my life, so quickly?

The sun is starting to rise and I go into the break room to get some coffee. On my way back, I notice another interoffice envelope on Duke's desk. It's addressed to me. I really don't think much about it, since I am running a major corporation—life goes on. I open it and watch a note fall out. *Oh fuck!*

I run into my office, "Joseph, they've made contact!" I yell.

Joseph jumps up. "Wait, don't touch it!" He opens the letter using gloves so he might be able to get some prints.

"What does it say?"

Joseph stares at the note, his eyes going left to right as he reads. "They are giving you the boy back for a transfer of fifty million to an off shore account."

"But what about Raven?"

Joseph is pale and visibly shaken. "They say that 'the teacher goes to the highest bidder.' They are contacting all the major crime families and letting them bid on her. They'll allow you to enter the bidding, too."

I look at Joseph in total disbelief. I pick up the phone to call Michael and Bella, letting them what is going on before I call my banker and arrange the transfer.

Joseph is sitting here, blank look on his face, obviously in shock. He finally looks at me. "I understand you're going to pay the fifty million for your nephew, but what are you going to do about Cara?"

As I pour myself a scotch, I turn to Joseph, "I will do whatever I have to. I need her back safe with me. But something is bothering you, I can tell. What is it?"

Fear washes over Joseph's face. "Jax, this is a bad can of worms that is being opened, and it might not be that easy to get her back."

I never thought it would be easy, but I would never tell him that. "Why? I have enough money to outbid everyone, and I will."

He nods and shuffles a finger at me and my canteen of scotch. I pour him a glass. "Jax, it's not that easy." He takes a quick sip as soon as I hand it to him. "These families are ruthless. They didn't get to where they are today by playing by the rules."

"Neither did I." I raise both my eyebrows before taking another swig.

Before I know it, my whole family is back in my office, including Junior's dog, Vito. Apparently, Vito has not stopped crying since Junior's been gone.

Duke comes in to offer everyone some coffee and food, but Vito starts freaking out. Duke puts everything down on the table and backs out of the room. Vito is trying to get out the door, his fur standing up. Michael tries to calm him down, but he's not moving.

Max starts pacing and *I know* that's not a good sign. I pull him aside, "Max, what's the problem?"

He shakes his head. "I don't know, Jax, I just feel like something is off. I spoke to Jackie. She was supposed to be on that playground, not Raven. They switched at the last minute. They have a set schedule, which apparently, someone knew about." He resumes his pacing and intermittent shaking of his head.

I'm about to question him further when Max's right-hand man, Tony, comes barrelling into the office. "I've got them. I've narrowed it down to a one mile radius of warehouses in Trenton, New Jersey."

Michael and I jump up to go, but Joseph yanks my arm, pulling me back. "Where do you guys think you're going?"

Michael grabs Joseph. "My son is in there; where do you think?"

"Did you think I would leave it up to you to find them?" Max barks, gaining Joseph's attention. " You're welcome to come with us, Joseph, but stay out of my fucking way!"

THE AREA IS DESERTED. No cars. Nothing. Max has a heat sensor that can detect body heat. Focusing on a row of abandoned buildings, the screen suddenly lights up with two body figures. One looks to be the size of a child, and the other could possibly be a woman. This gives me hope. Joseph grabs his radio, alerting his team and the paramedics which building we are at. The strange part is, there are no other figures. Before we can question it, Max is storming into the building. Michael, Joseph, and I are right behind him. All the rooms are empty until we get to a small room in the basement. That's when we find them huddled together. *They're not moving.*

Max yells, "They're alive, just drugged! Get the paramedics in here now!"

So much is happening so fast: yelling, pushing, and men holding us back. They set up IV's, put them on gurneys, and they're out the door in record speed with Michael and I running behind them.

When we arrive at the hospital, I have them put Raven and Junior in the same room. The doctor examines them both carefully and says they'll be fine—little dehydrated, but the IV will fix that. All we can do is wait until they wake up. The room fills up with family. The nurse starts to protest but Joseph just gives her a death glare that even makes me shiver.

Raven starts to stir. She is whimpering, "Daddy, don't die, please don't die."

My heart goes to my throat and I glance at Joseph. He's got tears running down his cheeks. I realize this is reliving a nightmare for him, losing his best friend and partner. I want to say something to him, but what could I possibly say?

I look over to Junior, and his eyes flutter open. He sees everyone and smiles, but then he springs up in bed, "Miss Raven, where is Miss Raven?" he yells.

We move so he can see her sleeping in the bed over from him. "Daddy, is Miss Raven okay?"

He strokes Junior's face. "Yes, son, she's just sleeping, same as you were."

Just then, Raven's eyes open and she yells for Michael. Quickly, it seems to register with her where she is, and Junior calls to her that he's okay. This seems to calm them both. Raven spots Joseph. Her eyes fill with tears, as do his. Their silence, I think, speaking volumes for both of them.

Finally, Joseph picks up Raven's hand. "My beautiful, Raven."

"Joseph, it's been so long. I'm sorry . . . so very sorry," her voice, soft.

"Shush, I will hear none of that *sorry* nonsense. None of this is your fault, not the first time and not now!"

Raven turns to me, and I get hit with those beautiful eyes. Violet to blues. "Hey, no more tears, sweetheart."

Before anymore can be said, Joseph starts asking questions and then Marco steps up doing what he usually does—lots of fussing. It hits me, just then, that Raven doesn't know that Marco works for Joseph.

Just as that realization hits me, Joseph grabs my arm. "Step outside with me, Jax, now."

We step into the hall, and before he can say anything, "This is the part where you're going to ask me to keep my mouth shut about Marco." I beat him to the punch. He raises his eyebrow as if he is surprised. "Joseph, I didn't get to where I am today by being a fucking idiot. I'm a leader, not a follower, and I'll decide what I want her to know. For now, your secret is safe, but I can't make any promises. Now, I'm going back to my girl."

Michael is not letting anyone question Junior right now. He is taking him home, which sounds good to me.

"Raven, the doctor gave the all clear, so I'm taking you home now." Before I can say anything more, she starts laughing and so does Junior.

All eyes turn to the two of them, but they just keep laughing. Bella looks at Junior. "What exactly went on with the two of you?"

"Uncle Jax, which doctor gave the all clear?" Junior tries on a curious tone but starts chuckling again.

Bella turns to Raven, "Please, don't tell me my brother got you into *Doctor Who*, as well?"

Raven and Junior are too busy laughing to even answer. I'm glad they found a way to get through this together.

I DECIDE TO TAKE Raven to the Ivory Tower tonight. "You know, Jax, you don't have to carry me I can walk."

I cradle her in my arms even tighter. "I know you don't need to be carried, but right now, I need this."

She lifts her head, "Oh."

"Yeah, *oh*," I whisper. I head right to the bathroom so we can have a shower. I want to check every inch of her beautiful body.

"Jax, I have a confession to make." I put her on the vanity and look into her eyes. I'm nervous about what she might want to confess.

"I had a dream the other night about your shower and I have to say, I think I had an orgasm in my sleep, dreaming about it."

Okay, well, not quite the confession I was thinking. "Raven, I would like to think that it was the man in the shower with you who gave you the orgasm and not the shower!" I start to undress her and she is smiling at me—pulling at that fucking ear. I pull her hand away from her ear and start kissing her wrist. I feel the jolt go right through her. *Oh yeah, gotcha, sweetheart.* We step into the shower. I want to kiss every inch of her beautiful body and she lets me. I kiss her cheek where a bruise has formed, and my blood starts to boil.

"Jax, it doesn't hurt much. I'll be okay."

"It slays me to think someone hit you, sweetheart." *She is so strong.*

"I'm okay." She kisses me so tenderly and I just want to be inside her. Right now though, it's not about what I want. It's all about her and my girl needs comfort, so I do just that. I put her into bed and head to the kitchen to prepare something for us to eat. My housekeeper was in today and left macaroni and cheese—now that's comfort food. I head to the bedroom with a tray of food and wine, but when I enter, I find Raven asleep in the throes of a nightmare.

"Please don't die, Daddy, Pleeeeeease!" My heart is in my throat. I take her in my arms and rock her. Finally, she wakes and starts crying. "Jax, I'm sorry, so very sorry."

I hold her tighter. "Raven, if you keep saying you're sorry, I'm going to lose it. You have nothing to be sorry for, you're so strong and so brave. You put Junior's life ahead of your own. I'm in awe of you."

She tilts her head back to look into my eyes and I know she gets it. Little by little she is knocking down my walls. "You need to eat. My housekeeper made mac and cheese."

She sits up, takes a sip of wine, and a few bites. "Jax, I was so scared, not just for me, but for Michael. He's the same age I was when I was kidnapped, all those years ago."

I need to keep her talking so she can try and get past this. "I know you were being brave for him. They sent a video. You were both laughing. It surprised us all. Why were you laughing?"

She gifts me with the most beautiful smile. "I had to distract him, he was getting very quiet. We talked about the things that he loved: his dog, Vito, and *Doctor Who.* You know he loves that show almost as much as you do, but, Jax, I think what he loves more is the bond the two of you have over it."

I don't know when it happened or even how, all I know is, I'm in way too deep to turn back now. I have fallen in love with this woman very hard. There's no going back and I don't want to.

"I'm glad that I have that connection with Junior. Family is very important to me. I cherish and respect it. I know how fragile it is, I've seen it disappear overnight. I think that's part of why I'm a little overbearing. Enough with all this talk; you need to eat."

Just like that, the conversation was done.

MORNING COMES AND I'M having the best dream. My cock is hard and warm, wet kisses are caressing it up and down like soft light flutters and it's the most amazing feeling. I slowly open my eyes and see Raven between my legs, slowly licking my cock up and down. Oh fuck, I died and went to *cock heaven,* if there is such a thing.

She locks her violets on my blues and takes me deep; really deep. My conscience thinks I shouldn't be doing this, she just got home from the hospital, but my cock has other plans. I'm about to stop her when she bares her teeth. I grab her head. I've lost all control. I'm screaming, slamming into the back of her throat, and start coming hard. The tidal wave finally slows down. I try to pull her towards me, but she shakes her head. She pleads, "No, Jax. I need this, please." She crawls up my chest, kisses me, and impales herself on my very firm cock.

"Sweet Jesus. It's okay, sweetheart, take charge." I understand right now she needs that, it was something that was taken away from her and she's reclaiming it. She takes my hands, leans in and licks and nibbles each of my nipples, back and forth, just like I do to her. She's riding me hard and I know I'm not going to last. I tilt up to meet her, and my cock hits the tip of her cervix. She starts bucking and screaming. "Eyes on me, baby, now!" *Fuck me!* Our eyes lock, and we crash together. I pull the comforter back over us and hold her tight, letting us drift back to sleep.

We wake and it's about an hour later. I'm still buried balls deep. I start to stroke her back, and she hums, "Thank you, Jax."

"Sweetheart, why on earth are you thanking me? As I remember, you gave me quite the fab morning!"

She giggles, and it's such a beautiful sound. "Yeah, I can feel you're ready to go again. Are you even human?"

Hmm. "Oh, believe me, I'm human. It's just the affect you have on me." I tilt my hips up, down, and around again.

"Jax, you have such a beautiful body. How often do you workout?"

"I do some sort of exercise six days a week, including weights. I eat healthy, so I'm able to have little indulgences without the guilt."

She slowly runs her tongue around my lips. "Six days a week is a lot. I've never seen you workout."

I can't help but laugh at her. "Sweetheart, you've been giving me my daily cardio!"

She smiles at me as she's working herself up and down, and I know I'm not going to last long. We lock eyes, and I know she's there. Then she does it! She does that fucking clench thing and I swear she needs to patent it. I explode so hard, I swear by all that's holy, the tip of my cock is going to burst!

"Jax, are you okay?"

I can't put two words together and she wants to know if I'm okay? "Sweetheart, when you do that clench thing, I swear—let's just say you need to patent it." I sigh "Cock heaven," I add in a whisper.

"We need to get ready. We're supposed to meet with Joseph this afternoon to answer questions."

She's not moving, and I can sense her apprehension. "Jax, I just want to put this all behind me and move on. Do we have to go?"

I feel sorry, but we don't have a choice. I know this is not over, and there's stuff she isn't even aware of yet. "Yes, we have to go, Raven. We can't just move on because there are more questions than answers. I'm not willing to take a chance that this might happen again. We were very lucky this time. I won't give them another chance. Done. In the shower you go, and I'll be in shortly."

Raven heads to the shower and I call Max. "Max, have you found out anything yet?" I know he's working non-stop on this, but he knows, when it comes to information—I want everything yesterday.

"Not just yet. However, there are a few things that are really bothering me."

Knowing Max, he's probably pacing. "Yeah, I could tell yesterday in my office. What's going on?"

He's distracted by something. "I'm not sure yet. I want to check a few more things. I'll meet with you before you see Joseph."

I hang up and head into the shower. *My girl is so beautiful.* She renders me speechless. I realize, yeah, she is my girl and there is no going back—*ever!* I just need to convince her of this. I stand in the doorway, watching her. She has her back to the door, her head tilted back, and water cascading everywhere. Fuck it, I'm hard again! Stepping into the shower, I trail kisses down her back, slowly turning her, dipping my fingers in and out, nibbling, and licking. She starts to quiver. She yells my name; a benediction from her beautiful mouth. I work my way up her gorgeous body, worshiping every inch of her and lift her up. "Wrap your legs around my waist." My beautiful girl doesn't hesitate as I lower her slowly onto my cock.

She throws her head back. "Ohhhhhhh."

I sigh, "Yeah, baby, *ohhhhhh.*"

She knows I need this slow right now, and she lets me. Up and down then, a swivel of the hips. First to the right and then to the left. She leans in and nibbles on my lower lip. "Jax, I can't hold it much longer."

I pull her in tighter. "Show me your soul, baby."

Her violets lock onto my blues and we're gone. I slide down the shower wall and just sit with my girl in my lap, my cock throbbing in cock heaven. "Jax, we need to get going."

"Hmm…"

"Is that all you're going to say? Hmm…?"

I can't even open my eyes, let alone move. "Sweetheart, my cock is enjoying being in cock heaven. I can't deny him this pleasure, don't you agree?"

She laughs at me. "I can't believe you call your cock *him,* and what the hell is cock heaven?"

All I can do is smile. "It's the happy place. Not everyone finds it—it's reserved for the special ones, a soul mate."

She gets up and offers me a hand. "Jax, once again you have rendered me speechless."

Raven

AS WE FINISH GETTING ready, I look over at him. He still has that crooked smirk and faraway look on his face. I realize, yep, I love him. Done.

Chapter Twelve

Jaxson

AS WE HEAD TO my office, Raven calls her school, reassuring them that she is fine and will be back to school on Monday. *Not if I have anything to say about it, but that argument is for later.* Right now, we have to meet Max and then Joseph.

We walk in, and Duke is at his desk. He informs me that Max is already in my office. He stares at Raven. *The little fucker better keep his eyes off her or I'll cut his prick off and kick him to the curb.* Duke gets back to work when he notices *me* watching him. Satisfied, I lead Raven into the office. Max jumps up when we get inside. "Miss Raven, please except my apologies. I'm so sorry."

Raven puts her hand up. "Max, it was not your fault. They knocked you out with something. I saw you trying to fight them off to get to us."

He shakes his head. "Still, Miss Raven, I'm sorry." She hugs him.

"How is Mick? He was trying to help us." *My girl has such compassion.*

He sits her down. "They are releasing him today from the hospital. What do you think we can do to help his situation without offending him?"

She looks so lost in her own thoughts. "I need to see him, Jax. I need to let him see that I'm okay. I hope this didn't escalate his nightmares."

I can only imagine what this has triggered off for this man. "Sweetheart, I will do whatever you feel is necessary to help him."

She smiles. "Thank you, both of you. What Mick needs most is to not be judged by anyone. People look right past him and they don't take the time to just listen. He's a proud man and very strong. He's just needs time to heal and someone to listen to him."

I sit in one of the club chairs and I smile at Raven. She returns with one more mischievous, confirming she knows I'm remembering that afternoon, in this very chair. *My cock springs to life.*

Trying to give my thoughts a different direction, I turn to Max, "Okay, mate, what's bothering you? What else have you found out?"

He looks at Raven. "First, Miss Raven, what did the kidnappers say?"

She takes a steadying breath. "They knew that Michael and I got out of the duct tape, and they said it saved them the trouble. The voice was the same as the man that was outside the gym. Their faces were covered the whole time. They came into the room one time, when Michael and I were laughing. They videotaped us, and walked out without a word."

"Jax, here's what's bothering me. First, Miss Raven wasn't supposed to be on playground duty that day. Second, when we got to the warehouse, there was no one there, almost like they knew we found out where they were and didn't have time to move them. Third, the interoffice envelopes are bugging me. We saw the first one being delivered, but not the second one. Fourth, they knew everything about Miss Raven's past, stuff that was classified. How were they going to sell her to the highest bidder? By the ransom they demanded when they asked for Michael, they knew you would pay. So, why not just offer you Miss Raven, too. It would be easier that way. This is about something more. I can tell you now; this is a puzzle that we don't have all the pieces to."

My eyes shoot back and forth between Max and Raven. I still hadn't told her about her being offered up for auction. She is white and shaking. I jump up and grab her. *Fuck.*

"I'm sorry, baby. I didn't get a chance to tell you everything. Fuck!"

"Jax, is there anything else you haven't told me?"

I run my hand through my hair and rub the back of my neck as I glance over at Max. He gives me a knowing nod, gets up and steps out of the room, allowing us some privacy. "Sit."

"This must be bad, Jax ,if you're telling me to sit."

Fuck, I could snap Joseph in half right now. "I didn't want to be the one to tell you this. It should be Joseph, but you need to know everything." I proceed to tell her everything Joseph told me about her, the half-brother, and finally, about Marco. She's shaking and very pale. I scoop her up and wrap my arms around her, holding her tight. I'm worried; she's being so quiet. "Baby, you're safe now. I promise you, no one will get to you."

There is a commotion outside my door. Joseph barrels through it while Max tries to hold him back. "Max, if you don't fucking let me go, so help me, I'll shoot your fucking Scottish ass and kick you over the pond!"

Raven jumps up and runs to Joseph. She reaches back and smacks him so hard across the face that even Max and I wince. I want to stop her, but I realize that she needs to have closure. She closes my office door and leans against it, not saying anything. She walks back up to Joseph, "Why?"

He has the decency to look ashamed. "Cara, sit, I'll answer your questions."

I see fire in her eyes. "My name is Raven, and I never want to hear that other name again."

He has the grace to look embarrassed. "Okay, what do you want to know?"

She starts to pace instead of sitting like Joseph suggested. "Why didn't you tell me I have a half-brother?" She stops and glares at him.

"Raven, I honestly felt it was for the best. He was a product of your father's evil brother; a brutal, vicious and jealous man." He pulls a handerkerchief out from his back pocket and wipes his brow before sitting.

She steps in front of him, leaning into the chair with her arms on each side, trapping him. "He was also part of my mother; a beautiful, kind, and tender hearted woman. Don't you think I should have had the right to know that there is someone out there? That I *actually* have a family member somewhere? Do you know how hard it was, after my adoptive mom died? Did you know my adopted father tried to rape me?! Is that why you put Marco into my life? After all this time, I thought he was my best friend—a brother—only to find out he is your *fucking* employee!" I see her fighting the tears and I want to take her in my arms, but she needs this more.

"Raven, I promised your father that I would protect you, no matter what. Hate me if you have to, but I would do it all over again. Antonio was not just my partner—he was my best friend, and he saved my life!"

"What do you mean; my father saved your life?" She asks through her tears.

"Raven, that day we rescued you, your father pushed me out of the way, and took a bullet that was meant for me."

I reach her just as she's about to hit the floor. "Fuck, Joseph, anything else you want to do to fuck up her life even more?" I snap. Max gets a cold towel for her head and she starts to come around. "I'm not letting you out of my arms, so don't even ask, sweetheart."

She nods, "That's fine. I don't want you to."

Max looks over his shoulder at Joseph. "Jax and I will keep Miss Raven safe. You need to find out who your leak is—and fast."

Max turns back to me, "Jax, that's the other thing I wanted to talk to you about. There has to be a leak somewhere. First, the Lansing office conveniently lost all traces of the kid. Then, the second interoffice memo was already here, yet the tapes don't show anyone delivering it; not like the first one. I told you . . . *something* is off. I need to have you stick to Miss Raven until we get to the bottom of all this."

Raven gets up. "Jax, I need to go back to my place and get some stuff. And I need to see Marco."

I don't want to bulldoze her, so I do my best to remain calm. "Sweetheart, everything you need, I can have brought to the Tower. We can deal with Marco, later."

"Jax, I know you just want to protect me, but I need to do this and I need to do it alone."

"Sweetheart, I'll take you to talk to Marco. However, I plan on being there the entire time. Deal with it!" I know I'm yelling, but this woman drives me fucking crazy. She takes in a deep breath, gives me a curt smile, and nods her head in agreement. *Good.*

Just like that, we're out the door. As we were leaving, I hear Joseph and Max arguing, but we're not sticking around to find out why. "Duke, I'll be out of the office for the rest of the day. If you need anything, I'm on my cell." We ride the elevator to the parking garage in silence. Maybe it will give us *both* a chance to calm down. "We'll stop by the hospital to see Mick before we go to your place, okay?"

She hits me with that smile. "Thank you. I know you're trying to protect me."

I pull her into my arms. "Stop thanking me. I would move heaven and earth to keep you safe and happy. I just wish you would let me." I kiss the top of her head and breathe her hair in.

"Do you think Mick would be open to working with Max in security? I could have Max put him downstairs as security for the building. Maybe if he has a job, it would be something for him to hold onto—a lifeline. I'll have Max talk to him about it." I ramble on without letting her get a word in edgewise. She doesn't really attempt, either.

I wish I knew what she was thinking right now.

WE GET TO THE hospital just as Mick is being discharged. He lets Raven give him a hug, which, I'm guessing, is such progress for him. "Mick, thank you for trying to help us. I'm so sorry they hurt you." She pulls away and gives him another once-over. As I watch their interaction, I realize how much Raven means to this man. It's a friendship she forged on kindness and respect.

"Raven, I'm sorry I didn't get to the school sooner to stop them."

She sits next to him rubbing his arm, offering him comfort. "Why were you at the school?"

He drops his gaze to the floor, seemingly uncomfortable with my question. "The other day, when we walked to the school, I noticed the van. It felt off to me. So, I thought I would keep a closer eye on you. Like I said, I'm just sorry I didn't get there sooner."

I extend my hand to Mick. "I'm grateful that you tried to help my girl and my nephew. I would like to help you, and before you say anything, please listen to me." I hold my other hand up to emphasize. We could use a man with your proven courage. You stepped up to the plate to help, when nothing was expected of you. A lesser man would have turned away. Just promise me you'll think about it." I reach into my back pocket, pull out my business card wallet, and retrieve one for him. "Here is my card; when you're ready, call Max or me. And again, thank you."

"Thank you." Mick extends his hand out for another shake. With that, we say our goodbyes and leave him to finish anything that needs finishing with his discharge.

Raven

WE HEAD BACK TO Jax's car in silence. This man has rendered me speechless. He is willing to take a chance on a man that most people walk past every day without a second glance. It's all the little things that make up a person. He might not show it, but he is tender hearted, and at this moment, I realize how deeply I love this man.

Jaxson

"I NEED TO CALL Max and let him know what Mick said about the van."

She takes my hand. "I wonder how long they were watching before they made their move. I was not supposed to be on playground duty, I took Jackie's place."

"Yeah, she told Max. She was distraught; she thought maybe it was supposed to be her. Max has been keeping a close eye on her." I reassure her.

"How long have you been friends with Jackie?" I decide to change the subject a little bit.

She smiles at the mention of Jackie and their friendship. "We were roommates in college. She is my best friend, and her family treats me like I'm their daughter. I could never ask for a better friend." Her grip on my hand tightens when I ask her why Jackie doesn't like Marco. "I'm not sure. I just know they don't get along, at all. I wanted the three of us to live together, but once they got to know each other, I knew that would never happen. Jackie looks sweet—almost submissive, but she is very intelligent and always observant. I think it has to do with the way she grew up. Most of her formative years were spent at her family's compound in Switzerland. She always had at least one, sometimes two, security guards."

"I'm sure growing up with such tight security made her more cautious when meeting new people," he states. "I better let Max know right away; what Mick said."

While he calls Max to tell him what Mick said, I think I'll check in on Jackie. "Hey, Jackie, I'm checking in."

She squeals, "Oh my God, Raven, I'm sorry. It was supposed to be me!"

I take a deep breath. "Calm down, we don't know any such thing. I'm just glad everyone is okay." *She really is like a sister to me.*

"Raven, can we get together tomorrow? I need a girl talk."

"Only if you bring the chocolate!"

She laughs. "I knew I loved you for a reason. It's a date!"

WE GET TO MY place in record time, which I notice, is the usual for Jax. I'm not even sure Marco will be home.

"Raven, do you know if Marco is even home?" Jax asks as if he's just read my mind.

Part of me hopes that Marco is home and part of me hopes he's not. I don't know if I'm ready to face him and his betrayal, just yet.

"Sometimes he works from home, but I'm not sure where he is today." We get upstairs to find the place empty. "Jax, I'm just going to pack an overnight bag. It shouldn't take me too long." I put my purse down on the counter and notice some of my magazines came in. I grab them and a pad out of the junk drawer before heading down to my room. I decide to leave a note for Marco, letting him know that I'm staying with Jax and also informing him that I've spoken to Joseph. *"We need to talk,"* is what I finish the letter off with. I walk out of my bedroom and Jax is leaning against the counter. Dang it, he is so beautiful. Before I leave, I have to dig out a picture I promised Michael, so I quickly go back in. I see Jax coming into my room out of my peripheral vision and he watches me dig through a shoebox.

"What are you looking for?" He comes over to see what I'm doing.

"I promised Michael I would show him a picture of my dog."

Jax is looking at the pictures in my shoebox. He finds a picture of my real mom and dad. "You look like a combination of both parents."

I'm about to comment but then I see it. "I found it! Look, this was my dog, Winston."

"Raven, that is not a dog, it's a grizzly bear!" he says wide-eyed.

I laugh, "He was a very protective Newfoundland, and he scared away many of my dates. That's probably why I never had a boyfriend in school."

Jax is stroking my arm, making me feel safe with his constant touch. Part of me wants to close the door and walk away from here, never looking back. The other part of me is determined to live my life without fear. He pulls me into his arms, and I need him. "Raven, you don't ever have to come back here or see Marco if you don't want to. I can handle it all for you." He understands my fear without having to tell him.

"This is my home and I love it. I'm not ready to let it go, and as far as Marco is concerned, I don't know what I'm going to do. I would like to see Michael today. Do you think that's possible?"

Jax smiles, then he calls Bella, informing her we're on our way. I have to laugh, he just does whatever he wants, whenever he wants, and watch out if you're in his path . . . *my bulldozer.*

*J*axson

WE PULL UP TO Bella's and Vito comes out to greet us. Raven kneels down, petting him and he loves it; licking and nuzzling her. I find this amazing since that beast only likes Junior. Junior comes running up to Raven as soon as we get in the door. I'm guessing he's excited to introduce her to his dog.

"Michael, he is just as sweet and strong as you described him."

We head into the living room where Bella, Michael, and my mum are waiting, but it's Junior I'm worried about. He's clinging to Raven, not wanting to let go. She kneels down so she's face to face with him. "Hey, buddy, you okay?"

He seems embarrassed, looking down at his feet. "Yeah, I was really worried about you. Mom said you're going to be fine. Will you still be my teacher?"

She smiles at him. "Miss Jackie will take over for a couple of days while I sort everything out, but then I'll be back. No worrying, okay?" She palms his face. This seems to pacify him, but I can tell something is not right with Raven. "I stopped at my place and found that picture I promised you." She retrieves it from her purse. "This was Winston."

He gasps. "Wow, Miss Raven, he really was huge and he does look like a bear."

My mum comes up to Raven and embraces her, and the tension in the room seems to ease.

"Hey, Junior, why don't you take Vito out back?" I suggest.

He laughs, "Uncle Jax, if you want me out of the room, you could just ask."

"When did you become such a wisearse?" I growl. Raven is giggling.

"Um, sweetheart, what's so amusing?"

"Well, it seems to me that Michael Jr. has inherited the Phillip's gene for directness."

Michael Sr. looks at Raven and throws his arms in the air. "Welcome to my world!"

After Junior leaves the room, my mum asks if we found out anything new. "Mum, the only thing we have right now, is more questions than answers." I let out a big sigh of frustration. Raven takes my hand like it's a lifeline. "It seems that the kidnappers were after Junior and Raven was only a bonus. The problem is, they now know who Raven really is, which puts everyone around her at risk. Max thinks there is a leak, possibly at the FBI and also at Raiders Inc."

Bella turns to Raven, "I hope you understand that I'm not saying this to be mean, but you can't go back to teaching at my son's school. Until you can get to the bottom of this, you should stay away from my family, including my brother."

"Bella!" I jump up.

Before I can say anything more, Raven grabs my hand and pulls me down. "Jax, please."

"No, Raven. No one will tell me who I can or can't be with, not even my family."

Everyone is yelling until my mum stands up and tells us all to be quiet. "First, my grandson is upstairs and can probably hear everything. Second, son, I understand your need to protect Raven and Bella, I understand your need to protect your family, but this is *my family too*, so please listen.

"Raven, you can't possibly go back to school until all of this is resolved. Too many children would be at risk and I don't think you would ever want that on your conscious. We know that my grandson was the original target, so that means he will still need more protection. Sending him back to school might not be the best thing right now. I think the best thing would be for you to home school Michael until this gets resolved. This house is locked up tighter than the White House. When a message was left here, Vito scared the person off.

I think Raven should stay here. She home schools Michael, and we add tighter security. Everyone will be safe. Michael will continue to get the education that he deserves and Raven will be doing something, rather than nothing. I already spoke with Maxwell, and he thought it was the best idea." she finishes her rant (a logical one, at that) and all we can seem to do is stare at her, speechless.

Bella stands up and takes Ravens hand, "Come, I'll show you to your new room."

Mum goes with them, leaving me and Michael, stunned at what just went down.

Michael looks at me and starts laughing. "What's so fucking funny?"

He's now in hysterics. "Raven's room has a twin bed and it's right next to Junior's. You poor bastard, you're so not getting laid!"

My fucking dick hurts at the revelation—*no cock heaven anytime soon.*

Chapter Thirteen

Jaxson

I CHECK IN WITH Duke, all is quiet at Raiders. So I call Joseph to see if he found out anything new, but nothing has changed. I head to the kitchen for coffee. I find Mum in there, already having her afternoon tea. "Hey, Mum, is Raven all settled in?"

Her breath quickens as her spoon rattles against her cup. It breaks my heart that she is afraid. "Jaxson, I'm worried, very worried."

I try to comfort her, "I know, Mum."

She shakes her head. "No I don't think you really do." She stirs her tea.

"Mum, I understand, but she wasn't even a target. It was Junior, all because of me, and now they're both targets. Unfortunately, I'm the one who started this ugly ball rolling and I'm the one who has to figure out how to stop it. I don't want their lives ruined because of me."

A tear escapes her and she quickly wipes it away. "You're a good man, don't ever forget that."

Raven comes in, I can't help but hug her; she's so brave. "You okay, sweetheart?"

She seems to be trying so hard to keep it together. "I guess. I just called Jackie. She's going to come by with stuff for me so I can homeschool Michael. I still haven't heard from Marco. Have you heard from Joseph?" She leans against the counter, crossing her arms. My mum quietly excuses herself, grabbing her teacup and saucer, nodding towards the living room.

I offer my mum a meek smile and turn my focus back to Raven. "I called him, but he has nothing new to report. I'm going to head back to the office for a little bit, then I'll come back here."

She shrugs her shoulders. "You don't have to do that. I know you have a lot of work to do."

Christ, this is killing me. "Sweetheart, I'm going to be stuck to you like glue, so just get used to it." She starts to cry. *Oh, fuck!* "Stop, *right now*. just stop. I can't take it when you cry. It tears at my soul, so please don't." I plead. She throws herself into my arms and holds on tight, kissing me like I'm her lifeline. "Raven, we need to stop this, like *right* now." She looks at me like a wounded puppy. "Oh fuck, Raven. Michael informed me that your room is next to Junior's, and it has a twin bed, so my dick has been booted out of cock heaven. If you keep doing that, I won't be able to control myself!"

"Follow me," she whispers, grabbing my hand. She leads me to the washroom off the kitchen and locks the door.

"Now, Jax, you'll do as I tell you, because after all, I am the teacher."

I nod, "Yes ma'am!"

She rubs her delicate hands under my shirt, and my cock has jumped to attention—he's such a greedy bastard. She brings her hands back out, reaches for and slowly unbuttons her blouse. She lifts each one of her breasts out of her bra. I go to reach for them, and she backs away.

"Did you forget that I'm the teacher? You have to do what I tell you." She rubs each one of her nipples until they are hard. Throwing her head back, she licks her lips. It's taking all I have just to watch. She undoes my pants and my cock springs to attention. "Sit down."

I hit her with my Jaxson smirk, "If I don't, will the teacher punish me?"

She moans, "Jax, is that something you want to find out, right now?"

I sit down and my head is level with her chest. She opens my legs and gets on her knees between them. She takes my cock in her hand, and it takes everything I have to control myself from just ramming my cock in her right now. *Oh, Sweet Jesus.* She takes me in her mouth; it's so warm. She licks up and down and then around. *How the fuck does she go so deep?* She finds that spot, just under my sac, presses, and just like that, I'm losing it.

"Oh fuck, baby, deeper . . . bare your teeth for me." I growl, "Fuck—harder!"

That's it! I'm coming from the depths of my soul. It's endless and she takes it all.

When she finishes, she places my cock between her breasts, rubbing up and down. Oh, fuck all that's holy; I'm hard as stone, again! She takes off her bra, tossing it onto the floor. She gets up, taking her jeans off real slowly, and then she slides her knickers down. She stands before me in nothing but heels. I know I'm growling as I try to reach for her. But she backs away, shaking her head. She takes the clip out of her hair, letting it cascade down, brushing her nipples. She slides her hands down her chest, playing with her nipples. Then she continues sliding her hands down and reaches between her legs. Her head tilts back as she dips her fingers deep into—what I like to refer to as—my cock heaven. She lets out a low moan and I think I could explode just from watching the show—giving herself pleasure the way I do. *What a lucky bastard I am!*

"Oh, Jax, oh, baby. . . so good." I'm fighting with myself not to touch her. She takes her fingers out and slips them into her mouth. Fuck, this is so erotic. I don't know how much more I can take. "Jax, I'm so wet for you." She puts her finger in my mouth and I taste her arousal. Sweet Jesus! She straddles me and slowly, lowers herself onto my cock. I'm back in my happy place. It is the most beautiful place in the world. She starts riding me really slow. "Jax, you're going to make me come really, really hard. Do you feel how wet I am for you? Just for you, baby, and your wonderful cock." Wow, she's picking up my habit of dirty talk, and I've got to say, it's beautiful . . . just fucking beautiful.

"Raven, look into my eyes. Are you there yet?"

She leans in. "Almost, baby. Play with my nipples, please." She doesn't have to ask me twice. I nibble each one and that's all it takes. She's falling, and I'm right behind her. Her forehead rests on mine, and she clenches my cock like an iron fist. I think I will definitely have to thank her Pilates instructor! She kisses me long and slow. "Jax, are you feeling better now that you've been to cock heaven?"

Hmm. "All better, baby, and you?"

She smiles. "I'm good now, but I hope no one missed us." We get cleaned up and sneak out with the hope that no one was looking for us.

Duke

AFTER EVERYONE LEAVES, I call Erica on my cell phone. "Erica, I need to see you. Please call me back!" I don't know how I let myself get *this* deep into this mess. I don't know what I need more, to get out of Michigan or inside Erica's warm cunt. Either way, I'm in way over my head. I sit at my desk, happy that I planted the bugs she gave so I could hear what was being said. Jax is too busy, fucking Raven, to think about anything else. But that guy, Max?— He scares me. Not even Joseph scares me like Max does. Max is not thinking with his dick; he's looking at the big picture, unlike Jax. How the fuck did this guy make so much money anyway, when he can be so easily distracted by the opposite sex. Erica said he is shrewd, but damn if I can see it.

I'm gathering up my stuff to leave for the day when I turn around and find Max, standing there, in the shadows, just staring at me. I nearly jump out of my skin. I'm not set out for this kind of shit! "Oh, I'm sorry. I didn't see you there. Can I help you with anything?"

Maxwell

MY TINGLE SENSE IS firing up. "Actually, Duke, I have some questions for you. Let's step in to Jax's office." I suggest. I can tell he's apprehensive.

"Is this going to be long because I have an appointment I can't miss?"

"I'm sure you do, Duke, but this is important, please follow me. Would you like some water? You seem to be a bit nervous."

He shakes his head. "I'm fine. I just can't be late for my appointment."

I walk right up to him, invading his personal space. I love to do that when I want to throw someone off balance. "I'll get right to the point then. Do you know how the second interoffice envelope was delivered to your desk?"

He shrugs his shoulders "How would I know? I wasn't here."

I take another step closer, and he steps back. "True, but it might have been delivered the night before and only found in the morning. I'm just covering all the bases."

He shakes his head. "I never saw anything. Now, if that's all, I really need to go."

I back up. "Sure, Duke. Sorry to keep you."

THAT GUY IS A little fucking weasel. I need to call Jax, but first, I want to sweep the office. I decide to call Tony, I'm sure he's still here. "Hey, do me a favor. I know Jax sweeps this place weekly, but something is bothering me, so do it again."

Tony never questions my tingle sense. "Sure, Max."

As I wait at Jax's bar for the all clear, I see Tony coming towards me, motioning me to be quiet. He holds up a bug but doesn't give me the all clear. He pulls out a laser and some spray before motioning me out of the room. He walks through the room spraying some stuff.

I've never seen anything like this. He backs out of the room leaving the bug, turns on the laser and the fucking room lights up like a Christmas tree! He closes the door and turns to me, but still motioning me to be quiet. Now, he begins spraying around Duke's area—nothing. "Max, it's fucked up in there,"

I'm in shock. "Tony, this makes no sense. Jax sweeps this place every week. He had special lead put in the walls. The only place to get a cell signal is in front of the window, and since it's all glass, a bug could easily be seen." I throw my hands out, miffed. Tony shows me one of the bugs, and it's the size of a grain of rice.

"Max, the reason there are so many is because of the lead in the walls. They are bouncing off of each other. There has to be a place in the office that doesn't have lead walls, where someone is listening with some hi-tech shit."

It's time I call Jax and get his arse here, now!

JAX GETS TO RAIDERS in record time. "Okay, I'm here now. What is so earth shattering that I had to rush here?"

I motion him towards the office. "We need to show you something, but please, be quiet." I open his office door, and Tony hits the laser. Jax turns to me, and I can tell he is going to lose it. He steps back and closes the door. He motions to Tony if the area we are in has been swept, and he nods yes.

"Max, what the fuck is going on? We sweep that office weekly, plus the added protection of the lead walls. How is this even possible?"

Tony clears his throat, "There has to be a weak spot somewhere in that office, and with the new technology that's out there, they are bouncing from one transmitter to the other. We need to find the 'mother', which is what they are all feeding into."

Max is pacing. "Are the private bathroom walls lined, also?"

I shake my head. "I honestly don't know. I never thought about it. Heck, I didn't even think about any of this until everything went down with Erica."

Tony instructs us to wait while he goes in to sweep the private bathroom. He comes back out, letting us know the device is, in fact, in the restroom.

"It is the size of a capsule. I can deactivate it or we can leave it on. Now that we know it's there, we can monitor what we let them know." He sits on top of Duke's desk, waiting for our thoughts.

"Leave it for now." Jax finally decides. I take a deep breath. "Tony, please go and sweep Max's office."

"Please don't tell me you think I'm involved?" I feel my eyes practically bulge out of their sockets in disbelief.

"Max, don't be ridiculous. I just need a safe place to work and think." He gives me a look as if I'm crazy.

Jaxson

AFTER WE GET THE all clear from Tony, I inform him that I want Max's office swept two times a day. And no one is to know but me and Max. "Max, I don't want anyone to know what we're doing, understood?"

"What about Joseph and Raven?"

I shake my head. "Until we get to the bottom of this, no one."

"Okay, understood," he agrees.

"All right, Max, bring me up to speed."

He starts his pacing and surprisingly, it is calming me. "Jax, you know that second envelope is bothering me, so I questioned Duke today about it."

"But, Max, you know he wasn't even here."

He stops pacing. "I thought of that, but who's to say it wasn't delivered the night before? And why was there no footage like the first one? There are too many questions and not enough answers. I know we did a check on him before you hired him, but I'd like to dig further, if that's okay with you?"

"Sure, but what reason would he have?"

"Try fifty million of them, Jax. Let's not forget the original ransom was fifty million for Junior. Raven was a bonus. The whole truth about Raven's family came out in your office, which we now know was bugged, between the last sweep and today. So who ever was listening, learned about her family when Joseph showed up."

I feel like my fucking head is going to explode. "Okay, Max, we need to find out who bugged the office and stop them before they auction off Raven's information to the highest bidder."

He starts pacing again. "Jax, I've been thinking about that. I think the key lies with the half-brother."

"I agree. I want to see the file on the kid. See if Joseph will play ball. If not, I'm not opposed to calling in favors. I'm going back to my place to pick up a few things and then I'm headed to Bella's. Any sign of that fucker, Marco?"

He shakes his head. "No, but when he shows up, do you want me to keep him there?"

"Yeah, Raven needs to confront him, and I plan on being there." I tap my finger hard on his desk.

I HEAD TO MY place to pick up some stuff. Max put a guard on me, even though I don't think I need one. Right now, I'm so distracted that, it's probably for the best. The doorman informs me that there was a delivery for me which is strange since, I don't advertise where I live. He hands me an envelope that was messengered over. On my way upstairs, I call Max and tell him about the envelope. He tells me not to open it, and he's on his way. I throw the envelope on the bar and pour myself three-fingers of Johnny Walker Platinum and wait for Max. Max shows up with Tony and asks him to sweep my place. "Max, is this necessary? This place is like Fort Knox with security."

Tony waves at us to get our attention and puts his finger to his lips to silence us. When he is done, he tells us all is clear, but do not bring anything from the office into the house.

Max puts on gloves and opens the envelope. Inside is a file, which contains everything about Raven/Cara, her mother, father, and her half-brother. The only thing that is conveniently missing is a picture of the brother.

There is a note:

We know it all. The starting bid fifty million. We'll give you first crack at it. We'll be in touch.

I stare at the folder. Words just aren't coming.

"Jax, there is that number again. I just don't like it."

My heart is driving the bus and not my head, which is never good. "I have to protect her. I can't let this fall into the wrong hands. Did you pull reports on her real parents?"

He pulls out a folder. "Her mother, Gabriella, was an only child. Gabriella's father was a prominent doctor in Virginia and Gabriella's mother was a district attorney. Her parents died in a car accident while she was away at college. A drunk driver hit them. There was a large settlement that was invested for her." He shuffles papers around. "Antonio's family is really bad news. They can be traced back to the early 1900's, to a Sicilian immigrant. Antonio's father, Dion, was the 'Boss of Boss.' Antonio had an older brother, Monti, who died before Antonio did. Monti died in a bar room brawl. There's a younger brother, Vincent, and a sister, Annabelle. Annabelle was a surprise because Joseph never mentioned her. It seems when Dion died, Vincent took over the business, which includes a lucrative, drug business.

"You remember when John Gotti was in power in New York? It seemed none of the charges ever stuck to him, earning him the nickname, 'Teflon Don.' Well the same could be said for Vincent."

"Max what are our options here?"

He pours a scotch, "Well, I think we need to play ball until we can figure out who the moles are."

"You think there is more than one?"

He downs his drink. "Yeah, I do. I think there's one within the FBI, which is obvious by this file, and I really think there is a leak in your office."

"Max, take the file and lock it in your office safe. I already have the money ready, but I need some guarantee that this is the only file. Other than you and me, who else has the combination to the safe?"

He shakes his head. "No one and I plan on keeping it that way." He takes the file and puts it in the safe, locking it up. I can't believe all this is happening. I gather my stuff and head to Bella's. I really need my girl right now.

WHEN I GET TO Bella's, everyone is in the family room watching a movie. I snuggle up to Raven, holding her as close as possible. "What's the matter, Jax?"

I shake my head. "Nothing, I just need this right now." She doesn't press for information, which is good because I'm on overload.

"Jax, did you eat dinner?"

I look into those beautiful eyes, "No."

She takes my hand, "Okay, come in the kitchen."

I know I have a look of shock on my face. "Why, Miss Raven, are you going to cook for me?"

She looks offended. "I may not cook, but I'll have you know that I make the best peanut butter and jelly sandwich this side of the Mississippi!" She swats my arm. Raven pulls out everything she needs to makes me a PB and J and surprises me with a chocolate egg cream.

"Wow, okay, how do you know this is my favorite drink ever?"

"Jax, when you watched the video of Michael and I being held captive, did you wonder what we were laughing about?"

I forgot about that. "Tell you the truth, I barely had time to process everything, but now that you mention it, what were you two laughing at?"

She smiles at me. "You."

I freeze mid bite of my PB and J. "Excuse me?"

She repeats. "You."

"I heard you, but I don't get it. Why were you laughing at me?"

She takes a deep breath to steady her nerves, I think. "Well, I realized that I was the same age as Michael is when I was kidnapped, and I felt I needed to distract him from the situation. First, we talked about his dog and I told him about mine. Then I asked him about television shows, and it was right at that moment he told me that his favorite show is *Doctor Who*. Needless to say, I could not control my laughter. He told me how the two of you have a ritual of watching *the doctor* while you eat PB and J, drinking chocolate egg creams, and all while wearing bow ties."

"Oh." I give her a shy grin.

She leans in and kisses me. "Yeah, *oh*." She puts her head on my shoulder. "So, Jax, are you ready to tell me what's going on?"

I shake my head, "No, and before you jump all over me, I know you need to know, but I really only have bits and pieces. Right now, I want to block everything but you, out of my head, just for tonight, please."

"Okay, but tomorrow we talk," she states, adamantly.

I kiss her, "Okay, it's not like I'm going to cock heaven tonight, right? I'm just making sure." *This is going to kill me I just know it.*

"Well, if everyone goes to sleep early, you might get to visit your happy place."

I swear my cock has ears because he has just sprung to life! "Sweetheart, maybe we can slip sleeping pills in their drinks? Oh relax, I'm joking." Okay, maybe I'm not joking but I would never tell her that.

It's getting late and everyone is getting that end of the day, glazed over, look. Michael carries Junior upstairs. Bella and Mum finally go up, too. Raven curls up into my side, and I realize, there is no way I'm going to the happy place with everyone under the same roof. I want my girl, and I want her screaming. That's just not going to happen tonight. I look down to break it to her and realize she is out cold. It's okay. She's safe in my arms. It's not cock heaven, but it's still my happy place.

Chapter Fourteen

Duke

I WAIT ALL NIGHT for Erica, and she doesn't call or show up. This is so fucked up. Finally, I get a text message, telling me to meet her at the coffee house on 52nd street again. When I show up, she is already there waiting. "Duke, you need to calm down."

I glare at her. "Calm down? You don't have Max breathing down your fucking neck!"

She starts stroking my arm. "What did Max ask you?"

I'm trying to remember everything, but I'm not cut out for this shit. "He was questioning the second envelope and how it got there. I told him, I wouldn't know since I wasn't there. I made sure Jax found it before I got there, just like you said. How did they find the warehouse, Erica? You said they would never find it?" I ramble on. I can't help it, I'm in panic mode.

She looks pissed off. "Raven had a second cell phone that Jax was making her carry. The crazy motherfucker put a tracking app on the phone."

I just want this over with. "So what now? We've got nothing; no kid and no money."

"We have something worth a hell of a lot more."

I swear I'm going to crack soon. "What do we have, because I'm not seeing it?"

She smiles. "We have your sister's true identity that we are going to sell to the highest bidder."

I grit my teeth, "I'm too nervous. I'm not cut out for this shit!"

She grabs my arm. "Nonsense, your father is a cold-blooded killer. That same blood is running through your veins!"

I feel bad for Raven, but I can't let Erica know that. "What about my sister? I read the file. What happens to her through all of this?"

She studies me for a moment. "Up until a couple of days ago, you didn't even know you had a sister, now you're worried? I hope whatever happens to her, torments Jax for the rest of his fucking life!" With that, she gets up and walks out. I just sit here, not knowing what to do next.

Jaxson

I WAKE UP IN The same spot I was in when I fell asleep last night, with Raven still curled up next to me. I'd like to enjoy this for a little bit, but then, my cell phone starts vibrating. There's a text from Max, "Get to my office, stat." I look at the time and it's only 6:30 am. I place soft kisses on Raven's face, when all of a sudden, I feel very hot breath near my head and hear a distinct growl. *Oh shit.* I'm not an idiot. I stop moving. Raven starts to stir, I tell her that Vito is behind her, very upset, and to please not move.

Raven looks back at Vito, "Hey, big guy, everything's good. Down."

He lies down at once. Wow, that dog never listens to me. As a matter of fact the only one he ever listens to is Junior. "I can't believe how he listens to you, it's truly amazing." I sigh.

"Well, I need to jump in the shower and pop over to work for a little bit."

She smiles at me. "Why don't you use the shower in my room? I can meet you in there."

I scoop her up and race up those stairs with only thoughts of the happy place. "Sweetheart, we still need to be really quiet, so no screaming."

She steps into the shower. She is so beautiful, I could just look at her all day, but there are other priorities. However, cock heaven is at the top of the list! I pull her towards me. "Wrap your legs around my waist."

She grabs my hair and pulls my head back. Our eyes lock and I slam into her—hard! She kisses me to stifle both of our screams. "Hold on tight, baby, this is going to be hard. I need it to be hard." I pull back and hit her cervix again and again. I feel myself starting to shake and my cock feels like the head is going to explode! "Oh fuck, oh fuck, oh fuck, Raven! I'm there, are you there?"

I don't have to wait for her answer—she locks on to my eyes, and it's the peak just before the fall, the look into her soul. We fall together. I slide down the shower wall with Raven still latched onto my cock. I thank all that's holy for my girl and cock heaven. It really is a very happy place.

WHEN I GET TO Raiders, I head up the back way to Max's office. "Hey, sorry I took so long."

He's fuming. "Sit down, Jax, I have some video to show you, and you're not going to be happy."

He turns his computer towards me and hits play. I can't believe what I'm seeing. All I can do is stare at the screen in shock. *What the fuck?* Erica and Duke, sitting in a coffee shop together.

"Where are they now, Max?"

He takes a deep breath. "I have someone tailing Duke, but I don't know where Erica went. The security guy thought he should stay on Duke since that was his assignment, however, he e-mailed me the video so I could get a heads up."

Fuck, this can't be happening. "I want to rip him from limb to limb, and forget what I want to do to her!"

I look at Max and admire how he remains so calm. "Jax, you need to calm down."

In one sweep I throw everything off the fucking desk! "Don't fucking tell me to calm down! This fucker has caused so much trouble and danger, and for what? Money! And that *bitch*—I should have sent her to prison when I had the chance! Was this all about revenge?"

"Jax, I don't know, but again, you need to calm down if what I'm suggesting is going to work."

I take a few calming breaths. "Okay, what's your plan? It better involve a lot of pain for these two fuckers."

"We leave Duke in play—let him think we're idiots. Duke is the low man in all of this. We need to find the leak at the FBI and then we need to figure out what to do about Raven's family. Jax, I have a feeling that Duke could possibly be the half-brother."

How the fuck did this get so out of control? "Are you fucking kidding me?"

He shakes his head, "No, I'm not kidding. The background report only said he was adopted and that's not a crime. His adoption records are sealed and he has no police record, no flags at all. I just think it's all too neatly wrapped."

I know he's right. "Okay, I trust you with my life and the lives of my family. I'll go along with the plan. What do you want to do about Joseph? Should we tell him about Duke or should we wait?"

I know the answer before I even ask the question. Max plays all his cards close to the vest, always has. "I'm not in a rush to tell anyone anything, Jax. Let's just sit back. In the meantime, I have my guy following Duke, and I'll put someone on Erica, as soon as we locate her. I really think she is the key to this mess. Has Marco shown up yet?"

"No, which also seems very strange. First, he was up her arse all the time, and now, he's nowhere to be found."

Hmm. "Do you think Joseph might have him stashed away?"

Max begins his ritual of pacing. "Well, Jax, maybe you should meet with

Joseph. You don't have to tell him everything—just enough. I don't want to you to meet him in your office."

I stand up to look for my keys in the mess on the floor. "I'll tell him I'm working from the penthouse."

"I'm going to give you a small camera device. I want you to film him. Just humor me, Jax. There are things that I'm trained to look for, plus, I'm not emotionally invested like you are."

Who am I to argue with him? I call Joseph and get back to my place to set everything up.

WHEN JOSEPH GETS TO my place, I pour him a scotch, making sure I keep him in camera range. "Joseph, I'm going to get right to the point, where is Marco?" I spit out.

Joseph stares at me blankly for a moment. "Jax, I have no idea. He hasn't checked in, and he hasn't been to his day job, or back to the apartment. We also haven't heard anything from the kidnappers, have you?"

I watch his every move, trying to read his body language. "Everything has been very quiet, Joseph, almost too quiet.

Have you been able to get the file on the brother from Lansing?"

He looks embarrassed, as he should be. "It seems to be lost."

If I didn't need this man right now, I think I would just kick his arse out. "You're the director of the *fucking* FBI and you can't even find a *fucking* file? I'm really feeling very safe right now!"

He slams his glass down. "Don't be sarcastic, Jax. I'm doing the best I can. I will keep you in the loop, and you do the same." With that, he gets up and leaves.

I upload the video to Max before I go to pick up Raven, we need alone time.

Raven

I'M HAPPY THAT JACKIE is on her way, I need girlfriend time. As she gets here, I notice she has a guard, too, and I feel so guilty about it.

"Hey, Jackie, I'm so sorry you got dragged into this mess."

"Don't worry about it, It's been interesting for me."

Hmm. "Oh really. Okay, chocolate, coffee, pastries, and girl talk!" I saw the sparks flying with her and Max. "So this is about Max?"

"Jump right in, Raven."

"I've been hanging out with Jax and his family; they pull no punches," I giggle. Jackie joins in but then begins to tell me everything that has happened with Max, leading right up to his kiss. "Oh my God, he kissed you, and?"

She throws her hands up, "Nothing. That's just it, he doesn't do relationships."

This man is such a mystery. "Then why kiss you? Maybe he does want a relationship and maybe it's all new to him."

She pops another chocolate in her mouth and I have to laugh. She loves chocolate like I love Nutella. "Raven, he's thirty-eight, I doubt it's new to him."

I roll my eyes at her. "That's not what I meant. Maybe he never had the time for a relationship until now. I can't believe you were ogling him in the mirror!"

We are both laughing now. "I can't believe it either, but let me tell you, he has a wickedly, awesome body."

I put my hand up. "Too much information, girl. I have to look at him every day!"

Jackie gives me a look and I know what's coming. "Have you heard from Marco?"

I'm fighting the tears of betrayal. "No, not a word. I can't believe he was being paid by Joseph to look after me."

I can tell it doesn't surprise Jackie. "I'm sure he will be showing up soon with his tail between his legs. Are you going to continue to room with him?"

I don't even know if I want to live in my apartment anymore, but I'm not ready to share that. "At this point, I'm not sure what I'm going to do."

She pulls me into a big hug. "Well, you can always room with me."

I thank God I have her. "You really are the best friend anyone could ever ask for, Jackie. Thank you so much."

She picks up her stuff and pops another chocolate. "No worries, and on that note, I've got to run. Let's try and get together soon."

Raven

I'M GOING CRAZY JUST sitting around here. I decide to take Vito out for a walk—not that I'm alone, some huge guy that I have nicknamed ," Tank", is following me around.

I really need to talk to Marco. I just don't get it. I understand Joseph wanting to keep me safe and all. Here I thought I did so much on my own yet, I was being monitored the whole time! Add to that, the fact that I have a brother. I just can't believe that somewhere out there, I have a brother. And this information has been kept from him and me. Suddenly, Vito starts crouching down and lets out a low growl. "It's okay, boy, there's nothing there." He's probably just jumpy.

Marco steps out from behind the trees just as I turn around. Tank is on Marco in a second. *Holy shit.* I'm trying to control Vito and stop Tank.

"Vito, heel!" At least he stops. "Tank, it's okay, please let go of him."

Marco looks up at me. "Thank you, baby girl."

I put my hand up, "Please, don't call me that ever again." I just stare at him, not really sure where to begin. "Why?" It's simple, but it's all I can manage at the moment.

"I was young, with great computer skills, when Joseph recruited me. It was supposed to be real simple—just keep an eye on you and report to him over the years. I never expected to become friends with you, let alone, be roommates. I found myself getting in deeper and deeper, until there really was no way out. I was going to back away when you started going out with your ex, but then that relationship went terribly wrong, and I realized, I couldn't leave you. I thought with Jax, you had a chance at a real relationship, but then everything just got so fucked up."

All I can do is cry. "Do you know where my brother is?"

He shakes his head, "No, I never knew anything about that. I was only there to watch over you. Raven, you have to believe me, I would never hurt you. I love you like a sister."

We start walking back towards the house. I see Jax coming towards us and he seems really mad. He grabs Marco by the shirt, "What the fuck do you think you're doing here?"

"Look, Jax, I came here, in good faith, to make a mends with Raven."

"Good faith? Make amends?" Jax yells. "Do you realize how fucked up everything *really* is? Your and Joseph's lies have put Raven and Junior's lives in danger!" He reaches back, and in a flash, Jax takes one swing and Marco goes down.

"Jax! Was that really necessary?" I yelp.

He turns to Tank. "You're fired! You let this man—who is a potential threat—get close to Raven. He could have also gotten to Junior. Get the fuck out of my sight, and take this piece of shit with you!"

Tank picks Marco up and drags him away. "Don't look at me like that. I'm not a crazy man. I did what was necessary to protect you. I understand you wanted to talk to Marco, but I told you, I wanted to be there when you did."

I'm staring at him in disbelief. "I don't understand why you needed to be there. Tank was there and so was Vito. It's not like he was going to kidnap me or hurt me anymore than he already has, so why the need to be there?"

He growls, "Another threat has come through. I'm not saying anything to Joseph or Marco. At this point, the only one I know we can trust is, Max. That's why I wanted to be there."

I put my hands on my hips. "Well, maybe you should have told me, and I would have handled it differently. When you keep me in the dark, this is what happens."

Jaxson

WE WALK BACK TO the house in silence, both of us trying to regroup, I think. "Get your stuff, Raven." I have to calm down I don't want to scare her and have her pull another fucking runner on me.

"Where are we going?"

I pull her into my arms, "I want to spend the night at The Tower. Geez, now you have me calling it that!" I chuckle lightly. "I really need to be alone with you, no interruptions, and no worries. Just you and me."

She pulls me close and I think she gets it, "Oh."

I whisper, "Yeah, *oh*."

Raven

WE HEAD TO THE Tower. Midtown traffic seems to part like the Red Sea whenever Jax is driving. Thankfully, we arrive in one piece. When he pulls out the elevator key for the penthouse, it's just another reminder how removed we are from the outside world. Every time I walk into the penthouse, the view takes my breath away. I turn back around, Jax is right behind me. "Aren't you worried that someone can see in here?"

Jax graces me with that beautiful, crooked smirk. "Do you think I would ever let anyone see you? If it were up to me, I would lock you in here, forever! The windows are mirrored on the outside. We can see out, but no one can see in." He begins caressing my arms and then he lifts both my hands to plant kisses on the inside of my wrists, and there's that jolt—right between my legs! He starts to slowly remove my clothes and I'm left with just my bra, panties, and heels. He growls, "Undress me, sweetheart, real slowly."

I slowly unbutton his shirt, being real careful not to touch his chest. I know if I do, it will be game over before it even starts. I pull his shirt down and let it fall to the floor. Next, I bend down and take his shoes and socks off. *Even his feet are perfect.* I stare up at him. He's so beautiful. "I still have pants on, baby." I snap out of my trance and with shaky hands, undo his pants. He is left with his black, Calvin Klein, boxer briefs, outlining his delicious hard cock. I pull them down to expose my prize and what a wonderful prize it is. I lick the pearl of his arousal off the head. I kiss his cock. It's hard, yet so delicately soft. I take him deep in my mouth, and he growls, "Fuuuuuuccccckkkkkk!" Up and down, then swirl around the head, and back down again. I love that I can give him so much pleasure. He lifts me up before I can finish and kisses me deeply. He slowly removes my bra and panties, but not the heels. He trails kisses down my neck, stopping at each nipple along the way, slowly nipping and sucking.

"Oh, Jax."

"I know, baby, I know."

Kiss, nip, suck, and then lick, over and over again. He hits spots on my body I never knew were so sensitive. He finally makes his way between my legs. He does the kiss, nip, suck, and lick, but then he blows on my clit; I'm shaking and screaming. He guides me down to him and enters me very, very slowly. My legs wrap around his waist and my heels are digging into his ass cheeks. He takes both my wrists into one of his hands and holds them behind my back. He lifts one of my legs and puts it over his shoulder; oh fuck, he's so deep! I arch my back, raising my breast up and closer to his face. I can feel the slight graze of his scruff as he leans down to suck and nibble on my nipples. "Jax, I can't take it, it's too intense!"

"Hold it, baby, you know you can." He starts to slow down, giving me time to get some sort of control.

I need more; I want more, "Damn it, Jax, harder!"

He pulls my leg off of his shoulder, and now both legs are wrapped around his waist, again. I dig my heels into his ass, trying to push him in harder. He looks at me with that crooked grin and twinkling blues, "You want it rough, baby?" His accent so thick now.

"Yes!" I yell. Before I can even think, he has me flipped over.

He growls, "Put your hands against the window and lift that beautiful arse of yours in the air now!" He positions his cock, holding onto my hips and in one swift move, he rams into me.

"Fuuuuuuuccccckkkkkk me!" He's giving it all to me.

"Hard enough for you now, baby?" He backs out and rams in again, this time, smacking my ass over and over again. I'm on fire and at the same time, losing all rhyme and reason. I feel like I'm going to go right through the fucking glass! He gathers my hair into a ponytail in one hand and pulls it back, bringing me into a sitting position; my back to his front. He kisses my neck, nibbling painfully at my ear, and pounds into me, all at the same time.

"You're going to come, baby." He grunts as I clench. I turn my head to find his eyes. Blue to violet and he's done. Bam! His body is convulsing, shaking, quivering, and falling apart.

He turns me around, lifts me up, and carries me into the bed. He takes my shoes off and covers us with the comforter. The cool sheets on my ass feel good and I drift off to sleep in his arms.

I WAKE A FEW hours later and find that I'm alone. I hear some talking.. I put on one of Jax's shirts and head towards the voices. It's Max and Jax, they're talking about me.

"Have you told her yet . . . about Duke?"

"No, Max, I haven't told her that my assistant is actually her brother and that my ex seems to be working with him to sell Raven to the highest bidder," he replies. "I also didn't tell her that we think there is a mole at the FBI. Truthfully, I don't know how much more she can take. I know it's still bothering you that Jackie was supposed to be on the playground that day, not Raven, and that there were two cots in the room where they were held."

"Her father is a powerful man," Max says. "I mean, let's face it, someone who's able to negotiate a peace treaty, is not a lightweight. However, he's very well-liked and respected. Her brother, on the other hand, not so much. He owns a computer software company in Japan. He has had some questionable dealings. Tony is still digging. In the meantime, I am keeping a guard on her. I'll keep you posted."

I hear Max leave. They don't know I was listening, and I am in shock. Duke is my brother? Jax knew and didn't say anything? I'm being auctioned off to the highest bidder, like some prostitute or cattle. I run back to the bedroom. If I try to leave, he will know and then what? I get back into bed just as he comes in.

"Hey, beautiful, you're finally awake. You okay?"

I smile, "Yes, of course." I need some space, but I know that's not going to happen with this man. He is operating on the assumption that I can never be alone.

"What would you like to do?"

I need to distract him and I know just how to do it. "How about a nice, hot bath? Your tub is so much better than mine."

He leans in and kisses me. "Okay, I'll set it up."

He leaves. I throw on his shirt and my yoga pants, grab my bag, phone and shoes. I make a run for the door. I grab the elevator key, jump into the elevator, and finish getting dressed on the ride down. When I jump out, the doorman stops me. "Mr. Phillips asked me to hold you here until he gets down."

"I believe it is still against the law to hold someone captive." I yell in his face. I must look crazy, but I don't care.

He doesn't seem to know what to say and I run out the front door. I know I will never get anywhere with a cab in midtown traffic, so I decide to run through the park. I know it's dark, and I know it's a stupid thing to do, but none of that matters. Right here and now, absolutely nothing matters, but getting as far away as possible. I run through the park, and when I come out the other side, I hear my name. It's not Jax, but another voice I know.

Jaxson

WHAT THE FUCK? SHE'S gone. I get down to the lobby and the fucking doorman didn't keep her there. He said she ran into the park. It's night time and she's running through Central Park?

I do what any crazy man would do—I take off running after her. I'm yelling like a nut, and it's a wonder I don't get arrested. Just as I get out the other side, I see the back of her, getting into a black town car. And just like that, my girl is gone.

I pull out my phone and call Max. "Max, tell me you have someone on Raven?" I'm trying to breathe.

"Jax, are you okay?"

I'm going to lose it, "Do I fucking sound okay! Tell me you have someone on Raven?"

He growls, "Why would I have someone on her? You fired *Tank*, and you said she would be locked away with you."

Christ. "Yeah, well, she just pulled a fucking runner again! She got picked up by a black town car."

"Jesus, Jax, she's going to be the death of both of us! Where are you?"

I look around to figure out which exit I came out. "I ran out of my building and across the park, coming out on the other side, just as she got in the car."

I hear keys clicking. "Hold on, let me pull camera footage from the area." I don't even want to know how he is able to do that.

"I see her exiting the park and running towards the car but the person never gets out. She just gets in. I might be able to get the plate number from other cameras. I'll put Tony on this."

The fear hits me. "Max, she is out there with no idea about the danger to her."

"Do you know why she ran? Did she say anything?"

I start jogging back through the park. "She didn't say anything. The only thing I can think of is, maybe she heard us talking. If that's the case, she knows about Duke and Erica. This is so fucked up. I have to find her." I know Max will move heaven and earth for me. I just hope it's enough.

"Jax, maybe it was Joseph in the car. She's not stupid. She would never get into a car with a total stranger."

I know he's right, but it's hard not to panic. "Where's Marco?"

I hear Max ask Tony about Marco. "He's still at his apartment, never left, but he did have Chinese food delivered."

I need my girl back now! "Have you found Erica, yet?"

"No sign of her, and she hasn't hooked up with Duke anymore." This is so fucked up.

"I'm going back to The Tower. If you find anything out, call me." I hang up and head back into my building, hopping on the elevator. Once inside, I pour myself a rather large glass of scotch and down it in one shot. Definitely not the way scotch was intended to be enjoyed. Then I pour another and just sit on the floor in front of the window with the bottle. I can still see her handprints on the glass where only a couple of hours ago my cock was in his happy place. I down another, and I can smell her. Everything smells of her. I look down at my cock. Even he misses her. Poor, cock, you're never going to see the light of day again. Fuck me, now I'm having conversations with my dick! Oh bloody hell, how could everything have gotten so fucked up? There is so much I need to tell her. It's not just sex with Raven. It's *everything* with her.

Jackie

MY DOORMAN INFORMS ME I have a visitor. Maxwell Fleming is on his way up. I open the door as soon as I hear the knock. "Hey, Max, what's up?"

He comes in slowly, watching me. "Hi, Miss Jackie, have you heard from Raven?"

I shake my head. "Not since I saw her this morning, why?" I can tell he wants to tell me, but he is so used to not saying anything, it's hard for him.

Maxwell

"SHE WAS AT JAX'S. But she pulled a runner, and then got into a black town car" I inform her and quickly take her arm as she gets a wan look about her. "Miss Jackie, maybe we should sit down."

She's shaking. "I know she was very upset about Marco and the lies. Raven bases everything on honesty. I think that is why she likes Jax and his family so much—they are brutally honest and direct."

I have to laugh. "Yes that they are. Sometimes it's a problem."

She cocks her head. "Why is it a problem?"

"People don't always like with they hear," I whisper. I can't help but grow more concerned the worse she looks. Damn, I can't get involved. I decide to make her some tea. That's what Mrs. Phillips always does, and that seems to work for her. "How about I make you a hot cup of tea?" I wait for her answer but am met with tears, instead. "What? It's just tea," I say in a panic over her reaction. Oh fuck, her lip is quivering. *No, no, no.* Her eyes get wide and she looks right at me, almost as if she can see through my walls. This is not good.

"Raven is my best friend. She's the sister I never had." She takes the tissue, I'm offering, out of my hand. But it's no match for her impending sobs. Oh damn it! I scoop her up and cradle her in my arms. "Please find her, I can't lose her."

"Miss Jackie, what do you know about Marco?" I ask as I hold her tighter to me.

She looks up at me, "I know I don't like him, and Raven knows how I feel."

I don't know why I feel this is important, but for some reason, I feel it is. "Why?"

She shrugs, "I don't trust easily, and something about him is off. I can't explain it, but he's the reason Raven and I don't share a place."

I hold her tight because I know this next one might do her in. "Do you think he would hurt her?"

She gasps, "When people are pushed, anyone is capable of anything. He knows I don't like him. So when I'm at Raven's he makes himself scarce. Do you think he is involved in any of this?"

I wipe the tear rolling down her cheek. "Well, I know that he was able to hide the truth from her for a very long time, so that tells me, he is capable of anything. What do you know about Mick?"

She smiles at the mention of his name; seems everyone likes this guy. "Mick is a good guy, Max. He just suffers from the horrible side effects of war. He worships Raven and would never hurt her."

At least there is some good news about the people around these women. "Okay, that's what I thought, but since you've known him longer, I thought I'd ask."

The tears fall and I decide to just hold her for a while, so she can find some comfort.

"Please find her," she whispers.

Chapter Fifteen

Jaxson

I FEEL THE SUN on my face. I try to open my eyes but it feels like they are filled with sand. I need to get a grip and try to find my girl before she gets hurt or—God forbid—killed. I pry my eyes open. Oh fuck and all that's holy, I drank the whole fucking bottle of scotch!

I check my phone for messages; nothing. It's 6:30 in the fucking morning. I decide to head to the shower. I look around the bath and am reminded of my girl everywhere. I don't know if I can ever take another shower in here again. Everywhere I look, I see myself fucking her, every way possible.

I walk out and use the guest bathroom. I call her, but it goes right to voice mail. I decide I'm going to e-mail her. *I need her.* Fuck me, I've never bloody needed anyone! I pull out my laptop and just stare at the blank screen. I don't know what to say or how to start. The elevator door opens and I jump up, thinking its Raven, but it's my mum. Without saying a word to her, she knows I'm hurting bad. "I'll make the tea, lad, and you can spill your guts." I really want to laugh—Raven is right, all the Philips have that direct gene.

"Oh, Mum, I really fucked up royally."

She puts the tea down and takes my hand, "Sit down and tell me what happened."

I spill my guts; my mum has a way of making people do that without even trying. "Well, son, it sounds to me that she is probably more upset that you kept the truth from her than the actual truth."

Now I'm confused. "Mum, why do you think that?"

She takes a deep breath before continuing. "Because no matter what has been thrown at this girl, she still plugs along. She's very strong, but you don't see that. All you see is someone you need to protect. A relationship is: trust, communication, compromise, and forgiveness. It's like a juggler, who is trying to balance all of these balls, and if he drops one it cracks form.

"First order of business is, to find her and make sure she is safe. The second order of business is, to sit down and tell her how you feel," she states and I jerk my head back. "Don't look at me like I have three heads. I told you she would be my daughter-in-law. When you face the fact that you love her, then you'll know what you need to do next. Have you called Maxwell?"

I nod, "Yes, Mum, he's working on finding her, too." Before I can even say another word, she gets up and leaves.

Sitting here, thinking about my situation and how to handle it, I realize there's only one thing I can do; how I can explain what's in my heart. I always write stuff down. From when I was a kid, I found, that if I wrote it all down, then I could make some sort of order out of the chaos around me.

Raven,

My beautiful, violet-eyed girl. I'm so sorry I hurt you. I never set out to do that. I only wanted to protect you from more pain. I realize that I should have told you everything as I learned it, so that we could handle it together. For that, I am so very sorry. Please know that I only wanted you safe. My world has been off kilter since that wonderful morning, when you dumped your coffee on me, and it will never be the same. We can get to the other side of this, but only if we are together. Please come home to me, sweetheart. I need you.

Your Jax xo

I decide to text it to her and see if she answers me. Now, all I can do is wait. Something I've never been good at. I get dressed and decide to go see Marco. If he really cares about her, then he will be concerned that she is out there somewhere.

"MARCO, IT'S JAX. LET me in, we need to talk."

After a lot of pounding, he still doesn't answer, "Marco, I'm not going away, so open the fucking door now!"

Finally, he opens it a crack, "Jax, I'm not alone." *Like I give a fuck.*

"Do you know where Raven is?" I ask. He seems genuinely surprised by my question. "By the look on your face, I gather she hasn't tried to get in touch with you."

He shakes his head, "No, I thought she was with you. What the fuck happened?" He has the audacity to ask me. I swear I just want to punch the fucker.

"She found out some information and she is upset. She pulled a runner through the park and then got into a black town car. I haven't seen or heard from her since. Marco, think. Do you have any idea where she might go?"

He looks down. "No, have you tried Jackie?"

"No, I'll call her next, but if you hear from her, please contact me." He doesn't even answer. He just slams the fucking door!

When I get downstairs, I call Max. "Hey I just left Marco's place, he said he hasn't heard from her. He suggested I call Jackie."

Max is silent, "Um, don't bother. I've been with her all night, and she hasn't heard from Raven."

I've noticed the way Max looks at Jackie but, he doesn't do *relationships*. I've been so preoccupied with everything going on, that I never took the time to talk to him about her. What kind of friend does that make me? "Oh, okay, I think we need to talk to Joseph. I'm going to call him to come to The Tower. I'll meet you there as soon as possible, please."

I know there is something I'm missing. It's just floating around in my brain, but I can't put it together.

Max and I reach The Tower at the same time. "Max, did Tony find out anything on the car that she got into?"

"He got a partial plate, and we're running it now."

Joseph finally shows up. And I ask him in an accusatory tone. "Do you have Raven?" Max is watching Joseph's every move.

"Jax, maybe if you told me everything, we wouldn't be in this position that we are now!" Joseph seethes.

"I'll take that as a yes. I just need to know that she is safe."

He nods, "I have her in a safe house, but she is refusing to tell me anything other than she needs time to think. I disabled the tracking app you put on her phone, and when she is ready to talk to you, she will. For now, just wait. Having her locked away and safe will give us time to figure out what to do next. I know you don't believe me, but I really just want what's best for her. Putting her up for adoption was one of the hardest things I ever had to do, but if I had kept her with me, it would have only put her in danger."

"Max pulled files on her family. They are a nasty bunch, and apparently, there is a sister. Did you know about her?"

He shakes his head, "No, I didn't find out about her until after Antonio died. You need to understand. He disowned his whole family and cut all ties. He never spoke to them, or of them. It was one of the conditions for joining the Feds. His knowledge of the inner workings of the Mafia was beneficial in bringing down key players in the organization, but that also brought enemies."

Max shoots me a look. I understand what he's asking and I nod. He turns to Joseph, "Listen, we found out some interesting stuff that might be beneficial, but you need to understand, this is for your eyes and ears only; trust goes both ways." He pours Joseph a drink.

"Okay, Max, what do you have that requires me needing a drink first?"

"For one, you need to know about Erica."

He nods. "That would be Jax's ex, correct? My understanding is that she was a real piece of work; corporate spy shit. You really know how to pick them."

Max doesn't give me a chance to respond, he knows I'm teetering on the edge.

"You also need to know that we found out who the half-brother is. And he's right here, in Manhattan."

His eyes light up, "Really, who is he?"

Max starts pacing. "He's the same person who bugged Jax's office. That's how they found out that we knew where they were being held. We left the bugs in place, so that we can feed them what we want them to know."

Joseph puts his drink down, "So, who is he?"

Max takes a steadying breath, "That would be Jax's assistant, Duke. But there's more. He is working with Erica. Oh, and one more thing, there is a mole somewhere in the FBI, and that person is close to you. We need to find this third player."

Joseph stares at us like we have three heads. He's doesn't say anything, and then he gets up and starts pacing. I realize that like Max, this is his way to process the information..

He turns to us, "This is not some Hardy Boys mystery. We are talking kidnapping, extortion, and a slew of other shit. When the fuck did you find this out?!"

Max grabs his arm, "We just found out, and that is what Raven overheard. That's why she ran. I know you think she will be okay in the safe house. Now that you know everything, including the fact that there is someone near you who is a mole, do you still think she is safe?"

The realization on Joseph's face is a horrible. All three of us start running for the elevator.

Max jumps in the Rover's driver's seat and Joseph and I follow; me in the passenger seat, Joseph in the back. "Joseph, tell me where to go."

He shakes his head, "Max, I can drive us there."

I turn back to Joseph, "Trust me when I tell you, no one can get us there faster than Max, not even me."

It seems to register with him to just let Max drive. "Okay," he gives Max the address. Max is flying around the traffic and then decides to cut through the park, where cars are not allowed. Joseph has a death grip on the seat, and he's starting to sweat. "Good God, man, where the fuck did you learn to drive?!"

Max never even breaks a sweat. "I spent my summers in Italy, working for Lamborghini."

Max looks over at me, "Jax, get the light from under your seat and put it out, so the coppers don't bother us." I do so and now we have lights and sirens to clear the way. And Joseph looks to have aged quite a bit.

We get to the house. The door is wide open and Raven is gone. The agent that was guarding her is dead—shot in the head at point-blank range. Now, we have to add murder to the list.

We drive back to the tower in silence, each of us lost in our own thoughts. My girl is gone, and in so much danger. How could this have gotten so out of control?

WE HEAD UPSTAIRS AND try to form some sort of plan. We need to go through all of the events leading up to Raven's most recent disappearance. I just know we are missing something. Max makes coffee and starts with Joseph. "I need you to start with when you picked up Raven last night."

"I was on my way here, to see her. When I saw her run out of the park, I stopped my car and opened the door. I called her name, and she got in. We drove to the safe house, but she didn't want to talk. So, I got her settled in for the night, then this morning, I got the call from you and came here."

Max starts pacing, "Was your driver the dead agent at the house?"

"Yes, when you called, you said to come alone and not to tell anyone where I was going. I left my guy there to guard Raven and came here."

Max takes a deep breath. "Did you tell anyone else that you had Raven at the safe house?"

All the color drains from his face, "Yes, I called Marco when I found her running from the park. I told him I was going to take her to the safe house. I knew he was worried about her. The only other person who knew was the agent who was shot."

Max turns to me, "Okay, Jax, you're up next; what did you do?"

I have to organize my brain. "My mum came by and after she left, I texted Raven. Then I headed to Marco's place to see if he had heard from her."

"What exactly happened at Marco's?"

That fucker. "I kept banging on the door until he opened up a crack, then I told him about Raven."

Max's hands fly up! "Hold up. What do you mean, he opened the door a crack?"

"His exact words were, 'Jax, I'm not alone.' Then I told him about Raven. He was shocked and suggested I call Jackie, and I left." I run through. I'm confused. "Max, what's the problem?"

Max turns to Joseph, "Joseph, Jax had me pull a file on Marco, and he is squeaky clean. However, before Raven, there is nothing on him; what do you know?"

Joseph is now as white as a ghost. I pour him three-fingers of scotch. "Drink this. You look like you need it."

He takes the glass, but he is shaking. "Max, Marco was a street kid who was a wiz with a computer. The Bureau nailed him for hacking, and rather than prosecute him, we decided to go with hiring him."

I run my hand through my hair. "Max, it couldn't have been Raven with Marco. She was still at the safe house with Joseph. He knew Raven was at the safe house when I was there. You said he got a delivery of Chinese food last night. Did anyone see the guy leave?"

"Jax, he would never hurt her." Joseph pipes up.

I growl, "I'm not prepared to take any chances."

"Jax, I can get a warrant, within the hour, to pull footage from the cameras around the building."

Max is already on the phone to Tony, "I'm not waiting around while you get a warrant. Max is getting the footage now."

Joseph starts to protest, "If you get the evidence without the warrant, it will get thrown out of court!"

"Joseph, get your head out of your fucking arse, I'm not waiting on some fucking warrant. I want my girl back *now*, and God help anyone who gets in my fucking way!"

Max grabs me. "Jax, where's your laptop?"

I go get it from the back office. Max opens my MacBook and before I know it, he has all the footage from last night. Max freezes the frame and blows it up.

I just stare at it, in shock. Staring back at me, from the footage, is Erica, dressed as a delivery man. Max and I are frozen, staring at the screen. *It can't be.*

"Who the fuck is that?" Joseph yells.

Max looks at him, "That, my friend, is Jax's worst nightmare come to life, Erica."

I can't move, I can't think, and I'm holding my breath. It's amazing what stupid random shit comes to light in your brain when you're in shock.

"I thought Marco was gay?" Even after it left my mouth, I knew what he was going to say, and personally, I could give a royal fuck who he's shagging.

However, my girl's life is in danger by a woman who despises me, and a man whom, by all accounts, she thought was gay.

"Well, not that it has ever come up in conversation, but I believe him to be bisexual. Why do you ask?"

"Well, we all thought he was gay. Marco with Erica changes things. Erica is a predator; she uses sex to get what she wants. Raven trusted Marco. Did he know where the safe house was?"

Joseph grabs the bar, his wan appearance only getting worse as he probably just came to the same realization that I did. Marco had to be the one that shot the agent, point blank—the kill shot.

Neither one of us is paying attention to Max, but then I hear him talking on the phone while he starts to pace. "Hold on, Tony, let me ask him." He pulls the phone away from his ear a bit. "Jax, you know that tracker app you put on Raven's phone?"

"Yeah, but Joseph said he deactivated it."

He grabs me. "Do you remember which version you purchased?"

"Yeah, the deluxe, but it's only because she kept running away and I wanted to find her. I was not being all stalker-like."

Max looks pleased that I was acting like a crazy stalker. "Tony, did you get that? Yeah, thank Christ the crazy fucker got the deluxe package. Can you do it?" He takes a deep breath, "Okay, mate, call me back, as soon as you know."

Before I can say anything, Max hands the phone to Joseph, "Call the clean team you have at the house and make sure they didn't find a cell phone."

He heads over to me, "Jax, the deluxe package comes with a code that enables you to remotely turn on the tracker app from any computer. With the access code, I had Tony hack your account and he is turning it on now. Hopefully, she had the phone on her and didn't leave it in the house."

Joseph hangs up his phone. "No cell phone was found at the house."

All we can do now is wait. Something I've never been very fucking good at doing.

Chapter Sixteen

Raven

JOSEPH HAD TO GO out. And now, suddenly, Marco shows up with a girl. How did he even know where I was? Joseph said no one would know I was here. I see Marco talking to the agent. He puts his arm around him in a loving gesture, puts his gun right between the agent's eyes, and pulls the trigger! I scream. Dear God, no please I can't believe this is happening, again.

"Marco, please no, not you, too! What the fuck are you doing? Why, Marco, why?!" I cry. The smell of blood and gunpowder fills my nostrils, catapulting me back to that one moment in time—the moment that changed my life forever. I scream a silent scream; the shrill sound, only in my mind. I'm seven, frozen with fear. Blood is everywhere. The metallic smell, turning my stomach. I'm trembling. I can't breathe. *Help me, Daddy, please don't die.* Marco slaps me out of my haze. His eyes are dark and he's wiping blood splatters from his face.

"Raven, this is my friend, Erica. She is going to help you deal with everything."

I look at him confused, "What do you mean, help me deal with everything? I don't even know this woman, and at this point, I'm not even sure about you anymore!" And without another minute going by, I suddenly realize—Erica is the same corporate spy that Jax was in love with. My knees give out and I hear the most evil laugh right before I pass out.

When I wake up, I find I'm tied up, in the back of a van. Sitting next to me, is Duke; the other player in this mess. My eyes engage Marco's, and I feel my tears pool again just before they start to fall. I have to look away. I feel beyond betrayed. At this point, I have no idea who to trust or what to do next.

We get to a small house in a quirky town. The sign says, "*Welcome to Woodstock, we're all here 'cause we're not all there.*" I almost want to laugh at the truth behind it. Slowly, it's starting to snow. Erica asks Marco if he was able to stock the house with all the needed supplies. He just nods. We get inside the small house and Marco unties me. "Don't think of going anywhere. It's snowing and dark out; you'll get nowhere fast."

Marco comes in with tea. He knows me so well. Stupid me, I thought it was because we were friends, but it was his job. I thought I knew him, but I really don't know him, at all. Duke is glaring at Erica because she is hanging all over Marco. The fog is clearing, and I'm realizing so much that I really don't want to know. "Marco, is Joseph in on this, too?"

He shakes his head, "No, Raven, he is clueless, although he did call me last night to tell me he found you running out of the park, apparently away from Jax. He said he was going to take you to the safe house and he would disable the tracker app on your phone. He practically gave me the keys to the kingdom."

"Oh," I whisper.

He smiles at me. "Yeah, *oh.*"

I avoid his eyes. "I don't have my phone. I left it at the safe house." It's really in my pocket, but maybe he won't figure that out.

"It doesn't matter. You couldn't get a call out from here anyway."

I sip my tea while I watch the three of them. Erica keeps eyeing me up and down. Finally, she stops and looks me in the eye. "Raven, you're a smart girl, have you figured out why this is happening yet?"

I'm so overwhelmed, I can't think straight. "I have an idea, but why don't you enlighten me."

She laughs, "That day at school, when we took Michael, you were just collateral damage, and I was prepared to kill you."

My whole body tingles. "So, what stopped you?"

Marco smirks. "I did."

"Why did you stop her?"

He takes a deep breath. "I stopped her because you're worth a lot more money alive than dead to the right people."

I'm shaking. "So, it has nothing to do with friendship or loyalty?"

He throws his head back and laughs, "Oh, baby girl, get your head out of the clouds. You're a high maintenance bitch and I'm tired of being your babysitter. I have been watching your ass, for the past twelve years, and now you're my golden goose; my ticket out."

"I wasn't supposed to be on the playground that day. If it was Jackie, what would you have done?"

"She would be dead right now. Although, her father would have paid big bucks for her safe return," he informs me. I believe him, and I'm happy she switched places with me.

"I don't understand how Duke comes into all of this? I think I deserve to know how my half-brother, that I never knew about, was brought into this plan."

He takes a deep breath. "You're right, you deserve to know the truth. Six months ago, Joseph was diagnosed with advanced stage prostate cancer. He was worried what would happen to you when he died—ironic, I know. So, he sat me down and told me the entire story of your life and your parent's lives."

"I was already with Erica, and she wanted revenge for being blacklisted from every major corporation, thanks to Jax. I had a friend, in the Lansing office, pull the file for Duke. After reading Duke's file, I realized that he would be a perfect mole, just like I was Joseph's perfect mole. Poor Duke didn't know anything about you. He's in it for the money and the sex. We just needed to get him into Raiders Inc."

"Erica still had some contacts, so she reached out to the ones that were burned by Jax. It didn't take long for one of them to help us. Duke was supposed to find out everything he could about Junior, imagine my surprise when I found out that you were his teacher!" He throws his head back and laughs. "After that, all the pieces just fell into place, which started with you dumping your coffee all over Jax."

I'm in shock. I can't believe this man, sitting in front of me, is the same man, that I have been friends with, for the last twelve years.

"But they didn't fall into place. We got away from your kidnappers."

He nods. "Yeah, well, thanks to the bugs that Duke put in Jax's office, we found out that your phone had a tracker app. Believe me, I would much rather have gotten the fifty million wired to my off shore account, then having to abort that mission. Instead of sitting on a warm beach, drinking champagne, and living off the interest, I'm now sitting in a cold house, with snow all around me, and still dealing with your high maintenance ass!" He gets up, kicking the chair as he leaves the room. I look at my tea, betting it's cold. Duke is still glaring at Erica, and she is smirking at me. *Ugh!*

Jaxson

"MAX, WHEN THE FUCK is Tony going to have this done?" Now, I'm the one pacing.

"He's working on it. There are a lot of security walls in place."

I look over at Joseph and he doesn't look good; his skin has almost a grayish tint to it. "Joseph, can I get you some water or something."

He nods, and as I hand him the glass, I notice his hand is shaking. Max turns to him, "Joseph, how long do you have?"

I'm floored. How does Max know anything? *Oh fuck, what am I thinking?* It's Max, for Christ sake. He knows if the wind shifts. "They told me I had a year, that I should get my affairs in order. That was six months ago."

"Is that when you told Marco the whole story?" Max asks.

Joseph laughs, "Max, you amaze me. You really should be working for us."

Max chuckles. "Joseph, I could never work for the Feds. I need things done yesterday, and you guys have too much red tape. Not to mention, in your world, too much information is put on paper. I'm thinking that's when Marco went off the rails, but you can't sit here and blame yourself." Joseph has a grave expression on his face, apparently Max's words don't seem to help him.

The phone rings and Max puts it on speaker; It's Tony. He's narrowed it down to the Catskills Mountain range. Max orders Tony to pull everything he can on Erica, Duke, and Marco, to find their connection to that area and get a better pin point of what their location might be. I grab the phone off the cradle before he can hang up. "Tony, Erica had a quirky uncle that became a recluse. He moved up to Woodstock. He wanted to live the rest of his life with nature and weed. Pull whatever records you can find. She used to joke that Flynn was flying without leaving the yard. We're going to start heading that way now. When you get the information, call me."

"Jax, we need the Rover. It's snowing here, so it will probably be heavy up there."

I toss him my keys, and I see Joseph flinch. "Don't worry, Joseph, Max also drove for the Royal family." I don't think that helps. We race out of the penthouse. The elevator ride down to the garage seems to take forever. We get to the Rover, Joseph gets in the back seat, double checking his seat belt. Max's driving through the blinding snow. All I can do is pray we can get to Raven in time.

"Jax, what did you do to this woman that she would want this type of revenge?"

I don't like to reveal too much of what I do, let alone to a Fed. "Joseph, my business is complex, but I'm good at it. I'm able to see the big picture and all the little pieces at the same time. Erica wanted in to my world, but she used sex, not brains. That was her first mistake. I was young and used to think with my cock, so I was vulnerable. When I realized what she was, I sent her packing."

"Why didn't you prosecute her?"

Right now I'm wondering the same thing. "The justice system here is for the rich and not the poor. She would probably have gotten off with a slap on the wrist, so I opted to blackball her from the only industry she knows. Because of it, her family also blackballed her, and her grandfather took her out of his will. We're talking millions here, Joseph."

He stares out the window for a while, "You said her *first mistake*. What was her second?"

"Crossing me and putting the people I love at risk."

He says nothing more as we speed through the night.

Raven

ERICA SITS ACROSS FROM me, her eyes glued to me. "I can't believe you're the girl that landed my Jax. You're so simple. You fucking teach second grade kids for Christ's sake!"

I just want to bitch slap her! "I think it's safe to say, if he was *your Jax,* we wouldn't be having this conversation."

She bangs her fist on the table and it makes me jump. "I would watch your mouth, bitch. I can fuck you up royally, just remember that."

As she walks out, she kisses Duke's cheek. Duke is being taciturn. My guess is, he doesn't know what to say or do with me.

"Duke, why are you doing this to me? I don't even know you."

He sits down at the table. "I wouldn't say that, Raven. We have the same blood running through our veins."

My eyes instantly fill with tears, and I have to fight to hold them back. "If you really feel like that, then why are you doing this to me?"

He takes a steadying breath. "I got sucked in real quick and deep, first by Erica, and then Marco. I don't see this ending well for any of us." He looks away.

"Duke, look at me, please don't look away. If you really believe that, then do something to end this."

He laughs. "What? Like going to the police? Marco shot that agent right in the head while Erica just stood there, talking to the man!"

I shake my head. "Just call, Jax. He'll know what to do."

I see such pain in his eyes. "You don't get it, Raven. Erica and Marco, they are just the tip of the iceberg. I did some digging, on my own, looking up our family tree. Even if we do get out of this, we are both fucked. They're all ruthless. I mean, Jesus, apparently my father killed your father, his own brother, and then raped our mother. If that's not fucked up, then I don't know what is."

I sit there for a while, thinking about all of this. "Duke, what do you think our family would do to us, when they find out about us?"

He shrugs, "They might embrace me, but for sure, they would kill you. It really doesn't matter, because they already know."

"Oh." I whisper.

We both sit here, watching the snow falling outside. I wrap my arms around my body and I can smell Jax on this shirt. *I wish I had never run.* As

I watch the snow, I wonder how something so peaceful could be happening in the mist of such evil.

Jaxson

WE STOP IN KINGSTON for gas, when Max's cell rings. He's pacing. That's never a good sign.

"Okay, Jax, Tony has an address. It's just off of Route 212, past the elementary school. Tony is worried. There's been some chatter and internet hits about the Chicago family, they might know already."

"Fuck! Okay, just keep driving. We will have to take our chances."

Joseph's phone rings. The caller ID says: Marco, and we all freeze. "Put it on speaker."

He takes a deep breath before he answers, "Hello, Marco, where are you? What the fuck is going on?"

Marco laughs, "Joseph, I want seventy-five million wired to my off shore account. You have thirty minutes from when I hang up."

"Hold on, Marco, how do I even know she's still alive? There is a lot of blood at the safe house." Joseph yells.

"Joseph, she is of no use to me dead, but I'll let you say, hello. Raven, say hello to Joseph, I'm sure he has you on speaker and Jax is probably sitting right next to him."

"Hello, Joseph. Jax, I'm okay. Please protect yourselves, I'll be okay," her voice quivers. What I hear next, slays me. He slaps her and she's crying.

"Marco, touch her again and I swear I'll rip you from limb to limb! You'll wish you were never born!" I yell. My adrenaline is so high; I can hear my blood pumping through my veins.

He laughs "Now, now, Jax, you need to play nice with me or I'll mess her up good. I've been babysitting this bitch for the last twelve years. I'm done."

"You listen to me, arsehole, I'm the one with the seventy-five million, so harm a hair on her pretty, little head and you will royally fuck yourself!"

"I just sent you a text with wiring instructions. As soon as the money hits, you'll get her location." He hangs up.

Raven

"MARCO, WHY ARE YOU doing this to me? I thought you loved me?"

He laughs, "Yeah, well you thought wrong, baby girl. I was just waiting for my cash cow to come in, and now it has."

"So, what about Erica, what happens to her?"

"You're so wrapped up in all your own drama, you stupid, little girl. Erica's my wife, what do you think is going to happen to her?"

My mouth falls open. "Wife?! When did this happen? I thought you were gay?"

He glares at me. "So many questions, and of course, you're so behind. I'm bisexual, and Erica is fine with that."

Suddenly, there is yelling between Erica and Duke, and he's shaking. "I loved you! I thought you loved me, and now I find out that you're married to him!" He's waving Marco's gun. Marco keeps his focus solely on the gun and where it's being waved. This is bad . . . real bad. Erica doesn't look as nervous as Marco does. She's laughing lightly and taunting poor Duke.

In the same moment, I see Duke snap. He turns towards Marco. "Duke, just put the gun down, and let's discuss this."

"I'm done talking, Marco." Duke shoots him, "That should, finally, shut you the fuck up."

Duke turns to Erica, "Now you're a widow."

I can't breathe. Duke just shot Marco in the head. Erica is looking at Duke, and then finally, she looks down at Marco's body. There is no grief, no crying—not even shock. Nothing but a blank stare.

"Well, Duke, I guess that leaves just you and me." She smirks. Is she serious? What kind of psycho was Jax and Marco involved with?

Duke glares at her. "Do you really think I want or need you?"

She laughs, "I think you do want me, and I know you need me to get out of this place."

There is some noise from downstairs. That must be the police, here to rescue me, thankfully. However, I notice neither of them panicking at this and I can't shake the sudden feeling that my first assumption could be very off. Duke scoffs, "I don't want Marco's leftovers and I, sure as shit, don't need you to get out of here."

Fear finally registers on Erica's face just as the door opens and in walks a man who could be my father's twin. "You gonna do her, son, or should I?"

Duke glances over to him but he turns back to Erica, "I wish I could stay, but our ride is here, and your number just came up!" He puts the gun right between her eyes and pulls the trigger. Her life is over, just like that. I'm left, looking into the face of a killer, my father's brother, and his murderer. "Raven, let me introduce you to my father and your uncle, Vincent."

My heart switches back and forth between racing and breaking all over again. "We met twenty years ago, when I watched him kill my father."

Jaxson

MAX IS SPEEDING INTO the night. The snow is coming down hard. Joseph is staring out the window, lost in his thoughts until he tells Max that the local police are on their way and should be at the house in twenty minutes. Max looks back to Joseph. "Do you really think I'm waiting for them? We will be there in five."

He takes a shaky breath, "Max, I know that you're a former Special Ops with the Royal Army, I'm sure you can handle yourself. I'm armed. I'm sure you are, but, Jax, you're not, and you need to stay in the car."

Max looks back at me, "Jax, under the seat, pull the panel down."

Joseph's mouth opens as if he's in shock. . "Are these even licensed? Fuck, are they even legal?"

Max just raises his right eyebrow at Joseph. "Jax, load up and get ready. We're here." Max tells Joseph that he will go around back and that he and I should cover the front. Just a few minutes and I'll have my girl back. We all step in at the same time. It's quiet—too quiet. We start searching room by room.

When we go up to the upstairs, the scene that awaits us makes me want to hurl. Two bodies. The first one is Erica, shot right between the eyes. The second body is Marco. He's been shot in the head. Their bodies are still warm. There is no sign of Raven and I can't help but feel paralyzed. I turn to Max, "Who?"

He looks around. "I venture to say she and Duke are together, and the family knows who they both are."

"God, forgive me, what have I done?" Joseph places his face in his hands.

Max grabs Joseph and throws him up against the wall. "Joseph, what the fuck *did* you do?!"

Just when I think things can't possibly get any worse, Max starts pounding on Joseph. I try to pull Max off of him. If he kills him, we'll never know.

"Joseph, before anyone gets her, you need to tell us *everything*."

"When I found out I was dying, I told Marco everything about Raven, and why I felt so protective of her. *Her father died for me!* Antonio jumped in front of me, *just* as Vincent pulled the trigger. Cara saw the whole thing. That's why she stopped talking. He convinced me that he would take care of her, and that for her safety, he needed to know where her half-brother was staying. I was blinded by loyalty, and that will probably get her killed."

My rage is rising to the surface as I hear his words. "So let me get this straight, you hired Marco twelve years ago to work his way into Raven's life? You then told Marco everything you knew about Raven's family, about her half-brother, that she wasn't aware of, and you told him where the brother was located?"

He nods, "Yes."

That's it. I look at Max, and before he can stop me, I punch Joseph in the face. Judging by the amount of blood, I've probably broken his nose. Max and I walk out, leaving Joseph with the mess he helped create.

"Max, where do you think she is?"

"Well, it's safe to say, that she is with Duke and he probably contacted his newfound family."

"So, Chicago?" I stare out the window.

Max is quiet for a bit. "No, Jax. That would be too easy. They don't want you finding her or Duke. With the amount of snow that is falling, it's safe to say, they are driving, not flying. I just don't see them driving back to the city, to get a flight out. It's too risky. Even Logan airport, in Boston, is too close. They'll still have the weather to deal with. I think they'll drive south. If it were me, I would drive to Atlanta. It is the largest international airport in the world. I'll have Tony check all the private airports from here to Florida. I also have him working on Duke's computer." Max puts a call through to Tony. "Hey, Tony, you're on speaker. I need you to check all the private airports from New York to Florida and look for any last-minute flights, heading out of the country. Did you find out anything from Duke's computer?"

Tony sounds excited. "I did find something interesting, but not from Duke's computer. Who's in the car, Max?"

Max gives him the go ahead to talk freely. "Okay, I hacked into Marco's computer. I just felt there might be some clues as to where they were taking Raven. I found out that Marco got married six months ago, but here's the shocker—he was married to Erica. It seems they've been together for almost a year. Oh, and it seems Marco has a very expensive, online gambling habit. That's how he met Erica, in one of the gambling chat rooms."

I can't speak, and I can't think. My entire world has been thrown off kilter so many times, over the past three weeks. I'm glad Max still has his brains, because mine are fried.

"Tony, were you able to access the logs from the chat room?"

He sighs, "Yeah, they are an interesting read. Really shows how twisted they both are."

"Well, Tony, they're both dead." I pipe up, finally finding my voice.

Max tells Tony to get on the airport search and pull the files for the

Chicago crime family as we head back to the city. I sit in silence, lost in my thoughts.

Raven

THREE WEEKS AGO, THE biggest thing I was worried about was parent teacher conferences. In that short time span, I have been kidnapped, for the fourth time in my twenty-seven years. I have seen four people murdered, right in front of my eyes. I have been lied to and manipulated, emotionally, by the people I trusted the most. Why is this happening to me, when all I want to do is teach my second graders?

As we are driving through the night, I notice that we are heading south. Where we're going really doesn't matter to me; I'm sure my life is over. Poor Jax, I think about him and feel so sorry. His life was somewhat normal, up until I came into it, although, the crazy ex and the assistant was his. We were both manipulated by people—the trusted ones. I think about Marco and the fact that Joseph put him into my life. How much of the last twelve years, with Marco, was real? How much was staged? I think about Joseph, and I know he blames himself for so much, starting with my father getting shot. He's dying, and I can't be there for him. So much pain and sadness, and for what—money? Is it worth it? I think I really understand, now, why Jax keeps himself tucked away in The Tower. I can't believe that Jax was ever involved with someone like Erica. She was so cold, and she had such a hardness to her, that I would never have expected someone like Jax, to be attracted to the likes of her. How could I not know that Marco was bi-sexual? Marco said that he married Erica six months ago, but when was he seeing her? Every time I saw Marco with someone, it was a guy. Pulling out of my thoughts, I realize we've already passed through Virginia. "Duke, where are we going?"

He doesn't answer. In fact he is just staring out the window, almost in some kind of trance. I know he is a killer. I've seen what he can do, but I don't think he was always like that. I honestly believe he was manipulated and just snapped. In the past twenty-four hours, three people were murdered, and I'm probably next.

As I sit here and reach back into the deepest, darkest parts of my mind, I close my eyes and I'm back to that horrible day, twenty years ago. I was coming home from school when a man picked me up, telling me that my parents were in an accident and I needed to go with him to the hospital. That day changed my life forever. That day changed the lives of so many people, actually, from the grandfather I never knew, to me—a clueless, little seven-year-old girl, just playing with her dolls without a care in the world. That day when Joseph and my father rescued me, I saw the man that shot my father, and now I'm looking at him again, sitting in the front of the car. *Talk about life, coming full circle.* I don't know if Joseph realized that I saw the man pull the trigger. I saw my father jump in front of Joseph, when that shot rang out. I wonder how much Duke really knows. I can't ask him now, not while his father is in the car. We all sit in silence. I finally fall asleep, but it's not peaceful, and it probably never will be again.

Duke nudges me awake. "We're here, you need to wake up."

I look up. "Where's 'here'?"

He points to the plane. "We're at a private airport in Charleston, South Carolina."

Oh God, this is it. "Where are we going?"

He doesn't answer. He just pushes me out of the car. If I get on that plane, I will never be found, but I don't know what I can do. "I need to go to the bathroom."

Vincent gives me a look. "You can go on the plane."

We climb up the steps, and I head into the restroom. I realize I still have my phone in my back pocket. I have very little battery left, plus Duke is right outside the door. I notice I have a message from Jax. He says he needs me. *Oh Jax I need you more, so much more.* What I wouldn't do to turn back the hands of time. I decide to text, rather than call Jax.

Jax
They don't know I have your phone. The battery is low, so I will shut it off, after I send this. Duke killed Marco and Erica. Duke's father, Vincent, showed up and took us out of the house. We are taking off from a private airport in Charleston, SC. I don't know where they are taking us. This madness needs to stop. I have seen three people murdered today, and I need to know that you're safe. Please don't look for me—this needs to end. I'm probably going to die, so I guess I'm not running anymore. You need to know, I only ran because you made me feel too much and it scared me. For the first time in my life, I've experienced pure love, and I will die, knowing that, for a little span of time, in my life, I was really happy, and it was all because of you.
Yours always
Raven xo

I hit Send. When it's done, I shut off the phone and go back to the cabin.

Vincent is looking at me, and then he smirks. "You look just like my brother, and we all know how that ended."

A chill runs through me. "Cara, I see in your eyes that you remember me. I was not aiming for Antonio. I was aiming for that prick, Joseph. But leave it to my goody-two-shoes brother to jump in front of him."

I glare at him. "Vincent, my name is Raven. Is that little confession supposed to make me forgive you for murdering my father?"

He laughs. "I see you have your mother's fire in you."

My eyes fill with tears. "Where are we going?"

"Some place far away from here." he replies. He looks like pure evil. I close my eyes. I can't look at this man, let alone talk to him. I drift off to sleep as we jet through the night sky.

Jaxson

WE WALK INTO MAX'S office, and my phone beeps. I pull it out, and it's a text message from Raven!

"Jax, what is it?"

I can barely breathe. "A text from Raven," I read them the message. Does she really think I won't look for her?

"Tony, you need to start checking the airports in Charleston for flights that have left tonight. Max, we need to go through the stuff that Tony found."

I see a look on Max's face that scares me. "Jax, if she doesn't want to be found, it will make things much harder."

I mentally count to ten. "Max, I'm going to find her—no matter what."

He starts pacing. "Jax, I didn't say we wouldn't. I'm just telling you, it will be harder."

I take a deep breath. "Then I guess we better get started."

Raven

DUKE NUDGES ME AWAKE, "Buckle up, we're getting ready to land."

I look across at Vincent and he is just smiling at me, making my skin crawl. "Cara, I'm looking forward to getting to know my niece."

I just close my eyes, fighting the bile that is rising in my throat. "Duke, where are we?"

"Italy. Sicily, to be exact."

There is a driver waiting for us when we land. Vincent is speaking to him in Italian. There's no need to let them know I understand what they are saying. When Joseph sent me to boarding school, I was housed with children from all different parts of the world. I learned Italian, Spanish, French, German, and a little Norwegian. I never thought this would be how I would use my language skills. We drive in silence, until we reach a beautiful villa on the coastline. Under different circumstances, this would be breathtaking. The gates open, and we drive up a long driveway that wraps around the cliff, to the top of the hill. The colors are magnificent; so many pastel shades, set against the blue Mediterranean. As we step out of the car, Vincent looks at me. "Welcome to your new home, Cara. You are free to wander around the grounds, but there is no escape. There are armed guards that have been told to shoot you, if you try to leave. All your needs will be taken care of during your stay."

He turns to Duke. "Son, come with me. We have lots to discuss." He takes Duke into the house, and I'm left standing here.

I walk into the villa. A housekeeper introduces herself as Maria and she shows me to my room. I look around the room, and it is beautiful. So much attention was paid to even the smallest of details. I decide on a bath, and then I need to figure out if there is any way out of here. The closet is filled with clothes. They are the right size, but they are dated. The bathroom is also well stocked. As I soak in the huge tub, I try to think of what to do next. I won't turn on the phone. I can't put Jax's life in danger anymore. I don't know when, or how it happened, but I realize, that I not only love him, but I'm *in love* with him. *He is a part of my soul.* I put my head back, trying to block out everything but his touch. His touch rendered me speechless. His kisses on my wrist were like a lightning bolt, jolting me right between my legs and curling my toes. That crooked smirk that could launch ships. When we were ready to fall and he would demand we lock violets to blues—that's the moment I knew I loved him. I found his soul, and he found mine. Before Jax, I thought I made a nice life for myself, just teaching and enjoying life with my friends. Now I know, there could have been so much more. I close my eyes and let the tears fall. I wonder about Jackie. I saw the way she looked at Max. What's not to like in him? Marco was right, he is very Daniel Craig like. My thoughts wander to Marco. The betrayal just blows me away. How stupid and foolish am I? I loved him like the brother I never had, but now I do have a brother—well, a half-brother, and he's a killer; a cold-blooded killer just like his father. How much more does Joseph know that he hasn't told me? Twenty years ago, I stood in that room next to my daddy and Joseph, just watching and listening to Vincent and Daddy yelling. After it was over, I blocked the whole thing out, never wanting to remember. Joseph sent me to therapy, but I never talked about it—what was the point? It wasn't until Marco came into my life and convinced me that telling someone might help me find closure. It was Marco, I told about my darkest days. Those days died with Marco. My skin is pruning. I need to get out of the tub and find something to eat. I find a pair of jeans that fit, but the t-shirt is snug for me. Time to explore my prison and figure a way out of here.

As I head downstairs, I see Vincent and Duke having coffee. It's amazing how Duke just fell right into place with Vincent. As I pour a cup of coffee, I feel their eyes on me.

"Cara, I see you found your mother's clothes." My eyes fill with tears and the bile, that I was fighting to keep down, is back. "Your mother loved it here. I don't know what Joseph told you, but I'm here to set the record straight."

My mother's clothes. That's why the styles are so dated—they're twenty years old. I have nothing that belonged to my mother. How ironic is it, that I'm being held prisoner, in the same clothes that she was?

"Vincent, I was told that you held my mother for two months, after my father died. I was also told that you raped her repeatedly before she was rescued. She was pregnant with Duke. I was sent away to boarding school, and she gave birth. My mother could not look at Duke and hung herself. Joseph put him up for adoption. That about covers it." I ramble through the information like bullet points on a paper.

He looks at me with fury in his eyes. "Well, Cara, I think you'll be surprised by what I will show you."He gets up from the table, leaving Duke and me alone. We have a stare down. The family resemblance is amazing, and I can't believe I didn't notice it before.

"Duke, please tell me you're not buying into all this family crap."

By the look on his face, I know he is. "Raven, this is our family, and you need to understand that. Joseph was not your family—we are."

Oh my God, he really believes all of this. "What about your adopted family, don't you love them?"

He sighs, "They tried, but there was always something missing, and now I know what that something was; my blood and my heritage. I'm where I need to be . . . where I want to be. I hope that will come for you, too."

Vincent returns and hands me a photo album. "This was your mother's, when she was here, and maybe it will help you."

I take it and decide to head outside to look at it alone. As I sit on one of the lounge chairs, I slowly open the book, and it's like going back in time. The book is like a diary with photographs, attached to her deepest, most private thoughts. I feel like an intruder, but I have to read this. No, I *need* to read this.

I arrived here two days ago, after the surgery I performed failed. He was just too far gone for it to work, but I had to try for my Cara and Antonio. After the surgery, Vincent showed me a videotape of Antonio being shot; taking the bullet that was meant for Joseph. All of this, while my Cara looked on. I don't think I will ever forget the look on her scared, little face. It will torment me always. I was told that Antonio died and if I wanted to keep Cara safe, then I needed to remain here, so here, I sit.

Oh my God, my mother watched the video of Daddy being shot, and she thought I was still being held! Does Vincent think this will somehow make me feel better or makeup for all he took from me? I need to keep reading.

The views here are tranquil; there is a peace that the sea brings with the incoming tide. Vincent is back. I don't want to see him or deal with him, but I must. For the sake of my daughter, I will do whatever he wants.

"Gabriella, you look so well rested today, I'm glad I brought you here."

"How long will I be held here, against my will?"

"You're free to go wherever you want; explore the grounds."

"I just want to go home to my daughter and get on with grieving Antonio."

"I can have Cara brought here. if that would make you feel better."

"I'll do whatever you want. but you must promise me that you'll stay away from Cara."

He smiles and walks away. He is pure evil. How could my Antonio have been cut from the same cloth?

I never knew my mother was an artist. The next few pages are filled with etchings of me. It's like she was doing them to try and remember me. They are beautiful and very detailed.

It's been a week, and I'm realizing I might never get out of here. I miss my Cara. She was just finding her independence, and it was beautiful to watch her. It's funny what little things you remember most. Whenever Cara was deep in thought, she would tug at her ear lobe. When she is angry, her eyes get the deepest violet color, just like my mother's eyes would. Daddy would say my mom's eyes could render him speechless, and I never understood what he meant, until Cara.

The next few pages are filled with violet eyes, all different shades.

Two weeks have passed and Vincent said, he is not waiting for me any longer. I realized I had no choice. I tried fighting him off, but he's much stronger than I am. My life is over, even if I do get rescued from this place. My tender-hearted husband is dead, by the hand of his brother. My husband's brother has repeatedly raped me. Every time he finishes, he looks up to heaven, laughs and says, "That's for you big brother." He thinks Antonio is watching this nightmare. I can only hope that Antonio is too busy watching over Cara.

I've had enough for today. Reading about my mother's abuse is gut wrenching, and I am just too nauseated to continue. As I walk up the steps to my bedroom, I have a moment of clarity. I realize I never got my period and I never took my pills that last week. I'm usually so good with them, but getting kidnapped could render a person a little dense. I'm sure I will be fine, but then I remember how much Jax loved to go to cock heaven, and I smile for the first time in a long time. It figures it's because of Jax and his wonderful, dirty bedroom language.

I decide to take a nap. I enter my room, and Duke is sitting in one of the chairs. "Why are you in my room?"

"Raven, I'm not a monster. Well, maybe to you I am, but I'm really not and I want to know more about you. I mean, after all, you are my half-sister."

I take a calming breath, "So, you choose now to find out about me?" I'm looking into his eyes, trying to understand him.

"Raven, we have the same mother, so I would like to think that some of what I'm seeing in you, is part of her. Vincent said he would tell me all about the family, but he has only told me his side, I want more."

I sit across from him. "Okay, what do you want to know?"

"What was she like? I really want to know all the little things you find out about a person over the years."

The tears fall; I can't stop them. "Duke, she died when I was seven, so I don't know much. My memories are faint, at best."

He takes my hand, "Please, Raven, whatever you can remember would be great."

I wipe away my tears. "Okay, well, she loved to sing and dance. She was very graceful and beautiful."

"Vincent showed me some pictures of her from when she lived here."

My anger is back. "Duke, she didn't live here. She was held prisoner here and raped repeatedly by Vincent." I can tell he doesn't know what to believe, as he picks imaginary lint off of his pants. Maybe if he sees the real Vincent he will understand how evil and vile Vincent really is. "Let me show you something that he gave me today." I pass him the book. "Please read this passage."

He starts to read and his eyes fill with tears. I know he murdered two people, but I also see how tormented he is, and how used he must feel.

"Raven, thank you for sharing this, but I just can't take any more of this." He hands me back the book and walks out.

The rest of the book is filled with all of the torment that my mother went through for the two months she was held captive here. Maybe Vincent gave me this book to show me what I can expect. Except, no one will be rescuing me. I'm so tempted to turn on the phone, but I won't put Jax in danger. I can't put him in danger. *I love him.*

I get up, and am hit with a wave of nausea. I'm very dizzy. I really hope it's not what I think it is, this could be really bad if it is. There's a knock on my door, and it's Maria asking me if I want lunch. Judging by the look on her face, I must look really bad. She helps me to bed and says she will bring tea and dry crackers.

I spend the next two weeks going from my bed to the bathroom, throwing up my guts all day, every day. Vincent calls in a local doctor to look at me, and Maria is translating for him. I won't tell him I understand what they are saying. I just don't know if that will come in handy.

I know I'm pregnant, and I have to fight for my child to get out of here. The doctor confirms what I already know, and says I am dehydrated. I need fluids, and I'm suffering from 'hyperemesis gravidarum,' which is severe morning sickness. He wants to put me in the hospital, but Vincent just sends him away.

I curl up into a ball and cry. I'm crying for my baby, that has to go through this, and for Jax, who will never know that his love created another life. I'm crying for all the time I lost with my parents, but most of all, I'm crying because I can't see a way out.

Maxwell

I'M SEARCHING EVERY LEAD that comes through and calling in all kinds of favors, but they all lead to dead ends. I've never seen Jax like this. He really loves Raven, and now she is gone. I can barely look at him. I keep trying to be positive for him and for Jackie, but they are both lost without Raven. Jackie keeps looking at me like she knows I'm going to save Raven. I don't have her faith that there will be a happy ending. I lost my faith in happy endings years ago. The longer time goes on, the less faith I have that we will find her alive. I can only imagine the kind of torture she is enduring at the hands of a madman. Time just keeps dragging on, and I have no answers for anyone. I know Jax's pain, I've lived it. It's a pain that slowly kills a man, one day at a time. I'm reliving a nightmare, except this time, it's Jax's nightmare, and I can't stop it. I try to distance myself from Jackie, but I just can't do it. I know it is best for both of us, but I'm losing all reason here. Three months since that horrible day, and it's like time has stood still for all of us.

Isabella is getting ready to send Junior back to school, but I know she is scared to let him out of her sight. We are all just going through the motions of life, but not really living.

Mick accepted a job, as a security guard, in the Raiders building. He seems to be getting his life back, one day at a time. Sometimes, I go and have a coffee with him, and his first words are always about Raven. Raven doesn't even realize the impact she has had on so many lives, without even trying.

Jax's mum is all over my arse about Raven and Jackie. I know she likes Jackie and maybe she thinks I should have a relationship with her. I swear, sometimes I think she thinks I'm Superman. I'm trying everything I can to find them, but nothing pans out. They have to be running low on money. There are no hits on any credit cards or at any ATM's. I've contacted a friend that specializes in wire transfers. I have Tony working with him to look for anything that will tie it to the family.

I find myself making all kinds of excuses to spend time with Jackie. Sometimes we silently run through the park. There is such ease with her. I really don't need to talk and yet she understands. I don't know when it happened, but she slowly broke through the barrier around my heart, and for me, this is not good. I decide to head to Raiders and try and go over a hunch I have with Jax. I need to put Jackie out of my mind, unfortunately, that is easier said than done.

Chapter Seventeen

Jaxson

IT'S BEEN THREE MONTHS since I lost my beautiful girl on that horrible winter night. There has been no contact, and all leads have gone dry. I have Tony hacking every computer that I can think of for some sort of potential lead. We know they left the country. They had to, after the murders. Max wants me to prepare myself for the possibility that she might not be alive, but I won't believe that. Every day, I bring Mick a coffee and check to make sure he is doing okay in his new job. He lets me just be miserable. He understands the loss, he loves her too.

"Don't give up on her, Jax. She is a lot stronger than you think."

I find comfort with his words. "I will search forever, Mick."

I head upstairs to try and do some sort of work. I'm barely running my business, and I am seriously thinking of selling it. I have a new assistant, and bless her for being patient with me. I made sure that I hired someone that I felt I could trust. I had Max check her all the way back to her birth hospital. Her name is Mrs. Osla. She's a fifty-five-year-old widow, originally from Edinburgh, Scotland. I think Max and I are the only ones, other than my mum, that understand her when she's talking. I know my mum is happy with her. She feels like Mrs. Osla takes good care of me and my business.

Mrs. Osla buzzes me, letting me know my mum is here. I love my mum, but my family has done nothing but hover over me since the incident. My mum flies through the door announcing it's tea time. *Really?*

"Mum, can I ask you a question?"

She smiles at me. "Of course, you never had to ask before."

"What do you think I do all day long?"

She opens her mouth to speak, and then shuts it. "Well, you don't have to get all snippy just because I'm your mother, and I was only in labor with you for twenty-six hours. I am worried about you and thought I should just pop in and have a spot of tea with you. However, if you're too busy to make time for your mum, then I'll just go see what Maxwell is doing." She clasps her hands in front of her. I knew the guilt trip would come, but what's even funnier, is Max, walking in at the end of her speech and realizing he was next on her list! He tries to quietly back out of the room, and I swear that woman must have eyes in the back of her head. "Maxwell, don't even think of leaving now!"

He is so busted, and I laugh a good laugh, which I haven't had in months. I lean in a kiss my mum. "Thank you."

She points to the sofa "Tea. Both of you, now." Max sits right down, and I'm trying not to laugh at him.

"Now, I have questions for both my boys. Maxwell, how is Jackie doing?" She inquires. He looks surprised that my mum knows about him and Jackie. "Don't look at me like that, Maxwell. I'm a mother, and I know."

He shrugs, "Um…she's doing okay. She misses Raven, and she hasn't heard anything, if that's where you're going with this."

Oh boy she's giving him the eye . . . that's never good. "Don't smart mouth me, young man, I'm just concerned."

He takes a deep breath "I'm sorry, ma'am."

She smiles, "That's better. Isabella sent Junior back to school today. The doctors suggested that he gets back to a normal routine."

I know I need to spend some time with him. "Mum, I will pop over there tonight and see if he is up to a *Doctor Who* night."

"How is Mrs. Osla working out?"

I laugh, "Good, Mum, it's like having another you around the office all day."

As I hit her with my Jax smile, Max laughs until Mum pulls his ear. "Maxwell, will you never learn?"

I love the look of fear on Max, "Sorry, ma'am."

"Hmm, that seems to be the story of your life, lately." With that, she leaves, just like the whirlwind that she blew in with.

"Max, you know she is going to be on you about Jackie. Mark my words, it's only a matter of time."

"Not that I need any more motivation to find Miss Raven, but that would do it."

"Speaking of which, what do you have for me today?"

"Well, I took your advice about the money trail, and now I have Tony working with my contact that deals with wire transfers that are questionable. What about you, Jax, do you have anything to report?"

I take a deep breath, "Yeah I paid off the mortgage on Raven's place."

Max has the grace not to say anything. I know I look like a lovesick puppy, but going into her home every day, I can still smell her, and I feel close to her. Fuck, I really need some help.

"We already went through Marco's stuff that first day, but you know I think I want to pop over there and take my time looking through his stuff again. I just have a hunch that we missed something. I also had all of Duke's stuff sent to Tony so he can double check it all." Max gets up. "Come on, I'll drive."

As we head over to Raven's, Max's phone rings. "Tony, you're on speaker. It's just Jax, you can talk freely."

"Okay. First, Joseph died today. Second, a notice just came that both of you have been requested at the reading of the will, along with Raven. Third, I found a money trail leading to a small town in Italy. Before you ask, I have the plane getting ready for the international flight. You leave in four hours from Teterboro."

Max finishes the call, since I'm just sitting in shock. Could it be that there is some hope to find my girl? Do I even dare hope? We pull up to Raven's, and I can't tell Max how much I come here just to be near her. When we get inside, I just sit on the sofa and think about all of our times together. It was fast and furious. I miss her so much, it hurts. Even my cock—who is usually always on alert—has gone dormant.

"Jax get in here!"

"Max, I don't want to be in this fucker's room."

"Jax, just shut up and get in here."

Okay, Max is pacing. "Jax, when I walk into this room, the hair on my neck tingles. Okay, I know it sounds strange, but something is off. Do you remember the day that Junior was kidnapped and Vito was in your office?"

I'm thinking, "Yeah, he was flipping out as usual. Only Junior and Raven can control that dog."

"He flipped out when Duke and Marco were in the room. He knew something was off with them, just like I feel something now. We need to rip this room apart. There has to be more, especially since Marco was a poker player. They always have an ace up their sleeve." He taps my arm with the back of his hand. We start at one end of the room and rip apart every inch. Nothing. Max turns to me. "Bathroom next."

I just want to get on that plane. "Max, I don't see anything."

"Look, Jax my *tingle* sense has never been wrong, keep looking," he raises his voice.

I pull apart the medicine cabinet and I pull out a box of condoms. I open it, and inside there is a thumb drive. "Max, I think I just found the ace."

He grabs his keys. "Okay, Jax, we need to get this to Tony, and we have to be at the airport.

Where is your passport?"

I have to think a minute. "It's in my office."

We race to the car and, of course, Max drives. "Jax, call Mrs. Osla and have her get your passport and mine. Tell her to give them to Tony and have Tony meet us at the airport."

"Where is your passport?"

"It's in my office safe."

I'm confused "I thought only you and I have the combination?"

He nods. "You can give it to her."

My shocked face registers with him. "Jax, there only two people I fear, your mum and Mrs. Osla."

I almost bust a gut laughing. We just make it to the airport, and Tony is waiting. Max gives him the thumb drive. "As soon as you know something, call me."

"Tony, where in Italy are we going?"

Tony hands me the passports. "Sicily."

I look at Max. "Who knows where we are going?"

He reads me better than anyone. "Only Tony and the pilots, and that's the way it will stay."

We get on the plane. I sit back and put on Raven's iPod. She has such a wide variety of music. I put it on shuffle. The first song that comes on is by Nickelback called "I'd Come for You". Hang on, baby, I'm on my way.

Raven

EVERY DAY, THE SICKNESS gets a little better. So today, I decide to leave my room to get some fresh air. When I go downstairs, I hear Vincent, yelling in Italian. He is talking fast, but I get most of what he is saying. He's telling someone that they should have hid the wire transfer better. The American and European bank system was hacked and no one knows where Phillips and Fleming are.

Oh my God, I hope Max and Jax are not coming here; it's not safe for them. Vincent turns around and hangs up when he sees me. "Cara, do you know what is going on?"

I barely look at him "Vincent, I have been in bed for weeks, I have lost all track of time. I don't speak Italian. What are you talking about?"

He changes the subject. "So, my brother's special baby girl is nothing more than a common whore, getting knocked up by the biggest tycoon in New York. At least your mother was married when I fucked her."

"Don't you mean—when you raped her—you pig?!"

He bangs his fist on the table. "Don't try my patience, little girl, or you will be very sorry."

I know I shouldn't egg him on, but I can't control how much I despise this man. "What has you so riled up, Vincent?"

Duke walks in. "Vincent, stop yelling at her. How she chose to live her life is none of your business." He snaps lightly. Vincent glares at me and walks away.

"Thank you for defending me to Vincent."

"I wasn't defending your choices, I was standing up to Vincent. He's not your father, and he can't tell you how to live your life. You're looking better. How are you feeling?"

I sigh, "I'm weak, but holding down some light food and more liquids than before." I sip some juice. "How long have I been here? I seem to have lost all track of time."

"You were pretty sick. To answer your question, we've been here for three months."

I'm in shock. I can't believe I've been in and out for so long. I've missed so much, yet life keeps going on, whether we want it to or not. "Duke, do you know why Vincent is so mad?"

He shakes his head. "No, but whatever it is, it must be bad because he went in his office to call the States. When he talks here, it's always in Italian because we don't understand it, but when he calls the States, he has to speak English, so he goes in his office."

My eyes fill with tears. "Is Vincent holding you here against your will, too?"

His mood turns bleak as he looks down at his hands. "Raven, I have nowhere to go, so it really wouldn't matter. If I went back to the States, I would be in jail or executed for murdering a federal agent. I mean, even though Marco went off the rails, he was still an agent."

I still feel like there is more to the story than I know. "Duke, how did you ever get mixed up with them?"

"Erica was the key. She used me. She was like a black widow spider, and I fell for her hard. I didn't know about Marco or you, until later on. It was a fluke that you were Michael's teacher and Marco's roommate. I think if Marco thought he could turn you, he would have, because, let's face it, you would have been the perfect mole. No one would ever suspect the teacher, but you're a good person.

"You weren't supposed to be on the playground that day. I guess Jackie was lucky that you were otherwise, she would be dead right now. Then, when you met Jax and started a relationship with him, the plan had to be escalated.

In the end, Erica and I were supposed to take the money and live off the interest on some small island. I never knew she was with Marco. I was told he was gay, and I believed them. It's hard to believe they were not only together, but they were married!"

Vincent steps back into the room and he doesn't look happy. "Cara, I have a question for you. Do you think that it was right that Joseph hid my only son's existence from me?"

I look at him and then Duke. "Duke, is this the garbage he's filling your head with? Joseph gave you the chance at a normal life. If you would have grown up in his world, you would be the same ruthless animal that he is."

Before Vincent can answer, Duke gets up. "Maybe I already am."

"Vincent, I would like to go for a walk. Am I allowed to get some fresh air?"

"Cara, there are guards throughout this place; you can walk around outside."

I decide to walk out back, through the gardens. They stretch to the cliff, and below the cliff, is a white sandy beach and the beautiful Mediterranean Sea. I stand at the edge and let the wind blow through my hair. The warm sun feels so good on my face after being in bed for so long. I walk over to the cluster of chairs and sit for a while.

Before I know it, my eyes close and I let my mind wander to a happier place. I look down at my tummy and smile. " My little one, you're causing quite a ruckus, and you're not even here yet. I wish you could know your daddy; he is such a beautiful man. He has the bluest eyes, almost like the Mediterranean Sea. There isn't a thing about him that isn't beautiful, inside and out. You have a cousin too, Michael Jr., and he is very tender-hearted. He has the coolest dog. His name is Vito. I hope someday if we get out of here, you'll get to meet them all." At least I can still dream that maybe my baby and I will make it out of here alive.

Jaxson

AS WE TOUCHDOWN IN Italy, I have a sense of urgency that I didn't have before. The minute Max turns on his phone, Tony calls.

"Max, are we on speaker and is it safe to talk freely?" That's usually means Tony did something illegal.

"Yes, Tony."

He's excited. "Good, I was able to hack Marco's drive and, considering he was a hacker, that is pretty impressive. Anyway, I have big news."

We both stop dead in our tracks. "Go on, Tony."

He takes a deep breath. "I know what Joseph had in his will, and it's big. Gabriella did not kill herself. She is currently at a clinic in Switzerland, and Joseph pays all her bills using a trust fund from her parents."

Will this ever end? "Hold on, Tony. Joseph said that he used that money to set up a fund for Raven?"

"I know, Jax, but what he did was take the money that was from Gabriella's parents, plus the settlement money from the accident, and he set it up to pay for her care. He then took the money from Antonio's insurance, and putting his own money in with it, he created a fund for Raven. She has no idea that her mother is alive. I also obtained a copy of Joseph's will. It names the two of you co-executors. You are both to take care of Raven and Gabriella. He named you both in the event that one of you dies." Max's jaw becomes tight and he grimaces. He has a white knuckle grip on the phone, probably trying to gain his self control.

"Jax, he left three sealed letters. One is for you, one for Max, and one for Raven. I also pulled Gabriella's medical file. It appears that after she gave birth to Duke, she had a mental break down. Joseph had her sent to the clinic."

I turn to Max, "Why would Joseph hide her?"

He shrugs, "Look, Jax, I venture to say this has to do with Vincent. The first order of business is to rescue Raven then, we go for Gabriella."

Tony informs us that he back traced phone calls going from Sicily to the bank in Chicago. Then he cross-referenced that with holdings that Vincent has, and he was able to find a villa that was under the great grandfather's name. He sent the coordinates to Max's phone.

I thank God that I have Max; he is fluent in Italian and knows his way around this country like the back of his hand. Max being Max, is making some calls; calling in favors and reinforcements, I'm sure.

"All right, Jax, I have everything arranged. The villa is at the top of a cliff. It is surrounded by beach, which will work to our advantage."

"How does that work to our advantage?"

We head to the car. "We'll be coming in by sea, just like regular tourists. Let's go, we have to be at the marina in an hour."

Waiting for us when we get to the marina, is by far the brightest, loudest monstrosity of a speedboat I have ever seen! "Max, first, what the fuck is that? And second, they will see us coming from ten miles away!"

He laughs. "Relax. Jax, your right. It's loud and that is what I'm hoping for. It's the perfect distraction. This boat is called *Phenomenon*. It's the world's fastest speedboat, going up to 250 mph. People will have all eyes on the boat, which gives us the perfect distraction."

It looks like a bright orange submarine that rides on top of the water. "I trust you, Max. So what's the plan?"

"Diving gear and every kind of artillery is already loaded. We head out now and anchor off shore. After sunset, we move in with backup."

Waiting till sunset will kill me, but the thought that my girl is coming home is all that really matters. "Okay, let's go!"

WHEN MAX SAID FAST, he wasn't fucking kidding me! This boat is going so fast, that it glides on top of the water. We get to the anchoring location, and I'm in shock. I know Max said the villa was on a cliff, but it is so high up. I have no fucking clue what he's thinking. Max looks over to me, "Jax, I have some ideas so, just keep an open mind. The cliffs are very high, and with shear rocks. How do you feel about BASE jumping?"

I don't answer him. I'm just looking through the binoculars stunned at the sight before me. *It's Raven!* She is just sitting in a chair looking out to the sea. For a split second, I swear we lock violet to blues. I have to be mistaken. She can't possibly lock eyes with me from here, but then, my dead cock springs to life! What the fuck, now you decide to make a fucking appearance?

"Jax, are you with me?"

"Sorry, Max, but I see Raven." I yell over the sound of the engine.

He grabs the binoculars from me. "Well, at least she is allowed to walk around and is not locked up."

I jump up, "Max, let's go. I need to get to her."

He grabs my arm. "Hold on, buddy. I understand, but we have a plan and we need to stick with it. The goal is to get her out of there alive. Stop thinking with your cock, mate."

I hate it when he is fucking right! "Okay, what's the plan?"

Raven

THE BREEZE IS SO nice. I love to look out over the sea and wonder what it would feel like to be swimming with Jax. My mind wanders to him always, but today something seems different. I feel him around me. It's probably the baby.

A really ugly looking boat just pulled up. *Who would ever want a bright orange boat?* I try to see the people on board, but I can't. I decide to close my eyes for a little bit, but all I can see are the bluest eyes. God, I miss him. As I drift off, all I can think of is how much I love that beautiful man.

Maxwell

"OKAY, JAX, HERE IS the plan. You and I are going back to shore. We'll glide toward the villa. When we are above it, we parachute in, landing on the roof, in the dark. We rappel down the backside where the bedrooms are located. We get Raven, and then we'll BASE jump out towards the boat."

I'm looking at Max like he has three heads. "Jax, just hear me out. I know you have done BASE jumping before, and I have done it enough that I can tandem Raven with no problem. Once we get to the boat, they won't be able to catch us."

I sit back, trying to think of the different options, and there really aren't any. "My concern is, finding her once she is inside the villa, Max. What if she's not in her room or what if we pick the wrong room?"

"The men on the boat are watching her, and they have determined that her room is on the back, left corner. She has a balcony."

I sit there, stroking my chin. I wish I could come up with something else, but we're out of options. "Okay, but I don't have to tell you I'm not leaving without her. I will lay down my life for her."

He hands me my chute. "Jax, I promised your mum and Mrs. Osla that I would bring you both home, and they scare me a hell of a lot more than Vincent and his goons."

Raven

THE MORE I READ the book, that my mother made, the more upset I get. She believed she would never see me again. Vincent, mentally and physically, tortured her daily, and yet, she found a way to go on. I don't understand why she killed herself. Joseph said she couldn't look at Duke, but she gave him up for adoption. She fought to stay alive through two months of nonstop torture, yet right after she gave birth, she killed herself? Something isn't right, but I guess I'll never know.

Joseph knew about Duke, and yet, his answer was to ship me off to boarding school? Maybe if I was around, my mother might have survived. Joseph did all of this, thinking he was protecting me, but all he did was make this mess even bigger.

I think about Marco, and part of me wants to grieve for him while the other part of me is still in shock by his actions. I still can't believe he did all of this for money, trying to kidnap poor little Michael. If he really needed money, I would have given him all of my trust fund with no questions asked. Now, so many people are dead, and lives have been changed forever.

I skipped dinner tonight, feeling nauseated, but now I'm getting hungry. I get up, but I hear a noise on my balcony. I turn just as the doors swing open. In walks the most beautiful sight; two men, all in black.

My eyes only lock on to one thing, the bluest of blues. I stifle a yell and feel my knees buckle. He is on me in a second. "I've got you, sweetheart; I will always have your back."

I throw my arms around him, flooding him with kisses, and then I realize he put himself in danger when I specifically told him not to. I don't know what gets into me, maybe the fact I'm pregnant and highly emotional. I reach back and smack him across the face! He gets a shocked look on his face, and Max is trying not to laugh.

"You crazy man, I told you not to put yourself in danger, but you just don't listen to anything! Do you think you're Superman or something? Do you realize how dangerous this is?"

He grabs me and kisses me hard. Oh fuck, I'm done! "Sweetheart, as long as there is life left within me, I will always come for you!"

"Jax, Raven, this is all nice and stuff, but we have to go now."

I'm trying to catch my breath. "Just how do you boys plan on getting me out of here?"

"Well, right now, everyone is asleep, including the guard that I hit with the tranquilizer dart. We are going to rappel down to the garden and BASE jump out to sea, where a boat is waiting for us."

I freeze. They both turn and look at me. "I can't do this."

Jax's eyes bug out, but Max is calm. "Miss Raven, I understand your fear of heights, however, I promise, I will get you to that boat safely."

This is not how I would have ever pictured telling someone something this important, but I don't have a choice. "I'm pregnant."

They both stop, and I swear both their chins are on the ground. I instantly see the fear in Jax's eyes and I realize what he is thinking—that Vincent did to me what he did to my mother.

"Jax, it's your baby. I'm a little more than three months along; Vincent never touched me, especially when he found out."

"Miss Raven, do you trust me?" Max asks.

"Yes, without any doubt, I do."

He puts his hand out "Good. Give me your hand. This might be a little bit unconventional, but I need to have you wrap yourself around my front like a monkey hold. Can you do that for me?"

Jax is frozen.

"Okay." I climb on Max.

He heads towards the balcony, "Hey, Jax, snap out of it, we are leaving now! Jax, I need you to go first and guide us down," he calls softly.

Jax doesn't say anything. He just does everything Max tells him. When we get to the bottom, Jax unhooks us, and we head towards the cliff. I think I'm going to puke. No, I know I'm going to puke. Jax is holding my hair back while I empty my stomach.

"Miss Raven, we really need to go. Climb back on me. If you have to puke again, just do it, I won't care, believe me I have seen a lot worse than that."

"Raven, you're jumping with Max. He's trained for tandem jumping." Jax finally finds his voice.

We hear yelling and running. "The party is over, we have to go now!" Max grabs me under my ass and takes off running. I close my eyes. Now I understand the statement 'take a flying leap.' I swear I scream the whole way down. I look up, and Jax is above us, gliding.

Max is gliding us towards the boat, and I realize it's the ugly boat I saw this morning. I hear gunshots, and they are whizzing past us. I feel something hot and wet, but it doesn't register that it's blood. We all land. The men from the boat get us on board, and in seconds, we are off.

Jax unhooks himself and comes running towards us, and I realize Max is shot. "Max, don't you dare die on me!" I yell at him. I don't know what that is supposed to accomplish.

Jax unhooks us, "Raven, you're shot!"

I look towards Max. "It's not me, Jax. Max is shot in the shoulder!"

"Make this fucking boat fly!" Jax yells to the captain.

Jax starts to take off Max's shirt, and they both look at his wound before turning to look towards me. "What, why are you both looking at me?"

They both jump up and grab me, but I don't understand why. I feel that wave of nausea, and the world starts spinning. "Max, it's a fucking through and through and she's hit!" I hear them yelling and my shirt being ripped off.

Then, nothing, but a quiet hum.

Chapter Eighteen

Raven

I'M SLEEPING AND HAVING the most wonderful dream, those beautiful eyes are staring at me, and I see that crooked smirk. I love when I dream of Jax. I go to stretch, and I have a sharp, burning pain in my left shoulder. My eyes fly open, remembering what happened and I'm instantly hit with the bluest, most calming eyes. "Jax," I whisper.

He grabs me. "I'm here, sweetheart, always here."

I try to jump up. "Max!" I'm looking around, but I don't see him.

"He's fine, just rest."

Realization hits me "Oh my God, the baby!"

"Hush, the baby is fine, everyone is good." He's really here smiling at me.

Jaxson

"LOOK, I HAVE SOMETHING for you." I hand her the scan of the baby. "See, the baby is just fine."

She stares at the picture, smiling. "I want to see Max. Where are we? How did you find me?"

I have to keep her calm. "One thing at a time, okay?"

"Okay."

I open the door and call Max and Jackie in her room. "Oh, Miss Raven, you're awake. I'm so sorry."

"Max, what on earth are you sorry for? You risked your life for me and you were shot! If anything, I'm sorry for putting you in that position."

Raven

BEFORE I CAN SAY anything more, the door flies open and Mrs. Phillips comes storming in.

"Maxwell, you should be sorry. I told you to bring her and Jaxson back safely. Jumping out of planes and leaping off of cliffs is *not* bringing them back safely. Plus, you were both shot!"

Max is looking down at his feet. "Yes, Ma'am, I am very sorry."

Oh my God, Max is afraid of Jax's mom. I start laughing and I can't stop. Everyone turns towards me, probably thinking I have totally lost my mind, and I realize I need to say something. I snort, "I can't believe big, bad Max is afraid of you!"

Max turns beet red, and I start laughing again. I really can't help it. Max grumbles, "Miss Raven, you should be too, she's really tough."

Before I can answer, she reaches up and pulls him by the ear! "Maxwell, you'll mind your manners, if you know what's good for you!"

Jackie hugs me, "I'm so happy that they found you, and you're safe."

"I missed you too, Jackie." I have so many questions for everyone. I look around and I realize that I'm not sure where I am. "Jax, where are we?" I ask.

He squeezes my hand. "We're back in New York. Max's wound was a through and through. Yours, however, was not. The doctor got the bullet out, and I had a plane on standby to take us back to the States. The doctor said you could go home tomorrow."

Wow, I can't believe we are already in New York. "Jax, we need to talk."

He's shaking his head. "No we will talk when we get home. Right now, I need you to rest; you've been through too much." He brings my hand up to his lips and plants a kiss on the back. I allow myself to be distracted by his affections for a moment, but I need some answers.

"What about Duke and Vincent, where are they?"

The mention of their names makes Jax grip my hand even harder. "Vincent escaped but Duke was apprehended, however, the Italian government has not decided what they are going to do with him. Now, enough! I said rest, Raven, and I mean it."

I can't even argue, my eyes feel so heavy, and I fall back to sleep, knowing for now, my baby and I are safe. Safe with Jax.

I WAKE AGAIN AND look at the clock; its 3 am. Jax is beside me, asleep. He is so beautiful, and I can't help but stroke his face. I hope the baby has his chiseled cheekbones and his soft lips. He has such long eyelashes, and they are so dark. I take my finger and run it along his cheek, so very beautiful. I let my fingers roam down his chest and slowly make my way down his happy trail.

"Busted, sweetheart," he whispers.

I yelp, "Jesus, Jax, you scared daylights out of me."

I can see him smile at me via the moonlight shining through the window. "You're supposed to be sleeping, and yet, my beautiful girl is copping a feel."

"I was not copping a feel, mister!" I squeal. Then, he opens his eyes and hits me with that crooked smirk and I can't help but giggle. "Yeah, I was, but it's your fault."

He laughs at me "Wait, I'm sleeping, you're copping a feel, and it's my fault?"

I'm never getting out of this one. "Yes."

He takes a breath. "Okay, how is it my fault?"

I stammer, "Well I can't explain it, but trust me, it just is."

He looks in my eyes and growls, "Don't look at me like that. I'm not taking advantage of you in a hospital bed, and besides, you were shot! Curl up next to me and I'll stroke your back so you can go back to sleep."

As I drift off to sleep, I hear him sing in almost a whisper, and it is such a beautiful song, one of my favorites, "Little Things" by One Direction.

MORNING COMES. I OPEN my eyes, and Jax is gone. *Oh no.* Was last night a dream? I start to panic. My body trembles and my breath quickens. Please dear God . . . please don't let it be a dream. I've got to get up. What if Vincent finds me? I'm half out of bed when the door flies open, and Jax comes in. "Where do you think you're going?"

I take a few steadying breaths, "I woke up and you weren't here." My teeth are chattering, "I was going to look for you?"

He's in his 'take charge' mode. "I was just outside, signing you out of this place. The nurse will be in a few minutes to take out the IV."

All I want to do is get clean. "When can I take a shower?"

He laughs. "I know you are in love with my shower, however, when we get home, you can soak in the tub, no shower until the stitches come out."

I am just about to ask him about work, when the nurse comes in. After she leaves, Jax gets me dressed and then the nurse comes back with the wheelchair. Jax ignores her, scoops me up, and walks out with me in his arms and the nurse following behind us, yelling about rules. I just laugh. Jax and rules don't mix well.

When we get outside, Max is there with an SUV. "Hi, Miss Raven, how are you feeling today?"

I smile, "I'm good, but how are you?"

Max is worried about me, but he was shot too. "I'm fine, nothing to worry about, just another chink in the armor."

After we get into the vehicle and drive away, my mind wanders to Marco. I feel so hurt, and tears fill my eyes. I'm trying not to cry in front of Jax because it really makes him crazy. "Aren't we going back to my place, Jax?"

Jax's jaw gets tight "Raven, we're going to The Tower."

"Oh."

"Yeah, *oh*," he whispers.

In the usual record time, we arrive at The Tower. Max comes upstairs with us, so they probably have some business. "Max, has the place been swept?"

Max nods as Jax steers me towards the bedroom. "I'm going to get you set up in the tub, and then I have some stuff to go over with Max. Are you okay?"

I'm searching his eyes "Yes, I'm fine."

He fills the tub and puts in some mandarin spice bath oil. The bath feels wonderful. I think I may have had fallen in love with Jax's bathroom even before I had fallen in love with the man! I open my eyes when I notice the water is starting to get cold, and find Jax, leaning against the counter, watching me.

He smiles, "I'm here to wash your hair for you. Scoot forward a little"

I do as I'm told. He turns on the water, wets my hair, and works in some shampoo. He is so gentle. It's a simple thing, but it is such a turn on! He conditions, then rinses, and then he towels me dry with heated towels. A girl could get very spoiled with all of this attention. He seats me at the vanity and dries my hair. "Jax, are you ever going to talk to me? You haven't said much of anything, since yesterday. Why?" I need him to be his usual bulldozer self.

"You're right. We have a lot to talk about, but I don't want to overload you or pressure you. I'm trying to figure out what you need. You are my *main* focus. As for me, it's simple; all I need is you, sweetheart."

We lock violets to blues. "Jax, what I need is your usual fast and furious self. I need the Jax that asks whatever he wants, whenever he wants, and damn anyone to hell that gets in his way."

"Okay, let's start from the beginning then. Why did you run away that night?"

I let out the breath I was holding. "I heard you and Max talking. I was hurt. You can't keep stuff from me; only telling me what you think I can handle. That's not life, and it's not fair to me."

He nods. "Okay, you're right, but you never gave me a chance. I only just found out that stuff, and I would've told you, but you ran, again," he defends himself then lets out a big sigh. "I thought you were on the pill, so how did you end up pregnant?"

I don't want him to think I got pregnant to trap him. "I was on the pill, but when I was kidnapped, I missed them, but we never abstained. I didn't plan this. I expect nothing from you. Look, maybe I should just go back to my place."

His jaw tightens. "There you go again, deciding for me what I can or can't handle! I didn't say I didn't want the baby, so if that's what you're thinking, just get it out of your head! Those three months you were gone, I died a little every day. And then to find you and find out you're carrying our child; It's overwhelming.

"Raven, so much happened in three months, but I don't want to overload you, so can we take it a little at a time, please?"

"Yes, but you must know I have so many questions, and I need to talk to Joseph," I plead and watch him quickly turns pale. "Jax, what happened?"

Jaxson

I HAVE TO TELL her. I just don't know how much more she can handle. "Joseph died three weeks ago from prostate cancer. That's part of why everything happened with Marco," I lay it out for her. I take her in my arms and just let her have a good cry. I don't know how the fuck I'm going to tell her that her mother is alive. "Joseph told Marco he was sick, and Marco convinced Joseph to tell him who your half-brother was and where he was living. Marco was heavy into gambling, and he hooked up with Erica in a chat room. They plotted to kidnap Junior, and when Marco found out you were his teacher, it just made things easier for him. It made it easier, that is, until he realized that Junior's uncle was also your Starbucks guy."

Raven

I WIPE MY TEARS. "Jax, if Marco wanted money, all he had to do was ask me. I would have given him my trust fund. When we were in that cabin, Marco said Joseph was sick, but I didn't know the difference between truth and lies with him anymore, when he was trying to justify his actions."

He's takes my hand, "Oh, sweetheart, there is so much more that you don't know."

I need to know it all. "Go on, Jax, just get it all out, so we can get past this and close the book."

He closes his eyes and lifts his head back, seemingly fearful of what he is about to tell me.

"If only it would be that easy." He has a really tight grip on me and I see fear in his eyes.

"Jax, what is it? What is so bad, that you're afraid to tell me?"

Jaxson

I'M SILENTLY PRAYING FOR her to have the strength to deal with this whole mess. "Raven, your mother is not dead. When she gave birth to Duke, she had a breakdown. Joseph had her put in a clinic in Switzerland. He took the money your mother inherited when her parents died and invested it. That money is used for her care. He took the money you received when your father died and put that, plus some of his own, into a trust fund for you."

She suddenly loses color to her face and starts shaking, her bottom lip is quivering while the tears spill out of her eyes.. "My mother is alive?"

"Joseph left Max and me in charge of the estate, and the care of your mum was left to Max."

She wipes away a tear, "Why would he do that?"

"We don't know. He made these changes the week before he died. I do know that he admired Max's tenacity; he called him a 'bull dog' when it came to never giving up. He also left three envelopes, one for each of us."

She clutches my arm, "I want to see my mother, is she safe?"

I nod, "Max flew there the other day and increased her guards. He is in constant touch with her doctors, and he is going to have her moved to a facility here. He is just waiting until he feels it's safe to move her, and he gets the go ahead from her doctors. Raven, we only found out when we landed in Italy. I don't want you to think that I kept this from you."

She takes a steadying breath. "Where are the letters that Joseph left?"

Raven

HE JUST KEEPS STROKING my arm, and I'm not sure if, it is for his benefit or mine. "They're at his attorney's office."

I stand up. "I need to talk to Max. Please, Jax, I need to see him now."

"He's here. He knew you would want to talk to him."

He stops me as I start to head for the living room, "Raven, you need to put on something, other than a towel, or I will lose it."

"HI, MAX, PLEASE TELL me what happened when you went to see my mother."

"Miss Raven, I don't know all the details about why she is in her condition. I'm hoping there is more in the letters that Joseph left. I can tell you, that she is comfortable. She seems to have understood me when I was talking to her. I did not tell her anything about you. I felt it would just be too much, too soon. However, she doesn't speak at all. I gave all of the proper paperwork, that grants me guardianship of your mother, to the Swiss doctors, and as soon as everything is filed with the authorities, she'll be moved to a facility here in New York. I promise you that I will take the upmost care of her."

I smile. "I know you will. Do you know how long it will be before we can move her here?"

He takes a deep breath. "I'm hoping for the end of next week. We do, however, need to get to Joseph's attorney's first. I took the liberty of making an appointment for tomorrow morning at ten."

I'm tired, but I need to know everything and then, process it, so I can move forward. "What about Duke and Vincent? I remember Jax telling me that the Italian authorities have Duke, but Vincent got away. Has there been any more news on either of them?"

"I am in contact with the Italian authorities. They move very slowly, but as far as Vincent is concerned, I was able to track him into Greece and then to Los Angeles. Miss Raven, for now, that is all I have, but be assured, as soon as I know anything, I will advise you and Jax. Is there anything else you need?"

I shake my head, "No, Max, thank you. I could never repay you or Jax for all that you've both gone through for me."

He gets up to leave. "Miss Raven, you are very welcome, and now, I will let you rest. I'll be by tomorrow morning at nine, to pick you both up."

"Jax, there is so much we need to talk about, but right now, can you just hold me?"

"Sweetheart, always. Come here." He pulls me into his lap, and I curl up into a ball in his arms. I don't think I have it in me to shed another tear. I cried so much, when I thought he was gone from my life. I cried for Marco, Joseph, and a mother, whom I thought was dead. I have gone through and witnessed more in my twenty-seven years than most people will ever experience in their lifetime. I know there is so much more to come, but just for tonight, I need to forget the rest of the world.

For tonight, I just need Jax. "Jax, will you please take me to bed and make love to me?"

I feel his cock twitch underneath me. "Raven, you just got home from the hospital. You've been shot and you're exhausted…"

Before he can say any more, I look up and kiss him. I lock violet to blues "Jax, I need you—*now*."

He gives me a slow nod. He lifts me in his arms and carries me to the bedroom. He, slowly and beautifully, makes love to me all night long.

JAX IS STILL BURIED within me when I wake up, his hands are latched on to my ass. I can't help but giggle. I take a peek at him, but his eyes are closed. I like to look at him when he's sleeping; he is just so beautiful. He always has scruffy facial hair, and it's such a contrast to his deep blue eyes. He has such long eyelashes, and his mouth with lips soft as pillows. Thinking of all the things he can do with that mouth, makes me instantly wet. I trail my finger along those lips, down his chest, around his nipples.

"Sweetheart, are you done taking inventory?"

I hum, "I thought you were sleeping."

His eyes are still closed, but he tilts his hips up, and his morning erection has sprung to life.

"Jax, he is always ready for action. Oh my God, now you have *me,* referring to your cock as a *he!*" I can't help but laugh until Jax lifts my hips and then pulls me back down.

"Raven, he is in cock heaven, so, of course he is ready. Feel free to talk to him whenever you want." He gifts me with that crooked smirk, and I start to move up and down, slowly.

"Take the lead, Raven, and ride me however you like."

I love that he doesn't always have to be in control. "Really, Jax? Anything?" I continue up and down, real slow.

I stop, and he watches me like he's waiting to see what I will do next. I lean down and run my tongue along his lips. I follow it with kisses. Traveling to his neck and down to his nipples, taking each one in my mouth—sucking and nibbling—just like he does to me. I lift myself up really slowly and then come down even slower, feeling every inch. I lift myself up again, but this time I climb off of him. I work my kisses down his happy trail. I nip and lick up and down his V. He is so hard. I kiss the top of his cock. I can taste myself on him, and it is so erotic. Nothing like I thought, as I swirl my tongue around the top and down to the base, I take him in my mouth and latch on to him, hollowing out my cheeks. I take him deeper than I ever have before, and I can see by the look on his face he is in shock. I start to slowly move up and down, going deeper with each pass.

He's moving his hips with me now, "Oh, Raven, what you do to me."

As I bare my teeth, his head flies back, and his hips shoot up. He screams and comes the hardest I have ever seen him come. I devour every drop of him that he offers up. I climb up his beautiful body real slow, leaving soft kisses in my path. When I reach his lips, my eyes search his. "I love you, Jax, heart and soul. And I always will."

"Raven, sweetheart, I never thought I would hear those words. The three months without you almost killed me." He lets out the deep breath that he had sucked in.

I kiss him. "Jax, the only thing that gave me any hope was, knowing that your baby was a part of me. I needed to stay strong to keep our baby safe. What were you doing while I was gone?" Once I ask, I see him avert his eyes like he is ashamed or embarrassed. "Jax, you can tell me," I stutter, "Did you try to move on?" I lower my eyes unable to look at him.

"Raven, *Look at me!*" he bites. I return my gaze. "I was dead inside without you. Even my cock didn't want to be bothered with me. I do have a confession for you, though. I purchased your apartment."

"Why?" I widen my eyes.

That glaze of embarrassment washes over his face again. "Well, I needed to keep the place to feel close to you somehow." He admits and I furrow my brows. "Don't look at me like that. I know I wasn't thinking like a normal guy. Hell, normal flew out the window the day you doused me with your coffee. I couldn't take a shower here. I couldn't sleep in my own bed. I wouldn't even let my housekeeper clean the living room because your handprints were on the window. I practically lived at your place for three months so I could be close to you, and while we're at full disclosure, I was seriously considering selling Raiders, Inc."

I just stare at him, in total shock. "Why would you sell your company?—you love it!"

Jaxson

"I LOVE YOU MORE." It was just a whisper, but I know she heard, and I know she understood. I told her once that those words are said too much, that it's a person's actions that speak louder than those words ever could, but I know she needed to hear them. "Raven, what happened for the three months you were held prisoner? Did they hurt you?"

She shakes her head. "You want to know if Vincent raped me like he raped my mother?"

Raven

HIS GRIP TIGHTENS AT the mention of Vincent's name. "I want to know everything you want me to know. I want to help you get all of this behind you, so we can move forward together."

I know he needs to hear this as much as I need to tell him. "On the first day, Vincent gave me a book that was left there by my mother. It was her account of what Vincent did to her while she was held at the villa. Every time he raped my mother, when he was done, he would look up to the heavens and tell my father that he did it for him. It was also her thoughts about my dad and me. There were pictures that she drew. I never knew my mom was an artist. She kept it almost as a diary. Unfortunately, we left it behind when we escaped. But to answer your question, Vincent never touched me."

I see relief in his eyes. "What about Duke, what did he do while you were there?"

I'm sad to think I have a brother and I will never know him. "Duke came in my room one day to talk to me. It was after Vincent gave me the book. He wanted to ask me questions about my mother. He needs to know she is still alive."

He shakes his head. "I'm not sure that's possible, especially if he is in contact with Vincent."

I know he's right, but what does that make me if I withhold that from him? "Jax, I need to talk to him."

"Please explain why, because right now I'm trying not to lose it."

I take a deep breath "When Duke came into my room, he was looking for answers. Jax, he was lied to and manipulated. I'm not excusing what he did. I mean, he did murder two people. I saw him pull the trigger. There was no remorse in his eyes, but he protected me from Vincent."

His grip on me tightens "What do you mean, protected you from Vincent? I thought you said Vincent didn't do anything?"

I stroke his arm to calm him. "He didn't physically attack me, but he did flip out when he found out I was pregnant. Duke stood up to him in my defence. Vincent called me a 'common whore, that was knocked up by the big New York City tycoon,'"

Jax winces. "Jax, please don't."

"Don't what, Raven? Don't get pissed off that you were made to feel like filth, for no reason? Our child was not conceived out of common, everyday lust. Our child was conceived from two halves becoming whole, two souls that are meant to be together. The fact that you had to go through this, makes me sick!" He gets up and heads to the bathroom. "I'm going to jump in the shower before we need to head out. Do you want me to set up the tub for you?"

"How about setting up the tub for us?" I can tell by the way he's stroking his chin that he's thinking. "Jax, what's the problem?"

He's staring at the tub. "Um, well, okay, so here's the thing, I've never had a bath."

I gape at him. "You mean you never used that beautiful claw foot tub?" Oh my God, he is blushing and looking down. "Jax, why did you even have such an elaborate tub installed?"

"For resale purposes."

"Did you design this bathroom?"

"No. Bella did, she loves baths. Even as a child, she was always soaking in the tub."

"Well, I will have to thank her. She did a wonderful job."I don't know what to say, I have ever met anyone who never had a bath. "What about when you were a child?"

He shakes his head, "No. As far as I can remember, my mum always left me to shower on my own. I've always been very independent. Plus it seems such a waste of time to just sit there, doing nothing."

Wow. "Okay. Well, Mr. Phillips, I am going to introduce you to the wonders of a big, beautiful tub. You wait here."

I go about filling the tub with that wonderful vanilla spice that I have come to love so much. I can't believe it. If I had this tub, I'd be soaking in it all the time. I love a good book, some soothing music, and a soak in the tub. I'm so excited that I'm going to give Jax a first.

Jax walks in and smiles at me, "What's that look for?"

I must have the most ridiculous smile on my face right now. "I just realized that I'm going to be giving you a first, and there is not too many firsts that I can give you."

He pulls me towards him "You're giving me another first—my first child."

Realization hits me at that moment, he's right. "Oh."

"Yeah, *oh*." He climbs into the tub, and I watch as he sinks into the water. "Are you getting in too?"

He is so beautiful; I could watch him all day long. "I just wanted a minute to look at you."

He opens his arms for me and I climb in. "Jax, can I ask you a question?"

"You can ask me whatever you want, you know that."

I turn and face him, "I understand that you love *Doctor Who*, but you never said why?"

He strokes his chin then, stops to move my hair from my right shoulder to my left. He places several soft kisses in the crook of my neck.. "I knew you would eventually ask me this, and I don't want to hold anything back with you but I have to say, this may be a little hard for me to share." He takes in a deep breath. "When I was a kid, the only thing I ever shared with my father was sitting down with him once a week to watch the show. I don't have very many memories of my father, but that is one that is so clear. My sharing it with Junior, I guess is, in some way, my sharing his grandfather with him. I hope that he will share it with his children, and I know, I will share it with ours."

I throw my arms around him. There are no words left to say. Oh, how I love this man.

Chapter Nineteen

Raven

MAX IS ALWAYS ON time and today is no different. "Max, where did you learn to drive?" His driving is fast, but not reckless.

"Miss Raven, I spent my summers in Italy working for Lamborghini. Why are you laughing?"

"When Marco first met you, he said you reminded him of Daniel Craig. Then when you and Jax rescued me, I realized, not only do you look like him, but *you are* James Bond. If I had any lingering doubts, your driving proves it." I lightly smack his shoulder. Max gifts me with a very large smile, which is so rare for him.

Jax leans over, "Sweetheart, don't encourage him, his head is big enough."

We arrive at the attorney's office right on time. We're ushered in, and then we have to wait. Finally, a man enters and introduces himself as Joseph's attorney. He looks to me, "Raven, I am sorry for your loss. Joseph left three letters with a codicil which names, Jaxson James Phillips and Maxwell Fleming, as executors of his will. Mr. Fleming has also been given legal guardianship of your mother.

"All of Joseph's assets were put into the trust, which controls both your trust and that of your mother. Your mother's trust is to be used for her care. In the event of her death, everything rolls into your trust. If you should precede your mother in death, then your trust would revert to your mother's trust, unless you have children. In that case, everything would revert to the children. Under no circumstances is anything supposed to go to Duke Jensen. Do you have any questions for me?"

Questions? Probably a million, but I doubt that he will have the answers. "Yes. Why?"

"Pardon me Miss. Anderson why, what?" He asks me in an uncertain tone.

I have tight grip on Jax's hand. "Well, first, why did he name Max and Jax when he really didn't know them? Why did he hide my mother from me? Why did he hide my brother from me? Why didn't he tell me he was ill? I guess the list of questions is really endless."

He nods. "Well, there really isn't much I can tell you, because I really didn't know the man very well. I can tell you, he made the changes in the last weeks of his life. The letter to you has been here for a long time, although he did add to it. The letters to Mr. Phillips and Mr. Fleming are new. Maybe the answers you seek are within these letters." With that, he has us sign some paperwork, hands us the letters, and then asks us if we wanted to use his conference room.

"Jax, I would like to go home," I say. Jax nods his head and excuses us from the meeting and the law office, letters in hand. We drive home in silence, the three of us lost in our thoughts. I really want to ask Max to stay. I want to know what Joseph wrote to him, but it's is personally addressed to him. Jax and I sit in front of the fire, and he pours a scotch for himself and water for me. We put the envelopes on the bar and stare at them. I just can't do this now. "Jax, I'm going to lie down for a while, I'm just not ready yet."

He kisses me. "I'll be here for you when you get up."

Maxwell

WHEN I GET BACK to my place, I check my voicemail. I have a message from Jackie, letting me know she's there for me. She's a sweet girl. Too good for me, but I can't walk away from her. I just don't get why Joseph did this; he hardly knew me. And at our last meeting, Jax smashed his nose and we both left him in a broken heap. I decide to pour myself a hefty scotch and sit down with my letter.

Dear Maxwell,

By now you're wondering . . . why? Well, it's what I saw in you, when we were searching for Raven. I saw a man that would not give up, a man of morals, and principals. When I pulled a check on you, I was impressed with your military record. If the Queen can trust her grandchildren to you, then I feel comfortable trusting Raven and Gabriella with you.

When I rescued Gabriella from Vincent, I had to choose to rescue her, knowing he would escape. I never forgave myself for that. She told me that every time he was done raping her, he would look up to the heavens and tell Antonio that it was for him. The man is a vicious pig. If he knew Gabriella was still alive, I don't doubt that he would come after her. When I got her back to the States, I had the doctors examine her, and that's when she found out she was pregnant. She would never have an abortion, so she opted to give the child up for adoption. If Vincent had found out, he would have come back for her. I had to protect Raven, and the best way to do that was to send her to boarding school. My plan was that I would keep Raven at school until Gabriella gave birth, then she could come back, and I would relocate both of them in the Witness Protection Program. You know what they say about best laid plans. Every day that Gabriella carried that child, she was driven more and more mad. She felt Antonio was looking down at her with disgust. I tried to get her into counseling, but she refused. Doctors really do make the worst patients.

By the time she gave birth, she was withdrawn, and then, she was hit with postpartum depression. She tried to hang herself. It was a fluke that I came by that day to find her. She never fully recovered, and I couldn't trust her to take care of Raven so I sent her away to the Swiss clinic and had Raven adopted. I had to do it this way. I needed everyone to think that Gabriella and Cara were dead. With the help of the former director, we staged a car accident in California and then announced to the world that they both died. If Vincent knew that they were both alive, he would have come after them. If you decide to bring Gabriella back to the States, you must protect her from Vincent. If he finds out she is alive, he will come for her and torture her; all in the name of his brother. He has a sick obsession with her. That night when you left me at the Woodstock house, my biggest fear was Vincent. I saw what he did to Gabriella, and I feared what he would do to Raven.

I know that Jax really loves Raven, but I know what you're capable of doing. I know what happened to your family, and I know you understand. So, please, protect them with all that you have.

I trust you with my family; they are all I ever had.

Joseph

I sit here, staring at the letter, and I decide to pour another scotch. What the fuck was Joseph thinking by making me Gabriella's legal guardian? Why does he think I'm such a stable person? I'm a loner. I have been since my Gram died. My mum was a weak person, and gave her life to drugs. I never really knew my father; my Gram raised me. I've had more heartache than one man should have to bear. He knew what I went through. So, what? He thinks I'm stronger because of it?

I'm not stronger because of it; I'm shattered. My only friend is, Jax, the man I trust with my life. He's the brother I never had, and now we're in this together, past the point of no return. He loves Raven, and she is sweet. She's good for him. She doesn't care who he is and how much money he makes. She loves him for him, and all his craziness. This, though, is a huge responsibility.

I don't know that I can do this. I don't know if I have it in me to be this responsible person that Gabriella and Raven need right now.

I consider calling Jackie, but then opt for another scotch. The last thing Jackie needs is me blowing her world apart. I look up at the clock; it's late, and I have finished half the bloody bottle.

Yeah, Joseph, I'm so fucking responsible.

Jaxson

I HAVE NO CLUE what the fuck Joseph was thinking. I'm glad Raven decided to try and lie down for a while. I just don't know what to say to her. I decide to pour another scotch and read the letter.

Jaxson,

I never thought I would have to have this discussion with you, but in light of recent events, I guess I must. I have asked Maxwell to be legal guardian for Gabriella. However, I would like for you to manage the trust fund for Gabriella and Raven. I feel that you would be the best person for this task, since you seem to have a golden touch when it comes to money. I know that you love Raven, and I hope you and Maxwell can get her back safely. I know I should have been more up front with you, but I have always played it pretty close to the vest.

Everything I did was to protect Raven and Gabriella from the horrors of Vincent. I know firsthand how sick and twisted Vincent is, which is why I chose to hide Raven from her mother. I promised Antonio that I would protect her, even if it meant my own life. I put Marco into her life to watch and protect her, I never expected him to turn on her. After her adoptive mother died and her adoptive father did what he did, I felt if I stepped back in to her life, Vincent might find her location. That's why I put Marco with her. I would much rather have kept her with me, but I couldn't take that risk.

Vincent had a jealous streak where Antonio was concerned that is like nothing I have ever seen before. If he found out about Raven, I have no doubt, he would have hunted her down and do to her what he did to Gabriella. When I rescued Gabriella, she told me things . . . things I would not want Raven to know. He did things to her, some very sick and twisted stuff. It was then, that I knew, I had to let the world believe they were both dead. With the help of the former director, we announced that Gabriella and Cara died in a car accident in California, when their car plunged off of the Pacific Coast Highway.

In the eyes of the world, they were dead. I knew Raven told Marco about her adoption and what little she knew about her family. It was not until six months ago, that I revealed to Marco that Raven was the niece of one of the most feared and vicious crime lords in the country. I told him about Duke, but I never told him about Gabriella. I hope you can bring Raven home safely, and that you will protect and love her forever.

Joseph

Wow, I understand the man had all the best intentions, but what a cluster fuck! I don't even know where to begin. I have learned that. no matter what, I have to tell Raven the truth about everything. I will not have her running away, ever again. No one is safe until Vincent is found. I have some thoughts on where Vincent may be, but I need to talk about them with Max. First and foremost, I need to check on Raven and feed her. I walk into the bedroom, and find Raven in the throes of a nightmare. Jesus, when she hurts like this it, slays at my core. I crawl in bed and pull her close, stroking her back.

She wakes and looks up at me, and I use my thumbs to wipe her tears. "Raven, what can I do to help you?" I keep stroking her back, trying to sooth her.

"You're doing it. Just being here with me means so much."

I kiss her soft lips. "I wouldn't be anywhere else, sweetheart."

I take a deep breath, "Did you read your letter from Joseph?"

"Yes I did. What about you, do you want to read yours now?"

She shakes her head. "No, I'm not ready. I'm not sure my heart can take any more."

I pull her tighter. "I will be here with you when you're ready." I need to start going over details with her, but I know I can't overwhelm her. "There is a lot we have to talk about, starting with your security."

"I agree, and I've been thinking, I don't think I can go back to work. It would be too dangerous for the children."

Finally, I feel like we are on the same page. "Agreed. You need to understand that I'm not letting you out of my sight." Fuck, if I could, I would lock her in here with me and throw away the key.

"Jax, that's unrealistic, you have a company to run and a life to live."

"My life is with you. From that day you doused me with your coffee, I knew my life would never be the same. I finally came alive. I agree I have a company to run, but your safety is first on my list. Maybe you should work for me. What do you think about that?"

Oh no. She's looking at me like I'm nuts. "Do you have second graders at your company?"

I thought about this everyday she was gone, and I actually think this might be a great idea.

"Actually, I have an idea that you might find intriguing. I was thinking of creating onsite childcare for the employees, ranging from infancy to elementary. I have been doing some research, and I found out that the cost of daycare is almost as much as a mortgage payment. If I had a school here on the premises, I could keep the cost down, and my workers would be more productive." She's listening, so that's a plus.

"I wouldn't know how to set such a thing up, Jax, I teach."

I know it's all in how I pitch it. "I understand that. I have done all the research, and I have a business plan already done. I got all the specs from the school board. I wouldn't need funding from the City, which means, we could get things done much quicker with no red tape. We can go over it later, but just keep an open mind." At least she didn't say no. It's all about negotiation and me getting my way.

"When can I go back to my place?"

Okay, I need to be calm here before I answer, "Sweetheart, Vincent is a major threat to you and your mother. I don't want to discount your feelings, but . . . never." Okay, maybe that didn't come out the way I intended, because the way she is looking at me I can swear I see fire in her eyes.

"Jax, I have a home and I would like to go back there. I will agree to protection, but I'm not a prisoner."

I need to calm down or I will lose it on her. "Let's talk about this later, okay?"

She shakes her head, "No, not okay."

I'm not good at calm, never one of my finer points. "Are you sure now is the time to do this?"

"Yes, Jax. Now is as good a time as any."

I take a deep breath and try to prepare myself not to come across as a bully. "Okay, Raven, here it is. You have been kidnapped numerous times, you have been shot, you were in the Witness Protection Program, all of this and you're only twenty-seven. Call me crazy, but I think you should be about done with all of this drama now."

She glares at me, "Jax, I was done with it all when I was seven! If I give in to all the drama then, the drama wins. I can't give up, and I won't give up. You can't keep me locked up here forever. I understand I can't go back to the school. I would never put anyone else in danger, but I can, and I will, go home!"

Does this woman think I would actually let her go back there? She doesn't get it. When it comes to winning, I'm a ruthless, fucking bastard. I will win! I pace around the room, no shirt, with my hands in my hair. Yeah, I know I'm good looking and I'm not opposed to using it to my advantage when needed. Her eyes are running up and down my body. Oh yeah, sweetheart, keep looking. I'm making a show of undressing, trying to distract her.

"Jax, don't think that you can flash your good looks and I will bend to whatever you want. Not this time, mister."

Fuck it all to hell! "Well, sweetheart, not only do I own your place, but I purchased the entire fucking building. If I wanted to, I could find a way to keep you out of it for good!" She has no idea how far I would go, and locking her in here is looking better and better.

"You wouldn't!"

We are nose to nose and I growl, "Watch me!"

With that she goes into the bathroom and slams the fucking door.Okay, I'm not a fucking moron. I do realize that I was probably over the top when I purchased the whole building, but in my own defense, I was not thinking clearly at the time. However, now I am thinking with all my pistons firing. There is no fucking way I'm letting her live anywhere but with me. Now, I just need to convince her of that.

I NEED TO GET in touch with Max. "Hey, Max, call me back. I need to go over Raven's detail with you."

I turn around, and I'm hit with her violets. "Where do you think you're going?" I ask.

She smirks at me. "For a run, so if you plan on being stuck to me like glue then, get your ass in gear, bucky."

It's got to be the hormones, it just has to be. I remember Bella was a nut case when she was pregnant. I need to call my sister later.

I change with the upmost speed, and before I know it, we are in the park. She's a runner in more ways than one, but if she thinks for one minute that she will ditch me, she can guess again. Her biggest problem is that she really doesn't know me. Not only am I ruthless when it comes to winning, I'm like a crazy man when it comes to safety. I've watched over my mum and sister my whole life. I'll be damned if this woman thinks she will rule me! Well, at least when I'm not thinking with my cock.

"Will your detail run the entire time with us, Jax, or will you have mercy on them?"

I turn to her and give her the Jaxson smile. I cock my head, "Not only will they run the entire course with us, but I have men stationed throughout the entire park, and at all the various entrances."

She glances over at me, her chin on the ground and eyes as wide as the moon. I reach over with my finger and close her mouth. "I told you, I'm a ruthless bastard, sweetheart. You've just touched the tip of the iceberg." We do the rest of the run in silence, and for once, I'm happy about silence.

Max is waiting for us, and of course he's not happy. Lately he's never happy. I need to talk to him. "Jax, why? Just please tell me why you chose to make my life harder?" He looks at Raven next, "Miss Raven, I understand your need for your independence, but please, can you try to work with me, instead of against me?"

Her eyes fill with tears "Max, what have I done other than go for a run?"

"Well that's just it, Miss Raven. There's a very sick, vicious man on the loose out there, and he is gunning for you. I'd like to get through this without getting anymore kinks in my armor, if that's okay with you!"

I grab his arm. "Cool it, Max. She's not use to this. Dial it down."

Max paces. "Jax, I'm trying! I mean. I'm really trying. However, I can't have unnecessary risks right now. I'm trying to deal with finding Vincent, keeping you and Miss Raven safe, figuring out what to do about Gabriella, and keeping watch on the rest of the family. I just need some sort of cooperation from everyone! Just until, I feel I have gotten a handle on Vincent, is that so much to ask?"

Raven gets up and hugs Max. "Okay, Max, I will do whatever you need me to do."

My head swings around so fast, it's a wonder I don't snap my own fucking neck. "You're listening now?"

"Well, Jax, maybe it's the way Max laid it out rather than bulldozed me." She arches her eyebrow as if to challenge me.

"Miss Raven, I have some things I need to talk to you about; they are personal. However, I know you want no secrets. I have to ask, do you want Jax here?"

"Yes, I have nothing to hide from him." He takes a deep breath. God, what else are we going to have to deal with?

"Okay, when Tony was looking through Marco's thumb drive, he found a letter addressed to you, along with pictures of the two of you. Tony put them all on here for you to decide what you want to do with them." He hands them to her and I can tell by the look on her face, she is in shock.

"Sometimes, good people do bad things. Sometimes they can't help it, but other times they don't think it's bad. Life is complicated, at best, Miss Raven. Have you both read Joseph's letters?"

"I did, but Raven didn't read her letter yet." I sigh. Max paces again. Oh boy, not good.

"Miss Raven, you can read my letter if you want, I have nothing to hide. You need to understand that Vincent hated your father his whole life. What he did to your mother was because of that hatred, and if he knows she is alive, he will go after her.

"After she gave birth to Duke, your mother snapped. She probably had a bad bout of postpartum depression on top of it, plus months of blaming herself for your father's death. It was too much for her. She tried to kill herself. Joseph found her and got her the help that she needed. His plan was to have you both declared dead from a car accident and then move you both within the Witness Protection Program."

"After your mum's attempted suicide, Joseph realized that your mum couldn't take care of herself, let alone you. That is why you were adopted. Joseph wanted to keep you himself, but he knew the danger. He did what he thought was the safest thing. He had you both declared dead, you adopted, and your mum moved to a clinic out of the country. The danger lies in moving your mum to the States. I can't let Vincent know she is alive."

She nods. "Max, I knew how sick and twisted Vincent is my first day as his prisoner, he made me wear my mother's clothes."

My mouth drops open in disbelief. She didn't tell me this, only about the book.

"He also gave me a book that belonged to my mother. Inside of it was a detailed account of what she went through. There were also some beautiful pictures that she drew. Vincent made my mother watch a video of my father getting shot and me being held prisoner. He physically and mentally tortured her for two months. So, what is it that you need from me, Max?"

Max takes her hand, "First, I need to read your letter from Joseph. I need to know if there is anything in there that might help me. Second, never ditch your detail. Don't even think about trying. I'm assigning you two people, whom I vetted personally.

"Dominika is your female guard. She is originally from Russia and she is former KGB. Your male guard is Daniel, and he is former Secret Service. You will also have a dog. His name is Bo. Bo is listed as a service dog. I don't have to list which service he falls under. You just need to remember never leave this house without him, and he must at all times wear his vest. The vest has a tracker and a weapon in it. No one ever checks the dog. Also, I want you to wear this bracelet. It looks like one of those magnetic ones, but it is also a tracker." He puts it on her wrist.

"Okay?"

"Jax, you have your standard detail that you usually have, however, I am giving you a bracelet to wear too. I have increased the coverage on all the family. Everyone is currently wearing a bracelet. I also put the same protection in place for Jackie and Mrs. Osla."

Raven looks at me, "Jax, who's Mrs. Osla?"

"She is my new assistant and Max is afraid of her."

Raven looks between the two of us. "Really, I thought you were only afraid of Jax's mom?"

I'm trying so hard not to laugh at Max right now. "Miss Raven, you will see for yourself, but heed my warning, she is scary. Okay, Miss Raven, let me introduce you to your new detail."

Raven

I TAKE TO BO right away. He is such a sweet boy. "Max, what type of dog is he?"

He loves getting his ears scratched.

"He is a mix breed, part German Shepherd and part American Pit Bull. He is strong, loyal, and has the best of both breeds."

"Was he bred for security work?"

"No. Bo is a rescue dog. When I was a young lad, my grams told me that the measure of a real man was what he gave of himself, unconditionally. Grams insisted that I volunteer my services to wherever I felt needed. I spent most of my youth at a rescue shelter. It was at the Battersea Dogs and Cats Home that I learned about the loyalty of a rescue dog. I can see that you and Bo will get along fine. Daniel will walk you through the different commands for Bo while I go over some stuff with Jax."

While Raven is working with Bo, Max and I go into my home office. "Jax, what did your letter say?"

"Nothing that you don't already know. He asked me to manage the money, of course, and the standard warning about Vincent. What did your letter say?"

"Just more of the same." Max leans back against my desk.

"I understand the concern about Vincent, but are you being extreme about the security?" I squint, rubbing the back of my neck.

"No, the man is sick and twisted. He repeatedly raped Gabriella, and when he was done he would look up to the heavens and say, 'that's for you, Antonio.' That is not someone to take lightly." He begins pacing again.

To think my girl was alone with this fucker for three months! "Any news on where he might be?"

"I have a lead. I'm leaving in an hour to head down to New Orleans to follow it up."

"What was in the letter from Marco?"

He stops pacing. "Just the ramblings of a tormented person. I think he was sorry for what he was doing, but the gambling and Erica just twisted him. You need to encourage Raven to go for therapy. Have you talked about her place and the baby?"

I stroke my chin before I go into a full frustrated, face rub.. "Max, I can't overload her. We already had a *come to Jesus* about her going back home. I venture to say, that every step will be a challenging one, when it comes to Raven."

"Did you tell her that you now own the entire building?" He raises both eyebrows.

I growl, "I can't hide anything from you. I did, and let's just say, she wasn't happy."

"You know you can't keep her from there forever." Suddenly, he gets a suspicious look on his face. "Jax, what the fuck did you do, mate?"

I can't hide anything, fuck! "I'm having the entire building tented for termites."

"You're dead serious, aren't you?" His mouth opens only to throw his head back and laugh hysterically. "Jax, you really are a crazy fucker. Does she know?" He finally calms down.

"Of course not. You know she'll hit the roof when she finds out."

"Will you ever learn? What about all the other tenets living in the building?"

I take a deep breath, "I put them all up at the W."

He shakes his head. "Before I leave, I need to see that letter."

Max reads the letter and then puts it back in the envelope, a stolid expression on his face.

"Max, anything I need to know?"

He nods, "There is a key in here for a safety deposit box."

I throw the letter on the desk. "Fuck, will this ever end?"

Max exhales loudly through pursed lips, "Not until Vincent is taken care of. I need to get to the airport. I will call you later to let you know what I found out. Monday morning, we go to the bank" Just like that, he's gone.

When I get back into the living room, I see Raven has made coffee for her detail. She needs to stop thinking of them as company and pretend they are not even in the room. They at least look embarrassed that she is serving them coffee. Bo leaps up and starts growling at me when I step closer to Raven. Daniel turns to Raven, "Miss Raven, you need to introduce him to Mr. Phillips. Teach him that he is not a threat to you."

She issues a command "Bo. Down. This is Jax." I don't know what else she's telling him, all I know is, both my hands are covering my crotch, protecting the *Crown Jewels*. He calms down, and then, Raven tells me all about the dog and the different hands signals she can give him in case she is unable to talk.

"Let's go inside and talk, please. We have a lot to go over." I lead her into the bedroom for some privacy. "I know you never had detail before, but you need to pretend they aren't even in the room."

Her violet eyes show a hint of sadness. "Why?"

I kiss her hand. "That's what will help them do their job effectively, by blending in without being noticed." I explain. "I promised you I would tell you everything as I find out about it. Well, Max just left for New Orleans to follow a lead. If you want to go to your place to pick up stuff, I will concede to that, but I will not let you out of my sight, until Vincent is caught."

I brace myself for the fight of my life. I've learned she can be like a pit bull, but so can I.

"Are you telling me that I am living here, or I'm just staying here temporarily?"

I need to dial up the charm here. "I want us together for the rest of our lives. Is that such a bad thing?" I bring her hands up to my chest. Tears fill her eyes. Okay, fuck me, what did I do wrong now?

"Jax." She jumps up and runs into the bathroom crying. For Christ's sake. I decide to call Bella.

"Hey, sis, you busy?"

She takes a deep breath, "Jax, oh my God, I have so many questions, and I need to see you."

Maybe she can make some sense of what I'm doing wrong with Raven. "Can Raven and I come over?"

"Why are you asking? You never ask." She's talking fast, her voice almost a shrill.

I sigh, "It's Raven. I can't seem to do anything right. I keep reducing her to tears."

She laughs, "Jax, she's pregnant. And the hormones will do it, plus all the additional stress. It's a wonder she can even put two words together."

See, I knew she would understand. "Okay, we will be over in a little bit. How's Junior doing?"

"He's quiet, and I'm worried. Maybe seeing Raven will help. Max came by with bracelets and more guards for all of us. Jax, none of us are fighting this. We won't give you a hard time, not even Mrs. Osla!"

I can't help but laugh, "Don't tell me you're afraid of her, too?"

She laughs, "Shit, yeah, aren't you?"

I don't get why Bella and Max are so afraid of her? "No, she's like Mum on steroids."

"She's scary. Even Vito cowers when she's around."

"Well, part of Raven's detail is a dog, and let me tell you, he will scare you."

Bella laughs, "I'll cook something. Come around six. Love you, bro."

God, I love my sister. I can understand how lonely Raven must feel without a sibling to lean on. "Me too, Bella."

I go back inside the bedroom and find Raven, staring at the laptop, crying. "Sweetheart, what's the matter?" *I can't take the tears.*

"I want to look at the flash drive that Tony sent, but your laptop is password protected."

I throw my hands up. "Is that why you're crying?"

She nods, "I realize I don't know anything about you."

She has a point here. Everything has been so fast, and then she was gone. "You know I love you."

Now she's really crying, fuck! "What do you want to know?"

There must be a hundred tissues all over the bed. "Jax, you don't understand, it's not what you can tell me. When you know a person, you know all the little things that make up that person. I sat here looking at this screen, and I realized, I have no idea what you would choose for a password!" She sobs.

"Raven."

"What?" She blows her nose.

I lean in and kiss her, "That's my password—*Raven.*"

"Oh," she whispers.

I kiss her. "Yeah, *oh.* Sweetheart, just know I love you and would do anything for you. I promise you, the rest will follow. Now, I'll leave you alone to read what's on the drive, but we need to leave in two hours to go to Bella's house for dinner. Junior really needs to see both of us. I'm worried."

"Jax, what's going on with Michael?" She straightens up, her focus, seemingly, anew.

I love how much she loves Junior.

"He went back to school, but he's very quiet. Bella is worried, and so am I. I think seeing the two of us will help."

She nods, "Okay, I'll be ready." I offer to bring her coffee, but she's already lost in what's on the computer, so I back out of the room as quiet as possible.

Raven

Raven,

If you're reading this, then I know you must feel really hurt and betrayed. When I was seventeen, I got caught up in a FBI sweep of hackers. I was really good at it, and I used my skills for illegal shit. Joseph saw something in me that, he must have felt, was redeeming. He put me through the Academy, nurtured, and mentored me. My parents threw me out when I was thirteen. They were extreme religious freaks and felt my being bi-sexual was the work of the devil. Joseph had been dealing with a bunch of personal stuff, but he still made time for me. Then one day, he came to me, and told me about you. He said, "Just keep an eye out for her, because I can't." He never told me anything more. That day, I showed up at the shelter, I felt like I found the most precious thing in the world—a friend. I was just supposed to keep an eye on you, but before I knew what was happening, we were roommates. Joseph only gave me one rule, and that was not to sleep with you, no matter what. It was by far the hardest rule to follow, especially after the ex-boyfriend. I just wanted to hold you in my arms forever. I think that's when I started to gamble. I'm not blaming you. I'm just trying to help you understand.

I'm sorry, I never meant for anything to hurt you. I got so caught up in gambling. Oh sure, it starts out simple, but it never ends that way. Before I knew it, I was in really deep. I was going to tell you and ask you for financial help, but then I met Erica. I fell in love for the first time. At least, I thought it was love. She made me believe I was her end all, but I realized too late that I was not and by then, we were married. My gambling was getting worse and I was about to come to you again, but Joseph came to me first, to tell me he was dying. He sat me down and gave me more details about your adoption than you knew. He also revealed everything about Duke. I had a friend in Lansing and had him pull the file on Duke. Erica came up with a plan to get Duke hired on at Raiders, Inc. She told me all about her affair with Jax and why it ended. She told me about her plan to seek revenge against Jax and how I can get out of the mess I was in. It was all supposed to work out, until that fateful day you met Jax. The entire plan became one big cluster fuck, all because fate had to bring you and Jax together.

Baby girl, I was in love with you, no matter what you think. I really did love you. Somewhere along the way, the lines were blurred for us, but I did.
Marco

I am in shock. I can't believe he was in love with me. *How could I not see this?* What fucking planet was I on? Am I that so self-absorbed that I couldn't see what was right in front of my face? There is another file on the drive labeled *pictures*, so I open it, and I am hit with one man's total obsession of me.

I pick up the laptop and fling it across the room, breaking it to a million pieces. Jax comes flying into the room. Bo, and my detail are right behind him. Jax looks to me and then to the computer, but he stays quiet.

"Jax, say something!"

He takes a deep breath. "I have always imagined throwing my computer across the room, but never quite had the nerve to do it."

He opens his arms, and I run into them. He nods to my team and they leave—all except Bo.

I hand Jax the thumb drive, "Here please put this away for now."

"Okay," he whispers. He's not even upset.

"That's it? Okay? I throw your computer across the room and its trash now. I just read something that obviously upset me greatly, and all you can say is *okay*?"

He kisses me. "Yep." *What the hell?*

"Why?"

He takes another deep breath. "Well, when you're ready, you'll tell me what you want me to know. I trust you with my heart and soul, and when you're ready, you'll trust me with yours."

The tears are trailing down my cheeks. Oh, how I love this man. "Oh."

"Yeah, *oh.*," he whispers. "Let's get ready."

Chapter Twenty

Raven

I DECIDE TO WEAR my black pencil skirt, red sweater, and my favorite stilettos. I figure I better enjoy this now, since it won't be long before I can't wear any of this. We head out to Bella's house, and I don't know why I'm nervous—I shouldn't be. "Jax, who knows I'm pregnant?"

"What do you mean, who knows?" He glances over as he lowers the volume on the radio.

For such a smart man sometimes I just want to smack him. "Just what I said, who did you tell?"

"My mum, sister and Michael, why?" He looks at me strange.

Like I wasn't nervous enough. "I'm nervous, and I don't want them to think I got pregnant on purpose. I'm an educated adult and should have been more careful."

Jax presses a button and the privacy glass slides into place, and then he turns to face me. "I won't even dignify that with an answer. I'm very close with my family, and I can only hope with time, you will come to feel close to them, too. We created a new life together out of love, and I will not have you taint it with anything else."

Wow, I hit a nerve. "I'm sorry, Jax, I just don't want anyone to think that I'm after..." Before I can finish, he's on me. He kisses me, our tongues doing a slow tango. He nibbles his way across my chin to my ear. He loves to nibble on it. He kisses my neck, following the trail down with his tongue. My nipples are instantly hard.

He leans me down, and as he does, he sees my thigh high's and garter. "Oh, bloody hell! Oh, fuck me!"

"You okay, Jax, can you breathe?"

He takes a steadying breath. "Barely, sweetheart, I can come just from the sight of you!" His eyes keep roaming up and down my body.

"Jax, you can touch me, I promise, I won't break."

He takes my hand and places it on his heart. "Raven you take my breath away. I just need a minute please. If I don't take one, it will be like a teenager, when he gets his first shag. Do you feel my heart? It beats wildly, just for you. If I died right now, I would die a happy man.

You have taken me to heaven and there is no going back. You gave me a life worth living."

My God this man renders me speechless. "Oh."

"Yeah, *oh,*" he whispers.

He takes a few more steadying breaths, and then he lifts my sweater, nibbling my nipples through my bra. He reaches over and presses the intercom, "Keep driving around Bella's house until I tell you differently." He lifts my breast out of my bra and latches on to my nipple—nibble, lick, suck. Oh wow, they are so sensitive. On to the next one, all the while he's humming, which radiates to my core. He pushes my skirt all the way up to my waist. "Are you wet for me?" he asks as he travels down my body.

I nod, "I'm always wet for you." *Holy, he just snapped my thong!* "I want to taste you now." He's nibbling and licking me, one finger in, and then another. Oh my God! He pulls his fingers out and offers them to me for a taste. It's so erotic, and it's all in the back of a limo. I taste myself on him, mixed with his Vanilla spice and I moan.

"My cock needs to be in the happy place," he breathes. I close my eyes and hear the sound of him working at his zipper. My heart races and my core aches for him. Suddenly, his cock is sliding up and down my wet folds. A moan escapes my throat as he enters one inch at a time. When he is all the way in, he stops. "Look at me!" My eyes shoot up to his. "Do you feel that? We are a perfect fit." He doesn't move but holds us at this intensity; so full . . . so perfect. He leans down and starts kissing me, slowly. He rests his forehead on mine. He's not moving his hips at all, and he's just locked onto my eyes. "Raven, you have unraveled me. Do you feel me? Do you feel how deep I am? I just have to be inside you, locked onto your eyes, and I will explode." Just like that, his cock starts to throb and pulse right before he floods me. "That's what you fucking do to me." Then he pulls back, and he's still rock hard. *How the fuck?* But before I can think, he slams into me with all he's got. "I could go all night in cock heaven. All night." He growls, "Fucking better than anything in the world."

I'm not going to hold it much longer. "Jaxxxxxxxx!"

He yells, "Fuck, baby, I'm falling with you!" Our breathing starts to slow down. He nudges my nose with his. "Never, ever enough. Never." He leans down further, kissing my neck and nibbling my ear.

"Jax, we need to be at Bella's." He gets up and it looks as though he is going to clean us up, but then he takes an ice cube and pops it into his mouth. He leans down and takes a nipple in his mouth with the ice. "Jax, holy hell! Oh my… oh, Jax." Then he takes another ice cube for my other nipple. The sensation is crazy! First hot and then cold, oh how is this even possible? He put one in his mouth and goes right between my legs. And I lose it, screaming, coming, and swearing like I never had before. I'm fisting his hair. It's a wonder I didn't pull it out in chunks.

"You're all clean now." And with that, he tells the driver to go to Bella's!

As we pull up to Bella's house, I am very aware that I have no panties, and that Jax loves it.

"Bella, thank you for having us on such short notice. How's Michael doing?"

She smiles, "Better now that I told him you were home safe."

"How much does he know?" This family has no secrets from each other, which is refreshing, however, he is just seven.

"We told him that you were away for a while. I didn't want him to know you were kidnapped, again. I think his fear is that the men are coming back."

I nod. "Okay, well that makes sense since it was always my greatest fear." When we get to the living room, Michael comes running right to me. I assure Bo it's okay, and then Michael leaps into my arms. This is what family is about—unconditional love; and I can't stop crying.

"Miss Raven, are you okay?"

I nod. "I'm more than okay."

He looks at me confused, "Then why are you crying?"

"I'm very happy to see you." That seems to do the trick. He takes me by the hand and leads me to the dining room for dinner. After dinner, the men go to the living room, and I'm left with Bella and Mrs. Phillips. I know what's coming next. With this family, there is no subtlety.

Mrs. Phillips starts the questions. "So, Raven, have you spoken with the doctor about the baby?"

I shake my head, "No, Mrs. Phillips, only what Jax told me at the hospital. I have a follow-up appointment this week with an OB."

She smiles at me. "Can you please call me An? After all, you're family now." She gets up,

"I'll leave you with Bella," and she heads into the living room.

"Bella, did I do something wrong? She seems upset."

Bella takes my hand, "I was pregnant with Michael before I was married, and now you're pregnant before you are married. It's just Mum is old school in many ways."

Oh what this family must think of me. "I'm not after Jax's money."

She stops me. "Hold up, Raven, no one said you were after his money. We are just concerned about him, that's all. My brother is a very strong and proud man, and I know, in some way, he blames himself for what happened to Junior, and then to you. Anyone just has to look at the two of you to see how much you love each other. I know that none of what happened was your fault, however, you have the ability to bring my brother to his knees."

I'm really confused. "I'm sorry, Bella, but I don't understand."

She takes a deep breath, "Look, Raven, Jax doesn't do anything half-arse, that's why he is so successful in business, when you run, it kills him. When he couldn't find you for three months, it was really bad here. Not even Max could help him. He blocked out his family and his business, he was always distracted, and he bought your building. He would stay in your apartment every day. He doesn't think any of us knew what he was doing, but we did. If you left, there would be no coming back for Jax. For the first time in his life, he loves someone so completely." She lets out a big breath. I don't know what to say to her to assure her I'm not running. "I know you're very emotional now with the pregnancy, but you need to cut him some slack if he is overbearing. It's just coming from the fear of you running or being in danger. As far as Mum is concerned, just know that she is worse than Jax when it comes to family. If you need me for anything, call me. Remember, I've been pregnant. I know all the crazy stuff you're feeling." She gets up and hugs me. "Let's get coffee and dessert." Just like that, she is done.

As we head back to The Tower Jax tells me that he heard from Max and New Orleans was a dead end. "Now what do we do?"

"Well, first, you need to read Joseph's letter. Apparently, there is a key to a safety deposit box in it."

Jaxson

THE REST OF THE ride is in silence. I don't know how much more stress she can take, but we agreed—*no more secrets.*

"Monday, we'll be at the bank when it opens and you can see what's in the safe. You also have a follow-up appointment with the OB at noon, same day. Raven, are you listening?"

She nods. "Yes, Jax. Are you planning out my life for me? Do I get any say, at all?"

I'm trying not to flip out on her, but it's really hard. I decide not to say anything for the rest of the ride home.

"Raven, would you like to be alone when you read the letter or would you like me with you?" I ask as we walk through the door.

"Can I use your office?" She takes the letter and Bo, goes into the office, and locks the door.

I decide to go next door to Max's place and vent to him. When I get there, I realize he's not alone, Jackie's with him. "Hey, sorry to bother you, I just needed to vent, no big deal."

As I turn to leave, Jackie stops me. "Jax, when can I see Raven?"

"You know what, she is next door reading Joseph's letter. I'm sure she will need you after that. Why don't you both come back to my place?" I hope I didn't just ruin Max's night with Jackie, but I need my best friend right now.

"Jax what's up? You're crazier than usual!" Max slaps me on the back.

He's right, I am. I know it. "Look, mate, I know I'm nuts right now, but I don't know any other way. I am operating out of fear and I don't know how to control it. I want, no, I *need* her safe, and I don't know how to stress that to her without scaring her or having her pull a runner."

"Jax, I really understand your fear, but you don't want to push too hard, otherwise it will have the opposite effect. You might want to give her a little breathing room. She's a smart girl, and she saw firsthand how evil Vincent is. Put yourself in her shoes—she's pregnant, she has been kidnapped four bloody times. She found out she has a half-brother who is psycho, and her mother that she thought was dead for the past twenty years is alive. Think about it, how would you feel?"

I pour another scotch. "I guess now is not a good time to demand that she marry me."

He just rolls his eyes and laughs.

Raven

I KNOW I NEED to talk to Jax, but right now I need to read this letter.

My Dearest Cara,

I have so much to say to you, but unfortunately—time is up. We live our lives, thinking we have all the time in the world, only to have it end so quickly. I'm sorry you had to find out about your mother like this. Everything I did was for your safety and for Gabriella's peace of mind. You need to understand that she agreed to your adoption to protect you. She knew how evil Vincent really was (still is); she experienced it firsthand. I can't stress enough, how much danger you and Gabriella are still in.

I made promises to both your parents to keep you safe, no matter what the sacrifice. I brought Marco into your life because I could not be there. I know that you saw what happened that day Vincent shot Antonio. The bullet was meant for me but Antonio pushed me out of the way. There is a reason he did that. Ten years before that night, Antonio and I were working undercover. The perp realized who Antonio was, he had him dead to rights, but at the last second, I stepped in front of him. I was shot, and years later your father did the same for me. In the weeks that he lingered, I asked him. 'Why?' He said, 'If you didn't take that bullet for me, then my greatest gift to the world, my Cara, would never have been born.' In the last few weeks of his life, he made a recording for you and Gabriella. It's in a safety deposit box, along with some precious mementos from your parents and grandparents.

When the time came to move you, I chose your new name because of your silky black hair. I hope in time you can forgive me. I hope someday, it will be safe for you to reunite with Gabriella. Life is short, so make the most of each day. Jax is a good man, he comes from a good family, and I believe, that with him, you will blossom into the woman that your father knew you would be. I have total faith that Jaxson and Maxwell will keep you and Gabriella safe.

God Bless you, I love you always.

Joseph

I decide to go find Jax, and I see that Jackie and Max are here. I throw my arms around Jackie. I really need her now. "Jackie, I'm so glad you're here. Let's go inside."

"Raven, what's the matter, I can tell something is bothering you."

She knows me so well. "I love, Jax, but he is such a take charge type of guy that I don't have a chance to think for myself. It can be very overwhelming, at times."

She hugs me again. God, I need her around more. "You need to just tell him. He can't read your mind. Maybe he thinks he's helping to relieve some of the stress. He was a total basket case when you were gone. No one could get through to him. I think he fears losing you more than pissing you off."

I know she's right. "Let's talk about you. What's going on with you and Max?"

"He doesn't do relationships, yet he is always trying to be with me. For the three months you were gone, he came by to see me every day. I just don't know what to think. Something stops him every time, and it is frustrating."

"Well he is under just as much stress as Jax is, so I think maybe you need to cut him some slack, as well."

Jackie starts laughing. "What's so funny, girl?"

She smiles, "We just gave each other the same advice."

We head back inside, and the guys are having a scotch by the fire. I stand there and enjoy a second of normal. Max and Jackie leave, and I decide to talk to Jax about what's bothering me. "Jax, can we talk?"

He hugs me. "Of course. If I did something to upset you, I need you to tell me."

I have to try and explain his overbearing way, and I'm thinking, *good luck.* "I just feel overwhelmed by everything. I know you're trying to manage everything, but I need to be in on making the decisions. I feel like you're dictating my life." He's looking at me and stroking his chin, so I know he is thinking about what I said. "Maybe I don't want to go to the doctor that you picked. I just want to be part of the decisions."

He takes a deep breath. "Okay, you're right. I tend to just pick up the ball and run with it. That can be over powering, if you're not use to it. If you want to pick another doctor, that's fine, but you need to get the follow-up quickly."

I sigh. "I'm sure you picked the top doctor in New York, and that's fine. I just need you to understand my feelings."

He kisses me, "Come here, I need to hold you, sweetheart." I crawl into his lap and find instant peace.

"What was in Joseph's letter?"

"Well, apparently, there is a video and some mementos in the box."

He's softly rubs my back, and it calms me. "Did he say what's on the video?"

I shake my head. "The video is a recording from my father. Apparently, Joseph took a bullet for him ten years before, and that's why he stepped in front of Joseph when Vincent tried to kill him. When Joseph asked him why he stepped between Vincent and him, he said, If Joseph didn't take the bullet for him then, his greatest gift to the world would have never been born."

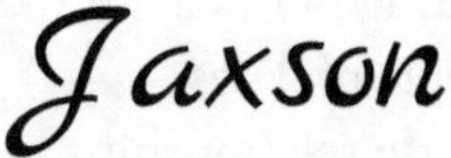

Jaxson

CHRIST, HOW MUCH MORE shit is going to be thrown at her. "Wow, that's some heavy stuff. How do you feel about all of this?"

She cuddles into me, "I have so many mixed emotions, but in the end, I love Joseph for all he did to protect us. I'm proud of the parents I had. I need Max to find Vincent so I can get some closure, and maybe have some sort of relationship with my mother. I'm going to try and be the best mother I can be. I want our child to know he or she is loved, and wanted. I knew my adopted parents loved me, and I believe my adopted father was just grieving. To know that my mom has been alive all these years makes me feel sad. We lost so many years that neither of us will get back.

I wipe the tear, trailing down her cheek. "I know you're going to be the best mum ever. You're kind hearted and very loving. Our child will know true love. Maybe having a baby around your mum might help her, especially if she sees you're happy and made a good life, even after all the shit you've gone through."

"Jax, can I ask you something?"

I smile. "Anything, you know that."

"What do you think about Max being with Jackie?"

I see this is bothering her, but why? "Why are you asking me this?"

She starts twirling her fingers, "I just worry about Jackie. You know, she is old fashioned and innocent. I don't want to see her get hurt. Max is older than she is, he's um—more experienced."

"What are you trying to tell me here, Raven?"

I growl, "Jax, why are you being so dense?"

He laughs, "I'm not being dense. I know there is a large age difference, but age is only a number. As far as experience, are you trying to tell me something here? Oh my God, she's a virgin, isn't she? You don't have to answer that. Your face just said it all. Well I can tell you that Max is a man of honor. He would never use her or be abusive. The Royal Army has awarded him numerous medals, and he guarded the Queens grandchildren. As far as financially, he is set for life. I hired him away from the Queen, and I had to make him an offer he could not refuse. He has no mortgage, no car payments. He owns a 20% stake in Raiders Inc. He has unlimited use of the private jet, and has full medical coverage for life. Does that make you feel better?"

Oh God, how I love this man. "Wow, Jax, that's impressive, but I'm more worried about her getting her heart broken. She has never shown an interest in anyone past a couple of dates.

Max told her he doesn't do relationships, why?"

He shrugs. "I honestly don't know. All you can do is just support her in her decisions about Max, and everything else will fall into place. Enough about them, I think I need to be kissing you all over."

"MAX DO YOU THINK Raven is safe?"

He takes my hand, "Miss Jackie, as long as she follows protocol, and doesn't try to ditch her detail, she will remain safe."

He's like a dog with a bone! "You're never going to let us forget about that, are you?"

He smirks at me. "Nope. Do you know how worried I was, and how much danger the two of you were in? Vincent is a very dangerous man. Now that I know what I'm dealing with, I have increased security."

I know I should be afraid, but Max has a way of taking away the fear. "I promise I won't ditch my detail, and I will be extra careful."

He pulls me close. "Thank you." He begins to kiss my neck. I want this man, but I'm scared. He is so much older than me and very experienced. I've had a couple of boyfriends, but no one that I ever wanted to give myself to.

"Max I need to get home."

He stops and looks in my eyes, "Are you sure?"

I nod. "Yes, I have to go." I reiterate. He doesn't push me. When we get to my place he, of course, has to come upstairs to make sure I'm safe. As he is leaving, he turns around pulls me close to him.

"I'm a patient man, and I will be here for you when you're ready for me."

He kisses me and is out the door. I'm so confused. I want this man, but I'm scared. God, I really need to talk to Raven, but it's too late now to call her. I decide on chocolate and a glass of wine. This man is going to break my heart, and there is nothing I can do about it. I'm about to go to bed when I receive a text message.

> **Raven:** I need to talk to you alone. I need to get away from Jax. He's too protective. Will you help me, please?—Raven
>
> **Me:** Raven, you seemed okay earlier. What went wrong?
>
> **Raven:** Can't talk now, will you meet me in an hour, coffee shop on 52nd street and 3rd?
>
> **Me:** Okay.

The one thing I'm not, is stupid, and it makes me mad when people think that a woman is stupid. I call Max and he answers on the first ring. "Are you okay?"

I take a deep breath, "No, Max, I'm not. I need you back here now. I just got a text, and I don't think it's real."

His mood changes instantly. "Do not leave your place. Do not answer the door. I'm staying on the phone with you until I get there!"

I hear him running, "Hold on, Max, someone is buzzing me."

"Fuck, Jackie, do not answer!" he yells.

I get back on the phone. "Max, calm down. The door man said there is a package for me."

"Jackie, I swear if you open that door, so help me woman… Go into your bathroom and lock the door, *right now!*" He's scaring me. Maybe I shouldn't have called him.

"Why?" I yell back.

"Why? Why are you fucking trying to put me in an early grave?!"

He sounds nuts. "Okay, please calm down. I'm in my bathroom, the door is locked, but someone keeps buzzing. Max, are you still there?" *Oh my God, there are gunshots!* "Max? Max? Please answer. Please."

"Miss Jackie, I'm outside your front door. I'm alone, look through the peep hole first," he instructs.

I let out the breath I didn't realize I was holding. "I can come out of the bathroom, then?"

He growls, "Yes, please let me in."

I open the door, and I can't help but throw my arms around him. "Did you look through the peep hole?"

Crap. "No. You said to let you in."

"I could have had a gun to my head, you should have looked."

I realize that I'm wrapped around him and holding on for dear life. He walks inside carrying me. "You can put me down now, Max."

But he doesn't. "Maybe I don't want to." He walks over to the kitchen, placing me on the counter.

"Max, what happened? I heard gun shots."

He takes a deep breath. "There was no package. The doorman was knocked out. Someone was waiting to take you. He pulled his gun on me, and I retaliated. Pack your stuff. You're coming home with me now."

"I thought I was safe with my detail?"

He shakes his head. "Your guard is on his way to the hospital. I'm trusting no one, but myself, when it comes to you."

"What about work?"

His jaw is tight. "You tell me. What do you think would happen, if you were at school, and all of this went on?"

Of course, what am I thinking? "I would never put any of the children in danger. I'll pack up. Maybe I should go home. My father has tight security, and right now, he is at our Switzerland compound."

"The only place you're going is home with me, right now." Max has a tight grip on me with a lost look on his face. Wow, I've never seen this side of him before. We head back to his place in silence. When we get upstairs, he shows me to his guest room. "I need to see your phone." As he reads it, he's heading over to Jax's door.

Maxwell

"JAX LET ME IN now!" I don't think this is from Raven.

"This better be fucking good because I was really happy until you banged on my door."

I push past Jax. "I need to see Raven now."

"What's going on, Max?"

I pace. I can't help it. "Jackie got a text from Raven."

"Mate, that's not possible. We've been a little tied up for a while."

"Get me her phone, it might have been cloned."

Raven comes to the door, "Hey, Jackie, what happened?"

Her chin quivers, "Someone pretending to be you, tried to lure me out of my apartment alone."

Jax is looking at the messages, and then hands the phone to Raven. "Jax, I never sent these messages."

He pulls her into his arms. "I know, sweetheart."

I pocket both phones, "Okay I'm taking this phone, and Jax will give you another one. You will have a new number, and so will Miss Jackie. These have been compromised. I'm concerned as to when this happened. Miss Jackie will be staying at my place, and will not be at work."

Raven takes Jackie's hand "Jax, I'm going into Max's with Jackie to help her get settled in."

He nods, "Take Bo with you, sweetheart."

Jaxson

"MAX, WHAT THE FUCK is going on?"

He paces. He seems to be doing this more and more lately with all that has been going on. "I left Jackie's place, and was almost home, when she called me. She said she got a text that she thought was fake. I stayed on the phone with her while I raced back to her place. While I was on the phone with her, the doorman was buzzing her that she had a package. I made her lock herself in the bathroom until I got there. When I walked into the building, the doorman was out cold and so was her guard. The guy that was there pulled a gun on me, and I shot him. He's not dead, and he is in police custody now."

I'm so tired of this. "Max, this shit has got to stop already."

He nods, "I agree, but it won't stop until we get to Vincent. I just have to figure out a way to draw him out."

"What's going on with you and Jackie?"

"Jump right in, Jax."

"Yep, you know me too well to think I would do anything else."

He takes a deep breath, "She's a sweet girl, Jax, and I'm just too distracted right now. I can't concentrate on anyone. Besides, you know I don't do relationships. What's bothering you, Jax? I can tell you have something on your mind, so spill it, mate."

Now I'm pacing. "Raven asked me about you today."

He cocks his head. "Really, why?" I hate this. I want to just come out and tell him, but Raven will be pissed at me, and I manage that real well on my own.

"She is worried about Jackie. Jackie is young, and innocent, especially when it comes to any kind of relationship." His stolid expression tells me that he's not "getting" what I'm trying to tell him.

"She's twenty-five, Jax, so what's the problem?"

I give him a look and then all of the sudden, I see it finally hitting him like a fucking brick. "Oh, bloody hell, no fucking way, mate. Are you serious! She's twenty-five. How is that even possible in today's world?"

I finally stop pacing. "Look, Max, I shouldn't even be saying anything to you, but I don't want to see her hurt. She's old fashioned, and she has dated, but no one she would give herself to. Don't you dare say anything, otherwise, I'll be in the fucking doghouse, for sure."

Max gets up. "Jax, I have to go." Oh boy, he's pissed now.

"What about the phones?"

He growls as he's running out the door. "I'm giving them to Tony in the morning. Right now, they are both shut off."

Jackie

"JACKIE, I'M SO SORRY that you have been dragged into this mess."

I hug her. "Raven, it's life, I'm okay. Things are going to be very different for us until they catch this nut."

"What about you and Max? Are you okay staying here? If not, you can stay in Jax's guest room."

I want to be here with him, that much I do know. "I'm okay here, he is the perfect gentleman. My problem is, I usually call my parents every Sunday night, and when I don't check in, they are going to be worried."

Raven

I'M TRYING TO FIGURE out a way around this. "Can you check in via email?"

She shakes her head. "No they will know something is up, we always Skype on Sunday."

I take her hand, "Okay, let's ask Max and Jax what they think we should do."

We head back next door just as the guys are finishing up, but Max looks lost in thought.

"Hey, guys, Jackie needs to check in with her parents. She usually Skype's with them every Sunday night, but the problem is, they will know something is wrong, especially when she doesn't call from her phone."

Jax turns on the fireplace. "Jackie, can you tell them you're on a ski trip with Raven, and we'll sit you and Raven in front of the fireplace?" Max is very quiet, more so than usual.

"Jax, I need chocolate." Jackie announces.

"Excuse me?"

She laughs, "When I'm nervous, I eat chocolate. It calms me. Do you have chocolate?"

"Yes, I do. Bella keeps a stash here," he chuckles.

"Jax, don't laugh. I bet you don't know Raven's vice?" She baits him.

Jax looks at me. "Oh my God, you're blushing! Do tell, sweetheart. What's your vice?"

"Well, aside from coffee, warm Nutella will bring me to my knees."

Jax smiles. I wish I knew what he was thinking right at that moment. "Okay, let's get this phone call done."

Jackie

MY PARENTS ARE VERY happy that I'm on a trip with Raven; they want us to visit soon. We let them know that we will on our next break from work. I miss them and really need to get out there soon.

"I'm glad the call worked out okay, but on that note, Max, Jackie, you need to go home now." And with that, he ushers us out the door.

Raven

I CAN'T BELIEVE HE'S pushing them out the door. What is he up to? "Jax, why did you push them out the door? That was rude."

He doesn't say anything, but he is doing something in the kitchen. "Raven, you can wait for me in the bedroom. I have a present for you." He pushes me along and runs back to the kitchen.

I'm in bed, waiting for him, when he comes in totally naked with his arms behind his back.

He jumps into the bed and he hands me a jar of warm Nutella! "Sweetheart, tonight I'm a canvas just for your pleasure."

I dip a finger in and lick it off, he moans. "Oh, please tell me you're going to slather that all over my cock and slowly lick it off."

I have to laugh at my beautiful crazy man. "Is that what you want me to do?"

His eyes grow wide with anticipation, "Yes, please!"

I dip my finger into the Nutella and spread it all over the head of his cock. I lean down and lick it off, and he's moaning. I do it again, this time making a trail all the way down to the base. I slowly lick up from the base to the tip. When I get to the tip, I nip a little, and he's screaming for more. Okay, I do it again and when I get to the tip again, he holds my head there, begging me to nip him harder. Just as I bare my teeth he loses it. "Oh fuck, fuck. Harder! I'm coming. Fuck!" I think he might pass out! "Jax, you okay?" His eyes are closed, and he's breathing heavy. "Jax?"

His breathing is becoming more normal, and I'm trying not to laugh. "Give me a minute to come back to earth."

"Jax, what happened, you look dazed?"

Oh my God, he's panting! "The warm Nutella, and then when you nibbled on my cock it just sent him to orbit. Why are you laughing at me?"

Oh my crazy man, "It's just the way you constantly refer to your cock as him." He gifts me with that crooked smirk and his twinkling blues.

"Come here, it's time for *the happy place*." With that, I'm gone.

Chapter Twenty-One

Jackie

WE GET BACK TO Max's and he is very quiet. "Max, are you okay?"

He nods, "Yeah, just a lot on my mind. Do you have everything you need?"

Wow I feel like I'm being dismissed. "Yes."

He nods, "Okay, I'll see you in the morning."

Maxwell

SHE HEADS TO HER room and closes the door as I take a bottle of scotch and sink into the couch. Fuck, what am I doing? This girl is too young and too innocent. I don't do relationships. I hate drama, and I won't ever give my heart away again. *Oh, who am I kidding?* I've got it bad for this girl and that's the problem. This is all Jax's fault. He couldn't get involved with someone who had a simple life. If I understand Jax, which I usually do, Jackie is a virgin, and I'm me, a man who is far from innocent. The fear came flooding back tonight when I thought they would kill her. I can't live through it again, not that this is living.

Jackie

I DON'T UNDERSTAND WHAT happened, it's like Max just flipped a switch. What do I say to him? Why did I have to fall for someone like Max? He's out of my league, but who am I kidding? Like Raven, I don't have a league! This is so messed up. Maybe he figured out I'm a virgin. It's not like I can say *hi, my name is Jackie, and I'm a virgin*, but maybe he figured it out. He probably thinks I'm too young, and he doesn't know how to tell me. I'll back away gracefully; giving him an out. I would leave, but I have nowhere to go. Maybe I should go to my parents' place. I'll pack up and have the guard take me to the airport. I'll call my dad to have his plane waiting.

I pack my stuff and head towards the front door when I hear him growl. "Where the fuck do you think you're going?"

I look at him. "Are you drunk?"

He takes a deep breath. "I asked you a question."

I step closer, "I asked you one, too. Are you drunk?"

He shakes his head, "Not drunk enough."

I take a step back, "What's that supposed to mean?"

He takes a step towards me, "Where are you attempting to go?"

I look into his eyes, "Home, to my parents, where I know I'll be safe, and you won't have to worry about me."

"What makes you think I would stop worrying about you?"

I take another step back. "Max, I'm a burden to you." He's searching my eyes, and I don't know for what.

"And you determined this all on your own."

I take a deep breath, "You're trying to take care of Jax, Raven, and now you have to worry about me. I saw the change in you when you had to bring me back to your house. I'm not a charity case, and I'm not a child that you need to watch over. I'm a grown woman who has been put in a bad position. I can have my dad's jet ready by the time I get to the airport. I'll be safe at his compound in Switzerland. I'll be out of your hair, and you can go about doing whatever it is you need to do."

Maxwell

I CAN'T BELIEVE HER. Yet I knew from the first day I met her, that there was a fire buried deep inside, just waiting to explode, and it decides now to rear its head! I walk up to her and pull her up against my body. I'm hard, really fucking hard for this woman. "Kiss me now, Jackie."

Her eyes grow large, "What?"

"You heard me, fucking kiss me now!"

If she does, then I know she feels what I do. If not, she'll slap me and walk away. She grabs a hold of me and kisses me long and hard.

"Just like I thought. Jackie, I want you, but I needed to know that you wanted me. All reasoning tells me to walk away —that you're too young and too innocent, but fuck it all to hell. I can't walk away, I'm in too deep." I lift her up and carry her to my room, kissing her deeply along the way. "If this is going to happen, I need you to be totally honest with me. I won't settle for anything less."

"That's all I ask for, Max, is total honesty. I don't do secrets and I don't play games."

I take a deep breath, "Okay, Jackie, have you ever been with anyone?"

"No." She looks down, so submissive, and very quiet.

I'm searching her face for answers that I already know. "Are you sure you want this to be your first time?"

Again she gazes down, not answering. "It's okay, if you want to say no, I will respect your decision, whatever it is."

She looks up to me, "I want you. Max, I'm just scared."

I need answers. "Are you scared of me?"

She shakes her head, "No, never. I'm scared that I won't be enough for you. You're so experienced, beautiful, and worldly, and I'm just a second grade teacher."

"Look at me, Jackie." As I look into her beautiful golden eyes, I'm lost. "My past is just that—past. I can't change it. There is no one in my life for a reason, but I'm not ready to share that yet. I never had anyone in this bed. I want to be your first and your only. It is a very special gift that can only be given once. I want you to be sure, really sure."

She leans forward and kisses me. "I'm sure, Max."

"Okay, I'm going to undress you very slowly." He takes off my shirt, and I thank God I'm wearing nice undergarments. He slowly starts kissing me, long and slow, nibbling on my bottom lip. Oh, I want this man bad. He gets up and takes off his shirt and I gasp! He smiles, "We're going to take this nice and slow." He lifts me up and places me in the center of the bed. He straddles me, kissing me. His lips are so unbelievably soft, and I swipe my tongue across them. "You're so beautiful. I tried to resist you, but that day in the park, when you massaged my leg, I knew right then that I was done." He's kissing down my neck. His stubble is soft and speckled with gray. His eyes are the palest blue. He takes off my bra and is nibbling my nipples. I'm not big chested, but I'm not small. He pinches and tweaks them and I'm fidgeting while he's humming.

"Max, I don't know how much more of that I can take."

He gets up and starts to take off my jeans. "These legs are so long and so beautiful." He kisses my legs up one and down the other. Before I realize it, he is between my legs kissing and nibbling, working his tongue into me. I never felt anything like this in my life. My skin is burning and my mind is buzzing.

"Max, Max, I can't think."

He looks up at my face. "That's the best part. Just relax and let me take care of you. I'm going to take you to a place you've never been before."

He dives back in, and I think I'm going to explode—No, I know I'm going to explode. " *Oh my God!*" My body is quivering and shaking and I can't put two thoughts together. My nails dig into his shoulders, and I scream!

"That's not God, baby, that's all me."

I watch as he finishes undressing, and he has the most beautiful body. He is very lean and he has the 'Loin of Apollo.' He has no chest hair. Only a little down the happy trail. I get a look at his cock and he's huge. "I'll go slowly, and if it hurts we can stop," he reassures me. He must sense my fear.

I nod. "I'll be okay." I can only hope. He's back between my legs licking and now he is working in a finger, then two, *oh my…*

"I have to open you a little, or it will hurt." He's working his fingers in and out real slowly. Wow, this is unreal. He climbs up my body. "Are you sure you want this?"

I nod my head yes.

"I need to hear the words. Tell me."

I take a breath. "I want you, Max, please don't stop." He slips on a condom and starts rubbing his cock up and down my opening real slow.

"I'll go slowly, but it's going to hurt, there is nothing I can do about that." With that, he starts to enter me, and then he stops to let me acclimate to him. "Breathe slowly. I'm going to move again." He pushes forward. I feel a lot of pressure and then, something pops; he's in.

"Look at me, baby, I'm in. Are you okay?"

I nod yes.

"I need you to answer me!"

My eyes shoot up to his. "Yes, I'm good." He starts to move real slowly in and out.

"You're so tight, it's like you have my cock in a vice grip!" As he pushes in, he tips his hips up and down, hitting all the right places. He's nibbling and sucking my nipples while his fingers are fluttering up and down my ribs. *How can he do all of this at the same time?*

"Max, I'm… I, oh, Max!"

He kisses me, "You're going to come for me, baby, I can feel you quivering. Don't hold back on me, just let it go." His hand reaches down, and he swipes his thumb across my clitoris. That does it! I feel my core tighten and my skin is flushed. It's like a rippling wave taking over my body. I'm screaming my release, and he is right behind me. "Baby, are you okay?"

"You took my breath away."

He laughs, which is so rare. "I'll take that as a good thing." He ditches the condom and pulls me close to him. As he pulls the comforter over us, he barely whispers, "You sleep here in my arms, forever, baby."

Jackie

MORNING COMES, AND AS I stretch out, I realize Max has a grip on me, and he's not letting up. He's so protective, even in his sleep. I get to really look at him since he's not watching me. He has so many scars on his chest; they make me want to cry. Who would do such a terrible thing to such a beautiful man? He keeps his hair very short, and his dark-blond facial hair is specked with gray. There is not an ounce of fat on his body. He is breath taking to look at. His hands are strong and his muscles are rock hard. I run my fingers down the V and I notice he has a scar on his hip. Oh, what this man must have been through. I lean in and kiss one of his nipples and he groans, "Are you having fun, baby?"

I nearly jump out of the bed. "I thought you were asleep."

He sighs, "I figured that. I've been up for about an hour."

"Why didn't you tell me?"

"I wasn't going to deny you your fun."

I kiss one of his scars, "You have so many scars."

He's stroking my back, "Does it bother you?"

"It bothers me that someone would do that to such a beautiful body, I never want to see you hurt." He doesn't say anything more about the scars and so, I just drop it.

"How are you feeling this morning? Are you sore?" He brings his hand to my face, palming my cheek. I look down, sheepishly. "Hey, don't ever hide anything from me, talk to me."

I look back up at him, "This is all new for me, not just the sex, but the intimacy—I've never experienced it before. To answer your question, though, I'm not too sore."

He takes a deep breath, "Did you like last night? Was it what you expected?"

"Okay, I have to tell you, I only know what I have read. I only have one girlfriend, Raven, and it's not something we talk about. She only had one boy-friend, and he was abusive, so there really isn't much to draw on."

He looks at me. "Why do you have no other friends?"

I shrug, "My dad's work, and the constant security was a problem. By the age of sixteen I had already finished high school. We were always moving, so I was home-schooled. I could have skipped a year in college, but I wanted to enjoy the entire experience. Raven was my roommate in college. The other girls where either intimidated by the security or thought I was their personal cash cow. It's a sad way to grow up, but unfortunately, reality. Can I ask you a question?"

He pushes my hair behind my ear and runs his hand down my back. "Always, you might not like the answer, but you can always ask."

"You said you don't do relationships. So what is this?" I ask nervously.

"I honestly don't know. I never expected you to blow into my life and turn it upside down. I just want to get all of this stuff with Vincent behind us, and then let's see where the rest leads us, okay?"

"Yes, thank you for your honesty. It's what I always need. I hate sugar coating the problems."

He smiles, "Okay, well then let me tell you, we have a couple of hours before we *need* to leave, so I think we *need* to stop talking and I *need* to be buried deep inside you."

Just like that, we are done talking. He is all over me, and I love it.

Chapter Twenty-Two

Raven

MAX AND JACKIE ARE waiting in the living room with Jax while I finish getting ready. I'm nervous about what I'll find in the safety deposit box, but I have to do this, not just for me but also for my mother. As I step into the living room, I notice Jackie and Max are holding hands, and he's not letting her go. She looks at me, and I'm seeing something very different today than yesterday, and it hits me. Oh my God, she took the plunge! I wish I had time for us to just have a girl day, but we have to go. As I walk up to her, she blushes, and I have to stifle a laugh. If Jax noticed anything, he would never say. "Okay, everyone, I'm ready. Thanks for coming with us, Jackie, I could use the support."

She hugs me, "Later,." she whispers near my ear. Of course, Max has to drive us. Even Bo is getting used to his driving.

Jax is the banks best customer, so they're opening up early for us. After giving the manager all the proper paperwork, he takes me into a windowless room and puts the box on the table.

"Jax, will you please stay with me?"

He pulls me close, "Of course, sweetheart."

When I open the box, there is a VHS tape, some photos, two letters—one addressed to me, and one to my mother. There is some jewelry that appears to be very old. Maybe the letter will explain whose it was. "Jax, I don't have anything to play this on, do you?"

He takes the tape, "Let's stop by the office, and I can have Tony transfer it to a DVD."

As we head to the office, everyone is quiet and then Jax just starts to laugh. We're all looking at him. As I'm about to ask him what's so funny, Max starts to laugh too.

Jackie and I shrug at each other. "Okay, both of you, what is so funny?"

Jax turns to me, "You're going to finally meet Mrs. Osla."

Jackie's eyes get really wide and fear seeps in. "Jackie, by the look on your face, I take it you met her already?"

She gasps, "Raven, she is unexplainable, and good luck understanding anything she says. I speak six languages, and I don't understand a word of what she calls English."

"Wow, Jackie, I never knew you spoke so many languages." Jax says, sounding intrigued.

She smiles, "My father is Swedish and my mother is Japanese. We had to move around a lot, so it was more for survival purposes that I learned them. Once you master one, it kind of becomes a little easier."

Jaxson

RAVEN LOOKS OVER AT me with fire in her eyes. "You see, Jax, this is what I mean, we don't know anything about each other." She crosses her arms. Oh fuck, here come the tears again, I can't wait till she sees the fucking doctor today. "Do you know that I speak other languages?"

All right, she got me on this one. Now, how the fuck am I going to get out of this mess? "I was too busy wrapped up in your beautiful body to even think about anything else, sweetheart."

Then I hit her with the Jaxson smile. That should do it, but she just rolls her eyes.

"Really, Jax, that's all you can say? *Je vous jure que vous pensez que vous pouvez juste me donner ce beau sourire et tout ira bien!*" He's just looking at me and not saying a word. I wonder if he even knows what I said. "I said, I swear you think you can just give me that beautiful smile and all will be well!"

"*Je suis dur.* I speak some French, sweetheart. Oh, look, we're here. Out you go."

Jackie and I get hysterical, laughing. "This isn't over, Jax, not by a long shot."

Jackie leans over. "Jax, no matter what you say, you're fucked, so just take it like a man."

Max starts laughing. I grab Max's arm, "Keep laughing, Max, I'll get even just wait—Mrs. Osla." That's all I have to say. Everyone shuts up knowing how Max fears her. We head to the elevator in silence.

"Wait, Jax, is that Mick?"

Everyone smiles, "Oh, yeah, something good happened while you were gone. Mick now heads up security for the building, and he moved into his new apartment."

Oh fuck, here come the tears. "Jax, just when I think I couldn't love you more." She runs up to Mick and hugs him. His face lights up.

"Raven, I'm so happy that you're back and safe. We all missed you."

"I'm happy for you, Mick, that you're working and have a warm place to live."

He takes a deep breath, "I owe it to you, Raven. You believed in me, when no one else did."

She shakes her head, "No, Mick, you believed in yourself. I just helped you to see it."

He hugs her as we head to the elevators.

"Max, is the office clear?" I ask.

"Yeah, Tony swept it right before we got here."

As we walk into the office, Mrs. Osla is following behind us, giving Max a hard time about Tony making a mess of things. Boy, he really fears her. I'm about to laugh, and she turns on me. *Oh crap.*

Raven

"JAXSON, HOW DO YOU expect me to keep things in order if you don't check in on a regular basis? I don't mind running things in your absence, but a wee bit of help now and then. Have you called your mother today?"

Tony comes barrelling in, and before he can speak she's on him too. "Young man, have you no manners? I told you that you must learn to knock. Now go back out and try again!"

Oh, my God, he goes out the door and knocks!

"Jaxson, Tony needs to see you. Is that acceptable?" Jax bites his lip to control his laughter, I'm assuming.

"Yes, ma'am, but let me introduce you to Miss Raven Anderson, my beautiful girl."

She smiles. "About time you showed some manners, Jaxson. Pleasure to finally meet you, and I'm glad you're back safe. Maybe now you can get him to cooperate with me. Can I get you some tea, Miss Anderson?"

I nod. "Yes, thank you, and it's Raven, please."

Just like that, she is gone and all heads turn towards me. "Why is everyone looking at me?"

Tony steps up. "Can I get the VHS tape, please? And I don't know how you did it, but you need to work here full-time."

As I hand him the tape, I ask "Did what?"

"Tame the Shrew," he mumbles.

"Give me a half hour and I will have this transferred for you. Welcome back."

"Tony, I want to thank you for everything you did to help find me. I will be forever in your debt."

Jaxson

RAVEN HUGS HIM AND I swear I want to get all cavemen on the poor guy!

Mrs. Osla comes in with tea. She gives me all the business that I need to address. "Max, any new leads on Vincent's whereabouts?"

"Yeah, Tony is following the money trail. Since the guy only had so much liquid cash, I figure he would have to eventually move something and he has."

"Okay where is he?"

"He just got to a Miami compound that is owned by a top drug lord. He came by way of Cuba. I'll be leaving shortly. I'm taking the plane and a couple of DEA agents with me to pick him up. You stick with the girls, and I added another female guard for Jackie."

"Why am I not going with you to Miami?"

He gives me a look and it hits me, he wants to know that Jackie is safe, and he will only be comfortable with me.

"I get it, Max. Never mind, I'll stay and watch the girls, but you be careful."

Jackie

HE PICKS UP HIS keys. "Jackie, walk with me to the elevator, please."

I'm scared for him. "Max, I'm worried about you. Do you have to go?"

"Yes, but you need to promise me that you will do everything Jax says, and you will not ditch your detail."

I take a deep breath, "I promise."

He takes my hand, "Come here, babe." He pulls me into his arms. He gives me the most sensual kiss, and I almost forget where we are. The elevator opens, and just like that, he's gone. I stare at the doors. My heart aches and I lose it. It hits me that I might never see Max again. I crumble into a ball on the floor, the fear and the angst over the last few months comes to the top and the dam of tears breaks open. Jax lifts me onto the sofa and Raven holds me.

Jax starts pacing. "Raven, what should we do for her?"

She shakes her head, "Nothing."

"What the fuck do you mean, nothing? I can't sit here and watch her cry."

"Sometimes the only thing we can do, is nothing. We're here for her, and we will be no matter what. Max is smart and strong and, by your own omission, very skilled. We need to have faith that he will be okay."

Jax is stroking his chin and pacing. Neither is a good sign. "We need to go, Raven. You have a doctor's appointment, and, Jackie, you're coming with us—no arguments!"

Raven

I DON'T KNOW WHY I'm nervous, but my emotions have been all over the place, lately. I'm sure it's probably pregnancy hormones. As I look around the waiting room, I'm totally embarrassed. There are more security guards than patients.

"Don't. They're doing their job, and I will not make them wait outside. While we are in the exam room, Jackie, you will not leave this room," Jax says, flipping through a magazine.

"Wow Raven, is he always like this?" she asks.

I roll my eyes. "You don't know the half of it."

The nurse comes out to get us, and looks at the scene in the waiting room but says nothing. The doctor finally comes in, and I'm happy that it's a female doctor. Knowing Jax. I'm sure he is happy too. "Hello, Raven, I'm Dr. Leanne and I will be your OB throughout the remainder of your pregnancy. Looking at your chart, I see you had a rough start with morning sickness and then a gunshot. I hope all the drama is now behind us. I'm going to do an exam, and then an ultrasound. We'll get you started on prenatal care. Have you decided on what type of birth you want?" She hits me with all of this information, like it's a race to see how quickly she can freak me out.

By the look on Jax's face, I don't think he was impressed with that presentation, either, and I swear I think he's going to flip out on the doctor. I know he is trying, but he doesn't take orders from anyone, except maybe his mom. "Dr. Leanne, Raven, and I want a healthy child and a calm delivery, so you need to do your job to make that happen."

I'm about to apologize for him, but Dr. Leanne laughs. "Don't worry, Raven. I'm used to first-time fathers, they don't scare me."

The nurse is back with an ultrasound machine and Jax watches without saying a word as she sets everything up. "What type of ultrasound is this?" he asks when the doctor starts and the picture pops up on the screen.

"It's a 2D machine , since Raven has been through so much already, I just want to make sure everything is on track."

I'm holding Jax's hand, and I realize I have a death grip on it. He starts rubbing the inside of my wrist, and I instantly relax.

"Do you want to know the sex?" The doctor asks.

I shake my head. "I don't. What about you, Jax?"

He shakes his head. "No, I just want to know that everyone is healthy. Gender doesn't matter to me."

"I will note on your chart that you want to be surprised."

The sight of this baby just hanging out, all safe and warm, is beautiful. "Okay, everything is great and right on track. You're due the first week of August, and you need to think about what type of birth you want. The nurse will give you all the information when you leave. You need to put on a few pounds. You're a little too lean for my liking. I'm giving you prenatal vitamins, and I suggest you take them with some crackers."

"What about travel, and will my mood swings get any better?"

Her expression when she responds is compassionate. "I don't see a problem with travel and as far as mood swings. Honestly, they won't get better. I'll see you in four weeks for a check-up."

After she leaves, Jax turns to me, "Where exactly do you think you're going?"

"I would like to see my mother," I answer quietly.

"Raven, I'm not going to yell and demand. I told you as soon as it's safe, I'll have your mother brought to a facility in Manhattan." He pinches the bridge of his nose. Seems like he's trying anything to not freak out on me.

My eyes fill up, and I'm trying not to cry. "What if it's never safe, then what? I have been without my mother for twenty years. Don't I deserve to have her in my life again?"

He pulls me into his arms, "You're thinking of a mother that you had twenty years ago. She's not that same person anymore."

I finish getting dressed. "Don't you think I know that, Jax. This is just so fucked up."

"Don't curse, the baby will hear you."

Is he out of his mind? "Jax, let's get Jackie and go home." I know I'm mumbling under my breath how crazy this man is.

We head back to the tower, each of us lost in our own thoughts. "Jackie, I moved your stuff into the guest room in my place until Max gets back." Jax finally breaks the silence. Her tears start to fall, and silence is back again. I know Jax is worried about Max. I can see it all over his face. He keeps checking his phone, but it is silent. All we can do now is pray.

Chapter Twenty-Three

Maxwell

I HATE THAT I had to leave Jackie, but I need to do this. I can't leave it to anyone else. Six of my own men and four DEA agents just to bring in one man, but I know how vicious he really is. I'm sure we will be met with resistance and it doesn't matter that we are also working with the local agencies—anyone can be bought. As we approach the compound, I can see it's heavily guarded. I have everyone on the ground in place, and we will be coming in by air. The Coast Guard is also on alert. "I want him alive, if possible."

"Sir, we are over the target, are you ready?"

That's my cue. I jump. The compound is large, but I went over the blue prints, so I know where everything is. There is a lot of gunfire, smoke, and confusion. I keep my target in my head and nothing else—that's how I'll stay alive. I search room by room until I get to the wine cellar. I hear him before I see him. He's yelling in Italian for transport by air, telling them he'll be coming out the other side. I enter the room and he's gone.

Fuck. Think, Max. As I start my usual pace, I realize there has to be a tunnel. I find it behind a wine rack. The race is on. I can hear him running, and I'm pretty sure he hears me closing in. As I round the corner, he's looking right at me—his gun aimed at my head.

"Game over."

We both pull the trigger and everything goes black.

To be continued...

Darkness
INTO
Dawn
THERESA SEDERHOLT

Chapter One

Jaxson

IT'S A COLD WINTER day in New York City, but the sun is shining. I decide to take the ladies out for a bite to eat while I wait to hear from Max. I'm very distracted, and I know it's from the anticipation of his call. I'm not good at waiting, but I have no choice. I push my food around the plate while Raven and Jackie talk about our baby. I want to get married before the baby comes, but I haven't broached that subject yet. Lately, it seems I can't get anything right with Raven. As I look around the restaurant, I realize we must look ridiculous sitting here with six security guards and a dog, but what the fuck do I care? I would have a hundred security guards if it meant our girls were safe. As the waiter comes with the dessert menu, my phone chirps with a text from Tony to call him stat.

"Ladies, I need to make a call. I'll be out front." They are so engrossed in baby stuff, I don't even think they notice, but it's okay. I'm glad to see Raven having some normal girl time. I make my way through the restaurant and out the door.

"Tony, what's the problem?" I ask as soon as he picks up. He starts talking but I can't believe what I'm hearing. I'm in utter shock. Everything he's saying sounds like white noise. "Tony, my jet is in Miami. I need you to charter a private jet for me to leave within the hour—at any cost." Ending the call, I go back inside to collect the ladies and pay the bill.

"Jax, what's wrong?" Raven only has to take one look at me to know when something is terribly wrong. I think she can see the fear I'm feeling on my face.

"We need to leave now."

She brings her hand up to her throat, and her eyes instantly fill with tears. "Jax, you're scaring me. Please, what's wrong?"

Before I can say anything, Jackie turns white and starts shaking. *Fuck!* "Jax, its Maxwell, isn't it? I can feel it." Her tears start falling. I'm trying to hold onto both of them.

"Ladies, I need to leave for the airport—now!"

Raven, puts her hands on her hips as if ready to stand her ground. "We are going with you. No arguments, Jax!"

I want her with me, close to me. I need my lifeline, my beautiful girl. "I'm not going to argue; let's go."

WE RACE TO THE airport where the jet is waiting for us. I get everyone settled in the main cabin before heading to the office area. I need to make some calls. I know I should be strong for Raven and Jackie, comforting them. I can't. Right now, I'm best at setting up top doctors and dealing with the authorities on the ground. All I know is that Max and Vincent were shot, and it's bad. My phone rings, its Bella. I don't want to deal with her right now, but I have no choice. I know she won't let up.

"Bella, I'm really busy at the moment." I try to rush her off the phone.

"Jax, it's all over the news. Where are you?" she cries.

I take a deep breath, trying to steady my nerves. "I'm on my way to Miami with Raven and Jackie."

I hear my mum in the background, trying to say something. "Jax, hold on, Mum wants you." She doesn't even give me a chance to protest.

"Jaxson, you go get him and bring him home. And you tell him he hasn't seen mad!" Her voice cracks and she starts to cry. When my mum cries, it shreds me.

"Okay, Mum, I love you," I whisper. I hang up and sit in my chair with my head in my hands. I don't hear her come in, but I can feel her, my skin tingles whenever she's near. She takes me in her arms and holds me gently. I don't have to say a thing; she knows what I need and she knows that, right now, she is my lifeline. I need to be strong for everyone else, but with her, I can just be.

WE TOUCH DOWN AND there are cars waiting to rush our security team and us to Jackson Memorial Hospital. We head towards the ICU where the nurse informs me that only family members are allowed. I was prepared for this and hand her Max's HIPPA medical release form. We made preparations one night, in a drunken state, hoping they would never be needed.

"Let me go in and assess the situation, then I will be back to let you know what I find out. Please stick with Jackie and your detail," I beg of Raven.

I look over at Jackie and I realize, she's not said a word since we left the restaurant. I hope Raven can help her, because I don't think I can. As I walk into the room, what I see shocks me. It rocks me to my core. My best friend—the man that I consider my brother—looks pale and weak. "Nurse, when will the doctor be here? I want to talk to him now."

"Sir, I just paged Dr. Scott. He is with the other victim now."

I growl, trying to rein in my temper. "Vincent is *here?*" I think I just scared the shit out of the nurse.

"Sir, by law I'm not allowed to discuss other patients."

While I wait for the doctor, I call Tony. "I'm here. Apparently, they have Vincent in the next room. I want extra guards put on his room and around this whole fucking hospital! I want you to find out everything you can about the status of his condition." I inform the nurse that the man in the next room is a murderer, rapist, and kidnapper. She glances at me, but says nothing as she checks Max's vitals. Dr. Scott finally comes in. I get up and shake his hand. "Dr. Scott, I'm Jaxson Phillips, I have Maxwell's medical power of attorney. What's the prognosis?"

He looks over Max's chart. "The next twenty-four hours are critical. As you know, he was shot in the head. I was able to remove the bullet, but his brain is swollen. I had put him into a coma to give his brain a chance to rest. His heart stopped during surgery, but there shouldn't be any affects from that since we were able to restart it rather quickly. My concern, right now, is Mr. Fleming's brain. He was shot with a low-velocity bullet. It entered the left side and stayed there. We were able to surgically remove the bullet, however, there is a lot of swelling. If the swelling goes down, then I'm hopeful Mr. Fleming won't need any additional surgery. That's what these monitors are for, they measure the pressure in the brain,"

I'm not a betting man. I always need to have all the information. I leave nothing to chance. "What are his odds?"

He begins examining Max, checking his reflexes and pupil dilation. "I can't really say until the swelling begins to subside. The fact that he survived so far, tips the scales in his favor. He is in good health, although like I said, the next twenty-four hours are critical."

I growl again. I feel my frustration with this man growing by the second. "What about Vincent? The other man he was brought in with."

He nods, "I'm not at liberty to discuss the status of his condition with you."

I want to rip this guy in half; he is so fucking calm. "You have no idea how sick and twisted that evil man is."

None of this seems to matter to him. "Dr. Scott, I know Vincent was shot, is he going to live?"

"Mr. Phillips, all I can tell you is he has not regained consciousness yet."

I'm not going to get anywhere with this guy. "Okay. First, for security purposes, the two women outside need to be in here. Second, when can I move Max?"

"Sir, do you understand the gravity of this situation?"

Now this guy is really pissing me off. "Dr. Scott, let me explain a few things to you. First, I do understand the *gravity* of the situation. Second, that man in the other room kidnapped one of those women, out in the hall, when she was seven. He killed her father in front of her, raped her mother, and then kidnapped her again just a few months ago. So now I ask you, do you understand the *gravity* of the *fucking situation!*"

"Sir, I understand your frustration, however, I need to consider the well-being of both of my patients." He tries to calm me down but everything he say's only enrages me more.

My patience is at the end of its rope and I'm ready to just punch this fucker. "I think maybe, just maybe, you should be thinking about the welfare of *all* of your patients, since the man in the next room poses a major risk to this hospital. You need to understand that he is a major crime figure with his own army, gunning for him. So how fucking safe is everyone *now?*"

The fucker nods his head, and narrows his eyes, but concedes my point. "Let's see what happens in the next twenty-four hours. The two women can stay in here, but the guards need to remain in the hall. Is that understood?"

I nod. "If that's all you can do then, I guess that will have to do. I have ordered more guards in and around this whole place," I inform before he heads to the door.

"Okay, if you deem that necessary." He sighs then leaves me alone with Max.

"Max, I don't know if you can hear me, but Mum said you're in big trouble, so you better get your arse back to us quickly or she will probably be on the next plane out here. Jackie is here, and I know you probably don't want her to see you like this, but I'm sorry, I had no choice." No movement. Not that I was expecting any. I thought maybe the mum threat might do something though. Fuck. It's killing me to see my best friend lying here so defenseless. I need to be strong for him, no matter what happens. I pop my head out in the hall and wave them in. Jackie still looks deathly pale. Raven is hanging onto her, trying to offer comfort and support. They head over to me.

"Dr. Scott said that they've placed him in an induced coma, hoping to bring down the swelling of his brain. The next twenty-four hours are critical. Come." I put an arm around each of them, and bring them into the room. Bo follows closely behind us. Jackie moves away from me and sits on the bed, stroking his cheek. Raven is shaking and crying. Fuck, I don't know what to do for either of them. Raven pulls herself together, and goes to Jackie's side, offering her silent support.

Now, we wait—something I am never good at.

Chapter Two

IT'S BEEN A FULL twenty-four hours and nothing—no movement whatsoever. I have tried to get the girls to eat something, but they won't. "Raven, think about the baby, please eat something." I plead with her.

Suddenly, I hear a commotion outside. I leap up. "Raven, no one leaves this room!" I open the door, and standing there, trying to push her way through six guards, is my mother!

"What the . . . why are you here?"

Oh no. She's giving me that look . . . the same look she gave me when I smashed her new car. This is not a good thing. "Jaxson James, where else would I be? Now please tell these men to let me pass right this minute!"

I don't need to say another word, I nod and they let her in.

"Where is he?"

I put my arm around her for support. "Mum, he's in a coma, the doctor said the first twenty-four hours is crucial but it's past that now."

She pushes past me towards Raven and Jackie. "I have protein smoothies for everyone. Maxwell, I flew all this way; you need to start waking up."

All heads turn towards Max, and I have to laugh; we all expected him to wake up, just out of fear of my mum. "Jaxson, call the doctor in here. I want to talk to him right now. I'd also like a private moment with Jackie, please." Raven, Bo, and I step into the corridor while we wait for the doctor.

Anwan

I WATCH MY SON leave the room, his head down, bearing the anguish for all of us. I fight my urge to unveil so many things he doesn't know. I can't tell him. I made a promise so many years ago—a promise I won't break. All I can do is pray Max fights hard to find his way back to us.

I gently stroke her back, trying to offer her some sort of comfort and support. "Jackie, I know neither one of you are ready to admit this, but I know love when I see it. Don't give up hope; he will come back to us." As I squeeze Jackie's shoulder, I'm reminded of the pain this man has suffered; more than anyone should ever have to endure. I take her hand, "Jackie, you're his lifeline.

He just doesn't realize it yet." I sigh at the continued silence. "Jackie, please look at me." She lifts her eyes towards mine. "I've known Maxwell for a long time. He is a fighter—as tough as they come. I can see the love in your heart for him; he's such a good man. He doesn't give his heart away on a whim. Just give him all the love you have; he'll know." I can only hope my words are getting through to her.

Jaxson

"JAX, DID YOU KNOW your mom was coming?"

"No, sweetheart, but I figured she wouldn't stay away. Max is like one of her kids. She is very protective when it comes to all of us."

She stammers, "Is Vincent n-next door?"

My whole body goes tense. "Yes. As soon as Max can be moved, I will be taking him home. Since the hospital is not allowed to give out any information on Vincent's health, I had Tony do some digging. It seems Vincent was shot in the head, however, the doctor couldn't remove the bullet. It is uncertain if he will ever recover. And before you ask, there is not a reason in the world I would agree to let you see him."

"Oh," she whispers.

I'm not giving in on this one, "Yeah, *oh.*"

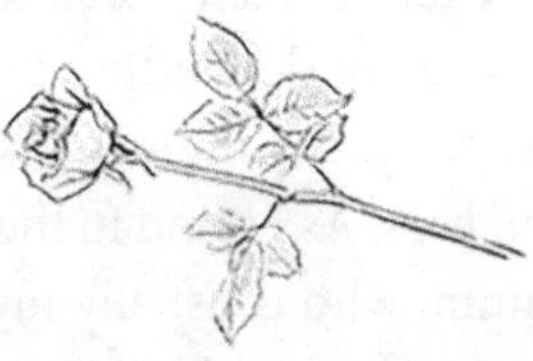

STEPPING BACK INTO THE room, I see tears streaming down Mum's cheeks. *Fuck.* I can't take this. *Fucking Max.* I swear I'm going to kick his arse. The doctor finally shows up, and I think my mum is about to rip him a new one. "Dr. Scott, I understand, from my son, that you put Maxwell in this coma. I'd like to know when are you taking him out?"

Dr. Scott takes a step back. He seems to be intimated by my mum. She has a way of demanding without demanding. She makes you think it was all your idea. I swear she should be running the government.

"Well, the pressure in his brain has decreased significantly. His vitals have been stable for the last twenty-four hours, so I will start easing him off of the sedation. Then, I'm afraid the rest is up to Mr. Fleming. He is strong and healthy. All the signs are positive that he can come out of this; however, you need to understand nothing is one hundred percent. We won't know if there is any damage or the extent of it until he wakes up."

My mum is stroking Max's arm, never taking her eyes off of him. "Jaxson, I want him moved from here, and brought home so I can look after him myself."

The doctor's eyes grow wide. "Dr. Scott, you heard my mum; when can we move him?"

He takes a deep breath. "Where will you be moving him to?" He raises his voice and takes upon a condescending tone.

The urge to punch this fucker is back again! "I will have him transported by private jet to a facility in Manhattan." *Did he just roll his eyes at me?*

"Lets give it another twelve hours, and then I will recheck him. How much notice do you need to arrange everything?"

I never flaunt who I am or how much money I have, but this is one of those times. "I have a jet on standby. Mount Sinai Hospital has been waiting for Max's arrival—they have been from the minute I received the first phone call. When we land, there will be a helicopter waiting to fly us to their rehabilitation center. Is that sufficient?"

He seems taken aback from all of this information; his eyebrows dart up and the corners of his mouth give a slight frown of contemplation. "Yes. Like I said, I will re-examine him in twelve hours to see what progress he has made." He leaves, and once again I'm left—waiting. *Fuck!*

I have three women who are depending upon me, looking to me for some sort of answers. I have none. My mum, bless her, finally gets Raven and Jackie to, at least, eat protein bars. As I stand in the corner, taking in the room around me, I realize my mum, who is usually my rock—tough as nails and so strong—is scared. I see it on her face; her lips are trembling and she seems to be fighting not to cry. It slays me that there isn't anything I can do. All the money and power in the world means nothing.

TWELVE HOURS PASS, AND the doctor is back again. He announces that the pressure in Max's brain has continued to drop and he can be moved in the morning, and the rest is up to Max. *What the fuck does that mean?* I swear I really want to punch this fucker. Raven must sense my frustration because I feel her take my arm, pulling me towards her.

"Jax, do you have a nurse to travel with us?"

"Yes, she's on the plane already, waiting for us."

Once again, I'm fucking waiting! Raven goes back to Max's bedside to be with Jackie. I decide to head out into the hall and see what is going on with Vincent. I see a flurry of activity, so I decide to pull one of the guards aside to get some answers. He informs me that Vincent is being moved to a federal facility—indefinitely. He will not be able to stand trial for any of the crimes he is accused of until he regains consciousness and is capable of understanding what he is being charged with. So my fucking tax dollars are now paying for him. Only Max can tell me what happened in that room. Why didn't he just kill the bastard?

MORNING COMES, AND I actually get Max and everyone else back to New York City without any drama for a change. While Max is being tended to, I pull Jackie aside to talk.

"I need to know what you need me to do for you."

She looks at me, but it's like she doesn't see me. "Jax, I just want to be with him, to help him."

I hug her. "I understand that, but what about work? Do you want me to handle that for you?"

"I can't think about anything but Max." *Oh fuck.* She's crying again . . .

"Okay, what about your parents? Just tell me what you need handled, I will take care of it all for you." I pull back from our hug.

She starts to shake uncontrollably. "My parents don't know about Max."

I get it. I'm not a moron; she hasn't told her parents about Max because they will probably flip over the age difference. "Okay, I'll take care of everything for you. Look, I had them put a bed in the room for you to rest, but you have to eat, as well. You will be no good to him if you are weak from lack of nourishment."

She shakes her head, "Jax, I can't."

I pull her close. "Here's the problem, when Max wakes up and he sees that you didn't eat, he will kick my arse, so please, eat."

I, at least, get a smile. "Okay."

She heads back into the room to be with Max. I don't know when it happened, but she's in love with him. And I realize I've been so busy with all the drama in my own life, that I didn't even see this happening. What kind of friend does that make me? Why has Max held back on this? Once again, I'm left with more questions than answers!

Chapter Three

Jaxson

I MADE SURE THAT Jackie's work understood what was happening, and they gave her a leave of absence. I paid her rent for a year, so she wouldn't have to be concerned with it. I then had to make the decision to move Max out of the rehabilitation center. I know Max, he would not want to be in there. More importantly, he wouldn't want Jackie there, so I moved him to his place. I put the nurse in the guest room, and I moved Jackie's personal belongings back to Max's penthouse. Now, it's back to a waiting game. My mum and Mrs. Osla come by daily to check on him and to make sure that Jackie is eating. As I head back across the hall to my place, I realize that Raven has a doctor's appointment tomorrow. It's been four weeks since Max was shot. For me, time has stood still. But for our baby, life goes on.

I walk in the door and smell something strange. As I head into the kitchen, I see the most beautiful sight—Raven is attempting to cook me dinner, and I must try *not* to laugh. Just then, she turns around. "Jax, I wanted to try and cook for you, but I'm not having much luck." *She bites her bottom lip; what a beautiful sight.*

She is standing in the kitchen, amongst a mess that I can't believe one person could possibly create. I am overwhelmed with my love for this woman. "Raven, I love you. I love everything about you. I love the fact that you have no clue when it comes to cooking. I love that you want to do this for me. But right now, I need you—*bad.*"

That's all I have to say; she drops everything and takes me in her arms. No words are necessary; she just gets it. She strokes my back, her simple touch offering so much comfort.

"Jax, whatever you need from me, just take it."

When did I become such a lucky bastard? I lift her in my arms and carry her to our bed. I slowly undress her, taking in her beautiful body. I kiss those amazing lips, and then nibble on her ear, slowly working my lips all over her body. Her skin is so soft and silky. I feel the subtle changes to her body as I glide my fingertips up and down her hips, and then reach up, and begin stroking her nipples until they peak for me. I reach up and nibble on *that* ear. *Fuck, I'm so hard.* I look into her beautiful eyes and slowly sink my cock into her warm body while cradling her in my arms.

"Raven, you have unraveled me layer by layer without even trying. I need this—us, in the *happy place—really* slow and gentle."

I move slowly, in and out, and I feel my heart race. I know I can't last much longer. She pulls my face towards hers, resting her forehead on mine. "Fall with me, Jax."

I'm there, the top of the cliff and I'm going to fall. All the tension and pressure I've been dealing with for the last four weeks comes rushing to the surface and I explode with such force, I think I might pass out. We lock eyes, and I know she understands everything I'm dealing with: my need to keep everyone safe, my impatience with Max's recovery, the baby, and all the unknowns. I don't do unknowns. We just lay here, enjoying a temporary moment of solitude together.

"Sweetheart, tomorrow you have a doctor's appointment, it will be four weeks."

"I know, Jax, it's also been four weeks that Max has been unconscious. He will come back when he's ready, not on your timeline but his."

I don't have to explain to her how important Max is in my life, how much I need him around me. She gets it, but more importantly she get's me. I smile thinking of her attempt at cooking. "Did you really try and cook dinner for me?'

She laughs, "Didn't quite turn out the way I planned."

My heart feels like it's going to burst. "Raven, I love you and everything about you . . . that's all."

Jaxson

MORNING COMES AND I'M still buried balls deep. *What a beautiful way to wake up.* As I watch her eyes begin to flutter, my cock jumps to attention. I swear that bastard has a mind of his own. *Calm down, buddy, she needs her rest.*

"Hmm, Jax, who are you talking to?"

Oh shit, did I say that out loud? "Good morning, sweetheart."

"Jax, were you talking to your cock, again?"

Need a change of subject—*quick.* "No, Raven, he was just saying good morning."

I tilt my hips up so he can give her a proper good morning.

"You know, Jax, talking to Mr. Cock will get you sectioned."

I throw my head back in a fit of laughter. "*Mr. Cock?* Is that what you've named him? I think you're the one who might get sectioned, sweetheart."

"Well, he may as well have a name, since you're always talking to him." She reaches up and kisses me with those puffy, soft lips. The taste of her is surreal. "How about if you and Mr. Cock give me a proper wakeup call," she suggests.

I tilt my hips up again, swiveling them around while I hold her firmly pressed against me. "Oh, sweetheart, I love proper morning shags with you."

I stop and watch her with wonder. "Jax, why are you stopping?"

I pull myself into a sitting position and bend my legs more. "I want to sit up and watch you gliding up and down my cock, so I can have this vision etched in my mind for the rest of the day." I tilt my hips up again, as her beautiful hair cascades around her bare breasts. I reach up to stroke her nipples, but she pushes my hands away.

"Just watch, Jax, and enjoy the show."

I'm such a lucky bastard. She's gliding up and down my cock, while she rolls her nipples between her fingers. I reach around and grab onto that fabulous arse, and slam into her. "Raven, I can feel you quivering. Come on, sweetheart, it's beautiful."

As she throws her head back and her lips part, I know neither one of us are going to last much longer. Leaning forward, I take one of those beautifully engorged nipples and drag it between my teeth. She clenches my cock from top to bottom, raking her nails over my nipples. That's it—her nails, dragging across my nipples is what throws me over that cliff. And my sweetheart is right there with me, screaming my name.

She sprawls across my chest as I stroke her back, both of us trying to steady our breath. "Jax, you don't have to come to the doctor with me. It's just a routine check-up."

My arm tightens around her. "Do you really think I wouldn't go with you? Really, Raven, I thought you knew me better."

She leans up and kisses me, "I just want you to know that I understand if you can't."

"Nothing will stop me—ever."

"I love you," she whispers.

I kiss those beautiful soft lips, "More, sweetheart, always more . . ."

Raven

WHEN WE ARE FINALLY ready, Jax and I head out to my doctor's appointment. Manhattan traffic seems to be light for a change. We arrive at the office right on schedule. We checked in, and get settled in the waiting room. I look around the room and take notice of all the women staring at him. I wonder if the feeling like I want to rip their eyes out will ever go away. He is so beautiful that words escape me. The women don't care that he is there with me, they stare at him; he pays them no mind. Just as I feel like I might combust, the nurse calls us back. The visit is as I expected pretty routine, that is, until the doctor informs me that I need to gain some weight. Jax actually asked the doctor for an approved foods list! I swear I want to ring his neck. *Oh whom am I kidding?* I love this neurotic, passionate, intense, over the top man. As we step outside, Jax turns his phone on, and it's going wild. His face lights up with the biggest smile, he doesn't have to say a word, I know—Max is awake.

Jackie

FOUR WEEKS, AND HE hasn't moved! I finally had to call my parents and tell them everything that has been going on. Come to find out, Jax had already spoken to my dad. He assured him I was heavily guarded.

I love Max so much. All I can do is hope that my love is enough to bring him back to me. I sit on the bed and hold his hand; I need the constant touch. "Max, when I was a young girl, my grandmother gave me a crystal pendant. She made me promise to keep it with me always. She said it would protect and heal me. I've worn this pendant everyday. I don't think my grandmother would mind if I gave it to you. I think you need this more than I do." I take it off, place it in his palm, and silently pray. Please, Grandmother, I beg you; bring him back to me. I won't survive without him. This man is beautiful, and I have fallen so deeply in love with him. I don't know when, or how it happened, but I know my life will never be the same again. "Please come back, Max, please." I sit back, getting lost in the sound of his breaths and the different thoughts that parade through my mind. Silence can be so loud at times.

Jax has been here everyday, and I realize that he and Max are a lot closer than I thought. I wonder if Max is aware how many people love and respect him. The nurse flutters around the room doing her work, she keeps humming and I swear I never hated humming until now. The only thing I want to hear is his heavy accent; it's low and as smooth as silky, dark chocolate. I love when he whispers in my ear. I'm so tired, but I will only take naps, just in case he wakes up.

His beard is speckled with grey and so very soft. I've decided to read to Max everyday. I found a book in his office, *The Wicked Wit of Winston Churchill* by Dominique Enright. It figures Max would have something like this; it's just short, funny quotes. As I read to him, I hold his hand. He starts to slowly move his thumb in circles over my hand, and I freeze. I take a deep breath and lean down to take a closer look at his face. His eyes are fluttering, and before I know it, he slowly opens them. I have to force myself to breathe before I pass out! Machines are beeping, and the nurse runs over to us.

"Please, step back while I examine him." She smiles and pats my arm before turning to him. "Welcome back. I'm your nurse, Nicky. Do you know your name?"

"Head hurts," he groans.

"What's your name?"

"Maxwell Fleming . . . head hurts . . . tired." He closes his eyes. I silently beg for him to please stay awake, but he's out again.

Within minutes everything in the room seems to come to life along with Max. After being paged by Nicky, the doctor shows up to examine him. He says it wouldn't be uncommon for Max to be in and out of it for a while.

Jax comes running in. "Jackie, what did he say?"

"Not that much, Jax, just that his head hurts, his name, and that he was tired."

"Jackie, he will come back to us. If he knows what's good for him, he better do it quickly." He tries to tease. "Did you eat at all today?"

"Yes. Your mom was here earlier; she brought sandwiches for everyone."

He takes a deep breath. "Jackie, can you give me a few minutes with him, please?"

"Sure, Jax. I'll go next door and visit with Raven for a bit," I say around a yawn. I hate to admit it, but I'm dog-tired.

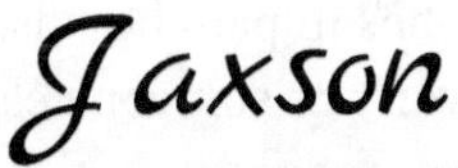

Jaxson

SHE LEAVES, AND NOW it's just us. "Okay, Max, if you can hear me, then you better start waking up, 'cause I don't know how much more I can take—and yes, right now, it's all about me. I'm doing your job and mine, plus dealing with Jackie, Raven, Bella, Mrs. Osla, and—*my mother!*"

Nothing. No response, *really, Max?!* "Okay, mate, have it your way, but don't say I didn't warn you." As I turn to leave, I could swear I hear him growl, but when I look back, he isn't moving.

I step out of the room and for the first time, since he was shot, Raven and Jackie are smiling. "Jackie, we are going next door. If he comes around again, please come and get me."

"Of course, Jax. Raven, you look tired; go rest. I promise, if there is any change, I will ring you." She heads back to Max's room as Raven and I go back across the hall. Raven is so tired. I pick her up and carry her to the bedroom.

"Jax, I can walk, you know."

"Sweetheart, humor me please. Have a nap, and if anything changes, I promise to wake you." I watch as she crawls into bed with nothing on but my dress shirt; she's so fucking beautiful. If I were a gentleman, I would buy her beautiful lingerie. But whom am I kidding? When it comes to this woman, I'm far from a gentleman. Seeing her, in my shirt, makes my cock stand at attention. If I don't leave the room now, she won't get her nap. I adjust my raging hard-on, knowing there will plenty of *cock heaven* later.

Maxwell

I HEAR EVERYTHING, YET I still can't bring my mind to the surface. Everything is cloudy; a dense fog. I wish Jackie would stop crying. I hear her sobs, and feel her trembling, but I can't pull myself to the top. Something is in my hand. I squeeze it tightly. My head hurts. I surrender into the abyss.

How much time has passed?

What is that God, awful humming noise?

Jackie is reading my Winston Churchill book. Her voice soothes the pain in my head. There is something in my hand. I vaguely remember Jackie putting it there to help me heal. Mrs. Philips is here, even though she scares me, I find comfort from her—but I would never tell her that. I must be pretty bad off if Mrs. Osla is here, too. "Maxwell . . ." she whispers in my ear.

I need to let Jackie go. She's in pain because of me. When did I let myself fall in love with her? I won't be someone else's burden. Raven will hate me for hurting Jackie, but I can't do this to her. She deserves to be happy, and she deserves to be loved. I'm nothing but a shell of a man.

Oh my head hurts, and the fucking humming has got to *stop!*

Jaxson

I DECIDE IT'S TIME to call in reinforcements, since Max has left me no choice.

"Hey, Mum, what's going on today?"

My mum never beats around the bush, and I don't expect her to start now. "Jaxson, what's the problem?"

She is as reliable as *Big Ben.* "Why do you always think there is a problem when I call you?"

"Jaxson James, I'm your mother, and I know that you don't call me in the middle of the afternoon for a chat. So, again, what's the problem?"

Fuck, middle name and all. "Okay, Mum, Max woke up, but then he closed his eyes again. The doctor said all of this is normal, and we just have to wait it out. I'm trying to deal with work, Jackie, Raven, the baby, and Max. He needs to wake up, Mum."

She laughs, "Don't you mean, *you* need him to wake up?"

"Yeah," I whisper.

She takes a deep breath. "I'm on my way. I'll bring Mrs. Osla again, that should put the fear in him." Before I can say anything else, she hangs up. Now I need to prepare for the floodgates that I just opened.

Jackie

ALL I CAN DO is wait and pray that he will come back to me. There was so much not said between us. *Why did I hold back?* I knew the danger. I should have gone with my heart, not my head. I close my eyes and let the tears fall.

"Max, I need you in my life. I don't know when it happened, but I'm putting it out there now—please come back to me, baby. I need your strong arms around me. I'm not going away, no matter what. Oh, Max, come home to me, baby, any way that you can, please."

Nothing. Not even a flinch. Time seems to crawl by. Nicky, the nurse, checks his vitals every hour, while Jax and Raven come in and out, all day long. Mrs. Phillips comes by once a day with food, usually around noon.

Today, she's been here twice and she brought Mrs. Osla again. They are probably here to try and scare Max in to waking up. I look at the two of them and I can't figure out why Max is so afraid of these sweet ladies. Okay—maybe Mrs. Osla—but I don't understand a word she says anyway.

"How's our boy doing today, Jackie?'

I smile. "He woke up for a few minutes, but then he went out again. The doctor said we have to wait, so wait, I will. You're here twice today, Mrs. Phillips, is everything okay?"

She nods, "Yes, dear. Please, call me An. I figured I would come back with Mrs. Osla and check on Maxwell again."

"Would you like me to step out?"

She takes my hand, "No, dear, you can stay. I just need to say something to Maxwell."

She leans down and whispers something in his ear, and then steps back. Then Mrs. Osla, takes his hand and says something, but I'm not sure what. I couldn't hear, and even if I did, Max is the only one who can understand her. They turn to leave and I can see tears in their eyes. "Oh, Max, I hope you realize how many people love you. You might not have any blood relations but you have something so much more, something people search for their whole lives, and it's right in front of you—pure love." I put my head beside his, trying to sleep, but the only thing that comes are more tears.

Raven

I WAKE FROM MY nap, feeling flutters. I realize the baby is moving! I go to look for Jax and see him sitting by the bar, staring out the window with a glass of scotch. He seems lost and so very sad; it breaks my heart to see him like this.

"I know you're there, sweetheart."

Hmm, "I know you do . . . you always do. I have something that might cheer you up a little." I walk up to him, take his hand, and place it on my tummy. His eyes widen as he gazes at my tummy, seemingly fighting to hold back the tears. "That's our baby, Jax."

He pulls me closely, "Sweetheart, it's so amazing that you have protected this little one through so much. I'm in awe of you."

I pull his head up towards mine. I need to see his eyes; they say so much. "Jax, what's got you so sad today? Max is starting to come to. I thought you would be happy."

"You know I'm not good at waiting."

I kiss him softly. "I knew you and Max were close, but I never really knew how close. How did you meet him?"

"I met him at a Pub in London."

"I know that already, but how?"

He takes a deep breath. "I closed a major deal, and I was *out on the piss.*"

"You were *what?*" I can't help my confusion. I have no idea as to what the hell that means.

He laughs. "I forget that you don't know all my slang. Drinking—you know—celebrating. I got into it with a group of people; booze was flowing and it soon became a brawl. Max stepped in to help me, and made sure I didn't get into it with the coppers. I offered him a job, and he joked that I couldn't afford him. He called me 'pretty boy,' dropped me off at my hotel, and told me to go back to the States. The next day, I saw him on the local news while guarding one of the Queen's grandsons. I stayed in London until I was able to find and convince him to work with me—not for me. We became closer than brothers. And honestly, I never thought friends, like Max, even existed. That man would lay down his life for me, and I would do the same for him. I have so few people that I trust; I can't lose him."

I hug him. "He will be okay, Jax. I know it."

"How can you know that?"

"I have faith."

"*Faith?*"

"Yes, Jax, faith."

"Jax, what else is bothering you? Don't say *nothing* because I can tell; your eyes give it away."

"I'm juggling a lot of balls right now, and I can't afford to have anything slip through the cracks. Lives are at stake. I usually have Max watching my back, but that's not an option right now."

"What do you need me to do for you . . . to lighten the load," I offer.

"Just having you here safe with me helps. God how I love you, Raven." The sincerity in his voice is almost too much for me to handle.

"What did the doctor say today after he examined Max?"

I feel his whole body tense. "Everything is positive."

I glare at him. "Jax, you are the most direct and honest person I have ever met, so what are you not telling me?" I search his eyes, looking for a way in. He leans in and gently kisses my lips, working his way towards my ear. *I can't let him distract me.* "Jax, you can't distract me with your kisses. What aren't you telling me?"

Jaxson

I KNOW I HAVE to let her in; it's just hard for me. I've only shared everything with Max. I swear I'm going to kick his fucking arse! "Nothing, I'm fine." I don't think she believes me, however, the alarm on my phone, indicating it's time for her to eat, has gone off. Perfect distraction. "Oh, time for you to eat, sweetheart."

She freezes. "Wait! First, you try to distract me with a promising visit to the *happy* place. Then, you have an alarm going off on your phone, reminding you to feed me? You're not going to answer my questions, are you?" She watches as I stroke my chin. I decide to distract her further and give her my crooked smile. It always seems to do something for her. This time is no different.

"Sweetheart, are we going to the *happy place?*"

"Not if you don't answer my questions."

I can be such a bastard if I have to be—she has no clue. "That's okay, sweetheart, I can hold out—can you?"

I lean in and nibble her ear, leaving a trail of soft tender kisses down her neck, smirking all the way down! I unbutton her shirt and latch onto one of her nipples, flicking it with my tongue. Slowly I release it and lift her hand towards my mouth and kiss the inside of her wrist—that does it—she leaps up and wraps her legs around my waist. I carry her to the kitchen and place her on the cold counter as I go back to kissing and licking one nipple, and then the other. I know I'm not going to be able to hold back much longer, so I stop.

"Jax, what the fuck? Why are you stopping?"

"First, no blue language; the baby can hear you. Second, I told you I can wait. You need to eat—doctor's orders."

She takes a deep breath, "Okay, so let me get this straight, you can swear up one side and down another but I can't?"

I smirk again, and I swear, I think she wants to pull my hair out. "Sweetheart, I only swear when you're taking me to the *happy place;* that doesn't count."

"Why?"

I need to make her see reason here. "Why, what?"

She huffs like she's getting more frustrated. "Why doesn't it count, Jax?"

"The baby is sleeping then."

Her eyes go as wide as saucers. I can tell she thinks I'm crazy. "Raven, don't look at me like that. I know what you're thinking."

"Oh trust me, Jax, you have no idea what I'm thinking right now."

I bite back a smile. "Let's eat. I have mac and cheese, tomato soup, or peanut butter and jelly. Which would you prefer?"

Raven

I OPEN MY MOUTH to speak, but nothing comes out so I shut it again. He's nuts. "What happens if I swear in my head?"

I watch as he mulls over my question. He cocks his head to the side, and gifts me with such a beautiful smile . . . *Oh fuck, I'm done.* "Raven, I don't want our baby's first word to be *fuck*. I don't think I'm being unreasonable." God bless him; he's serious.

I throw my hands up in the air. "Fine, I'll take the mac and cheese, please."

As he dishes out the dinner I go and curl up by the fireplace. We eat, both of us quietly lost in our own thoughts.

"Jax, since we've been back, our lives have been like a whirlwind. And then, everything with Max . . . we really haven't had any time to talk."

"Where would you like to start?"

I put my food down. "Well, maybe we can start with Erica."

"What about her?"

He's not going to make this easy. "How did you meet her?"

"I met her in a bar. I thought it was random, only to find out much later that she had set the meet up. Did she say anything to you while you were being held captive?"

"Only that she was surprised you would fall for someone like me. She still believed you belonged to her. What exactly did she do to you?

Jaxson

WELL, ASIDE FROM FUCKING with my mind, which she doesn't need to know. "She stole millions of dollars, and put me in a position that could have sent me to prison. It was only with Max's help that we unraveled everything she had done before it couldn't be reversed."

"How did you find out what she was doing?" She pushes her plate away, and I want to argue with her to eat, but I'm not going to push my luck.

I smile, remembering those events. "It was Junior."

Her eyes grow large. "Michael? What did he do?"

I push my plate out of the way, as well. "I went to take a shower, leaving Erica to keep an eye on Junior. She had to make a phone call when I wasn't around. She gave Junior my phone to play with, hoping it would keep him quiet. He didn't realize what he was doing, but he recorded everything. The next day I noticed there was a video on my phone. It was of Erica on her phone, plotting her next move. I gave it to Max and the rest, as they say, is history . . . a history I wish I could erase."

"Why didn't you prosecute her?" I watch her eyes pierce mine as she's trying to understand this cluster fuck of a mess.

"Joseph asked the same thing. With the American justice system and her money, she wouldn't have gotten much jail time—if any. I decided I was going to black ball her from the very thing she loved most—the business world. When her grandfather found out what she had done, he disowned her. She lost everything."

She seems speechless and I'm not sure if she's mad or trying to understand. "So she opted for revenge, and that's why she went after Junior and ultimately . . . me.

"I can't change the past, sweetheart, all I can do is go forward with the knowledge I have, and try to protect everyone as best as I can."

"Now that Vincent is in custody, do you think I can go home?"

Home? Is she out of her *fucking* mind?! Okay, I need to remain calm here. I don't want to freak out and scare her. "No."

"Why not?"

I have to pause, and take a few calming breaths. "Just because Vincent is in custody, it doesn't mean that you'll be safe. He is the head of a major crime family. There are other people out there that might think—to get to him—they should get to you. We don't know who else knows your true identity. We also need to consider your mother's safety and the safety of our baby. Vincent's people went after Jackie just to get to you! Why do you even want to go back to your apartment?" Her eyes burn into me.

"Jax, I would *never* put anyone else in danger. However, I need to get on with my life. I can't and I won't live in fear. You are the one who told me, *if I let fear rule me then fear wins.*"

I get up, "I need to go check on Max." If I don't, I know I will come unhinged.

I NEEDED TO WALK away before I blew a gasket. The last thing I need is for her to pull a *runner.* I need to make her see the light—*my light.* We will be together forever

Arriving over at Max's, I walk into his bedroom to find Jackie, diligent as usual. "Hey, how's he doing?"

She looks so sad. "No change, Jax. Do you want me to give you some private time with him?"

She really is such a sweet girl. "Yes, please. I promise not to be long."

"It's okay, Jax, I'll go next door to see Raven." And with that, she's gone.

I stand here looking at my very broken friend, and I can't help but feel so responsible for all of this. "Max, you fucker, you need to wake up. I can't handle this on my own." I pace with my hands in my hair. Suddenly, I hear him.

"At this rate, you'll pull all your fucking hair out."

I freeze. Is my mind playing tricks on me? I stare at him. His eyes are still closed. "Max?"

He growls, "Who the fuck else were you expecting, mate?" *Only Max would go from unconscious to fucking cheeky in no time flat!*

"How long have you been awake?"

He takes his time answering me. "I came to earlier and then went out again. Calling in your mum and Mrs. Osla? That was low, even for you, you bastard."

I laugh. "I was desperate. Why didn't you say anything to Jackie? She's been here the whole time, crying and praying for you. Who's the *bastard* now?"

He clenches his jaw. "I need you to do me a favor."

I step closer to the bed, "Of course, what do you need?"

He barely opens his eyes, "Help get rid of Jackie."

I'm stunned. Did I hear him right? "Why?"

He's fisting his hands, and I swear he wants to punch me. Which all things considered, it wouldn't be the first time. "Why can't you, for once in your fucking life, do what you're told without questioning it?"

I smile at him, "Because that's not me, and you know it. Now why, damn it?"

His breathing is becoming rapid; this can't be good for him. "She deserves to be happy and safe. I'm in no position to offer her either one of those things. I don't know if I will ever be whole again. I'm better off alone. This is another reason why I don't do relationships."

I'm searching his face for an answer I already know. "You love her, I know you do."

He doesn't say anything for a while. I think he might have fallen out again, but then he opens his eyes. "Just get her to her parent's compound. She will be safe there."

He closes his eyes and lets out a low growl.

Jackie

I WAS GOING NEXT door to visit Raven, but then I remembered I needed my phone for when my parents call. And that's when I heard it. Max was awake and talking to Jax about me. He wants me gone! My heart feels like it's shattering into a million slivers of broken glass. I run next door to Raven's. She takes one look at me, charging through the door and her smile drops.

"Oh my God, Jackie, what happened?"

I can barely get the words out. "I heard Max talking to Jax, but you can't say anything. He wants me gone, Raven." I fall apart in my best friend's arms.

"Jackie, no. What do you mean, he wants you gone?"

"He said he's better off alone, and this is another reason why he doesn't do relationships."

"Maybe that wasn't what he meant. He's probably scared he won't be himself again. I think you need to talk to him." She tries to comfort me.

"No. I will not be humiliated. I don't have to beg someone to love me. I can't believe I gave myself to him, and now he wants nothing to do with me? I thought what we shared was special. How stupid and naive was I?" I sob.

"You are no such thing. Are you sure I can't talk to Jax about this? Maybe I can find out what's really going on," she offers.

"No. I'm going to my parents for a while," I say adamantly.

"I'm here for you, no matter what you need, Jackie. Please don't forget that."

"I know, but right now, I think what I need is time and space. Can you arrange the flight for me?" I ask, wiping my tears away and trying to pull myself together.

"Of course." She hugs me.

Raven

MY HEART BREAKS AS I watch my only friend's life and dreams crumble around her. The worst part is, there isn't anything I can do about it. She heads off to the bathroom to freshen up and collect herself.

Jax comes back, and he looks about as bad as Jackie does. "Jax, I need you to do something for me, and please don't ask questions. Call your pilot and arrange Jackie's flight home."

His eyes shoot up to mine, "She knows?"

I nod, "Yeah, she knows."

"Okay," he whispers. He makes all the arrangements.

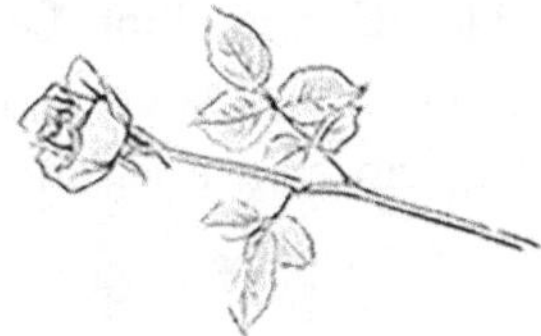

JACKIE AND I HEAD out to the airport. She's about to board the plane, when I take her hand and stop her. "Jackie, before you get on that plane, I need to know one thing—do you love him?"

Her eyes fill with tears, "Raven, what do you think? I've only ever given myself to him. I love him with all of my heart and soul. But I won't beg to be loved back; it's his choice." And with that, she is gone.

The ride back to The Tower is a long one. When I finally get there, I head upstairs to find Jax. I see him sitting in the dark, staring out the window. I walk up behind him, putting my arms around him. "Hey, do you want to talk?"

He shakes his head. "No, I just want to hold you in my arms all night long."

"Eventually, we will have to talk about it."

He sighs. "Eventually, doesn't have to be tonight. Tonight, I need to hold you in my arms, and make sweet, passionate love to you." He gets up and lifts me into his arms. He carries me to our bedroom, undressing me as we go. He lays me gently on the bed, cocooning me with his body. He sinks into me so slowly. When he's all the way in, we lock eyes. "Please don't ever leave me.

I think I would die." With that, I'm done. I pull him close and let him lose himself, knowing we both need each other.

Jackie

I PUT MY SEATBELT on, and listen to the flight attendant give me instructions about my safety. Can she give me instructions on how to save my broken heart? I watch the lights of New York City fade away into blackness; a blackness that clouds my heart and my soul. How could I have been such a fool? For the first time in my life, I actually wanted to give myself so totally to someone. Yet, he tossed me out like a pair of old shoes. I thought I really knew who he was. I thought he had morals, and valued the gift I gave him. He couldn't even tell me himself, he had Jax do it! I feel like such a fool. All those months, I shared so much of myself with him. All of my hopes and dreams, tossed aside. I've shed so many tears for this man; I don't think I have anything left. I feel so empty inside, like something died. I put my IPod on and hit shuffle. The first song that comes on is "Never be the same" by Red. Oh how true—I never will be. I curl up, close my eyes, and let the darkness take over.

Chapter Four

Raven

MORNING COMES TOO QUICKLY, and Jax is already getting ready for work. I have nowhere to go and no one to go with. My only friend is now thousands of miles away, hurt and shattered. There is nothing I can do about it—or is there? I'm lost in my thoughts when he barrels into the room, startling me.

"What's the matter, Jax?"

He smiles, "Nothing, just making sure you're real after last night."

I laugh, "No worries. I'm very real, and getting larger by the day. I need to go shopping for some clothes and I have other errands to run. I will take my guards and I know to always keep my guard dog, Bo, close, so don't worry, okay? I think I'm going to ask your mom and Bella to meet me for lunch." I'm not going to bring up going home right now; he has too much on his plate.

He smiles, "That's fine, just don't lose your detail. Make sure you have your phone turned on and with you. Your breakfast is ready. I will check in with you later." He leans down and gives me the softest kiss. "Oh, and just to remind you, I'm madly in love with you, that's all."

Just like that, he's gone. I head out to the kitchen and see breakfast is all set up with a single Abracadabra Rose left on my tray. I don't know how he does it but he just renders me speechless, even when he's not in the fucking room. *Oh shit!* I'm not supposed to think swear words.either. I can't believe I just thought that, and I can't help but laugh. Before I leave, I plan on visiting Max; this is not over by a long shot.

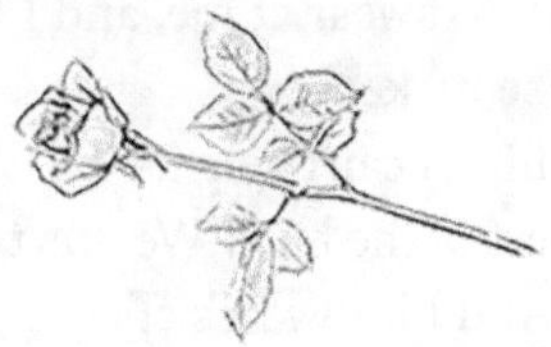

I GET READY AND head next door. I need to talk to Max; he can't possibly think that he can just dismiss Jackie like yesterdays news. I run into Max's doctor just as he's getting ready to leave.

"Hello, Dr. Steven, I'm Raven, how is Maxwell today?"

"He is awake and doing better. He starts therapy this afternoon."

Oh, I wonder if he will need any help with it? "What kind of therapy does he need?"

He gives me an impatient huff, "I'm sorry, but I'm not at liberty to discuss the matter with you."

And with that, he's gone. I walk into Max's bedroom and find him sitting in a chair, staring out the window. His back is to me, so I take the time to study this man. He's hurting just as much as Jackie is.

"I know you're there, Raven."

I smile, "How do you know?"

He lifts his hand, "Your reflection in the window. Don't worry; I don't have eyes in back of my head. I take it you're here to get some answers."

I'm not going to make it easy on him. "Actually no, I'm not. I already have all the answers I will need."

He turns and looks at me, his eyes wide. "Really? What might they be?"

I laugh, "You know, sometimes you and Jax can be such cavemen! I know you love her, and I know that you're pushing her away because of that love. You think your life is too dangerous and that she would be better off without you. You don't know if you'll be one-hundred percent again, and it has you scared. So you did what Jax would do, you shut down and block out all the people from your life who love you, the people who give a shit about you. Oh fuck. You see what you did? I'm not supposed to swear, or even think of swear words, and you have me swearing like a fucking sailor!"

His bottom lip is between his teeth, and his eyes look amused. "Well, Max, are you going to answer me? Or are you just going to sit there?" I ask and the amused look changes drastically.

"Raven, first, yes I love her, but look at me. Look at all I have been through. She is so innocent, precious, and pure; then there's me. I'm a broken man, for many reasons, but all the more—broken. Doesn't she deserve the best of the best? I love her enough to give her a chance at that. Secondly, I can't help it that you want to swear at me, and I find it very funny that you go along with the crazy arse fucker."

I know I'm glaring at him, I can't help it—he is so stubborn. "What makes you think you're not the best of the best? We don't get to pick our soul mates; I believe, God, does that. And I know he's crazy, but I love him, so no swearing in front of the baby!"

He seems to be at a loss for words. "I'm going to run errands, do you need me to do anything for you?"

"No, but don't lose your detail. Take Bo and your phone." He orders. I laugh and wave as I'm running out the door.

I HEAD DOWN THE elevator with everyone in tow. It's a beautiful afternoon, so I decide to walk. I call Bella to set up lunch. "Raven, is everything okay?"

I can't help but laugh. She's so much like Jax, it's funny. "Hello to you too, Bella. Yes, everything is fine. I wanted to know if you and your mom could meet me for lunch today? I need help with a project."

She's quiet for a minute, probably not sure how to deal with someone who isn't a bulldozer. "Sure, when and where?"

I give her the details on where and when to meet, and now I'm off to go clothes shopping. I get to Bloomingdales. I stand outside the store and cry. I should be doing this with my best friend, instead, I'm alone. Adding to that, I'm walking around with two guards and a dog! I try to go in, but then I'm reminded about the last time I was here with Marco. How did my life get so fucked up? As I stroll down the street, I find a small maternity boutique and head on in. I pick out some jeans, tops, and running clothes, figuring it's a good base to start with. As I go up to the counter to pay, I discover that one of my guards has already paid for me! "What do you think you're doing?"

He looks down at his feet, seemingly embarrassed by the situation. "Mr. Phillips requested that we get you anything you wanted."

I take my package and leave the store. This is ridiculous. I decide to head to Jax's office and give him a piece of my mind. This man has taken over my entire life. I can't go home. I can't shop without all eyes trained on me. I'm becoming a prisoner with invisible walls. I enter the *Raiders* building and walk up to the security desk. The guard, hands me a badge with my picture already on it. What the fuck is this man up to now! I get into the elevator with Bo and both guards positioning themselves in front of me. As we make frequent stops, people are getting on and off. A group of girls get on, and they are discussing their evening plans. It makes me want to cry. I miss Jackie, and even Marco; he was such a tortured soul. I didn't even realize that he was in love with me. As I watch these girls, I realize beautiful women surround Jax all day long, and soon, I will be a cow. I'm fighting my tears as the doors open and I head out towards Jax's office. Mrs. Osla lets me know he is in, but on the phone. I tell everyone to wait outside the door for me. The guard informs me he has to look inside the room first; this is stupid, but whatever.

As I go inside, I lock the door behind me. He's still on his call and he seems to be getting very pissed off. Oh, I don't want to be the person on the other side of that call. Wow, I don't think I have ever seen Jax this mad. He slams the phone down and opens his arms. I can't help it, I run straight into them. This man makes me crazy mad, and then crazy in love. Will I ever know what normal is?

"Sweetheart, this is a wonderful surprise. There's not something wrong though, is there?"

I'm fighting to hold back my constant tears lately. "Oh, Jax, everything and nothing."

"Okay, are you upset with me?" he asks apprehensively.

"Yes and no."

"How about you tell me what you did today, so far, and then we can take it from there." I can tell he's really trying to be patient with me.

"I had a talk with Max, and he really pissed me off," I say after finally calming down.

"I can understand that, he does it to me all the time. Sweetheart, you can't force him to face his demons, you can only support him."

"I know that, Jax, it's just that they are both hurting, and for what—stupid pride?"

"What else have you done today?" He leans back on his desk.

"I went shopping for clothes. I couldn't bring myself to go into Bloomingdales. The last time I was there was with Marco." A lump forms in my throat.

Jax picks up his phone and hits a button. "One second, sweetheart," he holds up a finger to me, "Mrs. Olsa, please hold my calls and cancel my next meeting. Thanks." He hangs up.

I can't believe he just blocked out that time for me out of nowhere. "Jax, you have to work. I'm a distraction; I'll go."

He pulls me tightly up against his chest, running his fingertips down my cheek. "You'll do no such thing. It shatters me to see you upset." He leans in, lightly brushing his lips over mine. "I'd stop the world for you, Raven."

"Jax, I want to go shopping, pay for my own stuff. Do you know how I felt when the guard paid for all my clothes? I felt cheap, like I'm being kept by someone. Let me tell you, it's not a good feeling." I watch his reaction, but he keeps a stolid expression. "Well, what do you have to say for yourself?"

"Sweetheart, every time I open my mouth, I make you cry, so please excuse me if I'm a little apprehensive here. While we are on full disclosure, I replaced all your credit cards with a Black American Express Card. There is no credit limit. I figured you might want to do some shopping for the baby."

I can't believe what I'm hearing! "So let me get this straight; you went into my purse, took out all of my cards, and then replaced them with one that you think I should have?!" I scream. He is so in the doghouse now. "Why, Jax? Why would you do that? You need to make me understand what the fuck you were thinking!"

He glares at me. "Don't swear, the baby will hear! I remember when we were preparing for Junior, it was very time consuming and expensive. I took care of everything for Bella."

Well that's news. "Why did you do everything for Bella? Why not Michael?"

He kisses my lips softly, and then leans in to nibble on my ear. "It's not my story to tell; it's Bella's."

"I want to see my mother; I think it will be safe. I would also like to check on Jackie. She's my only friend, Jax." I can't be made to feel like a prisoner.

He nods, "Let me run everything by Max first, and then we will figure out the next step, okay?"

"Okay, I have to go. I'm meeting your mom and Bella for lunch and probably some shopping. I'll see you later. I love you." I lean in and kiss him, he holds me so tight.

"Jax, are you okay?"

He smiles, "Yeah, just needed to make sure you're real, sweetheart. I love you more."

I realize that as strong and powerful as he is, underneath, he is still that little boy whose dad walked out on him, and my heart breaks.

Jaxson

I KNOW I'M NOT going to get any work done, so I head over to check on Max. I get to Max's flat. It's very quiet. I watch him sitting in a chair, looking out the window. How did everything get so fucked up for us? "Hey, Max, how are you feeling today?"

"Jax, if you're here to tear me a new arsehole, you're too late. Raven beat you to it."

I laugh, "No I'm not here for that. I'm here so you can tear *me* a new arsehole."

His eyes shoot up to mine, "What the fuck did you do now, mate?"

I have taken up Max's pacing. "That's just it, I don't know what the fuck I did. I don't think I'm unreasonable. I don't understand why she got so mad that I had the guard pay the bill when she went shopping. I then had to confess that I replaced all of her credit cards with the Black AmEx. She really went nuts over that one. I don't want to come across all crazy, but I just want to lock her in the fucking penthouse and throw away the key! Her emotions are all over the place; she cries easily. I feel like I'm walking on eggshells."

"Well, what are you going to do?"

"Fuck if I know what I'm going to do. Max, why else would I be here."

He laughs, "Oh, Jax, it's a good thing I know you so well; a lesser man might be offended by you. Maybe she needs more from you?"

I stop pacing and stare out the window. "Max, I'm not a total moron; I get that. *Fuck.* I've wanted to marry her from the first day I met her, but again, I can't come across out of control and possessive. If I ask her now, she will think I only want to marry her because she is pregnant. If I don't ask her now, she will think I don't want her. I'm so fucked either way. Maybe locking her away isn't such a bad idea." I sigh. " I know you don't want to talk about Jackie, but it's a problem." I wait for a reaction. His jaw gets tight and he closes his eyes, probably trying to gain some control. I can see his pain, both physical and emotional.

"Why is Jackie a problem?" he almost whispers.

Why do I have to spell everything out? "Jackie is Raven's only friend, and right now, she is held up at her parent's compound in Switzerland. Raven needs her friend, and I'm sure, by the look of Jackie when she left here, she is in need of Raven. Plus, Raven wants to see her mum, and I can't say I blame her. If it were my mum, I would be fighting tooth and nail to get to her. I told her I would talk to you and see if it's possible that we make a trip to Switzerland. What's your take on that?"

He takes a deep breath, "Well, I talked to Tony today and he brought me up to speed on everything. Vincent is still being held at a federal hospital. He hasn't regained consciousness, yet. Vincent's lawyer, Mr. Deveno, has been pushing the Feds to have Vincent moved to a private facility. Duke has been brought back to New York. He is being held in solitary at Sing Sing prison, awaiting trial. You know that no one is ever one-hundred percent safe, Jax, that's just life. If you want to get her out of the country for a little bit while she is still in the earlier part of the pregnancy, then I would say go for it. Make sure you have all the necessary security with you, at all times. I can't travel with you, but I will help with all the arrangements if you need me to. I can monitor things from here. As far as Raven is concerned, you love her—that's never been a question. So what are you waiting for? You go after whatever you want and damn anyone to hell if they get in your way . . . so, get the fuck out of your own way, mate."

"This is why you're my best friend." I slap him on the shoulder. I wish

I could help him figure things out; I know this is destroying him. But until he let's me in, all I can do is wait. I leave him to his thoughts and head back across the hall to plan my next move.

Raven

I MAKE IT TO the restaurant just as Bella and An pull up. When we're all seated, Bella jumps right in, "So, what did my brother do now?"

I can't help but laugh, "That's not why I asked you both here, but now that we are on that subject, he went into my purse, took all the credit cards out of my wallet, and replaced them with a Black AmEx card!"

Bella is laughing. "Raven, you need to understand that sometimes my brother can be an idiot. I'm sure he has no concept of how a women's purse is very private and personal."

Finally, someone who understands! "Well, I'm glad someone else sees how crazy he can be. He also told me that if I swear, or even think of swear words, the baby can hear it, and he doesn't want the baby's first word to be a swear word!" An is biting her lip, trying not to laugh, but even she seems to see how crazy her son's behavior is.

"Raven, my son can be a little intense."

Bella and I turn toward her and at the same time, we burst out laughing.

"You should have seen him when I was pregnant, you would have thought he was the father. He wouldn't let anyone come within ten feet of me. He wanted medical reports on everyone I came in contact with. I had three cleaning ladies quit because of him!" Bella reports before taking a sip of water. I want to ask her more about her pregnancy—where Michael was—but An is fidgeting and seems very uncomfortable, so I decide to drop it.

"I asked you ladies to lunch today to help me with Max."

"What's wrong with, Maxwell? I spoke to Jax, and he didn't say there was a problem." An's voice cracks and she turns pale.

I don't know how much Jax told her. "He pushed Jackie away. She went to her parents' compound in Switzerland. She is a total wreck; her heart is broken. I went to see Max this morning, and he's so lost. All he would say was that she's better off without him, and he doesn't do relationships. Jax told me to stay out of it, but I can't—they love each other. What has Max so rattled that he would push her away? He couldn't even tell her to her face; he made Jax do it. None of this sounds like Max to me."

An seems very upset, but Bella doesn't seem so rattled. "My brother and Max have been best friends for a very long time. They have relied upon each other for everything. They are closer than brothers; their bond is unbreakable. I'm sure he knows more than we think."

"An, what do you think we should do?"

"Raven, let me think about this for a little bit. You just be a good friend to Jackie. I like her a lot. Her parents raised her very well; they should be proud of her." *She seems really upset.*

I nod, missing my friend even more. "I'm sorry if I upset you, An, I just want to fix this."

She is so much like Jax, trying to be the strong one.

"It's fine, dear, please don't worry. I'm going to leave you here with Bella. Enjoy your lunch, ladies." She gets up and abruptly leaves.

"Bella, did I say something wrong?"

"No, Raven, it's not you. For some unknown reason, when it comes to Max, my mum can be very overprotective." She grabs a roll and butters it. I want to press her for more answers, but I don't have that comfort level with her, yet. God, I miss Jackie so much.

Pretty soon we are lost in all things baby.

WE FINISH LUNCH AND I decide to head back to The Tower to get ready to go for a run. I realize today will be the first time I go for a run with Bo by myself and I'm excited to see what he can do. I finally meet Jax's housekeeper, Sofia. I change so fast, even I can't believe it. I head out the door. I inform my detail of the route I want to take and get approval from them. We enter the park, and after a quick stretch, I take off; it feels wonderful. Running gives me the time to organize my thoughts. Bo seems to love it too.

As I acclimate to the pace I'd like to stay at, I think about Jax's housekeeper. I honestly can't believe this man has a housekeeper that looks like a cross between a Playboy Bunny and a Hooters waitress. No wonder he didn't tell me. He can't be so dense to think that I wouldn't be upset, especially since I'm going to look like a fucking cow soon. I need to figure out what I'm going to do.

I love Jax—heart and soul. I know that he loves me, but now there is a baby involved. I need to have stability, and so does my baby. I need to see my mother. However, I also need to consider her safety. I don't even know if she will know who I am. I could never forget her; her beautiful blonde hair and crystal-blue eyes.

It's amazing when you run through Central Park with two bodyguards and a big dog, no one comes near you. When we get to the end of the run, I head over to the vendor for a warm pretzel and water. I decide to sit on a bench and enjoy the sunshine. One of my fondest memories is of Marco and me, sitting on a park bench and people watching. We would make up stories about some of the people; Marco's were always funny. I still can't believe he is dead, and how little I really knew about him. Before I know it, the tears are flowing. I'm such a jumble of emotions. Bella said it wouldn't get better, so just deal with it and know that for the rest of the pregnancy, I will basically be *bat shit crazy.*

I get up to go across the street, and Bo stops. His hair is on end as he lets out a growl that freezes me to my spot. My guards are around me in an instant. I don't see any threats, only a very beautiful lady with long, black hair and dark glasses. She is watching me and it's making my hair stand on end. She takes a step forward. Bo crouches down, baring all his teeth! My guards lift me up and run me out of the park. Bo is walking backwards and growling, watching her every move.

We run into The Tower, and when I get upstairs, I head right to Max's place. I need to tell him what happened. He gives me his full attention as I relay the story. He gives the guards a quick nodding jerk of his head. They return it with a curt one and head out of the room. My guess is that was some sort of coded way to tell them to dig for answers.

"Raven, are you okay?" He brings his focus back to me.

As I calm my racing heart, I realize no matter how broken he is, we all rely on him so much . . . whom does he get to rely on? "Max, I was just rattled, you know Bo never did anything like that before. Who do you think that was?"

"Well, if I had to guess, I would say she is your father's sister, Annabelle. One of your guards took a picture with his phone and sent it to Tony. Hopefully, he'll have an answer soon. I know you think we are being hard on you with security, but do you see how danger can pop up anywhere?"

"Can this woman be as dangerous as Vincent?"

"Raven, even though women are generally not regarded as dangerous within the structure of a traditional organized crime family, Vincent structures his differently. He's an animal; the lowest of the low."

I walk over to the bar, and grab a bottle of water to help settle my nerves. "Max, what do you know about the structure of Vincent's organization? Does he have a wife or children?"

"Surprisingly, no. He relies heavily on Annabelle and his consigliere, Mr. Deveno."

I take his hand and squeeze it tightly. "Max, I understand about the security, but how am I supposed to live a normal life?"

He grimaces. "How do you think Jax would be able to live if something happened to you and the baby? Take it from me, he wouldn't. It would destroy him."

I'm not sure if he is talking about me anymore. "I get it, Max, and I'm sorry to unload this on you, especially with all the crap you are going through."

I reach in and hug him, I whisper "Thank you." As I leave, I turn and look back at him. He's facing the window, his shoulders slumped. My heart is breaking for this man.

I GO NEXT DOOR and find the place empty. I decide upon a long, hot shower. I set everything up, lighting lots of candles, and I put on Jax's IPod. I really can't imagine life without this shower. I sense him before I see him; I know when he enters the room. My body starts buzzing, and the closer he gets, the louder the ringing in my ears is. I turn around and I'm hit with those beautiful eyes. I pull him close to me, reaching up and running my finger over his soft lips. I need to be in control. He is always so dominate, but he knows when I need to feel in control, and has no problem giving it to me.

"I need you, Jax. I need to wash away the day. I just need you and me."

He leans in, slowly kissing me. "I'm here for you, baby, always." He runs his hands down the back of my thighs and lifts me up. I wrap myself around his rock hard chest. He just holds me so tightly.

"Tonight, baby, I'm your pleasure god, everything I do will be for your pleasure. Do you trust me?"

I don't even have to think twice, "Yes." And with that, he carries me into the shower. He starts massaging my back very slowly, and then, he balances me on one of his knees while he washes my hair. All of the tension I felt before flows out of me.

"I love your hair; it's so silky. When you drape it over my cock it's just—wow!" he breathes. He lets me down gently so we can take turns washing each other.

We get out of the shower; he wraps me in warm towels, and then starts to dry my hair. I study him by candlelight. When he is doing something, he is so focused and intense, unlike me. I hope the baby takes after him; he's so beautiful. He carries me into the bedroom, and I notice he has lit candles all around the room. He places me in the center of the bed.

"You are all mine, now and for always, my beautiful girl. I want to try something different with you. I'm not sure if you're ready for it, though. You have to tell me no if you can't, okay?"

My heart starts racing. "What do you want to do to me?"

He kisses me slowly, "I would like to blindfold you. I know from past experiences it might be too much to ask, so it has to be totally up to you."

I stammer. "I w-will try."

He strokes my back, calming me. "If it gets too much just tell me. I want you to experience pleasure without knowing what to expect; a total release."

He takes me to such new highs all the time. "I trust you, Jax."

He reaches over to the bedside table, and pulls out a blindfold made of silk. "Close your eyes." As he ties the blindfold around me, my heart beats wildly. I don't know if I can do this. I want to do this, to give him pleasure. More importantly, I need to do this for me. I will not let fear rule me; I rule fear. He kisses me long and slow, our tongues doing an erotic dance. "I want every part of you. I want to be your first and your last."

He's working his way down my neck, then back up to my ear, dragging his teeth as he goes. Just as I'm really getting into it, he stops. "Jax?"

"I'm still here, Raven, just getting some stuff."

Stuff, what stuff? I take a deep breath, releasing it very slowly. I trust this man.

"Are you still okay?"

I nod.

"I need to hear the words, Raven. Are you still okay?"

I let out a deep breath, "Yes. Yes, Jax, I'm okay."

He has the music on repeat; The Righteous Brothers singing "Unchained Melody." I feel his lips on mine and they taste like . . . Nutella! "Hmm, wow. So warm and silky." His tongue is full of Nutella, and he's working it around mine. This is so erotic, I don't want it to end. Now he's massaging my neck, his tongue follows wherever he's massaging. I realize he's massaging me with the warm, silky, chocolate hazelnut goodness. He works his way down my body until he's between my legs. I gasp.

"You okay, Raven?"

Every nerve ending is on fire. "Yes. Please don't stop, please. Oh my God, Jax."

His arms are locked around my thighs, and he is not letting up. The sensations are stronger because I can't see him. I'm pulling his hair and my hips are going wild. His grip on my thighs is strong like iron. "Are you really okay, baby, if not I'll stop."

I gasp, "Don't you *dare* stop! Jax, I . . . oh, fuck . . . Jax—I'm coming!" My core is shaking, and there is a buzzing in my brain. My body is so flushed; he's relentless. He works me down real slow as he kisses his way up my body.

"I'm not done, sweetheart, not by a long shot."

He enters me very slowly, so I can feel every rock hard inch of him.

"Oh yeah . . . do you feel that? Perfect, just fucking perfect, sweetheart. You're so beautiful. Enough of this blindfold, I need your eyes." He pulls the blindfold off and I'm hit with that beautiful smile. He has me totally cocooned with his body. In and out, then around to the right, and back around to the left. His arms reach underneath me, and he grips my shoulders, pulling me down as his hips push up—he's so fucking deep! Wow, this man has some killer moves.

"Look at me, Raven, now."

My eyes open wide and lock violets to blues. The depths I can see into this man's soul is . . ."Oh, fuck . . . oh, God . . . holy fuck, Jax!"

He slams into me, exploding with such force. He begins to slow down, giving me a chance to breathe. He rolls onto his side, taking me with him.

My brain fog begins to clear. "Jax, we should shower again, and clean up here."

He shakes his head, "Nope."

I look at him, "That's it, just *nope?*"

"Sweetheart, I could care less about the mess." He's in the *happy place* right now, and that's where I think he wants to stay. "Besides, I'm not done yet."

How could he possibly? "You're not done yet?"

As he laughs that beautiful raspy growl of a laugh, he tenderly kisses me, "With you, I know no end." He's moving slow and steady, in and out, but then he stops and pulls out of me. "I want to be in every part of you tonight." He crawls up to my chest and wedges his cock between my breasts, pulling my nipples, and pumping his cock.

"Oh, God, Jax, my nipples are on fire!"

He throws his head back, screaming and coming all over my breasts. "Raven, I. Love. You."

He leans down and kisses me real slowly. Working his way down my body, he enters me again.

"Jax, you can't possibly go again?"

He laughs, "No, now it's time for sleep."

I kiss him. "Shouldn't we shower?"

He shakes his head and gifts me with the most beautiful smile. "Nope, just like this—all night long." He pulls the comforter over us, and holds me in his arms, all while he's buried deep within me.

Raven

AS I SLOWLY OPEN my eyes, I realize Jax is still buried deep inside me. I laugh that this is the way this crazy, beautiful man loves to sleep. I have to wonder how he is going to manage that when I'm as large as a cow. We are stuck together and as I attempt to pull us apart, he tightens his grip.

"Where are you going?"

I never know when he's sleeping or just in, "Jax zone." "I was going to head to the bathroom, and then the shower. I thought you were asleep?"

There's that smile. "I've been up for a while, waking up like this is shear heaven."

"I don't understand how you're able to sleep like this."

"Sweetheart, knowing that you're safe, and locked onto me all night long is a beautiful fucking thing."

"Why are you allowed to swear, and I'm not even allowed to think a swear word?"

He opens one eye, "Hush, the baby is sleeping."

I open my mouth to speak, but only a squeak comes out. Is he serious? "I hope you know how absurd you sound."

As I watch his face, I realize he's serious. "I think it makes perfect sense. When Bella was pregnant, I made her listen to soothing classical music so Junior could relax. There are studies, showing that babies can hear stuff in the womb. Why do you think those Einstein CD's are so popular?"

"Bella said you were nuts when she was pregnant, that you wanted health checks on everyone she came into contact with."

He gives me that smirk then leans down and kisses me. God, only knows what else he did to poor Bella. "What else did my *wonderful* sister tell you?"

I can tell Jax doesn't like to delve into the past, his body tenses quickly. "We didn't go into it any further because your mom looked upset."

He takes a deep breath. "It was a hard time for my mum when Bella found out she was pregnant. She wasn't married to Michael, yet. My mum is a very traditional woman. She eventually came to terms with it, and no one could love Junior more. When he was kidnapped, and Joseph showed up at my office, she really tore into him. What else happened at lunch?"

"I spoke to them about Max. I'm worried about him and Jackie." I watch his face, gaging his reaction.

He's mindlessly stroking my arm. "Sweetheart, I understand you want everyone to have their own happily ever after, but that's not always possible."

I of all people know life is not all rainbows and flowers. "I know, but they are both so lost without each other. There has to be something I can do to help."

As he begins stroking my back, he leans in and kisses my forehead. "Well, we are going to Switzerland tomorrow. I contacted Jackie's parents and they are very excited that you will be coming. We are also going to see your mum and, if all works out, she will be coming back to the States with us."

"Please tell me these are happy tears," he pleads softly as I lose the battle with my tears.

I laugh, "They are. Just when I didn't think I could love you more . . ."

He kisses me. "Enough talk, sweetheart, its time for the *happy place.*"

He tilts his hips, and kisses my lips. Just like that, everything else is forgotten.

Maxwell

AS I SIT ON the sofa, staring out over the New York skyline, I realize how much I miss her. I knew it would hurt, but it would hurt even more to keep her chained to me. Suddenly, there's a commotion out in the hallway. I hear her before I can see her; the hair on my neck is standing on end. I knew she would be coming—it was only a matter of time.

"Maxwell, you tell these guards to let me in, otherwise you will be even more sorry than you are right now!"

I wave her in because to fight her would be fruitless. "Do you want a drink, ma'am?"

She sits next to me on the couch and pulls my ear. "Should you be drinking, Maxwell?"

"Probably not. I knew you would be coming by, so I figured you could yell at me for everything in one shot."

Her face becomes red, and her jaw is tight. She's really mad, and I hate that it's me that made her this upset.

"Don't get smart with me, Maxwell."

We are silent for a bit. "I made my decision and I would like for you to respect that."

She glares at me. "Not when it's the wrong decision."

I have to laugh, "No matter, it's still my decision to make, right or wrong."

She jumps up, "Are you afraid that history will repeat itself, Maxwell?"

I freeze, staring at her in shock. How could she possibly know? I've told no one. "How long have you known?"

"I knew your grandmother, and she told me everything—even why you went into Special Forces."

I can't believe she has known this whole time, never saying a word. "So you knew my grams before I even met Jax? Did you tell him? I mean, does he know the whole story? Is that why he tried to move heaven and earth to get me to work with him?"

Her eyes fill with tears, and she's losing the fight to hold them back. "No, of course not. It's your story to tell, not mine. Maxwell, it was a random act of violence, and there was nothing you could have done to stop it. Denying yourself love . . . is just so wrong."

"What if it happens again?" my voice cracks. "Look at what Jax is going through to keep Raven safe—all of you safe. I don't think I could live through it again. Jackie deserves a carefree happy life. She will never have that if she is with me, we both know that. The longer she is with me, the bigger the target on her back gets." I argue. She reaches down, taking my hand, and for the first time, I see such pain in her eyes. It breaks my heart, knowing that I'm the one causing it.

"Ma'am, some people are supposed to be alone."

She shakes her head, "Never, Maxwell, never."

"Either way, it's my decision and I need you to respect that."

"How about respecting Jackie. What you did to her was wrong. I understand your fear, but she didn't deserve that."

She squeezes my shoulder and heads out the door, leaving me to my thoughts.

BEFORE TOO LONG, JAX is back which is good. I need to be briefed on the trip. "Hey, sit down and run through your trip with me."

He's glaring at me. "Why are you drinking?"

I take a deep breath, "Calm down, Jax, it was just one scotch."

He growls, "I don't give a fuck! Are you trying to sabotage your recovery?"

"No, your mum was here earlier."

"Oh, do I need one of those, too?"

I nod, "Yeah, I need to talk, and you need to listen."

This is going to be so hard, but he needs to hear it all and it has to be from me. "Jax, there is a lot about me that you don't know."

"Max, whatever it is, it doesn't matter, mate. It's a little late in the game for this, don't you think?"

He's not going to make this easy. "Shut up and let me talk. This is very hard for me, and I never thought I would talk about it again, but then your mum came by and informed me that she already knew. Apparently, she was a friend of my grams long before we even met." I swirl my scotch around before bringing it up to my lips for a little courage. He sits down, his attention fully focused on me. "I told you my mum died when I was young, and I went to live with my grams in London. I went to the University on a full scholarship. I graduated early, and then went to work for Scotland Yard. I was young . . . about twenty. It was hard work, but I was good at it, always having an eye for the little details. Before I knew it, I was moving up the ranks rather quickly. During this time, I met a beautiful girl, Samantha; a Barrister. That was how we met. We worked so well together, I caught them and she put them away. We were married and she became pregnant shortly after. I felt that I had put everything with my mum to rest. And I was becoming a man that my grams could respect and be proud of. My son was born on a beautiful spring day in May. We named him Elliot, after my grandfather; he was a beautiful, blond haired, blue-eyed boy. Everything was going just as I planned. Well, you know what they say about that.

"One day in the early fall, Samantha took Elliot to the park; he always loved to be outside. When they were leaving the park, Samantha was taking Elliot out of his buggy, and two drugged-up punks' carjacked her. I was called to the scene, not realizing it was my wife and son. When I reached them, I found Samantha with Elliot in her arms . . . both of them were dead. I lost it. I was a crazy man, out for revenge. My whole world shattered that day. I quit my job, and took to the bottle."

Jax pours us another scotch. "My grams finally got me to a point where I could function and give up the drink. Then I joined the Special Forces. I didn't care about my life anymore. I didn't care where they sent me or what they asked me to do. I figured if I died, then I could be with my family. That's all I ever wanted—my family. The thing is, I never died. Oh, I was hurt a lot . . . probably should have died . . . but never did. One day, I was asked to guard one of the Queen's grandchildren. He was wild and they thought I would be able to tame him, or if nothing else, keep him safe. Then, you came along. I took your offer because I had nothing to keep me in the UK. My grams was there, but she pushed for me to try and get a life. As much as your mum scares the crap out of me, she is the closest thing I have to a mum," I finally finish and wait a while for Jax to say something—anything. "Jax, say something please, mate."

"Why are you telling me this now?" he asks.

I take a sip of my scotch, trying to steady my nerves. "Your mum knows the story, and I never knew that she did. When she came to me today, she made me realize that you have a right to know everything. You're all the family I have, and I don't want you to hate me because of Jackie. I love Jackie, and I know that I broke her heart. I don't think I have anything left inside me to give. I'm a broken man, Jax. She deserves only the best. She needs to move on with her life. I don't want this to be a problem for you. I know she and Raven only have each other. Raven and the baby, they're your family now. I will back away and give you back the portion of the company that you gave me. I am also going to move back to Scotland as soon as I'm healed. Tony can take over for me."

He jumps up, "So that's it? You think you have this all figured out. Just like that and you're going to write me off? Well, guess again, mate. You're like a fucking brother to me, not some random employee. We're in this to the bitter end—so, enough!" He throws his glass across the room and storms out.

Jaxson

I KNOW THE WAY I just responded to Max was not the adult way to respond to things. Ha—fuck that! I'm not feeling like one right now!

I go across to my flat, only to find it pretty lifeless. I check on Raven. She must still be shopping for the trip. I told her not to bother; we can get whatever we need when we are there. I think it is a way for her to settle her nerves, though. I'm glad she is not home right now; I need to be alone. I need to process all this shit and I know just where to start. I need to call my mum and find out exactly what she knows. I can't believe she has never said one word about this.

"Mum, I need to see you right now, where are you?"

"Why do you need to see me, Jaxson?"

I growl, "I just spent the last two hours with Max."

She lets out a deep sigh. "I'm on my way."

I always know I can count on her no matter what. I just wish Max could see that. How could everything have gotten so cocked-up for us? How did Max ever go on after his family was murdered? Three months without Raven nearly killed me. At least I had hope; hope that she was alive. Max had nothing.

The elevator opens, and my mum comes speeding in. "Okay, what happened?" She sits next to me. I see something in her eyes—fear maybe—I'm not sure.

"Max told me everything about Samantha and Elliot. He told me that you knew his grams. Why didn't you ever tell me?"

She fidgets with her bracelet, seemingly trying to find her words. "I made a promise to his grams, many years ago. Besides, it was not my story to tell, son, it was his heartache. He is like a son to me, and I want him to be happy. I tried to make him understand that what happened was a random act of violence. He can have love again, and a family, he just needs to open his heart to it. He's scared and lost. We need to support him."

She's going to be even more upset when I inform her of the latest development. "Well, you're not going to like this then . . . he has decided to go back to Scotland—permanently. He feels it would be better if he were out of all of our lives for good. What else did his grams tell you?"

Mum is visibly shaking. "She said it was Maxwell who was first on the scene; they were both shot in the head. He is in such a dark place right now, and I'm so scared. He said Jackie has a bigger target on her now. I can't imagine what he's feeling. He's hurting, we have to help him, son, *p-please,*" Mum cries.

Oh fuck. "I know, mum. I will. Family doesn't give up on family."

I know what I need to do. "Raven and I are going to Switzerland; she needs to see her mum and Jackie. I will keep you posted, but please keep a close eye on Max. As a matter of fact, just stay here."

She nods, "I will, son, this is far from over."

I GOT MY MUM settled in before Raven and I had to head to the airport, accompanied by more security than normal. I'm not taking any chances. When we get to Teterboro, we meet the pilot at the plane. Max always likes to do a walk around with the pilot, so I figure I should too. He informs me of the flight time and weather conditions as we board. Raven has a tight grip on my hand and she's not letting go. "Sweetheart, I know you're nervous, but I will be there every step of the way. Max and I have already spoken to the doctors, so they are expecting us."

She's holding my hand so tight. "I know, Jax, I'm just scared. I don't want to traumatize her anymore than she already is. I'm also very worried about Jackie and Max. I know something happened because your mom is staying close to him, which means you're worried. Why won't you tell me what has you so upset? I thought we weren't going to have any secrets?"

I look into those eyes, and I try to find the calm that she always brings me. "Yes, I'm upset. Actually, very upset. Secrets were kept for the past eight years, not only by Max, but also by my mum. It's Max's story that he should have told me eight years ago. Raven, Max thinks he can just walk out of my life, but he can't. I'm not about to lose the closest thing to a brother I have. I told you, I can be a real bastard, Max, knows this, and I will throw everything I have at him if necessary."

"Does this have to do with why he pushed Jackie away?"

"Yes, it does, and also why he is so overprotective."

She squeezes my hand. "I won't push for answers, but I hope you know I'm not giving up on Max and Jackie. I told you, Jackie and I were roommates in collage. She is two years younger than me, so I always felt like her big sister. Did Max tell you about her family?"

I shake my head, "Not much, just that she has an older brother, but there is a large age difference. When you graduated, why didn't you continue to room with her?"

"I got the job teaching at the school about six months before she did. Marco followed me up to New York from D.C, and we moved in together. I wanted Jackie to live with us too, but she didn't like Marco. At times it was difficult, but she would make herself scarce when he was around, so I wouldn't have to choose. Jackie's parents are very nice; her mother is a traditional Japanese woman, always putting her husband first. If I didn't know her father on a personal level, I would be very afraid of him."

Well that's a surprise. "Really, why?"

She bites her bottom lip. "Maybe I should let you experience him for yourself?"

I lift her hand and kiss her wrist, "Oh no, sweetheart, you opened this door; no turning back now."

She takes a deep breath. "He is a quiet man, but he is very powerful. When he walks into a room, he doesn't need to say a word; his presence demands respect and he gets it."

"Max said Jackie has an older brother that owns a computer software firm. Are they close?"

"No, Dylan is much older than her, he lives in Japan."

"When was that last time you were at Jackie's parents' house?"

"I usually went home with Jackie during Christmas break. I wasn't able to go last year, but I was with them the year before. It gave me some sort of family for the holidays."

She unlatches her seatbelt and crawls into my lap. She begins kissing me with those soft lips, very gently.

"You know you should have your seatbelt on?"

"Yep, I should." She kisses me again.

"You know the flight attendant can see us?"

"Yep, I know." Another kiss.

"You know there are quite a few people on this flight that can see us?"

"Yep, I know that too."

She swipes her tongue over my lips, and I moan. "You know I could make you get back into your seat and buckle up?"

"Yep, I know, but you won't." She deepens the kiss again, swirling her tongue around slowly.

"How do you know I won't?"

"Because I can feel how much you need me," she whispers into my ear and gives me a little wiggle and let's out a moan.

I smile and unlatch my seatbelt. "Did I tell you that there is an office on board and a master suite?"

"No, but I think it's time for a tour, don't you?" she laughs.

"We have at least another six hours of flight time, I'm sure we could find lots to pass the time, sweetheart." I lift her up and carry her into the master suite.

"Wow, Jax, this is beautiful."

I lean in and gently kiss her. "Sweetheart, you're beautiful, and all mine." I need to be buried deep within her, blocking out the rest of the world.

"Let me take care of you, Jax," she pants. She always knows when I need her like this.

I rest my forehead on hers, and I kiss her so softly. "Sweetheart, I'm all yours."

Maxwell

I SHOULDN'T BE SURPRISED, but I am. Jax had the balls to have his mum stay next door to watch me. He's such a bastard. It doesn't matter, my mind is made up. As soon as I can, I will be moving to Scotland. I don't know how she did it, but Jackie broke through all of my walls. I didn't realize it until the night Vincent tried to take her. Everything came flooding back that night, the fear of devastating loss; real pain. Thanks to me, Jackie's in more danger now than before. She needs to stay at her father's compound, where she will be safe. I was hoping to be gone by the time Jax returned. Now with his mum here, I doubt that will happen.

It's a nice day outside so I think I might go for a walk around the park; clear my head. I put on my gear and head out towards the elevator only to see Mrs. Phillips sitting in a chair with her book.

"What are you doing, sitting out here?"

She looks up at me, "Maxwell, what do you think I'm doing?"

I grit me teeth, "Spying on me for Jax."

"Where do you think you're going?"

I'm trying to be calm here. "I'm going for a walk in the park."

She gets up. "Did the doctor say you could?"

I'm so busted. "The therapist started me out in the gym. I'm bored; I know my limits."

She shakes her head, "You'll do no such thing, get back inside, right now."

I open my mouth to speak and she yanks on my ear. "Do I have to tell you again?"

I know better than to test her limits. "Ma'am, do you want to have tea with me? Or are you just going to sit out here and spy on me for Jax?" As much as I want to be left alone, I love having her here. I would never tell her that . . . but I do.

"Maxwell, I would love some tea."

She heads to the kitchen, and starts puttering around. "Ma'am, you know I'm quite capable of making tea."

"Yes, dear, I know that. But this is what I do, so behave and let me do it." I sit and watch her work her way around the kitchen with such ease. I will really miss her, but I have to do what's best for Jax; he deserves his shot at happiness. She sets everything up and sits next to me. She always gives me *Jammie Dodgers* with my tea, just like my grams did. "Jax, said you want to go back to Scotland, can I ask why?"

What do I say? I don't want to hurt her. "I was waiting to see how long it was going to take you."

She glares at me. "I was giving you some space."

I start to laugh, and I can't stop. Bless her, she is just sitting there with a straight face, waiting. "I'm sorry, ma'am, sometimes you're just too funny."

She rolls her eyes, "Well, I'm glad I can be your source of amusement, however, you still haven't answered my question."

I take a breath. "Jax has a shot at a happy life with a wonderful girl. He has a baby on the way. Raven's only friend is Jackie and vice versa. The situation with Jackie makes it hard for Jax, and he doesn't need or deserve that. He deserves to have his slice of heaven. Besides, if I'm in the picture, it puts a bigger target on Jackie."

She takes my hand and squeezes it. "What about you, Maxwell, what do you deserve?"

I stir my tea that's now cold. "That ship sailed a long time ago." We sit in silence for a while, sipping our tea. "Ma'am, can I ask you a question?"

She nods, "Of course, what is troubling you?"

I need to know this, but I don't want to upset her. "How did you know my grams?"

Her lip begins to tremble. "I knew it was just a matter of time before this story would have to come out."

A tear rolls down her cheek. *Oh bloody hell, what did I do?* "Please don't cry. I'm sorry. You don't have to say another word."

She shakes her head, "Unfortunately, it's not that easy. This story should have been told a long time ago, but I made a promise to your grams so I kept a lid on it. I knew who you were from a very young age. I was dating a young man, and I thought it was true love. I went against my parents' wishes and dated him. I fell in love; foolishness comes with youth. I found myself unmarried and pregnant. My father pushed for him to marry me right away, which he did. He said he was in sales and had to travel a lot. I was very young and very naïve, so I believed him. Things were good for a bit. He always made it home for the weekends to spend time with Jax. Then along came Isabella, and she was such a handful. After that, my husband came home less and less, until finally, he just never came back at all. I decided I would search for him, and what I found was his other family; you and your mum."

She stops talking, and watches me as if waiting for my reaction. Talk about dropping a bomb—Jax, Bella, and I are siblings!

"Your mum knew. He came home and told her everything, right before he left her, too. It wasn't too long after that, she overdosed. In the meantime, I decided to pack up my family and move to the States. When I found out about your mum's passing, I decided I wanted to take you with us. I wanted to raise the three of you together as a family. I went to speak to your grams; she was such a kind woman, Maxwell. Your grams was very gracious, but she wanted you with her. I couldn't blame her, you were all she had left. She promised me that she would keep me updated on everything in your life, and I kept her updated on Jaxson and Isabella's. When you married Samantha and had Elliot, she was so proud of you. Then when everything happened, she contacted me, thinking maybe I could bring you back to the States to live with us. She talked about maybe telling you the truth, but then you joined the Special Forces."

I take the rattling teacup from her hands. "Take as much time as you need, ma'am."

"Your grams wanted you to get to know Jaxson and Isabella. I think she wanted to know you had some sort of family before she died. You being in that bar on that night was not an accident, your grams and I arranged it. We couldn't think of any other way. And I knew how wild Jax would get after he closed a deal. We knew you would look after him."

I can't believe what I'm hearing; these two kind little old ladies totally pulled the wool over our eyes. "Does Jax know any of this?"

She shakes her head, "No. I would appreciate it if you let me tell him. He deserves the truth, and he deserves to hear it from me."

I stare into space, my mind racing, until I finally find my voice. "Of course, but why did you wait so long to tell me?"

"Shame." She looks down.

I don't know if I want to know this next answer, but I have to ask the question. "Of me?"

Her eyes grow wide. "Never, Maxwell! Oh, lad, never of you! Only of me."

"Why?"

I see her lip begin to quiver as she fights to hold back the tears. "No one likes to admit they were made a fool of. I fell in love with a man who was already married. I didn't know it, and I married him. My marriage was a sham, and my children would have to bare the shame of illegitimacy. It's my shame to bare—not theirs. I know in today's world it's not a big deal, but I'm from a different generation. Your grams never wanted him to know where you were, or anything about your life. I don't know where he is, or if he is even still alive. I really don't care. I made a promise to your grams that I would keep this secret as long as you needed me to. I tried so many times to convince her to tell you. Not just for you, but for Jax and Isabella. Your grams left a letter for you and told me that I would know when to give it to you. I have never read the letter. It's in a safety deposit box. When you're ready, I will give it to you."

We sit in silence, both of us not knowing what to say or do.

"Maybe tomorrow we can take a ride to the bank, ma'am, I would like to read that letter."

"Of course, and when Jax gets back, I will sit him and Isabella down and tell them the whole story."

I silently nod, not really knowing what else to say.

"Maxwell, I can only hope in time you will forgive me. I hope that by telling you this story, you will understand why you can't leave. Whether you like it or not, we are all family. "I'll leave you alone now."

I stay lost in my silence, soaking in all of this information, not realizing she's left until I hear a door shut.

Chapter Five

Jaxson

MY BEAUTIFUL GIRL IS fast asleep. It gives me a chance to do some research on Jackie's father. Wow, she wasn't kidding. This man is very influential. He holds a lot of power within the Japanese and Swiss governments. He's also very well insulated with security, which is a good thing. This is going to be a very emotional trip. I wish Max was here with me. I better check in with mum to see what's going on there.

"Hey, Mum, how's Max doing?"

"Well, he's not happy that I am sitting guard by the elevator, if that's what you mean."

I laugh at the thought. "Mum, of course I knew he would be mad, but how is he doing besides that?"

She sighs, "He's hurting, son, for many reasons. He needs us around him, now more than ever. You need to get through to Jackie and make her fight for him. I know she's hurt too, but she has no idea what this man has been through. It's his story to tell her, not yours, but she needs to be here."

"I get it, Mum, keep my mouth shut, but get her to come back with us. Just wish things would be easy for a change."

She laughs, "If it were easy, son, then it would not be worth fighting for. We will get to the other side of this, like everything else."

"Okay, I need to wake Raven up; we're getting ready to land. I will talk to you later, love you."

"I love you too, be careful."

I hang up and stare out at nothing, "When did life get so complicated?"

"Jax, your life got complicated the day you met me."

I jump up, "I didn't realize I said that out loud."

She strokes my face. "It's the truth, Jax. I understand your frustration and fear of the unknown. I feel it too, but all we can do is hang tough and lean on each other. Our love will get us through this, I honestly believe that.

I open my arms and she jumps into them, I'm holding her so tightly, that I'm afraid she won't be able to breath. "Raven, I need to speak to you about Max and Jackie."

She takes a deep breath, "Okay."

"I know why Max pushed Jackie away, but I can't tell you. It's Max's story. He needs Jackie, though, I know he does. But he needs to be the one to tell her why he pushed her away. I just don't know how to make it happen without revealing the things that should be told by him."

"Jax, I knew when you put your mom on as a watch dog that it was to make sure that Max didn't pull a *runner*. I also know that you are very worried and upset by all of this. I understand you can't tell me; I would never ask you to betray a confidence. Let me ask you this, with all your heart, do you believe Max and Jackie are better together or apart?"

I stroke my fingers up and down her back. The constant touch is comforting. "Together."

"Why?"

"I don't even have to think twice about it, Raven. Jackie got through walls in a matter of months, that I couldn't in eight years. She loves him for him, and not for what he could give her. She has brought my best friend back to life. His heart has been shut off since the very first day I met him, but with her, I have seen him come alive. I have seen him smile like he meant it, not because he had to. When I went to see him yesterday, it was the old Max, again—stone cold with dead eyes. It's not that I don't want that Max, I just want Max to be happy. Does that make sense?"

She kisses me, trying to sooth me. "Yes, baby, it does. I don't need to know what was said between you and Max. I will work on, Jackie. There is no way I'm going to let her give up without the fight of a lifetime. It's just not in me to see her give up, and I know it's not in her."

I love this girl with all my soul. "Okay, this is just another reason why I love you. We need to get back to our seats, we should be landing soon. We are going to check into our hotel first, and then I will check on your mum to see if she is up to visitors today."

"Thank you, Jax." She gives me another soft kiss.

"Sweetheart, you never have to thank me for letting me love and take care of you. It's my life's mission."

Maxwell

I'M STUNNED BY THE story that An has told me. Not only that she knew my grams, but the fact that Jax and Bella are my siblings. I knew that I probably had other siblings out there, but never in my wildest dreams did I think it would be Jax and Bella. We are tied together for life. Not just by friendship, but by blood. How could I leave now? When the one thing I always wanted is right before me—family. After I had Elliot, I thought about looking for my father and possibly, any other siblings. But when he and Samantha were murdered, I died that day, too, so why bother. I can't believe my grams kept this a secret from me. An should be here any minute to go to the bank with me. I don't know how I can look at her and not feel betrayed; she knew all this time.

SHE MEETS ME BY the elevator and we silently head to the car. The ride to the bank is long and quite. Both of us, staring out the window. I finally have to ask her, "Why?"

"Why, what, Maxwell?"

I don't want to get mad, but I don't understand. "Why keep this secret for so long?"

She turns her gaze towards me. "Perhaps you will understand more after you read the letter."

I snap back at her, "Do you really think being cryptic with me now is the way to go?"

"What I think is neither here nor there, it is what your grams wanted. I don't know what's in the letter, all I know is, I made a promise to your grams. In the end, Maxwell, the only thing we have, of any value, is our word. If I didn't keep my promise, then I would be no better than your father. You need to try and understand, I had to respect your grams wishes. I had to do what she felt was best for you, not me. She never wanted you to be tainted by the actions of your father."

We go into the bank and An retrieves the letter. She hands it to me, and then starts to step outside the room, but I stop her. "I would rather we went back home before I read this." She nods and we leave.

The ride is silent for both of us, and that's okay. Right now, I don't think I could handle much more. We step out of the elevator and she takes my hand. "Maxwell, I will be next door if you decide you would like to talk."

All I can do is nod and head into my place. I sit by the fire for a long time with a glass of scotch and the letter, trying to get the nerve up to read it. After I finish my drink, I open envelope:

My Dearest Maxwell,

If you are reading this, then An must have told you everything. You are probably wondering why I never told you about your family. I wanted to, especially, right after Samantha and Elliot were murdered, but you were in such a bad way that I thought one more betrayal would put you over the edge.

Your mum was a dreamer. She was beautiful and naïve, believing in her husband. James Phillips was a very good-looking charmer. Right before An came to look for her husband, James confessed everything to your mum. He told her all about his other family. Your mum's heart was broken, and she felt like such a fool. An is a very strong women who was able to pick up the pieces; your mum was not. She was young, so she brought you to me to take care of. She knew that I would love you with all of my heart. I blame myself for not realizing right then, why she brought you to me. She went home that day and killed herself. I tried to get in touch with your father, but I could not find him. It was at that point, I decided to change your name to Fleming, and erase all presence of Phillips from our lives. You need to understand, that man took away my only child, so I decided I would never let him near you, again. If he wanted to, he could have easily found us, but he never did. Right there, that should tell you the type of man he was. He never contacted An, either, which was probably for the best.

Don't blame An for your mum's death. I know she blames herself, but she came, in good faith, looking for a man that she knew as her husband. Unfortunately she was not his only wife. Your mum was not strong enough, and the betrayal is what killed her.

A few months passed, and An came to me offering to raise you with her children as one of her own. An is a tough woman, and even fiercer when it comes to her children. I knew that she would love you like her own; that was never a question. I really considered it, however, I needed you close to me. As selfish as that may sound, I just couldn't do it. The pain was too raw for me. I couldn't suffer another loss. You blossomed into such a wonderful man—a man I was so proud of. You met your beautiful Samantha, and then you gave me the greatest gift of all—my great grandson, Elliot. I thought life had come full circle. I wanted for nothing, until the world came crashing in around us. After that horrible day, I felt like I lost my child all over again. I realized that I needed to put my selfishness aside. I was ready to have An come, and we would tell you everything, but then, you joined the Special Forces. I really thought this would help you, until I realized you were taking ridiculous chances with your life!

Once again, I called An and we came up with a plan. She was worried about Jaxson, seems he was taking all kinds of risks when it came to business and women. An wanted him reeled in, so we set up a chance meeting that night. I knew you would never stand by and let someone be taken advantage of.

Please don't be mad at An, she was following my request to keep this secret. I told her she would know when to tell you the truth. Maybe I was wrong to keep this from you, but I didn't want you to blame Jax and Isabella for your mum's death. They're just as much the victim, in all of this, as you are. I hope that you will one day find love again. You have so much to offer someone, if you would just open your heart and get out of your own head. Life is too short, Maxwell, as you well know, so if you find that special someone, grab onto her and love her with all your might.

I love you so much, and I found peace in knowing that you will never be alone, again. I hope you can find that peace, too.

Love you,

Grams

I stare at this letter, trying so hard to wrap my mind around all of this. I understand what my grams was doing and why, but it doesn't make it hurt any less. The man I am today wouldn't blame anyone for my mum's death, but in my youth, I really couldn't say. I know I was bitter for a long time, that was until Samantha and Elliott came into my life. Having my own family helped me find some peace and stability in life. When they were murdered, I felt my heart turn to stone. I existed . . . one day leading into the next. Nothing ever really mattered, except keeping everyone safe. Then Jackie blew into my world, and everything has been turned upside down.

As I head next door, I see An sitting in a chair by the elevator and I have to laugh.

"Are you really sitting there, trying to hold me hostage?"

She nods, "Well, Maxwell, I'm trying to make sure you won't pull a 'runner' as Jaxson calls it. I'm also trying to make sure you are not doing anything stupid before you're one-hundred percent healed."

I smile at her. "You must be uncomfortable, sitting in that hard chair. Why not come in and we will have some afternoon tea."

"So you don't hate me, Maxwell?" her voice shakes.

I throw my arms around her, surprising us both. "I could never hate someone who would move heaven and earth to protect their loved ones. Come inside and make me some tea, I think we need to talk."

She reaches up and yanks my ear! "Ouch, what was that for?"

She laughs, "Manors young man—*please*," she emphasizes.

As we walk inside, I look at her and realize she has always been there. She's been like a mum to me no matter what. I sit at the table and watch her putting together the tea and Jammie Dodgers. I realize I could never walk away from this, the thing I treasure most—family.

I have so many questions for her, but I need to take it slow. "I know you said you were going to tell Jax when he got back, but what about Bella? Have you decided when you are going to tell her?"

She takes a deep breath. "Well, Maxwell, you tell me what would make you feel the most comfortable? I can tell them together or separately, the choice is yours."

I smile trying to make her feel more at ease. "I have waited this long for a family, I can wait a little longer. Tell them together, so they have each other for support."

She hugs me, "It will be no big deal to them because they already consider you their brother. I think it was a bigger deal for you. I think that might be what your grams was worried about."

I know she thinks it's no big deal, but I'm still worried. "Ma'am, it will probably be no big deal to Jax, but I worry about Bella."

She laughs, "Don't worry about her, she will be happy to have someone that she thinks she can pit against Jax! Maxwell, why are you pushing Jackie away? I know you love her, and I know you're scared, but let me ask you this, do you think it is fair to her? She is paying the price for a lost love."

I feel my heart tighten in my chest. "I don't know what's right or wrong anymore. I don't know how she did it, but she broke through without even trying. She weaved herself into my soul. What if something was to happen to her because of me? Look at that night, when Vincent's people tried to get to her. That night, as I was racing to her flat, I saw Samantha and Elliot—dead—all over again. I love her enough to want her safe and happy. And if it means that I have to let her go, then I'm prepared to do that. This whole mess put a huge target on her back, and I don't think I can live with that. I need to let her go."

"What if she's not prepared to let you go, have you thought of that?"

I need to change the subject fast. "Ma'am, why did you never get married again, have you thought about that?"

She glares at me. "Maxwell, I'm a very strong person, and you will not push me away, so if that's what you're trying to do, you should just forget it. Now to answer your question, I made my children my life. I experienced love, or at least what I thought was love. I never wanted to put myself in a position to get hurt or fail again. You know the saying, 'hind sight is always twenty-twenty'? Well looking back, I could have found a man, and have gotten married, if I really wanted to. Life would have been easier for me, but I wanted more."

I stare at her, totally confused. "What did you want, ma'am, that you don't have now?"

"A man who would love and respect me for who I am now, and the choices that I have made. I want to experience true love. I've never closed myself off from that possibility, can you say the same thing?"

I stare into my tea, saying nothing.

"Maxwell, I'm going to go back next door, but before I leave, I would like to ask you something."

I'm thinking this is a first, both her and Jax just say whatever the hell they want, whenever they want.

"I know that you had a mum that loved you very much. I would never impose upon that, but I have loved you like I love Jaxson and Isabella for your whole life. I have watched you grow into the man that you are today. A man I respect, a man I'm so very proud of. Your grams and I exchanged letters and pictures throughout your lives. I only hope one day, you will feel comfortable enough to call me something other than, ma'am."

With that, she leans in, kisses my forehead, gets up, and leaves. I'm on overload today. I just don't know how much more I can take. I love Jackie but what do I do about it? Can I really have someone in my life that won't leave or be cruelly taken away from me? Her safety is priority number one for me, and right now, I'm not one-hundred percent. It's time I make some phone calls, starting with Tony.

Jaxson

WE LAND AND THEN get settled into our hotel. I know Raven is scared and I know, if it were me, I would be too, but there is nothing I can do to make this any easier.

"Raven, I spoke with the doctors. They said Gabriella is having a good day, so we will be going after lunch. It's okay to be scared and nervous, but

I will be there with you every step of the way—no matter what. You need to prepare yourself that she might not even know who you are."

I see her eyes fill with tears. "Jax, what if she hates me? What if she sees me and is reminded of all the pain and loss in her life?"

I pull her close to me. "I don't think that will happen, but however she reacts, we will deal with it together. No matter what."

"Jax, did I tell you today that I love you?" She kisses me softly.

Those words make me smile, "Yes, but feel free to tell me as much as you want."

I lift her into my arms and nibble on her ear. I start to work my way down her neck when my watch alarm goes off. Oh fuck, she's going to pitch a fit now. As I stop, she looks at me.

"Jax, don't you dare, not now!"

I know she is going to flip out. "Sorry, sweetheart, you need to eat. Besides, the baby is up now."

"What makes you think the baby is not sleeping, Jax?"

"Well, if it's time to eat, the baby can't possibly be sleeping." I smirk.

She opens her mouth to speak, but nothing comes out. She closes it shakes her head. "Okay, Jax, what's for lunch?"

I lean my forehead against hers, "Do you see how much easier life is when you're agreeable?"

She rolls her eyes. "Lunch, Jax—now, because I'm not even going to dignify that with an answer."

"I'll order room service, what would you like?"

"The fruit and cheese platter with a cup of chai tea, please. I'm going to shower."

"I'll order, and then come in to wash your back."

"Ha, is that what we're calling it now?"

As I watch her arse sway, I know I'll be doing a lot more than washing her back.

I hurry up and order the food, then race to the shower, ripping my clothes off along the way. I open the door, and the sight before me brings me to my knees. *Oh sweet Jesus,* and all that is holy! She's standing in the shower with the water cascading down her back. She has one leg on the shower bench as she squats down. Her hands are clasped behind her back, pushing those beautiful breasts out. I'm frozen in place, staring at her.

"Um, sweetheart what are you doing?"

"Stretching after the long flight, Jax."

Stretching? She's not stretching—she's fucking trying to kill me!

Now she switches legs and I'm still frozen in place, mesmerized by her beauty.

"I thought you were going to wash my back for me?"

I snap out of my trance and race into the shower. I drop to my knees and worship that beautiful arse, kissing and nipping my way between her legs. Front to back and I'm not letting up. I'm working my fingers and my tongue; completely filling her. She's on the edge ready to fall, and watching her is a surreal experience.

"Jax, I'm there, please. I need you deep inside me now."

I get up and grab her hips from behind, slamming my cock deep inside of her. That's all it takes to tip her over the edge. She's shaking and screaming my name, over and over again. I pull out and turn her around, "My turn, sweetheart."

She knows what I want, and I can tell she wants it too. She kisses each one of my nipples before, dropping to her knees. She takes hold of my engorged cock and kisses the tip. She looks up at me before swirling her tongue around the head of my cock. I know she can taste herself on me and I can't begin to describe what that knowledge does to me. She works her way down very slowly, pumping me and taking me so deep.

"Deeper, please . . . *oh, God* . . . sweetheart."

My hips start to move, meeting her thrust for thrust. She squeezes the base of my cock to hold off my orgasm, while working my sac with just the right firmness. As she eases up on my cock, it swells, ready to explode.— She nips the head. I scream her name as I erupt fiercely. In one quick swoop, I reach down and pull her up.

"Turn around and put your foot up on the seat again now!" I bark then slam into her as soon as she does. I groan and nibble at her ear.

"Jax, how?"

"Fuck if I know, sweetheart, it's you, only you. I'm going to move now, are you ready, 'cause I need it hard."

"I'm there, Jax."

I grasp her hips for leverage and pound into her. I lose all control; I can't get enough. I want to be deeper, harder, further than ever before. "Fuck, Raven!"

We both explode. I pump into her a few more times, then collapse on her back for a moment before sliding out of her. I slowly turn to sit on the shower bench, bringing her with me to cradle her in my lap.

"Are you okay, sweetheart?"

"I can't move. Can we just sit here and nap for a bit?"

"Don't worry, I will wash us as soon as I find my legs."

I try to get up, but she's not helping at all. I look down and she's out cold. I need to get us up off the bench, and put her to bed. I get up without dropping her and rinse her off the best I can. I wrap her in towels, drying her off. I can't believe she's sleeping through all of this. I get us into the bed and tuck her into my side. When I get to watch her sleep, I realize how lucky I am. Now, I just have to figure out a way to convince her to marry me.

Chapter Six

Raven

WE HEAD INSIDE THE clinic in silence. My grip on Jax's hand is so tight. I'm scared to finally face my mother, especially since I read her journal. I know all that she went through, and the torment of losing the love of her life and a child. What she must have went through, being pregnant with the spawn of Satan. Knowing that I'm carrying a baby that was made from love, and feeling it growing inside me everyday, reminds me of that gift of love. My mother was reminded of horrific violence everyday that she carried Duke.

After signing all the necessary papers, the nurse leads us to a solarium where I see a beautiful woman with a sketchpad lost in her work. I realize that I'm shaking, and squeezing Jax's hand so hard I think I cut off the circulation. My God, she's beautiful. More beautiful than I remembered, with her: porcelain skin, crystal blue eyes, and golden blonde hair.

"It's okay, sweetheart, just be your beautiful kind self and take it slow."

Mom is busy sketching, and doesn't see Jax pull up two chairs. As we sit down, Jax introduces us, but she doesn't look up, she keeps sketching. I don't know what I was expecting, Max said she hasn't spoken since she was brought here. I guess I was hoping for some recognition; any sign of the mother I remember. I'm ready to bolt and Jax knows it; he puts his arm around me, slowly rubbing circles on my shoulder. I lean in to see what she is sketching and I freeze—it's me!

I whisper, "Jax, look at the sketch."

He leans in, "Hello, Gabriella, my name is, Jax. Would you mind if I looked at your sketches?"

She smiles and hands him the pad. As he begins to flip through the pages, she closes her eyes. I look over as Jax turns the pages, and all of the pictures are of me when she last saw me. I realize this must be her way of remembering me.

Mom looks down at her lap, not saying anything. I have no clue what to do for her. I feel so inadequate, but Jax is a take action type of guy. He reaches in and runs his hand down the side of her face.

"Gabriella, you are safe. Can you look at me?" he asks.

Her eyes shoot up to his, searching them. "Ma'am, I'm going to show you someone, and I need you to look into her eyes. Can you do that for me?"

She nods yes, and Jax lifts her head towards me.

"Gabriella, look into her eyes, do you know who she is?"

My eyes lock onto hers, and I see the moment when she realizes who I am. Her eyes become wide and she starts to shake. *"Cara?" she whispers through her tears.*

I gasp, "Yes, Mom, it's me, your Cara." I can't hold back my tears any longer.

She reaches her hand up to my face; they are so small and delicate. She brushes her fingertips along my cheek, "You're so beautiful. You have my mother's eyes," she whispers.

I'm in shock. "Jax, get the doctor—she's speaking!"

She smiles, "Your father, he loved you so much. You have his hair, so dark and silky, like that of a raven."

The doctors come running, but stop when they reach us, probably to avoid scaring her.

"Cara, where have you been? I've waited so long for you."

I'm trying to keep it together. I don't want to overwhelm her. "Mom, I only just found out that you're alive."

Her eyes grow wide. "But where is Joseph? He knew I was here."

I'm at a loss, I don't know how much she could handle in her fragile state.

Jax takes her hand. "Gabriella, let's start out slow for today. I promise you, we will answer all of your questions, but right now, the doctors want to talk to you. Is that okay?"

She squeezes Jax's hand, "Who are you?"

He gifts her with his beautiful smile and twinkling eyes. "My name is Jax, and I am the man who is madly in love with your beautiful daughter."

She reaches her hand to his face, and runs it down his cheek. "You're such a beautiful man, and I can see so much love in your eyes."

The doctors step up, and begin to ask her questions, but she wants nothing to do with them. "I assure you, I'm fine. I would like to talk to my daughter."

"Mom, this is such a shock, can we take it slow?"

She sighs, "I have been here for twenty years, how much slower do you want me to go?"

I fight not to cry. "I just don't want to lose you again. I need my mother in my life."

"You never lost me, Cara. I've been waiting here for twenty years to see you again. Where is Joseph? He promised someday it would be safe to bring you back to me." She reaches up and wipes away my tears. "Shh, Cara, no more tears. I will go slowly for you. But please, tell me one thing—tell me you're happy . . . that it was all worth it?"

I don't want her to know how much hurt and pain I've been through. I don't want her to have a setback. "I'm happy, Mom, very happy."

She looks back and forth between Jax and me. "I have so many questions for you, but first, where is Joseph?"

Just then, the nurse comes with a tray of food. I look at Jax and by the look of disgust on his face, I know what's coming. I take a deep breath and wait. He gets up and excuses himself. Okay, not what I was expecting. I figured one look at what was on that tray and he would flip out.

"Mom, are they taking good care of you here?"

She nods, "It's comfortable, but it's not home. Where is Joseph? He hasn't come back in a very long time."

Interesting. "Did he visit you often?"

She shakes her head, "He would usually come once a month. Those visits were becoming less and less."

I need information, but I also know not to push her. I need to keep it simple.

"What did he tell you, when he would visit?"

She has a faraway look on her face. "He would just sit here. Sometimes he would read, and other times, he would talk about a girl he called Raven."

I feel light-headed, and the faces around me are starting to spin. I hear yelling, and I realize it's my mom yelling for Jax, and calling out to me, right before everything goes black.

As I slowly open my eyes, I'm hit with those bluest of blues, I have come to love so much. I whisper, "Jax."

I see the fear in his eyes. "Hey, sweetheart, you're back. Don't scare me like that again, okay?"

I nod. "What happened?"

He growls, "You passed out."

I try to jump up, "The baby!"

He holds me tightly. "The baby is fine, but you need to rest. I guess now is a good time to tell your mum that we're having a baby."

My mom is kneeling next to me, "Is this why you came looking for me?"

Before I can answer, Jax takes her hand. "No, ma'am, we only just found out that you're alive. Once Cara knew, there was nothing that would stop her from getting to you. There is a lot that you don't know, but because of your health, we have chosen to take it one day at a time. I spoke with your doctors, and as soon as our business is finished here, we will be taking you back to the States with us. In the meantime, I need to feed our girl, and she needs some rest. If it's okay with you, I have ordered food to be brought here so we can all eat together. After, I will take Cara back to the hotel for some rest."

She smiles at Jax, "You're a take charge kind of man, aren't you?"

I can't help but giggle. "Oh, Mom, you don't even know the half of it!"

"SO, CARA, WHEN IS your baby due?"

I smile, my hands instantly go to my tummy. "Early August."

"Do you know what you're having?"

I shake my head, "No, I don't want to know, I just want a healthy baby."

She takes my hand and squeezes it tightly. "Did Joseph die?"

I don't know what to say, but I realize it's the truth that she needs right now more than anything else. "Yes, he died of pancreatic cancer."

She drops my hand and gets up. "I think I've had enough for today, and you need to rest. Will you come back tomorrow?"

I get up and hug her. "Yes mom, I will be here everyday until we move you."

"Thank you, Cara, and thank you, Jax, for all that you have done for my daughter."

Jax gets up and pulls Gabriella into his arms. "Ma'am, it's me that should be thanking you for giving me the most beautiful girl in the world."

She kisses us both. "Goodnight, I will see you tomorrow." And with that, she leaves.

As I watch her walk away, I think about the amount of information she *doesn't* know, and I'm not sure how much she can take.

"Jax, maybe I shouldn't have told her about Joseph?"

He strokes my arm, knowing that I need the constant connection. "Honestly, I think she needs the truth, right now. She is not as frail as you think. Everyone deals with grief differently. She mourned your dad, and maybe after the adoption, she grieved for you the same way. We need to take things slow with her. Giving her small amounts of information at a time. Remember, she has twenty years to catch up on, and we don't know what Joseph told her. Apparently, he spoke to her about you as Raven, but it seems that she didn't know that is your adoptive name."

I grab onto Jax. "I just want to scream, but what good will it do?"

He pulls me closer, "Getting upset is not good for you or our baby. Lets head back to the hotel, so you can get some rest."

I kiss him, so blessed to have him with me throughout all the madness. "Jax, right now, I'm so grateful that I don't have to think about anything. Have I told you today that I love you?"

He gives me that smile, "Yes, but you can never tell me too much."

Jaxson

WE GET BACK TO the hotel and Raven is so tired, I just want to carry her. She lets me. I put her on the bed and start to undress her.

"Sweetheart, I really need to get you something to sleep in other than my dress shirts." Her lip begins to quiver, and her tears are falling. "Hey, why the tears?"

"Jax, I love sleeping in your shirts. It's what saved me when I was kidnapped. I was able to smell you all around me. I didn't feel so lost and alone."

My heart aches for all she went through. "Well, that settles it, you can sleep in my shirts, and I will make sure I put everyone of them on before you do." I reach in and kiss her soft lips. "Do you want me to snuggle with you while you fall asleep?"

"Yes please, when I fall asleep within your arms, I feel safe."

"You don't have to explain, sweetheart. I love that you need me for the simple things." I open my arms for her and she crawls up into my lap. Before I know it, she is out cold. I could watch her sleep like this for the rest of my life. She is so beautiful. I wish I could shelter her from everything that would hurt her, but I know it's not realistic. Tomorrow is going to be another hard day for her. I haven't told her about Max, and what he is planning. I know if I do, she will push Jackie to come back and stop Max. I can't let Max leave. I know it's selfish but I never claimed to be a saint. Who am I kidding? I'm a self-proclaimed bastard when it comes to keeping my family together and safe.

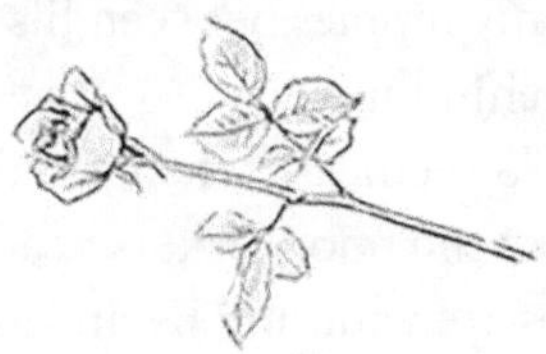

MORNING COMES AND RAVEN is still snuggled up next to me, awake and kissing my chest lightly. "Good morning, my beautiful girl."

Hmm, "Good morning, my beautiful man. Jax, I need you."

My eyes open wide. "Well, you don't have to tell me twice. Are you ready for me?"

"Oh, I'm always ready for you. I only have to look into those beautiful eyes and my whole body tingles."

I try to flip her onto her back, but she stops me. "Oh no, mister, today, I'm driving the car."

Raven

HIS FACE LIGHTS UP as I kiss down his chest. I lick the V that I have come to love, and then right down the happy trail. His cock is so hard, yet silky smooth. I love that I can give him this. I slowly swirl my tongue around the head. He closes his eyes and tilts his head all the way back. When I look at him in this position, I can see him coming apart; it's breathtaking to watch. I want to freeze this picture in my head forever.

"Raven, baby, real deep and slow for me, *please,* sweetheart."

I give him what he wants. I take his cock really deep, and then slowly work my way up. When I reach the top, I stop and watch him—he's really trying to hold it together.

"Oh sweet Jesus and all that's holy, ride me, sweetheart, please. I need to be buried balls deep inside of you."

I love when he gets like this; it's just so erotic to see. I crawl up and slowly lower myself onto his beautiful cock, and when he is totally buried within me, I stop. "Look at me now, Jax. You are all mine and only mine, now and forever." I run my hands up my chest stopping at my nipples, playing with them just the way I know he likes to. When he reaches his hands up, I push them away. "Not yet, Jax, just watch." I slowly rock my hips back and forth, still playing with my nipples. I look down at him, relishing how beautiful he is. I go up and down again really slowly, using my core to clench his cock. He leans up and takes one of my nipples between his teeth and I'm coming and screaming. Jax is not far behind me.

He's breathing heavy. "Sweetheart, when you do that clench thing around my cock, I swear it feels like the poor fuckers head is going to explode."

I look at him, my eyes are wide and begin laughing.

"What are you laughing at?"

I'm really trying to control my laughing. "Oh, Jax, I can't wait to see how you will explain the birds and the bees to your son one day."

The look of utter fear on his face is not lost on me. "Now, it's my turn to have some fun, sweetheart."

He flips me over and begins kissing my neck really slow, when all of a sudden, his watch beeps. Before he can say anything I jump in first, "Oh no you don't, mister, you're not stopping now."

He stops kissing me, "Raven, you have to eat."

I reach over, pick up the watch, and fling it across the room! "That's what I think about that fucking alarm, and before you say anything about my mouth, the baby is sleeping now, so quit teasing me. I want you and I want you now!"

His eyes grow wide and his chin hangs down. "Wow, I kind of like this side of you, but did you have to throw my twenty-thousand dollar Rolex across the room?"

Tsk. "Well, who in their right mind would pay that much for a watch?"

"Oh, my beautiful girl, right now, I'm going to feed you my cock and then later, I'll feed you some food."

Chapter Seven

Maxwell

I NEED TO GET out of this house, before I go crazy. I think it's time for a trip to the office for a few hours. I know I'm not up to working a full day, but the silence is killing me. I open the door and An is sitting by the elevator again.

"Ma'am, are you going to sit there all day, everyday until Jax gets back?"

She looks up from her reading. "Maxwell, what do you think?"

I need to stand my ground here. "I'm going into work for a couple of hours." *She's not budging.*

"Maxwell, again what do you think?"

I turn to the guard and notice my regular guard is gone, and Mick is here. "Mick, I'm going into work for a couple of hours, you can stay here with Mrs. Phillips."

"Sorry, sir, no can do."

So help me, I swear I'm going to kick Jax's arse! "What do you mean, *no can do?* You work for me. I want to go, so either we go or I fire your arse!"

He's shaking his head, "Sorry, sir, Mr. Phillips said you would pull that card. He said I work for him now, not you."

"What else did Jax say?" I yell. I know he's just doing his job.

He shuffles his feet and clears his throat. "Well Mr. Jax said that Mrs. Phillips is supposed to stay stuck to you like glue, and if you give me any trouble, I'm supposed to shoot you in the arse. His words, sir, not mine."

"You wouldn't shoot me!"

An stops reading and looks at the two of us. "Maxwell, if I tell him to, he will, because he has the good sense to be afraid of my wrath, something you're clearly lacking right now. I suggest you get back inside. Breakfast will be here any minute, and then you have therapy. I have the schedule, and you will do as you're told."

I shake my head and go back inside. The scary part of all of this, is Mick would probably shoot me in the arse, and An would let him!

I head inside, take a few calming breathes and call Jax. I need to find out what the hell he was thinking.

"Hey, Max, how are you feeling?"

I take a deep breath, "Jax, you really are a crazy fucking arse! What the bloody hell, you told Mick to shoot me in the arse?! You have your mum glued to me. Do you know that she put a chair by the elevator and just sits there? No matter what fucking bloody time I go out there, she's still sitting in that fucking chair! She has a schedule, a fucking bloody schedule!" The phone is silent and I look to see if the call was dropped.

"Max, you need to calm down. This can't be good for your recovery. Does she really have a schedule?"

He's got the nerve to be laughing. *What the fuck?* "Jax, if you don't stop laughing, so help me . . ."

"Calm down, where do you want to go?"

I'm a fucking prisoner. I can't believe I'm asking for permission to leave my home! "I was going to head into the office for a couple of hours."

"Why? You know you're recuperating, so what business do you have there?"

"I just want to get out of here for a couple of hours and check on things. I need a change of scenery or I'm going to lose it, mate!"

"Tony, is doing just fine, and there is nothing that you need to check on." Jax says calmly like he's trying to talk a jumper off a roof.

I grit my teeth and begin pacing. *Fuck!* "You're not letting me out of here, are you?"

"No, but I do have to talk to you about some stuff, so get comfortable. We went to see Gabriella yesterday."

I stop pacing and sit by the window. I need to keep it together for Jax; he's carrying my load right now.

"How is Raven?"

He takes a deep breath. "Well, I really wish you were here to see this. We found her mum sitting in the solarium, sketching. When we sat down with her, we realized she was sketching pictures of Raven, from when she last saw her," he starts to tell me about their visit. I listen for the next several minutes and get ready to interrupt him when he starts telling me the plans of bringing her back to New York.

"Wow, this has to be so overwhelming for Raven and Gabriella. I trust your opinion, Jax. I think we need to move her, but do a total name change and heavy guards on her at all times. Also, have the plane swept by your guards, not just the standard sweep. Do you think she is physically up for the move?"

"I do, and having Raven with her helps. She is opening up with Raven, speaking more and more. We had to tell her that Joseph died. She kept asking why he hadn't come back. Apparently, he would go visit her and talk about Raven, but never told her who she was."

"How did she take the news? Do you think it was too soon to tell her?"

"I don't think it was too soon, but it's hard to say. I'm clearly not a doctor, but I think, right now, its honesty that's needed the most. I don't think she's as fragile as we first thought, but I could be wrong."

I can hear it in his voice that something is off. "Okay, Jax, what else is going on over there?"

"Why?" he stammers.

I laugh, "I know you better than you know yourself, and I know you have something on your mind, so have at it. It's not like I have anything to do, that's for sure."

"Max, you know I really can't stand it when you're right. Okay, so here's the thing, I want to get married."

This is nothing new. "I know that already, Jax, what the bloody hell is your problem, mate?"

"I don't know how to go about this without being like a bulldozer. So help me, Max, if you don't stop laughing at me I will tell Mick to shoot you!"

"I'm sorry, Jax, it's just very funny that *big bad Jax,* who is always ten steps ahead of everyone else, is at a loss as to how to ask his girl to marry his sorry arse." *I can picture him pulling his hair out!*

"Come on, mate, how do I do this without being my usual bulldozer self?"

I can't believe I have to give him step-by-step instructions. "Well, first, you need to get a ring."

"Done. Max, I'm telling you, I've wanted to marry her from the first day I met her."

"Jax, dare I ask when you got the ring?" *I know this man, and odds tell me he got the ring the first day he met her.*

"No, let's just skip that part. What should I do next? I don't want her to feel like I'm pushing or dictating how she should live her life."

For such a smart man, he can be so clueless. I need to try and make him understand. "Jax, you are in essence asking her to change her life. Granted—she is pregnant, so her life will never be her own again, but you need to make her realize that you want to marry her because of her and not because of an obligation to your child."

"I got that, Max, but how do I ask her?"

I have to laugh, "Sometimes you can be such an arsehole. Just tell her how you feel without demanding she see things your way. Tell her what you see in a future with the two of you, together as a team for life."

Okay, I got it. I'm scared I'm going to fuck this up, and if you tell another living soul, I will shoot you myself!" he threatens. I reply with a chuckle. As funny and neurotic as he's being, I can't help but feel excited for him. It's good to see my friend . . . my brother so happy. "Max, later today I'm meeting Gerhard. I know you ran a check on him, is there anything I should be aware of?" Jax pulls me back from my thoughts.

I get up, knowing I need to quickly end this call. "Nothing that you don't already know. Jax, I have to go, your mum is back with breakfast." I don't give him a chance to ask anything else; I don't want to hear her name.

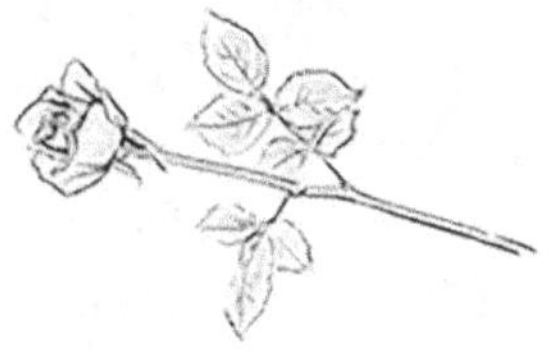

I DECIDE TO CALL Tony for an update. "Tony, I need you to bring me up to speed." This is what I do best; taking care of others.

"Max, what do you want first?'

"Start with Vincent and work from there." I hear the clicking of the keyboard, and I know that Tony is in his element.

"His condition hasn't changed, no better no worse. Apparently, Vincent's sister, Annabelle, went to visit him and Duke, however, they wouldn't let her see either of them. I was able to compare the picture from the park with a current one on the surveillance camera at the jail, it was a match."

"Did you tell Jax that Annabelle was the woman in the park?"

"No. I never had a chance, I was waiting on confirmation. When it finally came through, Jax and Raven were already on their way to Switzerland. I just got the confirmation and I sent it to the guards."

Hmm, "Is that all Jax said?"

He pauses for a few moments. "Look, Max, I don't want to get in the middle of anything."

What the fuck is he hiding? "Just fucking tell me what he said, Tony!"

"I'm not to let you leave—no matter what. Max, don't make me have Mick shoot you, okay?"

I could just picture Jax, ordering him to have Mick shoot me. "No, Tony. I might be stubborn, but Jax is the one that's crazy here, not me. Besides, there is a lot Jax and I need to go over, so don't worry, you're off the hook." I hear him let out a deep breath and I can't help but laugh.

"Goodnight, Tony, I'll probably come by tomorrow, if An lets me leave the house."

$\mathcal{J}axson$

RAVEN IS STILL SLEEPING. I'm worried if I can pull this off. Talking to Max helped; it always helps. I don't know why this man thinks he needs to get out of my life. My mum said he is lost and in a dark place. I just don't know how to help him. I do know that I need to be one-hundred percent honest with Raven and that means, I need to tell her everything.

"Hey, my beautiful girl, how are you feeling today?"

She looks into my eyes, "I'm good, Jax, but you seem troubled, what's the problem?"

She always knows. "I spoke to Max this morning."

She nods, "I won't press you for answers, just know I'm here for you, always."

I stare into her eyes and smile. "I told him about the visit with your mum. He agrees we should move her. I spoke with Tony, and there has been some noise from Annabelle, but he's not sure how much power she has, if any. He was trying to get an updated picture of her."

I see a look on her face that scares me. She instantly pales. "Jax, the day before we left, I was out running with Bo and my detail. There was a lady in the park, watching me and when she got up to come towards us, Bo freaked out. The guards got a picture of her and they were supposed to send it to Tony. Could that have been her in the park?" she asks. It's taking all of my control not to lose it.

"Why am I just hearing about this now?" I run my hands through my hair and pull at it. How could this have not been brought to my attention?

"Jax, I thought you were told. You know I wouldn't hold back something that important from you. Well, not intentionally." She sits up.

I get up, grab the phone, and put a call into Tony. "Hey, Jax, everything okay?"

I need to be calm—something I'm not good at. "No, why the fuck am I just finding out now about the woman in the park? Did you get a lead on her?" I seethe. I can feel the muscles in my arms and chest clenching, getting ready for a fight with an opponent that's not even in front of me. Raven's hands slide up my back and softly massage me, trying to calm me down.

"Jax, the picture was grainy and she had on large sunglasses. It could have been her, but we weren't sure. After she tried to get in to see Duke and Vincent, we got a better picture and compared them. I just informed Max, confirming that it was, indeed, Annabelle. I sent all this information to Raven's detail. They were supposed to give it to you. From what you're telling me, they didn't."

I take a deep breath. "Thanks." and I slam the phone down.

"Raven, please stay here and keep Bo with you. I need to talk to your detail."

I kiss her softly, I don't want to scare her, but I think it's too late for that. I step into the lounge and my eyes dart back and forth between Raven's guards. "Who took the information from Tony about the woman in the park?" They silently stare at each other until Daniel finally turns to me, "I did, sir, is there a problem?"

I mentally count to ten. "Did you feel that this was information that you should have withheld from me?"

I can't trust him. I know Max vetted him, but I can't trust him. I don't give him a chance to answer. "Collect your stuff, you're fired. There will be a ticket waiting for you at the airport. Now, get out of my sight."

I turn to my guards, "One of you take over for him. I will be fine with just one guard, and chances are Raven and I will be together on this trip, anyway."

I head back inside to assure Raven that I'm fine. I need to call Max, but before I can, he is ringing me. "What, did Tony call you?"

I know Max, and this can't be good for his recovery. "What the fuck, Jax? I vetted Daniel and Dominika myself. This is basic simple shit."

At this point, the only one I know I can trust is Max. "Max, I fired Daniel. What should I do about Dominika?"

"I think, for now, you should keep her so Raven has a female guard, but I would feel better if you never left her side. Try to finish up and get back here, quickly. I would rather have you here, where I have more control."

"We'll wrap it up as fast as we can and get home. If you find out anything else, please call me. I'll let you know when we are leaving."

As I hang up, I sit on the sofa and pull Raven onto my lap. She wraps her arms around me, holding me close. "Okay, Raven, let me tell you everything that I know to date about your family, so that you really get an idea of what we're up against. Your grandfather, Dion, was from Italy, and when he came to the United States, he brought his way of doing business with him. He had four children: Monti, Antonio, Vincent, and Annabelle. Monti was the eldest, he died in a bar room brawl. Your father never spoke of his family, and once he joined the FBI, he cut all ties with them."

She's tugging her ear, and I have to fight my urge to nibble it. "So, Jax, even though Vincent and Duke are in custody, there are other family members that could be a threat to us?"

I know it's a lot for her to deal with, but I realize she needs all the information. "Yes, but not just family members, these types of organizations are like roaches. You can never get rid of them. I think I would feel better if your mum was closer to us in the States. She has no family, her parent's died in a car accident while she was in college, and she was an only child. Having her close let's us keep an eye on her at all times."

She's searching my eyes as if she's looking for answers . . . answers I don't have. I can only hope I'm making the right decisions.

"Okay, I understand the risk, and I agree, I would feel better if she were close to us. But what else is bothering you? And don't say *nothing*, because I know better."

I take a deep, steadying breath. "Oh, my beautiful girl, I know sometimes you think you don't know me, but you really do know me so well. I'm going to tell you a story, and I need you to just listen. It's not my story to tell, but I think you need to know this before we go to see Jackie today." I proceed to tell her the entire story that Max shared with me.

"Do you see why it's really not my story to tell, and do you understand why he pushed her away? The murder of his wife and baby right before his eyes. I know I could never come back if, God forbid, something was to happen to you and our baby. It has to be Max's, decision to tell Jackie his story, not ours. She can't come back to him because of pity, she has to come back on her own."

I watch her, waiting for her reaction. She closes her eyes and pulls me close. "Look at me, please. Raven, tell me I'm doing the right thing here?" She opens her eyes and they seem distant. I'm watching her process everything I just told her. We say nothing for a long time. We just hold each other, lost in our thoughts. "Raven, I'm worried about him, he is in such a dark place. He wants to give me back his shares in Raiders, and move to Scotland. He thinks it would be best, so you can have Jackie in your life. I can't lose him, and I need to keep my family together and safe. I feel like I'm juggling so many things. I'm afraid of what will happen if I drop one."

"What has your mom said about all of this?"

My grip on her tightens, "That's just it, my mum is playing this pretty close to the vest. I know that there is something she's not telling me, but I can't force it out of her. My heart breaks for Max. I know he needs Jackie, even more now."

"Well, Jax, now that I know the whole story, it seems to me that Max is operating out of fear. Until he can realize that he can't let fear rule his life, then nothing will change for him. As far as your mother is concerned, I have to agree with you, there is definitely more that she is holding back. When I went to lunch with Bella and your mom, something was off. When I told her my concerns about Max, she could not get out of the restaurant fast enough. I knew she was going to head straight to Max. I think you need to have a sit down with your mom and get to the bottom of this. I know you felt Max should be the one to tell his story, but I think you did the right thing by telling me. I need to know, if I'm going to be able to convince Jackie to come home.

"Now as far as keeping Max hostage, will you ever learn your lesson? I know you want things done your way and on your timeline, but that's not how life works. You can't go around, threatening to shoot someone in the ass if they don't do what you want!" She smirks.

"How did you know that?"

"I heard you yelling this morning, but I figured you would tell me when you were ready."

As I stare at her, I try to keep a straight face (not easy here). "Raven, I wasn't really going to shoot him." *She is so not buying it.*

"No? Jax, somehow, I don't really believe that. What's even worse is you made your mother a watchdog, and we all know how much Max fears her. I'm surprised you haven't called in, Mrs. Osla."

As I watch her reprimanding me, I have to remind myself to stay focused on the problem, and not on that beautiful body!

"Well that was next on my list. Besides, I had to do something, and I knew he would never disrespect my mum. I told you I could be a real bastard when I need to be. I will fight to the bitter end to keep my family together and safe. Max, is the brother I never had."

"Max wanting to leave should show you how much you mean to him. He's willing to give it all up so you could be happy. Not many people would do something so selfless."

"Raven, knowing that only makes this hurt even more. How are you going to handle, Jackie? You can't tell her what I told you, that's for Max to tell." I pull at my hair again out of frustration.

She pulls my hands out of my hair. "I have no intention on breaking a confidence. I will have to convince her that running was a bad choice. Jackie and I have an unspoken trust between us. I have looked after her like a baby sister from the first day we met and I am not going to stop now!"

"Wow, this from the girl who spent the majority of our relationship running away from me. Well, I'm glad I made you see the error of your ways."

"Whatever, Jax, you just keep telling yourself that, if it makes you feel better. Now what is the plan for today?"

I hold up my shattered watch, "Well, first, I have to get a new watch, because someone flung mine across the room." I hit her with my usual smirk.

"Oh, don't smile at me, mister. I guess maybe you learned a lesson about trying to force me to do something I don't want to do."

She's got such fire in her eyes. "I'm just trying to keep you and the baby healthy, is that so wrong?" I grasp her hips and give her a hungry look that I know always gets her going.

"You really are a dirty bastard!"

"Oh, sweetheart, I love you!"

"Jax, while we look for a watch without an alarm on it, I would like to pick up some gifts to bring to Jackie's house. I know just the place to shop, it's called *Bon Génie*, have you ever been there?"

"Sweetheart, I hardly ever do my own shopping. If I really need something, I have my assistant pick it up. And as far as my clothes, I have my suits tailored from Savoy Tailors Guild in London. Everything else I have, a shopper at Barneys that takes care of me." I must have shocked her because her chin is practically on the ground.

"Wow, another first, Jax! There are seven floors of some of the most exquisite things in the world. Jackie and I would go every year, during winter break, and I would be honored to share the experience with you."

"Did you and Jackie travel a lot?" She smiles like she's remembering a happier time; at least she has those memories.

"We always came here for winter break and sometimes, her brother would come home if he knew we were going to be here."

I lean and kiss her, smiling at her beautiful face. "I'm looking forward to meeting Jackie's family, they sound interesting."

We get ready and head out.

WE PULL UP TO *Bon Génie*. Raven wasn't kidding, the place is huge! We spend the next three hours, tooling around and picking up some cool stuff for Junior and the baby.

"Jax, I'm hungry. I don't even need your watch to tell me that, so let's get something to eat." she says with a sarcastic undertone that makes me laugh.

"Very funny, sweetheart. Thank you for my new watch but you really didn't have to buy it for me."

"I know, but I really did feel bad that I pitched your old one across the room."

"I need to feed you, sweetheart, what would you like to eat?"

"A grilled cheese sandwich and a chocolate fondue. What? Why the face?"

I lean in to kiss her, "Raven, please tell me you're not going to eat them together."

She rolls her eyes. "Come on, Jax, let's eat. And no, the fondue is dessert. If you're really good later, we just might have some fun with chocolate."

Raven

AS WE HEAD OUT to Jackie's, I feel nervous, though I shouldn't be. Jackie is my best friend, I tell her everything. Having to handle this without telling her anything of Max's tragedy, I'm sure, will prove to be difficult.

We pull up to the compound and glancing at Jax, I see a look of surprise on his face. "You okay, Jax?"

"Well, Raven, I can understand now why Max said she would be safe here. There's a gated guard entrance, electric fence, attack dogs, and a slew of armed guards. Is this the way she had to grow up?"

When I think of all the stories Jackie shared about her lonely childhood, it makes me sad.

"Yes. It makes for a very lonely childhood. Plus, there are no neighbors; this estate sits on 250 acres. Jax, do you think Max sent her away because of the threat and not because of his past?"

He looks around, shaking his head, "Sweetheart, I honestly don't know. Now that I see this place, it might make more sense that he might have sent her here for her safety."

We pull up to the house and even though I've been here so many times, I'm still in awe at the shear size of the place. As soon as the car stops, I'm out and rushing for the door. Jax is quick at my heels. Just as we enter the house, Jackie comes flying down the steps nearly tackling us. "Raven, oh my God, I'm so happy you made it. How is your mom? Did you see her? Did she recognize you?"

I laugh, "Okay, girl, slow down. First, let me say hello to everyone." I gesture just as her parents come into the room, giving me hugs and kisses; they really are my family, too. "Jax, I'd like to introduce you to Jeffery and Emi Gerhard."

Jeff takes Jax's hand, "Please, just Jeff and Emi; it's a pleasure to finally meet you, Jax. My daughter has told me so much about you. How has your stay been, so far?

Jax gives his charming smile that I love. "Wonderful, Raven took me to Bon Génie today."

Jeff laughs "Ah yes, that is her and Jackie's favorite place to go; they can tool around there for hours! Come in and let me give you a tour of the place while the girls do their thing."

We sit down and Emi pours some tea. "Raven, I am going to leave you girls to catch up. I'm glad you're here and safe."

I smile, "Emi, you don't have to leave," I say but she smiles and waves for us to carry on before she leaves.

"Okay, Raven, you need tell me everything." Jackie grabs my attention back.

I look at her and I want to scream, *Max needs you,* but I have to do this right.

"Where do you want me to start?"

Jackie takes my hands in hers. "What happened with your mom?"

My heart instantly constricts in my chest, "First, I have to tell you for her safety, no one can know whom she is."

"I understand, I haven't spoken to anyone about her."

"Oh, Jackie, it was surreal. I mean, she was sitting in a chair sketching pictures of me as a child. It was like she was trying to keep my face in her memories. Jax realized it, and he made her *really* look at me . . . at my eyes. At that point, we could both see recognition register on her face. A single tear slid down her cheek and she whispered my name, Cara."

Jackie's eyes fill with tears, and she's rubbing her arms. "Oh, Raven, I swear you're giving me fucking goose bumps!"

I need to lighten the mood here. "Okay, I have to tell you something, and promise you won't laugh." I know she's going to laugh.

"Okay . . . you're acting weird, Raven."

I take a deep breath. "You can't curse in front of me. Don't look at me like that, I know it's crazy, but Jax has this idea that the baby can hear us. He doesn't want the baby's first word to be . . . you know . . . a bad one. Jackie, are you okay?"

She's biting her lip and I know she is trying not to laugh.

"I'm trying with all my might not to get hysterical! Raven, you can't be serious. Oh my God—you are serious! You know how absurd that is, right?"

I nod, "Of course I do, but he's so cute, I can't burst his bubble. Apparently, he was a real whack job when Bella was pregnant. He wanted health reports on everyone she came in contact with!"

Jackie laughs, "Okay, I will humor him. So what are you going to do about your mom?"

"We are going to move her to the States."

Jackie's face lights up. "Well, I think that's a good thing. Then, you can keep a close eye on her. Maybe she will even get to the point where she can get back into mainstream life."

Jackie knows how much family means to me. "I wish, but I don't think the threat against my family is going to go away anytime soon. My father also had a sister, and apparently, she is making herself known." I take in a deep breath and decide it's time to shift the conversation towards the topic of one Maxwell Fleming. "So, are you going to ask me about *him?*" I watch as she closes her eyes tightly. I know she's fighting back her emotions. "Talk to me, Jackie, please."

She shakes her head. "What's there to say? I heard what he said to Jax, there is no denying it."

I need to get through to her, and this is probably my only chance. "Okay, Jackie, I need for you to listen to me. I mean *really* listen with an open mind and an open heart. *Nothing* is ever what it seems in life. I, of all people, should know that. I mean, look at Marco. A lot has happened since you left. Apparently, Max is in a very dark place, for reasons I'm not able to talk about. Jax has put guards on him with orders to—and I'm quoting here—'*shoot him in the arse if he tries to leave.*' He has moved his mom into our place and apparently, she sits by the elevator everyday—all day—making sure he doesn't leave. He's hurting and he pushed you away. Maybe in his mind, it was for the right reasons, even though it was wrong. I always tell you, never make a decision without having all the facts. You, pulling a *runner?* That was acting out on a knee-jerk reaction. You need to come home and get all the facts before you make your decision. Otherwise, you will regret it for the rest of your life. You will always wonder *what if.* I don't want you to end up like some old spinster with a hundred cats!" She doesn't say anything, but I know she is weighing her options. That was my one shot, let's hope she listens.

"Did Jax really have his mom stay there? Poor Max. For him, that's worse than getting shot!"

"Exactly, Jackie. That has to tell you how desperate and worried Jax really is."

"What about his health? Is he going to be okay?" It figures the first thing she wants to know is if he's going to be okay. She is such a tenderhearted person.

"The doctor said he should be okay. He started therapy, but he's lost. It's like a part of him died, Jackie. He seems so empty inside."

"I need a change of subject, please. What is going on with you and Jax?"

Where do I begin . . ."The man is nuts, but we already established that fact. Aside from the whole blue language thing, I found out from Bella that Jax had my building tented for non-existing termites."

She's looking at me like I'm nuts. "Why did he do that?"

"Why, Jackie, that's a great question. All I can figure is he did it so I can't go home."

As she smiles, I can see she's going to be on Jax's side here. "Oh, Raven, that's so romantic."

Tsk "Not only did he have the entire building tented for termites, he put all of the residents up in at the W Hotel—all expenses paid! He doesn't even know I found out about it."

Her eyes are like saucers. "Are you serious?"

"Yes!"

Jackie is laughing so hard that she is crying. Right at that minute, the guys decide to come in and see what's going on.

"Okay, ladies, what has you both in a fit of laughter?"

Jackie smiles at him, "Well, that would be you, Jax."

"Oh really, what did I do now?"

"Nothing, just you being you is always very entertaining. Did Daddy give you the grand tour?"

"Yes, I didn't know you ride. I was quite impressed with all of your awards."

"Thank you, Jax. Riding is a great way to pass the day. It gives me the freedom to think without interruptions."

Jax picks up one of the pictures of Jackie on skis. "Raven said you also love to ski. I didn't realize you started so young."

Jackie looks at the picture and smiles, "Yes, I probably skied before I walked. I like cross-country skiing the most; it helps build stamina. My brother, however, likes snowboarding better.

My body tenses at the mention of Dylan. He's made me aware that he is attracted to me from the first day I met him, to the point where I'm uncomfortable to be around him. "Jackie, how is Dylan doing?"

"Actually, you can ask him yourself. He went to town for something but should be home soon. He surprised me with a visit."

I just hope Dylan behaves. "Wow. I haven't seen him in a while. I'm glad you'll get to meet him, Jax."

The front door opens with a bang. "Oh, speak of the devil, here's my brother now." Dylan comes barreling into the room, bypassing everyone and attempts to pull me into his arms. Jax pulls me up against him, staking his claim.

"Dylan, let me introduce you to Jax."

Jax reaches out to shake Dylan's hand. Oh boy. He's pissed. He has a tight grip on me.

"Hello, Jax. So you're the man that has finally caught our girl's heart."

Jax is glaring at him. Okay, need to change the subject quick before the man blows a gasket.

"So, Dylan, when did you get here?"

"I got in this morning. Once Jackie told me you were coming, I couldn't stay away. How long will you be here for?"

Jax's tension is not letting up one bit; the more Dylan speaks, the tenser he gets. "Dylan, our trip here is very short, and then I'm taking *my* girl home with me—where she belongs."

Wow, major pissing contest, going on here.

"So, Jax, what do you do for a living? My sister really didn't fill in any of the blanks."

Jax is glaring at Dylan, and I think he might snap his neck. "I own a company called, Raiders Inc."

This is not going to end well. I look to Jackie for help, but she just rolls her eyes.

"Don't think I ever heard of it? What does your company do?"

"I assist companies that run into trouble."

"Ah, so you're a *corporate raider.* Is that how you assist them? Hence the name."

Oh no, he's growling; a growling Jax is never good.

"Well, Dylan, if you really are interested, my company invests in agriculture, technology and clean energy. I don't go out and just pick apart companies for the heck of it. I focus on companies that have a good idea, but either no business sense or lack of funding. If it's just the funding then I support them. If the company can't be saved, then I try to place the workers within my existing companies before I break it apart. I'm not the bad guy, Dylan."

Dylan is smirking, and Jax's whole body is tight. "I didn't mean to upset you, Jax. I just need to know that our girl is in good hands, that's all. When will you be heading back to the States?"

I'm holding onto Jax so tight; I fear he might explode. "As soon as our business here is done. Which reminds me, Raven, we have a meeting; we need to get going."

We head towards the door and make our goodbyes. I hug everyone, but Jax makes sure I'm glued to his hip when Dylan tries to hug me.

"JAX, ARE YOU GOING to sulk the whole drive to the clinic?" He's pouting like a little boy, and for some crazy reason it's a total turn-on.

"No, but you should have warned me that the fucker has the hot's for you! Don't look at me like I'm nuts, you know he does."

My crazy man makes this so easy. I have to try very hard not to laugh. "First, watch your mouth, the baby can hear. Second, yes I know that Dylan has had a thing for me from when I first met him. And lastly, Jax, look at me, please . . . you are my end all. Raise the privacy glass . . . *now.*"

"I'm all yours, sweetheart, have your way with me."

I am wound up so tight I think I might burst! This man drives me nuts, but I can't seem to get enough of him. "Jax, I will never admit this to you ever again, so listen carefully. When you get all Alpha male on me, it makes me so fucking crazy, I just want to jump your bones. Even though you make me crazy mad, you also make me crazy hot. Now get naked and fuck me hard!" Oh bless him, his eyes are wide and his chin practically hits the floor.

"Oh."

I'm the one growling now, "Yeah, *oh.*"

Jaxson

WELL, I'M NOT AN idiot. I don't need to be told twice. I only hope the driver has headphones on because I will make her scream. I slowly unbutton my shirt while she watches. I roll my shoulders back so my shirt slides down my back. She's watching my every move. I place my finger in her mouth and she sucks it like it's my cock. I pull it out and run it over my nipples. She's holding her breath. *Gotcha, sweetheart, oh yeah.* She is still fully dressed and I know exactly what I'm going to do next. I release my cock from his holding cell and start to pump him up and down while my other hand is stroking my nipples, first one and then the other. She's losing it; squeezing her thighs together for friction. I take the first drops of my arousal on my finger, and place it in her mouth. She moans. That's it sweetheart, get really worked up for me.

"Oh my God, Jax, I don't know how much more of this I can take!"

I'm not stopping, "Sweetheart, do you think you're ready for me?"

She nods her head.

"Show me baby."

She starts to undress, never taking her eyes off me as I pleasure myself. All her skin is flushed. "Jax, do you know how beautiful you are? Seeing you like this takes my breath away."

I reach over and rip her panties right off of her. "Kiss me, Raven, now!"

She gently presses her soft lips to mine. "I need you inside of me, Jax."

I'm on my knees between her legs. I slowly rub my cock up and down her; still making a show for her. I don't think either one of us will last much longer. I slowly work my way in and then out. I reach down and play with her nipples applying just enough pressure to make them peak for her pleasure. Her skin is on fire.

"You want me, baby, you've got me heart and soul." I pull back and slam into her, causing her to scream. "Jax . . . oh God, Jax . . . please."

I stop. "Look. At. Me."

Her eye's fly up to mine.

"Raven, I love you. All that I am, and all that I will ever be, in this world, is yours for life. I'm baring my soul to you now."

Raven

OUR EYES LOCK. WE are both screaming and shaking. My release is like a wave of never ending pleasure, rippling through my whole body. I search his face and I can see something is off. I fist my hands in his hair and pull him towards me, kissing him so softly. I whisper, "I love you, Jax."

He keeps kissing me softly, and then he nibbles on my ear. "Jax, talk to me, please. What's wrong?"

His beautiful blue eyes are filled with such angst. He rests his forehead on mine, "Raven, marry me, *please*," he whispers.

I freeze. That was not what I was expecting. "Excuse me? Did you really just ask me to marry you while you're buried balls deep in me? In the back of a limo?"

He closes his eyes, "Well when you put it like that, it doesn't sound good."

"Jax, I think we need to get dressed." I try to move, but he holds me even tighter, pinning me beneath him.

"Raven, just stop for one minute and listen to me, please," he begs. "I know this is not the way I should be asking you this, trust me. I have been rehearsing what I wanted to say to you for a long time. I knew I wanted you for life the day I met you, but if I had told you then, you would have thought I was a nut." My eyes grow wide. "Don't look at me like that, I'm not a nut. Okay, so maybe a little, but still, let's put that aside for a minute. I love you with all of my heart and soul. You are my end all, and without you, I don't exist. I know this from when you were gone for three months. I was out of my mind, okay, maybe more of a crazy man. I sulked for three months, sat in your apartment, listening to your iPod over and over again. Some song called 'half a heart' every day for hours. I just sat on your bed, so lost without you. I can't go through life like that. I have so much love to give you and our child. I want to make a happy life for you and the baby. I want lots of babies. Okay, maybe we should get through the first one, but still, I see us growing old together. Geez, woman, I bought your whole fucking building and had it tented for non-existent termites, all so you wouldn't leave me! Okay, that didn't come out right, either. I really had no clue how to ask you this. I don't want you to think I just want to marry you because of the baby; I would marry you with or without a baby. When I asked Max what to do he said when the timing is right I should just bare my soul to you. Are you going to say anything?"

Jaxson

SHE LOOKS AT ME and begins to laugh, Not exactly the response I was expecting.

"I'm sorry, Jax, I shouldn't laugh at you, but really, you have to realize this will go in the history books as one of the funniest proposals ever. I don't think Max meant for you to be in this position, in the back of a limo, when you asked me."

"Well, Raven, are you going to answer me?"

She smiles and tenderly kisses me . . ."Jax, I already did, you are my end all. There could never be or will ever be anyone else but you."

Holy shit. I think she's saying yes! "You'll marry me? I need to hear the words, sweetheart, please."

She takes my face into her hands and stares into my eyes. "Yes, Jax, I will marry you."

I kiss him softly, "You crazy man. Make love to me now."

I instruct the driver to keep driving in circles until I tell him otherwise.

I lean in and kiss her tender lips; they are so soft. Our tongues begin a slow dance. I cocoon her whole body, and slowly begin to move. She needs me slow and tender right now. I'm giving her what she needs. In and out, holding her so close.

I search her face and I know she's there. I reach down and nip one of her nipples, and she starts screaming my name over and over again. That's all it takes, I explode with such force that I swear the head of my cock blew off. I rest my forehead on hers, both of us trying to catch our breaths. "Sweetheart, if it were possible to spend the rest of my life just like this, I would until my last breath on this earth."

Her eyes are filled with unshed tears. "Please, Raven, tell me those are happy tears."

She reaches up and kisses me, "Happy ones Jax."

I instruct the driver to head to the hotel, as we begin to make some sort of normal with our clothes.

"Jax, why are you staring down at your cock?"

Oh boy . . . I'm busted now. "I'm making sure he's still in one piece."

"Excuse me?"

"Okay, sometimes with you I explode so hard, I swear his head blows off," I admit. Her mouth gapes open. "Raven, are you going to say anything or just stare at me wide eyed?"

"I love you, Jax, and Mr. Cock is fine. You can put him away now."

She's amazing; she gets me like no one else ever could. "I love you more, sweetheart."

Chapter Eight

Raven

WE STOP AT THE hotel to get cleaned up, and Jax is pacing around the room. This is usually a sign that he is deep in thought, and that will mean trouble for me.

"Raven, if we didn't have to go to the clinic I would spend the entire day in bed ravishing your body."

We are all ready to leave when Jax takes my hand and drops to one knee. I look at him like he's a nut; I already said yes.

"Raven, I promise to fill every one of your days with all of my love. I will protect you and our baby. Everything I have, I give to you because without you I have nothing. I'm just a shell of a man. You're the half that makes me whole. When I look at us, I can see us growing old together. You complete me in a way that only you can. You get it; you understand me and all my crazy ways like no one else can. Will you please marry me and let me spend the rest of my life loving you?"

"You're my happy ever after, Jax . . . yes. Now and forever."

He slips the most beautiful ring on my finger. "I'm going to talk to your mum today about my intentions, I want her approval because I know you need it. But just know, no one will ever stand in our way."

We hurry up and get ready. I'm excited to see my mom today. I know I have to move slowly with her, but the sooner we are all safely back home, the better I will feel.

As we head to the clinic, I sit and think of how much my life has changed since that fateful morning at Starbucks. I can't believe I'm going to marry this intense, over the top, beautiful man. "Jax, when did you get the ring?"

"Do you really need to know this?" He strokes his chin.

"Yes, I do."

"The week I met you."

My eyes go wide and my mouth opens but nothing comes out.

"Raven, don't look at me like that. I just knew, that's all."

"You just knew what, that I would marry you? We had one date, how could you know?"

"I had purpose for the first time in my life. Everything I did or said mattered to me. That's how I knew."

Sweet Jesus, what this man does to me. "You'll always have purpose, Jax."

He kisses the inside of my wrist. "Raven, I never felt it until I met you."

There are no words left to say. I snuggle into him for the rest of the ride.

WHEN WE GET TO the clinic, I find my mom sketching again. This time they are of me now—not twenty years ago. "Mom, you're so talented; the likeness is unreal."

She smiles, "Cara, I never thought I would hear you call me mom ever again. Each time I hear it, it takes my breath away."

She seems at peace. I hope moving her is the right thing to do for her. "Mom, Jax and I have some things we need to talk to you about. Are you up for it?"

She grasps my hands, looking down at them. Upon noticing the ring, she looks at Jax and smiles. "Of course, what's on your mind?"

Jax and I take a seat next to her. Neither of us wants to make her nervous, but we really believe we are making the best move here for everyone. "Well, we would like to move you back to the States with us. What do you think about that?" Jax asks her.

Her eyes light up at the mention of it. "Jax, I want nothing more than to spend the rest of my days with my daughter and grandbaby, but is it safe for Cara?"

"Gabriella, for the rest of our lives, everyone will have to have constant guards. There is no way around it. Not just because of your situation, but also because of me."

I watch as my mother fights to hold back the tears.

"Jax, I don't understand, what do you mean *because of you?*"

It dawns on me how much fear Jax must have to live with everyday, not just because of my mom and me, but because of who he is and what he does.

"Gabriella, I am a very wealthy man. With wealth comes many crazy people, trying to take it away from me anyway they can. That wealth not only puts a target on my back, but everyone associated with me. I've come to accept that, and have made arrangements to always have protection." Jax pulls his chair closer and puts his arm around me.

"Jax, there are many wealthy people in the world. My parents were wealthy and we never had guards."

I need to give my mom all the information, so she can process it at her own pace.

"Mom, Jax's company, Raiders Inc., helps other companies that are struggling and sometimes the only way to help them is to dismantle them completely. You can make many enemies doing this, but unfortunately, it needs to be done."

My mom studies Jax. What she is looking for, I'm not sure.

"Jax, can I ask you some questions?"

He nods, "Yes, ma'am, just know that I don't sugar coat anything. If you want an honest answer, you will get it from me."

She smiles. "Wow, okay. Now what are your intentions?"

He hits her with the Jaxson smirk and his twinkling blues—God I love this man. Watching Jax is like watching a master artist at work. "Well, ma'am, hopefully with your blessing, I intend to marry your daughter, and love her endlessly for the rest of my days. I can provide nicely for her and our children. I want to support her in all of her dreams. I want to see the world through her beautiful eyes."

Okay, I'm officially crying. This man is so intense, he's so much more than anyone could ever imagine, and to think, that is what scared me away from him to begin with.

"Jax, you have my blessing. Now what's next?"

"Okay, the first thing you need is a total name change. I have all the security in place and they're ready to go as soon as the doctor gives us the green light. When we get back to New York, you will be at a clinic right near our flat. When the doctor says it's okay, you will be moved into your own flat. How does that sound for you?"

I hope my mom understands that Jax operates at one speed—his speed, and watch out if you get in the way.

"As long as I can be with Cara I'm okay. What name will I have?"

I know Jax is trying to slow it down a little, and bless him; it takes everything he has not to just dictate the way things will be.

"Gabriella, you can pick. Just keep it simple. You want something that will be easy for you to associate yourself with."

My mom looks to me. "Cara, what name have you been going by?"

I really don't want to upset her, but not being truthful would be worse for her. "Joseph named me Raven. He said my hair reminded him of a Raven."

She gets a faraway look in her eyes. "He would come to see me and talk about a girl named, Raven. I never knew it was you. I'm trying to remember all the stories he would tell me, but it's so overwhelming. Do you think he kept it a secret to protect you?"

I wonder what else he told her. "There is a lot that he hid from us, Mom. In time we will go through it all, but for now, let's concentrate on the here and now, okay?"

She smiles. I remember that smile. I'm trying so hard not to cry for all the years that have been lost. Years we will never get back again.

"Y-yes of course, and I must remember to start calling you, Raven. I decided upon my new name. I would like to be called Rose," she says and I can feel my eyes grow wide.

"Raven, you remember, don't you?"

I nod, but I'm speechless that she remembers something so simple.

"Jax, when Raven was a little girl, she would play a game called, 'Rose.' She and some of her friends, in the neighborhood, would dress up in their parents' clothes, pretending to be adults going to parties. They all called themselves 'The Rose Club.' They would drink juice out of champagne glasses and eat chocolates as Hors d'oeuvres."

Jax squeezes her hand. "Okay, it's settled. You are Rose Anderson. I will get the information to the lawyers."

"Jax, have you and Raven decided when you are going to get married?"

He shakes his head, "We haven't talked about that yet. She only said yes today."

My mom is laughing so hard she's crying. "Mom, are you okay?"

She smiles at Jax, "You're a very funny man. You may not have realized it yet, but I'm sure in the back of your mind, you have it all figured out. You don't seem like the type of guy who waits very easily."

I look to Jax, stroking his chin, and it hits me—she's right—he does!

"Jax, really, when were you going to tell me?"

His eyes grow large. He is so busted!

"Um . . . well, you see . . . oh crap. Am I in the doghouse now?"

I growl, "Yes you are! What did I tell you about dictating my life?" He gifts me with a huge smile, trying to charm me, I'm sure, but not this time.

"I know it's just—"

I grab his shoulders, "Just what, Jax? You're not getting out of this one—oh no, mister! Mom, stop laughing. You're not helping me at all here. You have no clue how nuts he is. Do you know that he went into my purse and took away all my credit cards, and then replaced them with one of his without even telling me?"

She's laughing even more now. "You two will be just fine."

Maxwell

I FINISH MY THERAPY and I'm starting to feel like myself again. Even my hair is almost back to normal. I would like to go for a walk in the park, but I know I won't be allowed to go by myself. I'm not going to fight it for now. I pick up my keys and head towards the elevator, and there she is, just like clockwork. "I am going for a walk in the park, would you like to come with me?"

She smiles. That's a first! Usually she's pulling my ear. "You know I am, but thank you for asking."

As we head down in the elevator, I figure I should tell her I spoke to Jax. "An, I spoke to Jax today, and everything is going well with Gabriella. He is making arrangements to bring her back to New York."

She seems happy about this. "Good. I think Raven will be happy having her mum with her."

The rest of the walk through the park is in silence. When we're done, I get pretzels and water from the vendor, and we head over to a bench.

"Thank you, Maxwell. I can never resist these warm pretzels. Have you thought anymore about your situation?"

I knew this was coming. I take a deep breath. "Actually, yes I have, I'm not going anywhere. I realize I really don't want to. This is where my family is. You were my family even before I found out that we *are* blood relations. I will have to find a way to make it work, now won't I." I take a breath, and close my eyes, knowing what she will ask next.

"Okay, Maxwell, but have you thought about Jackie, at all?"

I sit quietly for a bit. "I'm not ready to go there, yet. I hurt her very badly. She trusted me with her heart and I wasn't honest with her. I should have told her about my past. I shouldn't have gotten involved with her. The danger was too much, and now the target on her is even greater. Either way, I messed up. I'm not sure how to fix it, or if it can even be fixed."

She takes my hand. "Well, Maxwell, not that it's any of my business, but maybe you should start with a simple phone call."

I lean over and kiss her on the cheek, "Thank you."

She squeezes my hand, "What was that for?"

I fear this woman as much as I love her. "Just you, being you. I don't know where I would be without you. Now let's go back upstairs, I'm getting tired."

We get up to leave and I gather our trash, when I turn around I notice a woman watching us. I nod to one of our guards and he knows what to do. I lean in and whisper, "Come on, ma'am, we need to go right now."

I race her across the street and into the building. When we get into the elevator, I look over to An and see that she's as white as a sheet. "It's okay. I noticed a woman staring at us and it felt off. Our security is going to follow her and try to get some information, so don't worry." I try to reassure her. She takes a deep breath, and I feel bad that I scared her.

"Maxwell, I'm not good at all this cloak and dagger stuff. I wish Jaxson would get back sooner rather than later."

"I'll call Tony to get an update as to when we can expect them, okay?"

As we step off the elevator, she looks back at me, "Yes, and make sure you have a nap, then ring me for tea." She heads into Jax's flat, visibly shaken. Even if I was going to bolt, I would never leave An while Jax is out of the country and she knows it. I head into my flat, more pissed off than anything else. I'm worried about An. For the first time today, I saw real fear in her eyes. I grab my phone and call Tony.

"Tony, I just came back from the park with An. There was a woman following us, watching our every move. I sent one of our guards to follow her. Has he checked in yet?"

I feel bad that Tony is carrying my load, as well as his own.

"Not yet, but Jax checked in earlier. Gabriella consented to the move. Her new name is Rose Anderson. The doctors said she can be moved tomorrow, and I faxed you over some papers to sign for her release."

I walk over to the fax and flip through the papers. "Did Jax say anything else?"

He laughs, "He just reminded me that you're under house arrest until he gets home and you come to your senses, whatever that means."

"Funny, Tony, let me know when the guard checks in. I venture to say that it was Annabelle," I suggest. He only replies with a grunt of agreement before we hang up.

Next, I call Jax to find out the status of his return. "Jax, I just got off the line with Tony and he told me about Gabriella. I signed the paperwork and faxed it back to the clinic, so you are good to go."

"You sound better today, Max, does this mean that you have come to your senses?"

If he were here, I'd deck the cheeky fucker. "Jax, I'm not leaving you for many reasons. We'll save that conversation for another time. Right now, I need to fill you in on my day, so shut up and listen, mate." I tell him about the woman that was at the park, he's very quiet. "Jax, I have a feeling it's Annabelle.

Your mum has been a rock through all of this, but today. I could tell she was scared and I don't like it. You need to have the plane under guard twenty-four seven and check it twice before you even get on it. Do you understand? I already put a call into the attorneys and they are going to issue a restraining order against Annabelle." Ugh, I just want to scream. Can't we just get through a day without any fucking drama?

"Got it, Max. This is why I need you with me always."

"How is Raven doing?"

"Well, she said yes!"

Knowing Jax I fear he might have bullied her. "Great, mate, congrats. How did you finally propose to her?"

"Let's just say it was unconventional at best, but she said yes."

I really wish they were back home and not so far away. "Have you figured out when you are going to do it? Knowing you, like I do, you probably have it already planned." He's really quiet now. "Jax, you can't do that to her." He takes a deep breath and I know what's coming, typical Jax "get it done yesterday."

"Max, I want to get married Friday. That would give her two days."

I almost choke, "Jax, are you afraid she will change her mind?" He's slow to answer and I know I hit the nail on the head.

"Max, I really can't stand you sometimes."

"Get it through your thick head—she loves you! She will only change her mind if you push her, so stop bullying her. Getting married is a big step, and every girl has a dream of what her wedding will be like. You are just the bloke that has to show up at the church! Try not to bully her, get home, and I will help you, okay?"

"Okay, I will keep my mouth shut about wedding plans."

Jaxson

WE HANG UP AND I decide I want Raven, right now. God, I have no control when it comes to her. I come out of the office to look for her and I find a *fucking* note!

Jax,

Jackie is meeting me downstairs for coffee and chocolates. We are going to have girl talk. I have Bo and my detail. No worries.

Xo Raven

Yeah, no worries my arse. I wonder if that wanker, Dylan, is going to show up. Maybe I'll just sit in the corner and watch her. No, she will know that I'm stalking her, and there will be hell to pay if it goes anything like the credit card fiasco. I'll give her one-hour, and then I'm looking for her. When did I become such a fucking whack job?

Raven

AS I WAIT FOR Jackie, I watch all the different people go by. It suddenly dawns on me, I'm getting married. I never thought it would happen to me. *And* I'm going to be someone's mom.

"Raven, you look lost in your thoughts, everything okay?"

I smile, "Jackie, he asked me to marry him!" I show her the ring. She grabs my hand and gasps.

"Oh, Raven, I'm so happy for you. You deserve your happy ever after. We need to celebrate and I know just the thing." She calls the waiter over, and begins speaking rapid French. He smiles and leaves.

"Okay, what did you order? You were talking so fast, I only got snippets of the conversation."

The waiter is back with two cups; he places them down in front of us, and congratulates me.

"This is a liquid dark chocolate, hazelnut drink. There is no alcohol in it, but it's very addicting, so only one, my friend."

Words could never describe what I'm drinking, and I don't think I will ever find this anywhere but here. I begin to laugh, causing Jackie to look at me like I'm nuts.

"Raven, are you okay?"

I love her so much, and I know I can't leave here without her. "Oh Jackie, only you and I could drink liquid chocolate and make faces like we're having massive orgasms!" We're both laughing, and then Jackie takes my hand and squeezes it.

"That, my friend, is because you and I know the finer things in life."

"So, have you thought anymore about our talk the other day? Will you at least come back and talk to him?"

She clenches her jaw, and I can see the hurt in her eyes. I know if he would tell her everything, it would make a difference. In the end, it's up to Max to decide.

"Raven, you are becoming more like Jax everyday."

I smile, "Yeah, I know. It just works to get right to the point."

"I have and I've decided that I need to have some sort of closure with Max, before I can move on. I know you said there is a reason for his reaction, and I trust you. When are you flying back to the States?"

I bite my lip, trying to contain my excitement. "Well, if everything goes according to plan, we leave tomorrow. Will you be joining us?"

She nods, "Yes, if that's okay with you?"

I throw my arms around her. "Of course, you know I would do anything for you. Now, on another note, I would like for you to be my maid of honor." I hope she says yes, even if things don't work out with Max.

"I would love to. I'm sure Jax will have Maxwell as his best man. I want you to know, even if things don't work out, I would be happy to be a part of your special day."

I am so happy she's coming home with me. "Oh Jackie, I love you. You're the sister I never had." How did I ever get so lucky to have her in my life? "Okay, so next topic; what the hell was up with Dylan?" I know she didn't expect her brother to be such an ass. Heck, I know I didn't expect it.

"Yeah, I know. Raven, it hit him hard that you went and fell in love with the world's most eligible bachelor. I think he finally realizes that he will never have a chance with you."

I feel bad, but I never felt anything remotely like that for Dylan, and I hope I never gave him any ideas. "I'm sorry Jackie, but you know that I never had any romantic feelings for him."

"I know you never led him on. He will have to face it, and move on. Okay, so how did Jax pop the question?"

I start to laugh as I remember Jax's proposal. "Oh my God, Jackie, the man is crazy."

Jackie rolls her eyes. "Raven, we know that already, but how did he ask?"

I have to tell her everything; she's my best friend, but I know she is going to laugh her ass off. "We just left your place, having wild limo sex. While we were still deep in the throes of it, he asked me to marry him, followed by the most romantic declaration of love that I have ever heard."

Her eyes are huge, and she is trying not to laugh. "Do you think he was planning this?"

I take a deep breath. "Well, at first, no. But then, when we got back to the hotel, he did a traditional proposal with the ring."

"He already had the ring? Wow, he must have been planning this."

"Oh, Jackie, you don't know the half of it. Apparently he got the ring the first week we met!"

"Raven, you know he really is crazy and madly in love with you. I don't think that will ever change for him. It comes through in everything he does."

"I know, Jackie, I just need to find a balance we can both live with." I let out a long sigh and we glance at my ring again. When we look up, I see him. I knew he couldn't stay away long.

"Jax, congratulations on getting engaged, I'm so excited for you both."

"Thank you, Jackie, I'm sorry to barge in but I miss my girl."

Jackie gets up to leave. "It's okay, I'm leaving. I need to get packed."

Jax hugs her. I'm happy that he gets along so well with her, after all, she is my only friend.

"Oh, where are you going?"

She kisses us both as she leaves, "Raven will explain; love you both."

"Okay, Raven, what's going on?"

"Jackie is coming back to New York with us. She wants to talk to Max and get closure. She has also agreed to be my maid of honor, no matter what happens between them."

He kisses the inside of my wrist and I light up. "Wow, you have been a very busy girl. Well, I spoke to Max. He and Mum went to the park today and someone was watching them; a female. Max had one of the guards follow her to find out who she is. Tony and Max think its Annabelle. Max also contacted the attorneys, and they are issuing a restraining order against her. I told you I would not hide anything from you. We are leaving tomorrow, for sure. The doctor got the signed papers from Max, so we are good to go. Max has put the plane on a twenty-four-seven guard and it will be swept tomorrow before we leave."

Wow, this man thinks of everything. "Thank you for being honest with me. So, Max and your mom . . . in the park together . . . that's interesting."

He laughs, "Yeah, I don't even want to go there. What were you drinking?"

I know he is going to lose his mind when he finds out what this drink is. "Oh, you have to try this." I call the waiter over and proceed to order in French. "Jax, this is the most unbelievable drink I have ever had. You're going to love it."

He cocks his head and smiles, " You speak French beautifully."

I smile, trying to control the sparks. "Thank you. Now have a sip and tell me what you think."

He takes a sip and then calls the waiter over asking him to make it to go now. "You okay, Jax?"

He takes my hand and pulls me to my feet. "Yep, I'm good, sweetheart. We've been apart far too long, I want you now." He gently grabs me by the elbow. I throw my napkin down and rush off with him.

We get upstairs and he's trying to pull my clothes off, almost at a frantic pace. "Raven, please, just hurry okay—I need you now!"

Maybe I can take charge for a while. "Jax, you will do whatever I ask you to do, deal?"

He growls, "Right here and right now—*Yes!*"

"Well, then, Mr. Phillips, first, you have on entirely too many clothes and I need to rid myself of mine."

"I can help you with that, sweetheart."

I shake my head, "No, Jax, you get to watch." I make a show out of getting undressed. He's fighting his urge to touch me, fisting his hands and clenching his jaw. Now that we are both naked, I push him onto the bed. I open the drink and dip my finger in. I rub my finger over my lips and then slowly lick them. He tries to reach for me but I push his hand away. This is great; I finally have the upper hand!

"Woman, you're killing me. Please put me out of my misery."

Hmm, "Anticipation, Jax. You have to hold it."

He looks down at his cock, "You hear that, buddy? You need to just hold it."

"Oh my God, Jax, really? You know, having in-depth conversations with your cock could get you sectioned."

He's giving me the Jax smirk. "Well then, sweetheart, maybe you need to help him out here."

I dip my finger back into the chocolate. "Je tiens à lécher le chocolat hors de votre coq."

He takes a deep breath, trying so hard to let me have my way. "Oh fuck all that is holy, I have no idea what you just said, but I could blow just listening to you!"

I whisper, "I said, 'I want to lick the chocolate off of your cock,' now you need to breathe, Jax. If you pass out, it won't be fun."

"I'm trying sweetheart, but you are every fantasy come true, and then some."

I take the chocolate and trail it around his nipples and down the happy trail, making sure to not touch his cock. I look up at him and his eyes are wide.

"Sweetheart, please say something else in French."

As I slowly lick off the chocolate I tell him, "Je t'aime ma belle fou homme, which means: I love you, my beautiful, crazy man." I slowly cover his cock with the chocolate, and then swirl my tongue around the head. I don't know how much more of this he can take. He's really trying to keep it together as I work my tongue down to the base and back up to the head. When I reach the top, I nip it just the way I know he likes it. That's it—game over! He yells out my name, his hands squeeze tightly at my shoulders.

He pulls me up to him. "Come here, sweetheart."

He looks shattered. I love that I can do that for him. "You okay, Jax?"

He's nuzzling into my neck and giving me soft kisses. "Why wouldn't I be? You're my every fantasy, and then some. I need to make love to you, Raven, slow and easy. He takes his time entering me, and then stops.

"Open your eyes, Raven. Look at me."

Once I obey, he begins to move really slowly. Then he starts to grind into me the way that makes me crazy, I don't know how much longer I can last. "Jax, I can't hold it."

He softly kisses my lips, "Go, sweetheart, I need to watch you fall."

I look into his eyes and I can see the depth of the love he has for me and—I'm done. My body quivers and my heart begins to race. I'm riding the most unbelievable wave of pleasure.

"Oh, Raven, every time I watch you fall apart in my arms, I'm struck by how much love I have for you." he almost whispers before attacking my lips.

Slowly, we work our tongues into a sensual dance. He's buried in me, forehead to forehead, eyes locked. "You know what I want, don't you, sweetheart?" he asks.

I smile, "I know, Jax. Are you ready?"

He takes a deep breath. "Always, sweetheart."

I work my magic. "Oh my God, Raven . . . fuck!"

As he comes apart in my arms I whisper, "Jax, Je t'aime de tout mon coeur et de l'âme."

He pulls the covers over us, "I love you too," he whispers.

Chapter Nine

Jackie

I NEED TO TALK to my parents about my decision to go back to the States. I know they won't be happy, but in the end, I have to do what is best for me. I'm sure my brother will put his two cents in. Dylan's real problem isn't with me, it's with Raven. He's been in love with her from the first day I brought her home. I need to get this over with Raven and Jax will be here soon to pick me up. I head downstairs, suitcase in hand. My mother sees me, her eyes glance towards my suitcase and she begins to cry. I knew this would not be easy. However, I need answers and those answers are waiting for me in New York. I put my arm around my mom, "Let's go sit down, Mom."

My dad and brother are already in the drawing room, and I get the feeling that they know what's coming. My dad hands me an envelope.

"Jacqueline, before you make your decision to leave, that is a dossier on Maxwell Fleming. I'm not saying he is a bad man. All I'm saying is that he has a past, one that you should be aware of."

My brother is not as calm as my dad; he is fuming. "Jackie, he's thirty-eight and you're twenty-five. He is very experienced and you're not. Think before you jump in, blinded by lust. You're going to get your heart broken by this man, a man you know nothing about!"

I know I need to see this through and nothing anyone can say will stop me. "Dylan, life is about taking chances, and not always riding in the slow lane. Walking away from him broke my heart. There's not much more he could do to it now. I need to understand why. What ever is in the envelope means nothing to me. I need to hear it from Max."

"So, you're just going to up and leave? Do you even know anything about Jaxson or Maxwell? Do you know that Maxwell is twenty percent owner of Raiders Inc.? He might be Mr. Charming, but for fuck sake, Jackie, he's a glorified corporate raider—the lowest of the low!"

That's it, I've heard enough. I jump up, "Dylan, please stop. Your problem is not with me leaving. Your problem is with Raven. She fell in love with someone and it wasn't you. They are engaged, Dylan, and she is having his baby. It's time for you to move on."

I hated to throw that out there, but it's not fair for him to judge someone because he is hurt.

"Well, Jackie, are you going to follow in her footsteps and get knocked up, too?"

Before I can answer, my dad jumps up, "We have company."

I turn around and find Raven standing there with Jax. My father remains stoic not knowing how much Jax overheard. "I'm sorry, I wasn't aware that the housekeeper had let you in."

I think everyone is waiting for the explosion that is on the horizon. As Jax goes to step forward, Raven stops him. "Please Jax, let me handle this." She heads towards me and takes few steadying breaths. "Jeffery, Emi, you know that I love Jackie as if she were my own sister. I would never, knowingly put her in harms way. I promise you that I will look after her, and she will have round-the-clock security. Whether or not she decides to work things out with Maxwell is her decision and hers alone to make. Dylan, as far as your insinuations that she would get 'knocked up,' that is a very disrespectful thing to say about your sister. She has never done anything to warrant your behavior today. What I do with my life is my own business and none of yours. My fiancé, Jaxson, is a good man. He is kind-hearted, caring, and loving. Instead of disrespecting him, maybe you should strive to be more like him. Now, if you're ready, Jackie, we need to get going."

My dad pulls me into a hug. "I will let you go, however, you must take Samuel with you. The arrangements have already been made, since I knew what your decision would be."

"Oh, Papa, it will be fun, watching Samuel trying to adapt to living in New York City again!"

We say our goodbyes and head toward the door. Jax is very quiet, but his jaw is tight. I can tell he is fighting to control his anger. If Raven weren't here to diffuse the situation, Dylan would be in a heap, on the floor, right now.

As we head towards the door, Jax pulls my dad aside. "Jeffery, I don't know who Samuel is, and you're asking me to let him come on my plane with us. I hope you can understand why I'm apprehensive about this."

"Jax, I'm sure you understand how security conscious I am. I would never entrust Jacqueline's safety to just anyone. Samuel has been with our family for ten years, I trust him; he can't be bought."

"Jeffery, I need to make a call."

He nods, "Of course, Jax, we will wait for you in the drawing room."

"Raven, I need to call Max. I'll only be a few minutes," he informs her before we head back in.

Jaxson

"HEY, MAX, I NEED to run something past you." Before he can answer, I tell him what is going on with Jackie and this guy Samuel. I give him the guy's info, and I can hear him tapping away on the computer.

Finally he stops. "Jax, it seems that Samuel's info checks out. He has been with the Gerhard family for ten years. He was her guard when she went away to college. He has a very impressive history; he is former MI6. Have you met him yet?"

I stop pacing, "No, we are just getting ready to leave now."

Max, is quiet for so long that I have to look and make sure the call didn't drop. "Jax, I think it's okay but you have the final say. You need to trust your gut on this one, mate. In the meantime, I will pull a more in-depth report on Samuel and Gerhard. I'll also hit up all of my contacts at MI6 to find out what's not on paper. "

I just can't wait till there is some sort of normalcy in our lives. "Okay, talk to you later." I end the call. I walk into the living room and meet Samuel. He is nothing like I was expecting, that's for sure. He looks like he just stepped off the pages of GQ Magazine. *And* he is sitting next to Raven—chatting her up! Jeffery looks over at me and I nod.

"Jax, let me introduce you to Samuel Kent."

I step in and shake his hand, my eyes locked on Raven. "Mr. Phillips, pleasure to meet you."

As I shake his hand, I hear Max, in my head, telling me to trust my gut. "You can call me, Jax. We have a stop to make. I will brief you on the way."

Everyone says his or her goodbyes and finally, we are on our way. The ride to the clinic is eerily quiet.

"Jax, do I even want to know what is going through your mind right now?" Raven asks from beside me.

"Oh trust me, sweetheart, you'll find out soon enough," I reply in a hushed tone.

"Okay, stretch, spill. What the hell happened back there?" Samuel asks Jackie.

"Dylan was acting up and Raven put him in his place."

Samuel laughs, "Sorry I missed it. He's always had a thing for you, Raven. Guess you showing up with Jax burst his bubble."

"Sammy, I've never showed any interest in Dylan. Whatever thoughts he's had were manufactured in his own mind."

"I know, Raven, but I'm still sorry I missed it. So what's the stop that we have to make?"

"Sammy, I came here on some personal business for a friend. I have to pick someone up and bring her to the states. She has top-level clearance. I would never let anyone near these girls if it wasn't safe."

"Jax, why wasn't I made aware of this earlier?"

"For the same reason I was not made aware of your presence earlier. My plane. My girl. My rules. You can trust me or I can let you out now—your choice."

"Jax, wherever Jackie goes I go."

The rest of the ride is in silence.

Raven

WE ACTUALLY MANAGE TO get my mom, and settle in for the long flight without any drama. My mom is showing Jackie her sketches. Sammy is reading a magazine. I snuggle up to Jax.

"Raven, what's on your mind?"

I love that we are really figuring each other out. "How can you tell I'm thinking about something?"

He laughs, "Sweetheart, I can always tell when your wheels are turning."

"Do you think I was wrong for telling Dylan off in front of his parents? They have always been supportive and respectful of me. I feel like maybe I disrespected them."

His thumb travels up and down my arm. "Look at me, Raven." His thumb stops and he pats my arm. My eyes fly up to his. "What you said was the truth, and you said it a hell of a lot nicer than I would have. When you were telling Dylan, off I was so proud. Not for what you were saying about me; I could give a royal fuck what anyone thinks. It was your passion to defend, not only Jackie, but also our baby and me. I never thought I could love you more, but in that instant, I fell in love with you all over again."

I snuggle into him. "I love you, Jax."

He laughs, "More, sweetheart, always more."

Jaxson

EVERYONE IS ASLEEP, EXCEPT for Samuel, so I figured I'd go into the office and get some work done. First order of business is to check in with my mum. I only hope that Max survived being locked up all these days with her!

"Hi, Mum, what's going on over there?"

She huffs, "Well, it's about time you called me. When will you be home?"

"We are in route right now. We probably have another six hours of flight time. Is everything okay over there?"

"Well, what did you think I was going to do to him? I mean, really, son."

I'm trying to get a lead on what's bothering her, but she's playing this pretty close to the vest. "I know, Mum, is he any better than when I left?"

"Actually, yes, he is. Is Jackie with you?" she asks, her tone lightening up.

Of course she wants to know that. "Yes, Mum, but they have to work it out on their own, so no interfering."

"Really, son, I never interfere in anyone's business."

I damn near choke on that one.

"How is Gabriella doing?"

I know my family will embrace Gabriella. "She is doing a lot better than the doctors expected. I think she might not need to be in a clinic. I'm thinking of putting her in a flat in my building. Raven, can be close to her all the time; she deserves that."

"I think that would be a great idea, but are there any available?"

Ha! "Mum, if not, I'll buy the whole building!"

She's mumbling something under her breath—which she does a lot, when it comes to me.

I take a deep breath, preparing myself to give her the news. "Mum, she said yes!" I say quickly.

"Well, did you doubt it? I told you, from the first day I met her, that she would be my daughter-in-law, you just need to listen to your mum more often."

I am never going to live that one down.

"So, when is the wedding? You know, the baby will be here before you know it."

That's mum's way of telling me she wants us married before the baby gets here. "I know, I haven't spoken to her about it yet. If it was up to me I would marry her the second this plane touches the ground. However, I'm not sure what Raven is thinking. Oh, and we had Gabriella's name changed.

It's officially, Rose Anderson," I inform her. This is also my way of changing the subject.

"Okay, now when you get home we are having a family meeting?" I can hear the apprehension in her voice; it's so unlike her and I'm worried.

I have to ask, but I know she won't tell me. "Mum, is something wrong?"

"Never mind, Jaxson, we will talk about it when you get in. Be safe and I love you."

"Me too, Mum."

Something is off and I'm not sure what. I decided to call Bella. "Hey, sis, I'm about six hours out, what is happening with Mum?"

"Ha, hello to you too, bro. What do you mean? Mum is guarding, Max and he's not happy about it."

I tell her what mum said about having a meeting. "She only calls them when one of us is in trouble, and I don't think it's me."

I hold while she yells at Vito. I swear that dog is a beast.

"Well, that's news to me. I know I didn't do anything wrong, either, for a change."

This is bugging me. "Alright, maybe Max fucked up. I'll call him next. She said yes, Bella." I add in quickly. I can't believe I almost forgot to tell her.

She laughs, "Of course she did, she loves you. Sometimes, you're such a moron. When is the big day?"

I guess I really need to get this nailed down with Raven. "I don't know, we haven't talked about it."

Bella is quiet for a minute. "Well, if you want, we can have it here. The garden is in full bloom, and you know I can get it together really quickly. How's her mum doing?"

That's not a bad idea. I wonder if I can sell Raven on it. "She is doing great. I will talk to Raven about what type of wedding she wants. Sorry to cut you short but I have to go. Love you, sis."

She laughs, "Me too, bro."

Next on my list is Max. He picks up on the first ring. "Max, I see Mum didn't kill you, yet. How are you feeling?"

"I'm doing better, and I'm getting used to having my watchdog."

He must be better, he's getting all cheeky again. "You better not let her hear you call her that; she'll be yanking your ears!" That shut him up real quick.

"Where are you, Jax?"

I'm pacing again, something I find myself doing a lot since all this started. Usually, it's Max who paces. "In the air. We should be home soon and before you ask, I still haven't talked to her about what type of wedding or when."

"Mate, what is your fucking problem?" he yells.

"Max, what if she doesn't want to get married for a year? I will go nuts. I really wish you would stop laughing at me." *I'm glad my life is so fucking funny!*

"Oh, Jax, I can't help it. You really are very funny. You can negotiate million dollar deals, yet talking to a beautiful girl—who is madly in love with you—renders you speechless. Please tell me you see the humor in this?"

"Fuck you, Max. What is going on with Mum?" I shift the conversation. "She said we are having a family meeting. I called Bella; she hasn't pissed Mum off. And I've been away, so that only leaves you." He gets really quiet, and now I know it's him. Fuck! What is going on?

"Actually, it has been quiet here. An, and I go to the park for walks. Then we have pretzels, sit on the bench, and people watch."

I know when something is being kept from me, but I can wait a few more hours. "Max, I have a job for you." Maybe this will get him excited.

"Well, *finally,* I get to do something."

Ugh. "Wise arse. I need a flat in our building for Raven's Mum. Before you even make the suggestion, the answer is no fucking way, you're not giving up your flat." I can just picture him pacing.

"I thought she was going into a clinic? I made all the arrangements, Jax."

I know Max will agree she needs to be around Raven, not in some clinic. "When you see her, you'll understand. She really doesn't need to be in a clinic. Between regular doctor visits and having Raven around all the time, we both feel that she will be fine."

"If there are no flats, then what would you like to do? I don't know why I ask, I already know the answer. Just buy the whole building, right?"

Finally, he gets it. "You see, Max, you know me better than anyone. Oh and just so you know, you're my best man."

He's laughing, "Of course I am, mate, have a safe flight."

I GO CHECK ON everyone and find they're all asleep. I scoop Raven up and carry her into the bedroom. I'm such a lucky bastard. I know it. Now, if I can convince her that we should get married on Friday, all will be right in my world.

"Jax, where are we?"

I start by nibbling that ear. "We, my dear, are somewhere over the Atlantic, and I need you."

"Is everything okay?"

I laugh, "Oh it will be, just as soon as I get your clothes off." She slowly opens her eyes, "There she is, my beautiful girl." I nuzzle her neck.

"Hi." She kisses my lips so softly, I swear I could explode just from her tenderness. "Don't you ever sleep, Jax?"

I can't help but laugh, "Yes, but I sleep best when I'm buried inside of you." I love to kiss her tender lips and nibble on that ear. I don't know why it drives me crazy, but it does. "I need to make love to you very slowly, sweetheart. I don't know why, just know that I need it like my very existence depends on it." I enter her very slowly, and when I'm all the way in I stop and rest my forehead upon hers. "Raven, I have no control when it comes to you. I was so lost, and I didn't even realize it."

"Jax, I'm not going anywhere in this world without you—ever. I'm with you for life."

I take a deep breath, "I'm going to move now, and try not to explode, but I can't make any promises."

"Jax, flip me over. I want to be on top."

I'm a strong man, yet I don't mind giving Raven control in the bedroom. Sometimes she needs to take the power. It's a beautiful thing, watching her glide up and down my cock, taking me, as she needs me. Let's face it; I'm not a one shot man!

Wow, "I love when you get all demanding, it's a real turn on."

"Jax, everything turns you on."

"Okay, yeah. When it comes to you, that's true. I have a confession, but I don't know if I can talk right now while you're gliding up and down on my cock."

She takes both my hands and stops. "Tell me!"

I take a deep breath, "Okay, don't stop. When you were giving Dylan the bitch slap, I was hard as stone; very exciting stuff, sweetheart."

She throws her head back laughing. "Oh my crazy man, I love you. Now hold on 'cause I need to let loose." She goes up really slow and then, slams down on my cock. She clenches and goes back up again, then repeats her actions. That's it—I'm done. "Fuck . . . oh, holy hell, woman." She is digging her nails into my shoulders and screaming her release. *Nails and clenching; she's trying to fucking kill me!*

She's gliding up and down really slowly, as I try to catch my breath. I slowly caress her growing belly, trying to figure out how to convince her that we should get married right away.

"Jax, you seem perplexed, what's bothering you?"

I tilt my hips up to meet hers. "I can't keep anything from you."

"No, and you know I don't want you to. We are on this journey together, so no secrets."

I don't know why I'm so nervous to talk to her about this. I know I shouldn't be.

"We need to talk about the wedding."

She's staring at me, trailing her fingers up and down my cheeks. "Is that what you're worried about?"

I nod, "Well, yeah . . . Bella said the garden is in bloom and we can have it there, but Max said that every girl dreams of her wedding day, and I need to give you free rein with the details. But you know me; I don't want to make you feel like I'm bullying you into the wedding. I want to make all your dreams come true."

She leans down and kisses me really slowly. "Jax, calm down and let's talk. First, did you tell everyone that we got engaged yesterday, and when did you tell them?"

"You know me, I have to bounce things off of my family, it's just who I am."

"Jax, when do you want to get married? Let's start with that."

I cringe a little at the idea of telling her.

"Please don't tell me you already have it planned?"

"No, well, not yet. If it were up to me I would want to be married yesterday." I say quickly, and then wait for my words to register with her. "Raven, are you going to say anything, or are you just going to look at me like I've lost all reason?"

"Are you serious?"

I take both of her hands, holding onto them so tightly: afraid she might disappear.

"Of course I'm serious. I want to be married before the baby gets here. My life didn't start until you came crashing into it. I want everyone to know that I'm one lucky bastard—the luckiest in the whole bloody world. I want to experience life everyday through your eyes."

"Just how do you plan on pulling this off so quickly?

"Really, Raven, I don't like to throw my money around, but I'm one of the wealthiest men in the world. Surely, I can get a wedding pulled off in record time."

"Jax, how do you think I would feel?"

I chew on my bottom lip and squeeze her hands.

"Well, you see, sweetheart, there's my dilemma. I know how you would feel, I just don't know how to change that."

"Jax, I think a compromise is in order here, don't you agree?"

Suddenly, I feel a sense of relief wash over me. I think she may be onto something, here. "Okay, I can compromise . . . I think." Oh boy, not sure that was the right fucking answer. She looks like she's going to blow a gasket.

"You *think?* Jax, how the hell do you negotiate million dollar deals and not compromise? Please, I really need to understand this."

I give her my biggest smile, "I make them see the light."

"Okay, what do you mean by 'you make them see the light'?"

"Raven, I think you're making this a lot more difficult than it really is. I show the people what they can achieve when we all play nicely together, and then they see what life is like if we don't. It really is a no brainer, and I don't understand why more people don't do this for a living." *She's really quiet. I hope I didn't mess this up.*

"Jax, here is my list of *demands.* I would like a small wedding. I would like Jackie as my maid of honor. I don't have anyone to give me away, so I think I would like Michael Jr. to walk me down the aisle since this all started with him. I want one long stem Abracadabra Rose. I would love to have it in Bella's garden. I want you in a violet bow tie. Wow, you're not saying a word? I would've thought you'd interrupt me by now."

I smile, "I'm processing. How long will it take you to find something to wear?"

"After all of that, your only question is about my gown?"

"I can pull all of that off within a reasonable time frame. I love all of this *negotiating,* it's making me hard."

"Oh, for the love of Jesus, Jax, everything makes you hard!"

"Yep, when it comes to you, sweetheart, everything does."

"Oh, and, Jax, I want a prenuptial agreement. I don't want anyone to think I'm marrying you for your money. Bad enough, people will talk when the baby gets here."

"STOP. I will not have you talk about our baby like that—EVER! I don't give a flying fuck what anyone says or thinks, it's what I know in my heart. That's the only thing that matters, the only thing that ever will. Our baby—our flesh and blood—was created out of love. No more talk like that and no prenup!"

"Jax, I thought we were negotiating?"

I growl at her, "That is non-negotiable."

"Wow, you scared me. Are you like this with the companies you deal with?"

"Sweetheart, I know what I want, and what I'm willing to give up to get it. I don't waiver on the important stuff, I do on the stuff I could care less about and that makes them feel like they had a victory."

"Okay, no prenup."

"Good, now that we have that settled, do you think you can decide on a dress by Friday? If not, I can have someone make you whatever you want."

Her mouth falls open. "This Friday?"

I'm still buried inside her; I tilt my hips. "I told you I don't want to wait. If we do it this Friday or six months from now, nothing will change. I will make it exactly how you want it." I start moving slowly again.

"Jax, I will try—oh who am I kidding? You know and I know that we are going to get married on Friday, come hell or high water!"

I attack her neck with laughter and kisses. "Sweetheart, I love negotiating with you, we should do this more often."

"That wasn't negotiating, Jax, that was you getting what you want. " Look at me, please." I stop my attack on her neck and look up at her. "I love you, but I need you to understand that you can't always push me around to get what you want. If you want something, talk it out with me, first, okay?" she pleads.

"Okay, but you need to understand that this was real progress for me. Normally, I would just take the ball and run with it. Try to be patient with me and all my craziness and I will promise to try and negotiate with you on the important stuff. I'm not going to run to you with every little thing, and I don't expect you to run to me with the small stuff, either. I trust you and your judgment. I need you to trust me. Are we all good now?"

"Yes, we're good."

"Okay, baby, you know what I would love right now?"

"I know exactly what you want." She smiles coyly at me. I grind my hips into her just the way she likes and I can see she's getting close; her breathing becomes erratic and she quickens her pace. "Jax, you ready, baby?"

I take a deep breath and I feel need in me, climbing. "Oh God, Raven, I'm ready . . . do it baby, *please*." I beg. She clenches, squeezing my cock as she slams down. That's all it takes to send us both over the cliff.

I feel as if I'm about to pass out. "Jax, are you okay? Breath, baby, just breath."

I kiss her softly. "Raven, can we invite your Pilates teacher to the wedding?"

She laughs. "Go to sleep, Jax, I love you."

I whisper, "More, sweetheart, always more."

Maxwell

JAX WILL BE BACK soon, and then the calm, I've been experiencing, will be gone. There are no flats available in this building. I will see if anyone is willing to sell, otherwise, that crazy-arse fucker will buy the building, and then all hell will break loose. It's almost teatime with An; she keeps me on a tight schedule. I know she wants me to call her something other than ma'am, I just don't know what. Just like clockwork, here she comes.

"Maxwell, teatime."

I smile. She's so strong, yet she has let me see how vulnerable she really is. "Good afternoon, ma'am, how are you feeling?" She won't say it, but I know she's worried about telling Jax and Bella.

"I heard from Jaxson, they should be home soon. Raven said yes, so now we have a flurry of wedding events. Have you spoken to him?"

"Yes, ma'am, he called earlier. He was going to try and talk Raven into setting a date. You know what that means, he will move heaven and earth to get her down that aisle as fast as possible." I know she wants them married just as fast as Jax does.

"Well, I can tell you, I, for one, will be very happy on that day. I want them married and concentrating on my new grandbaby."

I'm more worried about Raven. "I know, but Raven has been through a great deal, and now she is taking on the responsibility of a mother, who, for all intents and purposes, died twenty years ago. I know she is thrilled that she has her mum in her life again, but it is an emotional time for everyone. And let's not forget that the threat is still out there."

Her face turns pale, and I feel bad that I even brought it up.

"Have you found out who that woman was? Did you think I didn't notice how worried you were?"

I laugh, "You're too smart for your own good, ma'am. I think it might be, Annabelle Gianconna, Vincent's sister. The attorneys are issuing a restraining order."

"Maxwell, we are going to have a family sit down later, and I would like you there. I plan on telling Jaxson and Isabella the truth about their father and you."

We are both quiet for a bit. "Are you sure you want me there? This is a very personal matter, maybe I should sit it out."

She's holding onto her teacup so tight I fear it will shatter. "Maxwell, you really don't want to be on my bad side. You are family, whether you like it or not, you are stuck with us. I know that Jax and Bella will be overjoyed to know what they feel, in their hearts, is in fact reality. Do you have a problem with us?"

I shake my head and just begin to laugh, "Oh, ma'am, you really are a mini version of Jax. Yesterday, you said you wanted me to call you something other than ma'am. What would you like me to call you?"

She smiles, "You'll know when the time is right. We are having the meeting here, so you don't have to go anywhere. I already let Isabella know."

I need to change the subject. "Jax asked me to find a flat in the building for Gabriella."

"Maxwell, don't even think about it."

Ha. "Relax, An, Jax already yelled at me. However, there are none available."

"Well, I'm sure Jax will convince someone to move out!"

We sit in silence for a bit.

"Maxwell, did Jax mention Jackie?"

"She is with them." My heart constricts as I whisper.

"I know. Have you thought about what you're going to do?"

"I don't know what I'm going to do."

"Well, you can't sit here, wallowing in self-pity, can you?"

"I'm at a loss here. What would you suggest I do? I really hurt her. I pushed her away without a word. The worst part is, I made Jax do my dirty deed. What kind of man does that make me? She deserves so much better than me. My head keeps saying she would be safer, if she stayed away from me. Yet, my heart beats stronger at the mere thought of her."

She just sits there, stirring her tea. "Well, are you going to say something or just stir that cold cup of tea?"

She finally looks up, "Well, you're right. She didn't deserve to be treated like that. When you were shot, she put all her fears aside and sat by your bedside twenty-four seven. I had to force her to eat and sleep. She was willing to stay by your side, no matter what the outcome. That is not someone to dismiss from your life, like you're throwing out the morning trash."

Well that didn't help. "I feel even worse now. I thought you were supposed to be here making me feel better?"

"No, Maxwell, I'm not here to make you feel better. I'm here to make you feel. I think you should start with an apology. And from there, maybe explain to her why."

I don't know that I can do this. "The wedding is probably going to happen on Friday. You know I'm the best man?"

She laughs, "Of course, did you think he would ever ask anyone else?"

I only have a few hours till they land. I can feel my heart racing. "I'm so much older than her, and she has so much life to live."

"Maxwell, please stop the pity party and get on with life. I'm not saying that what happened wasn't a tragedy, but don't you think Samantha would want you to be happy? If, God forbid, the shoe was on the other foot, wouldn't you have wanted Samantha to be happy?"

I growl, "You're right, and if you tell another living soul I said that, I will deny it to the bitter end!"

She reaches up and pulls my ear, and all I can do is laugh.

*J*axson

WHEN WE LAND, MAX has a limo and another group of guards waiting for us. I hope Gabriella is going to be able to deal with all of this craziness. Raven reaches up and pulls my hands out of my hair.

"Relax, Jax, we will be okay." She calms and grounds me. I don't know what I ever did before her.

Jackie seems very nervous . . . almost scared. "Jax, Sammy and I are going back to my apartment. I still have my tracking bracelet. Do you want me to have another guard?"

I know I can't stop Jackie from going home, but at least Sammy is with her.

"Okay, Sammy, take her back to her place, make sure the bracelet always remains on, and take another guard with you."

"Jax, he's gay. He's been in a committed relationship for the past seven years. His partner, Ian, has agreed to move and he will be joining Sammy soon." Raven informs me of this news. Though, she could of saved my nerves from being on edge hours ago, I'm glad she finally did say *something*.

"I love that you understand me, Raven. The whole ride, all I could think was *Max is going to kill me if I let her go off with him*."

She laughs at me but then glances at her mother and her smile fades. "Mom, are you okay?"

Gabriella closes her eyes and takes a deep breath. "I'll be fine, it's a lot to take in, all at once. I have been in that little clinic for twenty years. The world has changed so much, yet my life has stood still. Will I ever be able to catch up?"

Raven pulls her into her arms as the tears she was fighting to hold back begin to fall. "Mom, we will be here with you every step of the way. No one will hurt you, ever again. It's time you begin to live again. Daddy would have wanted you to be happy."

I watch my beautiful girl comforting her mum, and I realize this has to be so overwhelming for Raven too. She is so strong, and in this moment, I love her so much more . . . if that's even possible.

We pull up to The Tower and a confused look comes across Raven's face. "Jax, I thought we were going to bring my mom to a clinic?"

I take her hand, "I have been thinking that maybe it would be best if we got your mum a flat in our building. I would rather have her closer to us. I think it would be good for everyone. Until I can make the arrangements, I figure she can stay in our guest room."

"What if there are no flats available? Oh, why do I even bother asking such a stupid question? Don't worry, Mom, you will have a flat in this building if Jax has anything to say about it."

Chapter Ten

Jaxson

THE ELEVATOR DOORS OPEN, and my mum is waiting for us. One look and I know something is up. What else is going to be thrown at me? We make all the introductions, and Raven takes her mum to her room so she can get settled in.

"Mum, what's wrong?" I ask in a hushed tone.

"Jaxson, we are having the family meeting now at Maxwell's. Bella is already waiting for us. I would also like Raven to be there."

She really has me worried. "Are you ill?"

She shakes her head, "No, son, my health is fine."

Raven comes out takes one look at us, and she furrows her brows at me. "Jax, is everything okay?"

I take her hand, holding it tight. "We are having a family meeting at Max's and you have to come too." She strokes my back, trying to calm me. She is my rock, my light in the storm, and I thank God everyday that I went to that Starbucks a few minutes early.

We get over to Max's and Junior runs right into Raven's arms. He really is so attached to her. I glance over at Max, and I know something is up between him and Mum.

Raven is looking him over, "Max, you look wonderful, and all your hair is back!"

Bella laughs, "Raven, I was a cosmetologist before I met, Michael. I told Max I could make some crazy hairstyles if he wants, but he won't let me near him with my shears!"

"Why did you give it up?" Raven asks.

She kisses Junior's head. "When I was pregnant with him I didn't want to be around the chemicals. After that, I fell in love with being a mum."

My mum stands up. "Okay, everyone, please have a seat. I have something I need to tell everyone." My mum seems really nervous.

"This is a very hard story for me to tell, but the situation being what it is, it must be told. I was a young girl of seventeen, living in Wales when I met James Phillips. We fell in love, and I thought the world started and stopped with him. Well, I was caught up in the rush of the romance and found my-self pregnant."

Raven is squeezing my hand.

"My parents were very old fashioned and insisted that we marry right away. In the beginning, things were good. My husband was in sales and he traveled frequently, yet he always made it home on the weekends. When I found myself pregnant with Isabella, his time home became less and less, until finally, one day, he never came back. I decided to search for him. My search led me to Scotland . . . where I met his other wife and son. When I confronted her about her husband, I realized we were both duped. She said James came home and confessed everything to her, right before he walked out. I was stunned. I walked away that day a broken woman. So many lives were destroyed. The other wife's name was Cindy and their son was . . . Maxwell.

I leap up, "Are you telling me my father was nothing more than a bigamist? I never thought he was perfect, but a fucking bigamist?!"

"Jaxson, I'm sorry, son . . . so very sorry for all of this."

My mum begins to cry; she's trembling. I pull her into my arms, "Enough! Mum, I don't blame you at all."

"Please, son, sit down and let me finish. I left Scotland, went home to lick my wounds. I needed to figure out what I was going to do next. It was during that time that Cindy overdosed on pain pills. I reached out to Maxwell's grandmother, and we soon became friends. She never blamed me for Cindy's death, although, I will forever blame myself. She moved Maxwell to London and changed his last name to hers. I went to her, and pleaded with her to let me raise Maxwell as my own. I wanted to have the three of you grow up together, but his grams felt that he was settled in already. And she wanted him with her. I made her a promise right then and there that I've kept all these years. I walked away that day so sad. Sad that one man caused so much heartache. Sad that Maxwell would never know he had siblings. Sad that Jaxson and Isabella would never know what a wonderful brother they had. But mostly sad at the part I felt I played in Cindy's death. That day, I made my decision. I would move my family to the United States. It broke my heart to leave Maxwell but I never had a choice."

No one is saying a word, my mum is trying to keep it together and be strong, but I can see she is going to lose it. I get up and take her in my arms. "Mum, I am so very proud of you. You took a bad situation and made it better for everyone involved, always putting the children first. I, for one, am very proud to call you my mum."

She begins to cry, and it slays me that she went through all of this alone.

Max stands up, and takes her hands. His eyes, always on her. I don't know what happened when I was gone, but it seems like it was good for both of them.

"An, you should never have felt responsible for my mum's death. I'm so sorry that you carried this with you, all these years. You had no idea what you would find that day. You knocked on the door, looking for answers—answers you deserved. You were not there to hurt anyone. My mum just wasn't as strong. I've accepted that and you should too. Please stop blaming yourself. There is more to this story, and its time I told everyone."

Maxwell

I NEED TO GET this over with quickly. I know they need to know, but the pain in reliving it turns my heart to stone. "I did okay for myself. I met and fell in love with the most beautiful woman, Samantha. She was a barrister, and we worked well together. We married and soon after we had the most beautiful son, Elliot. I thought my life was complete, and I put the past behind me. Samantha would take Elliot to the park everyday. He loved to be outside. One day, while she was loading him into the car, some drugged up gang member's carjacked her. My wife and son were both shot. They died instantly. My life ended that day. I quit my job and drank myself into numbness. My grams was still in touch with An, and she told her what happened. An was getting ready to come and drag me to the States when I decided to join the Special Forces. I took every assignment there was, trying to get myself killed. I just wanted to be with my family. There is a saying: *'We make plans and God just laughs,'* well, God had his own ideas. I was then asked to guard the Queen's rebel grandson. I said okay, thinking the more danger, the better. Then one night I met Jax in a bar. I thought it was a chance meeting, only to find out, last week, that it was a set up by An and my grams. The rest, as they say, is history."

"Max, what do you mean, it was a set up?" Jax asks in shock.

I laugh, "Yeah, mate, your mum and my grams set the whole thing up. I was given a letter yesterday that your mum kept in a safety deposit box from my grams. She wanted your mum to give it to me when she felt I needed to know the whole story. If you want to read it, you can. Look, all of you, I've accepted that this is my life. I don't want your sympathy for what happened to Samantha and Elliot."

Bella jumps up and throws her arms around me, then smacks me in the chest. "You're such an arse."

We all freeze, watching Bella. "Of course we have sympathy, why wouldn't we? That's a terrible thing to have happen, and as a parent, I will never understand how you survived. When Junior was taken, I thought my life was over. I have loved you like a brother from the first day Jax brought you home and nothing that is said here will ever change that for me. What I always felt in my heart is real and I can use this to my advantage."

"Hey, Jax, why don't you come into my office and I'll give you that letter to read," I offer. He gets up and heads down the hall with me.

We get into my office and Jax is quiet. A quiet Jax is never a good sign. I'm worried about him I know this is a lot for him to deal with on top of everything else. "Jax, you're very quiet, mate, what's wrong?"

"Max, I have always thought of you as my brother. I'm blown away with the fact that you actually are. I couldn't be happier about that. I am in shock, however, to find out that Bella and I are illegitimate. I think I understand now why mum wants us married before the baby gets here, and why she was wild when Bella was pregnant before she was married. I know we live in a world where anything goes, but that's not how I fly, mate. You know I have morals and ethics that I live by, so how can I fix this for Mum's sake?"

"Jax, I honestly have no idea here, but I will do whatever makes it easier for everyone. Honestly, so much has happened since you've been gone. Your mum showed me a side of her I never knew existed. She acts all tough and brave, but she has been living with the fear that this will bring shame to her children. She's been carrying the guilt of my mum's death for all these years, a guilt she shouldn't have to bear. I think for everyone involved, we need to put this all away and move forward." I get the letter out.

Jax shakes his head. "That is personal, and I have no reason to doubt anything you tell me. Please put it away. What else happened while I was gone?"

As I put the letter away I take notice how tired he is. "Jax, we can go over this in the morning." He shakes his head no.

"No. Let's go over it now."

"Okay, if you insist. There are no flats available in the building. I put some feelers out to see if anyone wants to sell, but no responses. I got confirmation back from Tony, right before you landed, that the woman in the park was Annabelle. She has not made any more attempts to contact Raven. I am checking into new guards for Raven and Gabriella." I wait for a response from him. After a few moments, I lightly smack his upper arm. "Talk to me, Jax. I can't help you if you don't let me in." I open my drawer, pull out a bottle of scotch, and pour us each a glass.

"Will this cluster fuck ever end, Max? I want my family safe—safe and happy. Is that really too much to ask?"

"For everyone's sake, Jax, I hope so and soon."

Raven

THE GUYS ARE BACK and I see worry lines around Jax's eyes. My heart is breaking for this man. I need to get him to eat something and rest, and I know just what to do. "Jax, I'm hungry can we get something to eat?"

His eyes light up. "My girl is hungry, so I have to go feed her. I love you all, but this is a priority!" He is now pushing me out the door. Giving Jax purpose, and letting him know he is needed is what lights up his world. We go across the hall and everything is quiet. My mom is still sleeping, and I'm pretty sure she will be for a while.

"Raven, what would you like to eat?"

I reach up and kiss his soft lips. "Are you up for an adventure?"

He gives me that smirk I love so much. "As long as I'm with you, I will go anywhere."

Oh, how I love this man. "Jax, the only thing I need you to do is run a bath and I will meet you in there." He's about to argue, but I hold my hand up for him to stop.

" Remember, some things are non-negotiable. Right now, you need me to shut off your mind and let me take charge. Now, go."

His face lights up and his blues are twinkling. "Okay, you don't have to tell me twice."

I watch him stroll towards the bathroom, and I can't help staring at his beautiful ass. He stops just before the doorway and turns his head around, "Like the view, sweetheart?" I roll my eyes, so busted.

There is a little pizza place, not too far away, that makes a specialty pizza. I order it along with a ton of food, and give one of the guard's instructions where to pick it up. I head into the bathroom and there is my beautiful man, soaking in the tub. His head tilted back, eyes closed, and the room is filled with candles; vanilla and orange spice. I stand there and admire the view. I know he knows I'm watching, and I don't care. I get undressed and climb in with my back against his front.

"Jax, do you want to talk or would you rather shut your mind off, for the rest of the night?"

"I will take option B, thank you." He wraps his arms around me and pulls me tight. "Sweetheart, when we are locked away, just like this, I find a peace that I can't seem to get anywhere else. I'm worried about my mum, Raven, this shook her to the core."

Ah, so he does want to talk. "Give her time, Jax, she has held this secret for such a very long time. You know it had to be hard for her to admit everything. In her mind, she is afraid you and Bella will think less of her."

"I couldn't be more proud of her if I tried. To think, she put all of her pain and shame aside to give her children everything. Do you know what really got to me out of this whole situation?"

I turn in his arms so I can face him, "No, what?"

He pulls me tighter, "What really got to me is the fact that even though her husband was a bigamist, even though she was left with two very young children, she put all of that aside and offered to raise Max, along with us. That to me, shows what a strong and proud woman she is. I can only hope that I will set that type of example for our child."

I reach up and softly kiss his lips. "Maybe you need to let her know that, I'm sure it would help her." He doesn't say anything, but I know he gets it. I stand up, "We need to eat, and the water is getting cold." I offer him my hand, but he pulls himself to his knees, leans in, and kisses my growing bump.

"I love you, baby, and I love your mum, too." At this moment, I know I could never be without this man.

HE LEADS ME TOWARDS the kitchen. I stop. "I have a surprise for you, Jax, follow me upstairs." When we reach the rooftop deck, he looks at the spread and smiles. I know he's happy with the amount of food I ordered.

"Raven, this looks wonderful. I am starving, let's eat."

It's a beautiful evening, and this is the perfect place to enjoy the city, and each other. "Jax, do you think my mom is going to be okay, living in the city? I'm worried about her. This is such a change from where she has been living for the last twenty years."

"Raven, I know it will be an adjustment for her, but I think you being here, so close to her, will be a great help. I know you are fiercely independent, however, in this case, I think what would help her is to feel needed by you."

"I'm at a loss. How do I make her feel needed?"

"Sweetheart, your mum lost you when you were only seven years old. She missed out on all the milestones in your life. Yeah, she has you back, but you're a woman now, not a seven-year-old little girl. Helping you through the pregnancy, nurturing you, and helping with the baby will give her a sense of purpose. She will feel needed. Does that make sense?"

I nod, "It does. I can only hope that my pregnancy doesn't bring up any bad memories for her." Suddenly, Bo barks. I look over to see that my mom has wandered up to the roof deck. "Are you hungry, mom?"

"Yes, it looks wonderful."

Jax helps her to her seat. "Rose, I hope you feel comfortable staying here until I can secure a flat in this building. I know I can be a *bulldog,* so please tell me to rein it in, when I get overbearing." Jax is trying to make everything perfect for both of us.

"Jax, I'm excited to be close to Raven and the baby. Thank you so much for all that you are doing for all of us."

I know my tears will bring him to his knees, so I wipe them away quickly. Jax takes my hand and kisses the inside of my wrist, and I feel myself shudder. "Sweetheart, what's for dessert?"

I go about setting up the dessert, and I know he is going to lose his mind, but now that my mom is here I'm not sure how this is going to go over with him. I'm watching his face as I bring over a covered tray. "I hope you love it, Jax, it is one of my favorites."

I lift the lid, and the Jax's face is priceless. His eyes grow wide as he stares at the tray, speechless. I'm trying so hard not to laugh.

My mom smiles, but has a faraway look on her face. "Raven, do you know this is one of my favorite treats? Your father used to make this for me all the time."

I take a deep breath, to think that my mom and I both love Nutella. Something so simple, yet, so powerful. Jax still can't seem to muster a word. "My beautiful man, have I rendered you speechless?"

"I've never had a Nutella pizza. I am experiencing so many firsts with you."

I know Jax is trying so hard to control himself, but I can't help myself, he just makes it way too easy. I swipe my finger into the warm Nutella and pop it into my mouth. All the while never taking my eyes from Jax. I tilt my head back and let out a little low moan. He is frozen with a death grip on the sides of the table. Next, I swipe the whip cream and offer him my finger. He growls. I really don't know how long he is going to last, but I'm having way too much fun to stop now.

"Raven, I think I'm going to take my dessert and head back to my room. You both have fun." Mom giggles at us, shaking her head. I think she knows what I was doing to him just now.

My mom gets up and heads downstairs. The minute she is out of sight, Jax leaps up.

"I need you now."

I shake my head, "Nope, not yet, Jax. Tonight we are going to reverse roles here. I think it should be all about what *I* need." I inform him. His eyes grow wide, and he fists his hands like he's trying with all that he has for some sort of control.

"Sit, please." He does, but I can tell this is not going to be easy for him. I stand up and do a slow strip, just for him. I stand before him, wearing only my heels. He moans. I swipe my fingers through the pizza and smear the Nutella and whip cream on my nipples. "Oh my, Jax, this is wonderful. Warm Nutella and cool whip cream just making my nipples ache for you."

His eyes are gazing up and down my body, getting darker. I know he's not going to last much longer. I reach over and pick up his glass of Prosecco. I let it slowly drizzle down my breasts and between my legs. That's it—game over!

"Fuck all that is holy, woman!" he yells.

He leaps out of the chair, lifts me up, and runs with me to the cushioned chase lounge. He lays me down ever so gently, licking his way up my body, mumbling the whole way.

"You don't play fair, sweetheart."

He leans in to kiss me, but then leaps out of the chair. His eyes are wide with fear.

"Jax, are you okay?"

He stands there, silently, his bottom lip between his teeth. He runs both his hands through his hair, pulling it so hard I swear he will go bald. "The baby kicked me," he almost whispers in disbelief.

I have to try not to laugh but it's so hard not too.

"It's okay, Jax, the baby is moving a lot, lately." I take his hand. "Talk to me. What's the problem?"

"The baby moved just when I was going to have sex with you. I don't know; it freaked me out."

Oh my, he's really rattled. "Jax, the baby doesn't know what you're doing."

"But I know," he barely whispers.

How can I convince this man that it's okay? "Look, the doctor said we could continue to be sexually active." I watch him; he seems to be battling between his fear and his need. "I have an idea. Maybe it will help you if I'm on top."

He rests his forehead on mine. "Okay."

I lead him back down on the lounge chair. I need to get him to relax. I slowly work my way up his legs, kissing from one to the other. On my knees,

I stroke his beautiful cock up, twist, and then down. I lick the crown slowly, and he is finally relaxing. I climb over him and take my time lowering myself until he is sheath within me. "Give me your hands, Jax." I kiss one and then the other. I then place them on my breast. He's working each one of my nipples into a frenzied state. I pull myself up and slowly glide myself down, clenching all the way. His hips are coming up to meet mine. He puts my hands on his shoulders and he takes a hold of my hips. Leaning in, he takes one of my nipples between his teeth. I'm going to lose it real quick. Now he's onto the other nipple. "Jax, I'm not going to last, baby . . . Oh God, yes!" I can feel my whole body flush as I come, quivering and shaking. Jax's release soon follows.

I lie next to him and curl into his side. Both of us are quiet, and Jax is stroking my arm, lost in his thoughts.

"Raven, I don't know why I freaked out, it's just all of a sudden, the baby seemed so real."

I need to try and calm his fear, even though it's unfounded, it's real for him. " Do you think you're going to hurt the baby?"

"No, the doctor gave us the green light. It felt like I was walking in on my parents having sex."

I lean up, pulling his face towards mine. "Jax, the baby has no clue what we are doing. Making love with you is beautiful. Don't let the pregnancy take away from that."

He pulls the throw blanket over us, holding me closer. "I love you, and I love that you can take all my craziness, my beautiful girl."

"Jax, can I ask you for a favor?"

His smile is huge and his eyes are twinkling. "I would lay down the world at your feet, sweetheart, and just the fact that you need me for something is a total turn on!"

I can't help but laugh, "Oh, you're always turned on."

He's laughing and it's wonderful to be relaxed like this. "If we are getting married on Friday, do you think you can stay at Max's house, and Jackie can stay here with me and my mom?"

"We *are* getting married this Friday! You want me to stay away from you until Friday?" he asks. I kiss his soft lips and he smiles that beautiful crooked smirk. "Raven, I would lay down my life for you, surely I can do this for you. On one condition, you must keep your detail and Bo with you at all times— no matter what. That is non-negotiable."

Oh, how I love him and his wicked negotiating skills. "Deal."

He begins to move in and out really slow. "You had so much fun driving me nuts with the Nutella pizza, I think it's time I return the favor."

He helps me get onto my knees and puts gentle kisses up and down my spine. He reaches around and begins to roll my nipples with his fingers. They are so sensitive to his touch. He takes his cock and begins rubbing from front to back. He wants to consume every inch of my body, and I want him to.

"Push out for me, Raven, let me in."

As I push out, he slowly pushes through the barrier. He slowly begins to move. When he takes me this way, I can't think, maybe that's what he wants. The fullness is unreal, and my skin is becoming so hot. I know I can't last much longer. He leans down and slowly nibbles my ear. I'm trying so hard to hold it, not to fall too quickly. I want this to last forever. Then he takes his hand and goes right between my legs. Rubbing my clitoris and pushing his fingers deep inside me—every part of me is filled with Jax. I throw my head back, screaming. Jax is not far behind me. Time seems to stand still, both of us trying to breathe again. He pulls out and I'm tucked into his side, my head on his chest. When I finally open my eyes and I'm hit with the bluest of blues.

"There's my sweetheart, thought I lost you for a second. Are you okay?"

"Jax, are you even human?"

"Ha, of course I am, my beautiful girl. This is what you do to me. Let's shower, and then you need to get some rest."

He gets up with me in his arms. Pulling the throw around us, as he carries me downstairs. I'm so tired, but the thought of that wonderful shower makes me smile. I only hope I can stay awake long enough to enjoy it.

Chapter Eleven

Jaxson

I DECIDE TO GO next door and see Max. I left Raven a note in case she wakes up and I'm not there. I know Max will be up; it's been a long emotional day for all of us.

I find Max in the living room and I take a seat. "Hey, mate, I need to go over some wedding stuff with you. We are getting married this Friday, in Bella's garden. I need you to help me pull this off." He's sitting there, smirking at me. "Max, what is wrong with you?"

Ha, "I know you better than anyone, Jax. I knew you were going to go about this at lightning speed. I already started making the arrangements the day you left for Switzerland. Your mum has been helping me. You need to sign some papers for the license. The women need to get their gowns. Don't look at me like that, I needed something to do while you were holding me hostage in my own home."

He goes over to the bar and pours us both a scotch. "Jax, do you want to tell me what's really on your mind?"

"Max, I have more questions about our father, but on some level, I'm not sure I want the answers."

Max goes to his office and comes back with a file.

"Here." He passes it to me. "It's everything I know about the man. After he left, I vowed I never wanted to see or hear from him again. I carried on my life as if he were dead, because for me, he was. After I read the letter from my grams, I realized everything isn't always what it seems. I know that grams and your mum did what they thought was best for everyone involved, and I have only the utmost respect for both of them. I needed to know if he was still alive, and if there are other siblings out there."

I toss the file on the table and take another sip of my drink. "See, Max, I'm just not sure I want to go down that road. What made you feel you needed to know?"

He's pacing, which is comforting in a strange way, probably because it's Max's normal.

"Jax, we are as close as any family could ever be. What if there are more like us out there? I needed to know. I went from having no one to having a family, bound by blood, not just loyalty and friendship."

We sit in silence while I process this information. "Jax, now I need your help."

"Anything, Max. It's about time you ask me for something."

"Jax, can you help me with, Jackie? I know I really cocked the whole thing up. I hurt her badly, but in my defense, I was scared I wouldn't be me, again. My fear was that she would stay with me no matter what happened. She's so young, I just couldn't do that to her."

I sit for a moment, stroking my chin and thinking about all of this. "Max, do you love her, or is it just the sex?"

"I love her," his voice so low and vulnerable, I can barely hear him.

"Max, I know you love her, but are you *in love* with her? There is a big difference."

His jaw tightens and I swear he looks as if he's ready to punch me. "Yes damn it! I'm in love with her. There, I said it. Now, are you going to help me?" he asks almost angrily, fisting his hands.

I can tell he wants this badly, that's all I need to know. "Okay, mate, you work on the wedding and I will work on fixing this. In the meantime, what other information do you have for me? Don't look at me like that, Max, I know *you* just as well as you know me."

He pours us another drink. "Vincent woke up. They will not be able to operate; the bullet is in a spot that they can't access. I took my best shot, and the fucker still lived. The district attorney and the Feds wanted to meet with Raven tomorrow, but I put them off. I told you that we confirmed the woman in the park was Annabelle. She left an envelope for Raven. Before you ask, no I didn't open it, and neither will you. It's Raven's, and you need to let her decide what she wants to do."

I know he's right, and I can't bully her, but for fuck's sake, will there ever be an end to this?

"Max, we need to talk about Gabriella. I really don't think she needs to be in a clinic, however, I did notice that coming back to the city was hard for her." I change the subject, knowing I had no good argument on the other topic.

Max hands me another file. "Here is the file with the information on the flats in this building. I highlighted the residents that I reached out to, but so far, no responses. I think it's going to be hard for Gabriella, but she is stronger than you think. We just need to go slowly. Remember, it's not just Raven that has changed: the entire world around her has changed.

Everything from technology to terrorism. She might still think the World Trade Center is standing."

I thank God I have Max to calm me down and juggle some of this. "I never thought about any of that, I'm just so focused on Raven and the baby." I sit silently staring out the window, sipping my scotch until I finally get the nerve up to ask him. "Max, do we have any siblings . . . is he still alive?"

He's silent, and after a while he hands me the folder. "When you're ready, read it. I think you will find it very interesting."

I pick up the folder and the letter, heading back to my place.

I LEAVE MAX'S FLAT and head next door. Everyone is still asleep; you could hear a pin drop. I sit in the living room, looking out over the park. I keep staring at the folder, wondering how it will affect my mum. She's been through so much already, how could I possibly open this can of worms? Do I really want to know? I know the answer, no need to contemplate it any further. I have lived my life by certain rules. My very first rule is to never make a decision without knowing all the facts. That's probably why Max had this folder ready for me—he knew. Just as I pick up the folder, Raven comes into the living room. She just woke up, her hair is tousled, and she is in one of my dress shirts. She is hauntingly beautiful.

She sees me and strolls over. I thank God everyday for how lucky I am. I open my arms and she crawls into my lap. "My beautiful girl." I nuzzle into her neck. She giggles, and it is the most magnificent sound.

"Jax, I woke up and you were gone."

I take a deep breath, and prepare myself to tell her about the letter. "I left you a note, sweetheart. I went next door for a bit. Max gave me this letter that was delivered for you from Annabelle. Vincent woke up; they can't operate. The district attorney and the Feds want to talk to you, but Max put them off. I also have some papers you need to sign for the marriage license."

She is staring blankly at the letter. "Raven, I promised I would not keep any secrets from you. You don't have to read the letter if you don't want to."

Finally she takes her eyes off the letter and looks at me. "When do I have to meet with everyone?"

I pull her tight so she can feel my body envelop hers. "Max didn't say, and I would prefer to deal with this after the wedding. I only want you to concentrate on a dress."

She picks up the letter and hands it to me. "I don't want this letter. Nothing she says will change the fact that my father is dead and my mother was taken away from me for twenty years. I could never believe anything she has to say, and I chose not to read it. If Max needs to read it for security purposes, then he can. Now what is in the folder?" She gestures towards it.

"I wish in some ways I was as strong as you are. That file is from Max. It's a detailed report on our father and if we have any other siblings. Part of me wants to know, and part of me doesn't. There is my dilemma."

"Tell me first why you want to know, and then why you don't. I need a pad and pen, so we can make a Pros and Cons List." She picks up the file and I carry her into the office. I watch as her mind flips to teacher mode and fuck me—it's sexy.

"So let's start with why you want to know."

"Well, what if I have more siblings? I mean, look at Max, he's the best brother and friend anyone could ever want. What if my father is still alive? What if I could possibly find out why he did what he did?" I start to ramble out the reasons.

"Jax, would it make a difference if you knew why?"

"No, I don't think so. Nothing he could say would justify what he did."

She's writing every word down. "As far as why I don't want to know, probably because of my mum. This could open up a whole new can of worms for her. I don't want to see her hurt anymore. She gave up so much for all of us. She has carried the guilt over Cindy for years. It wasn't her fault, but she will never believe that. I've never seen my mum so vulnerable as she was tonight."

She gets up, takes the file and puts it in the file cabinet. "Here is what I think you should do. If I were you, I would talk to your mom first. You know she must have some feelings about all of this. If she wants to know, then look at the file, but if you feel she wouldn't be able to take it, then just burn the damn thing."

I smile, "You know, Raven, when you get all teacher mode on me, it makes me hard."

"Well, there's a surprise!" Okay, she does have a point.

She's in my lap, running her nails through my hair. I reach up and bring her hands into her lap. If I don't, it will be game over—for sure.

"I need to talk to you about Jackie. I spoke with Max and he asked me to help him get her back. He feared he would never be back to normal, and he knew that Jackie would never walk away. We need to come up with a plan." She gets a faraway look in her eyes.

"Jax, you need to understand we are dealing with two very stubborn individuals. We need to get them in the same room and get them talking. That's not going to be easy. When Jackie makes up her mind about something, she's like a bull."

"Well, sweetheart, I have a plan just how to do that. Let's go have a nice soak in the tub, and I will tell you all about it."

Raven

I'M DREAMING OF FRESH baked pastry. As I open my eyes, I realize it's not a dream. The entire room is enveloped in the buttery sweet smell. Jax is not in bed, so I decide to follow the smell. I head out to the kitchen and find my mom and Jax having coffee and pastry together.

"Wow, something smells wonderful in here." I take in another whiff and sigh. My mom passes me a dish with some of the most magnificent looking pastries. "Mom, did you make these?"

"Yes. Do you like pastries?"

"I don't think I ever met anyone who didn't. How did you learn to make all of these?"

"When your father and I first got married, we took cooking classes together. Do you like to cook?"

Jax almost chokes on his coffee. "Oh, Rose, your daughter has such unique culinary abilities. Let's just say, with you here, there will be more to life than peanut butter and jelly sandwiches."

"Raven, I could teach you how to make some of these."

I don't have the heart to tell her that I hate to cook. "That would be great, Mom."

"Ladies, before I head out there are a couple of things I need to go over with you. First, no one but my family knows who Rose really is, and we need to keep it that way. Raven, for now, please always address your mum as Rose. Sammy doesn't know her true identity, and I would like to keep it like that. I know you have a bunch of things that you want to do today, however, never lose your detail, and keep Bo close. Rose, Max gave me a bracelet for you to wear. It has a tracking device built in. Remember to be back here to put our plan in motion for Jackie and Max," He barks out his orders quickly, not giving any chance to be interrupted. He leans down and gives me a kiss. "I wish I could stay here forever. I love you, sweetheart."

"I love you more, Jax."

He grabs another pastry before running out the door. My mom makes me a coffee, and we curl up on the sofa. "He's quite the whirlwind, Raven."

"Yes, I guess you can call him a whirlwind."

"Raven, will you tell me about your childhood? Were your adoptive parents good to you? I have so many questions, but I don't want to upset you."

I don't know what to do. She is looking for answers and they are not all sunshine and roses. I don't know how much I should tell her. "My adoptive parents were good until my mother died from cancer. I left home shortly after that. I teach second grade at a private school in Midtown. Jax's nephew, Michael, is one of my students. Jackie teaches at the same school; her specialty is math. We roomed together in college. Mom, maybe we should stay focused on the present; the wedding and the baby."

"Okay, Raven. I only hope that in time, you will share what your life was like growing up."

I feel bad, but I don't want her to know how much I've been through. I don't want her to blame herself. "Mom, the past can never be changed. All we can do is look to the future."

"We can take it slow, Raven. Last night, I made some sketches of gowns for you and Jackie. I thought if we went to the seamstress with some sort of idea, it would help." She pulls out her sketchpad and begins to show me what she came up with.

"Mom, these are absolutely beautiful." Jackie's gown is a charcoal gray with silver running through it. She placed the accent on her legs, with a slit running up each side. "You captured Jackie's style so perfectly." Then she shows me what she came up with for my gown—it takes my breath away. It's exactly what I had in my mind, simple, yet elegant. The back has a low v with lots of little buttons covered in lace. The way the front is gathered, it doesn't show my bump. "Mom, this is perfect. I can't wait to show Jackie."

"Do you think the seamstress can pull these off on such short notice?"

"I'm sure Jax is paying a ridiculous amount of money to have them make whatever I ask for. I'm going to need your help with Jackie, today. After lunch, I need to get her back here so Jax and I can get her together with Max. Will you please say that you're tired and ask me to drop you at home?"

"Well, of course, if that's what you need me to do. But can I ask why?"

I don't know what to tell her, or how much she could handle. "They are two stubborn people that need to be locked in the same room. They love each other, but they keep getting in their own way. Max asked Jax to help him with this."

"Okay, Raven, I won't ask any more questions, for now. You need to hurry up and get ready or we will never get everything done in time."

Jackie

THE TIME CHANGE HAS really thrown my body for a loop. I need to go for a run, but not too sure how Sammy is going to react to that one. I get dressed and head out to the living room, only to find him already dressed for one. "Wow, how did you know I would be running? Especially, this early."

He gets up and disarms the alarm. "Stretch, after all these years, I know you very well. Let's head out, and on the way back, we can grab a bite to eat."

We head out the door, and Sammy informs my other guard where we are headed. I haven't run with Sammy for a while, but we fall right into step. There is an ease about Sammy and I realize I miss this. When we finish, we head to the local coffee shop for some breakfast.

"So, Stretch, do you want to tell me why this guy, Max, has the family up in arms?"

Do I want to tell Sammy? How much should I share with him? "Well, he's different than anyone I've ever dated."

He stares at me over the rim of his coffee cup. "I can wait all day, if that's what it takes. Don't even think of trying to blow me off on this one. I've known you for a very long time. You don't give away your heart that easily. So, what is it about this man that has your panties in a bunch?"

Ha, "Yeah, they are in a bunch—that's for sure. He is older, thirty-eight to be exact, and he . . . I don't even know where to begin."

"Okay, let me ask you this. Do you love him?"

I nod, "Very much so."

"So, what happened that sent you running across the Atlantic in the middle of the night?"

I trust Sammy. I know he would never betray a confidence. "I will tell you everything, but it is between us, okay?"

I take a deep breath and tell Sammy how Max came into my life. All the months of craziness that ensued up to Max getting shot in the head. "I stayed by his bedside the entire time, and when he woke up, he barely said two words to me. Then I'm outside the door, and I hear him tell Jax to help him get rid of me. I can't begin to tell you how much that hurt me. I love him, but I'm not sure if I can survive another rejection like that. I gave him all of me, Sammy, so what do I do?"

A lone tear slides down my cheek. Sammy reaches over and wipes it away. "Well, Stretch, it's like this. Part of me wants to snap him in two, and the other part wants to shake his hand. He sent you away, even though it hurt you and probably him, because he didn't want you burdened with his recovery. You know, what if he wasn't one hundred percent? Knowing you, the way I do, you would have stayed by his side—no matter what the outcome. What kind of life would that be for you? The other part of me wants to throttle him for hurting you. I think there are two questions you need to ask yourself: can you forgive him, and do you even want a relationship with this man?"

I have ripped my napkin into a million pieces. "You know he's Jax's best man. The wedding is Friday, so I guess I need to figure this out real quick."

We leave the café and head towards home. I still don't have a clue as to what I'm going to do. Maybe I will when I see him. As we round the corner for my place, I see the limo sitting there, and I know it's for me. Raven and Bo get out of the car. Bo sees me first, and his tail is going crazy!

"Raven, why are you here so early?"

She grabs my hand, pulling me into the lobby. "You need to shower and make it really quick. The wedding is tomorrow afternoon at three o'clock, and we have a lot to do. I'll be waiting in the car with Rose, so hurry!"

Okay, I can tell the next few days we will be operating the way Jax does—One hundred mph!

"OKAY, WHAT'S THE PLAN?" I ask, once Sammy and I climb into the limo, freshly showered and ready to take on the events of the day.

Raven opens up a box of my favorite chocolates and passes it to me. "Fuel for the adventure. Jax arranged a seamstress to make our gowns. She will be at The Tower later." She smiles over at her mom. Rose immediately pulls out a sketchpad. "Look what Rose did last night. They are unreal, Jackie."

My eyes grow wide as soon as I look. "Oh my God, Rose, they're unbelievable!" I'm glad I'm remembering to call her Rose instead of Gabriella. I'm sure it's hardest on Raven, trying not to slip up.

"I designed Raven's around her bump and yours, around your beautiful legs."

Sammy is laughing, "Now, you know why I've always called her 'Stretch'!" Everyone chuckles. I nudge him with my elbow, playfully.

"Jackie, I don't think the seamstress will have a problem having them done in time. I'm sure Jax is probably paying her a ridiculous amount of money for her to do it," Raven gets back to the topic at hand. "We have some errands to run before we meet with the seamstress. I need to go buy a gift for Jax." I'm not sure what I want to get him," she rambles. My friend is going to drive herself crazy if she doesn't calm down and take a breather.

Rose takes her hand. "What about a watch? You can get it engraved."

Raven starts laughing so hard, tears are rolling down her face. "Um, I had to buy Jax a new watch the other day because I took his twenty-thousand dollar watch and threw it across the room, shattering it. In my defense, he had the alarm set to feed me. It drove me crazy. *And . . .* who in their right mind would even spend that on a watch? Like really?!"

We are all laughing as we pull up to our first stop—Tiffany's. "I want to get a gift for An," Raven says before we get out, "and my mom," she whispers in my ear. She finds a beautiful diamond necklace with a little charm on it that says, 'Thank you for raising my happily ever after.' It's perfect for An. I help her to find a very delicate watch for her mom. She has them both engraved, 'Time to live again.' Now, it's off to Cartier, where she finds a special pocket watch for Michael Jr. She has them engrave the inside with, 'Future Time, Lord.' He'll definitely love that.

Maxwell

I DECIDE TO HEAD into Raiders for a bit. I have some things I want to look into. Tony should have the reports I ordered on Sammy and Gerhard. I'm not in the door five minutes and Mrs. Osla is all over me, asking a million questions about my health. I know I have to cut her some slack. She's worried, but I swear, she's like An on steroids! I don't have much time here before I need to be back to put Jax's plan in motion. I'm looking over the reports, when something pops out at me. *Fuck,* Sammy is still employed with MI6. Why would his file show that he's retired, yet, he is still employed? I need to get to the bottom of this. It helps that I still have many friends at MI6, even the Chief, himself, owes me. I call the Chief. After assuring him that I'm fine, he tells me what I need to know. I race out the door and head back to The Tower. I need to talk to Jax.

Raven

WE DECIDE TO TAKE a lunch break, which is good because I'm hungry. I take everyone to *S'Mac* for the best choices when it comes to Mac and Cheese. My mom is in shock when she sees there is a restaurant designed only around Mac and Cheese. I forgot that she has been isolated for twenty years; for her, time stood still.

"Raven, I've never been to a restaurant that only makes Mac and Cheese." Mom leans in and whispers in my ear.

I want to cry at the loss she has gone through, but instead, I decide it's time for a mental pep talk. I am going to enjoy showing her the world, seeing it through her eyes for the first time. "Rose, there is so much to see. A lot has changed since your last visit to the states." I try to play our conversation off like she just hasn't been here in a while and not hidden away for so long."

We order four different types of Mac and Cheese, each of us passing them around to sample. I check my watch and realize time is getting away from us. It's time to set the plan in motion. "So, Jackie, have you decided when you're going to see Max?"

"Raven, you're more like Jax everyday. No, I'm not sure what I want to do yet."

I sneak a peek to mom, and she knows what we need to do next. "Raven, I'm feeling tired. Do you think you can drop me off at home, and finish up without me?"

Jackie takes mom's hand, "Rose, Raven and I can finish up. We will take you back to The Tower."

As we head out the door, I quickly pull Sammy aside. "You need to go along with the plan, and trust me, don't interfere."

He whispers in my ear, "Raven, I knew you were up to something. Not to worry, I won't interfere with your plan as long as I know she's safe."

We all pile in the limo and as we head towards The Tower I text Jax:
Plan in motion. On our way. Make sure you're ready. XO

WE GET TO THE Tower, and everyone is very quiet on the elevator ride up. "Jackie, Jax and Max are staying at Bella's, so we can stay together until the wedding. We set Rose up in Jax's guest room, for now. We have lots to go over and we will need both places. Jax texted and said he set the seamstress up at Max's place." I know Jackie; she can be very stubborn, so I have to give her a push. We get off the elevator and Mick is there, waiting for us.

"Hey, there are my favorite ladies. Did you get everything done?"

I am so happy for him, He finally feels like he has a purpose; little by little the night terrors are getting better. "Almost, Mick, just a couple of gifts left to get." I introduce him to Sammy, and they take to each other right away.

"Raven, some deliveries came for you, and the seamstress is waiting in Max's place. I believe you're up first, Jackie."

She is hesitating, and I think it's because the last time she was there, Max wanted her gone. I pull her into my arms, "Come on, I will go in with you. You'll be just fine. He's not there; it's just the seamstress." We go inside and head down the hall, towards the living room. Max and Jax are both standing there. Max stares at Jackie—neither one—saying a word. I keep my arm around her waist, so she won't bolt.

Jax steps up towards us, "Jackie, Max, the two of you need to work this out. Please hear me out and then if you still want to leave, I will let you."

Max cocks one eyebrow at him, probably because he knows that will never happen.

"You are both stubborn fools, too blinded by hurt and misunderstanding to dig your way out of this mess. You both need me."

Jax gives them both the biggest smile, and I'm trying not to laugh at my man. He is really trying. I hold my hand up to Jax, "I think what Jax is trying to say is, you both need to sit down and talk this out. You might decide it's too much and walk away, but you don't want to ever wonder—what if. Jackie, when Max woke up, he was speaking out of fear and love. You know you're a very strong person and would have stayed by his side, no matter what the outcome. Max, you need to tell Jackie why you built walls around your heart. Then, you both need to be honest about your feelings. After that, if you walk, well there is nothing anyone can do about it." So far no one is moving. "Jax and I are going next door. We are going to leave the two of you alone to talk this out."

Jax takes my hand, "Sweetheart, can I talk now?"

Oh he's smirking at me. God only knows what he's up to. "Go ahead, Jax. The floor is all yours."

"Raven, is the nice negotiator, and she has been trying to help me with my *bulldog* style way of doing things, however, in this case, I have only one thing to say, you *will* sit down and talk this out. You *will* tell each other everything and, Max, I mean *everything*. If either one of you tries to leave here before that, I gave Mick instructions to shoot you in the *arse!* Okay, Raven, I'm done now."

Max is trying not to laugh and Jackie seems to be in shock.

"Jax, is Mick supposed to shoot me in the '*arse*' too, or just Max?"

He narrows his eyes at Jackie, "Seeing as your parents might get mad if I had you shot in the arse, I will have him tie you up until you listen to reason." Before anyone can say anything more, Jax pulls me into his arms and we are out the door.

Chapter Twelve
Maxwell

"JACKIE, WOULD YOU LIKE a drink?" I offer. Her eyes are glued to me and her silence is deafening. "Please, have a seat. I have a lot to tell you." I gesture to the seat next to me as I sit on the couch. She takes the chair. I push the coffee table in front of her and sit on that instead. Our knees are touching, and it takes all that I have not to pull her into my arms.

"I'm listening, Max, say what you need to," her tone, almost impatient.

I take a deep breath, preparing myself to relive this nightmare, yet again. "I have some things to tell you. Some of which, I only found out a couple of days ago. You need to know everything about me . . . why I'm so overprotective. Afterwards, if you hate me and decide to leave, I won't stop you." I wait a moment to see if she has any objection.

"My mum met a man from Scotland, got married young, and had me. He was in sales and traveled for business. His visits home became less and less, until one day, he just never came home at all. Shortly after, a young woman came to see us, claiming she was married to my dad. She had two children, Jax and Isabella." Just when I say that last bit, her face registers shock. "Yeah, I just found this out. It was not too long after that my mum committed suicide. An came right after that and offered to raise me as one of her own children. My grams kept me with her, but she kept in touch with An through the years. I made a life for myself. After graduation, I joined the Police Force and my career took off. Not too long after that, I met a girl and fell in love. Her name was Samantha, and soon we were married."

She leaps up, "Max, you're married? That's what this is all about?"

"No, please hear me out. In the end if you want to walk, I promise, I won't stop you."

She quietly sits back down and I take a deep breath to continue. "Soon after we married, we had a son, Elliot. I thought my life was complete, it didn't matter that my dad walked out. I had the family I always wanted. Then one day, Samantha took Elliot to the park. Afterwards, she headed back to the car and while she was taking him out of his buggy, two drugged up gang member's carjacked Samantha. They pulled a gun and shot them both. My Elliot died in Samantha's arms, along with her. My heart died that day, too."

"Max, my heart breaks for you and all that you have lost, but it doesn't explain why you've pushed me away. I gave you my heart, my soul, myself, so completely. And you sent Jax to get rid of me. You broke my *h-heart*."

I watch Jackie's face as the tears start to trail down. I want to take her in my arms, but she needs to hear it all, and then she can decide.

"Baby, you came into my life and you scared me. You blew my whole world apart."

She puts her hand on my knee and I jolt from the touch. "I scared you how?"

I take her hand and place in over my heart. "You made me feel hope, you made me feel love. You made me think of the future. That scared me half to death. The night that Vincent's men tried to grab you from your flat, I nearly died all over, again. I realized that night I was in deep. I can't take another loss. It's why I'm so over the top with security."

"That day I left you at the elevator to go after Vincent, I heard you when the doors closed. I heard the gut-wrenching wail, and I felt my heart crack in two. The whole time I was running through that mansion, searching for Vincent, I knew if I could just get this over with, I would be back in your arms. You're the light at the end of my tunnel, but then, my world went black." I squeeze her hands tightly for emphasis.

"I heard you at my bedside, crying. I heard Jax threaten me with bringing his mum to try and bring me around. I heard you and An, talking. Jackie, I heard you tell her that no matter what the outcome, you would sit by my bed and take care of me for the rest of your life. Do you know what that did to me?"

Her eyes grow wide and I can see she's shocked that I heard it all, that I could remember all of it. "It made me realize the best thing I could do for you, if I really loved you, was to force you to go, even if it meant that you would hate me. I didn't know if I would ever recover, and I couldn't, no—I wouldn't hold you back. You deserve to be happy and loved. When Raven was kidnapped for those three months, I would sit outside the school everyday and just watch you with the children. You love them, and they love you, how could I ever take that away from you? I just couldn't."

We sit there for a long time in silence. "Please, Jackie, you need to talk to me. At least tell me to sod off, if that's what you want, and I will."

She gets up and walks to the window, looking out over the park. "Would you have ever told me about your wife and son?"

I walk up behind her. "Jackie, please look at me," I plead. She turns and we're face to face. "Yes, I knew that I would have to when I felt the walls around my heart start to crumble. I knew I was in deep with you. You deserved to know my whole story."

She strokes my face, "How do you feel?"

I'm in shock. I pull her into my arms, "After all I told you, you want to know how I feel? I feel like I'm going to lose my mind if I let you walk out that door. I feel like my heart is beating again, now that you're in my arms. I feel like I've come back to life, like I've been given a second chance. I feel like I want to hold you, and love you all night long, never letting go. That's how I feel."

She leans up and lightly brushes my lips with a barely there kiss. "I meant your head, Max."

I lift her up, and carry her towards my bedroom; her long legs are wrapped around my waist. "Please stay, Jackie."

She kisses me again, "Not until you answer some of my questions."

I climb into bed with her still in my arms. She's sitting in my lap, her legs still wrapped around me. It feels so right, perfect. "Okay, you can ask me anything, and I promise to answer."

She searches my eyes, while stroking her fingers around my scar.

"How is your head? What did the doctor say?"

She's worried about my health? God this woman is beautiful inside and out. "I get headaches, but the doctor said that is to be expected. They are becoming less and less. I don't have all my stamina back, but I hope to soon. I have been doing therapy, and the doctor released me to go back to work on a limited basis. I do a full workout in the gym. I don't think I am ready to be back in the trenches, but being in the office, behind the scenes—for now—is fine."

She leans in and kisses me. "First, thank you for your honesty, it is something that I need. Do you know what happened to your father?"

I wasn't expecting that one. "Yes I do, I just learned the other day that I am related to Jax and Bella, and I wanted to find out how many others there could be out there. Our father was a bigamist, and poor An has carried this knowledge, silently for all these years. I gave Jax a file that has all the information in it, but he's choosing not to look at it. Do you want me to tell you?"

She shakes her head, "No, I don't want to know. What is going on with Vincent and Duke?"

She's not holding back. "Vincent came out of the coma yesterday. I'm not sure if he remembers anything that happened that day. Either way, the Feds and the District Attorney need to talk to both Raven and I. There will be a trial. And it will be messy. Raven's aunt has surfaced, and we will be bumping up security on everyone, including you. I don't see this ending any time soon. Duke is in Sing Sing prison. From what I've been told, the Feds don't think he will be beneficial to them."

I need to know how she feels, but I don't want to push her. "Jackie, talk to me, baby. Please tell me what you're feeling. Just like you, I need total honesty."

She puts her arms under mine and pulls me close to her. She leans in and kisses my heart. I swear to Christ, I don't know how much more I can take.

"Max, I love you. I don't play games, I know what I want and what I want *is you*. That being said, I'm not going anywhere, but we need to set some ground rules."

I let out the breath I was holding. "Okay, baby. I can live with rules . . . rules are good. Just tell me what you need." God I have missed this girl so much; my heart ached without her.

"Real simple, Max—no secrets. I'm not running away and neither are you. If you have a problem with me, then tell me. If you're scared, then tell me. If you need a timeout, then tell me. If you ever pull this shit with me again, the only thing you will be looking at is my ass walking away from you. We are equal here, and it's best you remember that."

I kiss her and she deepens it. "Will you stay with me tonight?"

She rests her forehead on mine and closes her eyes. "Sorry, I can't. Neither can you. You're staying at Bella's house, tonight and I am staying at Jax's with Raven and Rose."

I whisper, "Okay, I've waited this long, I can wait another day."

"Do you think it will ever be safe for me to go back to teaching?"

I wish I had all the answers. "I honestly can't answer that. Has Raven or Jax spoken to you about Jax's idea of opening a private school at Raiders?"

She smiles and kisses my lips. "No, but it doesn't surprise me. Jax is crazy when it comes to Raven."

Maybe if I can convince Jackie, then she will convince Raven. I'm getting as nuts as that crazy arse fucker. "It's a good idea for many reasons." She cocks her head and smiles. "Okay, don't look at me like that, just hear me out. If the workers had daycare and a school, within the same building, then they could be more productive. If the parents don't need to worry about after care or before care, then they would be more productive in their jobs. We could have all sorts of after school programs for the kids. The parents would know their children are safe and getting access to more opportunities they normally wouldn't. For safety purposes I think it's great. Now, as far as learning, we wouldn't be relying upon the state or the federal government for funding, so we could offer a much better education. I went to school on scholarships and it really helped not having any debt when I was done. It would make the workers more productive, and it could be part of the incentive package for new hires. There are other companies with the same business model." I'm not sure she is buying this, and I know I'm starting to sound as desperate as I feel. "There is a company in North Carolina that does this. They also have other things available for workers, such as dry cleaners or car maintenance. By doing this, they are creating less stress for the workers. In the end everyone wins."

She leans in, and kisses my neck. "It's also good for you and Jax, this way you both know where we are at all times."

She kisses me, and I don't want to let her go. "Baby, I know you said I have to go to Bella's with Jax, but please, just let me hold you for awhile."

"Only for a little bit, then the seamstress needs to measure me. There really is a seamstress, right?"

I kiss her neck, working my way slowly down her beautiful body. "Oh, baby, there's a seamstress. I can help her with your measurements. I could tell her, in great detail, about every inch of these beautiful legs."

"Maxwell, you'll do no such thing!"

She's blushing. Oh God, if I don't stop now, there won't be a wedding. "Come on, baby, let's go find that seamstress."

Raven

ALL IS QUIET NEXT door. I wonder what is going on. I know Jackie loves him, and she will listen, but she can be very stubborn. The seamstress got everyone's measurements but Jackie's. Jax is in the office, working on something, and I'm enjoying the quiet time, relaxing and gazing out the window. My mom is meeting with her therapist for the first time, today. I hope she takes it slow. I need to figure out what to get Jax. He has no clue what tomorrow is, and I decide I'm not telling him until after the wedding. I need to let him know that I would like to write our own vows. I head to the office and am taken aback at the sight before me. Jax is talking to himself, crumpled paper is everywhere, and he's practically pulling all his hair out. "Jax?"

He leaps up, "Jesus, woman, you almost gave me a heart attack!"

I'm instantly worried, seeing how frantic he looks. "What's the matter, Jax? You look very upset."

He pulls me into his arms, and scoops me up so tightly I can't breathe. "I love you, Raven."

"Jax, you need to be a little more gentle, please. I love you, you know I do." I brush my lips gently over his. "Why are you so frantic?"

My heart races. "I want to write my vows, and I don't want to come across as over-the-top crazy, but I want them to have special meaning for us."

I can't help but laugh, "I was just coming in here to ask you if we could write our vows. I also need to see Michael and ask him about giving me away." I gaze into his beautiful blues.

"Raven, we're not a conventional couple. I knew that you would want something different, so I'm glad you're on board with writing our own vows. I know I'm obsessing about them but I want them perfect. I also wanted to figure out the most comfortable and secure way to introduce your mum to my family. I figured if we had an intimate dinner here, your mum could get to know everyone in a more relaxed setting. You could also talk to Junior about giving you away. I called in a caterer to make it easy."

Tears spill from my eyes at this. He leans down and kisses them away. "Please, tell me you're happy about this?"

"Everyday I love you more than I ever thought possible, Jax. What time will everyone be here?"

He looks at his new watch and smiles. "You have about five hours. And I love my watch, sweetheart."

"I have an errand to run. I'll have Bo and my detail with me. Try not to worry, Jax, I love you." I grab my purse before he can try and talk me out of it and head out to finish up my errands before everyone gets here.

I RACE OUT INTO the hustle and bustle of Midtown Manhattan. The energy in this city is exactly what I need today. I have to get gifts for Jackie and Jax. I also need to make a stop to invite someone very special to the wedding tomorrow. I finally decide on a gift for Jackie. It's a charm bracelet, and the first charm is a diamond infinity sign; my best friend forever. I figured I could add to it for every occasion. Next, I need to get something for Jax. I have a great idea, so I head to a shop I love, in the East Village. I know they will make up what I want and have it delivered quickly. I decide to stop at Saks Fifth Avenue, and get some new clothes for my ever-growing bump before I head over to my final stop. I'm about to get into the limo to head home when Bo begins to freak out. My guards start pushing me into the car as a woman comes up to me. I know right away who she is, I've seen her before—Annabelle. She gets one look at Bo, baring his teeth and she turns away. We head back to The Tower. All the while, I try to calm my nerves; my adrenaline is pumping off the charts. Jax will freak out either way, but maybe if I were calm, it would help.

The elevator ride seems to take forever. When the doors finally open,

Jax is standing there. *Oh hell, this is not going to be good.* Before I can say a word he pulls me into his arms, he is breathing so heavily. "Jax, calm down, please. I'm fine."

"Raven, I know I'm not supposed to freak out. I know that you have security with you, but it doesn't help me, at all. I want to lock you in this Tower and throw away the key. If something ever happened to you, I would die."

I want to cry when I see the fear in his eyes. "Jax, if you live your life in fear then fear wins. Let's go inside and sit for a while."

We head inside, and we snuggle up on the couch. He methodically strokes my arm up and down. "Jax, have you given the letter to Max?"

"No, I was focused on writing my vows and planning the dinner."

"It's fine. I'm sure it's just more ramblings. I will give it to him tonight."

"I love you, sweetheart," he whispers, pulling me close.

"Jax, have you heard anything from Max and Jackie?"

"Max had the seamstress go in and measure Jackie. I have not seen or heard from either one of them."

" Maybe I should check on them?"

"Nope. They will be fine. I think I need to have my way with you before everyone gets here."

"Really? Is that what you think?"

"Raven, what I think is if you want me to stay at Bella's house, then we need to go to the *happy place,* otherwise, I can't be held responsible for my actions."

I lean in and run my tongue up the side of his neck. I know what will put him over the edge of sanity—dirty talk in French. "Je veux sentir ta bite au fond de moi."

Jaxson

I'M A STRONG PERSON with an iron will, but—fuck me—when she hits me with the dirty talk in French! I want to blow. I lift her up and head towards the bedroom. I'm ripping off our clothes as she's biting my chest. I might not make it to the bedroom. I put her down, and she begins to unbutton my jeans. She pushes them down as she drops to her knees. She takes my cock in her hands and kisses the tip. I'm trying to control the urge to push all the way in. I thread my fingers through her hair, slowly pushing my cock into her warm mouth. When I'm all the way in, I stop, willing myself to last longer. I finally begin to move taking my time filling and emptying her mouth. With each push in, I go a little deeper. I pull out, and she nips the tip—that's my point of no return. I'm groaning, totally unhinged. I reach down and pull her up into my arms; her lips are puffy and her hair is wild. *Fuck.* I'm hard as stone, again! I manage to get us to the bed without breaking my neck, making quick work of my jeans as I go.

"I'm not done with you, Jax."

She's hovering over me, rubbing my cock over her clitoris. I reach up and gently flip her onto her back. "I need you now, Raven." I slam into her, and then stop. Her eyes are wide and she's biting her lip. "Are you okay?"

"I need you, Jax."

"How do you want me, sweetheart?"

"Tender and slow."

I slowly pull back and then sink into her, taking her gently, mindful of the baby. I kiss her neck and then nip her ear. Working my way down to her sensitive nipples. I know she needs me to be gentle. I swivel my hips just like she likes it. I can feel her quiver and know she's close. I'm trying to go easy, but then she clenches and that sends me spiraling out of control. I pull back and slam into her.

"Jax, I'm there . . . fuck."

Watching her body turn crimson, and knowing that I've sent her to heaven, sends me falling. I roll us onto our sides and pull the sheet over us, both of us trying to catch our breath.

"Jax, I don't know what's gotten into me, but lately all I want is non-stop, crazy sex. Maybe I should talk to the doctor about it. Bella said the pregnancy hormones made her bat shit crazy."

I grin mischievously while still keeping my eyes closed. "I would love to know what you're thinking right now," she says.

"I'm thinking if this is the work of pregnancy hormones, then I need to keep you knocked up all the time." I open one eye to look at her and see that her mouth is hanging open. "Sweetheart, if you keep that mouth open much longer I might have to put something in it."

"Don't make promises you can't keep, Jax," she sasses back.

"Is that a challenge, Raven?"

I tilt my hips up, showing her that I'm ready to go again. "Are you human?" she asks.

"I told you, sweetheart—it's you." I tilt my hips again. "This is what you do to me. From that first touch outside Starbucks, I can't seem to get enough of you."

I work my way in and out, real slowly. I crook my neck and take one of her nipples into my mouth, nipping and licking. "It doesn't always have to be hard, Raven." I hold her hands above her head, and cocoon her whole body. I kiss her, working our tongues in a slow erotic dance. I swivel my hips to match my tongue. Right, then left. In and out, really slow as she begins to quiver and shake. "Eyes. Now, sweetheart."

So soft and tenderly, she falls apart in my arms.

Chapter Thirteen

Raven

THE CATERERS HAVE EVERYTHING set up, people are filing in. However, there is still no sign of Jackie or Max. I'm really getting worried. What if it's too much for her to handle? "Jax, maybe I should go next door, since we haven't heard anything from them."

He smiles, "Don't worry, they will be here. You need to introduce your mum to everyone. My family knows to only refer to her as Rose. And . . . Raven? I don't think I told you how beautiful you look tonight."

He's trying to distract me and I think I will let him, for now. I introduce my mom to everyone. They are making her feel very welcome and at ease. Finally, I see Jackie and Max come out of his place, holding hands. I look over to Jax and he has the biggest smile on that beautiful face. He mouths to me, "*Faith.*"

We all sit down, and Jax decides he wants to make a toast. "Thank you everyone for coming tonight and for sharing in our joy. Every single one of you has played a part in making this happen, and for that, I will always be grateful. Here is to good times and well-deserved happiness for everyone. God Bless."

The food is wonderful, but it's the company that makes this evening so special. I sit at the table, taking in each and every one of them. Jax has even invited Mick to join us. He always treats everyone with such respect. We all make our way into the living room for coffee and dessert. Jax has all different pastries. I laugh as I notice there is no Nutella. I look over to Jackie and she's laughing, she seems very happy. I think they will be okay. Max has been through so much. I know to survive he had to shut down. Jackie has loved him back to life.

It's time for me to talk to Michael. I excuse myself and I ask him to join me in Jax's office. I notice all eyes are on us as we leave the room, and I'm sure Jax will explain it. "Miss Raven, am I in trouble?"

Oh, how I love this little boy. "Not at all, Michael, I have something I need to ask you in private."

I don't want to sit behind the desk; it's to imposing, so we sit on the sofa.

"Michael, I need a very special favor, and since you're very special to me, I thought I would ask you."

He's watching me all wide-eyed, and I almost lose it when he starts to stroke his chin.

"With your uncle Jax and I getting married tomorrow, I'm going to need someone to walk me down the aisle and give me away. I would be very honored if you would do that for me." *Oh no, he looks like he's about to cry.* "Michael, are you okay?"

"Miss Raven, d-do I get to take you back after I give you away?" he stutters.

My eyes spring with tears before I can stop them. I love this boy with all my heart. "Michael, when we walk down the aisle and you hand me off to Uncle Jax, you are telling him that he gets to keep me in this family forever."

He gets it, his eyes become wide and his face lights up. "So, my mom said you will be my aunt, is that true?"

I hug him. "Forever, Michael. I have something to give you that I had made just for you. You have to wear it tomorrow at the wedding."

I give him the box, and he takes the pocket watch out. He opens it up, and when he reads the inscription he throws his arms around me. "I love you, Miss Raven, and I am your Future Time Lord! So, what do I have to do tomorrow?"

I stand up and take his hand. "We walk down the aisle together. When we reach the end, the priest will ask, 'Who gives this woman away?' You will say I do, and then you put my hand into Uncle Jax's."

He smiles, "No worries, Miss Raven. I got this."

We head back out to the living room, and Michael runs to show everyone his watch. Bella begins to tell him how his job is very important, but before she can finish he stops her. "No worries, Mum, I got this." He repeats to her what I just told him his duty was. "Then she becomes my aunt forever; piece of cake."

Everyone is laughing; he is such a sweet boy. "Uncle Jax, look what Miss Raven gave me."

Jax reads the inscription and he has the biggest smile on his face. It's the little things with this man that matter the most. I decide I will give everyone else their gifts right before the wedding.

I need to talk to Max about the letter, so I make my way over to him and Jackie. They look so happy together. I really hope they worked it out.

"Hey, Jackie, can I steal Max for a few minutes?"

She laughs, "Sure."

I take his arm and guide him into the office. I know Jax won't be far behind me. He has a seat while I get the letter. "Max, I need you to look at the letter from Annabelle. I don't want to read it. I don't want to be bothered with anyone in that family. I would just burn it, however, she tried to approach me today and—" Before I can finish, he is out of the chair.

"Why am I just finding this out now?"

Jax comes flying through the door. "Rein it in, mate; she's telling you now."

Max starts his usual pacing, "Jax, it's okay. Everyone needs to calm down." I hand Max the letter. "I know for safety reasons, you should read this. I don't want it back, nothing she can say will ever bring my father back."

"Okay. I am sorry that I flipped out," he apologizes.

"Apology accepted, Max, now go out there and have a good time." He grumbles under his breath, turns, and walks out of the room. "Jax, I have a question for you before we go back out there. Did you get Max a gift?" I can tell by the furrowing of his brows that he has no idea what I'm talking about. "Jax, you have to get him a gift for being your best man. I got something for your mom and mine. I got Jackie a beautiful charm bracelet and I got the watch for Michael."

"What should I get him?"

I kiss him, "Don't worry, you will figure it out." I think I have really thrown Jax for a loop. Just wait until tomorrow, when he finds out what day it is. I should probably tell him, but nope, I'm not going to. "Jax, what time do we need to be at Bella's house? Did you get the rings?"

He pulls me close to him, "Sweetheart, did you think I would forget the rings? They were delivered to Bella's house earlier today, and the limo will be here at 2 pm. Are you really going to make me sleep at my sister's house tonight?"

Oh I know what he's trying to do, but I'm not giving in on this one. "Just think how wonderful it will be when we go to the *happy place.*"

He's growling, and before he can say anything Michael turns to him, "Uncle Jax, are you going to Disney World too?"

Of course, I know exactly what he is thinking, and I turn a million shades of red, especially since Jax, has no clue.

"Junior, I'm not going to Disney World."

Michael looks up to Jax. "Mom said that we can go to Disney World on summer break; it's the happy place."

Jax's eyes grow wide, and I can't stop laughing. "Uncle Jax, what happy place are you going to?"

I bite my lip to squelch my laughter. "Junior, tomorrow I'm going to the happiest place in the world. I am marrying Raven, and my world will forever be the happy place."

I lean in to kiss him and whisper, "Nice save, Jax."

Raven

EVERYONE HEADS OUT, EXCEPT Jax and Max. They decide they can stay with Jackie and me, until one minute before midnight. Max pulls Jackie into his place, and I know she is thrilled. I'm tired, so Jax carries me to bed. "Sweetheart, you're so tired will you please let me take special care of you tonight?"

All I can do is hum. He takes off my shoes, sits on the bed, and starts to rub my swollen feet.

"Tomorrow night, at this time, we will be married. I know we can't go away right now, what between your mum and the pregnancy, but eventually, I would like to plan a proper honeymoon."

"Jax, you should have seen Michael's face when I first asked him to give me away. He was fighting to hold back the tears, he thought once he gave me away then I would be gone. After I explained it to him, and how important his role was, he was excited."

"That was a really cool gift you got him, what did you get my mum and yours?"

He's trying to get some ideas from me for Max! "Jax, you will know what to give Max, just think about your friendship and why it's special to you," I reassure him. He's stroking that chin and I know his wheels are turning. "Jax, did you finish writing your vows?" I figured after he was knee deep in crumpled paper, maybe I should ask.

"I assure you I will be at that alter and ready tomorrow. As much as I want to ravish you right now, I rather you and the baby get some sleep. Tomorrow is another busy day. Remember to keep Bo and the guards with you at all times. I will see you at Bella's, love you."

"I love you too."

Jaxson

RAVEN IS OUT COLD, so I cover her with a blanket and head over to Max's, but before I get there, Rose stops me. "Jax, can I talk to you for a minute?"

"Of course, come sit. What's on your mind?" I feel bad for her. This must be so overwhelming. I hope the therapy session went well.

"Are you going to be able to keep my daughter and grandbaby safe? These people are ruthless, Jax, and I'm scared—not for me, but for my family."

"I can assure you, I would lay down my life to protect them. What would really help is one hundred percent cooperation from everyone. One of the reasons why I pushed for the wedding to happen now was to build a barrier around everyone. If I could, I would lock Raven in this penthouse forever, but I know that's not realistic."

"No, Jax, that's not possible. So who is Annabelle? I heard her name mentioned tonight."

"Rose, I told you I would be honest with you. Were you aware that Antonio had a younger sister, Annabelle?"

She is quiet and I hope she can handle this. "Yes, Jax, I knew about her however, we never talked about his family. When he walked away from that family, he cut all ties with them. He hated the evil that surrounded them. Is she a problem?"

"Yes. She is coming around and trying to make contact with Raven. Vincent came out of the coma, but we are not sure if he remembers anything. The Feds and the district attorney need to sit down with Raven, but I want us to be married, first. There will be a trial, but we will cross that bridge when we get to it."

"Why was Vincent in a coma?"

I don't want to overload her, but I understand her need for the truth. "Max went after him and it didn't end well for either of them. They were both shot."

Thank you, Jax. After all this family has been through, what we need the most is honesty. I have so many more questions, but it's late, and we have a wedding tomorrow. Happy times are what we should be focusing on."

I hug her, "Get some rest and I will see you at the wedding."

Just as I head over to Max's, he comes out the door with Jackie. "Raven's fast asleep and I just sent Rose to bed." Jackie reaches up on her toes and kisses me on the cheek. "What's that for?"

She laughs, "Goodnight, see you at the wedding!"

"MAX, LET'S GO OUT for a drink." As we head out towards Bella's, we stop at a local Irish Pub.

"What's on your mind?"

"Did you read the letter? Part of me wants to know and part of me doesn't."

"Yeah, I read it. She is trying to sound like the wounded party, but I have no trust for this woman. I got the background check on her and she is very much like Vincent. I don't know how Antonio fit into this family."

"I spoke to Rose about Annabelle. She said she was aware that Antonio had a sister."

"What else is the problem, mate? After all these years, I can tell, so spill it."

"I found an island for sale, it's called *Jewel Cayle.* It's just off of the coast of Belize. It has two main houses, one on each side of the island."

"Jax, you can't hide her away on an island."

"Look, I know what you're saying makes all the sense in the world, but then there is the other part of me that wants to move us all there. You need to help me out here, mate, before I do something I probably shouldn't."

"Jax, take a timeout and think for a second. How would you feel if the shoe were on the other foot? You can't expect everyone to stop living his or her life, so you can feel safe. I, of all people, know that from experience. When my family was gunned down in the street like animals, I wanted revenge. Then after that, I didn't want to live any more. I closed myself off and shut down. I stopped living life even though life kept moving forward. I was stuck and determined never to let that happen to anyone, again. It almost cost me Jackie. Don't let your fear cost you Raven and the baby. We will work together, as a family, to keep everyone safe. I promise you, Jax . . . we will."

"So what am I supposed to do with this island?"

"Jax, you didn't, did you? Oh my God, you did."

I laugh, "Yeah, I did. Guess we have a new family vacation compound. Did you see Junior tonight? He was so excited." I then tell him about Raven asking him to give her away and what his response was. This reminds me to ask him, "Did dad ever watch 'Doctor Who' with you?"

Maxwell

WOW, THAT CAME OUT of nowhere, but I know Jax, and he's fighting both sides of the blade with this. "No, I was never really close with him. When he was around physically, he seemed distant. Did you read the file on him?"

"No, and I'm not sure I want to. I think we're doing okay. I don't need him, and if he came back into our lives now, I wouldn't trust him. How could I trust someone like him? I would always think he was in it for the money. You know what it's been like for me having money. Hell, you've had to step in on more than one occasion. You're a wealthy man, but we've kept your ownership in Raiders Inc. quiet. I've been the front man and that's okay, but I would never trust his reasons. I also have to think of mum, and how it would affect her. She gave up so much for us. I would never intentionally hurt her." We both sip our scotch in silence.

"Jax, while you were away, she asked me if I would ever feel comfortable calling her anything other than ma'am? I asked her what she would want me to call her, but she said I'll know when it's right. What does she mean?"

"Max, sometimes, for such a smart man, you can be such an idiot. I can say that because you're my brother, ha! Don't growl at me. She has loved you like a son. She is very protective of you. When you were in the hospital, she got on a plane and flew down to Florida, even though she hates to fly. She bullied her way past the guards, the police, and the hospital staff. She ordered the doctor around, and made sure you had everything you needed. She got the girls to eat, and held Jackie's hand the whole time. She never left that hospital. She slept in a chair, in the corner of the room, because she wouldn't leave you. When we flew you home, she suggested Jackie move in to stay close to you. She came by The Tower daily, for reports on you and Jackie. She hired the nurse, who by the way, annoyed the fuck out of us with her humming! Who do you think would do all of that, Max? Look, I know you had a mother, but she died while you were young. She felt responsible for that, and maybe her looking after you, all these years, was her way of honoring your mum by loving you as she would."

I don't know what to say, or even how to feel. It's too much, too fast; my head hurts.

"I get it, mate, but right now I'm so overwhelmed with everything. I need time to think and process it all. Give me that much." I close my eyes and rub my temples, hoping to ease the pounding in my head. "I need to talk to you about Sammy. I got a detailed report back, and it turns out he still works for MI6. I did some more digging, and found it's because of Gerhard. I spoke to the Chief this morning. He said, Gerhard was instrumental in peace talks. However, he's made some powerful enemies along the way. All of the guards that work for Gerhard are MI6."

He reaches over the bar and grabs the bottle of scotch. It's going to be a long night. "Is Vincent somehow tied into all of this?" he asks.

"Not that I can tell. Gerhard is clean, he's just a hard arse when it comes to getting his way."

"Max, no one outside of the family knows who Rose is, not even Sammy. I think we need to keep it that way."

"I agree. Let's get to Bella's house before it gets any later. We have a very busy day tomorrow. Did you get Raven a gift?" I ask. He's looking at me like I have grown another head. "Jax, you do know what tomorrow is, right?"

"It's my wedding day. Was I supposed to get her a gift? I could give her the island as a wedding gift."

Oh shit, he doesn't know. Fuck. "Sit back down, mate, we need to talk. Now normally, I would just mind my own business, but seeing how you are not only my best friend but my brother, I'm going to save your sorry arse." I look at my watch, "Today is Raven's Birthday." Oh I wish I could bottle that look: part shock and part horror.

"Why the *fuck* am I just finding out about this now?! Why didn't she tell me?"

I can only imagine her reasons. "Maybe because you're usually so over the top, and she doesn't want that. Maybe you could do something simple." He's really in shock and if he keeps pulling that hair, there will be nothing left.

"I'm at a loss here, Max. What the fuck am I supposed to do? *Fuck,* I'm getting married in less than twelve hours, and I need to come up with something special for her. It took me a whole day just to write my vows!"

"Come on, mate, we will figure this out." I get him outside and into the waiting limo. I tell the driver to head over to Bella's. "Jax, we are in the home stretch here. Don't give up now, trust me."

"I have an idea, but I'm going to need some help. We need to find an antique store."

I know I should probably tell him we can wait till morning but that won't work in Jax's world. I pull out my phone and find a dealer. Then, I do what I do best—track him down, in the middle of the night, and let Jax convince him to meet us at his shop now.

When we get to the shop, the man is none too happy to be here at four am. "Let me get this straight, you are going to pay me ten thousand dollars cash to open up my store, just so you can find your girlfriend a birthday gift?"

I tell the guy what I'm looking for, and it takes him all of ten minutes to find it. "Sir, here's an extra grand just for being such a good sport about all of this. And here is my business card, if you ever need anything, just call me."

The man seems in shock but I'm sure he's happy to have made a lot of cash for ten minutes of work. We head to Bella's, both of us lost in our own thoughts.

Raven

I WAKE UP AND have a wonderful stretch. When I open my eyes, there is a note by the bed with one Abracadabra Rose. I don't know when this man finds the time to do all that he does for me. I smell the sweet rose, and the baby starts kicking. I pick up the note. Behind it is a glass of orange juice and a warm croissant. Oh, even when he's not here, he drives me crazy!

> My sweetest girl,
> Today is a very special day. It is the day our family becomes one. I hope you love your breakfast. Please eat it all! Don't worry, I didn't sneak in and peek at you. I had your mum help me out this morning with all of this. I miss you and I love you.
>
>   Jax

Okay, I need to stop daydreaming about my beautiful, wonderful man, and start working on some personal notes for each gift. Everything was delivered yesterday, and Mick put it away for me. He really has become such a good friend. I head out to the living room to collect everything, and my heart skips a beat. I stand here, so overwhelmed by the sight before me. The man is nuts! I can't help my tears that are falling. There has to be, at least, thirty dozen Abracadabra Roses! They are everywhere. Every time I turn around, there are more. My mom comes in, hugs me, and wipes away my tears.

"He is extreme, but he does love you, Raven."

I'm speechless. I have no idea what to say.

"Raven, today is a special day. It's not only your wedding day, but it's your birthday too. I never thought I would get to spend another birthday with you, so this is so very special for me. When your father and I got married, my parents were already deceased. I had no one to give me any motherly advice, or pass any traditions down to me. I know that Jax loves you so completely. That man's love for you is in his eyes. I know he can be extreme and overpowering, just remember to stay true to who you are. Love him with all that you have. Life is full of compromises—some harder than others—that's just the way it is. If I can offer you only one piece of advice, it would be to never compromise on your love for each other. Hold onto that with all that you have and all that you will ever be. On my wedding night, your father gave me this Italian horn. He made me promise to wear it everyday, and I have. Even at the lowest point in my life. I think he would be happy to know that on this special day, I'm passing it on to you. I am so very proud of the beautiful woman you have grown into, and I know your father would be too. When I look at the woman you have become, I know that everything I have endured was worth it." She hands me the necklace and my heart swells from the significance of it.

"I'm going to give you some alone time while I start to get ready."

"Wait, Mom, Joseph left some stuff for me in a safety deposit box. There were some old pieces of jewelry in there, can you tell me about them?"

I hand her the box, but she hesitates. "Mom, if it's too much, we can wait."

"It's okay, dear, I just need a moment. I know what's inside the box. They were some of my mother's favorite pieces of jewelry. I asked Joseph to keep them safe for you. It seems like a lifetime ago. I'm sorry he's not here to see how happy you are."

She opens the box and pulls out the Cameo pin. "This belonged to your great-grandmother; she was French. The amethysts and diamond bracelet was your grandmother's. Your grandfather gave it to her on their wedding day, it was the color of her eyes."

I pick up the bracelet, and it glistens in the sunlight. "I will wear it today, in honor of her."

I hug my mom so tight. "It will be okay, Mom, we will get through this together."

"I know, Raven, let's focus on today, making a lifetime of memories for tomorrow. I'll leave you alone."

My mom gets up and goes inside, leaving me alone. I look around at the dozens of roses and I'm floored. I take one of the cards and open it.

I love you, sweetheart.

I go to the next one.

I will always have your back.

You rendered me speechless.

Looking at you takes my breath away.

I love negotiating with you.

Lock on, baby. Violet to Blues.

I hope I invaded your dreams like you invaded mine.

Sweet Jesus, and all that is holy—NUTELLA!

I'm laughing and crying at the same time.

Finally I find the last card.

> *My life began with you.*

I'm in shock; he captured all the craziness. I have to stop daydreaming. I need to get the gifts together. I pull out his gift, certain that he will love it. I got him a beautiful, chestnut box, with a violet bowtie to match my eyes. I had the artist carve one of my favorite quotes by Chae Richardson, '*Courage is not living without fear. Courage is being scared to death and doing the right thing anyway.*' With everything that is going on right now, all we have is courage.

Jackie comes in from Max's place and grabs a cup of coffee. "Holy crap, Raven! It looks like he bought out the florist shop!"

"You know how crazy he can be. I'm surprised he hasn't done more."

"Raven, you didn't tell him, did you? You know when he finds out, he'll go nuts."

Oh, now I feel bad. "Jackie, I didn't want him to make a big deal. He's so over the top sometimes and I just want simple."

"Raven, simple left, the day you crashed into him at Starbucks. Where did Mick go? I heard him leave."

"He went to pick up, Ashlyn, my Pilates instructor. I invited her to the wedding."

"I'm so happy for Mick. His life is really coming together. Has he ever told you what his life was like before the war?"

"No, and he might never be able to talk about it. I wish there were more services for the men and women like Mick; those who end up falling through the cracks. So, totally changing the subject here, but . . . what happened with you and Max?"

"He explained why he pushed me away. I understand his fear, but it still hurt. I can get past it, as long as he is honest. I do love him."

"He loves you, Jackie, very much. I don't know if I would have ever been able to come back from what he went through."

Jackie nods, then jumps up. "We need to think happy thoughts today. Mick should be back any minute now, and we need to get going. Where is Rose?"

All of a sudden it's a flurry of activity. My mom gathers up all of my stuff just as Mick and Ashlyn come in. We are all off to Bella's house. I can't believe in a few hours, I'll be getting married.

Chapter Fourteen

Jaxson

I FINALLY DECIDED UPON a gift for Max, and I know the girls are going to stroke his ego over it. I don't know why I'm so worried about today, but I am. I decided to give her the island as a wedding gift. Yeah, she'll freak out, but it will be a good family vacation spot. Everything is set. I just need to find Max.

Bella's garden is beautiful, so many different colors. I find Max on the back patio, having tea with mum. I think having her guard him for a few days really did a lot of good for their relationship. They have a closeness and an ease that they didn't have before. I pull up a chair and mum pours me a cup of tea.

"How are you this morning, son?"

"I'm happy. I wish everyone could feel this way; it's different. Mum, before this day gets away from us, I just want to tell you how proud I am that you're my mum." Just as I say it, Max starts to get up to leave. "Max, stay please. Mum, you're the strongest person I know, and I love you."

"Thank you . . . both of you . . . for all of your support. Enough of this. Maxwell, what happened with Jackie?" She waves away the emotions threatening her eyes.

Max leans in and kisses her cheek while I'm laughing. "An, you're the best. We are working it out. She has accepted my apology, and informed me that she will not accept anything but total honesty. We have a lot to get through right now, and I want to take it one day at a time."

"I need to finish getting ready; I will leave you two boys alone." Just like that, Mum is gone.

"Max, I can't imagine this day without you standing by my side. You've helped make it all possible." Before he can say anything, I pass him a box. "This is a little something to remind you of today. Don't let it go to your head, mate."

"Jax, we got here together and we will face everything that comes our way together. You didn't have to get me anything, I will never forget today."

"Max, shut up and open the bloody box."

"Jax, this is fantastic."

"Yeah, well, the girls all think you're Bond, so now, you have Bond cufflinks that turn into USB drives. You better not let this go to your head." I laugh and swat his knee.

Bella comes running out to the patio in a flurry. "If you two are done with your little bromance, you need to finish getting ready; the girls are here."

Raven

I NEED A MOMENT alone. I sit on the bed, and run through the events since I met Jax. It has been a whirlwind. So many lives changed. So many lost. I can't dwell on the negative. I need to stay positive, and focus on our baby.

"Raven? Oh. There you are, dear!" An comes in, seemingly happy. I think not having to keep her secret anymore will help her move forward.

"Hi, An." I greet her with a kiss on the cheek. I give her the gift I have for her. "I got you a little something to thank you for welcoming me into your family. I know there is so much stress and turmoil right now, and for that, I'm so sorry. I promise you, I will love him with all my heart—forever."

"Raven, it's me who should thank you. You have taught this old lady quite a bit these past few months. You've shown me that real strength comes from deep within. If it wasn't for all this craziness, I might have taken my secret to my grave."

"I'm glad you didn't. Max now has the family he always should have had. I know times were different, but no one should be alone."

There's a knock on the door. "It's almost time, Raven." Mom calls out.

An hugs me, "I'll give you some time with your mum."

"Mom, come sit for a minute, please." I hand her the present. "This is something for you to remember this day always."

She opens the box, and reads the inscription; *'Time to live again.'*

"Oh, Raven, it's beautiful. Today is so special for me. I never thought I would be here with you. I only wish your father were here to see what a beautiful, kind woman you've become."

I help her put it on. "Please don't cry, Mom. Today is a new beginning for all of us. I know my dad is watching over me. He is in my heart always."

"I will try not to cry, but I can't make promises." She smiles. "Now, you need to finish getting ready. I'll send Jackie in."

Jackie steps into the room, taking my breath away. "Jackie, you look beautiful." I slip the bracelet on her wrist. "This infinity charm represents my friendship and love for you, always. Don't even think of crying! Where is Michael?"

"Breathe, Raven, it will be fine. Michael is waiting right outside the door for you. Are you ready?"

I hear the music start and I know it's time. I whisper, "Yes."

Jaxson

I STAND IN THE garden—my nerves shot. I hope I can make it through this without passing out. Michael Sr. has the job of getting everyone seated. There is more security here than there are guests.

The music starts and it's the song I chose just for Raven. "How long will I love you?" by Ellie Goulding. Within a second, a fear that I will forget my lines comes over me. Max wraps his hand around my arm.

"Steady, mate, you'll be fine. Just remember to breathe."

Easy for him to say. Jackie comes into view; she's stunning. I look over at Max, and he's got a full fledge smile. Jackie reaches us, and then steps to the side. I finally get a full view of my beautiful girl. She takes my breath away, and my heart skips a beat. Junior is guiding her towards me. I'm so proud of the little guy. He whispers something to her, causing her to laugh. She is getting closer; my heart beats faster. I need to remember to breathe. I look up to the heavens and thank Antonio for this gift, a gift I will treasure with my life.

As they stand before me, the priest asks, "Who gives this woman away?"

Junior places her hand in mine and declares, "I do, Father."

She leans down and kisses Junior, turning him a million shades of red.

I'm holding her hand, staring at her in wonder.

The priest begins, "Raven, Jaxson, I understand you have written your own vows. Jaxson, please begin."

Hand in hand, she turns to face me. "Raven, the feeling hit me the moment I looked into your beautiful, violet eyes, the very first time. It was so immediate and powerful—far deeper and inexplicable beyond any calculation of time and place. You don't describe a feeling like that. You can't replicate it or force it. You just let it flow in and around you. You go where it takes you. I promise to love you with all that I am. I will support you and negotiate with you. I will challenge and protect you. I promise to grow old with you, every second of everyday. I will hold your hand through the good times and the bad. You are my lifeline in the storm. I'll love you beyond my last breath."

She brings my hand to her lips and kisses my palm. "Jaxson, my beautiful, intense man. Our love will transcend through all of time. I need you beside me, always, as my best friend, lover, and my soul mate. I will love you, honor you, and respect you. I will negotiate with you, and rein you in, when I have to. Through sickness and health, good times and bad, I will forever be your companion. You are my end all."

As we exchange the rings, there's not a dry eye in the house. The priest finally gets to the part I've been waiting for. "You may kiss the bride."

I lean in, "My beautiful wife, kiss me, please."

Raven

EVERYONE SEEMS TO BE having a good time. My mom is relaxed and laughing with Mrs. Osla. I almost forgot, I have to introduce Jax to my special guest . . . if I can drag her away from Mick.

"Jax, I would like to introduce you to someone very special. This is Ashlyn Adair, my Pilates instructor." I think he stopped breathing. I whisper, "Breathe."

"Ashlyn, let me tell you what a pleasure it is to finally meet you. Raven has shown me how wonderful Pilates can be. I ordered a Reformer for our personal gym."

Thank God Ashlyn is taking it all in stride. "Well, Jax, if you need any personal instruction, I'm sure Raven can show you. I also give private lessons and lessons for couples." Jax's chin is officially on the floor.

"I just might take you up on that. How long can Raven continue to do Pilates while she is pregnant?"

"As long as the doctor says it's okay, then up until delivery."

"Well, good to know, Ashlyn, I'm pretty sure we'll be taking you up on those private lessons." He smiles with a mischievous glint in his eye. I shake my head a little and bite back the giggle that wants to escape. "I can't tell you how happy we are that you could share our day with us. Please, make yourself at home. I need to dance with my wife, and then feed her. God, how I love the sound of that." He beams.

Jax pulls me into his arms, and the music suddenly changes. "Raven, I chose this song for you. The first time I heard it was on your iPod, 'Never Stop' by SafetySuit. The words say it all for me, wife. I love you."

The music starts, and my tears fall. It's such a beautiful song. As Jax glides me around, he begins to sing. His deep, smooth voice telling me how he'll never stop losing his breath when I look at him. You could hear a pin drop. My eyes lock onto his, and time stands still. It's a true declaration of everlasting love. I love this man, and all his crazy, intense ways. I wouldn't want him any other way. When the music finishes, he scoops me into his arms and carries me over to a table. I'm glad to finally eat and pick my feet up. Jax is slowly rubbing my neck, and I feel all the tension melt away. Max and Jackie come to join us.

"Hey, Max, you look wonderful. How are you feeling?"

"I'm doing better everyday, thank you, Raven. Did you see the gift that Jax got for me? They are Bond cufflinks that turn into mini USB drives."

"Wow, Max, I told you—Bond all the way!"

Jax rolls his eyes, "Please, sweetheart, don't fill his head."

"Max, Raven and I are leaving. I need you to take care of her mum while we are gone. We will be back for the deposition on Monday, but for now, we are heading out to Cape Cod for a long weekend."

"That's fine, just keep the detail with you both, at all times. Make sure you're back here for court at ten am, Monday. Jackie and I will keep Rose busy. You look very tired, Raven, go now, and we will handle the goodbyes."

"Thank you, Max." Jax scoops me up and practically runs out the door.

Maxwell

WHILE JAX AND RAVEN make a quick exit, I have other things to tend to, starting with Sammy. Jackie is talking to Rose and An. This is the perfect time to talk to Sammy. The guy's got the looks, but my understanding, from Jax, is that he bats for the other team, and is in a committed relationship. Lucky for him, otherwise, he wouldn't be staying at Jackie's.

I head over to him and slap his shoulder to get his attention. "Hello, Sammy, I think it's time we got to know each other. I understand from Jackie, that you have been her guard for a long time. How long do you plan on staying in New York?"

"I'm staying indefinitely, Max. Let's have a seat. I have questions, and I'm sure you have some for me."

"Okay, Sammy, what are your concerns? We are both in the same line of work, with similar backgrounds. I won't bullshit you, so ask away."

"Thank you. I'm sure you know I ran a check on you, so I know about your past. I never said anything to Jackie. I felt it was something that she needed to find out from you, not me. I understand why you pushed her away, but just so we're clear here, if you break her heart again, I will kill you."

Is he serious? Does he think he can intimidate me? "I assure you, my intention was to always keep her safe. Even now, I worry. Jackie will be staying with me. I have a guest room, and you're welcome to stay, also. We have to be in court on Monday for a deposition. I would appreciate you being there for Jackie, while I'm being deposed. I want eyes on her at all times."

"Let's get a few things straight, Max. I don't work for you. I'm here solely for Jackie's protection. That being said, I don't have a problem combining resources when it comes to her safety. Jackie has brought me up to speed on what she knows about Raven's situation. I also pulled everything I could find on Vincent. He's a real piece of work and I wouldn't be surprised if the Fed's offer him a deal."

I can play nice with others when I have to and now is one of those times. I will bite my tongue and let him feel like he has control. "I agree. At this point, I think his only option would be to turn state's evidence. That could possibly open a bigger can of worms. I heard today, from the district attorney, that Vincent's attorney is claiming it was self-defense for shooting me. He is also saying that Duke was responsible for kidnapping Raven. I'm not surprised that he would throw his kid under the bus." He's quiet, probably trying to absorb it all.

"What is going on with the case against Duke? Do you think he is going to fight the kidnapping charge or just go along with the father?"

"Sammy, this whole thing is so cocked up. Raven believes Duke is a *tortured soul,* but she sees the good in people. I think the kid did snap, however, he still needs to be held accountable for his actions. He killed two people at point-blank range. I think he deserves to be locked up forever. Either way, this is going to get a lot worse before it gets better."

"I notice there are many different guards here, but Mick seems to be a constant, and very protective of the girls. What's his story? I already ran a check on him, I want to know what's not on paper."

"Sammy, the one person I don't worry about is Mick. He loves those girls, and proved it when Raven was kidnapped. But I'm sure you already know that. He's a veteran, and a fine bloke. It looks like everyone is finally starting to leave, I'm going to collect Rose and Jackie."

As we head over to collect everyone, Mick pulls me aside. "Max, just want to let you know that Jax and Raven arrived safely. If you don't need me tonight I would like to take Ashlyn home."

I'm so happy that he is getting his life back. There is no one who deserves it more. "Mick, enjoy your weekend." I watch as he escorts Ashlyn out. I think she will be good for him.

I gather Rose and Jackie before we make our goodbyes. I want to get Jackie home, and spend time with her. God how I missed her. She calms me. I haven't felt this way in so long. I pull her close; she's my lighthouse in this raging storm. The entire ride is in silence. I focus on her slowly rubbing her thumb in circles over my knee.

When we get to The Tower, Jackie makes sure Rose is settled in next door. Sammy pulls me aside, "Max, I'm going to hang out in Jax's place with Rose. I have calls to make and some things I want to follow up on. If you decide to go anywhere, please let me know."

"Don't worry, I don't plan on leaving that flat, or Jackie, for the next few days. If Rose needs anything, let me know. I'm sure Jackie will want to check on her daily. Is there anything else you need from me?"

"No. I am, however, going to reach out to my contacts and see if I can get any further information. If I come up with anything, I'll let you know." And with that, he turns to walk away.

I take Jackie's hand, and we head next door. Finally, alone, at last.

Ashlyn

I SIT AND WATCH Mick drive. I realize there is a lot to this man that is unknown. He is always so quiet. I wonder if it's because it's his job or something else. "Mick, thank you for picking me up today."

"You're welcome. Would you like to go grab a cup of coffee?"

"I would love to. There is a local coffee shop, across from my house."

This man intrigues me. He's different. He's very quiet. Maybe he needs time to feel more comfortable with me. We pull up to the coffee house, and head inside. Mick orders our coffee while I find a table. It's not that busy and I'm able to get a quiet table near the back. He's back with the coffee, but he seems quiet again.

"Mick, how long have you worked for Jax?"

"Less than a year. I met him through Raven. How long have you been teaching Pilates?"

"I've been teaching for almost nine years. I also volunteer my studio and my services to veterans. I try to help them get some mobility back. I usually do that on a private basis. Makes them feel more comfortable."

He seems to tense at the mention of my work with veterans. "What about you, Mick, what did you do before this?"

"I was an Air Force pilot. I did six tours in Iraq before I was injured."

"Wow, six tours? That was a lot. What did you do prior to your service?"

"I only ever wanted to be a pilot. That ended the day of my accident. You don't have a New York accent, where are you from?"

"I was born in Los Angeles. My mom is a nurse at Children's Hospital in LA. My dad was a ship builder in Belfast. He met my mom when she was on vacation in Ireland, and followed her to the States. He died last year of a heart attack. Do you have any family?

"I am an only child, and my parents are both gone now. I was raised in Nebraska. When I got back from Iraq, I thought I would try big city living. I was living on the streets, when I met Raven. She helped me turn my life around. Showed me I still had purpose."

"Mick, everyone has purpose, you only need to believe you're worth it. If you're interested, come by my studio and I will teach you how to stretch out your muscles and work past the pain."

"I'd like that, Ashlyn, but for now, I better get you home."

He walks me across the street to my building. I don't know why I'm nervous. I hope he takes me up on my offer to train him. When we reach my door, he takes my hand in his and I feel all of his callouses, yet he's gentle.

"Thank you, Ashlyn, you're very easy to talk to. I'd like to get together again, if you would like to."

"Give me your phone, Mick." I hold out my hand. He reaches into his pocket and pulls it out for me. I call my cell from his phone, "Now you have my number. I would like to get together, again." I lean in and kiss his cheek. Finally . . . he smiles.

Chapter Fifteen

Jaxson

"MRS. PHILLIPS, WE ARE alone here, well, except for the guards and Bo, until Sunday evening. I expect you to take advantage of me in every way possible. Before anything, though, I want to wish you a very happy birthday." The look on her face right now is *priceless.* "Did you really think you could get something so important like a birthday past me?"

"I'm sorry, Jax. I didn't want you to make a big deal about it. You can be a tad over the top sometimes."

"Well, sweetheart, this time I think you will be surprised to know that my gift is not over the top." I won't tell her what I paid the guy just to keep things simple; she doesn't need to know that part.

"When I was in school, my teacher gave me an assignment. I had to write a small poem. It had to be something that I would want to give to someone someday. When she gave it back to me, she had me put it in an envelope and told me to keep it, until the day came when I would need it. I had no clue as to what she was talking about, but my mum did. My mum has held onto this for me all these years." I hand her the box, letting her unwrap it. Inside is a violet, antique, heart-shaped, glass bottle with a scroll inside. She pulls it out and begins to read:

"Jax, words escape me. This is precious and so special." Her eyes fill up.

"Sweetheart, those are good tears, right?"

"Yes, they are good tears. This came from your heart, so pure. It means more to me than anything, thank you. Right now, Jax, I need you. I mean . . . I *really* need you."

"Oh, you don't have to tell me twice." I scoop her into my arms and carry her to the bedroom. "I want to slowly peel you out of this dress and worship every inch of you all night long," I say as I place her back down on her feet.

She runs her fingers through my hair and brings my lips close to hers. "No one is stopping you, Jax."

I turn her around and start to unbutton each of the very frigging tiny buttons that are covered in lace. My crazy side wants to just rip it off, but my gentleman side is telling me to slow it down. "Sweetheart, how attached are you to this dress?" She tilts her head back and her lips are parted. Her silky hair, cascades down her back as her beautiful eyes lock onto mine. Fuck all that's holy—game over! I grab each corner of the dress and rip it right off her. *Fuck, I'll have the seamstress make her another one for keeps!* SShe spins around, standing before me—hands on her hips—in nothing but high heels, white—laced thigh highs, a sheer, white bra, and lace thong. She has fire in her eyes and my cock is screaming for freedom.

"Raven, I'm sorry . . . I um . . . I'll buy you another dress. I'll get this one fixed. Say something, sweetheart, please."

"You, Mr. Phillips, are extremely overdressed. You said I wouldn't have to ask you twice, yet, here I am, asking—again."

I grab her and kiss her wildly as I try to rip my own clothes off. She gets me, all my crazy ways and she loves me. *How the fuck did I get so lucky?*

I snap her thong and make fast work of the bra, but leave on the heels and thigh-highs.

"Breathe, Jax, close your eyes and breathe. I'm not going anywhere without you."

She pulls me in for another kiss. Our tongues are doing their slow dance. My heart feels as if it will beat right out of my chest. I grab her face between my palms, deepening the kiss further as I back her up to the bed. I slowly guide her onto it before spreading her legs and sliding my cock inside of her. She throws her head back and closes her eyes like she's relishing in the feel of every hard inch of me. Balls deep, I freeze. She opens her eyes. "Jax, are you okay?"

"If I could spend the rest of my life in this moment, I would be a happy man. As strong as I am, is as weak as you make me. I love you so deeply, so truly, yet there is always more with you. You understand me like no other, even when I don't understand myself. My heart and soul is in your delicate hands."

Raven

HE DOESN'T HAVE TO move; he's throbbing deep inside me. He throws his head back and my name is his benediction as he floods me. I'm right behind him.

After a few minutes, he gets on his knees, takes off my shoes and stockings, all the while, buried deep within me. This is my over-the-top, intensely wild husband, whom I love with all my heart and soul.

"I need you, wife—again and again. Always more, never enough." He leans back down, careful not to place all of his weight on me. He nibbles on my ear, and I feel his magnificent cock pulsing inside of me.

He tweaks my nipples, both at the same time. "Oh, God, Jax, I need more."

He growls in my ear, "More what, sweetheart?"

He's swiveling his hips, "You don't play fair."

He takes both my hands and holds them above my head with one of his. He lifts my leg over his shoulder, so he can go deeper. "Jax, please."

"Tell me, wife, what do you want?" He's not letting up, he pulls out slowly and I'm trying to push him back in, but he's in total control.

"I want it hard."

"Want what hard, wife?" *Oh he's smirking.*

"Fuck me hard, Jax—*now!*"

"Yes! I love when you talk dirty, sweetheart."

He rolls onto his back and guides me patiently to climb on top of him. Once I am positioned above him, he grasps my hips and slams me hard onto his cock. He's holding onto one of my ass cheeks, pulling and digging his fingers into it, and then, he smacks my ass. This sets me off in a wild frenzy of riding him like my life depends on it. After several minutes, I feel him grasping harshly at my ass again. Smack! "Come now, Raven! Holy fuck, woman! he grunts. The explosion for both of us is endless. He's slowly bringing us back down, guiding my hips on him, his cock slipping in and out. I have nothing left; I'm totally and utterly spent. I can't even open my eyes.

"Sleep, my precious one. I will love you past the heavens and the stars. I will need you beyond this lifetime," he whispers to me as he lays me down and covers us up. I spoon back into him and fall asleep to the sound of our synchronized breathing.

Maxwell

ROSE AND SAMMY ARE settled in next door, and now I get my Jackie . . . finally! It has been a test to my strength and patience, waiting to take her completely. "Jackie, you look beautiful." I wrap my arms around her and nuzzle her neck. God, she smells wonderful, I want to bury myself in her forever.

"Thank you, Maxwell. We need to talk."

Talk? She wants to bloody talk now! "Okay, baby, what's wrong?"

"I know you're worried about Monday, but I can tell something else is bothering you. You seemed more on edge than usual at the wedding. Was it just the wedding or did something else happen?"

How does she do it? "Let's sit, and I will tell you everything. You know we are keeping Rose's identity a secret? Even from Sammy."

"Yes, Raven told me. I would never want to put her life in jeopardy."

"I got a call from my attorney. Vincent's lawyer is claiming he shot me in self-defense. He is also claiming that Duke kidnapped Raven."

I see her shock turn to rage like the flip of a switch. "Max, it's absurd that anyone would even believe him."

"I know, baby, but I think he is setting himself up for a plea deal. His best bet is to turn state's evidence. I'm worried how this is going to play out for all of us. On Monday, while I'm giving my deposition, I asked Sammy to stay with you."

"Maxwell, I will do whatever you need me to do. I don't want you worrying about me. I understand the danger, and I promise you, I will not take any chances."

We sit quietly for a while, gazing out over the park. "Max, if you squeeze me any tighter, I might snap in half."

"Oh my God, did I hurt you? I'm so sorry, baby."

"Relax, I'm fine, but you on the other hand, need some attention."

I smile and kiss the tip of her nose. "Do I now? What type of attention are you offering?"

"The kind that requires a lot less clothing."

"Well I wouldn't mind removing your dress."

She stands up in front of me, but my eyes are focused solely on her legs. "Max, if you don't take your eyes off of my legs, we are not going to get anywhere."

"Oh trust me, baby, I know exactly where we're going."

Jackie

HE GETS UP AND sweeps me into his arms. "The first thing I want to do is dance with you."

He puts on a beautiful song, 'Pieces' by Red and takes me in his embrace. He's a fantastic dancer; light on his feet. He nuzzles into my ear, and begins to sing. Max is singing. I might faint. Real slow style dancing with Maxwell Fleming, singing in my ear. I'm about ready to pinch myself when the music ends. "Max, you have a beautiful voice." Before I can say another word, my dress is a puddle around my ankles.

"I'm going to kiss you from head to toe, and I'm not stopping."

His kisses are soft, yet firm. He flutters them down my neck. His soft stubble, tickles in the wake of his kisses. "Oh God, Max, if you're going to do this to my whole body, I don't know that I'll be able to take it."

"Hmm, oh, you'll take it, baby, and then some."

My bra and panties have somehow managed to end up with my dress on the floor. He's kissing my arms, and I can't move. Every spot he kisses sends chills up my spine.

As he latches onto my nipple he brings me down to the floor. He nibbles and licks, followed by kisses. Just when I think I might burst, he goes to the other one. His fingers are fluttering down my ribs. He's kissing me everywhere. I'm so overwhelmed.

"Max, I don't think I can take it much longer." I know I sound whiney and desperate, but at this point I don't care!

"Baby, you are so responsive to me, and I love that I can give you such pleasure."

As he's kissing his way down my hips, his clothes are being tossed everywhere. He holds my legs open with an iron grip, leans down, and swipes his tongue over my clitoris. I'm screaming and riding a wave of unexplainable pleasure.

Maxwell

"I NEED TO BE inside you now, baby." I crawl up her body and take my time entering her, treasuring every movement, until there is nothing between us. I can feel myself all around her, and slowly begin to move. It's been so long since I've been deep inside of her. She's tight and warm. I trail my fingers up her legs; they are so long and lean. Her skin is soft and smells sweet. I need to slow it down. I can't let it end. I roll her nipples between my fingers then I stop. Her eyes open wide and she begs me for more. I give her what she wants, taking one of her nipples into my mouth, very gently sucking. She's yelling and I need to focus on her, what she wants. I pull her nipple between my teeth, biting down with just enough pressure while I roll the other nipple between my fingers, pinching and tugging. I can feel my blood racing through my body; every part of me is tightening up. She begins to shake and quiver, dragging her nails down my back. "Oh, bloody hell."

She throws her head back and digs her heels into my arse. She's screaming, and clawing her nails into me. I lose all control. I feel a dam inside me open. All of the stress and the loss, floods to the surface. I explode like I never have before. I hold her close, knowing that she is the one who has brought me from a world of darkness. She's the one who put together all the shattered pieces of my heart.

I carry her into bed, realizing that I could never be without her again. Cradling her in my arms, I fight to hold back all of the emotions that I've kept buried for so long. I pull the comforter over us. I'm never letting her go.

$\mathcal{J}axson$

MORNING ARRIVES WITH RAVEN and I in a tangled heap. I smile and watch my wife sleep. Everything I need is right here in my arms. I don't want this peace and comfort to end, but come Monday morning, the craziness will start all over again. Mrs. Osla is overseeing the renovations on the island, which I've yet to tell Raven about. I love the mornings when I can hold her in my arms. The quiet and the feeling of knowing she is safe, overwhelms me.

"Jax, can you loosen your grip a bit, please. Are you okay?"

I pull her on top of me still buried balls deep, and I tilt my hips. "What do you think, sweetheart?"

"What's bothering you?" She narrows her eyes at me like she's trying to figure me out.

"I don't want this to end. I want to always have this feeling of total bliss."

"It will only end if you let it. We can't give up, and we won't give up—ever. Why do you fear it will end?"

I close my eyes and take a deep breath. "I'm worried about court, and everyone's safety."

Her fingers trace over the little lines at the corner of my eyes. "Have faith, think of *Die Hard* and how the good guy always wins."

I throw my head back and laugh. "Raven, I love you."

I tilt my hips again; she's so beautiful. Her hair is tousled, her eyes are bright and her lips are puffy. I'm a lucky bastard. "Ride me, sweetheart, take charge."

"Not just yet, my beautiful husband, first I want to kiss you everywhere." With that, she begins the slow process of kissing me over every inch of my skin. I know I won't last long. As she kisses each one of my nipples, I tilt my hips and grind into her the way that she loves. I don't think either one of us is going to last. She lifts her hips and slowly glides down. "Oh, it's so full this way," she whimpers before rising again and clenching as she slowly comes down. My eyes roll back, and I fist the sheets, trying to control the tidal wave. She does it again and I lose it, completely shattered. The sight of my undoing sends her over the cliff, I believe. She picks up the pace, the sounds escaping her keeping me hard for her finish. With one last guttural scream, she collapses into my arms. Neither of us move, we are barely able to catch our breath. Both of us silently lost in the intensity of our lovemaking.

She lifts her head after a few moments. " Are you okay?"

"Why wouldn't I be? My beautiful wife—who just gave me quite the morning shag—is sprawled naked across my body. I'm more than okay, sweetheart."

"Well, that same wife needs to crawl off your body like this. It's getting harder and trickier to do certain things with this growing belly. The same belly that is also rumbling for food." She climbs off. I jump up after her, lift her up, and head towards the kitchen. "Jax, you can put me down, I can walk."

"Nope, I'm spending the entire weekend just like this."

"You're out of your mind, we are not spending the entire weekend like this. Besides, I want to walk on the beach, what would the neighbors think?"

I frown. "I don't want to share you with anyone, is that so bad?"

"Jax, it's not bad. It's just not realistic. Let's look at it this way, when the baby is asleep we will be like this, and when the baby is awake we will let Mr. Cock take a snooze."

I stroke my chin. "Sweetheart, I'm really loving this negotiating stuff."

She rolls her eyes. "Jax, put me down, please. I want to give you something," She begs, but I don't give in. "Jax, the baby is up." And with that, I put her right down.

"I'm going to freshen up and you are going to get breakfast going."

"What would you like me to make you?"

"Surprise me." She kisses me and leaves me to it.

Raven

WHEN I GET BACK to the kitchen, after my shower, I see he has breakfast all set up on the patio. It's so beautiful here; the sound of the waves and the smell of the ocean. I sit down. I'm starving and before I realize it, I'm halfway through my omelet.

"Wow, sweetheart, you really were hungry. I can't let you get that hungry, anymore."

I have learned in life you need to pick and choose your battles wisely. I have come to know which ones I can win with Jax, and which ones are best left alone. As long as I don't let him dominate me all the time, I know we will find a balance.

"Jax, I really like the beach, and I was thinking maybe we can get a beach house for vacations. It would be nice with the baby to have a safe place to just be."

"Well, sweetheart, it's funny you should mention that."

He lifts his napkin and hands me an envelope. "My wedding gift to you."

I open it up and begin to read. I'm floored, but yet, I'm not. I look back up at him and see fear in his eyes, his jaw is tight, and I know . . . there is so much more to this than just a gift. I fold it up and say nothing, deciding to give myself time to calm down. I hand him a box. "My wedding gift to you, Jax."

He opens the box, his eyes becoming wide like a little boy. He looks at the bowtie, and smiles, but then he reads the quote by Chae Richardson. *"Courage is not living without fear. Courage is being scared to death and doing the right thing anyway."*

I brush my fingertips down the side of his beautiful face. "Now, Jax, do you want to tell me the whole story about the island?"

"Raven, I don't even know where to begin."

I get up and crawl into his lap. "Start at the beginning," I suggest. He says nothing. "Jax, when did you buy the island, how about that?"

He takes a deep breath and closes his eyes. "The same day I tented your building for non-existing termites." He opens one eye, probably to see if I'm going to flip.

"Why did you buy it? Go back to that day when you decided this was a great idea, and tell me why."

"You were always running away from me. Every time we were together, things would pull us apart. I just wanted to have someplace where we could be together and safe. I wanted to lock us away from the rest of the world. I know it's crazy, but in my defense, I wasn't thinking clearly."

"So, while we're locked away on this island, what about everyone else?"

"Full disclosure; my plan is to have houses built at all different points of the island. Everyone gets a house; we all live there. Mrs. Osla is overseeing all of the renovations."

"So, you're having houses built, and then you're going to lock the entire family away on this private island. Do you not see how crazy that is?"

"Honestly, up until the night before the wedding, it seemed perfectly normal to me."

I don't need to ask this, I already know the answer, but maybe if he hears it. "What changed? What, or should I say who, made you see how crazy this is?"

"Max made me see how unrealistic it was."

As I listen to his reasoning, I finally get it. This all goes back to the day his father walked out. Jax's fear of great loss came then. This is why he operates the way he does, so he never has to feel such pain, again. This is what drives the man.

"Jax, you have to stop operating out of fear. It's not good for you, and it's not good for everyone around you." I pull his face towards mine and kiss him. I hope that in time he will understand not all love comes with pain and loss. "Thank you, Jax. I guess we have a new vacation destination for the entire family."

"Let's go for that walk on the beach, maybe the baby will get tired and go back to sleep." He offers me the mischievous smile he's been sporting a lot lately.

Jackie

I TRY TO MOVE, but I can't. I open my eyes and Max is staring at me. He has an arm and a leg, locking me into place. "How long have you been staring at me?"

"I haven't been staring; I've been *watching* you sleep. Do you know when you're sleeping you look like an angel? I could watch you all day, but I've only been awake for ten minutes."

"Max, I need to check on Rose. What time is it?"

"It's eleven and I checked in with Sammy a couple of minutes ago. Rose is still asleep. What would you like to do today? I know you like to run, but honestly, I'm not up to a full blown run, yet."

"What I would really like to do is have a quiet, relaxing day alone with you. I still have more questions. And now that the flurry of the wedding is over, I just want a normal day. There is one thing we need to get cleared up right away. I'm not running away and I'm safe, so can you please loosen up your grip on me."

"Geez, I didn't realize I was holding you so tight. Did I hurt you?"

"I'm fine. Let's get something to eat."

WE HEAD TO THE kitchen where I sit and watch Max pull together a delicious breakfast. "This is amazing. I wouldn't even know where to begin."

"I take it, then, you don't cook?"

"No, I can make coffee and I can throw together a salad. Do you cook out of necessity, or do you enjoy cooking?"

"I never really thought about it, I guess a little of both. Let's take our coffee up to the rooftop deck, it's beautiful outside."

We head upstairs and I'm floored. "Max, this is so beautiful. I would be up here every morning."

"Sometimes I come up here just to think and forget, in a city this big, it's peaceful."

I pull him onto one of the lounge chairs. "Max, burying your head in the sand and trying to forget is never going to help you heal. Part of the healing process is talking about it. It's eating away at you like a cancer."

He's holding me and stroking my arm. "Elliot would have been ten. God, he was so beautiful."

Thank God he's talking. It's a start. I curl into him, wrapping my arms around him tighter. "It's okay, baby, take all the time you need."

"He was only eight months old. Seeing my wife and baby shot in the head is an image I will take with me to my grave."

"Don't focus on that, focus on the positive. Tell me about him, tell me what you remember."

"I remember his smell; sweet, so very sweet. His laugh would fill my heart. He loved music, and I would sing to him all the time. He didn't care what I was singing, just as long as I was singing. Samantha was good with him. She was fierce at work, but when she walked in the door, she was *mum*; she knew how to leave work at the door. I never could. I see danger everywhere and anywhere. After everything happened, I became worse."

"The healing process is different for everyone. You will probably be over-protective for the rest of your life. If you and Jax are honest with Raven and me, then we know the risk. We won't take stupid chances. Information is key. I never knew you sang, you have such a beautiful voice." I change the subject to something lighter.

"I haven't sung since my son died, at least, until last night. You're putting me back together, one shattered piece at a time. For the first time in years, I have hope."

"There is always hope, Max. First, you have to stop living to die and live to live. You need to realize that there are many people who love and respect you. You have been surrounded by so much love, but your heart has been closed to it all."

We sit in silence for a while. "Max, I would like to talk to Jax about setting up the school we spoke about. I realize I'm not going back to my job, and I need to do something."

"I have some questions for you; turnabout is fair play. What do you know about Sammy? I will admit, when Jax called me from your home, I pulled a file on him. I want to know what's not on paper, how you feel about him, and his partner."

"Sammy is very loyal to my family. I do know his partner, Ian, has agreed to move here. I'm very comfortable with him. He doesn't get along with my brother, Dylan, but in his defense, no one does."

"Are you close to your brother?"

"No. I tolerate him, at best. There is a large age difference, and he has been in love with Raven from the first day I brought her home. It's very awkward."

I lean in and kiss him softly. "What is it, Max, tell me what has you so twisted up inside?"

"I'm thinking of semi-retirement."

I see something in him, something beyond fear—I see hope. "Why would you want to do that, give up control? I thought you enjoyed what you're doing, making order out of chaos."

"I don't think I can go out in the field anymore. I'm not one hundred percent, and in my line of work, that could cost lives. The past six months, I've learned so much from you and Raven. All of this is just materialistic stuff, and if it went away tomorrow, it wouldn't really matter. I want to take a back seat and do more behind the scenes stuff. I'm ready to come back to the land of the living, and I want to start and end my days with you."

"Max, whatever your decision, I will support it."

He pulls me close to him and seems to be relishing in the peace he's newly found in life . . . with me.

Chapter Sixteen

Jaxson

THE LONG WALK ON the beach is wonderful, but my wife is tired. I scoop her up in my arms and carry her the rest of the way.

"Jax, I can walk."

I kiss her forehead and she nuzzles into my chest. By the time we reach the house, she is out cold. I put her to bed and decide to call Max. I want to check on Rose before Raven wakes up.

"Hey, Max, how's everything going?"

"Why are you calling me? Shouldn't you be spending quality time with your wife?"

"Relax, mate. She's sleeping, I wanted to check on Rose and I have questions that I want answers to before Monday."

"Well, Jackie just went next door to visit with Rose, so ask away."

"Okay, let's start with this one. Do you think Vincent knows that Rose is alive?"

"No, I don't. I think if he knew, he would do everything he could to get to her. His obsession with her was sick and twisted."

"Do you think he will turn state's evidence?"

"Yeah, I do. What worries me is Raven is the only living person who witnessed Vincent shoot Antonio. I've been trying to find the video that Raven told us about, but no luck. The statute of limitations for kidnapping in D.C. is six years, but there is no limitation on first-degree murder of a federal agent. Joseph left more questions than answers."

"What do you mean? What kind of questions?"

"Well, like why he didn't go after Vincent once he had Rose and Raven back. He was always preaching about following the rules and the laws, yet, he did none of it. The only thing I can figure is, Vincent's reach is far beyond what Joseph led us to believe."

"Max, do you think it would be better or worse if he turned state's evidence?"

"It would depend what kind of deal he gets. The best thing would be if he turned and received maximum jail time. Both D.C. and New York do not have the death penalty. If he does turn, it could incite a mob war. We will have our hands full, for quite some time."

"What about Duke?"

"He'll probably get life without parole, unless they can prove mental incompetence."

"Max, I'm worried about a trial. There will be a media circus, and rival families to think about. Who's been running his business while he's been in a coma?"

"From what I've heard, Vincent's consigliore has been running things. Vincent also relies heavily on Annabelle, which is unusual."

"Maybe it wasn't the best thing that I brought Rose back here."

"Jax, if someone were to dig hard enough, they would have found her. Joseph never even changed her name! Honestly, he was too emotionally invested to think everything through."

"How long do you think we can keep Rose's identity secret?"

"I honestly don't know, but as long as everyone co-operates, we have a fighting chance."

"How is everything going with you and Jackie?"

"Everything is good. Really good, actually. She's willing to try and so am I. Just need to take baby steps, something you know nothing about, mate. What happened with the gifts?"

"Fuck, Max, I'm not in the doghouse. I really thought she was going to flip out and tear me a new one, but she surprised me."

"Did you confess everything?"

"Yep, even when I purchased the island."

"Really, and when was that?"

I'm never going to live this one down. "When I tented the building. Stop laughing. I even told her about the houses that are going up on the island and how Mrs. Osla, is overseeing the project."

"Wow, you really did confess everything. How is she feeling?"

"She won't say it, but I know she is scared about Monday. I would feel better if Mick also stayed with Rose, on Monday. He's a good guy, and we all trust him. I think it would make Raven feel better, too."

"That's fine with me. I'm going next door. Let Raven know all is well here, and I will see you soon."

"Okay, thanks."

Maxwell

I'M THINKING THAT ISLAND is sounding better by the minute. Maybe Jax isn't *completely* off his rocker. Jackie and Rose are watching some mindless television show and Sammy is on the computer.

"Hey, Max, glad you're here. There's some stuff I want to go over with you."

"Why don't we go in Jax's office; it's quiet back there." I lead the way.

"Okay, Sammy, what's up?"

"Are you planning for Jackie to go to court with you on Monday?"

"As much as I want her stuck to me like glue, I know she can't be in the room with me when I'm giving my deposition. I was thinking Rose and Jackie could stay here. I will have Mick stay with them, along with an additional security team. I would like it if you stood here with them, too. This place is secure, and the lift has a private key and code."

"Good, I was thinking the same thing. There is no reason for them to leave here."

"Sammy, tell me everything you know about the situation with Raven, so I can bring you up to speed."

"Well, I know about Raven's father. I know who Rose really is. I know how sick Vincent is. I know that Duke probably snapped, and that Vincent is throwing him under the bus. I did find out that Vincent has some pretty heavy political friends, which will probably help him with a deal. I heard through the grapevine that the Feds are talking a deal. I also found out that Annabelle had one husband and two lovers that all died under mysterious circumstances."

"How do you know about Rose?"

"Max, the Chief called and he told me that he spoke to you. So, you know I still work for MI6. He told me about Rose, he wasn't going to let me go in here without full disclosure. You know I've been a guard with the Gerhard family for ten years. I can tell you that Gerhard is a hard, but fair man. He has a way of bringing people to the table. The government wants him and his family safe at all cost. I did some digging around and I heard the Feds were probably going to cut a deal with Vincent. Let's face it, they would be crazy not to. When Raven was seven, Vincent kidnapped her. This was the catalyst for everything."

"Sammy, what you don't know is Vincent videotaped everything that happened in that warehouse. Somewhere, there is a video of Vincent shooting his brother, a federal agent, to death. If we can find that video, it could prove murder. Right now, all we have is Vincent, saying he shot me in self-defense. The memory, from twenty years ago, when Raven was a traumatized seven-year-old, is not going to get Vincent convicted. Raven is the only living person who witnessed the murder. Rose watched the videotape, which is why we know it exists. Vincent is claiming that Duke kidnapped Raven, and that he had no idea she was being held against her will. With out that tape it's a he said, she said, and no evidence to back it up."

"Max, so what you're saying is, without that tape, he is practically a free man. How long do you think you can keep Rose under wraps?"

"I honestly don't know. I don't know why Joseph didn't change her name twenty years ago. Even if Rose came forward, she only saw a tape, a tape that we can't find."

"If we can find it, the best thing might be to leak it to the rival families that Vincent is turning; they will do the cleanup work for us."

"I thought of that, but then, what about Annabelle?"

"So we have until Monday morning to find that tape."

"Yeah, and trust me when I say, I've been trying."

"Well, I would bet that someone as sick as Vincent, would keep that tape pretty close to him, at all times. We need to get into his compound and find it before Monday."

"Keep in mind, if we obtain it illegally, then it can't be used in court."

"Max, you know there is always a way around everything. I'm going to make some calls, if I need to leave, I will give you a heads up."

"Sounds good. I'm going to collect Jackie, and go back next door."

When I get back into the living room, the ladies are laughing and chatting. It's good to see normal when we haven't had that in such a long time. "What are you ladies watching that has you laughing so much?"

"Rose never saw Friends, so I introduced her to Netflix and live streaming."

I keep forgetting all the simple things we take for granted that Rose doesn't know anything about.

Rose gets up and heads towards me, taking ahold of my arm. "Maxwell, please sit. I have some questions for you."

"I don't know that I'll have any answers, ma'am, but I will try."

"I would like to know what the plan is for Monday. You want me to stay here, don't you?"

"Yes, ma'am, I would like you and Jackie to stay here with Sammy and Mick. I need to know that you're both safe. I am trying to keep your existence under wraps for as long as possible."

"Will Vincent stand trial for any of his crimes?"

"Unless we can find the videotape that you wrote about, in the journal, then I doubt it."

She gasp, her face registering her fear. "How do you know about the journal?"

Oh no . . . I didn't realize she didn't know. "When Vincent kidnapped Raven, he gave her the journal to read. I'm sorry. I thought you knew all of this."

She begins to shake. "When d-did Vincent kidnap Raven? Oh my God, did he . . ."

I stop her before she continues. "Rose, he never touched her, I promise. I'm sorry. I thought you knew." I pull her into my arms. *Oh fuck . . .* she's shaking so bad. Oh my God, what have I done?

"Maxwell, so much is being kept from me. I'm a lot stronger than you think. I agreed to Raven's adoption to keep her safe. I would do anything for my daughter, even if it meant giving her up. Joseph looked for that tape for years. I'm not sure if he ever found it. Did you go through his private safe? If he did find it, he would have put it in there."

"I only met Joseph right after Raven was kidnapped. I don't know anything about his personal belongings, or where they would be."

"He had a cabin that belonged to his great-grandfather. Antonio and Joseph would go fishing there one weekend a month. I don't think they ever caught any fish. It was more to unwind. Before you even ask the question, yes, I know where it is. Raven owns the place. Joseph had no family, and when Antonio made him godfather, he put the cabin in Raven's name."

I'm shocked, "When I pulled a report on Raven, it didn't show that she owned anything."

"It's under Josephina Giaconna, not Cara Giaconna, or Raven Anderson. He probably never switched it. Maybe the answers you seek are there."

Sammy comes in the room, "Rose, where is the cabin?"

"It's in a small Virginia town called, Old Rag. It's about an hour and a half from DC."

I grab my phone and call Tony, "Hey, I need you to access all records for a Josephina Giaconna. I'm looking for real estate in Virginia. Send me the coordinates now, and get the jet ready. When we land, have a chopper ready to go. Tony, be on standby, I need to call Jax."

Sammy is about to grab my arm, but Jackie stops him. "He's in Max mode, let him be."

I hang up with Tony, and quickly call Jax. "Jax, I need to talk to Raven. We might have a lead on the tape, and only God knows what else."

"Slow down, mate. Tell me everything." I bring him up to speed on everything that we found out.

"Max, I will call the attorney and make sure it still legally belongs to

Raven. I will have Tony coordinate anything that Raven needs to sign for the state, and have it sent it here. Physically, are you one-hundred percent able to do this?"

"Yes, and I will have Sammy with me."

"Double up security on Rose and Jackie. I will call Mick and have him head over there now. Max, am I on speaker?"

"No, what's wrong?"

"Head into my office and close the door."

Fuck, what else . . . "Okay, what do you want to tell me that you don't want anyone else to hear?"

He's quiet for a second. "When Raven and I went to Switzerland, I had the walk-in closet converted into a panic room. I didn't tell Raven yet, because she's been so emotional. Flip the light switch, next to the closet, and the door unlocks. Open the door and you'll see a number pad. The code is *violet.* You need to show this to Jackie and Rose. Everything they need to survive, for two weeks, is in there. Max, are you there?"

"I'm here. Just shocked and proud of you."

"Really, why?"

"Shocked that you pulled this off without anyone knowing, and proud that you did it. I'm taking Sammy with me. He knows who Rose is, Jax. It has to do with Gerhard, he's a powerful man, and his safety is priority one. I've got to run, I'll get the girls set up and call you when we land."

I head back into the living room and instantly see the fear in Jackie's eyes. I know what she's thinking, and I have to reassure her. She fights her tears back as I walk up to her. "Hush, baby, none of that. I'll be okay. It's nothing like the last time."

"Max, the last time I let you walk out that door, it nearly killed both of us."

"I'm not alone, baby. Sammy's got my back. I promise, I'll come back to you. I need you to be strong for my sake and for Rose's."

She walks up to Sammy, and grabs his shirt. "So help me, Sammy, you better bring him back to me in one piece, or there will be hell to pay!"

I pull her away from Sammy, and kiss her hard. With that, we're out the door.

Jaxson

I SIT ON THE deck watching the waves, wondering if this will ever end. That island is looking better and better. A text comes through from Tony, letting me know there are papers that Raven needs to sign, and that he's faxing them now. I turn around and she's standing in the doorway, watching me.

"What's going on, Jax?"

I open my arms and she crawls into my lap. "Apparently, you own a cabin in Virginia. Your mum said Joseph put it in your name when your parent's made him your godfather. The reason we didn't know about it is because it was in the name of Josephina Giaconna. Legally, you still own it, and I have some papers you need to sign. Max and Sammy are on their way down there to see what they can find before court on Monday."

"What are they trying to find?"

"The videotape that your mum spoke of. It could be the key to putting Vincent away for life. You're the only living witness to your father's murder. That puts you in a world of danger, sweetheart. " I hold her closer. I'm so worried for her safety and our baby's. A few minutes go by and I suddenly remember another tape that Tony had transferred for Raven and her mum. "Sweetheart, why haven't you watched the tape that Joseph left you?"

"I don't know if I'm emotionally ready."

"Have you told your mum yet that your dad left her a tape?"

"No, I was afraid to give her too much all at once. I was going to ask her therapist about it."

"I think, when we get back, you should at least tell her about it. It might be helpful for her.

I better tell her about the panic room before she finds out on her own. "I have a confession to make." Her eyes grow large, and she's tugging that ear.

"Go on, I'm ready."

"I had the closet in the office removed and a panic room installed. Jackie and your mum have been instructed on how to use it. I had it installed when we were in Switzerland. I needed some peace of mind," I admit. "Please don't be mad. I like order and organization. I never had to deal with so much crazy shit all at once. I felt better knowing it was there, in case we ever needed it."

Her hands tremble as they stroke my face. "Jax, I'm sorry that all this—"

"—Raven, never be sorry for something that was never your fault. I love you, and will move heaven and earth to keep you safe." I run my hands up and down her arms. "Hey, are you hungry?"

"Starving!" She widens her eyes. "Are you going to feed me?"

"Sweetheart, I'm going to feed you, and then I'm going to make love to you all night long."

"Well, while you're getting dinner ready, I'm going to have a relaxing soak in that beautiful tub."

I kiss her and push her along, while I figure out what to do for dinner. I'm so glad Bella taught me how to cook. She said it would come in handy someday, and she wasn't kidding, especially since my wife is totally clueless in the kitchen. I put the dinner in the oven and decide to go check on Raven. She is soaking in the tub. Her hair is pulled up, but some tendrils are cascading down. Her eyes are closed, and she's singing a beautiful song by Nickleback, 'Never Gonna Be Alone.' I don't know why she thinks she can't sing—her voice is beautiful. I climb into the tub and face her. Her eye's fly open with a look that makes my cock jump to attention.

"I never heard you come in, is dinner ready?"

"You were very relaxed, and singing a beautiful song. You have a fantastic voice, so don't get all embarrassed. Dinner is in the oven, we have time. Relax and let me rub your feet."

She leans back and closes her eyes as I lift her foot. I work my thumbs up and down her arch, and then I graze my teeth along her big toe. She grips the side of the tub and just when she can't take anymore, I move onto the other foot.

"Oh, Jax."

"Feel good, sweetheart?" I give her a slight smile. My thoughts shouldn't be anywhere but with her, yet, I can't help myself from worrying about Max. What if, this time, my brother doesn't come back?

"Jax, he'll be okay." She pulls her foot away and moves to straddle me.

I let out a deep breath. "How could you know I was thinking about him?"

"Know that Max will be okay, or know that you're worried?"

"Both."

"I love you, Jax. When you hurt, I hurt. When you worry, I worry. I feel what you feel. I know Max will be okay because I have faith. The same way I knew he would wake up. You need to do the same. Right now, I'm more worried about Jackie and my mom. Both of them are reliving a nightmare. Jax, can we head back home? I know that we were going to stay here another night, but I would feel better if I was there for both of them."

"I was going to suggest the same thing. Let's head back."

Jackie

ROSE IS MESSING AROUND in the kitchen, trying to keep busy. I am in dire need of chocolate. I know that Jax has a stash here somewhere. I find some and sit at the counter, watching Rose cook. "I didn't know you could cook."

"Actually, I love to cook. I find it very relaxing."

"Well, Raven didn't get that gene, that's for sure. Unless you consider a peanut butter and jelly sandwich cooking."

"Maybe that's something I can teach her now that we're together. Right now, I want to talk about you. You haven't been yourself since Max left earlier. What's going on?"

"The last time Max went after Vincent, it didn't end well." I cross my arms across my chest, rubbing at them to fight the chill I just got.

"We just have to pray that everything will work out, Jackie. Stay positive, dear." She offers me a warm smile.

Nothing else needs to be said; all we can do it wait. I decide to hang out with Mick in the living room for a little bit while Rose is busy cooking dinner. "Hey, Mick, how are you doing?"

"He'll be okay, Jackie."

"Am I really that much of an open book?"

He laughs, "Well, yeah, you are."

"What happened with Ashlyn? She's a very nice person, Mick. She does some great work with veterans."

"After the wedding, we went for coffee. I like her. We talked about getting together again, so we'll see where it goes."

"I'm going upstairs on the deck, for a bit. If you need anything, let me know. I'll let Rose know where I'm going, and my security, too."

I don't give him a chance to protest. I need to get out and get some air. I would love to go for a run, but not without Max. It's a beautiful night, and I can see stars, even with the lights of the city. I've decided to tell Jax I want to go forward with the school at Raiders. I need something to do. I never thought my life would turn out this way. I had it all planned out, but not like this. I want a life with Max, but I also need to be safe. Now that I know everything that happened to Max's family, I can understand the fear he lives with. I need to get him to a place where he can finally feel safe and loved. Suddenly, I hear a noise and nearly jump out of my skin. I turn, see Raven, and lose it. She is on me in a second, her arms around me, holding me tight.

"Jackie, stop with the ugly cry; he'll be back safely."

"If you believe that then why did you come back early?"

"I knew you needed me."

"Ugly cry, really?"

"Yeah, really ugly."

"Did you know your mom cooks?"

"Yes. The place smells wonderful."

"Raven, thank you for coming back."

"He will be back, Jackie, I have faith.

You ready to go back down?"

"Yeah, lets go."

Raven

WHEN WE GET DOWNSTAIRS, I see my mom setting up plates of food. Jax and Mick are deep in conversation. As we approach them, the elevator doors open and Max and Sammy step out. I let out a breath as Jackie runs to Max. The look on Jax's face is like a kid on Christmas morning. I walk up to him and whisper in his ear, "Faith, Jax."

Max lets go of Jackie, and kisses her forehead. "I told you I'd be back, no tears, baby." He then looks at Jax. "We got it. The videotape was in a safe, in the cabin. The authorities took possession of it, and I have a copy. It will be submitted Monday morning to the Feds. I'm not sure what is going to happen, but either way, we can use it to our advantage. If he turns state's evidence, we can leak it to the rival families, letting them know that he is a rat. Or they can use it to prosecute him for Antonio's murder. It is clear cut, and he can't talk himself out of it."

"Max, what else was in the cabin?"

"Nothing, Jax. It was just a basic fishing cabin, in the middle of nowhere."

"Let's all sit down and eat. Apparently, my mother-in-law is a wonderful cook."

Everyone sits down to eat Rose's wonderful food. Talk soon turns to all things baby. It's nice to see such normalcy for a change.

"Mom, what type of birth did you have with me?"

"I had a natural birth. My labor was very short, and you were early. Have you decided what type of birth you want to have?" She grabs her glass of wine and takes a sip.

All of a sudden, Max starts laughing. "Max, you already used up your one get out of jail free card, so if you know something, you better confess now," I order, having a hunch that his laughter was brought on by something Jax had done. That's usually the case.

"Raven, think of who you're married to. You should have seen him with Bella. I'm surprised we didn't have him sectioned."

Jax is very quiet, stroking his chin. I know he's done something. "What did you do, Jax?"

He's about to get up, but I grab his arm. "Don't even think about trying to worm your way out of this one."

"Thanks for throwing me under the bus, Max," he says with a bit of irritation "I rented a private suite at the hospital. I hired a team of nurses. I've been interviewing nannies and security guards. The baby never leaves our sight, and I hired a private Lamaze instructor to come to the house."

I'm reciting my mantra in my head over and over again. Pick and choose your battles wisely. I know it is fear that is driving him, but if I don't rein him in, it will only get worse.

I leap up and slam my hand on the table, and all heads turn towards me. "Jax, what about me? What about what I want, or don't want? I understand a lot of what you've done. I know the more private we operate, and then the safer we are. The one thing I will not go along with is a nanny. I'm not working. I will stay home and take care of our baby. Women have been having babies and taking care of them for years without the help of a nanny. I keep telling you the same thing over and over again. You have to talk to me before you go off and do all this crazy stuff. You just used up your last get out of jail free card, so like Max, you better think before you go off half-cocked."

You could hear a pin drop it's so quiet. I turn my focus to my mother. "Mom, how early was I?"

"You were only a week early, nothing to worry about. You do need to let the doctor know that I had a fast birth, as did your grandmother. It would seem to run in the family."

"How fast was it?"

"From start to finish, one and a half hours."

There's a loud clank as Jax drops his fork. He's frozen, my poor husband. If he survives this, it will be a miracle. "Mom, Monday afternoon I have a doctor appointment, will you come with me? It's the start of my last trimester. You can tell her the family history."

"Of course I will. Don't worry, Jax, I will be here to help with the baby."

Jaxson

I'm listening to everything going on around me, but all I hear is fast birth, over and over again, in my head. I never even thought it was possible, especially since my mum reminds me repeatedly how long she was in labor with me. I swear it gets longer every time she gets mad at me.

While everyone is cleaning up and getting dessert ready, Max, Sammy, and I head towards the office for a private chat. "Alright, bring me up to speed. What happened at the cabin? And thanks for throwing me under the bus, Max."

"Jax, you threw yourself under the bus. You need to dial it down, we will get through this together, mate."

He hands me a flash drive. "Put this in the safe. I had the tape transferred to a drive. There is no reason for Raven or Rose to ever see this. There were some papers in the safe, and among them was a letter to Raven from Joseph, explaining why he chose not to use the tape to go after Vincent. At first, I didn't understand it, until I watched the tape. I hope that neither of them will have to watch it again."

I take the drive and put it in the safe. "What's the plan for Monday?"

"I asked Sammy to help with security and transport. Jax, I know I'm not one-hundred percent for field work, plus I'm too closely involved to be clear-headed." He looks down. I can tell this is a hard adjustment for him.

Sammy steps up and begins to explain his plan. "Jax, I am going to stay here with Rose and Jackie. I have brought in some private security that I trust, and have used before for additional backup. They are all retired MI6. We will leave via the back entrance where a bulletproof car will be waiting for you. I emailed you both pictures of your driver and additional security that will flank you at all times. I also sent you additional pictures of Annabelle and her children. She has a son and a daughter; neither is in the business. The daughter is a director at a private school for the blind. The son is a research chemist for new drug development. Keep in mind; I never make changes to a plan. If anyone tries to tell you that I changed something—I didn't."

"Well, it sounds like you have everything covered. Where are you staying, Sammy?"

"I moved into Max's guest room, since Jackie is staying with him. After the dust settles, I will make arrangements for a permanent solution. Right now, I just want to get us all to the other side of this."

"Thank you. We better go back inside before I get into anymore trouble."

I look to Max, giving him a slight side nod of my head. No words ever need to be spoken, that's one of our many cues when we have something more to discuss in private.

"Sammy, Jax and I have some Raiders business to discuss, we'll be out in a bit."

I watch him leave, then go to my desk, bring out the scotch, and pour us each a hefty shot.

"Talk to me, Jax. What's going on in that crazy head of yours?"

"How did Sammy know who Rose is?"

"The Director of MI6 told him. I told you, Gerhard has quite a bit of influence." He takes a sip. "You never told me that Rose didn't know about Raven being kidnapped by Vincent. When Sammy and I were trying to figure out where the tape could be, Rose heard. I had to tell her. I assured her that Vincent never touched Raven. It's because of Rose that we found that tape."

"What was on the tape?"

" I would say, it is one of the most horrific things I have ever seen. The rage and pure evil from that man was sick. I would not have been surprised if he was really aiming for Raven, when he took the shot. Maybe Joseph told Raven the shot was meant for him to ease the burden of her father's death. We'll never know the answer; he took it to the grave with him. After watching it, I can understand what drove Raven into silence and Rose to recess into the darkest corners of her mind. Vincent made her watch this over and over again."

"What was in the letter from Joseph? Why didn't he put the bastard away?"

"Fear. He feared if it went to trial, Raven wouldn't survive, neither mentally nor physically. He feared Vincent would find out about Duke's existence, and that Rose was alive. He also knew that Vincent's reach was far and wide. That type of venom has connections in high ranking places."

"Max, are you okay with Sammy taking the lead on security for tomorrow?"

"I am. I know I'm too close to the situation, and I'm not one hundred percent. I'm still getting headaches, although they happen less, I never know when one will spring on me. The Chief said he would trust his children with him."

"Just one more thing, Max, before we go. I'm telling you this one time, and one time only. After what you put me through, getting shot in Miami, you're never going out in the field again. Your little stunt of going to that cabin when you knew I wasn't here to stop you—it really pissed me off. I have too much on my fucking plate! And yeah, right now, it's all about me. Pull that shit again and I'll shoot you in the arse myself!"

I slam my glass down and head out the door, leaving Max in silence.

Just as I head back to the living room, Mum gets off the elevator. *Could this day get any better?* "Hello, Mum."

"Don't you *hello, Mum* me, where is he?"

I'm so glad I'm not in trouble for a change. "He's in the office."

Before she can say anything, Max comes up behind us.

"I'm here, An, and I'm fine."

She reaches up and pulls his ear with no signs of letting go.

"Let me tell you something, Maxwell Fleming, if you ever do something like that again, so help me, Lord."

"Mum, I already warned him." I try to rescue him.

"Jaxson James, stop laughing, you're in just as much trouble as he is."

What the hell? "I wasn't even here, why am I in trouble?"

"You know the way he is. Next time, leave Mick here to guard him, and make sure he behaves." It doesn't matter how old I am, when she yells at me, I feel like I'm a kid all over again.

"An, I am an adult, and I can take care of myself. I was in no immediate danger, and I had, Sammy, with me."

Raven comes out, probably to see what all the yelling is about. She knows how to defuse a situation. *Must be all of that teacher training.*

"An, why don't you come inside and have some tea. My mom made some wonderful cookies."

"Honestly, Raven, sometimes they are like little boys in the school yard."

She is still talking away as Raven leads her inside. She looks back to me and I mouth, "*I love you, wife,*" while giving her a smirk. She rolls her eyes.

Chapter Seventeen

Raven

IT'S MONDAY MORNING, AND I open my eyes, only to find that the room is dark and I'm alone. I feel panic, but then I see him sitting in a chair in the corner of the bedroom. My poor, beautiful husband, he's so brave, yet so vulnerable. Everyone looks to him for strength and guidance, whom does he look to? I know he's watching me; I can feel it in my soul. I say the one thing that I know will make him come running.

"Jax, I need you." Without another minute passing, he's holding me, loving me, and consuming every part of me.

"I need you more, sweetheart, more than you'll ever know."

It's just a whisper, but I heard him. His fear about today is really off the charts. I know where he needs to be. The one place he can let go, the place that's reserved just for us. He's kissing my neck and nibbling my ear. I love when he is gentle, but I love when he is fierce. Right now, I know he needs fierce.

"Jax, I need you inside me now."

He stops and our eyes lock, "Hard and fierce, Jax—no holds barred."

He enters me slowly, his eyes still gazing into mine. When he's totally buried, just the way he likes to be, he stops. He lifts my legs up and places them on his shoulders. He slides his arms under my back grasping my shoulders. Our eyes never stray. He doesn't have to say a word; I see it in the depths of his beautiful blue eyes. He pulls back really slow and then slams into me, screaming my name. First fast, then slow. Time seems to stand still as I feel my heart pounding. He slows down, I think it's to give me a chance to catch up, but then he's swiveling his hips, first right and then left. He pulls back and then begins pounding again. I don't know how much time passes by; all I can concentrate on is his relentless pounding. He grabs my legs and pushes them towards me, lifting my pelvis to take more of him in. I grasp at the sheets, practically ripping them as he explodes, so fiercely, I fear he might pass out. He rests his forehead on mine, our eyes still locked.

"I love you, wife."

"I love you more, husband."

Jax loves to be needed, and taking care of me fulfills that for him. "I am jumping in that wonderful shower, and then I want oatmeal made with almond milk, with a poached egg on top, please."

"Raven, that's disgusting."

"Don't knock it till you try it."

$\mathcal{J}axson$

I SLIP ON MY sweats and walk towards the kitchen, all the while muttering to my cock about how lucky he is. When I round the corner I see Max, pacing.

"Hey, mate, is there a problem, or are you just nervous about today?" I walk up to him.

"I'm having a problem leaving Jackie here." His hands are balled up; I know he's on the edge.

"Max, she will be totally safe here. The guards will be here, and Mick is staying here, too. Don't forget we also have the panic room. Would it help if I made them stay in there?"

"No, Jax, the only thing that would help is if I was here with her, and that's not going to happen. That fucking island is sounding better and better."

"Good, I'm glad you feel that way. I decided as soon as the baby is born, we are all going there for a couple of months," I inform him. Of course, right at that moment, Raven chooses to enter the room.

"Where exactly are we going, Jax?"

I jump, "I'm not keeping secrets, Raven, I swear I just came to the conclusion that it would be good to go away after the baby comes. The homes on the island will be done, and I think we could all use some relaxation." *God, I hope she's buying this bullshit.*

"I'm hungry, Jax."

She's not saying anything, so maybe I'm not *totally* screwed here. "I'm on it, sweetheart."

$\mathcal{R}aven$

WHILE JAX ATTEMPTS TO make my breakfast, and get himself out of the doghouse, I walk up to Max. He is frozen in place, not knowing what to do with his raging fear, it seems. "Look at me, Max, please." His eyes shoot up to mine. "I understand your fear and I have an idea that might help you. You and Jax have every gadget under the sun. I know there is probably a camera in the panic room. You can watch her from your phone while Jackie and my mom sit in the room with the door open. I'm sure they can play poker with Mick and Sammy to pass the time. You will be able to keep your eyes on them without even being here, would that help?"

He throws his arms around me, and holds me tightly. "Raven, the best thing my brother ever did was marrying you. He really is a lucky bastard."

"Language, Max. Remember, the baby is up, right now."

Max laughs, then releases me so he can go next door to get Jackie.

I head over to the counter and sit down to eat. "Jax, this is wonderful," I say after my first few bites.

He makes a face of disgust at my oatmeal, and then shakes his head. "Are we going to talk about it, or are you going to let me squirm all day?"

"This is what you get when you don't talk to me. You can't just decide what we're doing without even giving me a vote. If you would have asked me, you would have known that it was my intention all along to go to the island, after the baby is born. I need a break, and so does everyone around us. My only concern is timing as it is hurricane season that time of year. Let's table this discussion for now. Right now, I just want to get to the courthouse; the sooner we get this over, the better."

I walk up to him and pull him into my arms. "I love you, Jax, and we will get to the other side of this together."

"Max is right, I really am a lucky bastard." He squeezes back.

WE GET TO THE courthouse without incident, and we're ushered through the back. Jax has an iron grip on me, and Max is glued to my other side. Security is tight and Bo is on high alert. We are led into a room where a well-dressed man is waiting for us, along with four federal agents and Jax's team of attorneys.

"Miss Anderson, please, have a seat."

Jax squeezes my hand tighter, "It's, Mrs. Phillips," I correct him. "Let's get this over with."

"I'm Leo Hage, Federal Prosecutor. I have watched the tape and I've spoken with your attorneys. Before anyone say's anything, I will not subject Mrs. Phillips to viewing it."

I let out the breath I didn't even realize I was holding, my voice barely a whisper. "Thank you, sir."

"I will tell you, up until we got that tape, there really wasn't a strong case against him. Now that his attorney has been given a copy, he is requesting a deal. No matter which way this goes, it will be ugly. He's claiming self-defense in the shooting of Mr. Fleming. He is also claiming that Duke was responsible for your kidnapping, and that he knew nothing about it. I, of course, don't believe any of it, however, it is a he said, she said situation. Duke is not saying a word, even after we made him aware that Vincent is blaming him for everything."

"Mr. Hage."

"Please, call me Leo."

"Leo, Duke shot Marco and Erica; I witnessed that. I also witnessed Vincent, pushing Duke, egging him on. I believe his exact words were, *'You gonna do her, son, or should I?'*

I think justice would be better served if Duke was institutionalized."

"I understand he is your half-brother?"

I hold my hand up, stopping him before he goes any further. "I only found that out right before he murdered two people. I assure you, I have no emotional connection to the man. Clearly, anyone could tell he snapped."

"Well, Mrs. Phillips, I have to look at everything and decide how I'm going to get the most out of this. If Vincent is willing to give up key figures in his drug cartel, then honestly, I might cut a deal."

Jax has my hand in a death grip. "What about my wife's safety, or is that not a concern of yours?"

"Mr. Phillips, we will do all that we can to protect, Mrs. Phillips. I'm not opposed to the Witness Protection Program."

That's the straw that snaps Jax. I see the exact second when the curtain comes crashing down. He jumps up and slams his fist on the table so hard, even Bo jumps.

Jax's attorneys are on him, trying to hold him back. The men in the back of the room come running towards us, and Max, instinctively, throws himself over me. I can't see him; I can only hear him.

"Do you even know what *the fuck* you're talking about? Do you realize she was in witness protection, and your bureau couldn't protect her? The Fucking Director of the FBI couldn't even protect her. We came here today in good faith. I won't tolerate your bullshit, Hage. I didn't get to where I am today by being some kind of fucking pansy arse follower. This is how this is going to play out, and trust me, you'll listen. You've got the fucking tape; use it to put that fucker away. If you don't use it, and you make some sort of deal,

I will release it to the media. I will break apart Vincent's business, brick by brick, and anyone associated with him will feel my wrath. I have billions of dollars at my disposal and nothing but time. Time to protect my family. And if you think I won't do everything and anything to protect them, then you better go back and research me again. For all intents and purposes, this fucking meeting is over. My wife and Mr. Fleming will not be coming back here, again. Any other contact will be done through my team of attorneys, whom could keep you tied up for *years*."

Before anyone can say another word, Jax is ushering us towards the door. Hage reaches out his hand to try and stop us and Bo nearly rips it off. Max whispers something to Bo and just like that, we're heading out the door, never looking back.

The ride back to The Tower is long and quiet. I look over to Max, watching his phone and smiling. "Max, why are you smiling?"

"I'm watching Jackie beat everyone at poker."

I laugh. "Max, she's a math teacher. She's probably counting cards. I'm surprised Sammy is even playing with her. He's never beat her at cards in all the years I've known them."

Max doesn't say a word, he only stares at his phone, smiling.

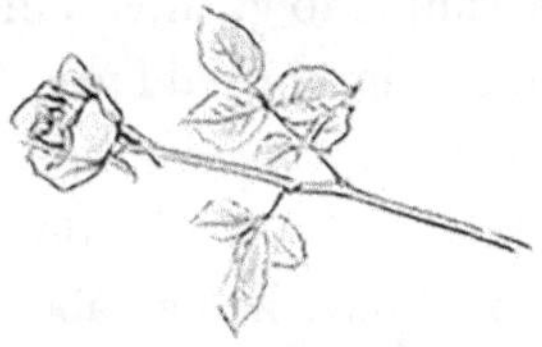

JAX IS QUIET—TOO QUIET. A quiet Jax is not good; it can only mean trouble. I witnessed fierce Jax, for the first time, today. I've seen so many sides to this man, and every side of him brings a different element that I love. It's when he's quiet that I worry the most. .

When the elevator doors open, Jackie flies into Max's arms. His whole body visibly relaxes as he scoops her up and carries her towards his place.

We head into the kitchen, and my mom is making tea. "Raven, come sit down and tell me what happened in court today."

Jax pulls me towards him and kisses my forehead. "I have to go to the office for a little bit. I will be back to pick you up for our doctor appointment. Please stay here and wait for me."

It's not a demand or a request, it's a plea, and it breaks my heart. "I will not leave the house today."

He's holding me tightly and whispers, "I love you, wife of mine."

"More, Jax. I love you more. Now go."

I watch as he and Sammy leave, and then my walls come crashing down. My mom is on me in a New York minute. We sit on the couch and she rocks me in her arms. I can't stop crying; I'm overwhelmed. This emotional roller coaster can't be good for the baby.

"Raven, please tell me what happened."

"Oh, Mom, I don't see an end to all of this." I'm about to tell her everything and then it hits me like a ton of bricks. I don't really know how much she knows about everything. Thank, God, for once in my life, my brain-to-mouth filter was working.

"What are you not telling me? Don't even think of lying. You, my dear, are someone who should never play poker. I'm strong, and I can handle whatever it is you're hiding from me."

"Mom, how about you tell me what you know and then I can sort of fill in the blanks?"

She is stroking my arm and I don't know if it's to sooth her or me. "Well, you know I watched that tape everyday that Vincent held me captive. He raped me, sometimes two or three times a day. I didn't fight him, Raven; I thought he still had you." Her tears fall and my heart is breaking. We're both holding each other; a lifeline in this raging storm. "Finally, Joseph found me. He told me that you were safe. He wanted to go after Vincent, but he realized, right away, how physically and mentally abused I was. He knew I needed medical attention, so he stayed with me. Upon examination and tests, they informed me that I was pregnant. I knew it wasn't Antonio's baby, and I didn't know what to do. I knew that I could have had an abortion, however, that's a personal choice. I decided to have the baby, and give it up for adoption. You have a half-brother, Raven. I'm sorry, but I couldn't keep him. Looking at him only brought up such rage within me. Joseph found him a nice home, and I prayed for him every day in hopes that he would never turn out like Vincent.

"I was overwhelmed by everything, and tried to commit suicide. Joseph found me in time. He made me realize that I needed help, and you needed to be safe. Your safety was everything to me.

"Joseph, found your adoptive family through a friend of his at the bureau. It was all done privately. He had the records sealed and marked classified. He staged the accident in California. And just like that, we were gone. I know that Vincent kidnapped you, Max and Jax rescued you, and Vincent and Max shot each other. I don't know much of anything else, but I figured, when you're ready, you will tell me. And if you don't, it won't change anything for me. You're my daughter, and I would do anything to protect you. You need to tell me what you're holding inside you that's making you so upset. Think of your child, this can't be good for the baby."

"Oh, Mom, I wish it was that easy. Life has been crazy, and I don't see any light at the end of the tunnel."

"Nonsense, there is always hope. Your father always told me that I was the strongest person he'd ever met. *Quiet tenacity* is what he would always say, and I see so much of that in you."

"Do you really think knowing everything will help? For all intents and purposes, Mom, you're like a prisoner, just released from a twenty-year jail term. Life has gone on and left you behind. The world's moral compass has changed, and not always for the better." I take in a deep breath then bring up something I've been curious about. "You stopped talking for twenty years, why?"

"Raven, dear, the world will always have both good and bad. It's about finding a balance we can live with. If we make positive changes in our own little circle, then it becomes like a splinter in a glass. I kept up with the changes in the world. I read the papers daily, and I know a lot of bad things have happened. I stopped talking because my heart was broken. I lost the love of my life. I gave both my children away to save them, one I never knew. I know you have so many questions and so many years to make up for. I promise you I won't break. Please, tell me what has you walking on egg shells around me."

I take a deep breath and tell her everything. I leave nothing out from my first meeting with Jax, to all the craziness that got us here today. I tell her about my life with my adoptive parents, and all about Marco. I even tell her about Duke. She sits in silence as if she's absorbing every word I say, until I tell her about the tape that my father made. She gasps, and then she begins to cry. I pull her into my arms and rock her like a mom cradling a child.

"Raven, have you watched the tape?"

"No, I don't think I'm ready to do that yet."

"Why not?"

"Fear, I think. My whole life, I put my father on a pedestal, my knight in shining armor. I don't want anything to happen that would make him fall off that pedestal."

"Oh, Raven, nothing ever will. When you're ready, if you want, I will watch it with you."

"There is also one that he left for you."

She begins to shake, "Oh, I need to see it right now, please."

"Are you sure you're ready for this?"

"I've existed for twenty years without hearing my beautiful Antonio's voice, I don't want to wait a second longer. The only images I've had playing over and over again were Antonio getting shot, and you, terrified. This could erase all of that. Of course, I'm ready."

I take her into Jax's office and sit her down with the laptop. "Jax's, tech guy, Tony, put them on a drive for us. I'll leave you alone, just click play."

I close the door and head towards the kitchen. I realize I'm really hungry. *Damn I wish I knew how to cook.* I promised Jax I wouldn't leave, and I don't know if ordering a pizza is a safe thing to do. What if someone tries to poison us, or the delivery person works for Vincent. Oh God, now I'm getting paranoid. I'm not about to bother Jackie and Max, not after they finally have some alone time. I'm just about ready to scream when the elevator doors open, and in walks Mick with pizza.

"Mick, how did you know I was hungry?"

"I didn't, but Jax said you should be hungry right about now. I figured I would stop and get your favorite pizza."

"Mick, do you know how wonderful you are?"

"Raven, its just pizza."

"No, Mick, it's more than that. Come and join me."

"Where's your mom? Jax said she was here."

"Don't panic, she's in the office watching something on the computer." His whole body relaxes. Everyone is on high alert, and I feel so bad about it.

"I'm just going to check on her, I'll be right back."

When I open the office door my mom is crying and hugging the laptop. "Mom, what can I do to help you?"

"Oh, Raven, you don't even realize what you've done for me. For the last twenty years, the last image I have of my Antonio was of him getting shot, and Vincent laughing. You have replaced that for me with my beautiful loving husband. I could never thank you enough for that."

"Mick brought pizza, would you like to join us?"

"No, I need some time alone. Can you make my apologies, please."

"Of course."

I head back inside to eat and I think, maybe it was a good thing that I showed her the recording.

"Raven, please sit and eat something. Is Rose okay?"

"Yes, Mick, she's is going to have a nap before we have to leave for the doctor. It's been a very emotional day for all of us."

We sit, eating our pizza and enjoying the rare quiet moment.

Rose

RAVEN GIVING ME THIS video is a gift that I will treasure for the rest of my life. I want to watch it over and over again. Maybe I can erase Vincent from my head, once and for all. I stare at Antonio's face on the screen and press play again.

"Gabriella, I'm so sorry, baby. The evil that I tried to shield you and Cara from has finally caught up to us. None of this was your fault, baby. He was too far-gone for you to save. I'm sorry that Cara had to witness any of this. I will love you beyond this world. My life may be short, but I've found what some men never do. You're my happily ever after, Gabby. Take good care of our Cara. I know it will be hard for you, but Joseph will always be there for you both. I love you, heart and soul, my beautiful angel."

I pause it, I can't breathe. Oh Antonio, how could things have gotten so messed up? His voice after all these years is still too raw for my heart to handle. I take a few breaths and hit play again.

"Cara will need you close after all of this. Hold her tight, and love her with all you've got. I will watch over you both. Always remember what I told you that day on the beach, when I asked you to marry me. My heart, my soul, my life is yours.

I love you, Gabby."

I love you Antonio, and I will be strong for our Cara.

Jaxson

SAMMY AND I GET to the office. I'm in a foul mood. I'm not here five minutes and Mrs. Osla is on me for not properly introducing her to Sammy. I swear she is my mum on steroids. "I would be more than happy to introduce you, if you could give me a second, please." I realize I snapped at her and I quickly apologize, and move on to more important matters.

"First order of business, what is going on with the buildings on the island?"

"Well, it seems they will be ready ahead of schedule, especially when I told them I was going to personally come down to oversee the progress."

God, I love this woman. She could put fear in the Devil himself.

"Is what happened in court today making you this way, or is it something you did that you got into trouble for?"

I'm rubbing my temples and growling. "Both."

"Will you ever learn? Call your mum before you get into trouble with her, too."

"Samuel, it's very nice to meet you." And just like that, she's out the door.

"Wow, Jax, where did you find her?"

"Max found her after the whole Duke thing. I wanted someone different, and boy is she ever."

"She's different all right; kind of hard to understand."

"Yeah, you'll get used to it. Sammy, I don't pull punches and I don't sugarcoat anything. I know you're still MI6. I understand the government wants Gerhard protected, no matter what. What I don't tolerate is secrets. No matter what, I need complete honesty. Jackie is staying here with Max, forever. He's not going out in the field ever again. I can't handle him out there, and right now, it's all about me. Before you say anything about that," I put my hand up. "Max is the one who suggested that he take more of a behind the scenes roll. I need a replacement for him, but to come on board here, you would have to give up your day job. Around here, it's one-hundred percent or nothing. I'll give you a tour, and then you think about it. Once the baby comes, I'm taking everyone to the island. We're going in complete lock down, until this cluster fuck is over with."

"Are you done, Jax? Can I get a word in?"

"Sorry, I know I bulldoze, as Raven calls it, but that's me."

"I knew about the island, and I actually think it would be a great idea. It will give us some breathing space. I would like to see more of what goes on here behind the scenes."

"I'll put you with Tony; he is Max's right-hand man and knows everything. Let's go, I'll give you a quick tour and then introduce you before I have to call my mum. We are a very close family. If you decide to come on board, be aware my mum . . . She's a lion in sheep's clothing."

I drop Sammy off with Tony, and they seem to hit it off rather quickly. . I head back to my office to call mum and find my attorney, waiting. This can't be good. Mrs. Osla is in a tizzy.

"Mrs. Osla, it's okay."

I lead him into my office. "Mathew, what's going on?"

"Who was that, Jax?"

"My new secretary. Trust me, you don't want to ever get on her bad side." I shake my head.

"Well, I met privately with Hage, after you left there today. They don't take threats lightly. However, I did help them see the light."

"Look, Mathew, I'm not letting any of my family anywhere near these animals. We are all leaving right after the baby is born. I have an island off the coast of Belize where we'll be staying for a few months. After that, if this is not under control, then who knows? I might start looking at other countries. Nothing and no one will stand in the way of my families' safety."

"I get it, Jax, but you need to calm down. Let me be your voice, that's what you're paying me for. I will fight any deal they offer that we all don't agree upon. They were surprised to find out you have a copy of the tape. They were trying to order you to surrender it, however, I squashed that. Make sure it's locked up and not on the premises. Keep duplicate copies at different locations; but you never heard that from me."

"What about Rose? No one but us knows she's alive, can we keep it that way?"

"I buried her name change paperwork very deep. I'm surprised Joseph didn't do it when he moved her to the clinic. I understand she was dead to the world, but that could have been a disaster for everyone."

"All answers died with him. I need to get going, Raven has a doctor appointment. If you need anything else, I can have Mrs. Osla help you."

"No thanks, Jax, I'm no fool."

As we head out to the elevators, Mrs. Osla is quick to remind me again to call my mum. "Mathew, stop laughing or I will have her work for you!"

Jaxson

ON MY WAY HOME, I call mum to check in. "Hi, Mum, how are you?"

"Jaxson, what do you mean how am I? I'm worried. You went to court today and never called me. I had to find out second hand what happened."

Do I even want to know how she found out? "Mum, whom have you been talking to?"

"Never mind that; how is Raven?"

"She's trying to keep it together. I'm on my way now to pick her up for her doctor appointment."

"Okay, well, let me know what happens. Bella is making a family dinner tomorrow, make sure everyone shows."

"Mum, is everything okay? Am I in trouble?"

"Everything is fine, and you're not in trouble. We just need some normalcy. Bring Mick; I like him."

Well, at least someone else, other than Max and me, is on her radar. "Okay, Mum, will do. Love you."

She's quiet for a minute. "Love you more, son."

We pull up to The Tower, and I see the woman that has been trying to get to my wife—Annabelle. I step out of the car and my detail surrounds me.

"I want to talk to her."

"Sir, please do not engage her. Go inside. It's for your own safety."

My guard presses something on my bracelet and within seconds, all hell breaks loose. Guns are drawn and pointed towards her and the two men with her. Max comes flying out of the building with his gun drawn, yelling for the detail to get me inside.

"Max, I'm not leaving you here."

"Jax, for the love of God, do what you're told and get inside now!"

"Annabelle, I suggest you take your men and leave here now, and never come back. If you ever come back here, or anywhere near this family, it will not end peacefully. Leave now before your family has to decide on an open or closed casket!"

In seconds, she's gone and Max is back inside. Only then, I realize he's barefoot and half dressed. "Max, what the hell? I wanted to talk to her."

"There is no reason to talk to her. Mathew issued a restraining order today. If you engage her then it opens a can of worms we don't want opened."

"How the hell did you get down here so fast?"

"Your bracelet was activated."

"That explains your state of attire."

"Don't be a wise arse, I was having a wonderful time and you cut that short. I will get even with you, mate."

When we get upstairs, I realize no one is around. "Where is everyone?"

"They're in the panic room. I didn't know what was going on, so I didn't want them out here."

Max radios the guards to let them know we're coming in. *Will this nightmare ever end?*

Raven runs into my arms. "I'm okay, sweetheart."

"Jax, what the hell happened?"

"Annabelle tried to pay a visit, nothing to worry about. Mathew got a restraining order issued today. We need to get going to the doctor."

"Jax, I would like to go with you to the doctor, but only if you think it's safe," Rose walks up to us.

"Rose, I would like you too, but right now, I don't think it's a good idea. I hope you understand that I need to keep your presence unknown."

"I do. Remember to tell the doctor what I told you about quick deliveries."

Raven

WHEN WE GET CHECKED in, the nurse weighs me. Jax is excited to see I've gained weight. "So have you decided what type of birth you're having?"

Jax's grip gets tighter, and I know the pressure is getting to him, Hell—it's getting to all off us.

"We are going for a natural birth, in the hospital."

I whisper, "Relax, Jax, please. Everything will be okay."

Doctor Leanne comes in, and Jax seems to relax a little. "Raven, I hear congratulations are in order. The nurse will update your name change and marital status with the hospital for you. Have you scheduled Lamaze classes yet?"

"Jax, will be scheduling someone to come to the house for the classes. I do have some new information about my family history. It seems my mother and grandmother both had quick, early deliveries."

"How quick and how early?"

"Both a couple of weeks early. As far as quickly, apparently, my mom delivered me start to finish in an hour and a half."

"Okay, I think we are moving along schedule here, so I'm not concerned. You have put on weight, so I'm happy about that. Your blood pressure is a little high, but I know you've been under a lot of stress. I would like you to watch your caffeine and salt intake.

The best thing you can do for the last trimester is to enjoy the change. Relax, prepare for the baby, and concentrate on you because once the baby gets here then everything changes."

Doctor Leanne is watching Jax, and I think she's worried about him. "Jax, get those classes scheduled soon, so that you can both feel comfortable. The nurse will give you a list of everything you need to have done before your next appointment."

Just like that, she's done, and we're left alone. Jax is quiet, too quiet. "Jax, what's the matter?"

He pulls me into his arms so tightly. "I want to go home and be alone with you. I need you, Raven."

I pull away and look into his eyes. I can sense the pressure is getting to him and it breaks my heart. He helps me get dressed and we get everything we need from the nurse. I need to get him home and have some alone time with him.

Chapter Eighteen

Sammy

TONY SHOWED ME ALL around Raiders and it's quite impressive. Jax is so much more then he lets on. Tony hedged on giving me any details, though; typical tech guy. I checked in with Jackie's detail and she is in Max's flat. I decide to head up to Jackie's, flat where I will have some privacy.

First order of business, I need to call Gerhard and bring him up to speed on Vincent. I might as well get this over with. I know he's going to flip when I tell him, but better me than Jackie.

"Sammy, what's going on with my daughter?" His voice loud, forcing me to pull the phone away from my ear a bit.

"Sir, she is safe, and under tight guard right now. I think Maxwell is not going anywhere, anytime soon, sir."

"This is not the news I wanted to hear. Does she know about his past?"

"Yes, she knows everything. He's a good man, sir."

"So now you're a champion for Maxwell?"

"No, I'm a champion for Jackie."

"What is going on with Vincent?"

"Sir, there is a good chance he will get a deal. There is a video of him killing Antonio." I pause, giving him a chance to let the information sink in.

"That should at least get him locked away for life. What happened in court today?"

"Jax ripped the Feds apart. He made all kinds of threats, especially when they offered protection for Raven."

"I'm not leaving my daughter's protection in the hands of the feds. Maxwell has put a huge target on my daughters back. So, what's our next move?" His voice is getting louder and I'm not sure how he will react to the rest of the information.

"Sir, Jax purchased an island off the coast of Belize. He thinks after the baby comes he can move everyone down there, Jackie included. Might not be such a bad idea. It will give us some breathing room."

"Sammy, Vincent needs to be dealt with, and a message sent to all the families."

"I understand, sir, I do. Timing is everything right now."

"How is Raven holding up through all of this?"

"You know Raven, she's a survivor; tough and strong."

"Any chance I can get everyone to come back here? There is plenty of room at the compound."

"Sir, Jackie would never go for it."

"Yeah, I know. Why did my daughter have to be so much like me?"

"Sir, before you go, there's something else I need to discuss with you. Maxwell is thinking of semi-retirement, more of a behind the scenes role. Jax asked me to take over for Maxwell."

Gerhard is really quiet, almost too quiet. "Sir, you there?"

"Yes, Sammy, I heard you. He's awfully young to retire."

"Well, he owns a percentage of Raiders, and from what I saw today, money is not a problem. Jax doesn't want Max out in the field anymore. This could be good for Jackie. Jax is also starting a private school for the employees at Raiders. He wants Raven and Jackie to head it up."

"Sounds like Jax is trying to tighten his ring around everyone. If my daughter is going to stay in New York, then I want you there. If you need to work for him, so be it. Make sure he is aware that where Jackie goes, you go; that's non-negotiable. Let me know when the Vincent situation is handled."

I hang up and now I need to figure out what direction I should go with Vincent. He has political pull and street muscle behind him. It would have been so much easier if Max had killed the bastard. First things first, I need to check in with the guard I have on Annabelle. Then, put a few more key pieces in place.

Hage

I KEEP WATCHING THIS video over and over. I know that no matter which way I go with this, someone will be on the losing end of the stick. If I cut the bastard the deal he wants, I will get some top-level scum off the streets, but at what price? What a cluster fuck this is becoming. It would have been a lot easier if Maxwell had killed Vincent. Maybe leaking the tape and letting the world see the animal he really is would be the best way to handle this. As I hit play again, my intercom buzzes.

"Mr. Hage, Vincent's sister is here with their lawyer, Mr. Deveno, demanding to see her brother."

Can this day get any worse? "Send them in."

Annabelle Giaconna steps into my office with Mr. Deveno. I can't stop myself from staring at her; she is beautiful. I quickly remind myself she is a Giaconna, and as ruthless as her brother.

She places her hands on my desk and leans towards me. "I want to see my brother, and I'm not leaving until I do," she demands.

"Which brother do you want to see, Ms. Giaconna? Your brother Vincent, in prison, or your brother Antonio, being murdered?"

"Do you think you can scare me, Mr. Hage? I don't believe that tape is real. Family is everything to Vincent. He would have never killed Antonio."

"Mr. Deveno, how about telling your client the truth. The tape has been authenticated, Ms. Giaconna." I flip my screen around and hit play. "Enjoy the show, ma'am."

I watch as she stares at the screen in silence. It has to have some effect on her. Watching her niece being scared and brutalized by that animal, and seeing Vincent gun down Antonio, all the while laughing about it.

"Hage, that's enough. You made your point, but it won't change. We're here to see Vincent and Duke." Deveno snaps.

Everyone has rights, even that piece of shit Vincent. "Fine, now that he's awake. Vincent has been moved to isolation. You have thirty minutes, so make it good. He's being held at Attica. One of New York's toughest maximum security prisons, so I hope you enjoy your ride upstate."

They leave just as quickly as the information shoots out of my mouth. And now, I'm back to figuring out what to do with this giant cluster fuck that's been dropped in my lap.

Annabelle

ATTICA: WHAT A GOD forsaken place this is. "Deveno, where is Duke being held?"

"He is being held at Sing Sing. The Feds wanted them kept separately."

I haven't seen my brother since they transferred him here. I have not been allowed to meet my nephew. After watching that tape, I hope Vincent has a plan.

"Annabelle, we only have thirty minutes. We have to see him together. I have stuff to discuss with him about the case. You know how crazy he can be, so don't push him. I'm also trying to get permission for you to see Duke." Deveno's jabbering pulls me out of my fog.

This whole process has been a giant *hurry up and wait*. If I ran my business like this, I'd get nowhere. Finally, he walks in. *Jesus, what the fuck are they doing to him in here?*

"Vincent, if you've got to be in here, the least you can do is take care of yourself. You look like shit."

"Well, hello to you too, Deveno. I'm in a tiny room for twenty-three hours a day, maybe you should shut the fuck up and try it."

I can't believe how much he's aged in the past few months. "Vincent, I saw the tape."

"So?"

"You killed Antonio. You swore to me that you didn't. It's all there, in black and white. How could you lie to me, of all people? Do you have a plan? What about Duke . . . have you figured out what to do about him?"

"Anna, you need to get Duke to go along with everything I told the Feds. If he's a true Giaconna, he will do this for his father."

"I haven't been allowed to see him, so how am I supposed to do that? I tried a couple of times to talk to Cara, but Jax's men were all over me. Then today, I was served with a restraining order. That guy is over the top crazy, Vincent."

"Deveno, what the fuck am I paying you for if you can't even get her in to see Duke?"

"Vince, I'm working on it. Once the Feds got the tape, everything went into lockdown. I should be able to get her in today or tomorrow, at the latest. Have you thought about a deal?"

"I'm not sure what I want to do yet. Why did this tape surface now? Why was that prick, Joseph, hiding the tape? I mean he had it and could have put the screws to me twenty years ago. What was he trying to hide? Anna, did you get a look at Cara?"

"Only from a distance. I told you, Jax's men were all over me. She looks just like Antonio, except for her eyes."

"She acts like him, too. She kept trying to help Duke the whole time we were in Sicily; filling his head with nonsense. If Duke had grown up under my roof, he wouldn't be a fucking pansy-ass pussy. Just another thing to thank that bastard, Joseph, for."

"I won't be able to get anywhere near Cara again, Vince."

"Anna, what I really want is that fucker, Max's head, on a silver platter."

"I understand, but for now, let's concentrate on getting you out of here."

"Deveno, what kind of deal do you think they will offer?"

"After today, I'm not sure that they will offer any kind of deal. Apparently, Mr. Phillips has a lot of power in all the right places. He made some powerful threats today. It seems that the Feds are taking him pretty seriously."

"What kind of threats did he make?"

"My source said, Phillips, has a copy of the tape, and he will release it to all the families and the press. He will say you've made a deal to snitch, basically putting the final nail in your coffin. Apparently, the only thing he will settle for, is you getting life with no chance of parole."

"That prick thinks because he has money, he can buy anything! Fuck that, I have more power than he could ever imagine. The difference is, I'm not afraid to use it."

"I wouldn't be too quick to count this guy out, Vince. He has a lot of power, and not just in this country."

"Couldn't have been too much power if I was able to get my hands on Cara."

"Do I need to remind you he was also able to find you, when no one else could? He infiltrated the entire United States and European banking system to do it. Does that sound like someone you should dismiss like a gnat?"

"Put some feelers out and see what they're willing to offer. Find out more about Phillips and that fucker, Max. Make sure you get back to me quickly. I'm paying you enough money, that's for sure. Now I want a few minutes alone with Anna."

Deveno gets up to leave, and I know to keep quiet until he is gone.

"Anna, we don't have much time left. Deveno is only as good as the money he's paid. He'd sell out to the highest bidder. Don't trust him."

"Then why are you using him?"

"I know what he's capable of. I want everything you can find out about Max. I need to know his weakness; everyone has one. The same goes for Phillips. Get your ass in to see Duke, and convince him to do the time for me. Find out what the fuck Joseph was hiding. Find out how many tapes this Phillips guy has and then get back here in a couple of days. I will get you a list of favors owed to me from other countries without US extradition. Now, go."

"How the hell do you expect me to do all of this, in only a couple of days? I know you want revenge, Vince. I get it. However, don't you think it would be time better spent to figure out how to get out of this mess and spend less time on revenge?"

"Anna, let me worry about that. Now, go!" Just like that, I'm dismissed. He wants all of this in a couple of days . . . is he fucking kidding me? As I get outside, I see Deveno on the phone, waving me over.

"Okay, got it. We're on our way."

"The permission for us to see Duke just came through. We are going to head over to Sing Sing now."

Could this day get any worse? "Now? I have some stuff to handle for Vincent. Can't we go later?"

"Look, we're up here and we're going, so deal with it. What else did Vince want?"

"Private family stuff that doesn't concern his case."

"If that's the way you and Vince want to play it, Annabelle, it's fine by me. I have work to do. If you need anything, tell the driver."

We get in the car and begin the long ride to Sing Sing in total silence.

WE PULL UP TO Sing Sing, and it looks like another hellhole. I'm finally going to meet my nephew today. I have to convince him to take the fall for Vincent, and I don't even know him. Security is very tight as we are ushered into a tiny dismal room. Just like the Attica, the table and chairs are bolted to the floor. I have no clue what to expect, but then he walks in and I'm floored. His dark hair and chiseled good looks were not at all what I was expecting. *Jesus,* he's so young. He seems lost and dazed.

"Hello, Mr. Jensen, I'm your attorney, Mr. Deveno, and this is your Aunt Annabelle. How are you holding up in here?"

"Duke, just call me Duke. How do you think I'm doing?"

"Duke, I met with Vincent earlier and there is a lot we need to go over. Vincent said you killed Erica and Marco, right before you kidnapped your sister."

"I snapped and shot both of them, but I never kidnapped Raven. So, it's true, then? This is the way he's going to spin this bullshit?"

"Look, son, we need to get the story straight and get the best possible deal for everyone involved."

Duke

THIS GUY IS AN asshole if he thinks I'm buying his line of shit. "Look, Mr. Deveno, you work for my father and you're trying to get *him* the best possible deal. Looks like I need a new attorney."

"Duke, calm down, please, and let me talk. You have more options than Vincent does. This is your first offense, and there are extenuating circumstances. Deveno can work it to your advantage—plus—we have unlimited resources. If you get another attorney, you won't have that. Please give Deveno a chance to see what he can do before you dismiss him," Aunt Annabelle tries to convince me. Funny I've never even met this woman before today, and yet she thinks I'm going to do whatever the fuck she wants.

"Our time here is short, kid, so what's it going to be? Are you going to listen to your aunt or do I walk?"

At this point, I really have nothing to lose. "Fine, for now I will listen, but at any point, if I don't like the way things are going, then all bets are off."

"Great, I'll be in touch over the next couple of days. Keep your mouth shut and let me work your case. I'll give you some private time with Annabelle." Deveno gets up and leaves.

I size up Annabelle—she wants something, everyone usually does. "So, Aunt Annabelle, what is it that you want from me?"

"What makes you think I want something? Maybe I want to find out who you are."

"Look, since I found my family, I've had nothing but trouble. I've had a lot to absorb in the past six months. I'm not looking for a warm, fuzzy family that television shows are made of; I'm looking to survive this nightmare. So, I'll ask you one more time, what is it that you want from me?"

"What did Cara tell you when you were in Italy? Did she talk to you about Joseph?"

And there it is . . . she's here to fish for information. I don't know what she thinks I could possibly tell her. "She told me who I was and that I was the product of rape. She told me a little bit about our mother. She gave me Gabriella's diary to read. Do you know what it was like to read about your father raping and beating your mother over and over again? Do you know how it feels to be considered the spawn of Satan? Raven never talked about Joseph or anyone, for that matter. Even if I get to the other side of this, I have no one—nothing."

"You have Vincent and me; you have a family now."

"Well, Aunt Annabelle, isn't that encouraging. Time's up, I've gotta go." I get up and give the corrections officer a nod of my head to let him know that I'm ready. He opens the door for me and I head out without hearing another word from my *loving* aunt.

AFTER THE RIDE HOME in silence, Jax and I are greeted by my mother as soon as we get off the elevator. "Mom, is everything okay?"

"Everything is fine, I was worried about you. What did the doctor say?" she asks after hugging me, her eyes on Jax.

"Everything is good. I told her about the family history and she was happy that I gained weight. Everything is going according to schedule."

"Jax, are you okay?" she asks him.

"I'm fine, Rose, just tired. I'm going to lay down for a bit, excuse me."

Before I can say anything my mom grasps my upper arms gently. "Go be with him, Raven. I think the pressure is getting to him."

I head into the bedroom, but he's not there. I hear the shower running. *That sounds really good right now.* I head into the bathroom and find him leaning against the shower wall, the water cascading down his body. I step in and notice his eyes closed and he's not moving.

" Jax, what's wrong?" I grab onto his shoulders.

"I'm very overwhelmed right now," he says softly, his eyes still closed.

"Damn it, Jax, talk to me! I know it's more than that."

He takes in a deep breath. "I'm beginning to doubt my decision to let Jackie come back here. Vincent is going to want to hurt Max in the worst possible way. Going after Jackie would do it. She is so stubborn; I know she'll never go for Max sending her back to her parent's compound."

"Jax, maybe we should go to the island now. We could all use an extended vacation . . . just until the Feds get everything sorted."

"Raven, have you forgotten something? You're pregnant?"

"Oh."

"Yeah, *oh.*"

"Jax, could I have a doctor on the island to deliver the baby?"

He's stroking his chin, which means he's either plotting or processing.

"I asked Sammy to join the company. I don't want Max in the field ever again."

"What did Max say about that?"

"It was his suggestion to bring Sammy on board. Max wants a more behind the scenes approach. He wants to spend more time with Jackie. Jackie is interested in heading up the school we talked about."

"Are you planning out everyone's life again? I warned you about that."

"I know, Raven. I'm not telling everyone what they should do. I'm practicing my new found negotiating skills with everyone."

I know how that goes. "What about me, what am I supposed to do?"

"I'm going to be real honest with you. I would like for you to be a stay at home mum. It was not something that my mum could do for Bella and me, and I would love to give that gift to our child. You could also use the time to get to know your mum better."

"You don't have to sell me on it, Jax. I want to be there for our child. Those years only come once, there is no second chance."

"Wife, have I told you lately that I'm madly in love with you?"

"No, my wonderful husband, you haven't."

"Well, sweetheart, I am, and I think I need to have my way with you.

In one fell swoop, he scoops me up and steps out of the shower. He pulls the towels off the warmers and wraps us in them as he heads towards the bedroom.

"Oh, my beautiful wife, I want to make slow passionate love to you for hours. Relax and let me take you to our *happy place.*" He places me in the center of the bed and slowly crawls between my legs. "I want to taste you and devour you."

He locks his arms around my legs, keeping me spread wide for him. He's nipping the inside of my thighs followed by a lick and a kiss. *Oh my God what he can do with that tongue; it should be illegal.* When he gets to the top he stops and switches to the other leg. When he finally gets to the center, he unleashes that tongue. Round and round, in and out. Swipe, nibble, lick, and kiss.

"Jax, I can't hold it . . . oh good God, Jax." My hands are fisting his hair and my hips are going crazy. I'm riding a wave of pleasure. Just as I begin to catch my breath, he enters me . . . every rock-hard, solid inch of him. My eyes fly open and lock onto his—violet to blues.

"Sweetheart, all that I am, and all that I'll ever be is because of you."

He pulls back and slowly enters me again. He's there but yet he's fighting it.

"Don't fight it Jax, let it go."

"No—I want more. I want it to last forever."

I do the one thing I know that will tip him over the edge—I clench. He throws his head back and begins to come, over and over again. "Oh, fuck all that is holy, Raven!"

Gently, he turns us so I'm on top. "Ride me down slowly, please."

Pacing myself, I glide up and down, watching a calm take over him. I lean down and kiss him softly.

"You don't play fair, sweetheart."

"Hmm . . . I never said I would."

"Well, my beautiful wife, neither did I."

As she's riding me down I'm pushing my hips up to meet hers, slamming into her clitoris. I lean up and take one of her nipples into my mouth, pulling and nipping. They are so sensitive to my touch. I gently roll her onto her back and I pull out of her. She whimpers at the loss of my cock, fuck it's so hot to watch. "I know what you want but not like this, baby."

I turn her and pull her up on her knees. "Hold onto the headboard." I command while taking my cock and spreading my wetness from front to back. I'm ready to take her again. "Push out, come on, baby, let me in."

I push through that barrier; she's so tight and so warm. I'm holding the base of my cock; prolonging my explosion. I take a few breaths and begin to move, slowly at first.

"God, Raven, you're so tight and warm."

"Faster, Jax, please . . . Oh, God . . . harder please, I won't break!"

I give her what she wants, what she needs. Taking her harder with each push. I reach around and glide my fingers in and out of her. "Raven, fuck I'm going, fall with me, *please.*"

I give her all I've got and she takes it, screaming my name with her release. I'm still throbbing deep inside of her. My legs and arms are quivering; it's never enough with her. I will always need more. I gently pull out of her and she rolls onto her side. Her eyes finally open and they are filled with tears. "Hey, beautiful, you okay?"

"Jax, that was so intense. I don't know what came over me, I was so demanding. Oh my God, I gave you a hickie! I'm so embarrassed." Her hands cover her face.

I look down at my chest, and sure enough, she gave my nipple a hickie. "Well, that's interesting. I love intense and it makes me even wilder when you get all demanding. Sweetheart, never be embarrassed for wanting more. You love me and you show it."

"I do love you, Jax." She smiles up at me.

"I love you more, baby. Let's go shower, and then I think I want to talk to Jackie."

"Have you figured out what you're going to say?"

"She's a very smart woman. I'm going to put all the facts out to her and see if she comes to the right conclusion."

"Don't you mean your conclusion?"

"Yep, the right conclusion."

Vulnerable Jax, is gone, and my take-charge husband is back . . . *poor Jackie.*

Jackie

IT'S BEEN ANOTHER CRAZY day. I'm glad Max is okay. There is a calm when I'm curled up into his side. He's finally asleep; today has taken a toll on him. He's getting better at letting me in, but I know it will take time. I very rarely get to watch him sleep, and I notice, even though he's sleeping, there is a worried look across his brow. As I stroke him there, he visibly relaxes. I tilt my head in and kiss one of his scars. He has so many both inside and out; my heart breaks for him. I trail my fingertips over his V. God he is so beautiful; imperfectly perfect. I lean in and kiss his chest very softly. I don't think I can ever get enough of this man.

"Hmm . . . I love to wake up from a nap like this, baby."

"I'm sorry. I didn't mean to disturb your sleep."

He pulls me on top of him. "Never be sorry for this. This is where I've finally found peace."

I lean down and kiss his soft lips. God, what this man does to me. "I'm worried about you, Max. You need to get more rest, and a lot less stress."

"What I need, is more of you, babe, just you."

"Then, more you shall have." I slowly work my way down his body. Kissing my way down his happy trail very slowly, I begin stroking his cock. I lean down and kiss the tip.

"Oh, baby, take me deep, please."

I take him in my mouth, swirling my tongue around as I go down. This is so new for me, but with Max, it's so comfortable. He lifts his head and watches me, chewing on his bottom lip as he fists his hands. He is *literally* coming undone, and it's all because of me. It's such a beautiful high, a high I've only known with him. He takes a hold of my shoulders and tries stopping me. I'm so lost in my ability to give him such pleasure. I don't want to stop.

"Jackie, if you don't stop now, I'm going to lose what little control I have left."

I'm not letting go. I want to know what it's like to take him all the way. I work my way down again as I'm pumping his cock. I take his sac and work it slowly and firmly. That does it for him. His head flies back and his hips are going wild. He's yelling my name as he explodes with such a powerful force. It's feels endless. I wasn't sure what to expect but then knowing that I can take him like this is such a heady feeling. He pulls me off of him and into his arms.

"Oh, Jackie, I'm never letting you go, baby."

"Max, we will get to the other side of this, I promise."

He strokes my back, carelessly. "Baby, what do you know about Belize?"

"I know about the island. Stop acting like Jax." I lift my head.

"I'm just thinking, after Raven has the baby, it would be good for all of us to go down for a break."

"Max, you have a *tell*. Everyone has one but yours is obvious, my love. Don't play poker."

"I'm really worried, Jackie. Why the fuck didn't that bastard die? There's an even bigger target on your back now. I was thinking maybe you should go to your parents' compound, just until the dust settles."

I can feel my body tighten as soon as he finishes his thought.

"Jackie?"

"I'm counting, Maxwell Fleming."

Maxwell

SHIT COUNTING *AND* FULL name. "How much trouble am I in?"

She climbs off of me and out of bed. She is standing before me, totally naked. That beautiful mane of golden hair and those legs—oh, dear God— those fucking legs are going to be the death of me. She's got one hand on her hip, and she has fire in her eyes. Fuck it all, I can explode right now from the sight of her.

"Let me tell you something, mister, I did not turn my life upside down for nothing. I will not be banished to the compound like I'm a child again. I knew the risk coming back here, and yet, here I stand. You will never ever order me to leave, and you will never decide for me what I should or should not be doing. I am an adult. I know what I want, and whom I want to be with. Do you understand?"

I've never seen this side of her, and fuck it all, she's really hot.

"Well, Max, if you have anything to say, you better say it now."

"Wow."

"That's it, wow?"

"Come here, baby." I lift her into my arms and place her in the middle of the bed. I begin kissing my way up those fucking legs, and I think I'm going to die. They seem endless as I work my lips gently up one side and down the other. There is a spot right behind her knee that I love to kiss, knowing every time I do, she moans. "I'm so fucking turned on right now, I'm going to take you every way I can . . . everywhere I can and when I'm done, I'm going to start all over. I want you screaming my name over and over again."

I reach over to the nightstand and grab a condom. Getting it on as quick as possible, knowing I need to be inside her now. I enter her very slowly and when I'm all the way in, I stop. I lean down and latch onto her nipple. Grating it with my teeth. "Oh God . . . more, Max . . . please."

I latch onto the other one as I slowly rock my hips up and down. Dragging myself across her clitoris with just enough pressure to make her quiver. I pull out and then slam into her again. I've got my arms locked around those fucking legs, and I'm not letting go. I feel it; dear God above, the wave that is coming over my body is going to fucking kill me. I'm looking down at her and she looks like an angel. I feel like I'm looking down upon the whole scene . . . everything, moving in slow motion. Her nails are digging into my arse, and she's screaming.

I rear back and slam into her, over and over again. "Oh holy hell, Jackie!" I explode with such a force and that's when it happened. Her eyes fly open and she knows it too. An explosion so forceful, the condom broke. The two of us are stunned. Neither of us knowing what to say or do.

"Jackie, it will be okay. Chances are, nothing happened. Look, we had so much sex the past few days, maybe they didn't really have time to re-group." I can't believe I just said that to her. She's too quiet. "Baby, talk to me, please."

"Max, I'm only twenty-five and no way am I ready for parenthood. We need to shower and then I need to get to the drugstore for the morning after pill."

I'm holding and kissing her, trying to calm my racing heart. "You go shower first, I'll be just a minute."

As I watch her walk away, I realize the broken pieces of my heart are coming back together. I want the whole deal with her, now I need to make her see the light.

Chapter Nineteen

Raven

WE HEAD NEXT DOOR to Max's place. Max let's us in and I see Jackie sitting in the living room, mindlessly flipping through the television channels. She waves at Jax, but she never looks up from the television. She seems really quiet. I know my friend and something is off. Before I can suggest that we have some girl time, Max takes Jax into his office for Raiders business. Jackie gets up and slips into the kitchen. I follow her, thinking maybe she wants to talk to me in private. She begins to put together a fruit and cheese plate.

"Jackie, how about you tell me what's going on with you."

"Oh, Raven, the condom broke!"

Okay, not what I was expecting to come out of her mouth.

"What did you do?"

"Really, what did I do? What do you think I did? I completely freaked out, that's what I did. I'm not ready for parenthood. Heck, I don't even know if that's on my radar. I made him take me to the store for the morning after pill. Condoms are supposed to have a low breakage rate, between 0.4 and 2.3 percent if used and stored properly."

"How many times have you read the box, Jackie?"

"A million times."

"Well let's stop worrying about how it went wrong, you can't change what happened. You took the morning after pill; maybe you will be fine. I do think that you should follow up with the doctor tomorrow, just to be on the safe side. Do you want me to call Dr. Leanne? I'm sure she will see you on short notice."

"Would you go with me? I don't want to go with Max."

"Of course I will go with you. Why don't you want to go with Max? You've been giving yourself to this man twenty-four seven. He is an equal partner in this and you need to realize that. You are both responsible adults, Jackie."

"This is all very new for me, Raven. I want to go on some sort of birth control. I'm not leaving anything to chance. And . . . you're right; Max should be a part of this."

"Good, it's your body, Jackie. You're in control, no one else. However, he is just as responsible as you are."

"Can you not tell Jax?"

"Jackie, I won't tell Jax but you know those two are joined at the hip, so there's no vouching that Max hasn't already told him."

"Let's get back inside, Jax needs to talk to you."

"That doesn't sound good."

"Keep an open mind."

Maxwell

JAX AND RAVEN CAME over and the timing couldn't have been more perfect. I need to bounce this off of Jax. I'm not that shocked that the condom broke. I'm shocked that I'm happy it did. I need to snap out of this, I know I said it was Raiders business but the reality is the condom breaking is the only thing on my mind. Jax and I head into my office, leaving the girls in the living room. I'm sure Jackie wants to tell Raven what happened. I pull the bottle of Scotch from the desk and pour us each a glass. He begins to take up my pacing and he keeps running his hands through his hair. "What's the problem, Jax?" I stare into my glass, dreading what's coming.

"I need to watch the video."

"Why? Jax, there's no reason to put yourself through that."

"I've put it off long enough. If that video needs to be released, then I need to stay ahead of it."

"Are you sure you want to watch this?"

"It's the last piece of the puzzle, Max, I need to see it."

I open my laptop and set it all up. He pours another scotch and hovers over the play button. "Do you want me to stay, Jax?"

"Yeah, please."

Jaxson

I HIT PLAY AND the screen comes to life. I gasp when I instantly see a seven-year-old Raven. She's so beautiful, even as a scared little girl. She's crying, her little lip is trembling, and my heart is breaking. Max goes to stop it and I grab his hand. "No, I need to see this through."

The evil bastard grabs her by her ponytail and puts a knife to her throat. *"Shut the fuck up or I'll slit your throat."*

Joseph and Antonio storm in the room. *"Vin, let my daughter go, it's me you have a problem with."*

"I've got the brat and Gabriella. The price you're going to pay for walking away from your family. You think you're better than us? Well, guess again. The blood that runs through us is the same that runs through her." He's gliding the knife down her neck. The lump in my throat tightens with each swipe of the knife.

"Let her go, Vin, Gabby will perform the surgery, you don't need Cara."

"You're right, I don't, but maybe I'll keep her all for myself. Think of the fun I could have with her. I could teach her all about our family; make her one of us."

The next few seconds happen so fast. Antonio looks at Raven, nods, and then say's something I can't catch. She kicks Vincent in the shin, bites his hand, and begins to run. He drops the knife, yelling. Vincent pulls a gun out of his back. Joseph jumps in front of Raven, and Antonio dives in between them. Vincent fires, hitting Antonio. Joseph blankets Raven with his body. Antonio takes aim at Vincent, but he's hurt and he's down. His shot only grazes Vincent's shoulder. Within seconds, agents are rushing in, shots are fired and Vincent is gone. The video is still running as Joseph gets up and Raven runs into her father's arms. There's blood everywhere, and Joseph is applying pressure to Antonio's wound. Then I hear her last words to her father:

"Daddy, Daddy, please don't die. I love you, Daddy."

"Cara, my beautiful, baby girl, don't cry. Daddy loves you, beyond this lifetime."

Then silence. She's rocking and crying in total silence.

Max stops the video and I can't hold back my tears any longer, I let them fall. She's so strong and brave. "Max, I never want her to see this ever, understand?"

"I understand, but it may not be up to us. We can try to shield Raven and Rose, as much as possible."

"Max, that bastard made Rose watch this everyday, it's no wonder she retreated into the darkest corners of her mind. I want him *dead*. The first time in my life I've ever felt like this. What does that make me?"

"Jax, after seeing that video, who wouldn't want him dead? It makes you human."

I take a moment to collect myself, staring into the glass of amber liquid in my hands. Finally, I take in a deep breath and look up at Max. "Rose watched the video from Antonio today. She thanked Raven for giving her Antonio, again. Raven still hasn't watched her video. I asked her why, and she said she might never be ready." I put my glass down, my hand still shaking from what

I've just watched. "When all this is over, I am going to see if she wants to go to counseling. I think we could all benefit from it."

"Jax, maybe a counselor will be able to help Raven deal with the video. I think the pressure and the stress is getting to all of us. Hell, I think we could all benefit from counseling after this nightmare." He throws back the rest of his scotch. "Jax, what happened with Sammy today at Raiders?"

"I spoke to him about working for Raiders. I think he's interested. We need someone in the field who can be trusted, and I'm just not sure, when push comes to shove, where his loyalty would fall. I know he is very protective of Jackie, which makes me feel a little bit better."

"Jax, what's your take on Gerhard?"

"He's smart and direct, but plays it close to the vest. The brother, Dylan, is a total arsehole. Apparently, he has a thing for Raven. When we went back to pick up Jackie, he was yelling, telling her she would probably end up knocked up like Raven."

"You didn't snap his fucking neck?!" He throws his hands out.

"Before I could, Raven gave him a total bitch slap in front of his entire family. I was very proud. Gerhard gave Jackie a complete file on you."

Max grabs onto the side of the table. "So she knew about Samantha and Elliot?"

"No, she refused to read it. She said, anything she wants to know she would ask you directly. She's tough, a lot tougher than she looks."

"Yeah, I know, but it's killing me that she's in danger because of me. God only knows how Raven feels."

"I met with Mathew earlier. He said the Feds were demanding we turn over our copy of the tape. How ridiculous is that? He said to keep a copy someplace safe, wouldn't be surprised if Vincent tried to destroy it."

"No worries, I've got multiple copies in many different locations, including one at the Yard. I called in a lot of IOU's."

"How connected is this fucker, Max?"

"He's got some judges in his pocket and he has some political connections. His lawyer, Deveno, handles a lot of his business, and surprisingly, so does Annabelle. You know money rules, Jax. He's got it and he's not afraid to use it."

"Yeah, well he just met his match."

"We need to be smart and operate without emotion, otherwise mistakes will be made."

"Trust me, Max, I understand lives are at stake here. No one fucks with my family or me. I'm going to break him into a million pieces. I'll rip apart his organization one brick at a time, until he's left with nothing."

"And what if he doesn't stop, have you thought of that?"

"He's made my family fair game, well, turnaround is fair play. He shot my brother, kidnapped my wife, kidnapped and raped Rose. By the time I'm done, he'll be begging for mercy."

I pour us each another Scotch. Something is bugging him, he takes care of all of us, it's about time he lets me take care of him. "So, Max, what's going on with you and, Jackie? Something seems off."

"I can't get anything past you. I brought up her going to her dad's for a while and before I could finish she tore into me like nothing I've ever seen before. It was actually quite hot, mate."

"What else?"

"The condom broke."

"Oh fuck, and?"

"We went and got the morning after pill, and I assured her I'm clean."

"What are you not telling me?"

He's quiet for a bit. "I never thought I would ever want another child again, but when that condom broke, I felt walls around me shatter with it. I want everything with her. I'm scared; there's a bigger target on her now than before, and I put it there. If I were a better man, I would have let her go. But God forgive me, I can't live without her."

I watch as Max picks up his glass and he's shaking. I realize I need to take charge here.

"Well, that settles it—we are going to the island. I will have a medical team brought in for the delivery. I need everyone safe. Raven knows this is what I want to do, and we came here tonight to discuss it with Jackie."

"Jax, you know she is going to fight you on this."

"I will negotiate with her. Stop laughing, mate, I've been practicing the art of negotiating. If that doesn't work, then, we go to plan B."

"What's plan B?"

"You don't want to know."

"How soon are the houses going to be done?"

"Well, now that Mrs. Osla told the crew she was going to go down to supervise, it seems they are ahead of schedule."

"I told you she's scary."

"Come on, I need to go negotiate with Jackie." I slap his back and we head out.

IN THE LIVING ROOM, the girls are deep in conversation. The look on Raven's face tells me all I need to know—she knows about the condom.

"Jackie, I need to talk to you about something important, and I need you to keep an open mind."

She jumps up, "Jax, before you start, I'm not going back to my parents."

"I understand from Max, that it's not an option. I have a plan and I would like for you to hear me out. Please, have a seat."

She sits next to Raven, and takes a hold of her hand.

"I know you're aware of the private island, I purchased, off the coast of Belize. I am having renovations done; adding cottages all over the island. I'm making it into a family retreat. I would like for us all to go down there for a while, until the dust settles. I'm having a medical team brought in for the baby."

"Jax, I understand that I'm at a greater risk now, but is running away really the answer? These people will know where we are. Do you really think you can stop them?"

"Baby, it's not running away." Max interjects. "We are trying to protect everyone and give ourselves some breathing room. It's not permanent, just until we can get a handle on the situation. The entire family will be there. Will you please do this for me . . . for my sanity?"

After listening to Max, she brings her focus back to me. "Jax, when would we have to leave?"

"Best case scenario . . . by the end of the week—at the latest."

Jackie grabs Raven's hand, and tilts her head as if she's unsure. "Raven, are you okay with all of this?"

"Yes, I think we all need a break. Security will be very tight."

"Jax, I have to let my father know what is going on before we leave."

"Of course. Max and I are working closely with Sammy on everything that is going on."

"Okay. Then, I will go."

I see a wave of relief wash over Max, and I'm happy my negotiating skills worked.

"Great, now that we've got that all settled, I'm taking my wife home."

I scoop her up and head towards the flat. "Before you tell me you can walk, I know, but humor me, wife. I need this."

Maxwell

STUDYING JACKIE, I CAN see how overwhelmed she is; rubbing her upper arms nonchalantly and staring blankly as if she's in a daze. "Talk to me, baby, tell me what's going on in that beautiful head of yours."

"I spoke to Raven about what happened with the condom. She's making a doctor's appointment for me in the morning. I would like you to come along."

"Were you afraid I wouldn't go?"

"I was unsure about asking you. It's my body and my responsibility, however, after talking with Raven, she made me realize that you're just as responsible as I am."

She's looking down and tearing up the napkin in her lap. "Look at me, Jackie. I would move heaven and earth for you. I am just as much responsible for taking care of this beautiful body as you are. We are in this together. Please, never feel that you have to hide anything from me." I open my arms, "Come here, baby."

She crawls into my lap, wrapping her legs around my waist. "I know that the next few days are going to be crazy, and very intense. I need you to understand that I'm not letting you out of my sight. I will get the doctor to come here. I know it's extreme, but I really need this from you right now. Please stay indoors, until we are on that plane. Jax has probably made all the arrangements, including the personal shopper to supply everyone with enough clothes for months."

"Maxwell, why was Jax so rattled when he came out of the office?"

I promised her complete honesty, I'm just not sure how much she can handle. "He watched the video of Raven's dad being murdered. You saw how rattled he was, do you understand why I need you to stay put?"

She's searching my eyes, not saying anything. She leans in and softly kisses my lips. "Okay."

I feel relief wash over me. "Thank you. Now, I need to make love to you all night long."

She leans forward and nibbles on my lip, "Max, I need it just as much as you do, probably more right now."

Raven

JAX IS STILL ASLEEP. I decide to make a cup of tea and watch the sunrise over Central Park. It has such a calming effect. The baby is so active now;

it feels like I'm growing bigger by the minute. I think Jax is right, escaping down to the island might be just what we need right now. I'm more worried about Jackie and my mom. If Vincent finds out my mom is alive, he'll come after her. I have no doubt about his sick obsession with her. Max has aged through all of this, and now his fear for Jackie's safety has brought all his pain to the surface again. I'm trying not to blame myself for any of this, but sometimes it's hard not too.

Staring out at the sunrise, I realize I'm ready to watch the video, I've put it off long enough. Mom is right; my daddy will always be on that pedestal and *nothing* will ever change that. I get Jax's laptop and plug in the flash drive. I close my eyes, take a deep breath, and hit play. The screen fills with my daddy in his hospital bed.

"Cara, my beautiful angel. The day you were born, my life changed forever. I finally understood unconditional love. I'm so sorry you were touched by all of this evil. Nothing that happened was your fault. You defended yourself exactly as I taught you to. Vincent just got the better of us; never blame yourself. You're strong, my beautiful girl. I might not be there to watch you grow into the beautiful woman I know you will be, but my heart will always be joined with yours. You take hold of your mom and don't let go. Joseph will always be there to catch you, if you fall. Live your life to the fullest and love with all your heart. You're Daddy's ray of sunshine, Cara, the best thing I have ever done in my life was help to create you.

Daddy loves you, Cara, always."

The screen goes black, and I'm frozen. All of the memories that I have kept buried so deep from that awful day come racing to the surface. *I can feel him pulling my hair. I can feel the cold steel knife scraping up and down my neck every time Vincent laughs. He's yelling at Daddy, and Joseph. I'm trying to be a big girl, but I'm scared and I cry. He yells at me to shut up, and presses the knife harder against my throat. He's dragging me by my ponytail, waving that knife around. Everyone is yelling: Vincent, Joseph, and Daddy. Then Daddy gives me the sign, that it's time to protect myself just like he taught me. I run it through my head, the mantra he would tell me whenever I was afraid. "Kick, bite, run, Cara, always remember that." Kick, bite, and run. Kick, bite, and run. I can do this. I kick him in the shin, bite his hand with the knife, and try to run towards Daddy. I did it just like Daddy taught me, but then Joseph leaps and all I hear are gunshots. All I smell is gunpowder and the metallic smell of blood. I'm rocking in my daddy's arms, crying,* "Please don't die, Daddy, please don't die."

$\mathcal{J}axson$

I OPEN MY EYES to find the other half of the bed empty. I know she can't sleep through the night without going to the bathroom—the joys of pregnancy I guess. As I head towards the kitchen to make coffee, I hear her crying. I race into the office, and find her, in a ball on the floor. Obviously, she became sick because she's covered in vomit. She's rocking back and forth, crying, "Please don't die Daddy, please don't die."

She finally watched the video that Antonio left her. It must have triggered the memories she's been fighting to keep suppressed. I scoop her into my arms, and carry her into our bedroom. She's shivering and I need to warm her up. I wrap us up in the comforter, holding and soothing her. "Raven, you're safe, sweetheart. I'm here with you forever, baby. No one can get to us." Finally the shaking stops. I pull her head up to mine. "Open your eyes, baby." She opens her eyes; there's my girl. "Hey, sweetheart, there you are. You're safe, I've got you, always."

"Jax, I watched the video my daddy left me. He loved me, and he didn't blame me for anything that happened."

"Of course he loved you, sweetheart, why would you think he would blame you for what happened?"

"He taught me to protect myself. He would say, 'kick, bite, and run' all the time. When he nodded to me I did it, only it didn't work; Daddy was shot. I thought I didn't do it right."

I have to tell her I saw the tape, and I know she was not to blame. "I watched the tape, Raven. You were a very brave little girl. You did everything right. You can't predict what will happen when you're dealing with a madman."

"You watched it? When?"

"Last night, when you were talking with Jackie. Max showed it to me. I needed to see it, to understand the depth of Vincent's depravity. It's another reason we are leaving for the island, sooner rather than later. Now that you've heard what your father said, maybe you can put your self-doubt behind you. We need to focus on the future with our growing family."

"I'm a mess, I need to get cleaned up."

"Let me help you, we'll have a nice hot shower and then some of that wonderful porridge that you seem to like."

"Okay, a shower would be wonderful and I do have some questions."

Great, anything to get her mind off of all of this. I carry her into the bathroom and put her on the counter, while I turn the shower on. I turn on the IPod and choose her favorite David Garrett song, "Bring Me Back to Life." The same one I played when we made our apple pie. It will relax and help sooth her. I lift her up and carry her into the shower, letting the hot water wash away all the angst. I slowly begin cleaning her up. She closes her eyes and let's me take care of her.

"What do you want to know, Raven?"

"I want to go over the arrangements you have made for us."

"Okay, but don't flip out on me. I need to be my usual self right now. I need you to understand it's for everyone's safety, and my own sanity. Everything for the baby is set up. Dr. Leanne has agreed to come down two weeks before your due date. I hired a nurse to stay with us for the next four months. I had a small hospital built and staffed. The staff has been triple checked. I arranged for my personal shopper to come and fit you, Jackie, and your mom for all the clothes you will ever need. Mick will be coming, as well as Sammy. I let Jackie's parents know everything that is going on, and when we will be leaving. Is there anything I missed?"

Oh dear God, she's crying. What the fuck did I do now? "Sweetheart, please, what's wrong?"

"I'm overwhelmed, Jax."

"Don't be, that's what I'm here for. Let me handle all the details, and you just be you. The kindest, most loving person I've ever known."

"I feel like I've disrupted everyone's life and put them in danger. Michael was looking so forward to going to Disney World this summer."

"Stop, just stop with the pity party. Junior will get his trip to Disney World, and I plan on surprising him with a very special trip in the fall to Cardiff Bay."

"What's in Cardiff Bay?"

Raven

HIS WHOLE FACE LIGHTS up like a kid on Christmas morning. "The Doctor Who Experience. Of course, we will take the baby with us."

Oh my God, he's serious. "Jax, the baby might be too young for that. Maybe it would be a good bonding trip for you and Michael."

"Turn around, Raven, let me wash your hair."

As he's massaging my scalp all I can think about is how much I'm going to miss this shower. He rinses out the shampoo and now he's working in the conditioner. I could get used to this really quickly. He's rubbing my shoulders and leaving a trail of kisses down my spine.

"Jax, I'm really going to miss this shower."

"No worries, sweetheart. I had the shower duplicated on the island. I would never deny my beautiful wife anything."

Oh how I love my beautiful, crazy husband.

Chapter Twenty

Sammy

MAX'S GUEST ROOM IS nice, but I need a private place to work. I decide to go back to Jackie's flat where I will have some privacy. I step into the hall and, as expected, Mick is sitting by the elevator, having his coffee. He's always there, and always on time. "Hey, Mick, let Max and Jax know that I went to Jackie's place to get some more of my stuff, and that I'll be back. My understanding is no one is leaving this flat until we head to the island. If something changes, please call me."

"Sure, Sammy, I'll let them know."

I get to Jackie's, and the first thing I do is update Gerhard. "Sir, Jax, has everyone on lockdown. No one is leaving the flat until the end of the week. Then they will be heading down to the island. Jackie has agreed to go with them. I'm going to arrange the transport for everyone."

"Jax contacted me and advised me of his plans. Have the Fed's decided what they are going to do with Vincent and Duke?"

"My contact said they are going to deal. They feel Vincent can give up some top level people."

"What kind of deal are we talking here, Sammy?"

"They are going to go with diminished capacity for Duke, and give him a reduced sentence. As far as Vincent, they aren't saying. I think it would depend on who he gives up."

"Sam, that animal can't get a deal, do you understand me?"

Oh, I get *exactly* what he's telling me. "Understood, sir."

"Did you get a list of all his dealings outside the United States?"

"Yes, sir. The list of his drug dealings, outside the United States, is quite extensive, along with his political connections. The Feds have got to know, if given the chance, he would flee. However, I think they're looking at the big picture, how much of a dent they can put into the drug trade. There like roaches, they keep coming back, no matter how much the government cuts into their business."

"Sammy, do you have any idea how quickly all of this is going to go down?"

"Not an exact timeframe, however, what I'm hearing is the Feds want this wrapped up pretty quickly. They're afraid the more time that passes the more problems they will encounter. They know that Jax has a copy of the tape, and there is probably nothing they can do to get it back."

"If that tape gets out—they will know Jax released it—then what?"

"They'd have to prove it, and Max had about a dozen different copies made. He stored them at various locations all over the world, including one at Scotland Yard. Apparently, he has a lot of friends in all the right places."

"Let me know when my daughter is safely on that island, and give me a heads up on Vincent."

I get what he's not saying, the further away from this Jackie is, the more plausible deniability he has.

I hang up with Gerhard, and check in with Annabelle's guard. Seems she has finally gotten in to see Vincent and Duke. Everything is going to move pretty quickly, now that the Feds have decided to deal. I need to convince everyone that they need to get to the island tomorrow, the latest. I have a few more arrangements to make before my team is in place. I get an alert that someone is looking into the Gerhard family, mainly pulling information on Jackie. They are following the breadcrumb trail I set, which is perfect. This will buy us a little bit more time, but we have to move quickly. There is only so long I can string whomever is looking along before they figure out it's a dead end.

Time to call Max, and get the ball rolling. Fucking phone goes right to voice mail. "Max, I'm on my way back to the flat. Get Jax, I need to meet with everyone now. Be there in ten.

Jackie

ANOTHER MORNING I'M UP before Max, which now has me worried. He's always up before dawn. He has an iron grip on my leg and his other hand is fisted and shaking. He is in a pool of sweat. Maybe it's a nightmare. If it is, I don't want to startle him. I stroke his cheek and whisper, "Max, it's okay. Everyone is fine. Please wake up, Max."

His eyes fly open and he leaps up, nearly knocking me on my ass.

"Oh my God, baby, are you okay? I'm so sorry. Did I hurt you?"

"Calm down, Max. I'm fine, but clearly, you're not. What is going on? And don't tell me nothing."

"Jackie, it's just the headaches, that's all."

I watch him as he checks his messages and I see he's still shaking. He might think I'm buying his excuse, but I'm not. Clearly, I'm not going to get anywhere with him on this.

"Sammy called, we need to get next door. The doctor called, she will be here at noon. Please stop worrying, Jackie, I'm fine."

We get ready and head next door, but this is far from over.

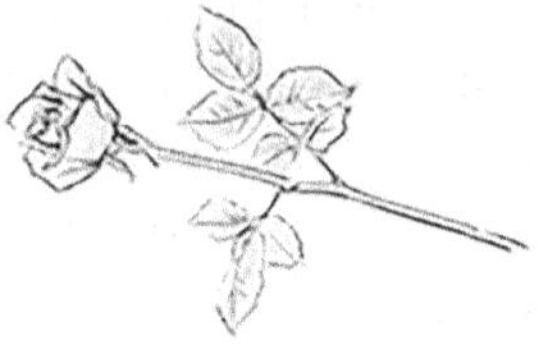

WE ALL GATHER IN Jax's flat. Rose has set up coffee for everyone. I know that we are all on edge right now, but not even Jax and Raven notice that something has been off with Max. Why am I the only one who sees it? I know we are all stressed and tired, but something is not right . . . I'm worried. Sammy comes rushing in and he seems very intense. Knowing him, as I do, this can't be good.

"Hey, everyone, there have been a few developments overnight that I need to make everyone aware of. First of all, the Feds are going to offer Duke a deal. They're offering him diminished capacity with life in prison. They are also going to offer Vincent a deal. However, they are not saying anything more until they find out what he is going to give them. Someone started looking into Jackie, but the only thing they got, right now, was the false trail I set up. I think we need to move to the Island today. I have transport and security already set up."

Jackie

I NEED TO MAKE a stand here. If this is what I need to do so Max will see something is wrong, then so be it. I stand up and all eyes turn towards me. "I'm not going anywhere, and before everyone starts yelling, please hear me out." You could hear a pin drop. Well, at least I know everyone is listening. "So much has happened, in such a short amount of time. I'm a strong person and I can endure quite a lot. What I cannot—no—what I will not do is sit around while the man I love is in physical pain, and hiding it from everyone. Until Max gets his head examined—literally—I'm, not going anywhere." No one is saying a word, however, all heads turn towards Max.

"Jackie, I assure you, I'm fine. It's the headaches, but they are getting better."

I roll up my pant leg, "Max, is this better? You gripped my leg so hard in your sleep that I'm bruised. You sleep past dawn; you never do that. You wake up in a cold sweat. You fist your hands in your sleep, and grind your teeth. None of this is normal. You get a complete checkup or I don't leave."

Before anyone can say another word, Jax leaps up and heads towards his gym. "I need a time out, please."

Raven gets up to go after him, but Max stops her. "Raven, please, it's me he's mad at, right now. Let me handle him."

Maxwell

I HEAD INTO THE gym. I see him beating on a bag, and I know it's my face he's seeing.

"Talk to me, Jax."

"Talk to you? You're the one who should be talking to me. Aren't you the one who's keeping secrets? What were you going to do, drop dead and leave me to clean up the bloody mess?"

"It's not that bad, Jax."

"Not that bad, did you see her leg? Did you see the fear in her eyes? Do you know what courage it must have taken for her to stand up in front of everyone, and put you before her own safety? Get your head out of your fucking arse, Max, or do I need to do it for you?! How fucking bad is it?"

"I thought it was the added stress."

"Well, apparently, it's not. I'm calling the doctor and getting him here now. You will do exactly what he tells you to do. Do you have any problems with that?"

"Okay. I will, but calm the fuck down."

"If you tell me to calm down one more time, so help me, you know exactly what I'll do!"

That shut him up real quick.

Raven

MY NEED TO BOLT has never been as strong as it is right now. My husband is on the verge of losing it. I can hear him screaming at Max. I would not want to be on the receiving end of his wrath right now. My best friend's life is in danger. The man she loves has been shot twice because of me. I brought my mom back into all of this, and now I'm questioning that, too. I have a baby to protect, and I'm in a world of danger. My heart is racing and my head is pounding.

"Raven, are you feeling okay?"

"I have a headache, Mom."

"When was the last time you ate anything?"

"Mom, you're starting to sound like Jax." I feel bad I just snapped at her.

"Well, maybe you should listen to him more. I'm making you some chamomile tea."

I pull Jackie into my arms, "He will be okay, and I'm not going anywhere without you."

Suddenly, Jax and Max are back. Jax pulls Jackie out of my arms.

"Thank you, Jackie, you're a very brave lady. The doctor will be here within the hour to examine, Max. No one gets left behind!" he says and he encircles me in his arms and squeezes me tight. "Raven and I are going upstairs for some fresh air. Sammy, can you brief Max and Mick on the transport, please."

We head up to the rooftop deck. The warm morning sun feels wonderful. Jax pulls me onto the lounge chair, and nestles me between his legs. "Talk to me, Jax, please."

"I need the peace of mind, right now, that only you can give me." He kisses the top of my head and takes in a deep breath. "Dr. Leanne, will be here soon to examine Jackie. I would like her to take a look at you again before we leave."

"Max told you about the condom but not about his head?"

"Yeah, go figure. I honestly don't know what the hell he was thinking."

"Jax, what's really bothering you? Don't look at me like that, I know there's more."

He's twirling a lock of my hair around his finger, not saying a word.

"What kind of person does it make me that I didn't even notice my best friend is in pain?"

"You can't blame yourself; you're juggling so many different things."

"I can't afford to let anything fall between the cracks, there are too many lives at stake."

"We'll get there, Jax, to the other side of all this madness. I promise you, we will."

"I wish I had as much faith as you do. Come, the doctor is probably here."

We get downstairs and I find my mom and Dr. Leanne, deep in conversation. My mom seems to be at ease with everyone she meets. I'm surprised how comfortable she is with other people since she was alone for twenty years. I think therapy is helping. Dr. Leanne pulls me away for a quick chat.

"Raven, I would like to give you another exam before you leave. I will be making periodic trips to the island to keep a check on you."

"I'm feeling good, except for a nagging headache."

"Your blood pressure was up the other day. I know you're under a lot of stress right now. When you get to the island, I would like the nurse to monitor your blood pressure daily. She can report back to me. Are you okay with that?"

"That's fine. Where is Jackie?"

"She went next door with Mr. Fleming; the doctor is here to see him."

"Dr. Leanne, I don't mean to be rude, but if we're done, I really need to get next door."

"Go, Raven, it's fine."

Jax is talking to Mick and Sammy, but his eyes are never far from me. I head next door to talk to Max's doctor. I don't have to turn around; I know Jax is right behind me.

Jaxson

"WHAT'S GOING ON, SWEETHEART?"

"Jax, I want to talk to Max's doctor myself. I'm not about to let Max sugar coat anything."

Right about now, I should probably feel sorry for Max. Raven has fire in her eyes, and for once, I'm not on the receiving end. Maybe he'll learn a bloody lesson.

"Hello, Dr. Steven, I'm Raven Phillips, we've met before. I want to know what is going on with, Max?"

"Well, that would be up to Max to share, not me."

"Well, Dr. Steven, if Max could be trusted not to hide when he's not feeling well, we wouldn't be having this conversation!"

"Raven, Dr. Steven, thinks it's scar tissue. However, he is going to run a few tests today just as a precaution. I promise you that's all there is to report."

"How soon will the results be in from the tests?"

"I will have them to Mr. Fleming later today."

"Okay, fine. We'll wait. Jackie and I will be upstairs. I'm sure you and Jax have plenty to go over."

I practically drag Jackie upstairs. I know something's not right with her; I can sense it. "What's wrong? I know when something is up with you, so spill—right now." She looks at me and begins to cry a full-blown, ugly-ass cry. "Oh my God, Jackie, what is it? Nothing is so bad that we can't fix it."

"Dr. Leanne said there is no guarantee that the morning after pill will work. She said many women still end up pregnant."

Okay, that's not what I was expecting to hear. "What did Max say?"

"That's just it, Raven, he said nothing—not one word! I can't start birth control until I know for sure. It's too soon to tell, yet. So, now, we wait. I'm not ready to be a mom. I might never be ready. What will my parents say . . . my brother, after he practically accused me of getting knocked up."

I pull her into my arms and let her have a good cry, rocking her and stroking her back. Jax comes upstairs. I lift my gaze to him and shake my head. Thank God, he gets it and backs away, giving us the space we need right now.

"Jackie, first, stop worrying about what everyone else will think, and worry about yourself. Secondly, maybe you need to talk to Max, find out what he's thinking. When is the earliest you can take a pregnancy test?"

"I can take the test the end of next week. I didn't get a chance to talk to Max because Doctor Steven was waiting for us."

"When Max gets back from taking the tests, I think the two of you need to sit down privately, discuss your feelings, and all of your options. Don't jump to conclusions."

"Okay. I think I'm going to lie down for a bit, my head is spinning from all of this."

As we head downstairs, I pray this works out for both of them.

I LEAVE JACKIE TO her nap and go next door to find Jax. I really want to be alone with my husband, but when I enter our flat I see it's filled with people. Everyone, that is, except for my husband. I find my mom. "Mom, where is Jax?"

"He went with Max to get some tests run. I made you lunch, come sit down, please."

"Well, whatever it is, it smells wonderful."

"I made salmon broiled with a mustard glaze and a salad. I know Jackie doesn't eat meat, and I wanted to make sure I had something to her liking."

I'm shocked how she can whip this stuff up. I'm lucky if I can make a sandwich. I'm starving, and before I realize it, I've cleaned my plate. Too bad Jax isn't here to see it. I decide to take a picture and text it to him:

> **'I cleaned my plate and thought this would make you smile. I miss you.'**
>
> **XO ~ Always**

My phone immediately beeps:

'Sweetheart, You were right! I miss you, too. How is Jackie?'

XO ~ More.

'She's trying to keep it together. How's Max?'

XO ~ More? I don't think so!

'He's not saying much. He told me what Dr. Leanne said, that's all. Is anyone there, yet?'

XO ~ Oh I know so.

'Yes, everyone is here and your mom is worried. You better warn Max. How much longer do you think you will be?'

XO ~ I need you.

'We're done here, I'm on my way, sweetheart.'

XO ~ Happy Place here I come! :)

Jaxson

DRIVING BACK, MAX SEEMS lost in his own head. I've never seen him this bad, not even when he sent Jackie away. "Max, if I'm going to be able to help you, then you need to talk to me." I say, then set my eyes on the rearview mirror to talk to Mick. "Mick, keep driving around the park until I tell you, thanks." I raise the privacy glass. "Well, talk to me, damn it! I know it's more than just the condom breaking. If she's pregnant, would it really be such a bad thing?"

"It is if she decides she wants to terminate it."

I freeze, "Do you think she would? It doesn't seem like something she would do."

His hands are fisted and his jaw is ticking. "Ultimately, it's her body and her decision, but it would be the final nail in my coffin."

"Well, then we just have to make her see the light."

"I can't bully her, Jax."

"Did you talk to her about how you feel? I know it's her body, but she needs to understand what you're feeling, too. This is a two-way street, you both took a dip in that pool and you're both responsible."

"I never got a chance, we had to leave to take these bloody tests."

"Raven texted. She said everyone is already at the flat. When we get upstairs, you head into your flat. I'll get Jackie in there and divert everyone's attention away from you. It will be okay, Max, I'm sure it was a shock for her."

I let Mick know to head back as we sit there in silence, both of us trying to deal with everything being thrown at us.

WE ARRIVE BACK AT The Tower and the elevator ride up seems to take forever. The doors finally open, and any chance of getting Max out of there quickly is gone. My mum is all over him.

"Maxwell, when were you going to tell me about the headaches?"

"Please don't worry, Dr. Steven ran tests and said its scar tissue."

"You still should have told me. Will you ever learn, Maxwell?"

"Where is she?" Max says under his breath when he pulls me to the side.

"Rose said Raven took her into your flat. Go, I got this."

"Mum, Max needs to rest and I need to go over some stuff with you and Bella; come."

Maxwell

JAX STEERS HER AWAY as I make a quick exit. I race inside and find her asleep on the sofa. Raven is sitting in the chair next to her, making sure she is there for her when she wakes.

"Max, she just fell asleep. Give her some time to come to terms with everything, besides we really don't know anything yet. What did Dr. Steven's tests show?"

"It's scar tissue, and this is as bad as it should get. Hopefully, with reduced stress the headaches will diminish."

"Good, I'm glad that's all it is. I'll leave you alone, but if you need anything, come get me." She gets up and gives me a warm smile before heading out.

I sit on the chair across from my sleeping angel. I know I'm only going to get one shot at this. I have to be honest with her. I need her to realize that my heart is in her hands. From this point forward, all that I will ever be is up to her. She can make or break me. I need to do all of this without scaring or bullying her. Her eyes are starting to flutter open; its time for my A game.

"Max, what happened with the tests?"

"Scar tissue, nothing more."

"What time are we leaving for the island?"

"We are not going anywhere until you and I get some things settled."

"Max, I'm on overload right now. I really don't want to deal with any of this."

I have to calm myself down or I will flip out. "You don't want to *deal* with this!" Maybe yelling is not my A game.

"Yelling at me, Max, is not going to help the situation."

"I'm trying to be calm, I really am, but I'm finding it a little difficult to be calm right now when my whole world is hanging in the balance."

"Your world? How the hell do you think I feel? I'm not ready for any of this. I thought I was being responsible. When that damn thing broke, I raced to get the morning after pill, now I find out I can still be pregnant."

"Jackie, stop. We used a condom and emergency contraceptive, no one is to blame."

Her lip is quivering and her tears are falling. "B-but I'm not ready for this, Max, I'm only twenty-five."

"What are you telling me, that you would terminate it?"

She stops, searching my eyes. "Max, is that what you want me to do?"

This is it, it's my do or die moment. I drop to my knees in front of her and lift her chin. "I would rather die first, Jackie. I never thought I wanted another child again, not after Elliot died. You cleared the muddy waters and showed me that I can love again. I want you, God how I want you with me for the rest of my life. I want to hold your hand and walk on the beach. I want to watch the sun rise and set with you in my arms. I want to watch you have our children—lots of them. I've watched you with Junior, and with all of your students, you're a natural born mum. I would be honored to have you be the mother of my children. More than that, I would be honored to have you as my wife. Before you say anything, please hear me out. I'm not asking you to marry me because of the possibility that you might be pregnant, believe me that would be a bonus. I'm asking you . . . no I'm pleading with you, because I love you. You've made me whole. You've taught me to finally live my life and not wait around to die. You've mended my broken soul. You complete me like no one else can. When the condom broke, I felt the walls around my heart fall like broken glass. Will you please do me the honor and marry me?"

She sits in silence and I'm holding my breath.

"Maxwell, I love you, I really do, but I feel like everything is spinning out of control."

"Baby, our love is the one constant thing through all of this. I won't rush you, but I'm not going anywhere without you. I can't."

"Can we have a long engagement?"

"My beautiful angel, if that's what I have to do to get you to say yes, then, hell yeah."

"And if I'm not pregnant?"

"Nothing changes for me, baby, absolutely nothing. We are all books, waiting to be opened, the pages filled with all of life's unknowns just begging to be shared. Please share the rest of your life with me."

"Yes."

I lean in and kiss her swollen lips. "Oh, my beautiful angel, you've saved me. God how I love you." I lift her up, and she wraps her beautiful legs around my waist while kissing me gently. She leans her forehead against mine, "I need you to hold me, Max, please."

"Forever, baby, always and forever."

Jaxson

RAVEN COMES OUT OF Max's flat, visibly shaken.

"Raven, how's, Jackie, doing?" I wrap her in a hug.

"About the same as Max is."

"They will be okay, sweetheart, I promise you they will be."

"How could you know that?"

"I know that because my wife's faith is rubbing off on me."

"Oh."

"Yeah, *oh.*"

"Jax, is Mick going to come with us to the island?"

"Yes. I gave him the option to stay here, but he was adamant about going."

"I feel bad that everyone's life is being turned upside down. Mick was just getting to know Ashlyn. Maybe I should talk to him about staying here. He needs routine and structure in his life, not all this drama."

"Would it make you feel better if you talk to him? I already did and he was adamant about protecting you and Jackie. If you want, you can ask Ashlyn to come, too."

"Jax, she has a business to run and then there's her volunteer work. I'm sure she would come for a vacation, but not an extended stay."

"Why don't we just take one day at a time? Let's get down there and settled in first."

"I think I'm still going to talk to him. Have you heard anything more from the Feds?"

"No. Only what Sammy told us this morning. Once we get to the island, I'm prepared to release the video, if necessary. We will be leaving later for the airport."

"Well you go check on Max and Jackie while I go talk to Mick."

I tighten my grip. "Jax, what's the problem?"

"No problem, but I need you to come with me for a few minutes, please."

"Go where?" She raises a brow at me.

"Um, office. Yep, that'll work." As we head towards his office, Bella try's to stop us. I make a quick U-turn and practically run into the bedroom.

"Jax, what the hell are you doing?"

I scoop her up and walk faster, trying not to judder her too much.

Raven

HE'S RACING TOWARDS OUR bedroom and in an instant he has me in our walk in closet. "Jax, why are we in our closet?"

"Look, sweetheart, when you get all demanding with me, it's so fucking hot, I can't think about anything but the *happy place*. It's been a crazy arse day and I need you, dear God, I need you now!"

I've never seen such urgency in this man before. It must be the stress, it has to be. He pushes the clothes on the pole aside.

"Hang onto the clothes bar for support, Raven."

I reach up and hold onto the bar. He quickly rids me of my pants as he drops to his knees. That beautiful strong powerful tongue hits me like a lightning bolt. He pushes my legs wider as his tongue is working front to back. His fingers are working their way inside of me very slowly but his tongue is moving with such urgency. Fast and slow at the same time. I can't take much more and he knows it, but he's not letting up. "Jax . . . oh, Jax . . . please."

"Please what, sweetheart? Tell me and I'll give you what you want."

"You know what I want, Jax."

He's slowing down! "*No!* Please don't slow down."

"Then, tell me what you want."

"I don't know how much longer I can hold on, Jax, please."

He grips my ass with both his hands and begins to lightly nibble on my clitoris. His fingers are moving in and out matching the tempo of his tongue

"Jax, baise-moi maintenant et me baiser dur."

I know what talking dirty French does to him and I swear he growls, his grip tightening. "Sweetheart, are you saying what I think you're saying?"

"Jax, fuck me now and fuck me hard!"

"Yes! Sweet Jesus, woman!"

He's off of his knees. "For the love of God, Raven, don't let go of the bar. Oh *happy place,* here we come."

He lifts me up so my legs wrap around his waist, which is not easy with my belly getting in the way. He takes his cock and strokes my clitoris with it, right before he enters me. I want him hard but he's determined to go slow. All the frustration and the fear from the past few weeks come flooding to the surface. He picks up the pace and finally gives me what I want. "Oh fuck, Raven, I'm going. You there, baby?"

He doesn't need to wait for me to answer; I'm screaming his name over and over again. Fast, furious, and so fucking hot. He's holding me up, and we're both shaking.

He finally finds his voice, "Oh, baby, you can let go of the pole now."

"Jax, I can't, my hands are cramped and stuck to it."

He pry's my fingers loose and we sit on the floor. I'm curled in his lap, both of us trying to catch our breath.

"My beautiful wife, I think you're trying to kill me."

"Jax, do you want to tell me what that was about?"

His eyes are closed, and he's got the Jaxson smile going full blast.

"I needed you, sweetheart. We were away from each other for way too long. When you get all teacher mode on me, it makes me crazy."

I'm snuggled into his chest and he's stroking my back. "Hmm . . . Jax, I could stay like this all night, but the baby is kicking like crazy. I need a shower and I'm hungry, yet again."

"Let's shower and then I'll get you something to eat. What would you like?"

"A toasted bagel with cream cheese, a cup of tea, and those wonderful cookies that your mom sneaks into Max's flat when she thinks no one is watching."

I sit up, "Wait, my mum is sneaking cookies to Max? What cookies is he getting that I'm not?"

"Some type of shortbread cookie with jelly in the middle."

"Oh my God! Max is getting Jammie Dodgers and I'm not! This is war, Raven, trust me."

"Sometimes, Jax, you're such a little boy. Let's go before anyone misses us."

Chapter Twenty-One

Annabelle

I GOT PERMISSION TO see Vincent, again, and he's not going to be happy with the news I have. My brother sits in front of me, on the other side of the glass. Every time I come here he looks worse. We both pick up our phones.

"Anna, what have you found out for me?"

"Apparently, Maxwell has gotten back together with Jacquelyn Gerhard."

"I thought he threw her out like yesterday's trash. When did this happen?"

"From what I can gather, Jax and Cara brought her back from Switzerland."

"What were Jax and Cara doing in Switzerland? I'm sure they didn't fly over there just to bring the little bitch home for Max."

"I'm trying to find out more, but right now, Jax has a wall up around everyone and everything. I did find out that he purchased a private island off the coast of Belize. There is some major construction going on there. Word is, that he is taking everyone there for a while."

"Anna, if he's planning on going to that island, then that means he's going to release the tape. Any luck on getting it back?"

"Apparently, Max has many friends in high places. That tape has been duplicated, and word is, Scotland Yard also has a copy."

"Anna, I thought Cara was dead. I only found out when Duke got in touch with me that she was alive, and that I had a son. Makes me wonder what else has been hidden from me."

"I don't know. All I do know is we need to figure a way out of this mess. I spoke with Duke and he is at least willing to listen. He will be keeping Deveno as his attorney, for now. I will tell you, Vince, Duke is a broken man with nothing left to lose."

"I know, and that's the most dangerous type of man. I'm meeting tomorrow with Deveno and the Feds to see what they are going to offer me. In the meantime, you need to stop Jax from getting everyone to that island. If they make it to there, then he'll release the tape. If that happens, then were all *fucked!*"

Duke

MY PARENTS HAVE TRIED to get in touch with me, but I declined to have any contact with them. I've fucked up their lives enough; they don't need to be part of this giant cluster-fuck. The Feds are on their way to talk to me, along with that weasel, Deveno. My father is willing to throw me to the wolves. At this point, who the fuck cares? I have my ace. I wonder about Raven and how she is doing. I hope her and the baby are okay; she deserves some sort of happiness.

I make my way toward the holding room, hoping my plan will put an end to all of this, permanently. I enter the room, and the guard locks the chains that are around my ankles and wrists to a ring on the floor. They act like I'm some sort of deranged serial killer. Maybe in their minds, I am. In walks the weasel and the Fed; let the games begin.

"Hello, Mr. Jensen, I'm Leo Hage, Federal Prosecutor for the United States government. I'm here to discuss your options. I understand you have retained Mr. Deveno as counsel?"

"Call me Duke and yes, Deveno is representing me at this time."

"Duke, as I informed Mr. Deveno, at this point, we are prepared to offer you diminished capacity with a prison term of twenty-five to life. Originally, it was life without parole, however, upon speaking with Mrs. Philips, I believe that you were under an extreme amount of pressure. Part of the agreement is you must sever all ties with the Giaconna family. You must also, undergo counseling. Do you agree to these terms?"

I'll play along with him, letting him think he's got a win. "So, Raven went to bat for me. When did she get married?"

"I'm not here to discuss Mrs. Phillips."

"Where will I be held?"

Deveno grabs my arm; the thought of him touching me makes my skin crawl. "Duke, does it matter to you where they hold you?"

"Well, seeing how my father is probably going to sing like a fucking canary, I don't think my life will be worth much. So, yeah, it matters, Deveno, it matters a lot."

Hage, shakes his head and mutters something under his breath. Clearly he despises Deveno, about as much as I do. "I've already made one concession on your sentence. Do you have something to offer me that would make me want to put you someplace easier?"

"Yeah, Mr. Hage, I do." Deveno's face turns red and he's about ready to stroke. Hage smiles, and I venture to say, he will be smiling even more.

Deveno jumps up, "Until I have time to talk to my client alone, this meeting is over."

"Mr. Hage, can you guarantee my safety? Not that it means much, look how well the Feds protected Raven."

"That would depend what you have to offer us, Duke."

"I have to object. Duke, stop talking, you're digging yourself into a hole. Let's talk about our options privately."

"Deveno, you're fired. I told Annabelle I would keep you, as long as you were useful. That usefulness just ran out."

"Hage, I'm filing an objection with the judge. Apparently, if you're willing to give him diminished capacity, you're aware he is unstable."

Hage's eyes light up, "Duly noted, Mr. Deveno. However, your client still fired you. Goodbye."

Thank God, that weasel is gone. I'm not going to rot here and be someone's bitch for the next twenty-five years.

"Okay, Duke, you do understand that you have the right to another attorney, and that you're waving your right to new counsel?"

"Yes, Hage, I understand. I will tell you what I have, but I won't show you everything, until I have a signed deal."

"What do you have that you think is so valuable?"

"I have the original FBI file on the entire Giaconna, family. I have Gabriella's hand written journal, detailing everything that Vincent did and said to her. He raped and tortured her. Made her watch her husband's murder over and over again. He made her believe he still had Cara, and he threatened to rape Cara if Gabriella didn't comply. I have journals and files that I lifted from the villa in Italy, when my father was fleeing the country. There are details of wire transfers, and lastly, there is a thumb drive. On that drive is a list of all of my father's business contacts; dealings and holdings that I conveniently copied. Hage, I've got the Holy Grail. You can lift your chin off the ground now and let's discuss what I want."

"How do I know you actually have all of this?"

"I have a sample saved in a drop box online. I will give you the passwords and you can confirm the information. I want total immunity, name change, and relocation. I don't trust your witness protection program. I've seen how well that worked for Raven. I want $20,000,000.00 in an off shore bank account and a clean passport. I also want safe passage out of the country to anywhere I choose. I want to stay in solitary until everything is done; it's my only chance to survive."

Hage

"GIVE ME THE INFORMATION and let me verify it. If it checks out, then we have a deal."

Duke gives me the information and heads back to his cell. This day just keeps getting better and better. I hope, for his sake, he can deliver the goods. I'm sure Deveno is on his way now to deliver Vincent the bad news. I would rather have Vincent locked away for life than give him any sort of deal.

Deveno

VINCENT'S GOING TO GO fucking ballistic when he finds out what went down with Duke. I don't have a clue what the fuck this kid has that makes him think he can get a deal. Time to face the music; Vincent enters the room.

"Deveno, what the fuck is going on? Hage, was supposed to be here today to discuss a deal and the last minute, he canceled."

"We met with Duke this morning. Apparently, he has something on you. He fired me and struck a deal with Hage. Before you even ask, I have no idea what the kid has. I have asked every one of my contacts at the bureau, but it's on tight lockdown. Whatever it is, it's big. Do you have any idea what it could be?"

"How the fuck would I know? I picked the kid up with Cara at that dump in Woodstock. We were at the villa the whole time, until I had to flee. I told the kid we would go our separate ways, and I would hook up with him in the states. Everything happened so fast; Jax and Max's men were all over the place."

"Was there anything at the villa he could have gotten his hands on?"

"There were some banking ledgers that I had to leave when we fled. I keep everything that's important on a thumb drive but I grabbed it when I left."

"Could he have gotten a copy of it?"

"I honestly don't think so. But if he did, then I'm fucked—which means—you're fucked too, Deveno. Everything you have ever done for me is also on that drive. All of my business dealings and contacts are on that drive. Judges, politicians, leaders in other countries, bank accounts—everything. You better fucking find out what the kid has, and then how to get your hands on it—now!"

"Why the fuck would you put everything on there?"

"Well, would you rather I kept written copies? It was easy and I could carry it everywhere."

"Where is the drive now?"

"I put it someplace safe before that fucker, Max, came after me and shot me."

"You're not going to tell me, are you?"

"No, there is no reason for you to know where it is. Find out what is going on and get back to me." Vincent gets up and walks away, leaving me sitting here, holding my dick.

Maxwell

I NEED TO TALK to Jax, something doesn't feel right.

"Jax, am I on speaker?"

"No, what's up?"

"Come next door, and bring Raven." I don't give him a chance to answer.

Within a few minutes, Jax comes flying through the door. "What's the problem?"

I begin my usual pacing which I find a comfort. "Jax, it's my tingle sense, it's firing up again."

"Oh *fuck,* no!"

Raven and Jackie have a deer in the headlight look. "Raven, Max's tingle sense was the key to finding you in Sicily."

"And I'm just finding out about this now!"

Max holds up my hand, "In Jax's defense, a lot has been going on, Raven."

Jax sits on the arm of the club chair and pulls Raven into his arms. "Go on, Max."

"I don't think it's safe to go to the island. I think we need to go with plan B. Let everyone think we're going to the island. And yes, Jax, I have a plan B." I hand Jax a scotch and the ladies water. "When Jax was holding me hostage, I was determined to leave here. With the help of a friend, I made a purchase abroad."

Jax looks like he's about to explode. "Who's the friend, Max?"

"Mrs. Osla."

The shocked look on everyone's face tells me that my plan worked. "I knew that above everyone else, I could trust her. With the help of Mrs. Osla, I purchased a 2700-acre equestrian farm in Angus, Scotland. When I realized I was never leaving my family, I figured, eventually, I would do something with it. Then when everything got crazy at the deposition, I knew I needed to do something. So I had the place updated. It has been equipped with everything we will ever need, including a clinic for the baby. It has its own airfield, and it has been completely staffed. I made the purchase in Mrs. Osla's maiden name. Vincent and Duke are getting a deal. The island is too isolated; we would be like sitting ducks." I look at Jax, and he's pulling his hair every which way. "Jax, if you keep pulling that hair, you will be bald, mate. Talk to me."

"Max, you're sure about the tingle sense?"

"One-hundred percent, Jax, I can't let the family go to the island, I just can't."

"Max, does my dad or Sammy know?" Jackie asks.

"No one but Mrs. Osla and us."

Jackie closes her eyes, "Will I be able to tell my father where I'm going?"

"Not until we are all safely tucked away."

"Max, how are you going to get us there, it's not like it's just the four of us." Jax brings my attention back to him.

"Well, we aren't getting on that plane tonight, that's for sure. I think if we do, it's game over. I called in a favor from a certain Turkish Prince. His private jet is waiting for us. I will let Mick in on what is going on. He can get the rest of the family to the hanger. We will be leaving by helicopter from the roof."

"What about Sammy? He's not going to be easily fooled." Jax throws his hand out.

"You're right, Jax, he won't be. Do you remember the night we first met? I was on assignment, protecting the Queen's grandson. Well I helped him out so many times that now, he has agreed to help me."

Jax gets up still keeping his arm around Raven. "Wait, Max, how will Mick know where to bring the family?"

"By now Mrs. Osla has everyone at Bella's house. Mick is on his way to pick them up and bring them to the airport. Mrs. Osla has his new instructions and a burner phone, so he can call me to verify."

Everyone is quiet, seemingly processing everything. "I'm sorry I had to keep everyone in the dark for so long. I needed to make sure I could get everything done as quickly and as safely as possible."

Raven lets go of Jax, comes over and pulls me into her arms. "Max, I could never repay you for all that you've done for my family and me. I know how hard this must have been for you. The added stress probably didn't help with your healing. Thank you."

"Raven, you're my family, I would lay down my life for everyone of you." I hit the remote and the TV comes on, showing the entrance hall.

The only thing we see is Sammy, and some of his guards waiting for us.

Raven gasps, "Max, when were these cameras installed? Are they all over the flat?"

"Raven, your privacy is intact. I had these installed after the night you pulled a runner on Jax. I'm sorry, but I had no choice; you were driving me nuts."

"Max, part of me wants to hug you and part of me wants to wring your neck."

"Well, Raven, I would much rather have the hug."

Jax and Raven are staring at the screen. We all see it at the same time, the elevator doors open and out steps the director of MI6 and a half a dozen guards. They block the door to my flat and that's our cue.

"Jax, grab Raven and Bo, we're heading up the back stairwell to the roof. NOW!"

Jaxson

SOMETIMES IN LIFE IT seems as if time is standing still. This is one of those times. Max scoops up a shocked Jackie as Raven gives Bo a hand signal to run. I realize Raven doesn't know where the stairwell is. Instinct kicks in as I reach down grab her hand to lead her. We run into the kitchen, behind the pantry door. We hit the stairs, taking them two at a time. When we get to the roof, there is a chopper waiting, along with a slew of men, guns drawn. I freeze, but Max grabs my arm. "They're ours, Jax, get in the chopper *now.*"

It seems like forever to get us in the chopper and airborne, but in reality, it's seconds. These men are trained for this sort of thing, we, on the other hand, are not. Max is co-piloting, which makes me feel better. All we can do is pray his plan works.

Sammy

I'VE TOLD THEM NO one is to divert from the plan, so what do they do? Divert from the fucking plan. Just as I get most of the family loaded into the van, Mrs. Osla tells me they are going back to Bella's house for some shit they forgot. That woman is a pain in the ass and she doesn't back down. I instruct their driver to take them to get whatever it is they forgot and head straight to Teterboro Airport and we will meet them there. The elevator doors open and I'm in shock. The Chief of MI6 steps off with an elevator full of guards. They form a barrier in front of Max's door. "Sir, what are you doing here?"

"Special request from the Queen. You need to stand down."

"Sir, what about, Miss Gerhard?"

"She's already been removed and is being transported to safety."

"Does Mr. Gerhard know, did he order this?"

"For everyone's safety, we are going dark. Let's go."

I've been at this long enough to know when to shut up, and now is the time.

Hage

WELL, THE LAST THING I ever expected was to walk out of Sing Sing with the gift that Duke just handed me. If this checks out, it's going to catapult my career. I open the drop box and there it is, a file and a video. The video is a short clip showing the FBI file and the Journal. I open the file and Bingo; it's a nice portion showing Vincent's holdings. Some of his contacts in other countries. Holy shit this is big. I need the rest of this list and I need to keep this all a secret, not just for Duke's safety but for my own, as well. This kid just bought himself a deal. If this is going to work, it needs to go down fast.

Duke

I'M BEING PULLED FROM solitary. Apparently, Hage is back already. For once, the tables of luck are on my side. They bolt me to the table, yet again, before they let Hage come in. "So, you're back? Guess you're happy with the information."

"You delivered, Duke, now how do I get the rest?"

"As soon as you get everything else I requested, then it's yours. Do you have the immunity agreement?"

"Yes, and the offshore account has been funded. You never said what name you wanted so I picked something simple. Patrick Brown, easy enough to remember. Due to the extent of high-level people in the information that you provided, only three people know of this deal: myself, the President of the United States, and the Prime Minister of Great Britain."

"How's Raven?"

"Mrs. Phillips is fine. You understand you can never have contact with her or any of the Giaconna, family?"

"Hage, I get it. Duke Jensen dies when I sign those papers. She was innocent through this whole mess. Even at the worst point, when she thought she and her baby would be a prisoner for life, she tried to help me. I just want to know that she's safe and happy."

"I assure you, with a husband like Jaxson Phillips, her safety is not an issue. How do I get the rest of the files?"

"I have a letter I want you to personally deliver to Raven."

"That was not part of the deal, Duke."

I slide the letter in front of him. "Yeah, well without this, there is no deal."

I grab the letter, "Fine, now give me the rest of the files."

"I'll give you the rest on the plane, let's go."

I sign the paperwork, giving birth to Patrick Brown, and leaving a world of hurt behind.

Jaxson

WE LAND AT A private hanger at Logan Airport in Boston. A car is waiting to take us to our jet. When we get on board, everyone breathes a sigh of relief. Max gives customs our passports, while Raven runs to check on her mum. Jackie's very quiet, and I'm worried about her. A lot has been thrown at this girl, today.

Max comes back and he seems relieved. "Jax, we're clear for takeoff. Let's get everyone seated."

It's only now that I take a look around and realize this is not a plane, it's a frigging resort.

Once we're airborne, everyone seems to relax. "Raven, I'm going to meet with Max for a bit. Try and get some rest."

"Come on, Max, we need to talk."

"There's an office in the back."

We get into the office, and I'm floored—this place is beyond words.

"Max, are we safe here?"

"Jax, this is the Turkish version of Air Force One. What do you want to know?"

"Why did you keep this from me?"

"Honestly, Jax, you had so much on your plate, and I wanted everyone to believe they were going to the island. I had to in order to pull this off."

"What about, Jackie? This girl has had so much shit thrown at her today.

"Don't you think I know that? Once we get to Scotland, she can contact her parents. I had no choice, mate. I had to keep everyone in the dark."

"What are we going to do about Vincent? Are we going to release the tape?"

Before Max can answer, his Blackberry buzzes.

"Apparently, Jax, we won't have to."

"What's going on now?"

"Text from Mathew."

"Stay away from New York right now. Shit hit the fan. Duke threw Vincent and the entire organization under the bus. Feds are NOT going to make a deal with Vincent. Don't tell me where you are. I will let you know when it's safe. Make sure Raven and Rose don't turn on the news; the tape has been leaked."

"Holy shit, Max, could this be the light at the end of the tunnel?"

Max turns on the TV and it's everywhere.

"Breaking news: Mafia Drug Lord kills his Federal Agent brother as agent's seven-year-old daughter watches."

"Jax, it's not just the tape. What the hell did Duke have on Vincent?"

"Oh my God, Max, it's that slimy lawyer, Deveno, being taken away in handcuffs."

"Jesus Christ, Jax, we got out just in time. Hage is slated to give an interview."

"I'll be right back I want to check on Raven."

"ARE THE GIRLS OKAY?" he asks as I walk back in. He hands me a scotch.

"Yeah, everyone is asleep."

Hage walks up to the podium:

"Hello, I'm Senior Federal Prosecutor Hage. Today will go down in history as the day The United States Government shut down a major Mafia crime family. It is also the day many people will be answering for their crimes. Arrests have been made, and many more to follow. If you've done any business with the Giaconna family, there will be no place you can hide. The United States Government is in possession of the Mafia's equivalent to 'The Holy Grail.' It's a list of anyone and everyone who has had any dealings with this family. Every payoff, every country, every government official is listed. Vincent Giaconna murdered his brother, a decorated Federal Agent, in front of the agent's seven-year-old daughter. He kidnapped, tortured, beat and raped his brother's wife everyday. You've seen the tape. At this time, Vincent Giaconna has been charged with murder, major drug

trafficking, and treason. All of these are punishable by death. No more questions at this time. Thank you."

Max and I sit here, stunned. How the hell did Duke pull it off?

"Max could this possibly be over for us?"

"We need to stay clear for a while, let the dust settle."

"We have to tell everyone. I don't want them to see that tape!"

"Jax, we might not have a choice. I'm glad we will be hidden away for a while; totally off the grid."

I'm swirling the amber liquid around my glass, trying so hard to keep it all together. "Max, do you think everyone will like this place?"

"Yeah, mate, it's beautiful. There is so much to do. I think Junior is going to love it there. Once everything gets settled, if anyone wants to leave, they can."

"Do you have everything set up for the baby?"

"Of course, that's the first thing I took care of. Hold on; let me pull up the pictures. The main house looks like an old castle and has enough room for all of us. There are a dozen cottages that are for the staff. There are stables, a lake, and an airstrip."

"What were you planning on doing there?"

"Do you really want to know this?"

"Of course, I want to know."

"I was going to make Scotch whisky. It's something I always wanted to try."

Jax is stroking his chin and sipping his scotch. I think the simple life I was dreaming of just got a whole lot more complicated.

"Jax, I have something else to tell you. I asked Jackie to marry me."

"And?"

"She said yes, as long as we can have a long engagement."

"Congratulations, mate, and to think, you owe it all to me and my negotiating skills. Did you get her a ring?"

"Jax, it wasn't planned from the first day I met her."

"Nonsense, that night on the dance floor, you were done. It just takes you longer to see the light."

"I have one question for you, why Mrs. Osla? For fuck's sake, Max, you're petrified of the woman."

"Have a seat, Jax. I've got something to tell you."

What the fuck else could possibly be thrown my way today? "You've got my full attention now."

"You've never once asked me how I found Mrs. Osla."

"That's because I trust you blindly, so why would I? Where are you going with all of this?"

"You know that she's a widow? Her husband was killed by a drunk driver, and she never had any children. What you don't know is Mrs. Osla is, Samantha's, aunt. When my family was murdered, it not only destroyed me, but Mrs. Osla, too. She was like a mum to Samantha, and she doted on Elliot. She came to see me when I was at the lowest point in life. It was with her help and support that I pulled myself together and joined the Special Forces. I never forgot her and when you were in need of a new assistant, I reached out to her. I knew I could trust her, and I respect her. In a way, it was like having a part of Samantha with me. She knew my past and never told anyone, not even your mum.

"Why are you telling me this now?"

"Raven and Jackie have taught me a lot, mainly that there can't be any secrets amongst us, our family. True love is about honesty, trust, and respect. I need you to understand Mrs. Osla is a very special lady, and without her help, none of this would have happened today."

"Have you told Jackie?"

"Not yet, but I will when Mrs. Osla feels comfortable with everyone knowing."

"One more question, are you really afraid of her?"

"Hell yeah!"

" After we land, we should let the family know what's going on."

WE ARE GOING TO be landing soon. Max and I watched the news all through the flight. So many people, arrested for having any dealings with the Giaconna family. The last one we watched was Annabelle. If I have learned anything in my life, it's that there is no easy way. Work hard and stay true to who you are, everything else will follow. Gaining power any other way but honestly only puts you at the top of the house of cards, waiting for it to tumble. Watching that tape, and seeing what Vincent did to Raven, made me want to kill him. If I personally went after him, it would have made me no better than him. I need to be better than that. I hope that I've set an example for Junior. I know I will for my own children.

I find Raven in one of the many suites in this flying palace. She's still asleep, in my dress shirt, of course. I undress and crawl in bed next to her, pulling her in my arms. Even in sleep, she wraps herself around my body. I know the next couple of months are going to be very emotional for everyone.

I can finally say I have faith, the same faith that she has. We *will* get to the other side of this. I gently kiss her lips and her eyes flutter open.

"Hey."

"Hey, yourself, sweetheart. We're going to be landing soon."

"Jax, you look different, are you okay?"

"Yeah, I'm great, actually."

She reaches up and kisses me, pulling my lower lip between her teeth. "I know you're great, but what happened?"

"It's over, Raven. The tape was released. Apparently, Duke had some sort of evidence that the Feds are calling, 'the holy grail.' They charged Vincent with numerous crimes, and they are seeking the death penalty. We don't know everything yet, but so many people were arrested, including Annabelle. We will stay in Scotland until the dust settles, unless you love it there and decide you want to stay." I look down and I see the stunned look on her beautiful face. "I know it's a lot sweetheart, but it's all good. We'll be okay, I have faith now." I smile and plant a kiss on her nose. "I have some other news. Max asked Jackie to marry him and she said yes. She wants a long engagement."

"I know she told me. So much has been thrown at her today."

"I know I was worried, too. I know that Max had Mathew check on her family, and they are fine." I rest my hand on her growing belly and I can feel my baby kick.

"Max showed me pictures of the place and it looks surreal. The main house looks like a castle. Junior is going to have a blast."

"Jax, is there anything else?"

God, she knows me even when I don't. "I decided I'm going to read the file."

"Did you talk to your mom about it?"

"No, it has to be my decision, not hers. I'm the one that needs to see this through. She's made peace with her decision when she moved to the States. I need to find that same peace."

I've made love to her in so many places, and in so many ways, but right now, I need her. Our room is beginning to fill with a golden hue as the sun starts to rise. I shift so she can climb on top of me and slowly lower herself onto my cock. She stops, takes my hands, and kisses each palm.

"God, Raven, how is it you always know what I need?"

"Because I need you too, Jax, just as much as you need me."

She kisses me, our tongues doing their dance. Maybe now, with all of this behind us, we can finally relax. I watch her as we unravel together. I'm buried deep within her, knowing that she can be safe, sends me over that cliff of extreme pleasure, taking her with me as I fall.

Were both quiet for a while, enjoying the calm, and watching the dawn of a new day on the horizon.

"Raven, how do you feel about making scotch?"

"Excuse me."

"Let me tell you a story."

Jaxson

ALMOST THREE MONTHS HAVE passed since we got to Scotland. Junior is in love with the castle. Everyday, I take him to explore the different secret rooms. Bella and Michael went to Italy to tend to Michael's winery, but I asked them to leave Junior with me. I love our private time together. Construction to add more homes on the estate has started. With Mrs. Osla in charge, I don't doubt they will be ahead of schedule. Between this place being so big and Raven, nearing the end of the pregnancy, I now have everyone carrying two-way radios. While Raven is resting, I decide to find Max and give him my decision. I radio him to meet me in the study.

He comes racing in. "Hey, Raven okay?"

"Yeah, nothing yet. Everyone in her family went early except for her. I want to talk to you about Raiders. I want to sell it. Before you say anything, hear me out."

"Go ahead, Jax, I'm listening."

"I'm tired of that lifestyle. We're young and I think we are due for a new adventure. I know that everyone loves it here. I spoke to Jackie and she wants to teach children with special needs how to ride and take care of the horses. I really want to get this Scotch idea of yours off the ground. It would also be easier for Michael to run the winery. Mum, Rose, and Mrs. Osla agreed to it, as well. Jackie would be closer to her parents, too. All the way around, I think it's a great idea. If you don't want to sell, you can buy my shares at whatever you think is fair. Are you just going to sit there or are you going to say something?"

"Well, it sounds like you have everything already planned out for everyone. How does Raven feel about this? Did you run any of this by her?"

"Yes, as a matter of fact, I did. I'm really trying hard not to bully anyone, Max. She wants to stay here. She loves the country. She wants to be a full-time mum."

"I'm okay with it, Jax. I would be very happy, living out the rest of my days here. We can keep the flats in New York for vacations, along with the island. What else is bothering you? I can tell, so don't even try to hide it."

"I also decided that after the baby comes, I want to read the file. I need answers."

"Jax, what if the answers you're seeking aren't in the file?"

"Then, we will find them out together, but either way, I need to know."

"What about, An, have you spoken to her about it?"

"She made her peace, now I need to make mine. Does that make sense?"

"Okay, get the ball rolling on everything."

"Have you and Jackie thought about setting a date? I know she was relieved that the pregnancy test was negative, but that doesn't mean she wants to wait forever. Bella can't have any more children, and I want lots of babies in this house. That leaves me and you, mate."

"Actually, Jax, we're thinking late spring. Does Raven know you want lots of babies?" he chuckles.

"Stop laughing at me. Yes, she knows. She probably figures after this one I might not want lots more. I think I've calmed down a lot since we've been here. All the arrests have helped to calm me down."

"Jax, you can't possibly be serious. You're a crazy arse fucker and you always will be!"

"Thank you very much, Max. On that note, I'm going to bring my lovely wife some freshly squeezed juice."

As I get up to leave my radio goes off, "Jax, help me!"

Max starts barking orders behind me as we're flying up those steps three at a time. As I burst through the door, I see Raven, kneeling on the floor. "What the fuck are you doing on the floor?!"

"I'm having a damn party, Jax! What the hell do you think I'm doing? I don't think I can make it to the clinic."

"What the fuck do you mean, you can't make it? You have to make it to the clinic, that's the plan! The plan is in place for a reason!"

"Max, please call my mother and the doctor."

"I already did, Raven, they are on their way. Jax, snap the fuck out of it and get her on the bed. Where is your labor bag, Raven?"

"It's behind the door."

Max grabs the bag and pulls everything out, finally finding a nightshirt and tosses it to me. "Jax, help get this on her now."

As I lift her up, there's a gush of water. Raven is screaming and panting. My heart is ready to leap out of my chest. I'm never going to survive this. Fuck all that is holy, stop this ride, I want to get off!

"Jax, what are you waiting for? Help her get undressed."

"Turn around, Max. Don't roll your eyes at me, I'm serious, mate, turn around."

He turns around and I quickly help her change. I get her comfortable in the bed with the sheet pulled up.

"Can I turn around now, Jax?"

"Don't be a wise arse, yes, you can turn around. What's the status on the doctor?"

"He's still a few minutes out."

"What do you mean, a few minutes out? He was supposed to be here on standby."

"One of the staff's children fell and broke her arm. He was tending to her. Look, forget about that right now, and start timing her contractions."

Raven is following her Lamaze lessons, doing all the breathing we learned. She has a death grip on my hand and the other on Max's.

When the contraction finally passes, Raven leans back into my chest. "Oh no, Jax, I feel like I have to push."

"What the fuck do you mean? The doctor isn't here yet! *The. Baby. Has. To. Wait. For. The. Doctor!*"

Max grabs my arm, "This baby is not going to wait for anyone, Jax, and that includes you. Get your head out of your arse—*now!* Raven, I need to see if the baby is crowning. I know this is not the ideal situation, but we are out of options."

"Max, do whatever you have to but please make sure our baby is safe."

"I promise, Raven, I will. I'm going to pull the sheet up and take a look at what is going on okay?"

Max rolls the sheet down and gently pushes her legs apart. His eyes become wide as he announces the baby is crowning.

"Looks like I'm delivering my niece or nephew. I've done this before, don't panic. Raven, I'm going to need you to pant and then push. Jax, you need to help her with this. Massage her back like you learned in class. Talk her through it. I'll tell you when."

"Max, can't we wait for the doctor, he should only be a couple of minutes."

Raven grabs my hair and pulls my face to hers. "So help me God, Jax, you do what he tells you to do. If you don't, I will pull every last hair out of that glorious head of yours!"

"If you two are done arguing, it's time to deliver. Raven, do you feel the urge to push again?"

"Yes."

"Start now. Jax, count it out for her."

"Raven, you're doing great. Now pant like you're blowing out a candle."

"Jax, you need to breathe. If you pass out, you'll miss this. You need to help her with the breathing."

"Jax, so help me, if you pass out, you and Mr. Cock are never going to *cock heaven* again!"

"Don't worry, I'm good." *Damn she goes right for the jugular.* I lean up against Raven's back and help her push. I look down to see what's going on and see a shock of black hair. I'm in awe of the sight before me.

"Jax, start counting for her again. One more push, Raven, come on you, can do this."

"I'm tired, Max, I don't think I can."

"You need to push the shoulders out. Come on, girl, you can do it!"

My beautiful wife gives it all she's got. The doctor and Rose come running in just as we hear the baby cry.

"Jax, Raven, meet your beautiful daughter." Max places her in Raven's arms and wrapping my arms around her, we cradle this angel together.

The doctor steps up and offers me the chance to cut the umbilical cord. I'm nervous but I give it a go, wiping my tears away, first, so I can see. The happiness I'm feeling is overwhelming. We fought hard for this and won. Life has come full circle . . . for all of us.

"So, does my niece have a name?"

Neither one of us is saying anything. We are too busy huddling together, watching her with wonder and love. Finally, I get up and hand the baby to the doctor and Rose to examine.

I turn to my brother. "Max, if it's okay with you, Raven and I would like to call her Antonia Samantha Phillips. You are my best friend and a great brother. You've been shot twice, protecting my wife and daughter. Now you've helped bring my beautiful baby safely into this world. I would be honored to give her Samantha as her middle name."

Maxwell

I'M STUNNED. "THANK YOU . . . both of you. I'm honored that you would do that."

I look over at Rose, coddling my niece, and I know that Samantha would be proud to have her name carried on. Proud of how far I have come. I back out of the room, giving them some privacy. I need to find Jackie, and let her know what's happened. As I head downstairs, Jackie, An, and Mrs. Osla come rushing in. "It's okay everyone, they have a beautiful, healthy, baby girl."

"Is Raven okay, and did my son survive this?"

"An, Raven is fine and yes, even Jax survived this, although, he might be rethinking his need for lots of babies right now."

An and Mrs. Osla head upstairs, but I pull Jackie back towards me. "I need you, baby."

"Are you okay, Max?"

"They named the baby Antonia Samantha Phillips. It was just a little overwhelming for me. Sometimes I feel like I've come so far, and then, I feel like I've hit a wall."

She pulls me into her arms and holds me tightly. "Max, there will always be a time when something or someone will stir up memories of Samantha and Elliot. Cherish the fact that you have some happy memories. Remembering them will always keep their spirits alive. It's okay to feel, Max, it's when you stop feeling that the walls go up."

I lift her head up to mine and look into those beautiful golden eyes. "Let's head upstairs, and you can meet my new niece. After that, I want to be alone with you for the rest of the day. Did I tell you I delivered the baby? You should have seen Jax. It's a wonder Raven didn't kill him."

"Why did you deliver the baby? What happened to the doctor?"

"Come, I'm sure Raven wants to tell you all about it."

We walk into the room and An is on the phone with Bella. The whole family is gathered around, and I realize, I've come back to life. It's taken ten years, but I've come full circle. I wish my grams were here to see this, to see I'm happy and loved.

I'm sure she's looking down on me now.

"Max, what are you thinking right this second?"

"I'm loved, baby; truly blessed."

Raven

AS I WATCH MY beautiful Antonia sleep, I look out over the sun rising in the meadow. So much has happened to me—hell—to all of us in this past year. Things I never thought or dreamed of, have become my reality. My mom is alive and getting stronger everyday. Jackie has found the love she always dreamed of, a true soul mate. Max is healing, one day at a time. He's feeling again, learning to live life. My Jax, oh how my skin tingles just thinking about him. I've finally figured out his over the top ways, but more importantly, why he does what he does. He's so wonderful with Antonia. I don't think any boy will ever have a chance with her. To think, I was worried that he would want lots of staff around to take care of her. He won't let anyone within ten feet of her. I'm glad he still wants lots of babies, this place is huge and I wouldn't want Antonia to be an only child.

He's been a little off, lately and I know it's that damn file. I wish he would just burn it, but that's not Jax. I know he has to see this through to the end, but at what price? I scoop up Antonia as she begins to wake. She has quite the appetite, which I'm sure, makes Jax happy.

"Hello, my beautiful Antonia." I watch her as she latches on. She makes a fist near her jet-black hair and I have to laugh, she really is her father's daughter. "There's a whole world at your doorstep, my sweet daughter, just waiting for you. I can't wait to explore it with you, one day at a time."

Jaxson

A COUPLE OF DAYS have passed and Antonia is already getting into a routine. Raven is a natural with her. I have a beautiful daughter, and rest assured, no man will ever be good enough for her. I pity the poor bastard that even tries. My wife and daughter are asleep. I know it's time; I can't put this off any longer. I head to my office and pull out the file. I've been waiting for the right time to do this and now seems as good as any.

"Are you ready for this, Jax?"

"Jesus Max, you scared the living daylights out of me."

"I figured you'd want to get started on this. Are you sure you really want to look?"

"Yes, I have to."

"Well, then, let's get started."

I open the file and there are pictures, lots of them. "Who are all these people?"

"The first picture is our father as he looks today."

"Who are these other people Max?"

"Read the file."

I begin to read and I'm floored. Our father is a career bigamist. He's lived off of all these women. When he is done with them, he moves on to the next one. Never caring about the devastation he's left behind. There are other children like us out there. "Jesus Christ, Max, we've done business with some of these people and never knew! Now what? Do we contact them?"

"Well, I don't think it is a decision we have to make right this minute. I think we need to talk to Bella and An about this. They need to be aware of everything. Jax, he's alive and well, living in Capri."

"Well, Bella will be home tomorrow. We will let her and mum know everything, and then I guess we're off to Capri."

Raven

I WAKE FROM A nap and look for Jax, but I know he's not here. I get up to find him, although I know I won't have a long search, he's never far from me. I stop outside Antonia's room and I hear him talking to her.

"My beautiful daughter, I am yours for life." He stares down at our daughter and I don't know what is going on in his head right now but he seems a little upset.

"My beautiful Antonia, you're so sweet like your mum. How could I go without seeing these little pouty lips everyday, or those beautiful crystal blue eyes? How can I leave Raven?"

What's this? "Jax, are you okay?"

He brings his focus to me. "No, sweetheart, I'm not. I read the file and, apparently, my father is a serial bigamist, living in Capri. I need to confront him and right now I'm struggling with leaving you and, Antonia."

"Are you worried about our safety, or something else?"

I watch his struggle as he tries to find the words, words I already know. My heart tightens in my chest. "Would it help if we went with you?"

"I thought of that, believe me, I have. I need to get a handle on these feelings. Feelings I've never had before."

"What feelings, Jax?"

He's quietly stroking Antonia's, cheek. "*Fear,*" he barely whispers.

My heart breaks for him, and I know that only I can help him through this. "What are you afraid of Jax?" Antonia, falls back to sleep and he puts her in her crib.

"I'm afraid this might all go away."

There it is, that little boy whose family was rejected for another. I take his hand and pull him towards me. "Look at me, Jax." His eyes shoot up to mine, "You are not your father. You're a kind and loving man. We made promises to each other, promises that I plan on holding you to, until my dying day. I will never leave you." I stroke my fingers across his worry lines, I see his angst. "I know your craziness stems from your father abandoning your family for another. That's an awful hurt for anyone, especially a little boy who idolized his dad. You're not your dad and you never will be, you don't have it in you.

You're a good man, Jax, one I plan on growing very old with. We have a long, full future ahead of us. A future we need to be working on."

"Raven, the doctor has not given us the green light yet, and I struggle with this every minute of every day."

I lean into his chest and kiss his heart. "My beautiful man, come back to bed, please . . ."

He lifts me into his arms and nuzzles into my neck. "Sweetheart, you don't play fair."

"I never said I would."

Maxwell

IT'S ANOTHER BEAUTIFUL DAY, and fall will be upon us soon. I know Jackie has already gone to the barn. She is so happy; her riding academy is a huge success. She's adding two new horses today. The kids love her, but what's not to love? I hate that I have to leave her, but Jax and I are supposed to be heading out to Capri today. I'm not sure either one of us can do it. Jax has put three guards on Antonia, one that Raven and Jackie call T-Bear. Mick is always within view, so I'm not worried about their safety. I just don't want to leave. I watch in the distance as Jackie mounts up. God she's so beautiful. Her golden hair, cascading down her back—and those legs! I watch, in a trance, as my mind wanders.

"Maxwell, are you sure you and Jax will be leaving today?"

"Jesus, An, you scared me half to death."

"Maybe your apprehension to leave is really a sign. What is it going accomplish anyway? The past is just that—the past. Nothing will change what was, only you can change what will be."

"For once, I agree with you, but Jax needs to do this and I won't let him go alone. Is there some other reason you don't want us to go?"

"No, I just don't see any good coming from it. Jax fears he is like James, but he's nothing like him."

"What about the other siblings out there, shouldn't they know the truth, An?"

"Maxwell, maybe they already do, have you thought of that? Maybe they know and they just don't care."

"I've thought about that, but I know Jax needs answers. Answers he can only get from our father."

"Do what you must." She walks away, leaving me to my thoughts. As I walk towards the barn, my phone beeps. It's Bella.

"Meeting. Now. Kitchen!"

She sounds upset. I better get over there now.

Isabella

JAX AND MAX TOLD me everything about my father. I have siblings I never knew about. They are getting ready to go to Capri. They think they can head out and leave me here.

Jax comes running into the kitchen, half out of his mind, as usual.

"Bella, what's wrong?"

"Calm down, bro, I'm fine."

"Then, why the meeting?"

Max steps into the room, "What's the urgency, Bella?"

"I'm going with you to Capri."

"Oh no you're not," Jax jumps in.

"Look, you can't stop me from going. I will be perfectly safe with the two of you. I need to do this just as much as you do."

"Your mum is upset that Jax and I are going, you going, as well, will be too much for her."

"Max, don't bring my mum into this. She doesn't need answers, I d-do." I stammer, trying to fight off my emotions.

"What kind of answers are you looking for?"

"Max, it was after I was born that he walked out, why?"

Jax pulls me into his arms. "I've heard enough, you are not responsible for his leaving. It was his choice to make. I tried to give you all the love and support I could, Bella, and I'm sorry if I failed you."

"Jax, you didn't fail me, but I still need to know."

"Well, then, I guess the three of us are going to Capri just as soon as I can pull myself away from my wife and daughter." He pulls back from me. My brothers and I all stare at each other in silence; this is going to be hard on all of us.

The End . . . *for now.*

FOLLOW YOUR *Dreams*

Jax

THE FIRST TIME I sent Raven the Abracadabra Rose, I had to have it shipped in from Germany. With the help of Mrs. Osla, I found a local shop that can get them. It wasn't the fact that they could actually get them that sold me on the shop; it was the name—*Bigger on The Inside.* Now don't get me wrong; I could ring up the shop or even order online, but with a name like that, curiosity has gotten the better of me. Besides, while I'm out, I can pick up the gift I ordered for Max.

I generally never head into the village area of the city, which is probably why I've never heard of this place. With everything going on right now, Max has put extra guards on everyone, including me. The sad part is, it's becoming the new normal for all of us. When we finally get there, I stand outside the door, trying not to laugh. Yep, the door to the TARDIS is waiting for me to open it and step inside. I pull it open and when I step inside, I'm taken aback. Right in the middle of the shop is a spiral staircase. The shop is very long and narrow with a couple of café tables and a sofa along one wall. It's so much larger then it appears. I know I'm in the right place, but I don't see a traditional floral shop. I'm engrossed in my surroundings until I realize that someone is talking to me. "Hi. I'm sorry. I thought this was a floral shop."

"You're in the right place. This used to be an old firehouse. I renovated it so now the front is a café and the rear is the floral shop."

My eyes quickly try to take it all in, including the pole in the middle of the shop. "What's upstairs?"

"That's where my darkroom is located." She steps forward and offers me her hand. "I'm Michelle, but everyone calls me Shell. I'm the owner of this fine establishment."

"Well, Shell, I'm Jaxson Phillips, but everyone calls me Jax. My understanding is that you carry different types of flowers that the average floral shops don't."

"Yes, sir, I do. Is there something in particular that you are looking for?"

"Call me Jax, please. And yes, I need fifteen dozen Abracadabra Roses. I would like them delivered in two days."

"Wow, okay let me make sure I can fill that on such short notice. Why don't you have a seat and help yourself to some coffee."

When I head over to the coffee machine, I notice a wall of photos. Each one seems to have been taken in this shop. Michelle is in most of them with some very impressive people. There are people from Henry Kissinger to Sofia Loren, very diverse. I hear her behind me, which snaps me back to attention. "This is quite a diverse wall you've got going here."

"Thank you. I'm able to fill your order. I will need the different addresses you want them to go to."

"They are all going to one person, my fiancée." It still sounds strange hearing me say that out loud.

"Wow, she's a very lucky girl."

"Truth be told, Shell, I'm the lucky one. I would like to put a card on each dozen."

"Why don't you enjoy some coffee while I get the cards for you. Maybe your security might want something to drink?" She winks at me, turns and walks away. I'm still so intrigued by the wall of photos—politicians to celebrities. They are very candid shots. Then I find a photo of Matt Smith. He wrote "*Shell, the universe is yours for the taking. With love, Matt.*"

"I gather you really like my wall of fame."

"I'm a huge *Doctor Who* fan, which is what brought me to your shop. I would love to know how you came up with the idea for this place."

She pours us each a cup of coffee, and we take a seat at one of the tables.

"I love photography; it's where my heart is, but I can't make a living doing that alone. I love flowers, so I thought maybe I could combine them both."

"And the coffee?"

"It's a way for me to get to know my clients better. It puts them at ease before they step in front of the camera."

"But what made you pick this place? I would think you would want to be closer to the larger retail areas in the city, like 5th Avenue."

"Of course, I would, but I needed to be realistic on what I could afford. I found this spot and, with a little imagination, I think I pulled it off."

"Yes, you have. I guess I'm a little bit surprised that such a diverse group of people adorns your wall. This place is not in the heart of the city, so how did they find you?"

"Well, Jax, you found me, didn't you?" She laughs and, for the first time, I notice she has the bluest eyes, very similar to Max's.

"I brought you a stack of cards to sign. I wasn't sure of the occasion so I brought a variety." Her quick change of subject tells me she doesn't like the spotlight on her.

"I want to flood my fiancée's room the night before our wedding."

"Wow, that's beautiful and very romantic. What made you pick the Abracadabra Rose?"

"It's unique and beautiful, much like her."

"Are you always this romantic?"

"No, I don't think so. I've never had a reason to be until now," I offer and lift my cup to take a sip. I notice her smile has faded. "Why such a sad face?"

"It's not sad—envious maybe. I think every girl dreams of finding that great once-in-a-lifetime kind of love."

"You hardly know me; how could you know that's it?"

She eyes me, thoughtfully, over the rim of her coffee cup. "Jax, the eyes speak volumes even when the mouth remains closed. It doesn't take a rocket scientist to figure out that you're a man totally in love."

I reach over, take her hand and give it a slight squeeze. Her slight gasp is not lost on me. "Tell me something, Shell, have you ever loved someone so completely that you would lay down your life for that person?"

She pulls her hand back and fiddles with her cup. "Honestly, no. And I'm not sure I ever will."

"What makes you say that? Everyone has a soul mate; it's just a matter of taking off the blinders. Sometimes it's right in front of us and we are so caught up in life that we don't even notice. You're a beautiful woman; I don't think you're going to end up like some old cat lady."

She nearly chokes on her coffee with laughter. "Well, good God, I hope not, Jax."

She's intriguing and I decide to press her for more. "Do you ever wonder how many people miss that opportunity? You know . . . that chance meeting of your soul mate?"

"I've never thought of it that way. Did you know right away she was the one or was it something that built up over time?"

"When I met Raven, she was running out of Starbucks and slammed into me. She doused me with her coffee and ran away. For me, it was instantaneous. Her touch sent unexplainable sparks through me. I knew, from that moment, I had to have her."

"You sound like a man who wanted to own her; how is that love?"

Her words sting. I don't think I'm like that at all. "I know that wanting to own someone is not love. The same way having all the materialistic things in the world is not success. But, I didn't really appreciate any of that until I met Raven. I've always been a man that sees what he wants and takes it. The one thing that I couldn't take is Raven. She is the first person to give me purpose."

She gets up, freshens up our coffee and puts a plate of cookies in front of me. "Do you think your relationship with her will always be like it is at this moment?"

"Yes and no. I believe it will grow stronger as time goes on. The days are not long enough when we are together and they are not short enough when we are apart."

"Wow, a girl could only dream."

I push the cookies back towards her. "Enough about me, I want to know about the pictures on the wall. I can understand Matt Smith finding this place, but Henry Kissinger—how?"

"He was looking for a particular flower and I was the only one in New York who was able to get it. He came in here to personally thank me. Once he was here, he fell in love with the quirkiness of the place. People find me for all sorts of different reasons. I must be doing something right; they keep coming back."

"Did you take all these pictures?"

"Yes, I did. If you're interested, upstairs is a gallery. You're welcome to browse around." She pushes the cards back towards me. "But for now, I'm going to leave you alone so you can work on these cards. If you need anything, I'll be in the back, working on your order."

She gets up to leave, but not before I notice the melancholy look on her face. I hope it wasn't caused by me. I spread out the cards and get back to the task at hand. With each card, I'm so proud of the love we fought for. I finally finish the last one: *My life began with you.* When I look up at the time, I realize I've been here for hours. I quickly gather everything up and go looking for Shell. I find her surrounded by boxes of flowers.

"I finished the cards and numbered them. I need to get going. Is there anything else you need from me before I leave?"

"Nope, I've got it all. I will personally make sure these get delivered for you."

"Thank you. It was a pleasure to meet you. I'll see myself out." I head towards the front of the store, but for some reason, I feel a pull to head upstairs. When I reach the top, I'm taken aback. Each photo is more beautiful than the next. The closer I look, the more it's like life was captured and frozen in time. One photo, in particular, captures my eye. It is a black and white photo of an older couple sitting on a bench in Central Park. Everything in the photo is kind of blurred except for the couple's hands. They are looking down at their clasped hands while some petals from a cherry blossom tree float around them. She was able to capture so much from that one snapshot. A deep love, frozen in time. I need to have this photo. They should really be on display for the world to see, not hung up in a room that, I'm sure, not too many people visit. I take it off the wall and head downstairs. I find Shell in the back, putting the finishing touches on my order.

"I stopped upstairs before leaving and found this photo. I would like to purchase it."

"Let me just wipe my hands and I will wrap it up for you. Can I ask why this one?"

"Sometimes, so little can say so much. This little photo speaks volumes. You have a gift, one that should be shared with the world." I don't really know this woman, yet, I find I can be comfortable and relaxed around her. Lately, that is a rarity.

"Well, I'm glad you found it along with all these flowers." She laughs as she waves her hand over a stack of boxes.

I know I can be a little over the top sometimes, but people generally see things my way after awhile. "Well, it was very nice to meet you and I wish you all the best with your shop. I need to get going; lots to do before the big day."

She wishes me well and I head out to pick up Max's gift. I'm sitting in the back of my limo, traveling uptown; my mind is still stuck on that photo. I unwrap it and study it. Maybe it's the way the man is holding her hand? Maybe it's because everything that is going on around this couple is blurred and the focus is only on their hands? I don't know what the answer is, but what I do know is that someone with this much talent should not be hidden away. I know just what to do. I pull out my phone and shoot a text to Matthew. What good is having a top attorney on retainer if I don't keep him busy?

> **Me: Matthew I have a small project for you to handle. I will have Mrs. Osla send everything over to you ASAP.**
>
> **Matthew: Shouldn't you be getting ready for your wedding?**
>
> **Me: That's why I'm having you handle it and not Max. Besides, for this, I need my attorney. Thanks.**

Three Months Later

Michelle

EVERY MORNING I HAVE a routine and I usually never veer off of it. I open up my shop and turn on one of the all day news stations while the coffee brews. Today seemed the same as all the others. That is until there is a breaking news announcement. *"Mafia Drug Lord kills his Federal Agent brother as agent's seven-year-old daughter watches."* Normally, I would continue setting up my shop for the day, but as the news is reporting, a picture of Jaxson Phillips comes up with a woman who must be his wife. He's the man who purchased one of my photos and all those roses for his fiancée. It really wasn't the purchase that stayed with me; it was the man himself. Not just the fact that his looks made my heart skip a beat. It's what he saw in my photo. He made me think. Am I really missing what I should be doing in life? The door chimes, pulling me out of my daydream and a very well dressed man steps in.

"Hello, can I help you?"

"I'm looking for Michelle."

"You're looking at her. What can I do for you?"

"My name Matthew Turner. My firm represents Jaxson Phillips. He asked me to personally handle this for him. May I have a seat?"

"Of course. I'm sorry, would you like some coffee?"

"No, thank you. This shouldn't take long. Apparently, you made quite an impression on Mr. Phillips. He purchased this building and gifted it to you, along with two million dollars in an account."

I know my mouth is hanging open but I can't seem to process what he's saying. "I'm sorry, he did what?"

"I'm sure after meeting him, you must have realized he is a force to be reckoned with. It's all legit and above board. My firm is will also be handling all the taxes on the building. You really have nothing to worry about. If you decide you need some help with managing the account, I can point you in the right direction. Do you have any questions so far?"

"Why?"

He passes me an envelope. "He told me to give this to you. Maybe it will explain more."

My grip on the envelope is so tight. I take a deep breath. When I open it, my own business card falls out. I flip it over and there are three words: *Follow your dreams.* I begin to laugh and then I cry. "Why on earth would he do such a thing for a total stranger?"

"Michelle, I have been Jax's attorney for many years. He sees potential in companies even when others don't. The same goes for people. I gave up questioning *the why* a very long time ago."

"How can I get in touch with him to at least thank him?"

"You can't; he's already left the country. Besides, he's not one to draw attention to himself. Enjoy your life, and pay it forward. If you need anything, please don't hesitate to contact me." He gets up, places his card on the table, and walks out. I can't take my eyes off of those three little words. *Follow Your Dreams.* I walk over to my wall of photos and place Jax's card on my photo of Matt Smith. I've sat on the invisible fence, too scared to take that chance. Maybe that's what Jax saw—my fear. I run my finger over those words one last time before setting out on an adventure that will change my life forever. *"Thank you, Jax."*

Follow Your Dreams

Shattered Lies

THERESA SEDERHOLT

Dedication

For Josiah Garcia, you are a brave and beautiful boy. I know you will survive and go on to do great things. Your kind and gentle way is an inspiration to everyone. It has been said that everyone comes into your life for a reason, even if it's only for a brief moment. I am honored and blessed that you have come into mine. Your faith and inspiration is a shining light. Thank you and God bless.

To everyone who has fought cancer, your battle has not been in vain. That moment in time, no matter how brief, will never be forgotten.

Chapter One
James Phillips

THE DAY HAS FINALLY come, the one I've feared the most. The day my oldest son comes to find me. I knew it'd be only a matter of time before my past would collide with my future. His family . . . murdered because of me. My grandson and daughter-in-law gunned down like animals. How can I face him, knowing what I've done? I've stayed away for their own safety, but what did that get me? They are *still* dead because of me. I have managed to keep the rest of them safe, but, for how long?

A knock on the door startles me out of my thoughts. I'm expecting my valet. "Come in, Reynolds." Reynolds has been my valet and confidant for twenty years; the keeper of all my secrets.

"Sir, I just received word their plane has landed. It's only a matter of time now. What would you like to do?"

"Well, Reynolds, what we won't do, is run anymore. The time has come to face my demons. I must own up to what I've done. They are not children anymore, and they deserve the truth, no matter how ugly it is."

"Sir, what about their safety?"

"Well, the better question should be, what about ours? When Maxwell finds out my role in all of it, I venture to say, I'm a dead man."

"Sir, you did everything you could, I'm sure he will understand."

I squeeze my eyes shut, trying to get that image out of my head. "Everything but save them," I whisper.

Ten Days Earlier

Raven

AS I WATCH JAX sleep, I see such anguish on his beautiful face. I wish I could take away his pain; I would bear it for him, if I could. I lean in and tenderly kiss him. I don't want to wake him, but I want him to feel me and know I'm always with him.

"Hmm . . . I'm awake, sweetheart."

"I can never tell if you're really asleep."

He tilts his hips and I can feel how aroused he is. I know he sleeps best when he's buried deep inside of me, but I haven't made it to my six-week post-partum checkup yet; my body's not ready. He keeps a tight grip around my waist while I snuggle up against him. For now, this will have to do.

"Jax, you know I'm not going to disappear; you can let go of me."

"Raven, you are so strong and so positive, even after all you've been through. How? How do you manage to do it?"

"I believe in us. Our daughter is a beautiful product of that belief. *And* I've made you a promise. A promise to be your companion, forever; beyond this lifetime. But most of all, I have given you my heart and my soul. I will fight to the bitter end for *us*." I lay a trail of soft kisses down his neck.

"I really am dreading getting on that plane tonight," he groans lightly. I lift my head up to catch his eyes. "Please don't look at me like that, you know I have to do it—I need answers. Now Bella has decided she is going with us. I think she blames herself for his leaving, and no matter what I've told her, she won't listen. She's so stubborn."

"Really, Jax? I wonder where she gets that from." He says nothing, only closing his eyes tightly.

"Sweetheart, Max and I have put extra security in place. I don't expect to be gone very long, however, I don't want you to be alarmed with all the extra guards."

At just the mention of his leaving, I feel his whole body tighten, his eyes still tightly shut. My heart is breaking for him. One of the many facets of this man is his need for the truth. "I understand having questions, but do you really need to know the answers? Will knowing change anything for you? Will it change any part of who you are?" I ask as he strokes my back in a rhythmic pattern like he's trying to find comfort.

"Raven, I've never shared any of this with anyone. I thought by keeping it buried, it would be gone. But things never stay buried, do they? Eventually, everything comes to light." He mindlessly twirls my hair around his fingers.

"I would sit by the window every Saturday, waiting for him to come home. Sometimes, I would set up our peanut butter and jelly sandwiches on a TV tray, hoping he would come back to watch *Doctor Who*. He never came back, but I kept setting it up . . . hoping. As I got older, I made sure I worked hard in school and helped my mum with Bella. I always protected my mum and my sister. I never gave into my fear that one day, I would wake up and they would be gone, too. I wanted to make him proud of me, just in case he came back to us. Instead . . . he just moved on to the next family. No matter how hard I tried, it was never good enough. *We* were never good enough," he barely whispers, "When is it ever good enough?"

Right now, my heart is breaking for this man. He's been through so much and yet all he ever wanted was his dad to love him, as he should have. "Jax, you were a little boy, trying to protect your mom and sister, the only family you had left. You did everything right. You carried so much of the burden. Anyone would be proud to call you 'son.' Don't ever think that you're not good enough; it's your father who's not good enough. He didn't deserve any of the wonderful children that he created."

"Sometimes I would make up stories about him. I would have him out, saving the world. I would pretend he was like *Doctor Who,* traveling through time and space, to save everyone like a superhero. It would ease the loneliness, especially for Bella. I thought I was helping her, but, maybe I didn't. Maybe I made things worse for her."

"Why would you think that you made it worse? It doesn't seem that she has put him on a pedestal or that she has any hate for the man. She seems almost . . . indifferent."

"What about her remark about dad leaving after she was born? That sounds like she blames herself and she shouldn't. For Christ's sake, she was just a baby. She wants to confront him, and honestly, I can't say I blame her."

"What about Max?"

"What do you mean?"

"Well, I understand why Bella wants to meet James and I even understand why you do, but why Max?"

"Sweetheart, I think he's going for Bella and me . . . to support us. I really think he has no desire to have any kind of relationship with him. He told me that when he married Samantha and had Elliot, he finally made peace with it all. I think in the beginning, he blamed dad for his mum's death. It's only with age and maturity that he's come to realize we are all responsible for our own actions."

"Your mom doesn't want any of you to go. She told me *'the past can't be changed and it's best to keep it buried.'* I think she is speaking as a mother, trying to protect her children. I know I would lay down my life to protect Antonia. Now that I'm a mom, I can understand that bond so much more. I think she chose to bury the past for survival purposes. It wasn't just for her survival, but for the survival of her children."

"My mum acts like she doesn't care one way or the other, however, I'm not so sure. What else did my mum tell you?"

"Nothing more about your dad. She does talk fondly of Max's grams. I think they became good friends over the years. Did you ever meet her?"

"Yes. I met her right after he came on board at Raiders. She passed soon after that. She always seemed like such a strong lady."

"Having lost a child and then having to raise her grandchild, I would think she was very strong." I stroke his face, "How long do you think you'll be gone?" I ask. His grip gets tighter, "Jax, really, if you need me to go, I will, but we will have to take Antonia with us."

He leaps out of bed and begins pacing and pulling at his hair. I'm watching his struggle boil to the surface. I'm shocked at his reaction; I never expected him to get this upset.

"Fucking bloody hell, woman! I can't do this. What the fuck has happened to me? Do you even realize what you've done?"

"Jax, calm down. Please, sit down and talk to me rationally."

"Calm? Rational? You can't be serious. Calm and rational flew out the window the day I met you. In one year's time, my entire life has changed. I have real love for the first time ever. I have a daughter, who I have to protect. I have a family that is growing daily. I've come alive, Raven, and it's all because of you. Now I have to leave this and confront the demons from my past. A past I thought was dead and buried. I really thought he was dead, and honestly, I didn't give a royal fuck until Antonia. Now everything I say and everything I do, matters. Every second, without you both, matters. What if she forgets me? Have you even thought of that? I know I have!"

"Jax, stop right now! You're not going to be gone that long."

"Raven, one day is too long. What if it takes a while? What if he doesn't want to see us? There are so many *what ifs*. I don't do *what ifs!*"

I need to keep it together for him, but he knows I'm just as apprehensive about him leaving. "Realistically, how long do you think you'll be gone?"

"I don't know. All I do know is every minute away is too long. I planned for two days; get in ask my questions and get out. Then, Bella demanded that she go. What if she wants to stay longer? I can't leave her behind—no one gets left *behind.*"

I open my arms, "Come back to bed."

He stops. His eyes gaze up and down my body as he seemingly struggles with his decision. "You're not going to tempt me with that beautiful body. I have enough to deal with, and not being able to go to the happy place for the past six weeks is fucking killing me!"

"You need me, Jax, but more importantly for you is the fact that I need you." He slowly walks toward me and just as he crawls back into bed, I hear the baby monitor come to life. I reach up and kiss him gently. "I'll be back in a little bit; Antonia needs to eat." The look on his face haunts me as I leave, so troubled and my heart is breaking for him.

Jaxson

I WATCH MY WIFE sashay out of the room and *now* my cock decides to come to life. Bastard has a mind of his own. I watch her on the monitor tending to Antonia and it's such a beautiful sight. It's pure and natural, which only makes me want her more. Right . . . like that's even possible. I head into the shower, trying to get my mind off of her, but it won't. As I go about washing, I look down at my cock and he's hard as stone. *Bastard.* "Look, I told you we are adults here and we need to have some sort of control. We don't have the all clear, yet. I told you no jumping about." I freeze—*shit* I'm so busted. I don't have to hear her; I feel it when she walks in the room. I turn around and I'm hit with those beautiful eyes. She's biting her bottom lip, trying not to laugh. "Go ahead, Raven, say it."

"Oh, my beautiful, sexy husband. I love that you have conversations with Mr. Cock. I love that you are trying so hard to follow the doctor's orders. Get out of the shower now, Jax, I think it's time you turn the reins over to me for a while."

I hesitate as I step out of the shower. "Do you trust me, Jax?"

"With my life," I say without missing a beat.

"Good, then trust me to give you pleasure tonight—my way."

"Wow. Okay, what do you want me to do?"

"Get into bed and wait for me. That's all."

As I look at my beautiful wife, I know, deep in my soul, that I am the luckiest man in the world.

Raven

I WATCH HIM HEAD into bed, and then, I begin to set stuff up for him. I gather a pair of my stockings to tie him with, some massage oil, and a glass of ice cubes. Anything I can think of that will bring him pleasure. I turned things over to him one night. I let him blindfold me, which not only ended up being very erotic, but also very therapeutic. I faced my fear and, in the end, it brought us closer. I need to do the same for him. He needs to know that he might not see me or touch me, but I will always be there. I head into the bedroom and I hear him talking to his cock, yet again. I love the playful Jax just as much as the intense one. So many facets, like a beautiful diamond; each one shining in it's own light.

"I told you, mate, if we waited long enough, it would happen."

"Good conversation, Jax?" I ask, grabbing his attention. His eyes grow wide like a boy caught swiping a piece of candy. "It's okay. I don't mind you talking to him, it's quite entertaining, actually."

"So . . . what are you going to do to me?" He presses his lips together and his hands seem to shake. He's hesitant in giving up so much control. Knowing that it's the control that grounds him makes this even more important for both of us.

"Do you remember the time you blindfolded me? I learned so much that night. I experienced what it's like to totally trust—unconditional trust. I never thought that was possible, and that's what I want to give to you. However, I want to take it a step further." I pause. "I want to tie your hands," I lay it all out. His jaw seems to tighten as he gets a wan look about him. "I know it will be hard for you. Your need to constantly touch me comes from your fear of loss. Just like I was able to put my fear of the kidnapping behind me, you can do the same with your fear of abandonment. The fear is never truly gone, but it's in a more manageable place where it can't hurt you anymore. You need to trust me. Do you trust me, Jax?"

"You know I do, but this is hard for me. I need that constant touch to keep me grounded."

"Will you try? If it gets to be too much, we can stop. If we don't try, you will always wonder *what if?*"

He bites his bottom lip and tightly closes his eyes. His skin seems to shiver and prickle at the thought of what I'm suggesting. I knew it would be hard for him; I just wasn't sure *how* hard.

He takes a calming breath, "I'll try," he whispers as he holds out his hands to me. The fact that his hands are shaking only makes me surer that what I'm doing is going to help him. I place my hand on his chest, and I can feel his heart racing. I swear it will leap out of his chest. I reach over to the nightstand and grab one of the black stockings to tie his hands together in front of him. "Breathe, Jax, it will be a good experience. If it gets to be too much, you can always tell me to stop." I take the other stocking and make it into a blindfold. "You'll need to rely on your other senses now. Take a deep breath and let it out slowly. Tell me . . . what are you feeling?"

"Fear, I can't see you or feel you."

"You know I'm still here and I'm not leaving you, *ever.*"

"My head understands everything you're saying but my heart doesn't."

I lean in and place kisses all over his chest, trying to get him to relax. "I made promises to you that I would never break." I continue kissing him gently up his neck and then kiss his lips. I can feel his jaw relax as I trail my fingers along the scruff of his beard. "I love when this scruff is between my legs. Use your other senses, what do you feel?"

"I feel your soft lips all over me. Your fingertips are following the trail of your tender kisses. I can smell our scents mixed together with a hint of sexual arousal, it's quite heady."

"That's good. Now take a few long breaths, like I taught you from Pilates . . . feel yourself relax."

I got edible, chocolate-raspberry massage oil today. I grab the bottle from the nightstand and put some in my hands. I rub them together to warm it up. I decide to start at his perfect feet. As I work his arch, he moans and the tension begins to slowly leave his body. "You're doing so good. I swipe my tongue up his arch and his cock leaps to attention. I try not to laugh— yep, Mr. Cock has a mind of his own. I work my way up his legs very slowly. Noticing his bound hands fisted, I bring them to my lips and kiss each one. Not being able to touch me or see me, is having a larger effect on him than I thought. He wants to do so much to please me and this really is one of the hardest things I have ever asked of him. I know the level of trust between us is so great, yet sometimes, the biggest struggle is with the littlest things. "It's okay, I'm here—always. Let yourself feel me."

"I can't; my hands are *bound!*"

"Feel me with your heart, Jax . . . your soul. You don't need your hands, I'm all around you." I reach down and plant a kiss over his heart. "Even if I left the room, I would still be in here." I tap gently with my finger before placing another kiss. "I will always be with you; that will never change."

His rapid breathing seems to be calming down. "Jax, are you okay now?"

"Yes, I'm good."

I take the glass of ice and pull out a cube. I slowly rub it around his nipples followed by my warm tongue. Hot and cold; back and forth. He's beginning to relax under my touch, ever so slowly. I massage every square inch of him— my tongue darting out to taste him—trailing with feather-light kisses. "Turn over, Jax." He complies and I begin the process all over again. I reach his ass and freeze. He has the most beautifully sculptured ass. I straddle him and try to continue, but as my hands work over this perfection, I moan. I reach down and kiss each cheek. My God, he takes my breath away. I swirl my tongue in circles and up his spine. I swear, I could have an orgasm just from the sight of him. My breathing has become rapid and I'm close to the edge. I can feel my body begin to tremble with every kiss. I know he can feel it too. He's always so in tune with me. He senses my needs before I do, knowing when to slow me down or let me have control. I hope tonight I'm doing the same for him.

"Sweetheart, are you okay?" he asks.

"More than okay." I climb off of him. "Roll onto your back and lift your hands above your head. Hang onto the headboard and no matter what happens, don't let go." God love him, he does it without question. I climb on top of him and kiss the tip of his cock before sliding my tongue up and down.

"Raven, I don't know how much longer I can last without touching you. I'm aching for you." There's a plea in his voice.

"Lift your head up, Jax."

Jaxson

I DO AS I'M told and I know exactly where I'm headed. I thank God for her and her willingness to explore the unknown with me. Her understanding and grace befuddles my own logical mind. What did I ever do right in my life to have been gifted with her? I lift my head up and my lips land right between her legs just as she takes my cock even deeper in her mouth. I know I have to be gentle with her right now, but it's hard to concentrate when she's working her magic on me. I lightly kiss her sweetness, followed with the swipe of my tongue. Still bound and blindfolded, I realize she's right; I don't need to see her or touch her. She is in my heart and my soul. As she gets to the tip of my cock, I beg her—no, I plead with her—to please do the nip that I love so much. She swirls her tongue around the head, then stops, hums, and goes right back down. *Sweet Jesus, and all that's holy, I'm gonna die.* When she gets to the top again, I hold my breath. I don't have to beg; she squeezes me and nips the head of my cock. She knows just how I like it. I explode with a force that I never thought was possible. Not having the sense of sight and touch makes my orgasm so much more intense. I shake uncontrollably and let out an animalistic groan that sounds foreign to my own ears. I know I should be giving her what she needs, but right now, I can't move . . . or even think, for that matter. Right now I'm just trying to breath. She climbs off of me and quickly begins to remove my bindings. "Jax, are you okay?"

I feel as if I'm in a daze. "Raven, I've never experienced anything like that before. It's like all of my senses were magnified." As she crawls into my arms, I glance down, taking a quick peek at my cock.

"His head didn't blow off, Jax; he's fine."

I laugh, "I can't get anything past you, sweetheart." My fingertips stroke her back slowly, "Let me love you tonight. I know we can't have traditional sex, but I can love you in so many other ways."

She reaches up and pulls my forehead to hers. "Nothing about us has ever been traditional."

I throw my head back laughing. "Oh, my sweet, sweet girl, let me show you exactly what I'm talking about."

Raven

I KNOW I'VE TOUCHED upon a fear in him that he's tried to keep buried. I can only hope that in time, he will see that I'm not going to disappear. Together—we're both unraveling—one day at a time. I reach up and run my fingertips down his face. " Love me tonight, before you go; slow and gentle, please."

"My beautiful girl, you'll never have to ask me twice." He plants a sweet kiss on my lips. "Now, let me show you something different tonight." He pulls the sheets over us, holding me tight. As he begins to lose himself in me, I feel a calm that wasn't there before. I know we will face whatever is thrown at us, together.

Chapter Two

Maxwell

I DECIDE TO GO over the file again before we have to leave. Something is bugging me but I'm not sure what. I know I don't want to leave, but I would never let Jax and Bella go alone. I wish I could figure out what is making my tingle sense act up. I had it that day I went after Vincent. I didn't listen to it, and I paid a heavy price. I thank God I listened and we didn't go to that island. We would have been sitting ducks, waiting to be plucked off. Sometimes, I can't seem to bring things to the surface of my mind, it's like a salmon trying to swim upstream. I close my eyes and rub my temples. I sense her before I hear her, I always do. My whole body seems to come to life when I know she is near. I turn around and what I see stops me dead in my tracks. Jackie is standing before me with fire in her eyes. I've only seen her this mad one time, *right before the condom broke.*

"Hey, baby, what's up?"

"Maxwell Fleming, don't you 'hey, baby' me!"

Holy fuck—full name; I'm in deep shit here. "Um, are you mad at me for something?"

She has one hand on her hip and she's pointing her finger at me. "Let me tell you what happened today. Maybe—just maybe—you will understand why I'm so pissed off. I went to see Mick today. I wanted to surprise you, so I asked him to teach me how to defend myself. I know you're going away, and you know I don't like guns, so I thought if I knew some self-defense moves, you would be more at ease. He informed me that he is not allowed to teach me because that would mean he would have to touch me. He said, and I quote, *'No one is allowed to lay a finger on you, Jackie.'* Really, Max, have you lost your ever-loving mind? I'm not a child, and you can't act like a crazy ass lunatic—that's Jax's job!"

"I could tell you that at the time I wasn't in my right mind, but in all fairness, that's not true. Honestly, the thought of anyone putting a finger on you makes me see red. If you want to learn how to protect yourself, I'll be the one to teach you."

"You don't see anything wrong with this, do you? Your fear is smothering me. I love you, but you're the one driving a wedge between us. My whole damn life has been turned upside down. I've constantly had to be the giver. I've given up my teaching career and my freedom. I'm only twenty-five and I'm being isolated yet again! My father isolated me, and I fought so hard to be free, but that's never going to happen for me is it, Max?"

"Please calm down, Jackie, whatever you need, please, just tell me."

"I need a life, Max, a normal life. I need to feel self-worth. I want to grow and be able to teach."

"I thought you loved your riding academy?"

"I do love it. You don't get it." She brings her hand up to her forehead and shakes slightly as if in disbelief. "I feel like I'm living in your fear." Her hand darts off, emphasizing her point. "Your fear that's overpowering me. I don't want to see doom and gloom around every corner. I want to love life. Maybe it's a Pollyanna way of thinking, but damn it, it's what I want."

I feel my heart constricting in my chest. If she leaves, I'll die—I know it. "Please, I need to leave tonight, but I can't leave you like this. I can't let them go alone. Please don't leave me."

"I'm not leaving you. I need you just as much as you need me. I need you to stop smothering me, though. Let me live and let's experience life together. I know you will always be overprotective—I get that—but let's work together as a team, Max. Love me like the woman I am, and not like the child you're afraid of losing."

I lift her up and she wraps those beautiful legs around my waist. I rest my forehead on hers. "Please, give me a chance, I'm really trying."

"Yes, you are, Maxwell."

"Well, at least you can still joke. Now let me be the one to teach you some self-defense."

"Is this going to be something I can really use?"

"Of course. But I think we need to be naked."

"Naked self-defense classes? You can't be serious."

"Oh trust me, I'm serious. I need to show you all the points on the body that you can cause damage to."

"Maybe we should wait till you get back. I have other plans for you tonight."

She stops me dead in my tracks, and I gently put her back down. "Really?"

"You see, Max, you have no idea what I'm capable of. You think I'm a fragile, porcelain doll, but you couldn't be further from the truth."

"I know you're strong and yet I love that you show me your submissive side."

She sighs and looks away from me as a flush spreads across her cheeks. "I want to experiment and try new things. You're the only man I've ever been with. I want more sexual experiences, and I want them with you." She says so quickly, as if trying to get it over with.

This has been my fear, that I won't be enough for her. My eyes are piercing hers, trying to figure out what she's not saying. She seems apprehensive and nervous, picking at invisible lint on her shirt. "Do you regret not having more sexual experiences?"

"No, of course not. I want to start and end my days only with you. I want to explore every inch of your body, take on new highs with you. I promised I would be totally honest with you." Her fingers are trembling as she runs them up and down my arm. "I don't want to fall into a routine. I want to experience loving you and being loved by you. I don't want to ever regret *not* having more sexual experiences with you. Does that make sense?" She leans into me and gently kisses my lips.

I lift her up and she wraps those fantastic legs around my waist. She wants different, I can do different. I gently place her on the kitchen table. "I fully intend on being the only one taking you to new highs. It's important for you to know that I will never hurt you, but I will push the boundaries with you."

Her eyes grow wide. "Um, will I need a *safeword?*"

My jaw tightens. "What do you know about that? What would make you think you need a safeword with me?"

"I might be inexperienced but I have read books, and I've seen movies. This is the twenty-first century, Max. I can tell you I don't understand getting pleasure from pain."

Her innocence is breathtakingly beautiful. "We are lovers and lovers will never need *safewords.* If we are doing something that you're not comfortable with all you ever have to say to me is *stop.* I get no pleasure from giving or receiving pain. What gives me the greatest pleasure is when you let me love you. Everything we experience together gives me the greatest pleasure." I realize that communication is everything for us. I'm determined to keep her forever and in order to do that, I have to let her in. "I will be more open with you, however, you must do the same. If you need something from me that I'm not giving you, then tell me. I promise to try to not treat you like a porcelain doll."

"Well, in that case, before you get on that plane, I need you—bad. You and me, babe—all night."

As my eyes gaze over her body, her nipples harden and I know this is going to be hard and fast. I lift her with one arm and yank down her yoga pants. "Hold on to the edge of the table and don't let go." I drop to my knees taking her pants all the way off. I kiss each foot as I place them on my shoulders. *Oh, these legs are my undoing.* I kiss them very slowly, working my way up one side and down the other. She's using her feet to pull me in closer. When

I finally reach my prize, I gently kiss her. I glance up and smile; the look on her face priceless. She's biting her lip trying so hard not to let go of the table while her legs begin to tremble. I push my fingers in deeper while my tongue never loses contact. That is until her hips begin to lift up and down. She's not going to last. I know she's going to come, so I slow it down almost to a crawl.

She whimpers, with such angst. "Max, why the *hell* are you stopping?"

"Anticipation," is all I say. She takes her hands off the table trying to push me, I stop completely. "Hands on the table or I will stop—*now!*" She grabs the table moaning, and fuck, it's hot! Very slowly, I use my fingers and gently, I spread her wetness from front to back and I feel her tense. "I will be gentle, and remember, you can always say stop." I feel her begin to relax. I work my tongue in and out of her as I push through her barrier with my pinky finger, matching the pace of my tongue. Sensing she's almost there, I take her clitoris between my teeth and gently tug while flicking my tongue. She tries to move her hips but I've got a lock on her legs. Her feet are kicking my shoulders. She is screaming my name over and over again, like the song of an angel.

I stand up and drop my sweats while lifting her off the table. "You can let go now, but wrap those beautiful legs around me!" I gently slide my cock up and down gathering the sweet essence of her. I enter her very slowly. But slow is not what I need, and it's not what she wants. "We're going hard and fast, baby," I warn her before I begin pounding into her. And she's taking it all. I feel the sharp piercing of her nails breaking the skin of my shoulders. "Oh bloody hell with the fucking nails, babe!" I slow it down, trying to gain some sense of normal. There is no stopping; I can't slow down. I pull back and pound into her, all the while, pulling her hips in hard to meet mine. My legs are shaking and I feel my blood surging through my veins. I look down at the sight before me, and that's all I need. "Oh, Jackie, fuck . . . I'm coming, baby." I explode with her like nothing I've ever experienced in my lifetime; we are both gasping, trying to gain some sort of control. "Babe, you okay?"

"More than okay," she hums.

"God, Jackie, I don't think I'll ever get enough of you. I'm going to try to move as soon as I can feel my legs again." Within a few moments, my legs come back to life. I carry her into our bedroom and crawl into bed. As I run my fingers up and down her spine, the thought of leaving tonight—leaving her—is killing me. I hold her in my arms until she falls asleep. Something is still bothering me with that file. I pull the quilt over her, while throwing on my discarded sweats, before heading into my office to look at it again. Spreading the file out, I take one document at a time. What the hell am I not seeing? Jax and Raven make lists for everything, but not me. I close my eyes and visualize each piece of paper . . . every word. Finally, it hits me, the piece of the puzzle that I've been missing. I've been so focused on his other families that I almost missed the most basic thing. I need to talk to Jax. I'm about to call him, when I hear her come up behind me.

"Max, I woke up and you were gone."

"I'm sorry. You fell asleep, and something has been nagging at me."

She sits in my lap and begins lightly stroking the scar on my head. She knows this helps with the tension. "Oh no, Max, your tingle sense?" *Just the mention of it freezes her in her tracks.*

"Yeah, every time I pick up that damn file. I finally figured it out. I was just about to call Jax, but it can wait."

She picks up the phone and hands it to me. "Call him right now. I know if you don't, it will be in the back of your mind."

"I love that you get me, babe. I'm going to head up to the main house; it shouldn't take too long." I gather up the file and run out the door, calling Jax along the way.

Chapter Three

Jaxson

I HEAD INTO THE kitchen and find Max waiting for me. "Hey, mate, this better be fucking good. I was having the time of my life, you know."

"Trust me, Jax, so was I," he grumbles. "Something was bothering me with that file."

"What's the problem?" I question.

"I was so focused on the other families he destroyed, that I almost missed it. Remember your mum said he was in sales? Well, when I looked into his past, the only thing it ever said was just that. It never said what he sold, or any companies he was affiliated with. It was all very vague. How did he make so much money to be able to live the life he's living? I checked to see if he was living off any of the women he was with, but they were not well off at all. Something's missing and it's bugging me."

"Max, what the hell could he be into? Do you think it's drugs?"

"Honestly, I don't know. I have to tell you, though—I'm not thrilled about this trip. I know you need answers, but at what price?" He paces.

"I would say wait but I'm not sure Bella will go for it. Aside from being a serial bigamist, nothing in the report showed any criminal activity."

"Don't you think I noticed that? There isn't even a fucking parking ticket! No one lives that clean, Jax." He throws his hands out in a frustrated manner. He pulls out the chair across from me and tosses the file in my direction as he sits.

"What are you thinking, that maybe he works for someone or some company that's keeping him clean?"

"Wouldn't be the first person to be a front man. I just don't like it." He rocks back and forth in his chair.

"Do you think we should take everyone with us?" I ask. Max knows me, he can figure out what I'm thinking without me having to say it. He must know I'm not comfortable with leaving my family behind.

"No way, Jax. I think it would increase the danger for everyone if they did come with us. I know you're struggling, so am I. Maybe if I talk to Bella, I can get her to wait a few days, giving me some time to dig a little deeper."

I rub my temples, trying to subside the headache I feel rolling in. "Good luck with that one. You know that Bella is like a dog with a bone." I'm looking at Max and he has a blank stare—shit. "She's right behind me, isn't she? Don't bother answering, I already know. Pull up a chair, sis; we need to talk."

She takes a seat next to mine, her eyes dart to the open file. "What seems to be the problem?"

Max, being the calmer of the two of us, gestures to take the reins. "Bella, every time I picked up that file, I felt like something wasn't right, I just didn't know what. I finally realized what's off. It says that he works in sales, but there is no company listed. He is squeaky clean without so much as a parking ticket. Something is off; no one is that clean."

"Look, I need answers, but I understand if you don't want to go. I'm going and I was looking for you to see if you think I should bring Michael Jr. He could meet his grandfather . . ."

All I hear is Bella wanting to bring Junior and my blood boils over. I pound my fist on the table, instantly silencing her. "It will be a cold day in hell before I let him anywhere near Junior! Never will he have an opportunity to meet him—*never!* He hasn't earned that privilege and I doubt he ever will. Do you think this is going to be sunshine and roses? He's a low-life, Bella."

"Then why are you going to see him?" she raises her voice.

"To ask one question . . . *why?*"

"*Why* . . . is that it? Ring him on the bloody fucking phone then, Jax!"

"No. I want to—no, I need to—look him in the eye."

"Are you afraid you're like him? Is that it, Jax? You want to see if the apple really doesn't fall far from the tree? Is that why you need to *look him in the eye?*"

Maxwell

I'VE GROWN UP ALONE, having no idea about how crazy brothers and sisters can actually get with each other. Bella really knows how to push all of Jax's buttons. She just hit the nail on the head.

"Enough!" An suddenly yells from behind us, grabbing everyone's attention. "If the three of you insist on going, I can't stop you. Although you don't always act it, you're adults. I will, however, draw the line when it comes to my grandchildren. Under no circumstances will James get anywhere near them. You're all adults and can make your decisions. You can deal with the consequences of those decisions, but they are innocent children."

With the silence blaring, I decide to be the first one to speak up. "Ma'am, can I ask you a few questions?"

"Of course, what's troubling you?"

"Well, there is never a mention as to what company James worked for, or what he sold. He's squeaky clean, almost too clean. Do you know anything that's not in the file?"

"Maxwell, my head was in the clouds when I was with him. I was a foolish girl who thought the sun rose and set with James. He said sales and I never asked. When I was forced to go back home with Jax and Bella in tow, my family disowned me. My brother called my children *bastards*. I walked out that day and never looked back."

I'm watching Jax; his jaw is tight and his fists are balled. I have a funny feeling I know what has set him off. "Why did you never tell anyone about your brother?"

"The day he called my children bastards was the day he died in my eyes. I would have given him the shirt off my back if he needed it. When it comes to my children, I will go to the depths of hell to protect them."

Bella stands up and takes a deep breath. "Max, you've got two days and then I'm on that plane." She walks out leaving an eerie silence behind her.

"Ma'am, is there anything else that you've kept quiet about? I understand why and I don't blame you, but now—for safety—reasons I need to know it all."

"I have no secrets. I never told you about my brother, Rhodri, because in my heart, he died that day. I don't know whatever came of him. I do know he was very active in his church. I don't even know if my parents are still alive."

"What did your parents say when you came home?" I push. She bows her head, keeping her gaze downward. She must feel like she is reliving the humiliation all over again. Jax and I glance at each other quickly over her disposition. It stops me dead in my tracks.

Jax grabs her hands, "Mum, if this is too much then stop."

"Are you sure you boys need to hear this? As painful and humiliating as this is, if it means that my family will be safe, then I will."

I look toward Jax and nod. "Ma'am, as much as you want this to stay buried, I can't, in good conscious, let any of us go there without all the facts. Safety always comes first. Would you rather tell me in private?"

"Maxwell, what I'd rather do and what needs to be done are two totally different things. Jax, please get your sister; she might as well hear it all. I will only tell you one time, and then I never want to speak about him again."

Jax goes to get Bella as I pour An a brandy. "Drink this; you look like you need it."

I watch her take the glass and her hands are trembling. She is visibly shaken by all of this. Jax and Bella are back and I see that they notice An's struggle. Hell, you'd have to be blind not to.

Bella puts her arms around An. "Mum, it's okay, you know nothing you tell us will ever change the love and respect we have for you." Bella gives her another squeeze before she pours herself a brandy. I set up my phone to record everything. Bella furrows her brows at me. "Is that really necessary, Maxwell?"

"Unfortunately, yes. I need to record this so nothing is forgotten. Take your time, ma'am."

She takes a few slow sips of her brandy, closes her eyes, and finally finds her voice. "As you know, I was born in Wales. My father worked in the shipyard in Cardiff Bay. My mother was a homemaker. I have an older brother, Rhodri. My parents were very proud of him; he was on track to become a minister. I wanted to become a nurse, so I volunteered after school at the hospital as a nurse's aide. One day, during my shift, your father came into the emergency room in need of stitches. I couldn't take my eyes off of him; he was so very handsome. We got to talking and he told me he was in sales. When I asked him what he sold, all he said was *'importing and exporting rare things.'* I asked him what kind of things and he spun a tale about rare artifacts. I could blame my youth; I was only seventeen. But the reality was, I believed him because I wanted to." She's tearing a tissue into a million tiny pieces.

I reach over and pull out a pad from one of the kitchen draws. I begin to make notes of questions I have. I don't want to stop her, having her lose her train of thought. I hand her a glass of water, "Go on, An."

"Thank you, Maxwell. Anyway, we started dating, but I didn't dare take him home. He was older than me and I knew my father wouldn't approve. I continued seeing him on the sly. Every week, James would go away for days at a time. I should have questioned him, but it created an air of mystery around him. Every time he came back, he would bring some sort of exotic trinket."

I take her hand and stop her, "Do you still have any of them?"

"I only kept a few. Are they important?"

"Everything, at this point, is important. We can look at them later. Go on, please."

"I think I knew he was trouble, but I was a naïve girl. He talked about all the places he visited and how he wanted to take me along with him. I believed every word of the tale he spun. Sometimes, he *would* take me on day trips with him. He always introduced me as his fiancée, which I found very exciting. He had lots of money and he always spent it on me."

An lifts her glass of water to take a sip, but her hand is shaking so bad, she gives up and puts it back down. "Ma'am, if you need a break then please stop."

"No, I want this over with. I don't want to keep reliving my shameful past."

Jax takes her hand, trying to offer his support. "There's no shame here; you were an innocent girl."

"Jax, I was not that innocent. I knew he was trouble, but I was excited with the mystique that surrounded him; he was so mature and worldly. He was my first love, and I was clueless about so much. I trusted him with my heart and my body in the short time we dated. I felt like I was on a secretive whirlwind romance and soon, I found myself pregnant and unmarried." She quickly looks away, avoiding any eye contact. "I went to him and told him and he said I should handle it."

Jax slams his fist on the table, startling everyone. "He told you to *handle it?!'* Was he expecting you to get an abortion?" His voice growing louder as he runs his hands through his hair, practically pulling it out of his head!

An quickly wipes away her tears. "Jax, he never said anything other than 'handle it.' I didn't know what to do, I was too afraid to tell my parents. I went to my brother first; I really trusted my brother and felt he would understand. Rhodri flipped out on me and went straight to father. My father had a lot of friends on the docks and they went and paid James a visit. It was right after that we were ushered in to the court house. And . . . just like that . . . we were married."

It's eating me up inside, asking her to relive all of this, but I have no choice. She is always the strong one. The one that we turn to, the one everyone leans on. I clasp her hands and try to offer some sort of comfort. "Go ahead, ma'am." I nod in encouragement.

She shakes her head lightly and takes in a deep breath. "We had set up house not far from town, and everything seemed to be fine. I finished school and began my studies as a nurse. Soon, I found myself pregnant again. James said he was happy and that he rather I stay home to take care of the children. His time home started getting less and whenever I would question him, he would always claim it was business. Sadly, I believed him. Besides, I was too wrapped up in my pregnancy to dig any further, if I wanted to. Once Isabella arrived, he seemed to be around even less. Isabella had a rough first year; she was sick a lot as well as colicky. When I think back to the time right before he left, he seemed distant and preoccupied. One day, he left and never came back. I needed to pay the rent and my children needed food, so I went to my mum for advice. She told me I needed to be strong and deal with it. She said, '*you're not a child anymore. You chose this path, now deal with it.'* That was the day I decided to look for him. I went to see Garth, a friend of mine from high school. He had just opened his own investigation business and agreed to help me find James."

I have a million questions, but right now, I need to take it slow. Before you go any further, I have quite a few questions. The records show he was born in Scotland—the Highlands, to be exact. How did he end up in Wales? How long was he in Wales before you met him? How did you track him down? Did he have any bank accounts that you were able to access? Did you ever hear him talking business? Where were these 'day trips' he took you on?"

She gets a distant empty stare and her bottom lip begins to tremble. Oh *fuck,* I want to kill the bastard. I pour her some water. She is shaking so much, the water spills out of the glass as she takes it.

Jax jumps up so quickly, his chair practically knocks over, "Enough! This is not a few questions!"

"No, Jaxson, this information might be helpful. It could mean everyone's safety."

Bella grabs Jax's hand and pulls him back down. "Jax, let Mum finish, it's important to all of us."

"I told Garth everything I knew about James, which really wasn't much. James said he was born in Scotland. He said he went away to university and never went back. He said his family was deceased. He was in Wales on business, and I'm not sure for how long before I met him. He had no bank accounts anywhere. Nothing was in his name; not the apartment or any of the bills. The last week we were together, I heard him yelling at someone on the phone, but I don't remember much. My focus was on you two." She glances at Jax and Bella, then back to me. "The trips were always by train around London."

"Tell me about the cut: how did he get it, where was it and how deep?"

"Maxwell, does it matter?"

"You know me, An—everything matters. Close your eyes and picture the cut. Describe what you see."

She closes her eyes and seemingly gathers her thoughts. "He walked into the emergency room holding a bandage on his right arm. I helped gather all the necessary information from him and then took him back to a room. The nurse pulled away the bandage to expose his wound. She informed him that it was deep and would require stitches. She asked him how he got it. He laughed it off, saying he was messing around with his friends. He needed twenty-six stitches. Now tell me, how does that help you?"

I get up and begin my pace. "It tells me he was in a knife fight and that he is left-handed."

"You're right, Maxwell, he was left-handed but, how could you possibly know that?"

"A wound that size was probably not from horsing around with friends. From where you described the location of the wound, it tells me he put his right arm up to block the knife, and his left hand would have reached for it. Did your friend find out anything else?"

"Yes, Garth found out he was married, but I didn't believe him. I could not imagine that the man I loved and trusted would betray me in the cruelest way possible. That's why I went to see for myself."

I stop pacing and pull her out of her chair and into my arms. This woman has become so much to me, I hope someday I will be able to express that to her. I hold her tightly as she begins to cry. "I'm so sorry that I had to put you through this. I'll need to see those trinkets now, please."

"Of c-course, Maxwell. I'll be right back." She leaves and I have a seat.

The three of us sit around the table, staring at each other . . . waiting. "Jax, believe me, mate, if there was any other way, I would never have put her through this."

He pours himself a scotch, staring at the amber liquid as if all the answers are buried there. "I know, Max. What the hell was this man into?"

Before I can answer, An walks in with a box. "Here is everything I kept. I really don't know why I kept it all, maybe to remind me of the fool I was."

Jax leaps up, startling all of us. "Don't ever consider yourself a fool; you did nothing wrong. I will have none of that, you hear?! The only person to blame is my father." Emotions are running high; we all need to dial it down a notch.

"An, maybe you could make us some tea, please." I quickly shoot a look at Jax that I know he'll understand. When An makes tea, it calms her. I walk over to the box and lift the lid. I'm quickly looking through the contents. Shock is all I can register; I know exactly what my father was into.

I begin to close the box when Bella gets up, "What's in the box, Max?"

She reaches in and lifts up one of the necklaces. I quickly take it from her and whisper in her ear, "Not now, Bella."

Jax follows An. "Mum, let me help you with the tea."

"Maxwell, is anything in the box useful?" An glances over her shoulder at me.

"It's too soon to tell, however I will go through it later. I think we've all had enough for today."

"Thank you. I would like to lie down for a bit, if you would excuse me, please."

The minute An is out of ear shot, Jax and Bella are all over me. "Max, what the fuck is in the box?"

"Calm down," I hold my hand up for emphasis. "I had my suspicion from the story An told, but I knew, from the moment I lifted the lid, what the old man was into. Both of you take a look and tell me what you see."

Bella lifts the lid and begins to pull them out. Each one is more spectacular than the last. When she pulls out the last one, she gasps. Her eyes are wide and as she opens her mouth to speak, but only silence is uttered.

Jax picks up some of the items. As he looks at them, his jaw becomes tight and his face reddens. He's going to lose it, and I might not be able to stop him. "Jax, please try and calm down; think of your mum."

"Max, are these real?" Bella finally finds her voice.

"One look at these, and even to a layperson, such as myself, I can see they are very valuable. I also venture to say that the '*day trips*' were for moving the merchandise around. I don't think An had a clue to any of this."

Jax closes his eyes and takes a few deep breaths. "Max, do you think he was a fence, a thief, or both?"

"I'm not sure. I'm going to look into some of these pieces and see if I can find out anything about them. In the meantime, I really think we should hold off for a couple of days. You've waited this long, a few more days to confront him won't matter."

Bella gets up and as she heads toward the door, she stops and turns on her heel. "I'll give you two days, but then I'm leaving. I want answers—answers that only *he* can give me."

With that, she's gone, leaving Jax and me alone. "You're very quiet, what are you thinking?"

"I'm thinking this is a big arse can of worms we've opened. I'm also thinking . . . if this is true, then there is a lot more danger than we originally thought. Are two days going to be enough? You know Bella; when she makes up her mind there's no changing it."

"I don't know what to think anymore. I wouldn't have believed it, but seeing all of this stuff with my own eyes changes that. I better get started figuring this out to meet Bella's deadline." I gather everything up and put it back in the box. "Go spend time with Raven and Antonia. If I need you, I will let you know." I leave him alone with his thoughts and head back toward my place. Right now, all I want and need is Jackie.

Chapter Four

Jackie

MAX HAS BEEN GONE a lot longer than I thought he would be. I gave up on him joining me for a soak in our beautiful tub. I'm hungry. Maybe I can attempt to cook something. Oh, who am I kidding? Unless it's salad or coffee, I'm screwed. I throw on one of his shirts and head into the kitchen just as he walks in with a box. His face is pale. "Max, what happened?" He closes his eyes and seems to be at a loss for words.

He puts the box on the table and lifts the lid. "Jackie, look at all of this and tell me what you see."

By the look of disbelief on his face, I'm almost too scared to look. I'm finally able to pull my eyes away from him and take a peek. "What I see are some very expensive pieces of jewelry thrown in a box." As I dig around some more, I find a few pictures and pull them out. They are of An and a man that I can only assume is James Phillips. "Max, what's this all about?"

"Well, I figured out what was bothering me. Nowhere in the file did it ever say what kind of sales James was in. I finally had to sit down with An and have her tell me everything she could remember about him. When she said she had some *trinkets,* I asked to see them."

"No! You think he was a thief?"

"As much as I don't want to believe it, yes I do. What other explanation could there be?"

"You don't think An knew this, do you?"

"At that time, I don't believe so; she was only seventeen when she met him. But now, I'm sure she realizes a lot more."

"What are you going to do? Are you still leaving tonight?"

Maxwell

WHENEVER SHE'S NERVOUS, SHE bites her bottom lip; her teeth are digging into it. "No, not tonight." I brush a few strands of hair off of her face. She closes her eyes, takes a deep breath, and when she opens them again, they are filled with tears.

"When will you go? Don't try and tell me you're not."

"Bella gave us two days before she's on that plane."

"That doesn't leave you much time. What's the plan?"

"Well, for starters, I need to figure out where these came from. I'm not sure if he's the middle man, the thief, or the fence."

I close my eyes and rub my temples. She knows I do this when my head starts to pound. She takes a hold of my hands and pulls them away from my head. "Max, come with me now."

"Gladly, baby." *God, she's beautiful.*

"I can't have you getting this stressed out. You know how I worry about you." She takes me into the living room and we sit by the fireplace. She wraps her arms and legs around me as I nestle between her legs.

"I think you're on overload right now. You need to organize your thoughts and make a plan."

"I think I'm going to take a picture of each piece and do a Google image search to figure out if there is any information on them. That could lead me to any reports of stolen jewelry and any insurance claims. I'm not an expert, but they look to be very expensive. An said she met him when he came to the hospital. She was studying to be a nurse and he came in with a cut. I've determined it was from a knife fight."

"How could you know that if you weren't even there?"

"He claimed he was horsing around with friends. He needed twenty-six stitches and, from where it was, it sounded like a defensive wound." I nuzzle in closer as she rubs my head.

"You only have two days and there are quite a few pieces there. I can help you with the search." She continues nursing my temples.

"I will take all the help I can get. I know Bella won't budge on the time-line. I swear, sometimes she is worse than Jax. I need to take my mind off of this for a bit. What happened with the new horses that came in today?"

"The colt seems to be pretty mellow and easy to work with. The filly is going to be trouble. I'm not sure she will work out. I'm going to work with her exclusively to see if she can be a good fit."

"You know I worry every time you go out there. All the reassurance and protective gear doesn't help me." My whole body tenses as I think about this. I close my eyes and sigh.

"I know, but I can't live in a bubble—none of us can." *If it were up to me,*

I would put her in a gilded cage, inside a plastic bubble if it meant she would be safe.

I turn in her arms and kiss her so tenderly. "Babe, I love you. I love everything about you. I love how you giggle every time you take your first sip of orange juice, and I don't even know why, yet, I still love it. I love the submissive side that you're not afraid to show me. I love your strength in everything you do. I love how gentle you are with the kids when you're teaching them about the horses. I love how you calm me, yet, I love how you make my heart race. I love falling asleep with you in my arms and waking up with you still there. I love how you tuck the blankets in around us like a cocoon. I love your endless legs—God, do I love them. I heard something one of the kids said the other day by Winnie the Pooh, *'If you live to be one hundred, then I want to live to be one hundred minus one so I never have to live a day without you'.*" I reach in my pocket and pull out a box that has been burning a hole all week. "I know you said you would marry me, but I need the world to know. I need them to know that you saved me when no one else could."

She opens the box and begins to tremble. I think this just became real for her. "Do you like it? I designed it myself. I wanted a heart-shaped diamond. My heart will always be in your hands." I take the ring and slide it on her finger and then, I kiss it.

"Max, I love it. You know all I really need is you. It's all I've ever wanted."

"I know but I need it." It's just a whisper, but I know she gets it.

"The first sip always tickles my nose."

"Really?" I chuckle at this revelation, and then give her a soft peck on the lips. "I know you said you wanted a long engagement, but how long are we talking here?" *I know I can't be like Jax, but I'm done waiting.*

She strokes the side of my face and I close my eyes. "Max, this is important to you, isn't it?"

"More than you will ever know."

"Dare I ask why?"

"Cards on the table, baby. Next month I'll be thirty-nine. I've lived half my life already. I'm at the top of the slope with the skis on. If we have a child next year, I'll be fifty-eight when the kid graduates high school, and that's just the first one. I want grandbabies and I want to enjoy them all. I want to experience so much with you." *Her eyes are wide and she is chewing on her bottom lip. I hope I didn't screw myself here.*

"Exactly how many babies are you planning on?"

"I grew up as an only child. I never want that for my own. All the responsibility falls to that one kid. You said yourself that with the big age difference between you and Dylan, it was like being an only child. It's lonely most of the time. I know that Junior and Antonia are here. And, knowing Jax, he is probably trying to talk Raven into having another baby already. But no one stays around forever."

"I agree with you about having more than one child, however, please understand, I'm not a baby factory! I get that you're going to be thirty-nine and you want to enjoy life. We said early spring; how about the end of May? My understanding is that Scotland, in the spring, is spectacular."

"Little more than six months; I can deal with that. I know you're not a baby factory, but at least two, please. Think of the fun we will have."

"I love you, Max." She gives me a squeeze then pats my back lightly. "Come, we need to get started on that jewelry. Two days is not a long time, and you know Bella."

I gather her in my arms and head toward the office.

Isabella

I TAKE MY TEA and head up to my room. It was a long flight from Italy and I know Michael is already asleep. I go into my sitting room so I don't wake him. I gave them two days to get it together. Reality is—I would give them more, if they really needed it. I don't think they do. I know that Max doesn't want to go, and now with Antonia, I'm sure Jax would put it off. I need answers, though. I need to know why he left. Was I to blame? I don't think so, but I need to ask. I thought maybe I could forgive him and try to have a relationship with him. But, after seeing my mum reliving her past all over again—a past that she felt shamed by—I realize that's impossible. He put her through hell. Poor Cindy made him the center of her universe; she saw death as her only option. How could she do that to her child? This family has been through so much, I'm not sure we can take another blow. Maybe I should forget about him, but now, I have *more* questions.

"Bella?"

I leap out of my chair, nearly spilling my tea. "Michael, I didn't hear you come in."

"I called your name, but you never answered. I didn't mean to startle you. Why are you sitting here, alone in the dark?"

"Max had some more questions before we could leave." I begin to explain everything that went down: all the new information we gained from Mum, the possibilities behind the trinkets, and my deadline. He sits there in silence. "Michael, did you hear me?! He's a thief!"

"I heard you, Bella. I don't want you to go. I don't see any good coming from this. You know what the man is, and meeting him will change nothing. Do you think you're going to have a warm and fuzzy family reunion? If he wanted that, he would have gotten in touch with you years ago. It's not like we were in hiding. You need to let this go, if not for your sake, then do it for Junior."

"Don't you dare throw Junior in my face; you know I would do anything for my son. I feel like if I don't see this through to the end, then I will always wonder 'what if.'"

"For Christ sake, what if *what?* He's a crook and a dead beat. He left because he wasn't man enough, not because of anything you did. I read the file, love. He finds his mark and fucks them; that's what he does. They mean nothing to him and, by what you're telling me now, he probably uses them as a front. Is that someone you want in your life? I won't have him anywhere near my son—*ever!*"

"How can you be so cut and dry, Michael?"

"Sometimes, it really is black and white—you just have to open your eyes and take off the blinders, Bella." He takes my cup of tea and sets it down. "Come back to bed, my love."

I reach for him and he pulls me tightly to his chest. I'm even more confused now than before. "Michael, I will think about it tomorrow, right now, help me forget . . . please."

Anwan

THIS HAS BEEN SUCH a difficult day, reliving the hurt and shame. My shame. A shame that I thought I kept buried for so many years. I don't know what to tell my children . . . to make them give up the idea that they will get answers from James. I know him better than anyone. I know they are going to walk away with more questions than answers. I learned the hard way how deceitful James was. It would be easy to sit here and blame him for everything, but . . . in reality, I'm just as much to blame. When Garth showed me everything, I was in shock. But, then looking back, I realize I had blinders on. I wanted this man to be all that I dreamed he was. The one positive that I took away from all of this was my children. I made them my world, and I don't regret one day of that. I have kept journals from the very first day I met James. Every day with him—documented in black and white. I can't show anyone; they are too personal. But, I still have the report from Garth. It's old;

however, knowing Maxwell, he will want to see it. I go to my closet and pull out my box of journals. I haven't looked at these in so many years; *a reminder of my many mistakes.* I thought about throwing them away, but they are a part of me, a part of who I once was. I pull out the first journal and begin to look at the entries; I was so naive. His good looks and charming ways pulled me into a rabbit hole . . . an adventure into the unknown; one that became a nightmare. As I flip through the journal, I come across a flower that I pressed between the pages: a beautiful, pink Armeria. It was from my wedding day. I don't want to read any of this, but I can't avert my eyes. *"Today I married my soul mate."* What a fool. *"Today James sang to me, he has such a beautiful voice."* The day of Jaxson's wedding, when he sang to Raven, my mind flipped right back to this day, reminding me of how beautiful James sang. I can't do this, putting myself through the hurt again. I flip through some more pages and find the report. I don't think it will be of any use, but I will give it to Maxwell in the morning. As I package up the journals, a picture falls out. It's of a group of men. I remember taking the picture for James. It was from one of our day trips. I will give it to Maxwell with the report. I really wish they wouldn't go. I might be able to convince Jax, but not Bella. She is so much like James and sometimes . . . that scares me.

I go through the rituals of getting ready for bed, but I know sleep won't come tonight. As I lie in bed, I close my eyes and silently pray that my children find the peace they are searching for, the peace that has eluded me for so long.

Chapter Five

Raven

JAX FINALLY CAME TO bed, but it was almost dawn. I could tell he was upset, but when he's ready, he will tell me everything. I have to tell him that I received a package yesterday from Hage; enclosed is a letter from Duke. I'm concerned that this will only add more stress on his plate. I look over at him and, even in sleep, he seems troubled. I am trying not to interfere but I think it's time I have a talk with Bella. She is the only person who can stop this before it goes too far.

Suddenly, I hear Antonia over the baby monitor; however, I knew it was feeding time before she announced her hunger. I reach over and kiss Jax before heading into the nursery with Bo quickly following next to me. I scratch his neck and sigh, not even Bo is getting a full night sleep.

Entering, I notice that Jax had set up the *Doctor Who* night-light and I giggle. He can be such a playful little boy and I hope he never loses that. I pick up Antonia, kissing her soft curls and begin changing her. When she first starts to eat, she always makes her little hands into fists. This is my favorite time of the day; it's quiet and I can enjoy sitting in front of the window with my daughter, overlooking the fields. I swear she has the best view in the house. Watching the change of seasons from this window will be breathtaking. I haven't looked at the letter from Duke, and I'm not sure I want to. I know Jax will say information is key, but—unlike Jax—I want to be done with the past. My mom is doing so well with her therapy, I've even started going with her. I need to find a balance with her. I've been so independent for so long that I find it hard to let her mother me in any way. I don't know how she survived all that she did. I need to find a way to talk my mom out of confronting Vincent. She thinks this will help her with closure, I think it will only poke a burning fire. I wanted to talk to Jax about it but, with everything going on, now is not a good time. Antonia is done nursing and is fast asleep. I need to talk to Jax. As much as I would rather wait, I know he will get upset if I don't tell him everything right away. As I get Antonia settled into her crib, I can't help but bask in her beauty. She really is a combination of the both of us. She has my thick, black, curly hair and pouty lips. She has

Jax's blue eyes and chiseled cheek bones. I'm so blessed that she survived so much before she even got here.

I head back to our bedroom, quickening my pace at the sound of strange voices coming from there. When I open the door, I see Jax in the throes of a nightmare. I know not to wake him, but my heart feels like it will leap out of my chest. He's never had one before and I know it's the stress that is triggering this. "I waited and waited. Please come back, I'll be good I promise!" he yells out while thrashing. My heart is breaking I can't stand here and listen anymore.

I go to the foot of the bed and try stroking his leg, "Jax, it's Raven, I'm here, Jax," I say softly. He leaps up and opens his eyes; he seems confused, looking around the room almost unsure of where he is. I'm still talking softly, hoping the fog clears for him. He finally hears me, and he must realize where he is.

"Raven, I'm sorry. Did I hurt you?"

"Jax, please don't be sorry and no, you didn't hurt me." I climb into bed and pull him into my arms. He's in a pool of sweat and still shaken. "Shh, don't say anything. Let me hold you, please." As I hold him and stroke his back, he begins to calm down. "I'm going to set up the tub, and then we will get cleaned up."

"I don't want to talk about it, Raven."

I pull his face up to mine and rest my forehead upon his. "When you're ready. And if you're not, that's okay too."

I get up and go set up the tub. I know it will be the best thing to relax him. He walks into the bathroom and he has dark circles under his eyes. " Come get in the tub, please." He climbs in and I climb in behind him so I can hold him for a change. I have so much to tell him about before he leaves, but now I'm not so sure.

"I'm sorry," It's just a whisper but I heard him.

"You have nothing to be sorry for."

"Sweetheart, I need to tell you what I've learned; nothing good, I'm afraid," he adds. I hold him tighter. "After a lengthy meeting with Mum, Bella, Max, and myself, we discovered some things about our father; none of them good."

"How did all this come about?"

"Max and his tingle sense."

"Oh, that's never good. What did he figure out?"

Jax proceeds to fill me in on their meeting and I'm shocked and saddened by what An had to go through, not just with James but her own family too. To know now that James is not only a bigamist but a thief as well. It's all too much to process.

"Jax, please tell me you're not going; clearly, you can see no good will ever come out of this."

"Bella gave us two days and then she is leaving. I can't let her go alone."

"Can't Michael talk to her? She has to see how dangerous this is; she's not a fool."

"I honestly don't think anyone will be able to get through to her."

"What's bothering you? And don't say 'nothing'—I know something is."

"I don't want to load you with anything else, but our deal is no secrets." I mindlessly stroke his chest.

He turns around so he can see me. "Go ahead, I'm listening."

"First, a package came yesterday from Hage, in it was a letter from Duke. Before you freak out, I didn't read it and I'm not sure I want to. Secondly, I went to a therapy session with my mom yesterday and she is talking about confronting Vincent." I wait for the storm that is coming. Surprisingly, he is very quiet. He closes his eyes and tilts his head back. He takes a few deep breaths, probably trying to gain some composure. "Jax, are you going to talk to me?" He lifts his head and opens his eyes. They are dark, very dark.

"Why? Please explain to me why she would want to confront Vincent? She is a smart woman and clearly, she can see no good would ever come of it. I know everyone is in jail. But still, Raven, you have to talk some sense into her."

"I have tried—believe me—I have. She is pretty adamant about it."

"What has the therapist said about it, or is that too personal to ask?"

"I honestly don't know; I wasn't in the session."

"What was in the package that Hage sent?"

"Besides the letter from Duke, there were some papers that Max and I need to sign. They have enough on him that Max and I won't have to testify. I really don't want to go back to the states, but if my mom goes back, I can't let her go alone."

"I understand, but your mum is not going back there. I will have to negotiate with her."

Oh Jax and his new found negotiating skills. "What if that doesn't work?"

"I will never let you anywhere near Vincent. If I have to, I will take her myself."

"I love you, but please go easy on her. Now let's get out of here; the water is getting cold and I'm hungry." I get up and give him my hand. He reaches for it and kisses the inside of my wrist. I shudder; his lips will *always* have that effect on me.

Maxwell

JACKIE AND I SPENT hours combing the Internet and the results weren't good. She finally fell asleep on the sofa. I need to head back to the main house and let everyone know what we found out. I love that we live close to everyone, yet we have our own sanctuary. I need both, more than anyone will ever realize. I look up from the computer and watch my sleeping angel. I can't wait to get married and start a family. I lift her up and carry her to bed; the bad news can wait a little longer. I need her softness, it's what grounds me. Through her, I see the good in the world. Through her, I see hope. That's what makes me want to have children again. As I carry her, she nuzzles into my neck. "Mmm, Max, where are we going?"

"To bed; I need to lose myself in your loving arms for a while."

She's kissing my neck and I might not make it to the bedroom. She begins to run her finger up the back of my neck, massaging my head. She knows I have a headache . . . she always knows. "How bad is your head, Max?"

"Nothing that an hour or two—lost in you—won't cure, baby."

"You never slept, did you? You can't keep doing this, Max. You'll be no good to anyone if your head gets worse. Promise me you will rest."

"I promise, just as soon as I have my way with you." I climb into bed with her still in my arms. She pulls me toward her and softly brushes her lips over mine. "Help me forget for a while, Jackie . . . *please.*"

She slowly kisses me softly, slowly . . . tenderly; feeling her touch relaxes me. "Lose yourself in me, Max."

I slowly peel away what little clothes she has left, leaving a trail of kisses in their wake. Gentle is what I need right now to wipe away all the harsh realities. I kiss up one leg and down the other; magnificent works of art that I will never get enough of. I lock my arms around her legs, spreading her wide for me. Her skin is so soft, and she smells so sweet as I work my way up to her core. I find my prize and she is so ready for me, but I need more. I work my tongue around her clitoris and gently tug with my teeth. She begins to shake and digs her nails into my shoulders. She knows what those nails do to me. She's there, so ready for me. I pull myself up to my knees and rub my cock up and down, stroking her very gently. When I know she's at the edge, I push my way in very slowly. When I'm all the way in, I stop. Her eyes grow wide and she bites her bottom lip. I lean down and brush my lips up her neck. I hold still—hard as stone—throbbing deep within her. I rest my forehead on hers, "Take me, baby."

"Flip me over, Max—*now!*"

My eyes grow wide with wonder. *Wow, demanding Jackie is hot.* I waste no time and follow her command. She's on top of me now and taking full control.

"Shut your mind off now, and give me your hands." She takes my hands and puts them on her breasts, helping me work her nipples, bringing her into a frenzied state. Neither of us is going to last much longer. She begins slowly gliding up and down my cock. My hips are rising up to meet her, slow and steady. Her body begins to flush and I know she's there, trying to take me with her. I start to shake and I know I can't wait any longer. I put my hands on her hips and pull her down hard to meet my upward thrust. That does it, I explode within her. She lets out a whimper and cries out my name. I pull her toward me, holding on tight, feeling her heart race next to mine . . . *beautiful.*

All I can do is whisper, "I love you . . ."

Raven

I GRAB THE BABY monitor and head downstairs to the kitchen. I told Jax to get Antonia cleaned up and meet me in the kitchen. I am going to, at least, learn how to make eggs. When I turn the corner, I find Max and Jackie are already there. *Thank God*—Max is making French toast. I grab a cup of coffee and have a seat. Before I can say anything, the monitor comes to life and what I see and hear next floors me. Max, Jackie, and I sit in front of the screen with our coffee, silently watching the show.

Jaxson

RAVEN ASKED ME TO get Antonia and meet her in the kitchen. I head toward the nursery, and I can hear my beautiful daughter cooing. I scoop her up and begin to change her. "My princess, I love being a dad. If your mum would consent, we would have ten babies. I'm realistic, knowing that will never happen, so I need to negotiate with your Aunt Jackie to get the ball rolling. After all, Uncle Max is not getting any younger. Okay, Antonia, your beautiful mum is attempting to make breakfast. Bless her for trying, but thank God we don't have to survive on what she comes up with. Now here is the plan. I need you to hang out with your Aunt Jackie, and be really good. I need you to make her want to start having babies right away. Now, I know you can do this for me and Uncle Max. Let's pick out something for you to wear that Aunt Jackie got for you. That might help the cause." I go about getting her ready and I can only hope my plan works.

Raven

I'M TRYING NOT TO laugh; even through all the madness, he can still be so playful. I look at Jackie's face, expecting to see her in total shock and instead, she is biting her lip and trying not to laugh. "Jackie, you know he's . . . well . . . he's just being Jax."

"Oh, Raven, I'm not laughing at Jax. I'm laughing because he thinks he wants ten kids!"

After hearing Jax's plan, Max silently goes back to making breakfast. "Max, you're awfully quiet. Please don't tell me you're a part of his crazy plan?"

"Raven, unlike my crazy arse brother, I don't want ten babies . . . five will do."

Jackie's coffee cup crashes to the floor. Max is on her in a second. "It's okay, babe, we can take it one at a time."

I don't think that helped her at all. It's at that moment I notice the ring. Maybe they finally set a date. I'm about to ask when I hear him coming down the hall.

Jax walks into the kitchen with Antonia. "Good morning, everyone." He smiles but it slowly fades as we collectively stare at him. "Okay, why is everyone staring at me? I've only just gotten up, what could I have possibly done now?"

I hold up the baby monitor, "Ten? Really, Jax?" I smirk. It's time for Antonia to eat, so I take her and leave Jax to work himself out of the hole he dug himself into.

Jaxson

"HOW MUCH DID EVERYONE hear?" I have to remember that damn monitor is always on.

Max hands me a cup of coffee. "Enough to screw us both; let's just leave it at that." He smacks my back. "I have information about An's trinkets." He grabs his mug and leans his back against the counter. "It appears they are all stolen. Insurance was paid, so legally, they belong to the insurance companies." he says before blowing into the cup, then taking a swig.

My mum walks in looking dog-tired. I pull her into a hug, "Let me get you some coffee, Mum." She nods then sits down and hands Max an envelope.

"Ma'am, what is this?"

" It's the original report on James from my friend, Garth, and a group picture from one of our day trips that I found in my journal."

I clench my jaw, trying to retain some control. "Mum, is there anything else you might have overlooked that you think we should know?" I try to keep my voice steady.

"Jax, All I have left are my personal journals. If I thought they would keep you from going, I would give them to you. However, I don't believe anything will stop you." She raises a brow as she takes her mug out of my hands.

I look at the baby monitor and see Raven is putting Antonia down for a nap. When I look up, everyone is staring at me. "Don't even say a word, none of you. Max, after breakfast, we have a lot to go over. We have a buyer for the company. And a package came yesterday from Hage. Where is Rose this morning?" I'm surprised Raven's mum isn't joining us for breakfast.

Max turns pale, "I don't think she is back from her daily run yet, is there a problem, Jax?" *I'm not sure Max could handle another thing.*

"I need to talk to her before we leave." I put my mug down and take a seat. Max begins serving up breakfast as Raven comes in with her mum.

"Ahh, Rose, just in time; Max made breakfast. Afterwards, I have some stuff to go over with you. How was your run?" I need to keep things light and my temper at bay.

"It was good. I've been exploring different sections of the property. I don't know if I will ever see it all," she says with exasperation then directs her attention toward Jackie. "Jackie, how are the new horses?"

"The colt will be fine but the filly will need a lot of work. Are you going to come down to the barn again today?"

"Yes, I enjoyed working with the children, that's if you don't mind."

"I would love the extra set of hands."

I take a step back and watch everyone laughing and just being a normal family and I wonder why can't we have this all the time? Is that so much to ask for?

Raven takes my hand, snapping me out of my daydream. "A penny for your thoughts?"

"I'm enjoying the normal for a change, sweetheart." I pull her tight, "Did you put the package on my desk?" I add.

"Back to reality. Yes, and go easy on my mom, *please.*"

"I will, if you promise to go easy on Bella." I lift her chin up and laugh, "I know you just as well as you know me." We finish up breakfast and I grab another cup of coffee. "Come on Max, we've got lots to discuss."

Raven

"CONGRATS ON THE RING; you did good. Now start making babies. You're not getting any younger, mate." I hear Jax talking to Max as they head down the hall.

My mom and Jackie head out to the barn, leaving me with An. "Did you get any sleep? You look tired." I shift in her direction, giving my full attention.

"Not really. I just wish there was something I could say to them to stop them from going. I have a bad feeling about all of this."

"Do you think I have a chance of getting through to Bella? I don't want Jax to go. I don't see any good coming from this."

"My daughter is more stubborn than all of them combined. She is the most like James in looks and temperament." She waves off the idea before picking her cup up for a sip of coffee. "What's going on with your mum? Something is bothering her. I tried to talk to her about it but she didn't say much."

"She wants to confront Vincent. I get why she wants to but I don't think she sees the big picture."

"Raven, do you honestly believe that my son is the best person to talk to her about this? Dear God, you know how he is; poor Rose won't stand a chance."

"I know, but he promised he wouldn't bully her. Besides, she won't listen to me."

"Well, let me know if there is anything I can do to help. I'm going to try and rest for a bit." An heads out and I'm left alone.

I need to piece together what I'm going to say to Bella. Lost in my thoughts, staring out the window, I jump as I hear a noise behind me. I turn and see one of the walls in the kitchen pop open; out steps Michael, Jax's nephew! I gasp, " How did you do that?"

"It's a secret passageway that Uncle Jax found. Come on, I'll show you." He holds out his hand.

I get up and head into the passageway. Michael turns on a flashlight and leads the way, with Bo right behind me. "Michael, how many passageways are there?"

"There are five that Miss Rose and I have explored. There is one that you can take from the main house all the way to the stables. Uncle Max showed me that one. Miss Rose and I were going through them, when we noticed strange carvings on the walls."

"You and my mom come through here?"

"Oh, Miss Rose loves to explore with me. She's the best!" he states enthusiastically.

I'm happy they enjoy spending time together, exploring. "Where does this one lead?"

"There is a spiral staircase up ahead. Once we climb that, we will be right outside my bedroom door. Isn't this great?"

I laugh at his excitement and I'm sure Jax was just as excited. "Michael, maybe tomorrow you can show me another one."

"Sure, Aunt Raven, that would be fun. If you look to the right, there is another tunnel. But, I haven't been down there yet."

We get to the top of the steps and he presses on the wall. It pops open. Sure enough, we are right outside his bedroom. "Thanks for the short cut, Michael. I need to talk to your mom."

"No problem. I'm going into my room to watch some television."

He doesn't seem to be his usual energetic self. He never wants to sit around and watch television, only if it's *Doctor Who,* of course. He seems a little off. I hope he's not getting sick. "Michael, you feel okay?"

"Just a little tired, Aunt Raven."

"Go get some rest." I watch him head off into his room and I go look for Bella.

Chapter Six

Jaxson

MAX AND I HEAD into my office to discuss business. I need to see what Hage sent and I know Max wants to tell me what he found out. However, first order of business is Jackie. "Max, what happened with Jackie?"

"Jump right in, why don't you, mate? I had the ring made and then I waited until I figured out exactly what I wanted to say. Of course when I started, it was like one giant run-on sentence. I persuaded her to get married sooner rather than later. I want a family, but I realized this morning that she's scared."

"What do you think she's scared of?"

"I don't think it's of being a mum; she is great with all children. I think it has to do with actually having the child. I need to figure out her fear and then fix it."

"Did you try asking her? I mean that just seems to be the logical approach."

"No, Jax, I haven't because I haven't had a minute to breathe."

"Well, the sooner we get this all done, the better for everyone. What did you find out about the trinkets?"

Max gets up and walks over to the window. He picks up the binoculars I keep close by and begins looking out over the vast property. "Jax, every piece was high-end and stolen. Insurance was paid on them. If he was acting as a fence, then why keep them? I think he is the thief. I don't know why he gave them to An. Based on all the reports and what An said, it's not like they were living in luxury."

"When were they stolen and from whom? Could the people or the places have had any meaning to him or Mum?"

"I don't know yet, but I do know that two days is not enough. We need to talk to Bella."

"Yeah, well, Raven was going to try and talk some sense into her today," I inform him. Max cocks his head and raises one eyebrow. "Yeah, Max, I know, but you got to love her for trying."

" How long is it going to take for the Raiders Inc. deal to go through and are you happy with the terms?"

"It should be closed in six months, possibly sooner, since it's a private company. I'm happy; I think we got a fair price. We need to look at whatever Hage sent over. Raven said there is a letter from Duke. But, we have a bigger problem to deal with, Rose wants to confront Vincent."

"Jax, we have to stop her. I know she thinks this will bring her some sort of closure, but it won't, trust me, I know. Revenge didn't help, it only added to the nightmares I have to live with."

I never asked him, but knowing Max, I didn't have to. "I'm going to try and talk to her today. I can't say it's going to be easy." I hand Max the package from Hage. "We need to deal with this. I thought part of Duke's deal was no contact ever?"

"Yeah, well, it says here that the only way Duke would agree to the terms was if this letter was sent to Raven. I'm sure, at that point, Hage would do whatever he had to do. At least Hage left Raven and I out of everything. The book with all the details of Vincent's dealings was enough for Hage to offer Vincent a plea deal; life—with no chance of parole in exchange for his testimony." I shrug. Max throws the papers on the desk, his face taking on a look of disgust. "What's the problem?"

"Who's to say that he won't be running his business from a jail cell? We have to talk Rose out of her plan to confront him. I'm sure if we explain to her that he can still be a danger to Raven, it would stop her."

"Max, I will negotiate with her. Don't laugh at me; I'm getting better at this every day. Do you think the papers Mum gave you will help in any way?"

"At a quick glance, the investigators papers seem pretty basic. It's the picture that I'm interested in. I'm not sure what it is about the picture, but I have to tell you, something seems almost familiar about it. I'm not sure, but I'm going to run it through an age progression program to see what comes up." He gathers up his stuff and heads out, leaving me to figure out how to stop Rose.

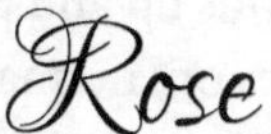

Rose

I ENJOY SPENDING TIME in the barn with Jackie. She is so comfortable to be around. She never pressures me; she just lets me be. Today, however, I can tell something is bothering her. She seems distant and troubled, quieter than usual. I take the brush from her hand and put my arm around her. "You look like you could use a hug. Do you want to tell me what's wrong?"

Her bottom lip begins to tremble and she starts to cry. "Shh, I've got you, Jackie; come sit down and tell me what's wrong. Nothing is so bad that it can't be fixed." We head over to a bale of hay and sit for a bit. I hold her in my arms, keeping my silence, I let her cry.

"Rose, I love him with all of my heart. But, I'm afraid." I'm glad that she feels comfortable talking to me. I try to be like a mom to her, knowing that she must miss her family.

"Tell me what you are afraid of? You know I would never judge you." I gently rub her back, offering her some comfort.

"Max wants a lot of children and I'm scared."

"Look at me," I demand softly and lean back as she raises her head. "It is natural to be scared of the unknown. I was scared when I was pregnant with Raven, and I'm a doctor." I wipe away her tears. "You can read all the books in the world, but until you actually do it, you won't know what to expect. That can be very scary. Gather strength from everyone around you. We are your family and we would never let anything happen to you. I promise you, every step of the way, I will be here for you, even if it's just to hold your hand. What else is bothering you, sweetie?"

"I was a twin. My sister, Madeline, didn't make it past a few hours. I was born first and apparently, I was the strongest. My mom is Japanese, Rose, and very small. The doctors were afraid she wouldn't make it to term. She went early and my sister just couldn't survive."

"Do you blame yourself for being strong? You know, logically, that's not true." She's very quiet, twisting her fingers in her lap. "Jackie, why haven't you told Maxwell?" She is biting her bottom lip, seemingly hesitant.

"What if something like that happens to me? Max will never survive and I don't think I would either."

I take her hands in mine. "Jackie, after I had Raven, I became pregnant again." Her eyes grow wide. "That's right. I was pregnant and I lost the baby at twenty-six weeks. It was very hard on Antonio, but even harder on me. I had to go through delivery and then bury my baby. We grieved, but we knew we did nothing wrong." I lift her hands up and place them on my heart. "Do you feel my heart beating? It still goes on, no matter what. The point is, you were not responsible for Madeline. Whatever happens, you will deal with it, and so will Maxwell. You can't try to stop every bad thing from ever happening; it's life. Be the best you can be and everything else will fall into place. You do, however, need to talk to Maxwell. He has the right to know your fears. You say you love him, well then trust him with your heart." I hold her in my arms and comfort her as her mother would. In the distance, I see Maxwell. "Jackie, Maxwell is on his way over here, and I think it's time you tell him everything."

"Okay," she barely whispers.

I wipe away her tears, kiss her forehead. Maxwell crouches down in front of Jackie. "Hey, babe, what's the matter?"

"I'll leave you two to talk." I'm not sure either one of them heard me, and that's okay. I start heading back to the main house to talk to Jax.

Maxwell

"OKAY, JACKIE, I'M NOT going anywhere, and neither are you, until you tell me everything. If I have to, I will lock you in the house and throw away the key!" I have to try and calm down. I can't scare her.

"Max, I'm cold; let's go inside and talk." Before she can say anything more, I put my arms around her and we head toward the house. I don't know why she is so upset, but I could never leave her like this. We get inside and she curls up on the couch, I cover her with a blanket. I light the fireplace and then make her a cup of tea. The ritual of making the tea has a calming affect. I snuggle up to her, pulling her into my arms. "Now, talk to me. Surely you know that you can tell me anything; I would never judge you."

She is chewing on her bottom lip and I gently pull it out from her teeth. "I'm afraid to have a baby." She says it so softly, but I hear every word.

"Is that what all this is about? Why now?"

"When you first asked me to marry you and said we could have a long engagement, I thought I could grow into the idea and settle my fears. It seemed so far off, but then last night, you wanted to nail down a date. You gave me a ring; it's real and it's happening. Now you're saying *five* children!"

"Why are you scared? You need to tell me everything, Jackie. I know you're holding back."

She's got a death grip on my hand. "I had a twin sister who died at birth. I thought you might have known when you ran a background check on me, but then you said you didn't look at anything personal, only what you needed for safety purposes."

"Wow, Jackie, I understand some of your fear but not all of it. Listen, you have to know it was not your fault that you lived." I squeeze her to me. "So, what else, babe?"

"Twins run in my family; what if it happens again? I'm afraid something like that would kill you." She looks up at me. Oh my God, she's worried about me . . . about my sanity.

"Babe, you are beyond words. Your kind and generous heart knows no bounds. Whatever is thrown at us, we will deal with together. Plus, medical science is much different today than twenty-five years ago. I don't expect you to be a baby factory. I would love to adopt, especially some of the children with disabilities that you work with. I love them all. But, babe, I really want to have a child with you; it would be a gift. I know how special you are and I want the world to know too. I promise we will do it together—one step at a time." I snuggle her into my arms and hold her tight. She is still so tense, and she's got a tight grip on my arm. I can sense there is something more.

"Hey, you might as well tell me everything, I'm going to find out anyway."

"I need to go home next week," she says quickly. My grip on her tightens.

"This *is* your home—for life."

"My birthday is coming up. Every year, I honor Madeline by having a cupcake at the repository where she's laid to rest. I try to spend the day with my mom, reflecting upon the last year. I have to go, Max."

"I know it's your birthday. I was trying to hold out giving you the ring until then, but it was burning a hole in my pocket. We go together—understood? I spoke to your father and asked for your hand in marriage. Now I can speak to him in person and settle any fears he might have, including that brother of yours."

"You spoke to my father?!"

"Of course, it's what any good gentleman would do. I assured him you would want for nothing in your lifetime, and that I would love you beyond the end of my days. I must say he was quiet impressed."

"What if you're not back in time?"

"I will be back, no matter what happens. I promise."

I pick up the remote and the music comes to life. As I hold her close in my arms, I know without her, I'm a shell of a man. I rock her gently and mindlessly sing to her. The lyrics are so beautiful about a man who is scared of the feelings a woman makes him feel. Stroking her back and softly singing soothes her. "I love you, baby, and I will do anything to make you happy . . . never forget that."

"Max, I've never heard that song, it's beautiful. Who sings it?"

"James Morrison. It's called "You Give Me Something." He's a young bloke, wickedly talented."

"What happened with Jax?"

"Well, we went over business stuff; nothing for you to worry about. He did say that Rose wants to confront Vincent. I don't know what the fuck she's thinking? I just want to keep us all safe."

"What was in the envelope that An gave you?"

"The original report that her friend ran on James and an old picture from one of their day trips. Which reminds me, I want to run the picture through the age progression software that I have. Everyone is so young, but something seems familiar." I sigh. "What's your plan for the rest of the day?"

"I want to go for a run and then, later this afternoon, I have a class coming in. Do you want to run with me?"

"Sure, let me load this picture and change." I get up and head to my office to load the picture. I'm staring at it and my tingle sense comes alive—*fuck!* As the faces begin to age, the locked gates within my mind open. A rage deep within me begins to boil. This can't be happening. The room is spinning out of control; down the rabbit hole, I'm falling. The program finishes, and I freeze on the face of my nightmares.

Raven

I NEED TO TALK to Bella and see if I can persuade her to give up this idea of meeting James, or at least giving her brothers more time. This house is so huge but I finally find her in the kitchen, making coffee. "Hey, Bella, do you have a minute?"

"Raven, I'm not changing my mind, so if that's why you're here, you're wasting your time."

"Bella, please don't get defensive. I would like to talk to you about the trip. Believe it or not, I do understand why you want to go. It took me a while to figure it out, but I got it. What I don't get is why the rush? If you value everyone's safety, why push them? Let them get all the information before jumping in blinded by emotions."

"How much time are we talking here? I will give them a few extra days, but nothing changes for me. I want answers that only he can give me. That man's blood runs through my veins and it disgusts me."

"If you really feel that way, then why go?"

"I look exactly like him. Mum has said many times that I have his personality. How do you think that makes me feel? Knowing what he's done, I need to know why."

"I'm not going to stop you, Bella, but give them some time if they need it, please."

"Okay, I'll go tell Jax." She gets up and heads out to find Jax. Now, if I could get my mom to agree, all would be right for a little bit.

Jaxson

I NEED TO FIND Rose and have a talk with her. I don't want to scare her, but there is no fucking way she is going anywhere near Vincent. I get up to go and as I turn around I find her standing in the doorway. "Rose, I was just coming to find you."

"I figured by now Raven told you and that you would be looking for me."

"Have a seat, please." *I need to try and remain calm.* "I need you to make me understand why you feel you have to see Vincent."

She is quiet for a bit, wringing her hands in her lap. "Jax, that man took so much from me." Her voice is soft and shaky. "I lost my soul mate. My daughter was taken from me and raised by others. I lost my career, which ultimately cost many people their lives. The procedure that I pioneered, had I perfected it, would have saved so many lives. I know that others tried to continue my research, but it was never the same. He destroyed Joseph's life. He raped and beat me. I need him to know that he didn't break me."

"How did he destroy Joseph's life?"

"Joseph was engaged when everything happened. He walked away from the relationship because he felt she would never be safe. He made Raven and me his family. He watched me slowly fade away, and there was nothing he could do about it. He took care of me throughout the pregnancy. He was there when I delivered Duke. I realized Joseph thought there was more to our relationship and, at first, I chose to ignore it, thinking it was only his need to feel needed. Then not to long after Duke was born, he professed his love for me. He built up a vision in his mind that we could live happily ever after. He wanted to keep Duke and raise him as his own. He offered to marry me and make a stable life for all of us. That was the day I tried to take my own life. I realized how much was lost for all of us. I couldn't hurt him."

Shock is all I can register. "Does Raven know any of this?"

"No. What purpose would it serve? It won't change the past; that is dead and buried forever. I know now trying to take my life was wrong. I was overwhelmed with grief, fear, and rage. I didn't know how to deal with any of it. I've had more heartache in my life than anyone person should ever have to endure. Now you tell me, how could I not face the man that was the catalyst for most of it."

I honestly don't have any answers for her. I get up and pour us each a drink.

"Jax, you're very quiet, this is not like you."

"You're right. I'm at a loss here, part of me agrees with you and the other part doesn't. I don't know how to deal with all of this. Have you spoken to your therapist about what you're planning?"

"Yes, however, she doesn't understand the depths of who Vincent is."

"What about safety? Vincent got a deal, Rose. He got life in prison without parole. My fear is that he will continue to conduct his business from jail. Once he knows you're alive, all bets are off. I have to think of everyone's safety. I'm sorry; you're going to have to figure out some other way to come to terms with this."

"You know, Jax, I could leave, if I want to. I'm not a prisoner here."

"You're right, Rose, you can walk out that door anytime you want, however, you won't. You love your daughter and granddaughter too much to do that. Think of their safety."

"I've always put Raven's safety first. You can protect her and Antonia."

"You're right, I can. But if you go, it will break her heart, and I can't have that."

Her eyes grow wide and I know before she says anything, I don't even have to turn around. "Raven, I think you and your mum need to talk." I get up and head toward the door, "I love you and I'm here for you." I kiss her and head out to find Bella.

I MAKE A QUICK detour past the nursery to kiss my daughter. Honest to God, I don't know how I'm going to leave. I make my way downstairs and find Bella in the kitchen. "Hey, sis, I was just coming to find you."

"I spoke to Raven. I will give you a few extra days if you need them. I will tell you, no matter what—*I'm going.* But, for safety purposes, I will give you what you need."

I'm floored, how the hell did my wife do it? "You will?"

"Yes. I want everyone to be safe, Jax. If that's what it will take, then I will."

"I love you." I grab her, pulling her into my arms. "You can't possibly know how much this means to me. I need to find Max, let him know what's going on, and see if he had any luck with that picture."

As I turn to leave, Bella grabs my arm, "What picture?"

"Mum had a picture from one of their day trips. It was a group photo of dad with his friends. Max was going to run it through an age progression program."

"I'll go with you."

We head out toward Max's. I'm surprised he hasn't contacted me yet. Maybe he had no luck with it.

Jackie

MAX WAS SUPPOSED TO change for a run but he never came out of his office. I wonder if he had any luck with the picture. I head toward the office and it's very quiet. *Strange.* I open the door and it's dark. I could swear he was in here. I flip the light on and what I see stops me dead in my tracks; Max, sitting in the dark, almost in a frozen state. I rush up to him, but he's pale and shaking. "Max, please, what's wrong?" He's not saying anything. I hear Jax and Bella come up behind me. Jax takes my arm "Jackie, what the hell happened?"

"I don't know. Please, Jax, help him.

Jaxson

I CROUCH DOWN NEXT to him. "Hey, Max, it's me, mate, what happened?" *Nothing.* I look at the screen to see what he's fixated on, but all I see is the picture that Max aged. I've never seen him like this, not even when his grams died. His eyes are dark and hooded. His fists are clenched and his jaw is tight. He's shaking, pale, and as he closes his eyes, he begins to sob. For the love of *Christ,* what the hell? "Talk to me, Max. I can't help if you don't let me in."

"I told you I was a man out for revenge when my family was slaughtered. I found the murderers and got my justice. I never found the leader . . . until today."

I freeze at his words. "Max, who?"

He points to the man that our father has his arm around, and I feel my heart hit the floor. He growls out the name Miguel Dominguez. Suddenly, Max lets out a roar and in one quick sweep, throws everything off the desk. He's screaming as I try to hold him back, afraid he'll hurt himself. "Max, stop! What the hell are you saying? Who is Miguel Dominguez? Are you suggesting that Dad was somehow involved in Samantha and Elliot's deaths?"

He glares at me, "What the hell else am I supposed to think? My father has his arm around a murdering, Columbian drug lord, laughing and my family is *dead.* Don't tell me it's a coincidence. I don't do coincidences and neither do you, Jax."

I hear my mum gasp right behind me. I look and Raven has her arm around her. I never even heard them come in. I can only assume Bella must have called them.

Her knees buckle and Max catches her. "All I have ever done is love you and protect you like any of my children. I don't know much about that picture; it was over thirty years ago! Please, you must believe me."

"I do. I'm sorry. Please, calm down."

She's very pale and shaking. "Mum, please, Mum. Raven, call the doctor." Before I can finish, Rose is pushing me out of the way.

Everything is happening so quickly, yet it feels like slow motion. I step back and let Rose take over while I call the clinic.

"AN, LOOK AT ME; focus on my voice. Max, get an aspirin *now!* Focus, An, push whatever you heard out of your head and focus on my voice. Think about Antonia, how soft she is. Michael took me on an adventure today. He showed me some secret passages. Has he taken you yet?" I ask as Max comes back with the aspirin. "An, can you chew this for me, please?" I place the aspirin in her mouth and she begins to chew it. I make sure to keep her in a sitting position with bent knees. I keep talking to her about mindless stuff, keeping my voice soft and low. Trying to keep her focused on anything but what happened here. I check her pulse and it seems to be steadying. Having a clinic on the property is a good thing. Within minutes, the doctor shows up with the ambulance. Max sits next to her and takes her hand. His voice is low and steady. "You listen to me, you will not die today. Not on my watch and never because of all of this."

She seems to be getting some color back, but I know she will probably need to be airlifted to the hospital for further care. I don't know what went on in here, but someone needs to take control. "Jax, go with your mom to the clinic, she will probably have to be airlifted to the hospital."

They all race out the door and follow the ambulance to the clinic.

Chapter Seven

Jaxson

ONCE AGAIN, I'M WAITING—SOMETHING I've never been good at. Finally, the doctor comes out, "Your mum's condition is stable but she will need surgery. She had a mild heart attack. She needs an Angioplasty, which will open the arteries. A deflated balloon is threaded through and then inflated. It's invasive and requires an overnight stay. It's pretty common, she is lucky whoever took care of her, when it happened, knew the right things to do; probably saved her life."

"When will you do this procedure and what are the risks involved?"

"We are prepping her right now. With any surgery, there are always risks," he rattles off the long list and I try my best to stay focused. "But this is the least invasive," he finishes then nods to the nurse who proceeds to hand me a clipboard. "You have some papers that you will need to sign before we can get started. You may see her before we take her in." He looks around the room at all of us and states, "Only one at a time and make it brief." He shakes my hand and pats my back before heading off to the OR.

"Thank you." I sign whatever they need and hand it to the nurse.

I head in to see my mum before they take her back. She looks so frail. The stress this past year has been unbearable and it's taken a toll on all of us. This however, is really bad. "Hi, Mum, you gave us quite the scare. Did the doctor explain what they are going to do?"

"Yes, how is M-Maxwell?" She begins to cry.

The monitors start beeping, *fuck*. "Mum, he will be fine. He's right outside the door, but they will only let one of us in at a time. We are all here for him, but if you don't calm down, I'm really going to lose it."

She clutches my hand, "Jaxson, I didn't know."

"Mum, he knows. Please, you need to calm down."

"Ma'am, we are going to give you something to relax you."

"Can you please give us one more moment before you give her that?" She nods and I call in Max and Bella.

I step back and let them know they need to make it quick before we all get thrown out of here.

Bella leans in and kisses Mum, "I love you, Mum."

She steps back and Max walks up to the bed. "Remember what I told you, not on my watch. I love you, Mum."

She smiles as the nurse puts a shot into her IV and she fades out. And now . . . we wait.

"I love you, Mum." I'm not sure that she heard me.

Raven

JACKIE IS ROCKING ANTONIA in her arms. I think it's more for her comfort than my daughter's. My mom is staring out the window, seemingly lost in thought. I put my arm around her and she smiles. "Raven, she will be okay, I spoke to one of the nurses and I think we got her here in time. What the hell happened to bring this all on?"

"Once again the past has reared its ugly head. I don't know all the details and honestly, I'm not sure I want to."

"Sometimes we don't have a choice. No matter how much we want to leave the past behind us, sometimes it's out of our hands. At least you can all lean on each other for support."

Her words remind me that she was alone for twenty years with no one for support.

They finally take An into surgery and the others have joined us in the waiting room. Waiting is not something any of them do well. Jax walks up and takes Antonia from Jackie's arms. He takes in a deep cleansing breath. "My salvation," he whispers. He kisses the tip of her nose. "You ground me."

"JAX, WHAT'S THE STATUS on your mom?" I ask as he heads back from the nurses' station. Before he can answer, the doctor comes out.

"Your mum did fine. She is in recovery and then they will be moving her to a private room. You can wait in there for her, if you like. Please try and keep the visitors to a minimum."

"Thank you. When can we take her home?"

"I will check her tomorrow. If all is well, she should be good to go home late in the afternoon. Expect her to be sore for a couple of days. She will have to follow up with a cardiologist. I'll give you a list when she checks out."

"Thank you."

Everyone heads into An's room, but I hold Jax back. "Before we head in there, tell me, do you think it might be possible that James could be involved somehow?"

"I have no idea and right now, I wish to God I never even saw that file, let alone the picture. I don't know what's going to happen next or how Max will want to deal with this. I just want it over with."

"It's no longer up to you; it's up to Max and how he chooses to pursue it. All we can do is support him."

"I'll support my brother as long as he makes the right decision. If not, I will negotiate with him until he does."

It's going to be a long bumpy road. "We will be okay. Come on, let's see if she's back in her room yet."

"Sweetheart, I wish I could believe that, I really do."

"I have faith, Jax . . . enough faith for all of us."

The nurses finally bring An in and get her settled in for the night. She's in and out of it, but it seems to register with her that we are there. I'm happy my daughter has no clue about anything going on around her. Life really does carry on whether we want it to or not. I put Antonia back into her carrier and take Jax's hand. We head out to the waiting room to be with everyone else. "Come sit for a bit."

He sits in the chair and I climb in his lap. I snuggle into him and close my eyes. Just breathing him in calms me. My heart is breaking for all of them. I know the worst is yet to come. I must have fallen asleep, when I open my eyes, daylight has filled the room. I look at Jax and he looks so tired, I doubt he slept. At least Antonia slept the entire time. The past few weeks she has been sleeping longer at night. "Hey, did you get any sleep?"

"No. Antonia is starting to stir, she probably needs to be changed and I'm sure she wants to eat."

"I'll take care of her." I get up, stretch, and head over to her. Her eyes are wide and she is kicking her little legs. After I change her, I begin to nurse her. I peek at Jax and he is smiling. "What are you smiling at?"

"It is so beautiful to watch you with her."

The nurse informs us that An is beginning to wake up. She reminds us that only two visitors at a time are allowed. We gather up all our stuff and head into her room.

Jax takes her hand, "Mum, you're fine. The surgery went well and we are going to try and get you released today."

"Maxwell, how is he?"

"He's fine mum, right outside that door. If you promise not to get upset I will let him and Bella in; you can only have two visitors at a time."

She waves her hand as if swatting a fly, "Nonsense, I want my family in here now."

I step outside and tell everyone to quietly slip into the room before we get into trouble.

She looks around the room at all of us, smiles, closes her eyes, and goes out again.

"Okay, everyone, she needs her rest; let's get some coffee." They all agree and head out the door. Jax takes Antonia. I kiss him and let him know I'll be out in a moment. I want to make sure she has everything she needs within reach. Her eyes open again. She is so sad and frail. She has been Jax's rock for so long. "An, look at me, please," I encourage. She begins to cry, and I wipe away her tears. "There will be none of this crying stuff. You are very strong and your family is looking to you for that guidance and strength. I know Max is hurting, we all are, but you know what? He will be okay. He has Jackie to lean on now. And I know she will support him and guide him through all of this. What this family can't deal with is anything happening to you. So pull it together and deal with the storm that is coming at us right now." I can't believe I just spoke to her like that, what the hell was I thinking?

"Raven, I could never want for a better daughter-in-law. You are all I ever wished for my son. With all you've been through, you still see the good and the happily ever after, *how?*"

"I have faith in my love for Jax and our family. It will see me through even the darkest of days. When Vincent held me captive, and I knew I was pregnant, I felt Jax all around me. I drew on his strength and now it's time this family draws on my strength and faith."

"You're a survivor, the strongest of us all."

"I don't know any other way. Now, how about I help you get cleaned up a bit. Before the others come back, I'm sure it will make you feel better."

"Thank you, my dear."

Jaxson

MICK WALKS IN. HE sees me and heads over. "Hey, Mick, is everything okay?"

He hands me two coffee carriers, "I figured everyone could use these right about now. How is Mrs. Phillips doing?"

"She had surgery and did fine. They will probably release her later today, barring no complications." I notice he's got a bag with him. "What's in the bag, Mick?"

"I know Raven grabbed the diaper bag, but I wasn't sure how long you would be here, so I brought some stuff for her. Do you think I can see Mrs. Phillips?"

I know I must have a look of disbelief on my face, but that was the last thing I expected him to ask me. He's looking down and picking an imaginary piece of lint off of his shirt. "Sure, I didn't realize you were close with my mum."

He lifts his eyes and smiles, "When you were in Switzerland, we would have tea and talk every day. She listens. She's a good friend and I respect her. I just want to see for myself that she's okay."

"Hey, you don't have to explain. My mum has that way about her. She will get you to tell her your whole life story in five minutes without you even realizing you're doing it. Come on, keep it upbeat, so she doesn't get stressed."

We head back to the room and my mum is awake, sitting up talking to everyone. She sees Mick and smiles. Wow, talk about me being clueless. "Hey, Mum, look who I found."

"Mick brought everyone coffee and some stuff for Antonia."

Raven hugs him, "You know . . . you're the best, Mick."

"Not really, Raven, I know how you are without your coffee. It's more for everyone's safety," he teases her.

I take Raven's hand and bring it up to my lips and kiss it gently. "Sweetheart, why don't we step out and give them a moment?" I glance over to Max and he ushers everyone out of the room.

"Mick, we will be out in the hall, if Antonia wakes, please let me know."

We step out of the room and Raven's speechless. "Sweetheart, I have no clue what is going on with them. All I know is, he said they talk a lot since our trip to Switzerland. I'm choosing to leave it at that."

"I don't think they are anything more than friends."

"Either way, sweetheart, I choose to keep my head in the sand on this one."

"Where is your mum?"

"She's at the nurses station, chatting up a storm."

"I have to tell you she might have been out of practice for twenty years, but her instincts kicked right in. She saved my mum's life."

"I know; I was amazed how quick and how accurate she was."

I pull her tightly into my arms, finding my comfort and solace. "I will always be grateful for all she has done."

"I love you, Jax."

"More, sweetheart, always more."

Anwan

"MICK, THANK YOU FOR coming. How are you? I'm sorry if I scared you."

"Ma'am, you can't get upset or it will set you back. If that happens, everyone will be all over me. Don't worry about me, I'm fine now that I know you're going to be okay."

I take hold of his hand for comfort. "Do you think Maxwell will be able to get past this? He was so close to having it all with Jackie, he can't let this set him back."

"I'm telling you; he will get past this. He has his family to lean on now, and, he has Jackie. Please trust me; he will be okay."

How do you know that, Mick? "

"If I can come back from the bowels of hell, he can too. Now, I'm going back to the house to get everything cleaned up and ready for your return. You need to follow doctor's orders."

"Okay, can you send Maxwell in, I want to talk to him privately."

I watch him head out the door, grateful for his kindness and friendship.

I need to talk to Maxwell alone, I know he will want to know everything I can remember about that bloody picture. I wish to God I never saved it, and then none of this would be happening. The door opens and he pops in, "Mick said you wanted to see me alone."

"I figured you would want to know everything I could remember about that picture."

"You are supposed to be resting, not getting upset over a picture."

"The sooner we get this over with, the sooner we can put this all in the past—where it *should* remain. I knew you would ask me for details. I tried to remember anything I could about it. I was seven months pregnant with Jaxson. I didn't want to go to London, but James insisted. There were four of them, and they were pretty good friends. James had me take the picture, but the man next to him, the man you called Miguel, refused to be in it. At the last minute, James pulled him in and I snapped the picture. Miguel started yelling, as did the man at the other end of the photo. James and the man next to him laughed. I don't even know their names. That is the only picture I have. I don't even know why I kept it. I have my personal journals, and the items I gave you. I assure you, I knew nothing about those men. If it will help you, I will give you the journals."

He takes my hand and squeezes it. "I don't need anything else. I know you were just as surprised as I was."

I can finally breathe a sigh of relief. I whisper, "I heard you call me mum, did you mean it?"

Before he can answer, everyone begins piling into the room. He's smiling, so I reach up and yank his ear.

"Ouch, what's that for?"

"You know perfectly well what that's for. Now, go find that doctor; I want to go home."

Everyone is laughing and right now, that is exactly what we all need. Max throws his hands up and starts mumbling while he walks out the door.

Bella begins gathering my clothes for me. "Mum, you know you really should listen to the doctor."

"The sooner I get dressed, the sooner I can get out of here."

Just then, Maxwell comes back in with the doctor. "Good morning, Mrs. Phillips, how are you feeling today?"

"I'm fine. I want to go home right now. I can assure you, we have a clinic at our estate with all the necessary equipment and a doctor on standby." That should pacify him

"You can go home. However, you need to reduce the stress in your life. I also want you to follow up with the cardiologist. He will probably recommend diet modification and exercise. I will sign the necessary paperwork, and then you will be good to go. You need to rest for this week and take it slow. You will be sore for a bit, but the rest will help. Do you have any questions for me?" He looks up from my chart that he had grabbed while he was talking.

"No, thank you so much for everything." I give him a curt smile. *Reduce the* stress—easy for him to say. No sooner does he head out and the nurse brings me my discharge papers, instructions, and a wheel chair. After all is said and done, we are out of here.

Jaxson

I MAKE SURE MAX and Jackie get back home without any distractions. When I get back to the main house, I find Bella is in the family room by the fire. "Hey, sis, how are you holding up?" She begins to shake and cry. Oh *fuck*.

"Jax, I feel like I brought this on myself. If I didn't insist on going, Max would have never found out. Mum never would have had a heart attack. What have I done?"

"Hey, stop . . . none of this is your fault." I take her hand and she immediately gives it the death grip. "It would have come out eventually; secrets always do. It's better that it came out now while we have a chance to get ahead of this. I don't want to go in there blind."

She gasps, "You still want to go?"

"Yeah, I'm going. I would feel better though, if you stayed here. Before you say anything, I *need* to go. Max will need me to stop him from doing something he might not be able to live with."

"Jax, *who* is going to stop *you?*"

Before I can answer, my wife steps into the room. "I will."

I close my eyes, knowing by the tone in my wife's voice she's not happy. "Raven, please give me a chance to explain."

Bella gets up, "I'm going to check on Mum. I will talk to you later."

She leaves us alone. Raven gives me the stare down and there is fire in those violets. Right now, I know I'm so fucked. Her hands are on her hips, her face is flushed, and—*Lord, help me*—all I can think about is how desperate I am to sink my cock deep inside her. "Jax, just so we are clear here. You will not be going anywhere without me." I'm about to object but she holds her hand up to stop me. I freeze, my eyes gazing up and down her beautiful body.

"We are a family, all of us. Max needs us to keep him from doing something that he will regret. We leave in four days; my mom will be taking care of Antonia. I've stocked enough food for her in the freezer. We will only be gone two days—no more. It's time to put all of this to bed so our family can move forward. The past is just that—the past. We can't change it. That past is what made Max who and what he is today, and we love him just the same. I will not let him make the mistake of a lifetime. It's not your job or Max's to carry the weight of this family. We are a team and we work together. Well, do you have a problem with this?"

"Am I allowed to speak, now?"

"Actually, no."

What the fuck?—she turns and walks out! "Raven, wait! Where the hell are you going?" I'm frozen in place, mesmerized by the sway of her beautiful arse. When she's halfway up the stairs, she turns, gives me a look that cuts to my soul. "Now, Jax."

As she turns to go up stairs, it hits me like a hammer right between the eyes. It's finally time, and I can't get there fast enough. I race upstairs and when I get into our bedroom, she is standing there in absolutely nothing. My heart skips a beat. "Raven, can we? I mean, I know it's only been six weeks—trust me I have counted every day—but are you okay? Did the doctor say it's okay?"

She smiles, pointing toward the chair. "Sit. *Now.*"

I don't know what happened to my wife but this is so surreal. I'm not an idiot. At this point, I'm not saying anything for once in my life; I'm doing what I'm told. She puts on the music, one of my new favorite songs by James Morrison, "You Make it Real," and I'm thinking how appropriate it is. She walks over to my chair and straddles my lap. My jaw is clenched it's been over six long weeks since I've gone to the happy place, and I'm praying I can last. She begins to slowly undress me. Every button of my shirt is sheer torture. She opens it, pulling it down my shoulders.

"Jax, you have the most beautiful neck. I love running my lips up and down it, nice and slowly. You're very tense—*relax.*"

"Sweetheart, it's easy for you to say. I'm trying to maintain some sort of presence of mind here."

"I want to take you past euphoria, past that presence of mind." Oh dear God, she's pulling my nipple between her teeth.

She stands up and bends down, pressing her lips against mine. "Take your jeans off, Jax, *now.*"

I find my scrambled brain, stand up, and, in one swift yank, I unbutton my jeans. "I'm all yours, sweetheart."

She lightly pushes me to sit again and then straddles me, slowly lowering herself onto my cock. "I want to own every one of your moans, your growls. I want to feel every inch of you. Every pleasure you experience, I want to come from me."

She puts her hands on my knees and arches her chest; those beautiful, full breast right in my face as she rolls her hips.

"Oh, Jax, *fare l'amore con me lento e facile.*"

"Oh, dear God, sweetheart, what the fuck are you saying to me?" She knows I can't take the dirty talk.

"Italian; make love to me slowly." She takes my hand and starts working it up and down her clitoris. She takes my other hand and glides it up her body to her lips. "Jax, *prendere me e fammi tuo.*"

I'm frozen like I'm in a dream.

"Jax, *take me and make me yours!*" She does the one thing that she knows will be my undoing, the one thing that will send me over the edge . . . *Clench.*

"Fuck all that's holy, Raven, please tell me I can move . . . that I won't hurt you."

"*Now!*"

I stand up and feel my legs wobble as I take her to the bed. I don't want to hurt her; I need to be gentle. "*Fuck . . .*" I begin to move slowly at first, trying for some sort of control. Oh, who am I kidding? I lost control the day I met her. I pull back and slowly glide in and out of her warmth; it's so wet. Every time I pull out, she clenches, making it snugger for my cock. My body begins to shake and I know this is going to be of epic proportions. "Dear God, please let me go longer, *please*. Raven, oh, sweetheart, I can't hold it."

She digs her nails into my arse and I'm growling endlessly. I don't care who hears. I can't stop—it's endless and mindless—it's euphoria. I look down and Raven opens her eyes and kisses me so tenderly. "Jax, I need more." It's just a whisper, but I know I what I heard.

"Really? How much more, sweetheart? Well, you know I'm not a one shot guy."

"It's been too long for me too, Jax."

"Well, you had a lot of fun teasing me earlier, I think turnaround is fair play. Will you let me bound your hands, like you did to me?"

She bites her bottom lip and pulls that ear. "I trust you, Jax."

"Okay, we will use your stockings, since they worked so well on me." I go to her drawer and get two sets, making a show of everything I'm doing. "Get on your knees, Raven." I bound her arms together and then tie them to the headboard above her head. I keep her spread wide for me. Now, I blindfold her. I take a moment to bask in my handy work, what a beautiful site. "Are you okay?" I ask her.

"Yes," she whispers.

I crawl on the bed behind her while on my knees, and rest my cock right between those glorious arse cheeks. Oh Jesus, it's like going home. Leaning down, I kiss my way up her spine. As much as I would love to reach around and play with her nipples right now I know they are too sensitive. I work my way down her back and nip at that beautiful arse. I swirl my tongue down further until I reach my goal and she lets out a low long moan. I take her clitoris tenderly between my teeth, tugging gently, followed by a kiss and a lick. I work my tongue deep inside her. She's fighting her restraints. "Raven, you still okay?"

"More than okay; please don't stop."

I spread her wetness, front to back, and slowly work my finger into her, while I unleash my tongue, quick and hard. She's right on the edge. I stop.

"*Noooo! Please, you can't leave me like this.*"

"I would never leave you on the edge." I get back on my knees and rub my cock up and down, stroking her softly. I enter her very slowly, one hard inch at a time. When I'm all the way in, I smack her arse hard enough to only tease.

"Oh, Jax, more please."

She's pushing herself back, trying to get me in deeper, harder. As much as I know she wants to, I know we still need to be careful. Instead, I reach around and run my fingers over her clitoris, applying more pressure.

"Yes!"

I smack her arse again and she is begging for more. Over and over again, right then left. "Sweetheart, are you there yet?" I don't need to wait for her answer, she is screaming and shaking. I explode endlessly within her. As I slowly bring her down, I untie her, gently massaging her wrists. She reaches up and pulls off the blindfold. I pull out of her and she turns over. She crawls into my arms and pulls me tightly. I'm holding her and trailing my fingers up and down her back. My mind flips back to why the argument started, and I need to make her understand that she should stay home. I'm about to say something when the baby monitor goes off.

"I need to feed Antonia." She gets up, puts on a robe, and goes to feed our baby. I watch her leave and I have no idea as to what I'm going to do.

Chapter Eight

Raven

I CHANGE ANTONIA AND begin to feed her. Tonight with Jax was wonderful. We finally went to our special place. I know what's coming and I will fight him on it. I can't let him go without me. I know he needs me there, even if he doesn't know it. I have to keep this family together, and I have to stop Max from making the mistake of a lifetime. I need to make Max understand that going after James will cost him Jackie. He'll never survive another loss.

I can sense that Jax is behind me, I always know when he's near. "Jax, if you think you're going to try and talk me out of going, you won't. I need to make Max understand what he will lose by doing this. We all go together or not at all. Don't think about pulling the Antonia card cause that won't work either. She needs to grow up with all her family around her. I'm making sure that's possible."

"Can I ask a question now?" he inquires as he walks around my chair so that we can see each other.

"Of course, I just wanted to make sure you're clear on where I stand."

"What happened? You've never been aggressive or domineering, yet today, I've seen a whole new side to you. Even when we were making love, you were different."

"Honestly, I don't know. What I do know is life can change on a dime. When I saw your mom go down, I panicked. I watched my mom come alive and yet, I felt myself shutting down. I won't be that vulnerable little girl ever again. You've carried all the weight of our family for so long. When your dad walked away, there was never time for you to be a little boy. You have been everything to everyone for so long. Now it's time for you to share the load." Suddenly, I realize the depth of his question and can't help but wonder if my new and improved confidence in the bedroom bothers him. I jerk my head up quickly. "Are you upset with me?"

"Well, I have to say it was hot seeing you take charge while making love to you. I love all the dynamics that make up who you are. I'm upset with the fact that you won't stay home. I'm also no fool, Raven; I know when there is no changing your mind. Tomorrow we will talk to Max, but tonight, I need my wife." He grazes my cheek with the back of his hand before helping me to get up. I put Antonia back in her crib, asleep and content. As we head toward our room, I mentally prepare myself for what I have to tell him next.

Jaxson

SHE HAS BEEN TUGGING on her ear—always a sure sign for something being on her mind. We sit on the bed, and I pull her hand from her ear. "Are you ready to tell me what's wrong?"

"I'm not on birth control. I was going to tell you to pull out but then I got caught up in the heat of the moment. My mind lost all reason."

"I thought you wanted to wait, why are you not on your pill?"

"While forms of birth control are discussed before having the baby, nothing is set in motion until after my six week postpartum visit. I can't take the pill until after I have my first cycle. The fact that I am breastfeeding might work to our advantage for birth control."

"Why were you afraid I would be upset about this? You know I want lots of babies."

"I know you do, I just didn't think it had to be right now . . . not that I think anything is going to happen, but I want you to know everything. After all, Antonia was a surprise. I want all cards on the table."

"Sweetheart, you know I don't want Antonia to be an only child. If it happens, then so be it. I'm glad you're not taking anything that would cause any problems. Please, don't ask me to wear a condom. If you want, I will attempt to pull out, but I can't guarantee I will have the presence of mind at the time." I lift her hand and kiss the inside of her wrist. I can feel her shudder as the jolt of excitement shoots right to her core. "Are we good now, sweetheart?"

"Yes, Jax, we're good."

I pull her into my lap and kiss her tender lips. "As much as I would love to go to the happy place, I know that we can't over do it. How about I hold you in my arms all night long?"

"I know you're right and before we know it, Antonia will be up again." She tries to stifle her yawn. I roll us on our side and pull the comforter over us. "Let's get some sleep, tomorrow is going to be another long day"

I look down and she is fast asleep. I kiss her gently, "There will be plenty of time for babies." I whisper.

Maxwell

I DON'T WANT TO go anywhere near my office. I want to shut off every-thing that went down. "Why don't we go in the living room and sit by the fire for a bit?" I suggest to Jackie.

"Of course. Would you like some tea?"

"That sounds wonderful, thank you."

While she is puttering around the kitchen, I stare into the fire. I don't know what I'm going to do. My mind is on a complete overload. Jackie comes back and sets the tray down. I smile . . . she even has Jammie Dodgers.

"Max, can I ask you a question?"

"Babe, you know you can ask me anything."

"What is the story with these cookies? I mean, when Jax found out that An was getting them for you, he went crazy. I don't understand."

"My grams always gave them to me with my tea. It's comforting to me, like in some small way my grams is with me. Jax loves them and when they were featured in that show he watches, it made him love them more. When we were living in the states, we couldn't get them. So, An had them shipped in. When he found out, he went a little nuts . . . probably just to give me a hard time."

"Are you still going to confront James?" She shifts gears.

"Would I lose you if I did?" I watch her face for all the signs that she will leave me. I see nothing.

"Max, I want you safe, and I want you healed. That's really all I've ever wanted."

"Babe, What are your thoughts on the whole situation?"

"Tell me everything you know. Sometimes having an outsider's perspec-tive can make all the difference."

"Are you sure you want to hear it all?"

"Yes. I know you've held back, but I figured that when you were ready to share with me, you would."

I give her a small nod of agreement, and then take in a deep breath be-fore I let it all pour out of me. "After everything happened, I fell into a dark place, filled with nothing but hate and revenge. I was out for blood, and I left no stone unturned. When I found the gunmen, I did what needed to be done. I vowed I would never let them see the light of day." Her eyes are fixed on me, and I know this is hard to hear—hell, it's hard for me to relive it. "The thing is, I didn't feel good like I thought I would. I have to live with that for the rest of my life. I know I'm probably going to hell and all the redemption in the world won't help me. I knew who the men worked for; Miguel Dominguez,

Columbian drug lord. I thought about going after him, but in the end, I knew revenge was not the way. It would make me no different from him. When I saw that picture, I knew the face looked familiar but I couldn't place it because he was very young. When I aged it, I realized who he was. The shock was seeing my father with his arm around the man, laughing. Does he know the man was responsible for the death of his grandson and daughter-in-law? Does he even care? Was he a part of it?" I've got a grip on her hand; twirling her ring around her finger. "Jackie, I need to confront him, but I'm scared."

"Scared of what?"

"Babe, I don't know if I can keep it together. It's not just me anymore. I have to think about the rest of the family. I can't lose them, especially over him. I can't lose you, you're my world."

"What makes you think you would lose your family or me? Max, at the end of the day, you know what the repercussions will be if you take matters into your own hands. He's not worth it. I can understand you wanting to confront him and call him out for whatever part he might have been responsible for. What you can't do is make him turn you into someone you don't want to be."

"How, baby? How do I do that?"

"You do what you do best, Max: gather information and facts, slowly build a case against him. Leave him to rot in jail, just like Vincent will."

"I don't know that I can do that? In my head, he is dead to me, but in my heart, he's my father. I'm so tired of all of this. I just want it over already."

"Max, you need to stop looking at him like a loving, caring father. He is nothing more than a sperm donor. He didn't make you the man you are today. Your real family is who shaped and loved you, no matter what." She kisses me and holds me tight. I know she's right.

"Max, when I was young, I had a friend that I trusted completely. She was one of my only friends. One day, she betrayed me really bad. Of course, it was nothing like this, but at that time, I was so upset and wanted to hurt her like she hurt me. My mom sat me down and told me I needed to forgive the girl. Well, I can tell you, I thought she was crazy. I told my mom she was absolutely nuts if she thought I would ever forgive her. My mom asked me if I thought I was better than Buddha. I told her, 'Of course not, what would make you think that?' She said, 'Buddha can forgive, so why can't you?' I really couldn't answer her. She gave me the best advice that day, Max. She said forgive the girl and move on. She doesn't have to be in your circle. She has to look in the mirror every day. And in the end, she has to answer to her God for what she has done. My point is, Max, if you reduce yourself down to his level, then you're no better than he is. Let him live with what he has done and let him answer for it. The more you hold onto the grudge, the more bitter you will become."

"Wow, what did the girl do?" I ask and she widens her eyes. "Don't look at me like that, you had to know I would ask."

"She slept with my boyfriend right before he came to pick me up for our date."

"So, what did you do?"

"I told the boy that I knew what he did, and I forgive him. I told him he could have her, and that he would never have me. I then went to see her, and told her that I hope they are very happy together. I wished her luck and walked out. I never spoke to either of them again. I knew if I didn't do that, I would become a very bitter person. Max, don't let James make you into a bitter person. Don't give him the power to take away what you have found here. Only you can stop this." She pulls me into her arms, wrapping those wonderful legs around me. I'm resting my head on her chest and I can feel her heart beating. It's what keeps me alive.

"Max, do you remember the crystal I gave you?"

"Yes, I carry it with me all the time. Do you want it back?"

"No, I want you to use it to help you concentrate on healing. Every time you feel that you are on the verge of losing it, rub the crystal." Her fingers are tracing the scar on my temple, and it has a calming effect on me. *Everything* she does calms me.

"I really got scared when I thought we were going to lose An. If something would have happened to her because of me, I don't think I would have survived it."

"Well, then I suggest you do whatever you have to do to put this whole situation with James to bed. He's eaten up too much of your life and, he's just not worth it. I think he should pay for whatever part he played, but not at the expense of anyone else."

I lift my head up and look at those beautiful golden eyes. "I love you."

"I know, Max." She presses her lips to my forehead. "Get some rest." I snuggle up against her, thankful that she's not letting go. Reminding myself that I need to stay focused on the present and not the past.

Jackie

MAX HAS BEEN ASLEEP for hours. The realization that James could have been a part of the darkest point in Max's life has taken a toll on him. If I was in his position, I don't know what I would do. I love this man heart and soul, but what am I willing to live with? I need to call my parents. As I try to wiggle free, his grip gets tighter. It's barely a whisper but I hear him plead with me not to leave. I close my eyes, giving in to his need to hold me tightly.

I OPEN MY EYES and realize I'm alone. I don't know how much time has passed but it's dusk outside. I get up and stretch before heading out in search of Max. I find him in his office, cleaning up the mess. "Max, can I help you with that?"

"No, babe, it's my mess, I can clean it. I'm sorry if I woke you." He seems solemn.

"You didn't wake me." I offer him a small smile. "When are you meeting with everyone?"

"I'll meet with them later. I wanted to clean up this mess, and form some sort of plan. Are you hungry?"

"Starving. Will you fix something, please?"

"Of course, babe."

I take his hand and pull him from the room. "Come, this can wait right now. I need food and you."

"Really? In that order?"

"Yes, in that order."

When we get to the kitchen, I watch him begin assembling dinner. My eyes gaze over to the table where just yesterday, I was having the time of my life. I feel my cheeks heat at the memory. I think it's time I try to turn the tables on Max, and get him out of his own head. His back is to me and I can't help but remember the first time I saw his ass, it literally took my breath away. I quietly get up and walk up behind him, slide my hands into his sweats, grabbing each ass cheek. He freezes in place. I lean in and kiss his shoulder, never letting go of his ass. He's still not moving and not saying a word. I grate my nails up his ass and then stroke them down. He drops the whisk. "If you do that again, dinner will be delayed," he whispers.

I pull my hands up but instead of stopping I grab the waistband of his sweats and yank them down. He tries to turn around. I grab his hips, "No."

He grips the counter and tries to steady his breath. I drop to my knees and begin lightly kissing his ass, all the while, admiring how sculptured it is. "Turn around," I command. As he turns around, I stand up. "Get up on the counter, hold on to the edge, and no matter what—don't let go." I giggle at hearing those words, the same words he used on me.

He's smirking and I know he is remembering too. As he climbs on the counter, I take off his sweats. Now . . . I'm going to have some fun. I have on entirely too many clothes. I take the hem of my shirt and lift it over my head. I watch his eyes grow wide and his knuckles turn white as his grip gets tighter. I slip my thumbs into the band of my yoga pants and peel them off. His jaw tightens and I know he is trying so hard to let me stay in charge. Sometimes I wish I had more experience. Hmm . . . what to do next? He must sense my apprehension, he growls. "*Touch yourself, babe.*"

I glide my hands over my breasts. "Talk me through it, Max, please."

"Play with your nipples, take each one and roll them between your fingers. Pull them to the point of pain, and then stop. Tell me what you're feeling? Does it feel good?"

"It feels different, not like when you do it."

"You like when I play with your nipples? What about when I suck and nibble them, do you like that?"

"I love that, Max."

"Slide your fingers down; feel the contour of your abs. Feel how lean and long you are. Glide your fingers into the folds of your beautiful sweetness. Enter real slowly, and imagine it's my tongue going slow and deep."

As I follow his instructions, I can feel my skin prickle and my heart race. He's not even touching me, yet, I feel him all over me—*how?*

"Talk to me, babe. Tell me how it feels."

"Powerful and erotic; I feel you all over me, yet you're not touching me. I want more, Max."

"Let your thumb swipe up and down your clitoris. Make the strokes faster, while your other fingers are moving in and out of your sweetness, spreading your arousal. Now, tell me what you want, Jackie."

"I want to come with you inside of me."

He leaps off the counter and comes toward me. He begins pumping his cock and when he reaches me, he takes my hand and brings my fingers to his mouth, sucking my taste off of them. This is so erotic, almost surreal. He takes my other hand and places it on his cock, keeping his hand over it as he begins moving my hand up and down. The movement of my hand, matching my fingers in his mouth. He takes my hand from his mouth. "Do you want me, Jackie? Do you think you're ready for me?"

I brazenly take his hand and guide it down until it's right between my legs. He's trying to hold me back from pushing his fingers deep within me. My eyes glance upwards and he's smiling. "You're not going to make this easy on me are you?"

"Babe, all you have to do is tell me what you want, what you desire . . . what you *need*."

He's watching my every move, waiting for my words. As he waits for my answer, he leans down and takes my nipple between his teeth. Oh dear God, I can't think, let alone form a sentence. "Max, I need to feel you inside of me."

He's sucking and pulling at my nipple, finally letting go with a pop. "My tongue, my fingers, or my cock?"

He's strumming his fingers over my clitoris and I think I might scream. "All t-three, Max."

He lifts me up and carries me out of the kitchen. "Where are we going?" I squeak.

"I want you everyplace I can have you, Jackie, but right now I want you in our bed."

He carries me into our bedroom and as he places me on the bed, he begins to kiss me slowly and tenderly . . . no sense of urgency. My body is wound so tight, I fear I might combust. He's kissing my neck and I know I can't take much more. "Max, please I need—" Before I can finish he slowly sinks his cock deep inside me and stops. "Why the hell are you stopping?"

His entire body blankets mine. He grips my hands above my head. His eyes are closed, and he's trying to slow down his breathing. I can feel his heart pounding. He rests his forehead on mine and I swipe my tongue over his lips. He opens his eyes. They focus intently on mine. He pulls back and finally starts to move. He's in total control as he cups my breast and pebbles my nipple. He nibbles down my neck and latches onto my nipple. It's a mixture of pain and pleasure, something I never thought possible.

"Max, I can't hold it." He nips me harder and I can't hold back. My release is so intense and I feel his body shake as his release floods me. "Max, are you okay?"

"I will be in a minute, as soon has I come back down to earth. Jesus, Jackie, what you do to me, I've never thought possible."

He begins to slowly move in and out, he's hard as stone again. He pulls out and works his way down my body, very slowly. As he nips my hip bone I giggle. His tongue circles my belly button as he continues downward. I can't take much more and I push his head down as I try to wiggle myself up further. He's teasing me, knowing what I want, what I need. He swipes me with his tongue and then works his fingers deep inside me. I'm almost there, his tongue so forceful. He pulls his fingers out and begins to work one very slowly into my rear. Oh my, it's tight but I can't focus on anything but that tongue. Flicking, nipping at my clitoris while his fingers are pushing inside of me. "Max, I'm . . . *coming!*" I'm shaking and kicking my legs as I dig my nails into his shoulders. He gets up and rubs his cock up and down, I'm nervous he will want anal sex and I'm not sure I'm ready for that.

"Not today, Babe, that takes control," he says as if he could hear my thoughts. "Right now I want to take you hard, you ready?" He hovers over me.

"Yes!"

He slams into me and God, it feels wonderful. It doesn't take long for both of us to explode. We lay here, neither one of us having to say a word. I love to mindlessly stroke his back as we both come back to earth.

"Max, are you ever going to feed me?" I ask after a few minutes.

"Babe, I'm starting to think you just want me for my culinary skills?"

"Well, that, combined with your sex skills, makes you my complete package."

He throws his head back and laughs. It's wonderful to finally hear that laugh again. "I love you, Jackie."

Chapter Nine

Raven

JAX IS STILL ASLEEP when I hear the monitor. I try to get out of bed, but I'm locked in his embrace. I hate to wake him, but I have no choice. "Jax, I need to take care of Antonia." He kisses me and mumbles something as I crawl out of bed. I get to the nursery and Antonia is her usual morning fussy. I get her changed and sit in front of her window while I feed her. This is my favorite time of the day, watching the sunrise with my daughter. I know it will be so hard to leave her, but I have to go with them to Capri. There is too much at stake here. An needs to recuperate; all the burden can't be on her. Antonia finishes and she is out cold. She always falls asleep when she is nursing. After I get her settled in her crib, I head out the door only to run into Michael.

"Hey, Michael, where are you off to so early?"

"I don't feel good, I was going to get my mum."

I feel his head and he feels warm. "What do you feel, can you tell me?"

"I'm tired and cold, Aunt Raven."

"Back to bed, little man. I will get your mom and my mom, too. Let's see if we can get you fixed up really quickly, okay?" As we head back to his room, he begins peppering me with questions.

"Aunt Raven, is it true that Miss Jackie is marrying Uncle Max?"

"Yes, where did you hear it?"

"My mum told me, she said Miss Jackie will be my aunt now. That's cool, cause she is really nice and we have lots of fun with the horses. The only bad thing about her is he doesn't watch *Doctor Who*."

I pull him close to me and kiss his head, even when he doesn't feel well, he still makes me laugh. "I'm sure we can work on that. Now, back to bed."

I go in search for Bella and find her in the kitchen making coffee. "Morning, Bella, I was looking for you. I ran into Michael, he was on his way to get you. He has a fever and said he feels tired. I sent him back to bed and told him I would find you and my mom to come and look at him."

"Thanks, Raven, he seemed a little off last night. I was going to ask Rose to check him but she was busy with mum. I'll ask her this morning. I hope it's not that flu that's running around. You know when school starts, kids pass everything around."

"How is An doing?"

"She will never say; you know mum. I heard her tell Rose she felt sore from the procedure. Rose assured me that was to be expected. She needs to rest, and she needs to reduce the stress in her life."

"Bella, we all need to reduce the stress. I'm hoping to try and talk some sense into Max, but I doubt he will listen."

The door swings open and Jackie comes barreling in. "Hey, Jackie, is everything okay?"

"Yeah, I wanted to talk to you before Max gets here, and before my class starts."

Bella gets up to leave but Jackie takes her hand. "Bella, please stay."

She is scaring me. Something is off, and I know exactly what Jackie needs. I get up, pour her coffee, and get our stash of chocolates.

I pass her the chocolates, "This should take the edge off of whatever it is."

"Oh, Raven." She begins to cry. Oh dear God, how much more?

I get up and take her in my arms, rubbing her back to calm her down. Bella takes Jackie's hand, "Hey, no matter what, Jackie, we are family and we will get through it."

"I must be at my parents for my birthday. Max knows this and promised me that he would be back in time. He made that promise before everything happened. I don't want him to confront James. I'm scared what the result will be for everyone. He has been rocked to the core. He's afraid he is going to lose the rest of his family over all of this. There are so many emotions and now the headaches have come back, along with the night terrors. I know if I go with him, that I might be able to help him maintain some sort of control, but I have to be at my parents."

I know why she has to be home, but Bella doesn't. It's not up to me to tell her, only Jackie can. I push her hair back and wipe away her tears.

She turns to Bella and squeezes her hand. "Bella, birthdays are a happy time for some, but not for me." She goes on to explain about Madeline. "I have to be there—*no matter what!* But, I'm really worried about leaving Max."

"Jackie, I'm sorry. I never knew. Maybe we can delay the trip till you get back. I will try talking to my brothers. In the meantime, I need to check on Michael; he's not feeling well."

"Bella, I'm sorry that I bothered you."

"Nonsense; we are family." She heads out to see about her son.

"Okay, Jackie, I know something else is bothering you, so spill."

"Max and I finally talked everything out. He wants to get married and start on a family right away. I told him I'm scared, not just for me but for him, too. Jeez . . . he wants five kids! I told him I'm not a baby factory. He wants to adopt a special needs child."

I'm watching her rip apart her napkin and I know there's more. "What are you afraid of?"

"What if we have twins and that happens to us? I don't think Max will survive. Raven he's barely hanging on now."

"I know your fear is very real for you, but not all multiple births end up like yours."

"My logical mind agrees with you, but my aunt's pregnancy ended the same way. Do the math, the facts don't lie."

"I know that, but you can't go through life afraid of *what if.* Whatever happens, we will deal with it together. Max has a great support system around him and he always will."

I hug her tight, knowing that's what she needs the most right now. "You need to get Max, and tell him there is a family meeting here in two hours. Let him know I've called it."

I don't give her a chance to question me; I know she will fight me on my decision. I quickly head out to find Jax.

I HEAD UPSTAIRS TO find Jax but run into my mom leaving Michael's room. "Morning, Mom, how is he?" She seems very distracted.

"He still has a fever. I'm not sure what's going on. I'm waiting for the doctor to get here. How is Jax this morning?"

"He's still sleeping. I was just headed in there. We are having a family meeting in two hours; please make sure you are there. Mom, before the day gets away from us, I just wanted to thank you for all you did to help An." I give her a hug, and she seems distant.

"Mom, what's wrong? You seem so sad."

"Raven, I felt myself come alive, and that made me realize how much I've lost. Sometimes it's hard to keep the nightmares from surfacing. I'm happy that all my years of school and training was worth something. My whole life, all I ever wanted to do was save lives. Then, that was ripped away from me. Everything I built my life around was gone in an instant. I need to find my place in the world all over again. Everything that happened brought that need back to the surface, deep from where I buried it."

"Do you think it's possible that you would be able to practice again?"

"I wouldn't even know where to begin. My license was in New York State and I live in Scotland now. I'm sure the laws and requirements are different now. You know, I'm not young anymore. So much has changed."

"Mom, never rule anything out. We should have Jax's attorneys find out the legal end of things and then lets take it from there. You can't let what happened dictate who you are. If you do that, then all the evil wins, and that's never an option."

"You are so much like Antonio that sometimes it takes my breath away. Your quiet strength is amazing. You never fall into that pity party mentality, how is that even possible?"

"Someone told me once, 'Pity parties are for fools. You can't change the past, but you can change your path for the future. Tell that pity party to kiss your ass goodbye, as you're walking away from it.' I live by that rule."

"Great advice, do I dare ask who?"

"It was Marco. Mom, I know he did a lot of bad things, but in my heart, I also know all the good he did for me. That's what I choose to remember, otherwise, I will become bitter."

"I'm glad that you are choosing to focus on the good from that relationship. I know, from what you told me, that he caused so much pain. But, he also looked after you. Joseph must have seen something good in him if he put him in your life."

"Your right, Mom. I will always try to focus on the positive."

"Oh, Dr. McCord is finally here. I want to talk to him about Michael. I will see you at the meeting."

She rushes into Michael's room. I hope he's going to be fine. I need to find Jax. Just then, I hear Jax on the baby monitor. I look at the screen and see them both. I love watching him with her. He is such a powerful, strong man, yet . . . so tender-hearted. Sometimes I feel like I shouldn't watch or listen to them, but I can't pull myself away.

Jaxson

I LIKE TO START my day with my daughter. Even if she's asleep, she has a calming affect on me. I lean in and she begins to stir. Well, at least Raven can't yell at me for waking her up. I scoop her up and breath in her scent. She smells so sweet and pure; my beautiful girl. I love talking to her, we have the best conversations.

"Oh, my sweetest girl, I don't know how your mum and I are going to leave you. I don't know how parents do it? Your Uncle Max is going to have some really hard times ahead of him. We need to keep him grounded and strong. I think I finally got through to Grandma Rose about the potential danger she could put the family in if she goes to see Vincent. At least I hope so. Your mum is so strong; I wish I had half the strength she does. Don't you let her fool you, little one, she holds all the power in this relationship."

I nuzzle my sweet baby. "Raven, how long have you been standing there?" She never has to say a word, my blood races whenever she is near.

"Long enough, Jax. Michael is not feeling well, the doctor and my mom are in with him now."

"I should go check on Junior. What have you been up to?"

"I spoke with Jackie and Bella. I let them know that I'm calling a family meeting, and to let everyone know."

"Wow, you called a meeting? Am I in *trouble?*"

"Ha! No, for once, you're not in the doghouse. We need to organize everything before we leave. We need to have a plan. We can't go running in their half-cocked." She stops rattling off her list, cocks her head, and furrows her brow. "Why are you looking at me so strangely?"

"I'm not; everything is fine." *Fine—my arse; teacher mode makes me crazy.* "What time is the meeting?"

"In about an hour; we have time. I need to feed Antonia, and I want to talk to you . . . have a seat."

I watch her getting Antonia settled in to nurse, and it warms my heart to see such beauty. She is a perfect mum: kind and loving. "God, I hope we made a baby today." Her eyes grow wide and she is staring at me. "I just said that out loud, didn't I?"

"Yes, you did. Before the meeting, I have to tell you something. It was never my story to tell, but since Jackie has shared it, I need to tell you. Jackie's birthday is coming up, and she must be back at her parents home to celebrate it."

"Why? Can't she go in a week or two?"

"No, it has to be on that day." She shakes her head and explains to me why. "Her mom is Buddhist and follows their teachings. Madeline's ashes are in a temple repository on the property. Every year, Jackie goes to the temple and then spends the day with her mom reflecting upon the year that passed. It is a tradition that is important to both of them. She explained it to Bella, and told her if we leave for Capri, we must be back for this or, if possible, delay the trip until after her birthday. I'm going to talk to everyone and see what would be best. Max cannot and will not go this alone. I will not allow it."

"Wow, sweetheart, that is so sad. I understand she wants to be there for Max. I would much rather we wait until she gets back, that would buy us a little more time to research what we are walking into."

"I agree, plus, I don't want to leave if Michael is sick."

She's tugging her ear and I know something else is on her mind. "What else is bothering you?"

"I spoke to my mom and thanked her, her quick actions saved your mom's life and probably Max's too. She is sad that she can't practice medicine any more. Do you think your attorneys can find out what she would need to do if she decided she wants to get back into the field? She sees all the obstacles in her way, whereas I don't."

"Oh, Raven, you never do. It's one of the many things I love about you. I will give Mathew a call today." I lean in and kiss her tender lips, and then lean down and kiss Antonia. "While you finish up here, I will check on Junior. Aside from the occasional cold, he never gets sick."

I head toward the door but look back at Raven who is softly singing to Antonia, while lightly stroking her head. God I love this woman.

Maxwell

THE HOUSE IS QUIET. Jackie is probably out at the barn. I head into the kitchen to get some coffee, and I find Mrs. Osla standing at the back door. I know I'm in trouble by the glaring look on her face. I open the door, expecting her to yell, but she surprises me by throwing her arms around me and begins to cry. "Shh, please don't cry, Mrs. Osla; I'm fine. Come in and sit. I'll make you tea."

"Lad, I leave you alone for a couple of days and all hell breaks loose. Please tell me from the beginning what happened?"

It kills me that she is upset yet again because of me. I relay everything that happened, including the fact that my father was associated in some way with Miguel. "When An realized everything, she had a heart attack. I thank God that Rose was here. She quite literally saved us all," I state with widened eyes. She listens, stirring her tea and so I continue. "Part of me wants to kill him while part of me just wants to know *why?* I know if I go after him, I might not be able to control myself. I know if I do that, it will cost me Jackie. I don't know how to deal with these emotions."

"Maxwell, only you can decide how much power you are willing to give James. How much more are you going to let him take from you? He's cost you so much, when will you say enough? Is knowing really worth the price of Jackie's love and respect? Your own self-respect? I love you, lad, but ultimately, it has to be your choice and yours alone. I'm going up to the main house to check on An." She gets up and heads toward the door. I watch her leave and think about all that has happened. I know what I have to do, what is best for everyone. I need to somehow convince them that we all need to walk away.

I'm about to get up and head to the main house when Jackie comes barreling through the door. "Hey, babe, you okay?"

"Yeah, we have a family meeting in about an hour at the main house. I need to jump in the shower so I don't go smelling like the barn."

I follow her into the bathroom, taking my clothes off along the way. "Who called a meeting?"

"Max, why are you naked? Raven, called a meeting."

"Babe, you said we are having a shower. Why did Raven call a meeting?"

"I said *I was* having a shower. If you come in, we might not get out. I don't know why she called a meeting, I guess we will find out soon enough."

"Jackie, I need to be in the shower with you. I mean, after all, you do need your back washed."

"I've been doing okay all these years, Max. Besides, we have to be at the house in an hour."

We step into the shower, and as she is about to unravel her braid, I stop her. My voice is low and my desire is high. "Not yet, babe, I need you now."

She said she wanted to try new and different things, well, now's her chance. Her back is toward me, and I blanket her with my body. I begin rubbing myself up and down her beautiful arse. I reach around to feel if she is ready for me. God, she is *so* ready. "Put your hands up against the wall and push that luscious arse toward me." She instantly takes my commands. I pick up her braid and looped it around my fist, pulling it just enough to sting. "I'm going to take you from behind. It will be hard and it will be fast, are you okay with that? Do you think you can handle me?"

"Yes," she whispers.

I smack her arse, and she yelps. "Louder, Jackie!"

"Yes, I can handle it, but if you smack my ass like that again, I might not last long."

Interesting that she likes the sting of my palm. I position my cock over her clit, slowly rubbing the head up and down, front to back. I can feel her beginning to shake and that's when I slam into her. I find a rhythm; as I push in, I pull her braid. She's almost there, but I want more. I slow it down, needing it to last. I feel my blood coursing through my veins, as my cock continues to get harder. I take a finger and work it into her beautiful arse. I want to fill every part of her. Now I work two fingers in, still going slow.

"Max, smack my ass again, please; I won't break."

Oh bloody hell! I smack her arse over and over again. It's turning pink and I fucking love it.

"Harder, Max, please."

"Oh fuck, Jackie, I'm coming." I throw my head back groaning her name, and she's following me. Beautiful . . . just *fucking* beautiful. I bend down and kiss that gorgeous, pink arse.

She pulls away and reaches for the body wash. "Max, we need to get clean or we will be late."

I spin her around and her face is flushed. "Babe, I don't care. I want to talk to you first. You said you wanted to try new things. Did you like what just happened? Did you find it pleasurable? Did it hurt at all?" I watch her face, trying to gauge her reaction. Her eyes cast downwards, so submissive—and, *fuck me*—she is so sexy. I lift her chin up so she's looking into my eyes. "No secrets."

"I liked it a lot. It didn't hurt, it stung a little, but then, it felt warm. I felt like I didn't have to be in control, yet I knew if I said stop, you would. I gave you power without giving up my power. Does that make sense?"

I pull her into my arms and kiss her long and slow. Our tongues, stroking gentle then hard. When I finally pull away, I look down at my cock and I know I need her again. I lift her up with one arm, while she wraps her legs around my waist. Slowly, I sink deep within her. I steady my legs and begin to move, taking my time—gently—until I can't take anymore and we both roll into a beautiful orgasm. When we finally come back to life, I let her down and begin to methodically wash her. Nothing needs to be said; she knows I love her more than life itself and I always will.

We finish getting ready and as we head out the door, I stop her, "Jackie, I want to let you know that I've decided that I don't want to go to Capri. I'm going to let everyone else know, but I wanted to tell you first."

"Can I ask you why?"

"Because I love you, babe . . . more than my own life. I don't trust myself in the same room with him. I'm not willing to take any chances. He's not worth it."

"What made you change your mind?"

"Mrs. Osla was here earlier and she asked me how much more power I am willing to give my father. She's right. I can't change the past, but I can protect my future, and my future is you. I will move heaven and earth for you." I look into her eyes, they are so bright. Her huge smile lights up her whole face, and I know—she understands.

"For us, Max, I love you and I will support your decision. Come, let's go find out what's going on." We walk up to the main house hand in hand. I feel good about my decision. Now I have to make Bella and Jax understand.

Rose

DR. MCCORD FINISHES HIS exam and assures Bella that it's probably the flu. I decide to step out and speak to him before he leaves. "Dr. McCord, I'm concerned about Michael. I know you said you think it's the flu, however, his fatigue has been building for days. He keeps bruising very easily and now he is running a 103 temp. I don't want to tell you how to do your job, but don't you think it would be wise to run a CBC panel?"

"Rose, I understand you are a doctor, but you have been out of practice for a long time. And so much has changed. He probably has the flu; this time of year it's pretty common. Let's not jump to conclusions. I'll check on him in a couple of days."

He storms off before I can say anything else. I'm about to go back into Michael's room when I see Jax coming and pull him aside. "Can I please talk to you for a minute."

"I was just going in to see Michael, can it wait?"

"No, please, it's about Michael."

"Of course, Rose, what's the problem?"

"You can tell me to mind my business, but I can't. Michael is fatigued. He has been bruising easily and he is running a 103 temp. I suggested to Dr. McCord that it might be wise to run a CBC panel. Michael never gets sick and he's usually so full of energy. Why not play it safe and run the panel?"

"What did he say?"

"He blew me off, telling me to leave it to him. I would, if I thought he was doing his job. He thinks it's the flu and I hope that's all it is, but I'm worried. If it is the flu, then I should have it too. I'm with Michael every day, exploring all the secret passages in this place. Why is he the only one who is ill?"

"Rose, let me look in on Junior and talk to Bella."

"Okay, I don't mean to alarm anyone. I'd rather be wrong than right." As I watch him head into Michael's room, I pray to God I'm wrong.

Jaxson

I STEP INTO JUNIOR'S room and he looks so pale. He looked tired yesterday, but nothing like this. "Hey, Junior, how are you feeling?"

"I'm tired, Uncle Jax, but I'll be okay. Miss Rose and I found another secret passage yesterday, it leads to a tunnel. We didn't go all the way yet."

"Well, when you get better, you will have to show me. Do you want to watch some *Doctor Who?*"

"I'm tired, Uncle Jax, maybe later, okay?"

"Sure, you get some rest. I'll be back later."

I step outside the room and Rose is waiting for me. I pull out my phone and call Dr. McCord. "Get your arse back here right now and run a CBC panel on Junior." I hang up, not waiting for his answer.

"Jax, you see what I'm talking about?"

"Of course, Rose, one look at him and I can tell something is off. He doesn't even have the energy to watch *Doctor Who*. Do you have an idea what is wrong?"

"I won't speculate, let's get the test run."

Before I can ask her anymore questions, McCord walks up. It takes all I have not to rip him apart. "Get in there and run the test now. One look at Junior, and you should have been able to see something is off. It's not like you've never met the kid before."

"Mr. Phillips, I think Rose is blowing this out of proportion."

Before he can finish, I grab him by the shirt. "Listen to me! This is not a fucking pissing contest. Get in there and run the test before I snap your fucking neck." I feel Rose pulling me back, and then she steps in front of me.

" Dr. McCord, I'm sorry if I offended you, please, just run the test. Thank you."

If Rose wasn't here, God knows what I would have done. McCord heads into Junior's room. I need to calm down before I go in. I don't want to upset Junior.

"Rose, how long will the test take to run?" Everyone knows I don't do well with waiting.

"It should take about two hours. Everything we need to run the test can be done at the clinic here. I will go back with Dr. McCord and oversee it. I know the nurses are capable to run the test, but I would feel better being there."

McCord steps out of the room, and I don't give him a chance to say anything. "Rose will be overseeing the test. Get me the results as quick as possible. Thank you, Rose."

I head back into Junior's room. I'm trying to avoid looking at Bella, if I do, she will know I'm worried. "Hey, Junior, I need to borrow your mum for a bit. Aunt Raven called a family meeting."

"Uncle Jax, are you in the dog house again?" At least he's laughing.

"Junior, have you ever known me *not* to be in the dog house? And stop laughing. Get some rest and I'll be back up later so we can watch the new *Doctor Who*."

We step out of the room and Bella begins to cry. I pull her into my arms and try to calm her down. "Bella, don't let Junior hear you crying, please."

"Why did you have Dr. McCord come back and run a test? You seem very worried."

"Rose asked McCord to run the test and he blew her off. She came to me and said she was concerned about Michael's fatigue and bruising. She asked me to demand a CBC be done. When I asked Junior to watch *Doctor Who* with me, he said he was tired. That was all the answer I needed. How long has he been feeling ill?"

"The fever only started this morning. Past couple of days he said he was tired. The bruising I put off to all the exploring he's been doing with Rose in those secret passageways."

"Where is Michael? Does he know Junior is ill?"

"He left early this morning before Junior was even up. He should be back by now."

"You need to keep it together, Bella, we have no idea what is going on. It could still be just a really bad case of the flu. The test should be back soon. Let's head downstairs and see what's going on."

We are about to leave when Michael comes up the stairs. Bella sees him and burst into tears again. I bring Michael up to speed on everything.

"Jax, he's been tired the past couple of days, but I figured he was getting back into the routine of school and stuff. Bella, this is just another reason why you can't leave and go to Capri."

"Michael, I already decided I wasn't going. Raven called a family meeting and I was going to let everyone know my decision."

"Sis, I'm going to head downstairs. I will let everyone know. You stay here with Junior."

She grabs my arm, "Jax, I'm not going because I can't put Max in that position. I realize that man is not my father; he donated his sperm, nothing more. Max is my brother and more important to me than that cold-hearted bastard could ever be."

I lean in and kiss her forehead, "I get it; stay with Junior."

As I head downstairs, I realize Bella is right; the past needs to stay there. This family needs to focus on the present. I have to keep my brother from making the biggest mistake of his life, no matter what it takes.

Chapter Ten

Raven

I GET DOWNSTAIRS AND hurry up, preparing for everyone's arrival. I put out some water and, of course, some Scotch. I've never been the one to call a family meeting—heck—I've only ever been to one. I silently rehearse all the points I want to bring up. I need to stress that the past needs to stay in the past. I only hope I can get everyone to listen. No one has shown up yet, and I'm about to go search out Jax when he walks in; his face is pale and his jaw is clenched. What the hell happened now?

"Jax, what the hell is going on?"

"Junior is sick."

"I know. I saw him this morning. Is his fever worse?"

" Dr. McCord thought it was the flu, but your mum doesn't think so. She had me order a test. The results should be back in couple of hours." He leans in near my ear, "I think he's really sick," he whispers.

Everyone else seems to show up at once. Before Jax can say anything more, Max and Jackie walk in. Max takes one look at Jax and freezes. "What's the matter?"

Jax brings him up to speed on what he knows so far. An is very quiet. The last thing she needs right now is any more stress.

"Son, when will the results be available?"

Jax sits down next to his mom and holds her hand. He's trying to keep her calm. "Mum, Rose is overseeing the test and will let us know right away."

I called this meeting, so it's time to get this done. "Okay, everyone, I'm just going to jump right in here and say that no one is going to Capri. Before anyone says anything, please hear me out." All eyes are on me and I have to make the strongest case. I'm only going to have one chance at this.

"There is no reason for any one of you to meet James. Nothing good will come of it. It is abundantly clear that the man is nothing but trouble. This family does not need any more drama or turmoil. We need to look to the future and build upon that. Jax, I get that there are three other men out there that are your half brothers. If you want to make contact with them, then that's a different story, but James breeds trouble."

Jax still has a grip on his mom's hand, I think more for his support than hers. "Raven, Bella already decided she is not going. She said he's nothing more than a sperm donor and I agree with her. Even though I want to know why, nothing will change. That boy will still be waiting by the window for his dad to show up. Max, if you want to go, then I will have to go with you. However, I don't think it's in your best interest to do so, but I would never let you go alone."

I can only hope we've gotten through to Max. If he doesn't go, then all this ends tonight and we can move forward. He's silent for a bit, holding both of Jackie's hands tightly in his. He lifts them to his lips and kisses them. "I decided today that I wasn't going to confront him. Nothing can change the past. I need to protect my future and the future of this family."

"Great, so it's settled then, hopefully Michael only has the flu and we can all go to Switzerland to celebrate Jackie's birthday. A vacation right about now sounds wonderful."

The baby monitor lights up and my daughter begins to stir. "I need to go nurse, please let me know when the results are back." I head upstairs praying that it's just the flu.

ANTONIA IS VERY RESTLESS today. I wonder if she can sense how stressed out I've been. I get her cleaned up and, once she starts eating, she seems to settle down. She has a great appetite and she seems to be sleeping longer at night. I can't believe she is almost two months old. I know Jax wants to have another baby right away and reality is I do too. I never want my child to be alone like I was. I look up and Jax is in the doorway. "Hey, are the results back yet?"

"Rose, just called, she and Dr. McCord are on their way."

Jax takes Antonia and gets her settled in her crib. We head downstairs and I pray it's only the flu. We sit next to Bella, and Jax firmly holds her hand.

"Sis, no matter what happens, we will get through it."

My mom walks in with Dr. McCord, and by the grim look on her face, I know it's not the flu.

Jax jumps up, "McCord, what are the results?"

I watch Dr. McCord; I notice he can't look Jax in the eye. I get up and put my arm around Jax's waist for support. Dr. McCord finally looks up from the papers he has clutched in his hands. "We just got the results back, Michael has Acute Lymphocytic Leukemia, commonly referred to as ALL."

Bella drops to her knees, crying and shaking. Michael drops to his knees stunned and silent, trying to hold his wife.

"Please, everyone, it's not a death sentence. Thanks to Rose's insistence on running the test, we have caught this early. He will need to have a bone marrow aspiration and biopsy, but that has to be done at the hospital. Once all of the tests are completed, treatment can start right away. I will outline it all for you. In the meantime, I want everyone to be tested for a possible bone marrow match. It's a simple cheek swab, but since Michael has no siblings, everyone needs to be tested. Rose will do the swabs and get them over to the lab right away."

We're all in shock; no one is making a sound. Absorbing everything being said but not believing a word of it, I look over to An and I realize, with her health so fragile, this could be her breaking point. I release myself from Jax's tight grip, grab some water, and offer it to her. Her hands are trembling so bad, she can't even hold the glass.

My mom comes over and immediately checks An's pulse. "An, please try to stay focused right now. Michael will get treatment, and he *will* survive. We have caught this early enough for the treatment to be effective. What this family can't handle is anything happening to you. I need you to calm down, take some slow, deep breaths, and concentrate on my voice." My mom, once again, is working her magic. "Raven, please make some chamomile tea," she asks me quickly then turns back to An. "Remember what we discussed; you need to focus on your health. Michael needs you to be strong and healthy."

I hurry up and put up the pot for tea. Jax finally snaps out of his shock and takes charge of the situation. "McCord, after we do the swab's, what's next? Where can he get the best treatment?"

"Mr. Phillips, the treatment is done in three phases. The first phase is called Remission induction. In this phase, the goal is to kill the leukemia cells that are in the blood and the bone marrow. The second phase is called consolidation or intensification. This starts when Michael is in remission. It's a specific therapy to kill any remaining leukemia cells that may cause a relapse. The third phase is a maintenance treatment. The best place for this type of treatment is in the USA. I have looked at the top five hospitals in the United States and I would suggest The Children's Hospital of Philadelphia. Dr. Torrence is the head of the oncology pediatric department. They are on the cutting edge of research for this type of cancer. I took the liberty of contacting them and arranged for Michael's admittance."

"What about this bone marrow that you're testing us for? When does that come into play?"

"It's not part of the initial treatment, it's used in the event of a relapse after treatment. I want to be prepared just in case. Usually a sibling is the best match, but since Michael is an only child, I want to start the search now. As long as everyone is healthy, then donating won't be a problem."

I bring An her tea and she seems to be calmer. My mom takes the swabs and begins to swab each of us. As she swabs the inside of my cheek, I'm reminded that something so simple can be a life saver to someone in need. When she gets to Jackie, she stops her. "I'm already a member of the Blood and Marrow Transplant information network. I've donated in the past, and if I'm a match, I would gladly donate again."

Max tightens his hold on her hands. "Thank you, babe."

"Max, please don't thank me. Everyone should be doing this and not just in a time of crisis. A lot of people know about donating blood, however, not everyone knows about donating stem cells."

My mom takes Bella's hand and pulls her to her feet. "Bella, listen to me, please. You are Michael's rock right now. His state of mind will be based on how you, and everyone here, react around him. It's very important to keep a positive outlook and, whatever you do, don't treat him any differently. I understand that I'm not Michael's doctor. I am, however, his friend. If it would be okay with you, I would like to go with him to the states and stay with him."

"Oh, Rose, I would love to have you there with us. I know how close the two of you have become, and I'm sure Michael would love having you there. Dr. McCord, when will we be leaving?"

"You will be leaving in the morning."

"Okay. Thank you, everyone. If you'll excuse me, I'm going upstairs to be with my son." Bella and Michael Sr. race upstairs to be with Michael.

My mom gathers up the swabs and hurries out to get them back to the lab.

The baby monitor comes to life but I already know it's time to feed Antonia, I can feel it. "An, I'm going upstairs to feed Antonia, would you like me to walk with you to your room?" I'm not really giving her an option; she needs rest.

"Thank you, Raven." I help her upstairs and let her lean on me for support, knowing the rough road ahead for all of us and silently praying we come out okay.

Jaxson

FOR THE PAST TWO days, my life has been spinning out of control. I hate the unknown, yet lately, that's all I have . . . a life filled with 'what ifs.' I don't do 'what ifs'; I don't leave things to chance. I snap out of my stage of disbelief, I need to make the rest of the arrangements. I hear Max on the phone, probably arranging security. I pour us each a scotch while I wait for him to finish his call. "Jackie, how long have you been involved with the donor network?"

"I became involved about eight years ago. My father had a friend whose son was also diagnosed with ALL. Like Michael, he is an only child, so my whole family was tested. I came up as the closest match, so when he needed the transplant, I donated. Jax, the little boy is fine. We've stayed in touch. He lives in the states and is getting ready for his prom."

"Thank you, Jackie. You are a very kind-hearted person and my brother is very lucky to have you in his life . . . we all are." I hug her. She brings so much to this family without even trying.

Max is finally off the phone. "Max, I need to get a place to stay near the hospital. I'll be leaving in the morning with Junior."

"Jax, we are all leaving in the morning. The plane is being prepared now. Mrs. Osla is setting up a place for us to live. Security is all set; we all go, mate."

I pass him his scotch, "Why did this happen to Junior? Is this something that runs through our gene pool? He has been having so much fun here."

Jackie gets up and hugs Max. "Max, I'm going to check on An and Raven."

"Jackie will go to her parents for a few days and then meet us in the states." He turns his focus back to me.

I let him know that Raven told me about her birthday. "That must be so hard for her. Birthdays are supposed to be a happy day. Can we do anything to make it better for her?"

He swirls the amber liquid in his glass; he seems distant. "I was going to go with her to her parents but, with everything happening with Junior, I'm going to the states with you."

"Go with her, and then you can both head over to the states together. It's only for a few days, and we will all be there. If you want, talk to Junior about it." I know he's torn and not just about Junior. "Max, what made you decide not to go to Capri?"

"Mrs. Osla and I had a long talk. She made me realize what I could lose if I go. I can't lose Jackie, it would kill me."

"I should have figured Mrs. Osla had a hand in it. Do you think she will ever feel comfortable letting everyone know her connection to you?"

"I told her that you know she was Samantha's aunt and practically raised her. The rest is up to her. Knowing her as well as I do, I imagine she doesn't want anyone to feel uncomfortable around her. "

"Was she upset that you told me? I've never said anything to her, I respect her privacy."

"She understood that I needed to tell you everything so that I could move forward in life. Ultimately, that's all she's ever wanted for me. When she's not scaring the living daylights out of me."

I look at him and he's really serious. I can't help but laugh. "Oh, Max, sometimes you really are my source of amusement. Let's go check on Junior, I'm sure Bella told him what's going on by now. I don't want him to be scared."

As we get up to head upstairs, Mrs. Osla walks in. "Jaxson, I need to go over the arrangements I made for tomorrow."

We both freeze in our tracks. Max is biting his bottom lip, trying not to laugh. "Jax, you stay here with Mrs. Osla and I will meet you upstairs." As he turns to leave his eyes meet hers and he stops dead in his tracks.

"Maxwell, he is your nephew also, so I suggest you both have a seat."

Heading back to the couch, I can almost swear I hear Max growl. She hands us each a folder. "I have compiled some information about the treatment that young Michael could expect, the length of time required to administer the treatment, and the possible side effects. The treatment and follow up could take up to three years. I secured an estate ten minutes from the hospital that is large enough to accommodate everyone. I understand everyone is in shock right now, however, please bear in mind this is not a death sentence. I have enclosed a packet on Dr. David Torrence, the oncologist that will be handling young Michael's treatment. If you look at the research I provided you with, the survival rate since 2005 is at 90.4%. That is something to stay focused on. It is very important that everyone stay positive and upbeat for the lad. Jaxson, I'm worried about the stress all of this is having on An. If it is okay with you, I would like to accompany her to the states and stay with her. She has been a very kind, dear friend and I would like to do the same. However, if you need me to stay here, I will."

I'm overwhelmed looking through all the research that she pulled. "Christ, Max, look at all the stuff Junior is going to have to go through. I had no idea it was going to be this much and this long." I thank God we have the unlimited resources to provide anything he needs.

"Neither did I. We will be there with him every step of the way."

"Jaxson, I also got the information from Matthew that you requested. I think you will both find this very interesting. In New York State, your medical license is for life, as long as you have not been convicted of a felony. When a physician's license is put on the inactive list, it must be updated every two years. Apparently Joseph had her license placed on the inactive list, and made sure he maintained the status for her. Matthew started the process to activate it and have her name changed on her license. If she wanted to practice legally, she could, however, she would be required to complete all updated course work and training. It won't be easy but it doesn't mean she can't do it. There are a lot of options available to her, but it is up to her to decide. Maxwell, as per your request, Matthew removed you as her legal guardian but you are still the executor of her will. Jaxson, you can't bully her to do something she's not prepared to do."

"Mrs. Osla, I wouldn't bully her." She raises one eyebrow and cocks her head to the side. "Did Matthew say how long it will take?"

"Surprisingly, once he submits the name change, only a couple of days."

"Thank you. I will sit Rose down and let her know what is going on. You can travel with my mum to the states and stay with her. I'm sure she would love the company and I appreciate that you would want to do that for her."

"If you don't need me for anything else, I want to visit with An."

"That's fine, thank you."

"What the hell are you thinking, Jax? She's been locked away for twenty years, she can't just go back to a life that doesn't exist anymore," Max pounces before Mrs. Osla even steps fully out of the room.

"Calm down. I'm not going to push her into anything. Raven, asked me to look into it. She said she spoke with Rose and it might be an option. She doesn't have to go back to being a surgeon, she could go into research. She needs to know that all her schooling and training wasn't for nothing. She still has a very full life ahead of her and we need to give her every chance possible."

"Jax, don't force her to do something she might not be ready to do."

"I promise I won't. Let's go see Junior. I promised him we could watch the new *Doctor Who.*"

"Jax, so help me, I'm not sitting through another hour of that show. Did you know Junior is trying to get Jackie to watch it with him?"

"Ha! I told you that kid is a genius."

Chapter Eleven

Raven

"AN, PROMISE ME YOU will try and get some rest. Michael needs all of us to be strong," I plead with her. I don't doubt she needs this reminder as she is still recuperating from surgery.

"Raven, I'm so scared. I've never had to deal with anything like this. How much more heartache will we have to suffer?"

She begins to cry and I pull her into my arms. "An, Michael is a very strong boy. We need to have faith. We need to be his rock to lean on." *Maybe if I tell her enough, I'll believe it myself.*

We head into her room and I get her settled in. "I'm going to feed Antonia, and then I will check back in with you. In the meantime, try and get some rest."

I'm heading toward the nursery when I run into my mom. "Hey, Mom, you're just the person I wanted to see. I'm heading in to feed Antonia, will you come with me?"

"I was going to check on An, can it wait?"

"Actually, I just got An settled in for a nap."

"Oh, okay, I will check on her later. We need to try and keep her calm. What do you need?"

"Let me get Antonia situated first."

We head into the nursery and my mom begins to change Antonia. When she's done, I take my usual seat in front of the window and begin to nurse.

"What's on your mind, Raven?"

"Actually, I have quite a few questions. What can we expect with Michael's treatment? Should Antonia be tested? What are Michael's chances of survival? How did he get this?"

"Raven, slow down. First, I'm not an Oncologist, and neither is Dr. McCord. These are questions that need to be addressed by Michael's Oncologist. While the test was running, I did some research and found The Children's Hospital in Philadelphia has a high survival rate, in the ninetieth percentile. We've caught this early, and that's also a positive for Michael. I don't have all the answers, I'm sorry. I only thought to check for it because I worked closely with an ALL patient who also had a heart condition. This is not going to be a quick fix and everyone will have to adjust to the changes, especially Michael. He is so active and full of life. I thank God that Jax listened to me and ran the test. From what I read online, the treatments can run for three years. We will have to adjust and live our lives around his treatments."

I sit quietly for a moment, letting all of this information sink in. Suddenly, I remember the letter I received the other day. "Mom, Jax got a package the other day from his attorney. There is a letter addressed to me from Duke. I didn't open it and, to be honest, I'm not sure I want to."

"What are you afraid of? You know he can't hurt you, Raven."

"Not physically, but how about emotionally? I've worked so hard to put the past behind me only to find out I have a sibling. My whole childhood, I dreamt of having a sibling, then that dream came true, except . . . he turned into a murderer. I'm sorry if this hurts you, Mom. I don't know what to do? I would have had Max read it, but I can't put anything else on him."

"Do you feel you have to read it? Why not just burn it?—he's not in your life and he never will be."

"I thought about that, but it's because of Duke that we are free from Vincent."

"Raven, it's because of Duke that Vincent knew you were alive. Don't paint him out to be the victim. From what you told me, he had a hand in your kidnapping and the kidnapping of Michael. One good deed doesn't wipe out all the bad. He walked away with a sweet deal, never having to answer for the lives he took."

"I wish I was as strong as you, Mom."

"Nonsense, Raven, you're a lot stronger than you think. I'm going to check on An while you finish up with Antonia." She squeezes my shoulder and turns to leave just as Jackie walks in.

"Hi, Jackie, I was just going to check on An, is everything okay?"

"Yes, Rose, I just wanted to see my niece." My mom leaves and I know something is bothering Jackie. I don't say anything, I know her; she will talk to me when she is ready. I put Antonia in her crib and take a moment to watch her sleep. I'm reminded that with all the turmoil around us, life still goes on. I turn around and Jackie is sitting in the rocker, staring out into the darkness. "I never knew that you donated stem cells. What made you do it?"

"A friend of my father's son had ALL. He is an only child, so we were all tested. I was a close match. The surgery is not bad; a needle is injected into the back of the top part of the hip bone. They harvest about 2 pints of marrow, and you're sore for a couple of days. Something so simple can save so many lives. Donating cord blood is very important and also so simple. When I have a child, I already plan on donating."

"I never knew that there were uses for the cord."

"Raven, there are a number of uses for the cord blood, but you have to have the baby in the hospital."

"Funny, Jackie . . . very funny. So what's bothering you, and don't say 'nothing.'"

"I told Max we could get married in May. Now with everything going on with Michael, I'm thinking of delaying it. I just don't know how to explain it to him."

I stretch out on the window bench trying to figure out a solution. "You know he is going to flip out if you delay the wedding. Plus Michael told me today how excited he is that you will be his aunt. We need to figure something out."

"I don't know what we could figure out, we are leaving in the morning for the states, and then I have to fly to Switzerland."

"Where were you planning on having the wedding?"

"I figured Scotland is very pretty in May, so I would have it here. Why, what are you thinking?"

"Now hear me out and keep an open mind."

She stops rocking and leans forward. "Okay, you have my full attention. What's the plan?"

"The plan is: you go to your parents' home and have a ceremony for them. You then come to the states and have a ceremony at the hospital, so Michael can be a part of it. When we get back and everything is settled, you can renew your vows and have whatever type of wedding you want," I declare. Her eyes are wide and her mouth is hanging open. "Well, aren't you going to say anything?"

"Are you nuts? I went from having no wedding to having three weddings. You want me to get married now?! Besides, Max is going to the states with Michael. I don't expect him to go to my parents with me."

"Look, you know you want your parents to be there. The entire family wants to be part of this day. You can't put everything on hold. Life doesn't stop, we have to adapt. This is us adapting. Max will never let you go to your parents' house alone. Face it, Jackie, he needs to feel like he is protecting you."

"Even if that's true, how do you intend on getting everything together so quickly?"

"Jackie, we have Mrs. Osla! That woman can move mountains if she had to."

"So, what do you suggest I tell Max?"

Right at that moment, Jax and Max decide to walk into the nursery.

"Tell me what, Jackie?" His voice is low and his jaw is tight, he takes hold of her hand.

I get up and take Jax's arm. "How about we give them some privacy? Besides, I need to see Michael." I pull Jax out of the room, not giving him a chance to answer.

Jackie

"RAVEN AND I WERE discussing Michael's treatment. I explained to her that it could take about three years. We were trying to figure out what to do about our wedding when you came in. Do you have any ideas as to what we should do?"

"The only thing I've figured out so far is that I'm going to Switzerland with you. Mrs. Osla made all the arrangements for Michael, and she set up a place for all of us right near the hospital. I know Michael's treatment is not an overnight fix, but I'm begging you please don't ask me to wait three years. Did Raven come up with ideas?"

"Max, calm down; we don't want to wake the baby. Raven's idea was for us to get married while we're in Switzerland. Then, we can have a simple ceremony at the hospital for Michael and the rest of the family. Down the road, if we want to renew our vows back in Scotland, we can. She suggested Mrs. Osla could pull this off." Max's face lights up and he gifts me with a huge smile. "I take it you like this idea?"

"I'll be your husband sooner rather than later, what's not to like? How do you feel about this? I know that every woman dreams of her wedding day. I want to make all your dreams come true."

"I've never dreamed of a big fancy wedding, maybe because I grew up so isolated. All I ever dreamed of was finding a man to love me honestly, heart and soul. I've found that in you. It doesn't matter how it happens, just make it happen, Max."

"Babe, I will get Mrs. Osla on it right away. Everyone leaves in the morning for the states. We will follow them over there as soon as possible. What day would you like to get married?"

"I would like to get married on my birthday. I think it's only fitting that I can mark a sad day with some happiness. My sister will be there in spirit, and that would mean so much to me."

"If you're really sure that's what you want, then I will talk to Mrs. Osla and have her make all the arrangements."

I reach up and kiss his tender lips. "Yes. Now, let's go tell Michael that I will be his aunt. I know he will be happy, even though I refuse to watch that show with him."

He puts his arm around me, and as we head out of the nursery, Antonia starts to fuss. Max walks up to the crib, reaches in, and rubs her tummy. He begins to sing very softly to her. I can barely understand what he's saying. It sounds like *hush ye, my baby, and sleep without fear.* Antonia falls back to sleep and we quietly step out of the room.

"Max, what were you singing? I could only understand part of it."

"It's an old, Scottish lullaby by Jackie Oates called "Dream Agnus." I would sing it to Elliot every night."

"It's beautiful, very soothing; she fell right back to sleep. Come on; let's go tell the others our plan."

Jaxson

AS RAVEN AND I head toward Junior's room, she fills me in on what's going on with Jackie. "So, what have you been up to since I left you alone?" she asks, changing the subject. I promptly relay all of the information Mrs. Osla gave Max and me.

"I asked my mom if we should have Antonia tested and she said we need to speak with Michael's oncologist."

"Mrs. Osla lined up the top oncologist to see Junior. It kills me that he has to go through all of this." As we get ready to step into Junior's room, I take a moment to put on a happy face and bury my anger. I know he needs only positive, upbeat people around him right now. As soon as we step inside, I notice he's upset.

"Hey, Junior, what's the problem here?" I ask then notice Bella and Michael looking grim.

"Uncle Jax, Mum told me what is going on. I don't want to leave here, and I sure don't want to get stuck with a bunch of stupid needles."

I feel like my heart is ripping to shreds. "Hey, Junior, we are all going to be there with you every step of the way. You know that, right?"

"Everyone? Even Antonia?"

"Yes, even Antonia. We are family and we stick together—no matter what. Why are you so worried about leaving here?"

"What if we don't get to come back here? Miss Rose and I have been exploring everyday and I love helping Miss Jackie with the horses. I have a lot of friends here, what about t-them?" He stutters and his lip begins to tremble.

I'm trying so hard to keep it together here. I glance to Raven for help. She sits down on the bed next to Junior and takes his hand.

"Michael, look at me, please. You know this place is over a hundred years old, it's not going anywhere. Your friends will still be your friends. I promise you will be able to Skype with them all the time. When we get back, I'm sure Jackie will have you right back down at the barn. I know you're scared, and it's okay to have those feelings, but we will all be with you every step of the way. You'll never be alone—I promise. Remember, when we were kidnapped? I promised you we would be rescued and we would be okay. I'm promising you now, we will be with you and you will be okay. Faith, Michael." She pulls him into her arms, "Faith," she whispers. The door opens and in walks Max and Jackie.

"Hey, Michael, Jackie and I need to talk to you about something."

"Sure, Uncle Max, what's up?"

"Everyone is flying out tomorrow with you to the States. Jackie and I have to head to Switzerland for a few days to see her parents. We will head out to you right after that. Are you okay with that?"

Jackie sits on the bed and takes his hand. "Michael, I promise we will be with you the whole time. I need to go to my parents for a few days, if it wasn't important, I wouldn't go. When we get to the States, your Uncle Max and I are going to get married. I was wondering if you would give me away like you did for Aunt Raven?"

"Miss Jackie, I will give you away and it's okay if you need to go to your parents. You promise you'll come as soon as you can?"

"I promise, Michael. Don't worry about the horses, I've got their care all arranged until we get back."

"There's just one thing, Miss Jackie."

"You're gonna make me, aren't you?"

"Yep."

"Michael Giaconna, I swear you are more like your Uncle Jax every day. Fine, but your Uncle Max has to, as well."

"Yes!" He throws his arms around her.

"Hey wait, what do I have to do? Jax, what's so funny?" Max smacks my arm as I chuckle.

Oh my God, I can't stop laughing. The kid is a genius. "You have to watch *Doctor Who*." I could swear he's growling.

Raven gets up, "I'll go make the peanut butter & jelly sandwiches."

Chapter Twelve
Maxwell

THE SHOW IS FINALLY over. I don't understand what the attraction is, but Junior was happy he finally got us to watch it. At least Raven made me popcorn. "Okay, Junior, you get some rest. You have to leave early tomorrow. Jackie and I will be out in a few days. Don't even think of complaining, we held up our end of the deal." I take Jackie's hand and we head out the door.

"Hey, Max . . . Jackie, wait up." Jax catches up to us.

"What's up, Jax?"

"I just want to thank you, Jackie. I know it's not the wedding of your dreams, but you made Junior very happy, and for that, I will always be in your debt."

"I love that little boy, and I would do anything for him."

"Thank you. Is there anything you need me to do for you before I leave?"

"No, I have arranged everything for the horses."

"Max, is all the security arranged for the trip and at the hospital?"

"Yes, I've got everything under control. Get some rest, you have another long day tomorrow."

"I will. I want to check on Mum first. I'll see you both in the morning, good night."

He leaves and now I want to talk to Mrs. Osla, before it gets any later. We head downstairs and find her in the kitchen. Jackie and I explain to her what we want to do and she assures us she can get all the arrangements made.

"I'm very happy for you both. It's time this family had some good news." She hugs us both and we head out the door. I need to be alone with Jackie. It's been a very stressful day, and my heart is breaking for Junior.

We walk back to our place hand in hand; this is what's special to me. "Babe, I understand that the treatment and follow up could last three years, was it like that for the boy you donated to?"

"Every case is different; everyone's body reacts differently to the treatment. He had a setback which is why he needed the stem cells. He's fine now, and odds are in Michael's favor. His attitude is a big part of the healing. He has to believe he will beat this, as do the people around him."

"I get it, so even though my heart is breaking, I will put on a brave face and treat him no differently than I do now."

"Exactly. That is very important. Michael needs to understand that it's not a death sentence and it's not a license to do whatever he wants. Love him as you always have and always will."

As we head in the door, I turn her around in my arms and kiss her very tenderly.

"Babe, I need you slow and gentle. I need to feel your delicate fingertips trailing all over my body. I need you to make me forget."

"How about we have a nice soak in the tub, and then I'll see what I can do to help you relax."

We head into the bathroom and Jackie sets up the bath. She lights the candles, lights the fireplace, and turns on some music. I sit on the counter, watching her and I'm amazed how graceful she is . . . even doing such simple things. She shuts the water off and announces the tub is ready. I watch in a trance as she undresses and slowly sinks in.

"Are you going to join me, or are you going to ogle me all night?"

I quickly snap out of my trance and take off my clothes. I climb in the huge tub, facing her. I begin to massage her feet, and when I get to the arch, I press and drag my thumb all the way up. She tilts her head back and moans. *Fuck me,* she is so beautiful.

"Max, that feels absolutely wonderful. Now, let me return the favor. Come sit between my legs and let me massage your shoulders."

I turn around and wedge myself between her legs, looping my arms around them, feeling totally surrounded by her. She massages my shoulders and I feel myself finally relax.

"Max, have you always loved baths?"

"Yes, even more now with you." I can feel my tension fade away. "Do you think your parents are going to be okay with the quick wedding arrangements?"

"Once I explain to them why, they will understand. My mom will be happy to have something so wonderful on such a somber day. I will warn you, my brother will probably have something to say about it."

"Jackie, you understand no one will get in our way. I will be respectful of your family, however, I know what he said to you when you left. I will not put up with that type of behavior toward you—*ever.*"

"It doesn't matter to me what he thinks, it's what's in my heart that counts. Nothing will ever change that for me. Now, I think this water is getting cold and I need you to fulfill your promise to love me tender and gentle."

I climb out of the tub and get the towels off of the warmer, wrap one around my waist, and then dry her off. I don't think I will ever get tired of touching her, or caring for her. It's all the little things that make our relationship special. She tries to stifle her yawn, but I know she's tired. We've both had a long and emotional day. "Babe, let's get some rest, tomorrow is going to be another hard day for all of us." We climb into bed and I pull her close to me. I laugh as she tucks the blankets in around us. I gently stroke her back and listen to the tempo of her breathing slow down as she drifts off to sleep. "Thank you for loving me, Jackie," I whisper and kiss the top of her head.

Isabella

I SIT IN MY son's room and watch him fall asleep. I feel another wave of fear rush over me. I have to be strong for him, I just don't know how. Why did this happen—he's never been sick—*why?* Michael comes back in to check on us. I know he's scared too, but I need to focus all my energy on our son.

"Bella, come to bed. You need to get some rest. You'll be no good to Junior if you get sick."

I know he's right but I can't bring myself to leave his side. "Maybe later, right now, I need to be here with him. I know he's scared and I want to stay here in case he wakes up." He scoops me up into his arms. "Michael, what are you doing?"

"Bella, if you stay I stay; we are in this together."

He sits in the chair and cradles me in his arms. I rest my head on his chest and let my tears silently fall, careful not to wake my son.

"Hush, Bella, I've got you. I'll always have you."

In the safety of his arms, I allow myself to finally get some sleep.

Rose

I WANT TO CHECK on An again before I turn in for the night. I know what lies ahead for Michael, but the last thing anyone needs right now is to be overwhelmed with too much information. I need to make sure she remains calm. She is very lucky to be alive right now, and I mean to keep it like that. I knock and Mrs. Osla lets me in.

"Hi, Mrs. Osla. I wanted to check on An before I turned in for the night."

"She is sleeping right now, but do you have a moment to chat with me?"

"Of course, what can I do for you, Mrs. Osla?"

"Well, you can start by finally calling me Rona. You saved my best friend's life and I will always be indebted to you. I did the research for Michael's treatment, so I know what is in store for the lad. I know it's not your field of study, but I'm grateful you insisted the test be run. Again, I wanted to thank you and to let you know I will be traveling to the States with everyone. If you need me for anything, please don't hesitate to ask."

"Okay, thank you, Rona. I'm going to do a quick check on An and then try and get some rest." I head into An's room and she is asleep, however, I want to at least take her blood pressure and pulse. Exhaustion must have finally hit, she barely moved while I checked her. I head out and I see Rona is still here.

"Everything seems good. I will check her again in the morning. Rona, your name is very unusual, what does it mean?"

She smiles "Wise ruler, very fitting, don't you agree?"

I laugh, "Yes, I would say so. You should get some rest; it's a long flight tomorrow."

"I will, thank you, Rose."

I head out the door feeling very tired and overwhelmed with today's events. I need to get some sleep. I only hope my mind will let me.

Raven

ANTONIA IS UP VERY early this morning, which is fine since I need to pack her stuff. It's amazing how much one little baby needs. Knowing Mrs. Osla, she's probably made sure the house is well stocked. I sit in front of the window, watching the sunrise probably for the last time in a long while. *I'm really going to miss this place.* It's become home; my daughter was born here. I promised Michael that we will come back and I intend to keep that promise . . . no matter what. He is such a special boy. I spent most of the night, praying to God to please give him the strength he will need to get through this. It's going to be a long road for everyone. "Good morning, Jax," I say as I feel his presence.

"Good morning, sweetheart. Is she done eating?"

"Yeah, but she doesn't seem tired."

"I'll take her while you get ready," he offers. I hand him the baby, but I don't get up just yet.

"It's going to be another long emotional day for all of us. I'm glad my mom will be with us. Watching her take charge of everything, so effortlessly, was very comforting. She was able to keep the panic at a minimal." He sits in the rocker and slowly glides back and forth as Antonia fights to keep her eyes open.

"Raven, I had Matthew look into your mum's license, like you asked. It's still good. Also, Matthew had her name changed and requested to have it made active, but that's only the beginning. There is a lot of other stuff she would have to do in order to practice. I'm not sure of everything that is needed, but Matthew is going to look into it and let her know. In the meantime, I am going to bring her up to speed on what we do know."

"Well, I wasn't expecting it to be easy."

"That's just the first hurdle. If she decides to practice, then I'm sure she would be required to do continuing education classes along with training to bring her up to speed. Maybe she would rather go into some sort of research; I don't know what that would entail. Ultimately, it's up to her. I'm just giving her the opportunity to make her own decision."

"Thank you. Just remember to go slow when you tell her." I get up to leave and bend down to kiss Antonia. I love her smell; sweet and fresh. He takes my hand and brings it to his lips, tightly closing his eyes. I know something is bothering him.

"What's wrong?"

"The letter; have you decided what you're going to do?"

"Yes. I'm going to read it before we leave today. It won't change anything, at least for me it won't."

"I'm here for you and, if you want me to be with you when you read it, let me know."

"I love you, Jax."

"More, sweetheart, always more."

I LEAVE ANTONIA'S ROOM with Jax mindlessly rocking her back and forth. She's asleep. He could put her in her crib, but this is his special time with her. While everyone is still asleep, I decide to head straight to his office and retrieve the letter. I need to get this over with and move on. I take the letter off the desk and curl up on his oversized, leather sofa. I close my eyes and take a deep breath. I know nothing he can say will change what happened. Jackie has always told me that the only way to move forward is to forgive and leave the past behind. *Easier said than done.* "I don't think I'm that strong."

"You're stronger than you think, Raven."

My eyes fly open and find Jax standing in the doorway. "I didn't hear you."

"I know. I didn't want to startle you, but I was worried. I'll give you some privacy, however, I won't be far away." He steps out of the room and closes the door. I muster up my courage and open the letter.

Raven,

I know you must hate me and I can understand why. I won't make excuses for what I did; I have to live with that for the rest of my life. When I first met you, I didn't know what to think. The only information I had was what Erica shared with me. I only found out you were my sister when you and Michael were kidnapped. I was not involved with Marco and Erica's plan to take you from that safe house. At that point, I was in too deep and had no idea how to get out. I thought by contacting Vincent, and telling him I was his son, that it would be a way out of that clusterfuck of a mess. When I explained to him who you and I were, and what was going on, he went ballistic. He told me not to panic, that he would help me. Little did I know the type of help he was offering would be even worse. I never killed anyone before. Hell, I've never even gotten into a fight! But that night, I took two lives. I will have to live with that for the rest of my life.

When we were in Italy, and you showed me our mother's journal, I realized what Vincent really was. I walked out of your room that day, knowing I needed to come up with a plan. I figured if I kept quiet, and let him believe that I wanted to be a part of his life, that I could figure a way out of that mess. The day the doctor came to examine you, Vincent stayed outside your room the entire time, waiting to find out what was wrong with you. That gave me the opportunity to go into his office and look around. I saw the program opened on his computer, so I downloaded everything. I knew that it must've been important, since he kept that drive with him all the time. When Jaxson and Maxwell came to rescue you, Vincent heard them and ordered the guards to go after them. He told them not to harm you, not that any of that mattered. He ran into his office and grabbed the drive. He told me to flee, and he would meet me in the states. I hid in the wine cellar until I had a chance to leave. I knew I would never get out of the country, so I took everything I thought was important and mailed it to a friend. I went to the airport, where I was picked up by the police.

Vincent sent Annabelle to see me, to try and persuade me to take the fall for everything. I knew then—I had to make a deal. I asked Hage if you were safe; I was prepared to include you in my deal if you needed me to. That's when he told me you and Jaxson were married. He assured me that Jaxson would make sure you were safe, and I knew this to be true.

Part of my deal is that I'm never to contact, or see you or any of the Giaconna family. I have no desire to see any of them, although, I would've liked to have gotten to know you better. You were always kind to me, even when I wasn't to you. I wish you and your family only the best; you fought hard for it and you deserve it.

I'm glad you're getting your happily ever after—you deserve it!

Duke

Wow, so much that I wasn't aware of. It doesn't change anything for me. I told Hage that Duke snapped that day. Anyone could see how played he was by Marco and Erica. Because of his efforts to get that drive, though, Max and I didn't have to testify. If my mom decides she wants to read this, I will let her. Maybe she can see some good in him. I take the letter and put it in the safe. I need to get ready. I want to make sure Michael is not scared. I open the door to head out and find Jax sitting on the floor.

"What are you doing?" I reach my hand down to him. He takes it, pulling himself up off the floor.

"I was worried about you and wanted to be here . . . just in case."

"I'm okay. I put the letter in the safe. He explained how he got the information and why. It doesn't matter, Jax; I closed that door for good. Now let's go check on Michael and then get started."

"Raven, you are, by far, the strongest person I know. I love you."

"It's the only way I know how to be."

As we head down the hall, he pulls me close. "You really okay with everything?"

"I really am. I know that whatever happened with Duke, he has to live with it. Jackie always tells me to forgive and then put it away. If I dwell on what happened, it would make me a bitter person. The past can't be changed, but the path we choose to move forward on can. I'm choosing only positive in my life."

"Sometimes your strength and faith befuddles my mind." We quietly head down the hall to Michael's room.

Chapter Thirteen

Junior

I CAN'T SLEEP AND I know it's cause I'm scared. My mum is trying not to cry but I can tell she's scared too. Why did this have to happen to me? I won't even have time to say goodbye to any of my friends. I wonder what the doctors are going to do to me? Vito slept with his head on my pillow all night. "Don't you worry, Vito, you go where I go." My door slowly opens and Aunt Raven and Uncle Jax stick their heads in. "I'm up; you can come in. You just missed Mum and Dad, they went to get ready to leave."

Aunt Raven crawls into bed next to Vito; he likes her. "Michael, are you ready to get going?"

I'm trying to be brave but I'm worried about Vito. I wipe my eyes as Aunt Raven pulls me toward her, which is hard with Vito in the middle.

"Michael, please tell me why you're upset. Maybe I can fix it."

"What a-about, Vito? What will happen to him, Aunt Raven?"

Uncle Jax throws his hands up in the air. "Junior, is that what this is about? I told you no one gets left behind and that includes the beast."

Aunt Raven and I start to laugh, "Uncle Jax, you know you love him."

"Whatever, Junior. Do you have everything packed? If you forget something, Uncle Max can bring it. I made sure Mrs. Osla ordered all our favorite DVDs. By the way, that was a slick move last night. You made me proud."

"Thanks, Uncle Jax, but I don't think they liked it. Oh, and why doesn't Uncle Max like peanut butter and jelly sandwiches?"

"I don't know; I never asked him. When you find out let me know."

"Uncle Jax, is Grams going to be able to come with me?"

"Just try and stop her! Now come on, you need to get ready. Be downstairs and ready to go in thirty minutes."

When they head out the door, I get up and throw on my clothes. I'm not going to some stupid hospital to get a bunch of needles. I looked it up on the Internet last night, and whatever this is that I have it doesn't look good. I grab my backpack and I'm thankful that I snuck into the kitchen this morning, using the secret passage to get my supplies. "Vito, come on, we have to go." He's not moving off the bed, but his tail is thumping. "Come on, Vito, we can't get caught." Finally he hops off the bed, and we quietly head out the door. I press the secret panel and just like that—we are gone.

Jaxson

"RAVEN, WHILE YOU FINISH tending to Antonia, I want to go over a few things with Mrs. Osla. I'll meet you downstairs."

"Ok, I shouldn't be too much longer."

I kiss her and head downstairs. I find Mrs. Osla and my mum having breakfast. "Good morning everyone. Mum, how are you feeling this morning?"

"I'm fine, son. Is everyone ready to leave?"

"Almost. Mrs. Osla, you got everything I asked for set up at the new house?"

"Jaxson, I assure you—all your favorite DVDs are already there. And, I even managed a surprise for young Michael. Before you ask, the answer is no; you'll have to wait and see."

Just then, Bella comes rushing in. "Jax, I can't find Junior! Do you know where he is?"

"I just left him in his room with the beast. I told him he had thirty minutes to be down here."

"I checked! He's not there and neither is Vito."

"Did you call his cell?"

"He left it on his nightstand. Michael went out to check the barn. I asked the guards and they said he never left the house."

"Bella, he has to be here . . . he didn't just disappear. It's a big house; let's get everyone together and start a search."

I call Max and inform him what's going on. We gather everyone into the kitchen and I hand out the two-way radios. "Rose, you've done the most exploring with Junior; is there any one of the secret passages that he likes the best?"

"He loves them all, but I know he really wanted to explore the tunnel that stretches from the backend of the house to the barn. There are so many that we haven't checked out yet."

Max comes racing through the door. "Hey, any sign of him yet?"

"No, Max, nothing. Why the hell would he do this?"

Max unfolds the blueprints and assigns each person a section to cover. "Maybe he's scared, Jax. Everyone take a flashlight along with your radio.

Please check in every fifteen minutes. Mum, you and Mrs. Osla wait here in case he shows up."

Raven comes in with Antonia, ready to go. "What's going on?"

"Junior disappeared. We are going to split up to search." She gives Antonia to Mrs. Osla.

"Jax, give me a section and a radio."

We each take a passageway and head out in search of Junior.

Raven

WITH BO RIGHT BY my side, I take the passage that Michael showed me. Instead of going up the staircase, I take the tunnel to the right. There are so many twist and turns. The tunnel seems to get a little wider and then suddenly, I come to a fork in the road. I stop and look in each direction. I have a gut feeling that I should go right. I go a few feet and I see Michael curled up with Vito, fast asleep. I pull out my radio to let everyone know I found him. "Jax, I've found Michael; he's asleep. Go through the passage way off the kitchen. When you get to the spiral staircase, there is a tunnel on the right. Go through the tunnel until you get to the fork, and then, go right. I will wait here for you." He assures me he's on his way. I sit next to Michael and try not to startle him.

"Michael, it's Aunt Raven, you need to wake up," I whisper as I gently stroke his hair.

He slowly opens his eyes, and widens them as if he's shocked to find me sitting next to him. "Aunt Raven, how did you find me?"

"I remembered you told me you wanted to explore this tunnel, so I thought I would look here first. Why did you run away?"

"I looked up on the internet what could happen to me and I got scared."

I open my arms, "Michael, come here." I hug him tightly. "You can't believe everything you find on the internet. I get that you're scared. It's okay to be scared of the unknown. I promised you we would all be there with you. You will never have to go through this by yourself. I need you to fight, Michael. I need you to be that brave boy that you were when we were kidnapped. You helped me get through that and I will help you get through this."

"How did I help you?"

"You gave me strength and you reminded me that I had a lot to live for. You also made me laugh even when I wanted to cry."

"I will try to be strong. My mum is going to be really mad at me."

"I won't lie, Michael, everyone is out looking for you. I radioed your Uncle Jax, and he is on his way."

"It's okay, Aunt Raven, I will apologize to everyone."

I hear Jax coming as he rounds the corner .Vito jumps up. "It's okay, Vito, it's only Jax."

"Junior, are you okay? What the hell were you thinking?"

"I'm sorry, Uncle Jax, I really didn't mean to make everyone worry about me."

He crouch's down in front of us, "Why did you run?"

He's looking down at his hands, seemingly trying not to cry. "It's okay, Michael, tell him."

"Uncle Jax, I'm scared. I don't want to do any of this."

Michael begins to sob uncontrollably, "Shh, don't cry, Michael, you'll be okay."

Jax pulls Michael into his lap. "I know you're scared, and, I won't lie to you—we all are. But, you are the bravest boy I know. You helped Aunt Raven when you were kidnapped. You moved out of the country; no questions asked. I know you can get through this, too."

"How?"

"Faith. Now we really need to get back. How about you climb on my back and we race on out of here?"

Michael climbs onto Jax's back and I gather up our stuff. We head back out the way we came in, with both dogs trailing behind us.

"Junior, how far back does this tunnel go? It's not on Uncle Max's blueprints."

"I don't know, this was the furthest I've ever gone. Uncle Jax, blueprints are like a map right?"

"Yeah, kind of like a very detailed map, why?"

"I wonder what else we don't know about? Do you think Uncle Max will let me see them?"

"Well, after he calms down about you running away, I'm sure he will give them to you. Hell, you got him to watch the *Doctor;* I couldn't even do that."

He laughs and the sound warms my heart. We get to the panel and press it open. When we climb back into the kitchen, Jax puts Michael down. Bella is crying, she grabs and hugs him, then lets go. "Michael, what the hell were you thinking? Why would you do this? Do you know how worried I was?" she begins to yell.

"Sis, cut the kid some slack. We had a talk and all is good now." Jax nudges him a little. "Go ahead, tell them."

"I'm sorry, everyone, if I made you worry. Last night I looked up on the

Internet what's wrong with me. I got scared and didn't want to go. I thought if I hid in the tunnels that you wouldn't find me. I guess I didn't really think it through."

Mrs. Osla steps up and takes Michael's hand, "Young man, I know this is going to be a long, hard journey, but you're strong. You need to ask yourself, what would the *Doctor* do?"

"Ma'am, he would accept the challenge and do his best."

"Well, then there's your answer. Now, I have a very special surprise waiting for you at the hospital, in the states, so I suggest you get ready to go." He gives her a big hug which surprises all of us, including Mrs. Osla.

"Uncle Max, do you think I can have a copy of the blueprints?"

"Why would you want blueprints?"

"They are like a giant treasure map, and I want to study them while I'm away. This way when I get back, I can search out all the secret passage ways."

"Okay, I will get a set and bring them with me next week. Now, we need to get going."

Max gives Michael a big hug "Let's go down to the barn; we will meet everyone at the plane."

"Okay, Jax, I need to feed Antonia. I will be back in a bit. Then we really need to get going."

I head out the door, and I can hear a flurry of activity behind me.

Maxwell

JUNIOR AND I HEAD out the door with Vito right behind us.

He sees the new golf cart waiting and he begins to laugh, "Uncle Max, when did you get this?"

"Okay, here's the thing. I was saving this for your birthday, but since you will be in the States, I thought we could take it out for a spin now. Do you like it?" I probably got this for the both of us, but I will never confess to that one.

"What's not to like?—a golf cart that looks like a Lamborghini! Can I really drive this?"

"Yes, you can drive this, but don't tell your mum. And whatever you do, don't tell your grams or you know what will happen. Hop in and let me show you how to drive this. You have to be careful cause I had it modified to get up to 70 mph." We hop in and he takes to it right away. I thank God he doesn't have his mother's coordination. We race toward the barn, and Vito is running behind us.

"Junior, pull behind the barn; we have to hide this." As he pulls behind the barn, we find Jackie standing there. *Oh bullocks,* I'm so busted.

"Uncle Max, looks like you're in trouble."

Jackie walks over to my side of the car, "Max, out right this minute."

I climb out; ready to make up some lame excuse, "Jackie, I can explain . . ."

She doesn't even let me finish. She hops in the car and begins to laugh uncontrollably. "Oh, Max, I wish you could see the look on your face right now. You're not having all the fun around here. Michael, hit the gas and let's take this for another ride."

Before I can protest, they are speeding away, laughing with Vito running behind them. I turn around and Jax is standing there. "Are you going to yell at me? I had it made for his birthday, and since he won't be here, I thought he should have a little fun."

"Why would I yell, he's having the time of his life. Thank God he doesn't have Bella's coordination."

"He's gotta be okay, Jax."

"He will, have faith. Do you know what Mrs. Osla planned for Junior?"

"Nope, but I'm sure it's special, she loves kids."

We watch them go around the field one more time and then they pull up to the barn. They climb out and Junior's cheeks have the most color I've seen in days.

"Okay, Junior, give me a hug. Jackie and I will see you next week. I'll hide this toy till you get back."

"Thanks, Uncle Max. Miss Jackie, I'll be ready to give you away next week."

She gives him a big hug, "I'm looking forward to it."

I watch Junior climb on Jax's back and as they head up toward the house, I feel my heart tighten, "I can't lose him, Jackie."

"You won't. We need to be strong."

I know she's right, however, it's not easy. "Hop in and I'll take you for a spin. I need to store this in the garage for now."

"You know, Max, I might want to get one of these in purple."

She can't be serious. "It will be a cold day in hell before I buy a purple Lamborghini golf cart." She reaches over and places her hand on my crotch, lightly tapping her fingers. I see where this is headed, but I'm still not buying a purple Lamborghini, it goes against everything manly. "Still not happening, babe." She removes her hand and places it in her lap. After a few seconds, she unzips her jeans, slowly shimmying them down. She slides her delicate fingers slowly into her knickers. What the hell is she trying to do, kill me?

"As you well know, Max, I've never had sex in a car before. I think it's something I might want to try."

I clench my jaw and white knuckle the wheel. I'm trying not to look but then she moans. *Fuck me.* I take a quick peek, holy hell! Her knickers are around her knees and her fingers are working in and out of her sweetness. She tilts her head back moaning. I avert my eyes from her and back on the road. I gave some thought to what she said the other day, how she wanted to have different experiences with me. I guess now is as good a time as any. Her breathing is becoming rapid and I know she is closing in fast. Two can play the same game. "Jackie, if you come without me, I will put you over my knee and spank your very beautiful arse until it's that very lovely shade of pink again. Remember how you felt the other day, the rush of power you felt. The heat from my hand . . . over and over *again?*" I glance over and she's biting her lip, her fingers are moving at a good clip. She's won't be able to take much more. I pull into the first building, which is the new distillery, and hit the brakes. After cutting the engine, I turn toward her. "Carry on."

Her fingers stop moving and her eyes are wide. "Max, I want you to—."

"You want me to what, babe?" She's practically whimpering and *fuck me* it's hot.

"I want it to be your fingers, not mine."

"Lose the knickers." I hold out my hand. She slides them down and places them in my palm. I rub the beautiful lace along my cheek and then shove them in my pocket for later. "You've been very naughty and I think now you need to understand what happens when you are naughty." I get out of the car and head toward her side. Opening her door, I offer her my hand. When she places it in mine, I can still feel her wetness. I lift her fingers to my mouth and brush them across my lips. "Place your hands on the car and stick that luscious arse out for me." Her breathing is becoming rapid as I slowly stroke my fingers over her arse. I start out with a few alternating light smacks. She takes her hand off the car and puts it between her legs. I stop her and pull both hands behind her back. I tie them together with her knickers. "I might have to give you some extra spanks for that one, babe." I lean her over and begin spanking her, one cheek and then the other. She's wiggling, and every time she does, I spank her harder . . . just enough to sting. When I dip my finger into her sweetness, she screams out my name. I drop my pants, take my cock, and enter her from behind. When I'm all the way in, I can feel the heat from her arse. I'm using her hands, tied with her knickers, to pull her back toward me as I push forward. "Oh God, Jackie, please tell me you're there."

"Yes, Max, harder, please! Don't stop! Oh God, again."

Everything in me tightens and I explode over and over again. When my scrambled brain finally comes back to life, I untie her hands and then bend down to kiss her beautiful pink arse cheeks. "Are you okay?"

"Now can I get my purple cart?"

I throw my head back and laugh, "You really want a purple cart?"

"Of course I do, if for nothing else, but to see you driving it."

"I guess I'm ordering you a purple cart."

She throws her arms around me and kisses me hard. "Yes!"

Chapter Fourteen

Raven

JAX HAS MANAGED TO get everyone from Scotland to Heathrow without incident. It's already been a long day for Michael. Jax told me about Max's present for Michael and how much fun he had driving it. I look around the cabin and everyone seems to be busy reading or listening to music. All, except An. She's so pale. Something is still off with her, and I need to figure out what it is. She is a very strong, proud woman, and getting anything out of her won't be easy.

Jax puts his magazine down and leans in near my ear. "Penny for your thoughts?" he whispers.

"I'm still concerned about your mom. She seems pale, and before you say anything, I know that she still needs to rest. It's just been a hell of a few days for her, for all of us."

"Raven, I know this has been exceptionally hard on her, and I can see it's taking a toll. I had Mrs. Osla arrange for the top cardiologist to tend to her while we are in the States. Come with me."

He unbuckles our seat belts and pulls me to my feet. "Jax, what's up?"

He's not saying anything as he leads me down the aisle to his office. He pours himself a scotch and offers me a drink. "I have some things I need to talk to you about. With everything going on, we haven't had a minute to ourselves. There always seems to be something going on, some fire to put out."

We sit on the sofa and I take his hand in mine. "Talk to me; what's wrong?"

"I've been thinking about your mum and her medical license. Here's my dilemma: what if she wants to go back into medicine? I mean, she was very well known in that field. You saw how she came to life when everything went down. Matthew might have changed her name, but it doesn't mean she's safe. Add to that her wanting to confront Vincent and I'm not sure what to do."

"What happened when you spoke to her about Vincent?"

"I have to say, Raven, she made a very compelling argument, but in the end, it's got to be about safety."

"Did you tell her any of this?"

"No, I haven't had a chance. And now with everything happening to Junior, all my focus has been there."

"Jax, let me try talking to her. Maybe I can get a feel as to what she might want to do. In the end, it has to be her decision. Now I have something I need some advice on." I put my glass down. He gifts me with a huge smile.

"Should I have my mom read Duke's letter?"

"Why would you want her to? Do you think any good would come of it?"

"At first, I thought no, but then after I read it, I realized he was just as much a victim as the rest of us." His grip on my hand tightens. "I'm not condoning what he did, Jax. I just thought if she read it, then maybe she could come to terms with everything. She might see there was some good in him. After all, he is a part of her."

"I get why you think it might help, but honestly, looking at this from a non-emotional side, I think it might do her more harm than good. She might feel guilty for what's become of him. Even though she's not responsible, as a parent, you will always take the blame for your child—no matter what."

"I never really thought of it like that, but I guess it makes sense." I take his glass from his hand and put it on the table, and then crawl into his lap. He wraps his arms tightly around me and I feel secure.

"What else is on your mind, Raven?"

"Do you know what arrangements were made for Michael's schooling?"

"No, I didn't get that far. My goal was to get him into that hospital as quickly as possible. What are you thinking?"

"I spoke to Jackie and we want to homeschool Michael. They probably offer the services at the hospital; however, we would feel better if we did it."

"Why are you trying so hard to sell me on this?"

"I promised you that I would stay home and take care of Antonia, but if I did this, I would be away from her for a couple of hours a day. I didn't think you would mind, but I don't want someone else to take care of our daughter. If I'm not there, then I want you to be . . . not a nanny."

"Oh, I never even thought about that. Okay, I will go along with it. Besides, Max will be there to help me. Speaking of which, I know Max is stoked that he is getting married in a few days. Is Jackie really okay with everything?"

"Jackie and I had a long talk before we left and she is happy that it will happen on her birthday. She feels it will help her mom the most to have the ceremony on that day. They are Buddhist and believe life is about helping and giving to others."

"How do you think Max is going to do with her family? I have to confess, sweetheart, I told him what Dylan said."

"I figured you did, after all, you and Max are joined at the hip. You met him Jax, you know as well as I do that Max will not do well with Dylan. Jackie already called him and told him she was coming home with Max. She won't take any bull from him."

"I could never repay Jackie for what she has done for Max. She mended his heart and she stopped him from making the biggest mistake of his life. I honestly don't think I would have been able to stop him without her. I would like to make the wedding they are planning to have in the States really special for her. Do you have any ideas what she would like?"

"Simple is what works for Jackie, always has been. Don't worry, I'm sure, knowing Max, he will already have Mrs. Osla handling all the details."

"Now, I think we've done entirely too much talking, don't you? I also think you have on entirely too many clothes." I turn in his arms and lean in to kiss him; he has the biggest smile on his face. "What are you thinking?"

He runs his fingers down my cheek and then pulls me toward him, gently pressing his lips against it. "My beautiful wife, I'm thinking that no matter how crazy the world around us becomes, we will always have us. Our sanctuary; so different from everyone else's."

I begin to unbutton his shirt, leaving a trail of soft kisses behind. The intercom buzzes. He reaches behind him and hits the speaker. My mom lets me know Antonia is awake.

"Raven, I'll go get her and bring her in here." Before I can say anything, he's out the door. I know he loves tending to her just as much as I do. He comes in the door with Antonia crying in her infant carrier and the diaper bag. He seems flustered as he tries to get her out of the carrier.

"Jax, are you okay?"

"Why the hell are these seats so complicated?" He's growling with frustration.

"It took me a little bit to figure it out, too." I quickly show him how it works and then go about changing her. As soon as she is clean, she stops crying and I'm able to nurse her. I snuggle up to Jax, and he puts his arm around me.

"Sweetheart, watching you tend to our daughter takes my breath away. We really need to make another baby."

I take my time before answering him.

"Raven, I can't help the way I feel. I love babies and love making them with you. I think you are the greatest mum ever. I want to enjoy my children while I'm young."

"Have you ever thought about adopting? Jackie said that Max wants to adopt a special needs child."

"Honestly, I've never thought about it. However, I wouldn't rule it out. Do you want to adopt?"

"I'm not sure. Actually, right before everything happened with Max, I started looking into the foster care program in Scotland. I was thinking it would be a good way to reach many of the children that are considered too old for adoption. We could take the money that the government pays monthly and put that in an account for the child. This way when the child becomes of age, they will have some savings to work with."

"Obviously, you've been thinking about this for quite some time."

"I always thought about being a foster mom or a big sister, but then everything got a little crazy. I've been watching Jackie work with the kids and the horses, so I decided to look into it. I know we will be gone for a while, but maybe we can look into it more when we get back."

"It sounds like a great idea, as long as you don't rule out making babies."

"Ha! Never, Jax." Antonia falls back to sleep and I put her in her carrier.

"You take the carrier and I've got the bag. I want to lock that contraption back into the seat and check on your mom."

We head out to the main cabin, and everyone is getting ready to eat. It smells wonderful and I'm starving. Nursing seems to make me want to eat all the time. Everyone is laughing except for An. I notice she's pushing her food around but not really eating anything. I decide to wait until I can get her alone later to see how she's feeling. I don't want to alarm anyone. Dinner with all of us together is always comforting, but I really miss Max and Jackie. I hope Max is going to be okay dealing with Dylan. Jax takes my hand and kisses the inside of my wrist. No matter how long we are together, I think I will always shiver when he puts his lips there. I rest my head on his shoulder "I think I'm going to try and have a nap while Antonia is sleeping. Lately, I'm tired all the time."

"Is it normal to be this tired? Maybe we should go to the doctor." His grip on my hand gets tighter.

"I think it's all normal. The hunger and the fatigue add to that all the stress that we've been going through. I don't think we have anything to worry about." I get up and excuse myself and Jax gets up, too. "What are you doing?"

"Sweetheart, I think I need a nap. All of a sudden, I'm feeling quite tired."

If I look at him I know, I will burst out laughing, so I opt to quickly head down the hall.

We get into our room and I'm so tired. I sit down to take off my shoes, barely able to keep my eyes open. Jax crouches down at my feet and begins to take off my shoes. He's starts rubbing my feet and I feel my eyes growing heavier.

"Raven, please let me take care of you. You're always taking care of everyone else."

I lie down and give in, too tired to help myself. I feel myself slowly fade out as he's massaging my feet.

Jaxson

RAVEN HAS BEEN SO tired, and doing so much for everyone else that I'm afraid she is going to get sick. As much as I always want to be with her, it's rest that she really needs now. She gives so freely of her strength and faith, I truly have no idea how she does it. I look at my watch and realize Max must be getting ready to leave. I give him a call before he heads out. "Hey, Max, are you almost ready to go?" I ask when he picks up.

"Yeah, everything okay there?"

"We have about three hours left before we land. I wanted to talk to you before you go. Now whatever you do, make sure you don't snap the wanker's neck, cause that would not go over too well with Jackie's dad."

"Is this why you called me?"

"I'm worried about you; I know I wanted to snap that fucker's neck. You will surely want to do more. Just try to remember you're there for Jackie."

"What else is bothering you? I doubt you called just for that."

"I feel bad that I'm not going to be there when you get married. You're always there for me."

"I know, but you'll be there for me next week. I just can't wait to make it official."

"Have you thought about a gift for her? I can help with it." I'm laughing and he is probably rolling his eyes.

"Well, I really wasn't too sure what to get, but then this morning, when she went racing around with Junior, she mentioned that she wanted a purple golf cart."

"You bought her a purple golf cart?" I'm laughing so hard, I'm crying.

"No, not a golf cart. I called my friends at Lamborghini and ordered her a purple one. They sent over a certificate with her name and delivery date. I wrapped it up."

"What about her birthday, mate?"

"When I had the ring made up, I also had a matching pendant made. Somehow, I knew I wouldn't be able to wait till her birthday. I'm going to have to get going, but before I do, how is everyone doing?"

"Everyone is doing okay, although Mum looks a little tired. Raven is keeping a close watch on her, so don't worry. I'll let you go, but make sure you check in with me." He hangs up and I'm still sad that I won't be there, but I know he's getting his shot at a happily ever after and that's all I ever really wanted for him. While Raven is still asleep I'm going to check on Junior.

I quietly leave the room, making sure not to wake her. Junior's room is right next door. I stick my head in to check on him, but he is asleep. I'm trying so hard not to let him see how scared I am for him. I close the door and go in search of my mum. She is in the main cabin having tea with Mrs. Osla. I take a minute to gather my thoughts before heading into the cabin.

"Hey, Mum, how are you feeling?" When she lifts her eyes toward mine, I notice how tired she looks.

"I'm fine, son, how is Raven? This has to be a lot for her to deal with, on top of a new baby."

"She'll be fine, Mum, it's you I'm worried about. You need to try and get some rest. I know we're all worried about Junior, but you getting sick will not help him. Bella is going to need a lot of support right now from all of us." *Oh fuck, she's crying.* I pull her into my arms. "Shh, stop crying, please."

"I'll be fine, son, really, I think I'm just tired. Plus, the realization of everything that James was into has been very hard on me. I feel like a fool—"

"—Stop, please! Just stop blaming yourself for things you never had any control over. We need to focus on the future and things we *can* control. My wife told me 'the past can't be changed, but the path we choose to move forward on can.' I believe she might be onto something." She stops crying, and I think I finally might be getting through to her.

THE FLIGHT ATTENDANT COMES over to inform me that we will be ahead of schedule and we should be landing in about an hour. The captain will make his standard announcement when we are thirty minutes out. However, she wanted to make sure I had enough time to tend to any of Junior's needs. I need to make sure everyone is up. "If you'll excuse me, ladies, I need to wake up Raven and let everyone know we are ahead of schedule."

I check on Antonia and she's still sleeping. I thank God that she is such an easy baby. I head into Junior's room and let them know to get ready to land. Now I just need to wake up my wife. I open the door and she's lying on the bed crying. I race over to her and realize she's in the throes of a nightmare. I know not to wake her. I get a wet washcloth and sit on the bed, softly calling her name over and over again. Finally, she stops and her eyes flutter open. I take the washcloth and clean up under her eyes. "Do you want to talk about it?"

"What's there to talk about?"

"Oh, I don't know, maybe the fact that I find my wife crying and thrashing about in her sleep has me worried. I know you're trying to be strong for everyone, but you need to let me in, Raven."

She sits quietly for a while, looking down, twisting her fingers. "I had a bad dream, Jax, a dream that seemed a little too real. Can we please let it go for now?"

I don't want to upset her anymore. "Sweetheart, I can let it go for now, but if they continue, you will need to tell me. We will be landing shortly and we need to get into our seats." I don't want to give her any time to dwell on it. We head out to the main cabin to check on Antonia and take our seats. As the wheels touch down, I close my eyes, making a silent prayer that Junior will be okay.

Chapter Fifteen
Maxwell

I'M PACKING EVERYTHING I think I will need, making sure I take the blue prints for Junior. The thought of him having to go through this is tearing me up inside. I just about have it together and now I need to find out what is keeping Jackie. I go in search of her and find her sitting on the floor in her closet, surrounded by shoes. I learned rather quickly that she has two vices in life: chocolate and shoes. It looks like someone took every pair of shoes she owns and piled them on the floor. "Hey, babe, what are you doing?"

"Trying to decide what shoes to bring." I'll never understand the need for all these shoes, however, I'm not an idiot—I know when to keep my mouth shut.

I sit on the floor next to her, always needing to touch her. "You could just pick a few and buy whatever you want in the States." That earns me a glare.

"Or . . . we could just take them all." Her bottom lip begins to tremble and something tells me this has nothing to do with shoes. "Talk to me, babe, what's really bothering you?"

"I'm getting married tomorrow. My mother has requested that I wear my grandmother's Kimono. My best friend isn't here, and you are going to hate my brother."

"Would you rather wait until we get to the States to get married. We can fly your parents out next week and do it with everyone there."

"I thought of that, but my mother doesn't fly."

"Wait then how were they getting here in May for the wedding?"

"They would drive."

"Jackie, that's over seventeen hours, you can't be serious. Why won't your Mum fly?"

"I asked her that once and she said she wasn't born with wings Really, after that, what could I say? The more I thought about it, the more I really want to have the wedding on my birthday, so I can have some happy memories, too."

I lift her hand to my lips, "I have one question? How hard is it going to be to get you out of this Kimono?" Her mouth falls open and her eyes grow wide.

"Is that all you're worried about?" she squeaks in disbelief.

"Babe, none of this matters to me. Out of respect for you, I will play nice with Dylan. I will have as many or as few ceremonies as you want. As long as there is one very quickly, nothing else matters. Hell, I'll even wear this Kimono thing if that will get you down that isle!" She takes my hand and begins to laugh.

"Okay, what's so funny?"

"Careful what you wish for Max. You have to wear the traditional men's Kimono."

She is now laughing so hard that she falls backwards amongst the shoes and she's holding her sides. I'm glad that through this nightmare, she can still find something to laugh about. I get up, take her hand, and pull her to her feet.

"Jackie, leave the shoes and I will take you on a whirlwind shoe shopping trip when we get to the States."

"Max, have you ever been to Bon Genie?" We head out of the closet and I begin to laugh.

"Jax told me about it when he came back from Switzerland. Not gonna happen, babe." She cocks her head to the side and gives me a beautiful smile. Who am I kidding?—*she* knows and *I* know that I'm going to Bon Genie; seven floors of shopping hell.

Jaxson

WE LAND WITHOUT INCIDENT and Max has a fleet of vehicles, with guards, waiting for us in a private hanger. We head directly to the hospital, only to find a dozen or so reporters camped out front. I've been so wrapped up with Junior that I forgot the sale of Raiders was announced today. I've been away from the press, hounding me on a daily basis, but Mick realizes what's going on and radios all drivers to go around back to the service entrance. We drive around back and there are some there, but not as many.

Before I open the door, Mick holds his hand up, stopping me. "Jax, I need everyone to go but Rose." He hands Rose a baseball cap and dark sunglasses. "Can you please put these on, ma'am? Jax, it's you they want pictures of, so I'm hoping once you're inside, I will be able to sneak Rose in without anyone noticing."

"Thank you, Mick. I almost forgot how ruthless the press can be."

We get out of the cars and make our way into the hospital with a limited amount of flashes going off. Junior grabs my hand and is squeezing it really hard. We make our way to the elevators quickly and the ride up is long and quiet. The doors finally open and we are greeted by two very kind looking nurses, Sarah and Janett. Sarah informs me that she works for the hospital, and Janett is the private nurse that Mrs. Osla has hired.

Sarah extends her hand out to Junior. "Hello, Michael. I know you are scared, but Janett and I will be here with you. There is another boy here named Josiah, he's very into superheroes and *Doctor Who*. I'm sure the two of you will become good friends. Let's get you checked into your room and then I will introduce you to him."

Junior's face lights up at the mention of *Doctor Who* and for the first time since this began, I can feel myself relax a little. As we approach Junior's room, Janett informs me to get the camera on my phone ready. I have no clue what she's talking about, but then it hits me, Mrs. Osla's surprise. Junior opens the door and steps inside. I'm so shocked that I can't even speak. Janett takes my phone and begins snapping pictures. The entire room looks like the inside of the TARDIS. Junior is laughing and running around the room, checking everything out. I finally snap back to reality, thanking Janett for taking the pictures.

Junior runs up to Mrs. Osla and throws his arms around her. Two hugs in one day must surprise her. "Mrs. Osla, you're the best! Thank you." Even the always stoic Mrs. Osla is teary eyed.

Sarah informs us that Dr. David Torrance is in charge of Junior's case and is waiting to meet with us first before he meets with Junior. While Janett and Sarah are showing Junior around, we step outside his room to meet with the doctor but find Rose and Mick waiting for us.

"Mick, were there any problems?" He's fidgeting and rocking back and forth on his heels. He seems on edge.

"Yeah, Jax, one guy was able to get a picture off. I pulled his SD card from his camera. He wasn't happy."

"Did you see anyone else? Did he try to find out who she is?" God, I can't wait till Max gets *here.*

"There were some reporters across the street, but I don't think anyone noticed us. I had her keep her head down with her hair tucked into the cap. He tried to question me about her but I cut him off. I'm going to have her change into scrubs when we are ready to leave. I will have you leave out the front and I will take Rose out the employee entrance."

"Thanks, Mick. We are about to meet with the doctor, can you please hang here with Junior?" Even though the other guards are here, I feel better with Mick around. He hangs back while we head to the meeting.

When I walk through the door of his office, I look around and I'm shocked. I was expecting a typical doctor's office. He has the usual medical books, but what surprises me the most is the wall of handmade cards. The wall has to be eight feet high and twelve feet wide, and the entire wall, from floor to ceiling, is covered in these cards. On the far wall is a shelf filled with superhero figures.

Raven is fixated on the wall with the cards. "These are amazing."

I take a closer look at them and I realize they are all survivors, thanking Dr. Torrence and his staff. The door opens and the doctor steps in, looking a lot younger than I had expected.

"Hello, everyone, I'm Dr. David Torrance, or Dr. Dave, if you will. I'm sorry; I wasn't expecting so many people; who are Michael's parents?"

Bella and Michael introduce themselves, and then proceed to introduce all of us to him.

"Mr. And Mrs. Vizzano, is everyone going to be involved with Michael's care?" He seems surprised.

"Please call me Bella. The answer is yes, and he also has another uncle and aunt that will be arriving from Switzerland, at some point. I assure you, we are a very close family." She leans her head on my shoulder and squeezes my hand. I want to make all her pain go away and handle this for her, but I know she needs to do this. I squeeze her hand back, giving her the support she needs.

"Okay then, Bella, let me lay out what I see will be our best course of action. We *have* caught this early, so that is in his favor. As far as the stem cell tests that were run, the closest match was you, however, I would have liked it to be closer. I hope we won't need it, but if we do, are there any other relatives that can be tested?" he asks. Bella is not answering and her lips begin to tremble. Michael pulls her into his arms, trying to calm her. My mum pales and Raven pulls her close.

I take a deep breath and slowly let it out. "Dr. Dave, Junior has a grandfather that we are not in touch with. If need be, I will take care of it. For now, why don't we focus on what we can do, please."

"Yes, of course. The first thing I want you to know is that his treatment will be over the course of three years due to the different phases it requires. I like to explain this to families first so that they can begin to mentally prepare for the commitment this unexpected illness will take." He pauses and looks around at every one of us in the room. Michael and Bella nod in understanding. "He will be allowed to go home for some periods of time. I understand that you reside in Scotland?"

"That's right," I speak up.

"Well, I would prefer, during treatment, that he doesn't leave the country." He grabs a folder off of his desk. "The first part of the treatment will take a month. It's called Remission induction. Remission doesn't mean he is cured, it is only the first stage." he says the name slowly as he pulls sheets of paper from the folder and hands us each one. I look down and see that it has all of the info on it for the first phase. "The goal of this first treatment is to kill the leukemia cells that are in Michael's blood and bone marrow. He will first get a blood transfusion, and then I will administer chemotherapy and steroids. I will give you a more detailed packet, outlining all the treatment. However, I would rather go over it with you before each one. It can be very overwhelming and he might not need all of it." He leans back on the edge of his desk and crosses one foot over the other as he tosses the folder down on it. His eyes soften as he looks around at all of us again. "Please know this is not a death sentence, his odds are very good. Bella, Michael . . . you did nothing wrong." He gives a nod of encouragement. "Now, what questions does everyone have?"

I put aside my fear and begin to go through my list. "Is this something that can be inherited? Should my daughter be tested? How much are you going to tell Junior? What do you need us to do or not do?" He seems to be listening intently. Not once has he treated us like just another number.

"Mr. Phillips—"

"—Please, call me Jax."

"Jax, there is no evidence that Acute Lymphocytic Leukemia is hereditary. As far as what I plan to tell Michael, I always explain the leukemia in a way a child can understand it. I also make them a part of the treatment every step of the way. Children are very smart and expect to be treated as such. When speaking with Michael, I will always refer to the cancer as ALL. What I need for every one of you to do is stay positive around him. He will sense your fear, and that is not good for him." He gives us all a slight stern look. "Now, it was brought to my attention that you will be providing his home schooling?"

"Yes, my wife, Raven, and his Aunt Jackie are both teachers."

"That's fine. I will provide you with his schedule. There will be plenty to keep him busy here. Between his treatment, schooling, and the different events we plan for the kids, I doubt Michael will get bored. Now if you don't have any other questions, I would like to go meet him."

"Actually, I have one more question. Why the superhero figures?" I couldn't help it; curiosity was killing the cat.

He puts his pen down and smiles. "Every child that comes through here gets to pick his or her favorite. That figure stays with them the entire time. They sleep with it, they shower with it, and they get their treatment with it. That figure becomes a very important friend. It's the friend that helps them fight to live. Through their journey, they learn all about the figure they chose and how and why they became a superhero. They become that hero. How about you take me to meet Michael now?"

We all turn and file out the door. I stop before leaving and look back at the figures. I freeze, and then a smile hits my face. I know *exactly* which one Junior will choose. "Jax, are you okay?" Raven calls me, snapping my focus back. All I have to do is point to the shelf, and she begins to laugh.

I put my arm around her and we head out the door with a little more faith than we came in with.

Junior

MY NURSES, MISS JANETT and Miss Sarah, are really nice. They asked me about my home in Scotland and what hobbies I have. I can't wait for Uncle Max to get here with the blue prints so I can show them the castle I live in. Miss Sarah is showing me what everything in the room is for. Everyone comes back in and there is a man with them who looks around the room and begins to laugh. "Hi, Michael, I'm Dr. Dave and I will be taking care of you. I'm sorry to laugh; I wasn't expecting to walk into a TARDIS. I haven't met many *Doctor Who* fans; who is your favorite Doctor?"

This might not be so bad after all, "I like the eleventh, Matt Smith, but my Uncle Jax's favorite is the tenth, David Tennant. Who is your favorite?"

"I think each one brings something unique to the role, but I'm partial toward the ninth, Christopher Eccleston. So, Michael, are you ready for me to go over what you can expect while you're here?"

"I g-guess so, Dr. Dave." I'm barely able to get the words out.

Jaxson

MY HEART IS BREAKING for Junior I know he is trying so hard to be strong. Dr. Dave takes Junior into an area of his room that has a table and chairs set up and some bookshelves. He sits down with him and begins explaining everything on Junior's level. He's not demanding or dictating. He tells him fear of the unknown is natural, but ALL is not unknown to him. For the first time, I feel myself relax a little. I pull Raven closer to me; her strength and faith are my rock right now. She reaches up and tugs her ear. I pull her hand away and bring it to my lips. I lean in and whisper, "Sweetheart, are you okay?"

"I'm very proud of Michael, he is such a strong boy. I wish I could shelter him from all of this, but I know Dr. Dave is right; Michael has the right to know what is going to happen. I'm just glad he is explaining it to him in a way that doesn't scare him more. I know he will be okay, but that doesn't make this any easier."

Antonia begins to fuss just as Raven finishes her thoughts. She takes her from Mrs. Osla and heads into the other room to tend to her, with Bo and her guards not far behind her. After setting Michael up with an IV, his nurses begin to administer the first blood transfusion. I decide to step outside his room to check in with Max.

Max picks up on the first ring. "Jax, is everything okay? How is Junior holding up?"

"Calm down, mate, he's doing okay. The doctor is really nice and doesn't pull any punches. He talked to Junior directly, explaining every step of the way, what will happen without scaring him." I inform him, then continue on to relay every bit of the conversation we had with the doctor prior. In regards to our father possibly being a closer match, I know Max, if needed, he'd probably remove the damn stem cells himself. "Max, if it comes to that, I will take care of it. What is going on with the wedding?" I look at the phone to see if the call dropped, "Max, you there?" Then I hear growling. Oh no, I hope he didn't snap that wanker Dylan's neck.

"Do not laugh, Jax, or I swear I will get even with you." He then lets out a big disgruntled sigh. "I have to wear a bloody Kimono."

I try—I mean, I really try not to laugh—but the thought of Max in a Kimono creeps into my head and I lose it. I swear I'm laughing so hard, I'm crying. It is at this very moment Raven steps out of Junior's room to find me. Max is yelling something in my ear and she is looking at me like I have two heads. Maybe it's the pressure that's finally gotten to me. She walks up to me and takes my phone.

"Hello, Max, it's Raven, please stop yelling. Is everything okay?"

"So help me, if he doesn't stop laughing, I'm going to kick his arse!"

"Can I ask why he's laughing so hard, he's crying?"

"No! Please put him back on the bloody phone."

I find some sort of composure and take the phone. "Okay, mate, I'm back, but you must promise me pictures." All I get is a growl and a quick disconnect.

Raven is waiting for some answers, guess I better explain. "I was checking in with Max, and he has to wear a Kimono. Surely you see the humor in that?"

Her face lights up with a beautiful smile. "Oh, Jax, I can't believe I forgot about that. I hope Jackie gave him a heads up before time." She giggles and it's such a wonderful sound.

"Sweetheart, I have a surprise for you. Well really, it's for all of us. I spoke with Jeffery Gerhard today, explaining the situation here and why none of us can be there for the wedding. He has agreed to surprise Jackie and Max by letting us SKYPE the ceremony. I can still be his best man and you can be Jackie's matron of honor. The entire family can be there for them."

She throws her arms around me, hugging me tightly. "Jax, as if it were even possible, I love you more than I ever thought I could. Your kindness knows no bounds." She kisses my cheek enthusiastically, and then pulls back. "When is the ceremony?"

"Jeffery said he would give us advance notice, so let's go let everyone know what is going on, and see how Junior is doing."

Chapter Sixteen

Vincent

I JUST GOT WORD that my new attorney is here to see me today. That's a surprise, since I already gave the feds what they wanted or, at least, as much as I was willing to part with. There's more—hell—there's always more. I've been moved to an underground facility in Colorado. This place is considered hell-on-earth and that's not far off in the description. I'm being led out to a special visiting room that has been set up for attorneys visiting inmates. The feds might think they got a win, but this is only the first round. As long as I'm not dead, I can't be stopped. I shuffle along as best I can, being led in leg irons and cuffs. Deveno is gone and so now I will have to train my new attorney. That's okay. Unlike Deveno, maybe this one will get everything I ask for done. When we get into the room, the guards attach my restraints to a bolt in the floor and step out. There's a knock on the door, it opens and in steps my attorney. *What the fuck?!*

"Hello, Mr. Giaconna, I'm Ms. Amelia Jade, I will be representing you. I know that you already have a deal in place at this time, however, I'm here to see if I can make it better."

"Who the fuck hired you?" Damn this girl is a looker; long, red hair and tits that I wouldn't mind burying my face in.

"Your sister, Annabelle, hired me to take a look at your case."

"Well, Ms. Amelia Jade, what makes you think you can do anything for me? I already have a deal in place with the feds. My long-lost son, whom I only knew for three fucking months, threw me, along with the entire family, under the bus. The evidence against me was pretty black and white, so I really didn't have a choice. Where did Anna find you?" Let's see her work with nothing.

"Well, Mr. Giaconna, I'm not going to dispute the deal, only the evidence that was used to make the deal. I believe there was a break in the chain of evidence—the video tape to be precise. When it was obtained, copies were made. The prosecutor said it never left the chain of custody, yet, Mr. Fleming had a copy. I believe we might be able to pull the deal and have a trial. Either way this goes, you will be going to jail, I have no doubt about that. As far as Annabelle is concerned, I found her."

"So, if it's not going to change my conviction, then why bother? Why contact my sister?" Her jaw is tight and her emerald eyes become very dark. She looks down at her hands and then back up to me.

"Revenge, Mr. Giaconna—pure, sweet, and simple. I want it and you're my way of getting it."

"Wow, who pissed in your corn flakes?" I jerk my head back. "What would make you think I would even go along with any of this?"

"You want to know who pissed in my corn flakes? Joseph Adessi, when he recruited my brother, Marco, to be his spy. Cara AKA: Raven, your niece, for turning my brother into some love-sick puppy. Duke, for putting a bullet in him. I can't get to Duke, at least not yet. Joseph is dead. So that leaves Raven. My way to her is through you, plain and simple."

"You think I'm going to go along with this? What's in it for me?" Why did my sister even go along with this broad?

"Oh, there are two reasons I know you'll go along with it. I might be able to get you something better than this hellhole and I can guarantee Jacquelyn Gerhard's head on a proverbial silver platter." Now this broad has my attention.

"The entire Phillips family has arrived in the States, with the exception of Maxwell Fleming and Jacquelyn Gerhard. It appears Michael Vizzano Jr. is ill and will be here for treatment for the next three years. He just happens to be staying at the hospital where a friend of mine works, which is why I was lucky enough to receive this information so quickly. Mr. Fleming and Ms. Gerhard are in Switzerland and will be arriving soon. Once they are back in the States, the target becomes more vulnerable."

She takes out pictures of everyone arriving to a hospital and places them in front of me. I flip through them, they seem mundane until I get to the last one; I freeze. No fucking way is this possible. "Where was this picture taken and when?!"

"It was taken this morning outside the hospital in Philly. I had no idea who that was, so I had the picture enlarged. With the hat on and glasses it's still hard to tell. Is there a problem? Do you know who that is?"

This can't be, is this why Joseph never came after me? I stare at the picture and there is no mistaking that beautiful jaw line and those delicate features. "I will go along with your crazy plan under one condition. I need to see the girl in this picture, find her and bring her to me." I fold the picture and put it in my pocket.

"Mr. Giaconna, if you can tell me who the lady in the picture is, that would help?"

"The lady in the picture is Gabriella Giaconna, the catalyst for all of this; the mother of my only child. Bring her to me and you have a deal." I've always operated on the theory that my friends and associates are there for me to use. My enemies are there for me to destroy. Ms. Jade just became my new friend. I will use her and even destroy her if it means I can get my hands on Gabriella—*again*.

"First I need to get you moved out of this hell whole and back to the East coast. I will be in touch soon."

She gathers up her stuff and walks out, leaving me with more questions than answers. I can't get them from Joseph, but I will get them from Gabriella. The guards come in, unlock my chains and I begin the trek back to my cell. Once again, it's a waiting game for me.

Amelia Jade

I HATE THIS PLACE and the man I came here to see. I have no choice, though. If I want revenge for my brother's death, then I will have to deal with the devil. I'm in shock; how could this be? There was never any indication that Gabriella was alive. If Vincent is correct, then what else was Joseph hiding?

My brother ran away when I was thirteen. Joseph should have helped him come home, not make him into a babysitter for Raven. She turned him into some lovesick puppy and in the end, it cost him his life. She might not have pulled the trigger, but she was just as responsible. I need to keep my end of the bargain. If Vincent wants Gabriella, then he will get her along with Jacquelyn's head as a bonus. I pull out my duplicate set of pictures and find the one of the woman. From this picture, it's so hard to tell who the woman is. Maybe Vincent is seeing what he wants to see. Staring at this picture isn't going to get me anywhere. I pull out my phone and send a quick text to my investigator in Philly.

Just left Vincent. It's a go, but only if we deliver the lady in the attached photo. He claims it's Gabriella Giaconna. This could be why Joseph didn't use the tape. I'm heading to the airport now. Will contact you when I land.

I instruct my driver to go directly to Pueblo Memorial airport, while I try to make some sense of this. Joseph staged that accident in California to look like Gabriella and Cara died, but why put Cara up for adoption if her mother was alive? Why not relocate them both? Gabriella already gave Duke away. I just don't understand what the reason could've been to separate mother and child? I decide to head directly to, federal prosecutor, Hage's office in New York. I'm sure by now he got my motion for discovery. Maybe I can find something in his files. We pull up to the airport and I rush out to catch my plane. All of this will have to wait till I touch down in New York.

Vincent

I SIT IN MY cell and pull out the picture, stroking my finger up and down that delicate jaw line. So fucking beautiful, but this can't be—*how?* I close my eyes and remember the first day I had her. She thought she was so strong. She thought she could fight me. That was until she found out I had her precious Cara. She did whatever I asked, and when she didn't, when she fought me, it was even better. Just the thought of it makes my blood surge all over again. I can feel the tenderness of her sweet pussy like it was yesterday. I close my eyes and slowly stroke myself. What a poor substitute my hand is for her warmth. I remember thanking Antonio with every thrust inside her delicious pussy. I need to get out of here and find her again. I close my eyes and kiss her picture. I need to have her—*I will have her.* Nothing and *no one* will stop me. The thought gives me that last push I need, forcing me to finally come. *"I'm coming for you, Gabriella, you'll never be rid of me."*

Maxwell

I'M GLAD JAX CHECKED in, letting me know that Junior was doing okay. And all the information I found on the doctor seems really positive. I know Jackie is nervous about today, but something else is bothering her. She was so quiet on the ride to the airport and now, on the ride to her parents' house, she seems anxious. "Hey, babe, talk to me, this can't just be wedding jitters."

"Max, we haven't seen Sammy since the day we fled the country. I spoke to my mother and she said Dylan is in a foul mood. I thought I could do this on my birthday, but now I'm not so sure."

Fuck me, she can't be backing out now! "Jackie, I promise you everything will be fine. I will talk to Sammy about why I chose to leave him in the dark. Your brother will deal with the fact that I'm not going away. You have a lock on my heart for life and nothing he says or does will ever change that."

Her grip on my arm seems to lighten a little, that is, until, we pull up to the guard gate. As we drive up to the house, I finally get a sense of how she grew up and the isolation she had to endure for so many years. Things are starting to make sense. I look around and notice there are a lot of guards and dogs. "Jackie, is security always this tight?"

"No, Max, something must be up. My father never has the dogs this close to the house."

We step out of the car and I pull her tightly into my arms. "Until I find out what is going on, I want you close to me, understand?" Before she can answer, the door opens and Jeffery Gerhard steps out.

"So happy you're here, Jacquelyn." He pulls her into his arms.

"Papa, this is Maxwell Fleming. Max, my dad, Jeffery Gerhard," she goes about introducing us.

"Please, call me Jeff. Your mother is waiting for you. Maxwell and I have a lot to discuss. Don't worry, I promise I will go easy on him."

I pull her close and kiss her cheek, "Go, I'm fine."

When she is out of sight, I turn towards Jeff, "You can call me Max. Why don't we go sit down, so you can fill me in on what happened?"

"What makes you think anything happened?"

"Extra security and the dogs are close to the house."

"Sam is in my office, waiting for us. He has some intelligence information that he wants to go over with you." He smacks my back and leads me to his office.

"Hello, Max, I have some information to go over with you." Sammy looks up from Jeff's desk as we enter the room.

"First order of business, Sam: no hard feelings. I'm sure you understand why I did what I did. The less people that knew what we were doing, the safer everyone was."

"I understand. I didn't like it but I get it. We have more important matters to discuss. A very creditable threat has come through on Jackie's life. I know that you have bumped up security, however, I'm not sure that going to the States is the best decision."

I feel my heart constrict and pound in my chest. "Show me what you've got."

"I found out that Vincent has a new attorney. She filed a motion for discovery. My contact said she is trying to get the plea overturned due to tainted evidence."

Just the mention of his name makes me lose all reason. "Why the fuck would anyone take his case and think they would win? There has to be something in it for the attorney."

"Oh there is, Max—revenge. Her name is Amelia Jade and she is Marco Green's sister."

I freeze "Sister? Since when did Marco have a sister? There was nothing in his file about any siblings."

"Amelia Jade Esq. was Amelia Green. She was thirteen when Marco left home. Soon after her father died and her mother remarried. Her name was legally changed to Jade and all her records were sealed."

"Sealed? Who sealed them? Please don't tell me Joseph."

"No, Marco sealed them. He was a hacker and damn good at it. Apparently, he sealed them without telling anyone. It was his way of protecting her from anything he did."

"Look, Sam, I get it. She is hurt that she lost her brother, but Duke shot him and he's gone in the wind somewhere. Why try to re-open a case that she has no chance of winning?"

"She is trying to get to Raven and to get to her; she has to get to Jackie. That is probably the only way she would get Vincent to go along with this. She knows she doesn't have a snowball's chance in hell of winning, but if she can force a trial, then you and Raven have to testify. Vincent wants revenge against you and getting Jackie is the ultimate revenge. He doesn't give a shit about you personally, only what he can do to make you suffer. You know his MO has always been about torture, Max."

"Raven didn't do anything to Marco. She honestly loved him like the brother she always wanted. I knew going to the States was a risk, but we had no choice. I have tripled security on everyone. Has Jax been informed of the latest developments?"

"No, this all came to light today when she sent Hage a request for full disclosure of every document pertaining to this case. I had MI6 dig into her past and that is when I found the sealed file. I had my contact get me a copy of the original file. That's when I found out exactly who she was. After that, all the pieces fell into place. I know Jackie and I understand leaving her here is not an option. We need to figure out the safest way to proceed. Max, understand I'm on board one-hundred percent. Jackie's safety and happiness is all I've ever wanted."

"Well, first thing I need to do is call Jax and bring him up to speed. If you wouldn't mind giving me a few moments to talk to him in private."

"Of course, Max, Sam and I will step outside. Let us know when you're ready for us." They leave and I take a few minutes to collect my thoughts. This is not going to be an easy call to make. I close my eyes and pray that—if there is a God—he would do what he *didn't* do before and protect my family.

Jax picks up on the first ring. "Hey, Max, what's wrong? Don't tell me one look at you in the Kimono and she ran the other way?"

"Very funny, Jax. Take Raven and go someplace quiet so we can talk. There's been a development that I need to go over with both of you."

"Give me five." He growls and hangs up.

Waiting for his call affords me the time to walk around Jeff's office. The man keeps pictures of his family everywhere. Jackie as a baby takes my breath away. All I can think of is how much I want babies with her. My phone rings, taking me out of my daydream.

"Jax, where are you and are we on speaker?"

"Raven and I are in a utility closet and yes you're on speaker. What the hell is going on?"

"Raven, did Marco ever mention a sister?"

"No, he hardly ever talked about his family; only that they disagreed with his lifestyle. Is there a problem?"

"Yeah, a big problem—for all of us. Her name is Amelia Jade and she is Vincent's new attorney, and she is out for revenge against you Raven. She knows to get to you; she has to get to Jackie. When we are locked away in Scotland, we can keep the animals at bay but back in the States, that buffer is gone."

"What kind of case could she possibly have? Vincent already accepted a plea deal; how does that get her revenge? Max, none of this makes any sense to me."

"I know, Raven. I thought the same thing but then I *really* thought about it. The first thing she did was file a motion for full disclosure of the evidence. Her focus is on the evidence, mainly that video tape. Since it is known that I have a copy, she is going to question the validity of the tape due to the chain of evidence. She will try to say it is tainted; she only has to show reasonable doubt. If she can force a hearing, that gets us out into the open and vulnerable. Killing Jackie would give her revenge against you, Raven. She would be taking away a person that you love, like she feels you took away her brother. Vincent would go along with this sick plan to hurt me where it matters most."

"Max, I didn't take away her brother, if anything, Joseph was the one who turned him into a puppet."

"Yeah, but Joseph is dead and no one knows where Duke is, so going after you is the next best thing. Raven, look I know it's a sick plan but a plan nonetheless, we need to deal with this." There is a long pause and I check to see if the call was dropped.

"Jax, are you still there?"

"Yeah, trying to wrap my head around all of this. What's the plan, Max?"

"I already tripled security, I'm not sure what other steps I want to take yet. I wanted to make you aware of what's going on. I'm also concerned about Rose. I know she wanted to confront Vincent. This threat might push her in that direction. He can't find out she's alive."

"We might have a problem, Max—a big one. When we got here, there were a slew of media. I realized the announcement came out about Raiders. Mick took Rose around back and put a hat and glasses on her, but a reporter took a picture. Mick pulled the guy's SD card, however, there were other reporters across the street. He can't say one-hundred percent that no one got a picture."

"*Fuck,* Jax! I'm going to have more security put in place. I also want to put security on Junior's doctor and nurses. I'm going to say that due to the announcement, I feel the need for additional security. Do you think they will give us a problem?"

"Not sure, mate, but I will have a talk with them. I would much rather move everyone to Scotland, but I don't think it's an option. The doctor told us that while Junior is having treatment he can't leave the state. When can we expect the additional security?"

"I will have everything in place within the hour. I'm pulling Sammy in on this; we need more people, people we can trust. Are you okay with that?"

"Yeah, I agree we need more help. Send me the files on the changes and I will update the hospital staff. What time is the wedding?"

"In a little while, but I need to get this handled first. I will send you everything and I will also send everything to Mick. Raven, hang in there. I promise you I would lay down my life to protect Jackie."

"Thank you," It's barely a whisper but I hear her. I'm barely off the phone and Jeff is back with Sammy. "I brought Jax and Raven up to speed on everything. I need to send copies of all the changes to him and Mick. Sammy, we might have another problem. With the announcement about Raiders today, there was paparazzi at the hospital. Mick brought Rose around back, one guy got a picture but he pulled his SD card. If it gets out that she is alive, all hell will break loose. On top of that, she wants to confront Vincent! Jax and I have talked her out of it for now, but I'm not sure how long that will last." I realize Jeff might not know Rose's true identity. "Jeff, have you been brought up to speed on who Rose really is?" He walks up to the window and quietly stares out, before turning his attention back to me.

"Yes, the chief filled me in—not Sam."

Sammy clears his throat, bringing our attention back to him. "So, you don't think Rose will consent to go back to Scotland?"

"Never. Look, we also need to add security on Junior's doctor and the nurses that are taking care of him. I'm leaving nothing to chance."

"I already ordered the additional security. I will send everything to Jax and Mick."

Jeff picks up one of the many pictures of Jackie that he has on his credenza. "Max, is there any way Michael's treatment can be done here in Switzerland? We have some of the finest medical facilities here; the University Children's Hospital Zurich has cutting edge research and could possibly have the treatment that young Michael needs."

"I'm not really sure. Everything happened so fast. Get me the research on what they have to offer and I will talk with the family about it. In the meantime, we have a wedding to get ready for."

Raven

"JAX, I'M SCARED. DO you think these people could get to Michael? What about Antonia and my mom? I'm so worried about your mom. I honestly don't think she can physically take another thing; she's so frail." I lean into him and begin to cry and I can't stop. The fear is overwhelming me. His arms around me are holding me up, supporting me, and I let him.

"I've got you, sweetheart, always. I think the added protection is necessary more for our own sanity. You need to pull it together, and I need to talk to the medical staff."

He wipes away my tears and kisses me so softly. "I'm okay; let's get this over with." We head out of the closet to find the staff, only to find Mick standing there, waiting.

Jaxson

"HEY, MICK, DID MAX get in touch with you?"

"Yeah, he brought me up to speed. Raven, Antonia is fussing, and there are no more bottles. Jax, I have Dr. Dave with Michael's nurses waiting to speak with us."

"Okay, Raven, go take care of Antonia; I will be in shortly." I watch my wife walk away and keep reminding myself, throughout all the madness, how lucky I am.

"Mick, how many new guards do we have coming on board?"

"Max said at least six for the family and then three for the staff. He wants me to stay on Rose twenty-four seven. He's worried she might try to confront Vincent if she finds out what's going on. Honestly, Jax, I'm not sure anyone will be able to stop her."

"I spoke with her about it before we left Scotland. I explained to her the danger she would be putting Raven and Antonia in. She is a smart woman, I think she would stick to the plan." I walk up to Dr. Dave's office and stop, taking a deep breath before entering; preparing myself to do whatever it takes to make this work.

Chapter Seventeen

Jackie

MY MOM IS IN the drawing room waiting for me, staring out the window, seemingly lost in thought. "Hello, Mom," I call out to her. When she sees me, her face warms with her beautiful smile.

"Kon'nichiwa, Jacquelyn. I didn't hear you come in. Happy birthday, and a blessed wedding day. Where is Maxwell?"

"Papa needed to speak with him right away. Come sit with me and have some tea, please."

We sit by the fireplace for some warmth and I pour the tea. "Mom, I know that everything is happening very quickly, but Papa did explain to you why, right?"

She's quiet for a bit but then she takes my hand, turns it over, and runs her delicate fingers up and down the lines of my palm.

"Of course he did, but I do have some questions for you." She usually never questions me. What she does do is make me think things through, look at all sides of a situation.

"How is Michael handling all of this?" She always thinks of others first.

"He started his treatments today. He was afraid, but we are all there for him and always will be. This family has been through so much, yet their strength is amazing to me."

"How is Raven holding up? Did you bring me pictures of Antonia?" I take out my phone and begin to show her the tons of pictures I have been taking of my beautiful niece.

"Mom, are you okay with me getting married on my birthday—"

"Stop, Jacquelyn, it will always been a double edge sword for me. I will always be sad that I lost a child. The grief is with me every day of my life, however, I will always be blessed that I have wonderful children. You and Dylan have exceeded all my dreams for you. Why don't you tell me what else is bothering you?"

How does she do it? I don't have to say a word, yet she always knows. "I love him and that's never been a question, but can I be all that he needs? He has experienced such great loss. He recently found out that his father was friends with the man behind that loss. Now Michael is fighting for his life and the threats against everyone have not gone away. Jax's mom had a heart attack. What if what happened to you happens to me? I don't know that he can survive any more. I'm scared mom, really scared for him, for all of us. I can't let him see my fear or he will lose it." I finally let it all go, I can't stop my tears and I really don't want to. I want my mom to hold me and keep me safe. I want her strength and support. She pulls me into her arms and holds me tightly.

"Oh, my sweet child, you are so brave and so very strong. A lot stronger then you ever give yourself credit for. Your father told me all about Maxwell's past. He has survived so much, don't doubt him now. He will always have your strength to draw upon. If you are blessed with children, you will love them and survive whatever God has in store for you. You love each other and you need to draw upon that. We don't always walk side by side; sometimes one must carry the other. That is what love is all about: compromise, compassion, and putting someone else before yourself."

I hear Max coming and I quickly wipe away my tears. I can't let him see me this upset or he will lose it. "Mom, let me introduce you to Max."

She gets up and embraces him. "Maxwell, welcome to our family. I hope Jeffery hasn't been to overbearing."

"No, ma'am, he has been giving me a tour of your lovely home."

"Thank you. I'm going to get ready for the wedding. Jacquelyn, I will meet you in your room shortly to help you."

My dad takes her hand, "Emi, I will go with you. Max, when it's time, I will be up to help you. Hopefully you won't need too much help getting into your Kimono." He chuckles as he heads out with my mom.

Maxwell

"OKAY, JACKIE, WHAT'S WRONG? Don't say nothing and don't tell me not to worry."

"I saw my mom and everything just hit me, hard. So much has happened in such a short time. Lately, there are never any carefree happy times. It's always so intense, and I'm worried all the time. Now I see your face, and I know something else has happened. I'm scared to even ask what's going on now."

My heart is breaking for all that she has had to endure. "I know you have been overwhelmed by everything, but you have to know that I will do whatever it takes for you to be safe. I won't give up—ever. There has been another credible threat. I'm bringing Sammy in on your protection. I have ordered more security on everyone, including the doctor and nursing staff. I won't hide anything from you, Jackie, ever."

"What kind of threat, Max?"

I update her on all of the info I had just received. "We are very well insulated, babe, and I won't let anyone get near any of us."

"You talked to Jax, how is Michael?" Of course she is worried about Junior, she is a giver and will always be.

"Jax said he is doing good, and the doctor is great. Now, I want you to put all that aside. We have a wedding tomorrow to prepare for, and apparently, your dad is going to help me get into my Kimono."

She laughs and it warms my heart. "Just the thought of you in the Kimono is funny, let alone Papa helping you." She gets up and extends her hand toward me. "Let's go. The sooner I become Mrs. Maxwell Fleming, the sooner I can have my way with you."

"Wow, you have plans for me, babe?"

"Big plans, Max." She leans in and whispers in my ear a little bit of what her plans are.

I feel the heat rush to my cheeks and Jackie giggles.

"Why, Maxwell Fleming, I do believe you're blushing."

"I might be blushing now, but your arse will be a lovely shade of pink later."

We race up the stairs. Not quite sure who is pulling who.

FINALLY MY WAIT IS over. Today, I will not only be her lover, friend, and protector, I will become her husband, too. After a quick shower, I attempt to figure out the Kimono. There is a knock on the door and Jeff comes in. "Hey, Jeff, I've got everything but this sash figured out."

He silently begins to tightly wrap the sash around me. "Maxwell, I know you love her, that's never been a question, but can you protect her? She's my life."

"Jeff, I love her more than life itself. When I pushed her away, it nearly killed us both. If I could keep her locked away, I would, but you know your daughter, hell would freeze over first. I promise you, I will lay down my life for her."

"Okay, I will give you a moment and meet you in the drawing room. Dylan is waiting for us."

I walk up to the window and look out over the estate. It really is very beautiful here and very lonely. I close my eyes, thinking about my first wife and silently pray. *Oh, Samantha, please know I loved you so much. I would have been with you for life, but God needed angels. Jackie loves me with all her heart. She is genuine and pure; I know you will be happy for me. Watch over her and keep her safe.*

I take a deep breath and head out to begin a new life. Now, I have to meet the wanker, Dylan, and try not to snap the fucker's neck.

Jackie

I RUN MY FINGERTIPS down my grandmother's beautiful Kimono, the same one my mom wore on her wedding day. It's soft and silky. The design has a thousand cranes stitched in gold thread, and when the light hits it, they sparkle like a thousand stars. I pray for my grandmother to watch over him again, just like before. *Keep him safe, all of them.* There's a knock on the door, it must be my mom to help me get ready. When I open the door, I'm surprised to see Dylan. Before I can speak, he pushes me in the room.

"I need to talk to you alone, Jac, now."

"Calm down and tell me what's wrong." I just wish he would, for once, let me have my time without butting in.

"You can't marry him, Jac. There is so much danger around him. I can't let you do this!"

He can't be serious. "Dylan, please just let it go. I love him and he loves me. He's a good man and he can protect me." He grabs my hands and tries to pull me toward the door.

"Dylan, let go of me; you're hurting me."

The door flies open and Max, along with my father, Sammy, and the guards, come racing in. Max puts his hands around Dylan's throat, lifting him off the ground. "Max, let go of him please." My father and Sammy finally pull them apart. Max pulls me toward him.

"Jackie, are you okay? Did he hurt you?" He's running his hands all over me looking to see that I'm not hurt.

"Max, I'm fine. It's just Dylan, being his usual self."

He holds me tightly into his arms, his breathing is heavy. "Please calm down, Max, I promise I'm okay." I feel his heart racing.

My father and Dylan are yelling. I've never seen my father this mad before. Finally, my mom steps into the room. Dylan sees her and immediately stops yelling. My mom then asks everyone to please leave except for Dylan and me. I feel Max tense up, and I know he's not going to leave me alone with Dylan.

"Max, look at me please." His eyes are locked on mine. "I promise you, I will be okay. I will keep Sammy in the room. You need to step outside, please."

"So help me, babe, if he touches you, all bets are off." He steps outside the room and I know he is just on the other side of the door.

My mom steps in-between Dylan and me, "Look at me, son. What has gotten into you?"

"I can't let her make the biggest mistake of her life. She might love him, but is that any reason to put her life in constant danger? He chose the life he has lived, but she has not."

I'm about to answer him when my mom stops me. "Let me ask you this. Would you feel the same way if you were marrying Raven, knowing all the danger that surrounds her? Would that be okay with you? You have had no problem letting your sister be friends with Raven as long as you thought there was a possibility that you might have a chance with her. Now that you realize that possibility is gone, can she no longer be friends with her, is that what you're suggesting?"

She steps closer to him, never giving him a chance to answer. "Since Jackie met Maxwell, she has come alive. She is growing into the woman I always knew she could be. I will not let you, or anyone stop her. I suggest you figure out how you are going to apologize to your sister, and, to Maxwell."

Dylan takes a step back "Mom, I'm sorry, but I can't be here for this. Jac, you are making the biggest mistake of your life. I love you . . . I honestly do. Quite frankly, when everything came out about Raven, I was glad that Max sent you packing. If he truly were the man you all think he is, he would have put you first. He would have never put you in so much danger. Everyday the threats get worse, and you're walking around with your head in the clouds. Jesus Christ, because of all of this, you can't even teach anymore. What are you going to do, sit around the house all day and do nothing? Or, is he going to knock you up every year to keep you locked away in that castle? I'm leaving, and if you actually live through all of this, you can call me when it's time to pick up the pieces."

He storms out of the room, leaving me alone with my mom. "Are we having a wedding here today, Jacquelyn, or am I to get Maxwell?"

"I would like a few minutes alone, please." My mom steps out of the room and I begin to cry.

"Hey, stretch, look at me." My heart nearly leaps out of my chest; I forgot Sammy was in the room.

"Are you going to let what Dylan said influence you? Don't listen to anyone but you. What is your heart telling you to do?"

I wipe away my tears. "I need to talk to Max." I open the door and he is standing there, fists clenched, and a look of angst on his face that breaks my heart.

Sammy takes my hand, "Jackie, I'm going to step outside and give the two of you a little privacy."

He is barely out the door and I throw my arms around Max. I'm trembling and I can hardly speak.

"Jackie, I heard everything he said. I don't care what he thinks, I only want to know how you feel."

I pull back and take his hands. "I want a life with you. I want to be your wife and best friend. I want to fill my days with us. I want a family with you. I want to be loved by you. I want to grow with you; into someone you will always respect. Marry me, and then I want to leave right away. I don't want to spend my wedding night here."

"That's all I need to hear. Let's go right now to the temple before anything else happens." As we race toward the temple, he notifies the pilot to have the plane ready to leave within the hour.

Raven

I HEAD INTO MICHAEL'S room, pick up Antonia, and go into the restroom. I change her and then begin to feed her. I love our quiet time together; it gives me a chance to think clearly about everything. I can't believe that Marco kept such a huge secret from me—then again—he, kept a lot from me. I wonder how much Max has told Jackie. I know that nothing and no one will stop Max from marrying her. I just pray that we can keep everyone safe.

Michael is exhausted from today; I hope he can stay awake to see the wedding. Antonia is falling asleep during her feeding as usual. I need to find Jax and make sure he didn't bully the staff. When I step outside the restroom, I see Jax lying in bed with Michael. The two of them look so tired. Bella is standing in front of the window crying. This is not what Michael needs right now. I put Antonia into her carriage and bring it next to the bed. I need to see if I can help Bella.

I walk up to her and pull her into a hug. "Hey, we need to keep it together for Michael. What's the problem, Bella?"

"Let's step outside, Raven."

As we step outside I glance over toward Jax. He's holding Michael while he falls asleep.

"Bella, what's the matter? Did something happen with Michael?"

"No, not really. It's just hard to feel so helpless. You're a mom now; imagine Antonia hurting and not being able to do anything about it," her voice trembles. "To start out in life the way he did, now this . . ." she trails off.

"What do you mean 'start out in life the way he did'?" I tilt my head, trying to think if there was something I'd forgotten about. *Was he a preemie?*

Bella takes in a deep breath before leaning in closer to me. "You're family now, so I'll tell you, but you mustn't say anything to Michael Jr.; he doesn't know." She pauses. I nod for her to continue. "Michael Sr. is not Junior's biological father. I was date raped before I met Michael. I didn't find out I was pregnant till after he and I became serious. It didn't matter to Michael; he loved me and anything that was a part of me. He talked me out of having an abortion and raised Michael Jr. as his own." She lets a small smile grace her face as she wipes her tears away.

"Wow, Bella." I shake my head in disbelief. "I'm so sorry that happened to you, but I'm so happy that Michael Jr. is here . . . that you have him and your wonderful husband." I grasp her upper arms and squeeze them gently. "Stay focused on that. We have to stay focused on the positive. There's enough love and strength in this family—*our* family—to get us through anything."

"You're right and that's what we're going to do—stay positive." She brings me in for a hug. "I love you," she says softly and she tightens the hug.

"I love you, too."

"Everything all right, out here?" Jax grabs our attention, breaking us from our hug.

"Yes, it is now." Bella reaches her hand out to him. "I've told her everything, Jax. She knows what happened to me." She squeezes his hand.

A mixture of anger and remorse flashes across Jax's eyes. "I blame myself. I was just making a name for myself. I didn't know enough to have guards on everyone. That's when I brought Max on board."

"Oh my God, none of you are to blame. What's important is everyone is safe and will remain that way. If Michael needs stem cells, we will move heaven and earth to get them. Let's try and focus on the positive. Jax, did the doctor say how close of a match you and Max are?" I try to change the subject a little, pull him away from the blame game; it won't help anyone.

"No he didn't, why? I know you, sweetheart; I can see the wheels in your mind turning."

"Jackie said something to me about donating cord blood. I don't remember what the hell she said other than the baby needs to be born in the hospital."

Bella gives me a look of utter shock. "Oh, Bella, don't look at me that way;

you know this crazy man wants ten kids. If the stem cells are needed, it won't be for a while," I finish. Jax begins to laugh a deep, hearty laugh.

Bella grabs my hand, "Raven, you would do that for me . . . for Michael?"

"I would do anything for that boy and, chances are, you might not have to wait that long. You're going to have to tell Jackie everything." On that note, Jax stops laughing and his eyes become wide.

"Don't look at me that way Jax, you know that Max is just as nuts as you are. Now, I believe we have a wedding that should be happening shortly," I say as I head toward the door. I turn around and they are both standing there, looking stunned. I smile and whisper, "*Faith,*" as I head back in the room.

Chapter Eighteen
Maxwell

JACKIE AND I RACE toward the temple. The sooner we do this, the sooner we are out of here. I know that's not the way one should look at their wedding day, but I can't let anything go wrong. Sammy stops us at the door, "Max, Jackie needs to wait here."

"It will be a cold day in hell, Sammy, if you think I would ever let her out of my sight."

"It's tradition; her mom has to walk her half way and then her father walks her the rest of the way."

"Where is Dylan?" I feel my heart in my throat.

"He's already gone, Max. You're going to have to trust me. I would never let anything happen to her."

I close my eyes and silently pray for some sort of strength and courage, but I know I can't do it. I whisper her name and pull her tightly in my arms.

She kisses me so softly, "Max, let's start our own tradition. How about you walk me down the aisle with both my parents."

I open my eyes and I whisper, "Thank you, babe."

We step inside and find hundreds of tiny paper cranes hanging from the ceiling. The lights in the room make it look like they are all twinkling. Emi comes up to me and takes my hand. "Maxwell, sometimes in life, one must make changes. I understand your fears and I am willing to make the changes you need. When you love someone, you must sometimes carry their fears for them to get them through the difficult times. I wish for you both only happiness and joy, but I am realistic; I know there will be tears. Love her with all that you have and all that you will ever be. Need her and want her always. Don't be afraid to share your fears with her, your tears, and your joy. They will help you to grow not only as an individual but as a whole." I'm floored; she is so quiet and reserved yet, when she speaks to you—it is profound.

I'm about to start up the aisle when Jeff stops me. "I have a surprise for both of you." He nods to Sammy and the television screen comes to life.

"I could not let you get married without your family to witness it." I'm speechless; I can't believe they pulled this off. Junior looks tired as he has stayed awake for this.

My grip around Jackie is even tighter, "You ready, babe?"

"Yes."

The music begins and we head down the aisle. I look up at the screen and I swear Jax might be crying. Everyone is there, glued to the screen. When we reach the front, Jeff sits next to Emi and we face a man that, I'm guessing, is some sort of minister.

"Hello, everyone, my name is Bill. I will be officiating your service today. I would like to start with a modified version of the Buddhist Declaration of Intent; if you agree then both say *we will.* Will you, in every way you can, allow your deepest self to be shown?"

"We will."

"Will you both take full responsibility for your own life and all of its dimensions?"

"We will."

"Are you committed to embrace all parts of each other, your deepest fears and bring them toward the light to heal?"

"We will."

"Will you always keep your hearts open to each other, even in extreme pain?"

"We will."

He hands us each a small bottle of sand, and now I'm really confused.

"Maxwell, every grain of sand in your jar represents every beat of your heart." He hands me a larger jar, "Please pour it into this jar." I'm still confused but I do as instructed.

"Jacquelyn, every grain of sand represents every beat of your heart. Please pour your sand into the jar with Maxwell's sand."

He puts a cap on it and shakes it, and then hands it back to me.

"The sand can never be separated again. You have become one heart and one soul—for life." I roll the jar in my hands, watching the sand swirl around; something so simple, yet, so profound.

"Jacquelyn, and, Maxwell, remember these words and carry them in your heart. It's the little things that matter the most in life. You are never too old to hold hands. Never go to bed angry. Put your lover before you. Say I love you every day. Don't expect perfection. There are no halos or angel wings attached to you. We are all a work in progress, so learn to forgive and forget. Keep family close to you. Do for each other out of joy not obligation. When you have to carry the load, do so willingly without regret," he finishes, giving us a warm smile. "Who has the rings?"

Oh my God, I can't believe I forgot the rings! Jeff gets up and hands the minister the rings. "Relax, Maxwell, your brother sent them." I look at the screen and Jax has a huge smile.

"Hey, I'll always have your back, mate—always."

The minister holds up the rings, "The wedding ring is the outward and visible sign of an inward and spiritual bond which unites two loyal hearts in partnership." Maxwell, please place the ring on Jacquelyn's finger. Do you promise to always love her with all that you are and all that you will ever be in this life?"

"I do."

"Jacquelyn, please place the ring on Maxwell's finger. Do you promise to always love him with all that you are and all that you will ever be in this life?"

"I do."

Before the minister finishes, I take both of Jackie's hands in mine. "Jackie, you saved me. Everything I will ever be is because of your love for me. You've made me want to have a life worth living."

"Max, I didn't chose you, my heart did. Wrapped in my arms you will always be home. Like the sands in the bottle, our hearts beat as one. Everyday with you is a gift I will treasure forever"

I close my eyes and rest my forehead upon hers, breathing in her sweetness. "Please tell me I can kiss you now?"

"Kiss her already!" I hear Jax yell.

I open my eyes and they connect with hers, making my soul burn with desire for her. I glance toward the minister and he nods, "You may kiss your wife now."

Your wife two words that I've longed to hear. I gently kiss her tender lips. I hear clapping and laughing. We both turn and look up at the screen. What a wonderful sight; everyone is celebrating.

"Thank you, everyone, for being here with us. Junior, our flight leaves in thirty minutes. We will see you soon." He looks very tired. I don't want to be away from him longer than I have to.

Jeff and Emi step up to congratulate us. "Let's head up to the main house before you have to leave. I will keep it brief; I know you need to be with your family at this time."

"Thank you, Jeff, for being so understanding."

I pull Jackie close as we head up toward the main house. It's been such an emotional day for both of us, and I know saying goodbye will be very hard for her.

We get to the main house and I'm glad to see that there is no sign of Dylan.

"Jeff, I know this has been a whirlwind for everyone. Please, understand it was never my intention. Unfortunately, sometimes life does get in the way of living. I promise as soon as everything settles down, we will come back."

"I understand and I never would have gone along with any of this if I wasn't sure of how much you love Jacquelyn. I know you will keep her safe, but so help me if something ever happens—all bets are off!"

He pulls Jackie into his arms. "My beautiful girl, everyday you have brought me so much happiness. I tried to think of what I could give you today, but what do you give someone who wants nothing? Finally, this morning it hit me like a lightning bolt—*shoes!*"

Jackie begins to giggle and, Jesus, I love that sound.

"Max, you must know by now that my daughter has an excessive amount of shoes, but have you ever asked her why?"

I'm about to ask when Jackie gasps. "Papa, you know?!"

"Of course I know, and don't glare at Sammy; he didn't give you up. You know I love a good mystery, so I investigated on my own. Max, Jacquelyn buys six pairs of shoes at a time, all the same, all different sizes. She keeps one pair for herself and she donates the others to shelters. She has been doing this since she was thirteen years old. I will match your donation to every shelter with whatever they need."

Wow, once again she has left me speechless. She always does something so simple that can mean so much to others. *Another facet of this beautiful woman to love.* I glance at my watch, "Jeff, we need to get going. I promise, first break in Junior's treatment and we will come for a visit."

Jackie pulls her mum into a hug. "I love you, Mom, and thank you so much for everything."

"Happy birthday, my beautiful girl; safe travels and let us know when you arrive." She places a pouch in Jackie's hand. "Please give this to young Michael."

We make our goodbyes and head out to the plane, with Sammy and six guards in tow.

Jaxson

JUNIOR HAS FINALLY FALLEN asleep with Bella curled up next to him. Michael is mindlessly channel surfing while Raven is tending to Antonia. Mick has taken Rose, Mrs. Osla, and my mum back to the house. My mum was so tired. I know Rose is worried about her. I know everyone was glad to see the wedding. I didn't see Dylan there. I'll get all the details from Max when he gets back. I'm glad my sister finally shared everything with Raven. I hate secrets. Leave it to Raven, though, to find a silver lining. I stare out the window, processing everything that happened today. I feel her arms slowly wrap around my waist. She presses her warm body against mine. I need her so badly, like nothing I could ever explain. I've never needed anyone, yet she completes me. Through all the sadness and the pain, she gives me hope . . . hope for the future . . . our future.

"Jax, what happened when you spoke to the doctor about the added security?"

I turn around and hold her tightly in my arms. "He understood and so did the nurses. I tried not to focus on the unknown danger, only what we know for sure."

"How long will Michael have to stay in the hospital?"

"The doctor said for a month, and then after that, he will come back and forth as needed. We can't leave the country; he was adamant about that."

"Have you looked into treatment in other countries?"

"No, sweetheart, everything happened so fast. What are you thinking?"

"I know that Mrs. Osla pulled the best places for treatment, however, I'm sure there are other countries that might offer the same and, possibly, something new and cutting edge. I'm not saying there is anything wrong with the treatment that he's receiving, I'm just saying we should get all the facts."

"I will have Mrs. Osla look into it. I would feel safer if we were out of the States. The staff is bringing in a bed for Bella and Michael. I think we will take turns staying here; it will make it easier for all of us. When he can get out of here, I will feel better. This past year, I've grown used to having everyone under one roof."

"When can we expect Max and Jackie to get here?"

"He texted me that he was in-flight and he should be here in about six hours. I need to get you and Antonia home. You are beat, and we will be back here before you know it. Besides, I really need to lose myself in you for a while, sweetheart."

I don't need to say anything more; she gets it. She gathers up Antonia and we say goodbye to Michael Sr. We head out of the hospital, flanked by six guards and Bo, into a waiting car. The house we are renting is a quick ride from the hospital, which I thought would be a blessing until I get a look around the neighborhood. The iron gates open and we drive up a short drive to a nondescript looking home. Given the increased threats, this is never going to work for us. We get out and head inside. Mrs. Osla is waiting for us.

"Raven, why don't you get Antonia settled in for the night while I talk to Mrs. Osla."

She looks between me and Mrs. Osla, "Go easy on her, Jax."

"Raven, the bedrooms are all upstairs. Antonia's room is the third door on the right; it's attached to your room. Don't worry about me, I can handle him."

"Thank you for everything, Mrs. Osla. Jax, I will meet you upstairs."

I watch my wife walk away and my need to lose myself in her is becoming even more intense.

Mrs. Osla clears her throat, snapping me out of my daydream. "Jaxson, I know this is not the best place, but you saw the same pictures I did. The area around us didn't look like this. The pictures made it look more secluded. I'm trying to find something else, but it's not easy."

"Let's go sit down. I need to bring you up to speed on everything." She leads me into a den and pours me a drink.

"Mrs. Osla, there have been some new security developments and I know this place is not going to be secure for us."

"I'm aware of the developments; Mick has explained everything. I looked to see if there are any other hospitals that have this level of treatment for young Michael; there aren't any in this area. There is St. Jude's Children's Research Hospital in Tennessee, but I'm not sure it would be any more secure then what we've got. I also looked into other countries. Until I get the reports back, this one still comes out the best. So, what do we need to do to make it safe for us to stay here?"

"Short of locking everyone up in here, I'm not sure. We'll stay here for tonight, and then I will get with Max in the morning. How is my mum doing?"

"The trip was a lot for her, but she is resting. And Rose is keeping a close eye on her."

"How much does Rose know?"

"Nothing, we got home, and then she was making sure your mum was settled in."

"Good, I need to have Max here with me when we explain everything to her. How many guards are here?"

"There are a dozen at different points of the house."

"Okay, we should be good for the night. Get some rest, tomorrow will be another busy day."

She gets up and I'm left alone to figure out what to do about this mess. Just then, Raven walks around my chair, pulling me from my thoughts. She crawls into my lap and nuzzles my neck. "Come to bed, Jax. Everything will still be here in the morning. Tonight, I need to cuddle up into your arms and have a peaceful sleep; we both do."

She doesn't need to say anything more; I lift her and carry her up the steps. My love, my salvation, the only place I truly have any peace is when I'm lost in her. "I love you, sweetheart, always and forever more."

Maxwell

WE ARE SAFELY IN-FLIGHT and I texted Jax to let him know.

My wedding night . . . not exactly what I was planning, but I can improvise. I take her hand and guide her into one of the large suites in the back of the plane. "My beautiful wife, God I can't get enough of that word. Happy birthday, Jackie; one of many we will share together." I hand her a small box. "I had this diamond heart made to match your ring; my heart next to yours—always."

"It's beautiful, Max, please put it on me." She turns and lifts her hair. I gently kiss her neck before putting on the necklace.

"Please, Jackie, get me out of this Kimono."

Her giggle is so sweet. "Maybe I like seeing you in this, then what?"

Her delicate fingers are trailing up and down my chest and I feel like I might combust. "Well, then I might have to get used to it, or maybe prove to you how much better it is when I'm naked."

She blushes and quickly helps me out of my Kimono. "Jackie, I need to figure out how to get you out of this. I don't even know where to begin!"

"Start by untying anything you can find. The wedding ones are more intricate, but I'm sure you will get me out of it. Keep in mind . . . this was my grandmothers, so please be careful."

Guess taking a scissor to it is not an option. There are so many parts to this, but I prevail. As the robes all fall away, I'm left staring at the most beautiful sight I've ever seen. My beautiful wife—in thigh highs, diamonds, and pearls . . . *nothing else.*

"Max, um, are you okay?"

Her voice snaps me out of my daze, okay? She is standing here like a vision and she thinks I would be okay! "I need a minute, babe. You took my breath away."

"I have something for you." She steps over to one of her bags and pulls out a small package.

"I wanted to give you something very special and it has to be now." She is chewing on her bottom lip and seems very nervous. I open the box and my eyes grow wide.

"What do you give a man who has everything? The one thing I know he really wants. I completely stopped them the day we got engaged. Honestly, with everything that has been going on, I haven't kept good track of them. I know I've missed several, so what's the point? As scared as I am, I know my life is with you and will always be, no matter what."

I pull her birth control pills out of the box. I'm speechless; she knows how much I want a child with her and she is willing to jump right in.

"It might take a while; it might not. I'm willing to go on the journey with you. We will face whatever life throws at us, together. I love you."

"I'm confused, I thought you were scared to have a baby?"

Her hand is trembling as she places it on my cheek. "Trust me, Max, I'm scared. But being around Antonia and the kids that I teach made me realize how much I really wanted one. I didn't want to tell you I stopped my pills until the wedding. I didn't want to put any more pressure on you. My hope is that, by your birthday, I will have a great present to give you. You are a very hard man to surprise, so I needed to do it this way. I knew we would be together forever; I wasn't being underhanded, Max. I wanted to make it special for you. Are you mad at me?"

With her, my needs are always first. How could she possibly think I'd be mad? "Mad? How could I ever be mad? You're making all my hopes and dreams come true. You, babe, amaze me. Come here." I pull her tightly in my arms. "You make me want a future, one that will never end. I promise you I will treasure our baby with my life."

I gently kiss her tender lips; they're so very soft. I don't want to rush this. I want to live in this moment for the rest of my life. I flutter my fingers up her sides, swirling up and around her nipples. They perk instantly to my touch. She looks down, following the trail of my fingertips. Her head is bowed but her eyes glance up to mine. She has a gift like no other, submissive and powerful in one single sweep of her eyes. "Kiss me, Jackie, *now.*"

She slowly lifts her head, her eyes keeping contact with mine. I feel desire burn deep within my soul. She softly brushes her lips over mine, followed by the swipe of her tongue. She takes her hand and glides it down her body. Slowly, she uses her fingertips to gather her wetness. She brushes her fingers across my lips and I taste her sweetness. I nip her fingertip. I consider myself a strong man, a man who is able to take a lot. When she tilts her head back and lets out a long, low moan, I lose it. I lean down and take one of her nipples between my teeth, pulling just enough to make her buck and yell. I lift her and place her gently on the bed and I wait.

She fists the sheets, "Max, what are you waiting for?—I want you now."

"Anticipation, babe, you can't always get what you want." She said she wanted to experiment and try different things. I plan on fulfilling every one of her fantasies, even ones she didn't know she had.

"Play with your nipples, Jackie." Her eyes flutter, and that shy submissive look is all over her face. She hesitates and that's what I want, that's what will intensify it for her. She brushes her fingers over them, causing them to perk. *Simply beautiful.* I kneel between her legs, lean down, and kiss each one. I slowly leave a trail of gentle kisses all over her. When I get to her clitoris, I barely let my lips touch and she gasps.

"Oh, Max, more please, I need *more.*"

Kiss, blow, nibble, and then swipe my tongue. She grabs my head, bucks her hips, trying to push for more. I've got my arms locked around her legs, holding her down. I work my tongue in and out, then stroke up and down. She begins to shake and her skin feels like it's on fire. As I work my fingers deep inside her, I keep a constant force on her clitoris. She arches her back and begins to beg me for more. "I know you want more, but not yet. I won't rush this night, our wedding night is once in a lifetime."

I need to slow her down. I slowly work my way off of her, taking my time nipping and kissing her everywhere. She whimpers at the loss of my tongue on her. Fuck me, it's beautiful. I head over to the dresser for some toys I got specifically for tonight. When I look back at her, she is rolling her nipples between her fingers.

"Does someone need a spanking?"

"No, please, Max, I need you."

I walk up to the bed and crawl between her legs. I pull her hands away from her nipples and put a remote in her hand.

"What is this for?"

"Babe, it's for your pleasure."

"What is that thing on your cock!?"

"You'll see, right now I'm going to enter you very slowly. When I tell you, slowly tilt your hand."

I enter her and she closes her eyes, I stop. "Open your eyes and watch, *now.*"

Her eyes fly open when I'm all the way in. "Oh my!" she gasps from the cock ring hitting her clitoris.

"Tilt your hand very slowly."

It begins to vibrate and her eyes grow wide. "Oh wow, what the hell?"

"Tilt your hand back and forth, you have all the power, babe. If you want more, move it more."

Every time she moves her hand, my cock grows harder. While she's having fun with her remote I roll her nipples into a perfect peak. "I have another surprise for you."

"O-oh this is so wonderful, I don't think I can handle any more surprises."

"You can and you will. Slow it down or this will end too quickly."

She slows down the vibrations and her rapid breathing is becoming more even. I reach down and grab her next surprise off the bed. I hold them up for her to see as they sparkle in the dim lighting. "What are they?"

"I had them made for you; diamond and gold nipple clamps." I need to start her slowly with these. I put them on, but make sure they are not too tight—yet.

"Wow, they are beautiful. They feel . . . different."

"Now you can use the remote again, but slow, babe."

She's getting into this and I'm trying not to explode. It's a mind game; concentrating on giving her pleasure. When she speeds up the vibrations, I tighten the clamps. Her eyes open wide and she doesn't realize it, but she's moving her hand more, which of course, makes the cock ring vibrate even more. I'm harder than I can ever remember being in my lifetime. "Oh, Max, you feel huge. I don't think I can take much more."

I tighten the clamps again and her whole body begins to shake. "Babe, you're shaking, what do you want?" Before she can answer, I release the clamps and it sends a surge through her. Right at that point, I release the cock ring and slam into her, over and over again. She finds her release and I'm right behind her—*beautiful.*

I slowly work us down as I nuzzle her neck. "I hope we made a new life tonight," she whispers.

I pull the covers over us and hold her close to my heart. "I hope so too, babe."

Chapter Nineteen

Leo Hage

THE CASE THAT MADE my career is now blowing up in my face. I'm looking at the order, demanding all documents in the Giaconna deal to go to his new attorney. Who is this attorney and why have I never heard of her before today? What does she think she can accomplish? The buzzing of my intercom snaps me out of my thoughts. My assistant informs me Amelia Jade, the current pain in my ass, is here to see me. Sending her away would be like poking a hornet's nest. "Give me a minute and send her in."

Within a moment, the door opens and in steps the most stunning redhead I have ever seen. I have to stay focused; I can't let her distract me. "What can I do for you, Ms. Jade?"

"I'm here to discuss Mr. Giaconna's case."

"Have a seat, Ms. Jade, and please enlighten me; I don't know what case you're referring to? Mr. Giaconna took a plea deal, *there is no case.*"

She doesn't sit. Her glare becomes more intense. "Mr. Hage, you must have received the order to turn over all your files in my client's case, by now. My client is requesting an emergency bail hearing and a trial. The tape was obtained illegally. You should have known that this would somehow come back to bite you in the ass. You obtained the tape without a warrant, and a proper chain of evidence was not followed. Therefore, all the evidence you obtained from Duke never would have happened without the video. It's called *fruit of the poisonous tree,* and you knew that but chose to ignore it. Mr. Hage, my client has the right to face his accuser; he wants his day in court."

She's got to be just as crazy as Vincent if she thinks this will ever fly. "You know and I know this is never going to happen, so what's your end game?"

"Everyone is entitled to justice, Mr. Hage, even Mr. Giaconna—whether you like it or not. We all have to play by the same rules. You can't write them to fit your needs. I want him moved, via U.S. Marshals Service, from ADX Florence to Daniel Patrick Moynihan United States Courthouse for a bail hearing. On my way here, I filed the necessary papers for the emergency bail hearing."

"Look, Ms. Jade, I don't know what your game is but no judge would ever grant that animal bail. You and I both know you don't have a leg to stand on. Drop it; find another way to make a name for yourself."

She gathers up her stuff and turns to leave. "Mr. Hage, I will see you in court." Just like that, she's gone. I sit back in my chair; total shock envelops me. What is her end game? Money? Making a name—what?

My intercom buzzes again, "Mr. Hage, papers just arrived for you from the court. It appears Mr. Giaconna has been granted an emergency bail hearing. I also sent Ms. Jade the files . . . sir?"

"I'm here. Get Mr. Phillips on the line for me immediately. " This is a call I'm not looking forward to making.

$\mathcal{J}axson$

LOSING MYSELF OVER AND over again in Raven last night was just what I needed. With her, I can release all my fears and frustration. With her, I find my safe place. I've got her locked up in my arms when my phone begins to ring. At this hour of the morning, it has to be a problem. I look at the display. And so the nightmare continues . . . Hage.

" Hage, what's the problem?"

"Vincent is being granted an emergency bail hearing." What the fuck?!

"I'll call you back in five." I don't want to wake Raven. I make my way out of bed and grab my sweats. I head downstairs where I know she won't hear me. I'm about to call Hage back when Max and Jackie come through the front door. Relief washes over me, and I pull Jackie into a big bear hug.

"Jax, you're smothering me; is everything okay?"

"Oh sorry, yeah, just very stressed out. Glad you guys got here okay." I look over to Max and nod. I never have to say anything with him.

"Babe, I'm going to go over some stuff with Jax, and then have a quick shower before we head over to the hospital. Would you mind getting everything set up for us?" he asks.

She kisses him and giggles, "If you want alone time with Jax, you just have to ask."

He is watching her head up the steps with a grin like the cat that ate the canary.

"Okay, Jax, besides this house, what's the problem?"

"Hage just called and said Vincent was granted an emergency bail hearing. I didn't ask any questions. I didn't want to wake Raven. I need to call him back now."

Sammy walks into the room. "Hey, Jax, I just hung up with my contact. The U.S. Marshal will be bringing Vincent from Colorado to New York. Hage requested that he be brought back via private plane due to the high security threat. The hearing is set for tomorrow. It's only a bail hearing so Max and Raven won't need to be present."

"Thanks, Sammy. Sorry about everything that happened when we left the States the last time."

He holds up his hand, "Don't worry, Jax; just business."

"Sammy, before I call Hage back, does he know who Amelia Jade really is?"

"I don't know, but I would tell him. Better to have all the cards on the table."

"Max, you ready for this?"

"Yeah, put him on speaker."

He answers on the first ring. "Hage, you're on speaker, and Max is here."

"Okay. As I said earlier, Vincent was granted an emergency bail hearing. He is already being processed and turned over to the U.S. Marshals office for transfer to New York City. Do not come to court."

"I personally won't be there, however, my attorney will be. My family's safety is at stake; I trust no one." I hear him growl and I really don't give a fuck.

"Hage, do you have any idea who Amelia Jade is?"

"I know that she is from Virginia and graduated top in her class. She knows she can't win the case. Vincent made a deal and now she wants him to back out of that deal. I can't figure out why. I thought maybe it was some sort of revenge but she is squeaky clean with no ties to the Giaconna family. Do you know something I don't?"

I run my hands through my hair, trying to keep my temper in check. Max holds a hand up to silence me before I snap.

"Hage, Maxwell here. Amelia Jade was formerly Amelia Greene, Marco Greene's sister. Marco, if nothing else, was a brilliant hacker and had her name changed with the records sealed. The motive very simply put: revenge. She wants a trial to get Raven out into the open. She wants to make Raven suffer the way she feels she has suffered. Vincent wants me to suffer, so there is a huge bounty on Jackie's head."

I look at the phone to see if the call has dropped as Max begins to pace. *The silence is deafening.* "Apparently, Hage, you knew none of this. My wife and Jackie will never step foot near that courthouse. My nephew is here for medical treatment and, as soon as I can make other arrangements, we will be leaving the country. What are the chances of him getting bail?"

"I didn't even think he had a chance at getting a hearing, so what do I know? I haven't been told what judge has been assigned to it yet. My understanding was that Annabelle found Ms. Jade, but now, after what you're telling me, I'm not so sure. Where is Miss Gerhard now?"

"She is safe, and that is all you need to know. When you find out who the judge is, let me know what his chances are." I don't wait for his reply—I can't or I might snap—so I just hang up.

I need coffee, but I don't even know where the kitchen is in this place. Bless her; Mrs. Osla comes in with a tray, bearing coffee and pastries.

"Welcome home, Maxwell, and congratulations. I'm sorry about this home, it's not as it was pictured. I'm trying to find something more suitable, however, getting close to the hospital is an issue."

"Thank you, Mrs. Osla. Please don't worry, we will figure something out."

"I will be upstairs if you need anything more."

As she leaves, the three of us grab our coffees and try to formulate some sort of plan.

"It's not her fault, Max, it seemed that the house was more isolated in the pictures. So, first thing we need is a safer place to stay. There are too many windows and too many neighbors. Even if I purchased every house around us, it would still take too much time to process and get them cleared out. How about a penthouse? We can isolate ourselves like we did in New York. The only thing that might be an issue is traveling to and from the hospital."

" We could ferry everyone by helicopter. I will look at the regulations, but that might not be such a bad idea. I sent Tony whatever information Sammy had on Amelia, so I need to get in touch with him and see if he found out anything else."

"How is he settling in? We gave him a sweet deal but, in the end, it's never been about material stuff with him," I ask. Max seems apprehensive as he pours himself another coffee.

Before he can answer, Sammy puts his hand on Max's shoulder. "I know more than you think, Max. You're going to have to get used to me being around and you're going to have to trust me. You know I only have Jackie's best interest at heart. I think I proved myself with Dylan."

"What the fuck happened with that wanker?!"

"That is a story for another day, mate." He shakes his head and rolls his eyes a bit. "It's not easy for me, Sammy, but in time, I will come to trust you more." He holds his mug up to Sammy in gesture before taking another sip. He puts his mug down and brings his attention back to me. "Tony is thrilled that at twenty-nine, he was able to semi-retire. But you know him; he can never be idle. He wired up the entire island, and now it's like a fort. He loves it there and has since taken up fishing. He was happy that I gave him some work to do."

"What are we going to do about Jackie? Every time she walks out that door, she is in danger. I know you want to be here, but maybe it would be for the best if you head back to Scotland."

"Trust me, I thought about that, but she will never go for it. She is the most stubborn person I have ever met—worse than you, mate. Jeff found a private clinic in Switzerland that is doing a lot of cutting edge work with ALL. He gave me the file, but I haven't had a chance to look at it yet. I'm going to have Rose look at it. I won't leave Jackie's side, Jax, ever. I just can't do it."

"I get it; I wouldn't ask you to. We will figure something out. What are we going to do about Rose? If Vincent gets wind that she is alive, he'll go crazy."

"Best case scenario, we are going to have to keep her locked up here until we can get her out of the country. We are going to have to tell her what's going on. I mean, we really don't have a choice."

"You think Jackie is stubborn? My mother in-law is worse!" I get up to get more coffee when I hear Raven scream. We fly up the steps and I find Raven with Antonia in her arms, and Bo attacking one of the new guards. Sammy pulls the guard out of the room, with Bo still trying to rip him apart. I push Raven and Antonia back into the bedroom.

"What happened? Why did you scream? Are you okay? Is the baby okay?"

"Antonia woke up and I went in her room to take care of her like I always do. When I turned around, that guard was in the room. He was staring at me and he started to close the door. I screamed and gave Bo his command to attack." She begins to shake and cry. *Fuck.*

I'm holding them tightly in my arms. "Shh, you're okay, sweetheart. Max is here now, and he will make sure we are all safe." The door flies open and Max comes barreling in with Jackie right behind him.

"Jackie!"

"Raven, it's okay, he's gone and no one will get near you. Are you and Antonia okay?"

"Yeah, Max, we are fine. I just got creeped out. Oh my God, Jackie, I'm so glad you're finally here."

"Me too, let's get Antonia cleaned up; I have lots to tell you." I watch my wife leave while trying to keep my temper in check.

"Where the fuck is he, Max?!"

"Come on, Sammy has him downstairs."

We race downstairs and find Sammy in the den with the guard strapped to the chair. Bo is sitting in front of the guy, growling. I'm about to step in and snap the fucker's neck when Max grabs me. "Don't; you and I will kill him. Sammy will get information first. After that, be my guest."

"This fucking bastard was going after my wife and child, Max!"

"Was he going after Raven because she is beautiful or because of Vincent? If you kill him, we will never know. Let Sammy do his job. After that, I'm going upstairs, and you can do whatever you want. I won't stop you."

Sammy

"I'M GOING TO MAKE this real easy on you. Tell me what you were doing up there. If you do, I will keep Jax out of here." He has the nerve to sit here and smile, *really?*

"Look, I was doing a walk through and when I got to the baby's room, I checked to see if everything was okay. She went nuts and sent that beast after me. I was just doing my fucking job."

"That would be all well and good if your job was to be upstairs, but it's not. You are supposed to be out back watching the perimeter. So, do you want to tell me the truth now?"

"I don't know what you're talking about. I was just doing my job. Look, just let me go and I won't press charges for that dog attacking me or you tying me to a chair."

"Do you really think I care about you pressing charges? You should be more concerned about staying alive and possibly being able to keep your balls firmly attached right where they are." I pet Bo as I glance down at the guy's crotch for emphasis.

"I don't know where you're from, but I have rights." Rights? Fucking scumbag I'll show him *'rights.'*

"I totally agree with you. I told you, you have the right to live and keep both your balls firmly attached. I think that's a great deal. Now, let's start again. Who do you work for?" He says nothing. The more he smiles, the more I want to unleash Jax on him. I'm done being nice. I reach in my pocket and pull out my new pocket knife. This bad boy hosts thirty-two different tools, very versatile. I make a show of slowly opening each tool, which is supposed to offer a firm grip and precision when cutting. I'm guessing it's time to find out just how precise. I take the large blade first and hold it up to the light.

"I just got this for my birthday and I've wanted to try it out. You know, the advertising claims that all thirty-two tools are very versatile. This one looks like it could cut through just about anything. The company says it's very precise; you better hope so." I slowly swipe it up his crotch, cutting through his jeans and boxers, still leaving his balls intact. He's breathing very heavy and beginning to sweat. Seems perfect to me.

"Wow, I guess their advertising is correct; one upward sweep and you still have your balls. So, are you ready to talk to me yet?"

"Go fuck yourself, pretty boy."

"Have it your way. No skin off my balls; just yours."

I take the little saw blade out and hold that one up to the light. His eyes are following my every move. I smile as I reach down and make a small, jagged slice right up the center of his balls.

"Are you fucking nuts? I don't know anything!"

He seems to be trying his hardest not to scream, but then I pull a bottle of booze off the shelf and he gets where I'm going with this. One pour of this on the torn up skin of his balls and he will either hit the roof or pass out.

"Are you going to talk to me now?" I unscrew the bottle and slowly walk up to him, holding it over his lap. I tilt it slightly, and his jaw is tight, as his eyes stay focused on the bottle.

"Okay, I freelance for a private detective firm. He hired me to find out everything I can about the girl with the baseball cap. I was upstairs looking for her when I saw the other one and she was so hot. Then she started nursing that baby and I lost it, I swear that's all I know."

"What is the name of the firm you work for?"

"Look, if I tell you that, I'm a dead man."

I look down at his balls, and blood is starting to pool around the jagged tears in the skin. I tilt the bottle a little bit more and his eyes grow wide. "Who?"

"Johnston Investigations; I swear that's all I know."

I tilt the bottle and watch the liquid land all over his balls. He is screaming and begging me to stop. "That's for being a filthy fucking pig." As I walk out, I see Jax with his fists clenched and Max trying to hold him back.

"I got what we needed. When you're done, if there is anything left, I will have him put into the prison system and his paperwork lost for quite some time."

Max let's go of Jax. "Don't go past what you can't live with. I'm going upstairs to check on everyone," Max growls. Jax heads into the den and closes the door as Max heads upstairs. I walk away, listening to the sound of the man begging. *All the begging in the world isn't going to help him.*

Jackie

RAVEN HAS ANTONIA TIGHTLY in her arms as we head into her bedroom to get her cleaned up.

"Let me take care of my beautiful niece," I offer. She gives me Antonia, sits in the chair, and begins to cry. I don't tell her not to—hell—I want to cry, too. The pressure is getting to all of us.

"I'm sorry, Jackie; this should be a happy time for you."

"Stop apologizing for something that is out of your control." Just then, Mick steps into the room. "Welcome home, Jackie, and congratulations. What went on here this morning?" He quickly turns his attention to Raven. "Are you okay?"

Rose, An, and Mrs. Osla come rushing in. "Raven, what happened? We heard yelling and Bo barking."

"Oh, Mom, one of the new guards freaked me out. Everything is fine now."

Swaying with the baby, back and forth, I glance up to Mick. He nods. "Ladies, I'm going to leave you all to catch up on the wedding while I find Max and congratulate him."

"Okay, Mick, thanks." I smile as he heads out.

An gives me a big hug. "Jackie, we all watched the wedding ceremony; it was breath taking. It looked like you were standing under a thousand twinkling lights."

"Thank you, An. It is a custom in the Japanese culture for the mother of a daughter to begin making paper cranes from the day she is born. They are then used to decorate for the wedding. She hung them from the ceiling; with the lights, and the breeze hitting them, they twinkled. The Kimono was my grandmother's wedding Kimono. I felt very honored to wear it, but I have to tell, you getting in and out of it was a challenge!" I laugh as I look down and notice Antonia is out cold. I swear she will sleep through anything. I put her in her crib and it hits me; I'm really ready. Not just for Max, but for me. I want a baby with Max.

"Come on, ladies; let's give them some time to catch up. An, it's time for your meds. I'll put up a pot of tea." Mrs. Osla barks out orders, ushering everyone out of the room.

Before she leaves, she pulls me into a hug, "Thank you," she whispers, and then wipes away a tear and rushes out of the room.

"Jackie, you okay?"

"Yeah, I wasn't expecting that from Mrs. Osla. She is usually very stern and reserved."

"She loves Max—hell, we all do. So, how did he react when you gave him the gift? Don't even think about holding out on me. Hell, I couldn't stop thinking about it all through the ceremony!"

We both begin to laugh and it feels good. "He was surprised and thrilled. I did warn him that it might not happen right away. He was okay with that."

"What happened with Dylan; don't think I didn't notice he wasn't there."

"Ugh, it was really bad. He tried to physically take me from the house. Max grabbed him by the throat and lifted him right off the ground! My mother stepped in and called him out on his feelings for you."

"Oh my God, you can't be serious?"

"He said I'm going to be isolated and waiting to get *knocked up*. Max knows how I feel about the isolation and I understand, right now, there are not a lot of options. I can see past that, though. Once all this craziness dies down, we will be able to have the life that we want and not the one we are forced to have at this moment in time. I was never able to see past any of that until Max. That's what Dylan doesn't get; with Max I see the future, not just the moment."

"Maybe in time he will come around. Don't give up on him. What happened when you saw Sammy?"

"Max apologized to him and he said he understood that it was business."

"Did Max bring you up to speed on the latest threats?"

"Not all the details; we were trying to get the wedding done, and then get here as quickly as possible. So, fill me in."

"I don't know all the details but, apparently, Marco had a sister who is now Vincent's new attorney. I know that was the reason for the increase in guards. That's really all I know." She shrugs then lets out a big sigh. "I think we should get ready and get over to the hospital."

"How is Michael doing? I bet the room cheered him up."

"He's brave and strong. You knew about the room?"

"I helped Mrs. Osla get it all together but you better never let Jax and Michael know, otherwise, I will get sucked into watching that ridiculous show."

"Your secret is safe with me. I'm going to get ready; will you stay with Antonia?"

"Of course, go."

Raven

I HURRY TO MY room to get ready. I want to get to the hospital as quickly as I can. I hear the water running; Jax must already be in the shower. I head in and find him with the water running over his hand. He has a grim look on his face. The sink is full of blood. What the hell? "Jax, what the hell happened?!"

"I think I broke the guy's jaw and possibly my hand. He was working for a private investigation firm, trying to find out who Rose is."

I can't panic, my husband needs me now. I rummage under the sink and find a first aid kit. I open the peroxide and pour it over his hand.

"Can you move your fingers?"

"Yeah, barely, but I can. Please bandage it for me." His plea breaks my heart. We are both silent as I clean and bandage his wound. I'm so afraid this is going to break him, his spirit.

"Where's the baby?"

"With Jackie, she is fine. Now talk to me, tell me everything."

He sits down and fills me in on everything that he found out. "How the hell was he given a bail hearing? Wouldn't he be considered a flight risk?"

"Sweetheart, my head is spinning from all of this. If he's granted bail, the last thing I would be worried about is him being a flight risk. He's fucking crazy and that's what scares me. This house is not safe; too many neighbors and windows. Jackie's dad found a private clinic in Switzerland that might be a good fit for Junior. Mrs. Osla is going to check that out today. If it's possible, I would like to move him there."

"Do you think Max and I will have to go to court?"

"I told Hage it's never going to happen."

"Maybe I should confront Ms. Jade, let her say what she needs to. Maybe all she wants is her day in court."

"Have you lost your mind?! She wouldn't go through all of this for a conversation. She wants revenge, not a fucking cup of tea and social chat."

"Beating people up might make you feel good, but it doesn't solve the problem. Maybe using something other than physical violence might help defuse the situation. Maybe a *fucking* cup of tea and social chat is just what she needs." I'm not about to fight with him about all of this. I go turn on the shower and step in. I hear him growl and he slams the door. I go about my shower, trying to calm down, when I hear him come back in. He puts the music on pretty loud and then steps into the shower.

"Jax, what the hell are you doing and why is the music so loud?"

"The walls in this place are thin and I want to negotiate with you."

Jax's version of negotiation is a lot different from mine. "You're getting the bandage wet."

"I don't give a *fuck* about the bandage. I need you to understand every move we make can be life and death. Think about the price that is hanging over Jackie's head. Think about your mum . . . our daughter. What would happen to Antonia if you were gone? This girl is out for revenge. She wants you to suffer, just like she feels she is suffering. That guard was hired to find out who the lady in the baseball cap was. If Vincent finds out, then all bets are off. Even if you try to explain to her that you are not responsible for what happened to Marco, she won't believe it. You can't reason with crazy. Please, I'm begging you not to fight me on this."

"Okay, I will not fight you on this, but understand I want Vincent held accountable for all the heartache he has caused me. I won't back down on that. Do you have a plan?"

"Yes, if the Swiss clinic can offer Junior what he needs, then we are out of here. I don't feel safe in this house or this city. Maybe I'm wrong, but I would feel better if we were not in the States."

"I agree. Now, let's get out of here; I need to re-bandage your hand." We begin to towel off and something he said just hits me like a brick. "Wait a minute! If the guy was here to find out about the lady in the baseball cap, what was he doing in Antonia's room?" His jaw gets tight and his body instantly goes ridged.

"He saw you begin to nurse and decided he wanted to see more." I barely make it to the sink and heave. He holds my hair back and hands me a wet washcloth.

"I feel violated, and I want to leave here."

"I know, sweetheart. I'm working on it. Let's get ready and get to the hospital. Max can't wait to give Junior the blueprints. How is Jackie holding up with all of this?"

"Honestly, we talked about the wedding and stuff. I did tell her the increase in guards is because of Marco's sister. However, I ended the conversation pretty quick since I'm not sure how much she knows."

"Well, now I need to talk to your mum and explain what is going on. I'm not looking forward to *that* conversation."

We finish getting ready and head out to face everyone.

Chapter Twenty
Maxwell

I NEED MY WIFE—*BAD*. I go in search of her and find her singing and dancing with Antonia in her arms. I stand in the doorway, taking it all in. They are a beautiful sight; Antonia is giggling and Jackie is singing a song I've never heard before. Jax and Raven come up behind me and they are trying not to laugh.

"She was like, come here boy, I wanna dance."

Jackie spins around and notices the three of us. "Oh my, um . . . how long have you been standing there?"

"Long enough, babe. What song were you singing; quite the catchy tune."

"Max, don't tell me you've never heard Luke Bryan? That was one of his most popular songs, "Play it Again." He's a country music singer. Anyway, I was entertaining my niece. Are we ready to go to the hospital?"

"Not just yet, I need to talk to you about some stuff before we leave." I take Antonia from her arms and give her a kiss before passing her to Jax.

"Max, you're scaring me; what's wrong?"

"I promised you no secrets. Vincent was granted an emergency bail hearing. He is on his way to New York right now. I can't keep you here and safe. We are going back to your parents' compound."

"You're 1-leaving me?"

"Oh, babe, never—I promise. I'm going with you. Remember your dad gave me that file on the Swiss clinic? We think it might work. Your dad said we can all stay there, and that way I'll know you're safe."

"What if you have to testify? You're not coming back here without me."

"I promise you I won't."

"What about Michael?"

"We will talk to him about it today after I talk with his doctor to find out how quickly we can leave."

"Raven, are you okay with this?"

"Everyone's safety is the most important thing. I don't see any other options."

"Okay, can I at least see Michael before we have to leave?"

"Yes. Jax and I just told everyone else what is going on."

"Oh my God, Rose." Of course she would put someone else before her own safety.

"Yeah, we haven't spoken to her yet. She had wanted to confront Vincent even before all of this happened. We can only hope she goes along with the plan. For now, let's go see Junior."

We head out to the waiting car; Sammy has us in one large Dartz Kombat. It's basically a bulletproof tank with two cars in the lead and two cars bringing up the rear. I'm glad we had brought him into the fold. He is proving himself with all the small details. Everyone is very quiet and I fear this is taking a toll on An's health. She seems frailer than when she came home from the hospital. I reach over and take her hand. "Mum, it will be okay, we will get through all of this." Oh bloody hell, she's fucking crying.

"Oh, Maxwell, hearing you call me 'Mum' . . ." she trails off.

I pull her into my arms. "Is that why you're crying? If you don't stop, I swear I will go back to calling you ma'am."

She reaches up and yanks my ear. "Manners, Maxwell." Everyone begins to laugh, and I'm glad.

We finally get to the hospital and pull around back to the employee entrance. Jax is about to open the door, but I stop him. "Don't.

He freezes. "What is it, mate?"

"Not sure. Mick, please drive around the block to the area that has the freight elevators." Even though the windows are limo tinted, I pull Rose down and throw my jacket over her. Sure enough, as we pull out, the paparazzi are running toward the car, trying to get off a few pictures.

Mick gets through security and to the service elevator, which is designed to carry large equipment. He backs up into the elevator and we are able to exit the vehicle right into the elevator. "You went through the employee entrance yesterday, so they figured you would come back the same way today. I'm not psychic; it's what I would have done."

Rose leans in and kisses my cheek and I swear I must turn a millions shades of red. "Thank you, Max."

The doors open, and I can't wait to see Junior. I race to his room and swing the door open. "Oh hell no! Jax, did you do this?"

"Nope, I was just as surprised as you when I saw it. Mrs. Olsa all the way, Max."

"Uncle Max, you made it! Did you bring them?"

He throws his arms around me and it feels like home. "Yeah, buddy, I got them. How are you feeling today?"

"I'm a little tired but I'm okay, promise."

"Good, I'm going to talk to your doctor." I hand him the blueprints and he quickly loses himself in them.

I pull Bella and Michael aside. "We need to meet with the doctor, we might be moving from here."

"What do you mean moving? Michael has already started his treatments."

"Bella, for safety reasons, we need to get out of here. We are going to be moving to a private Swiss clinic. Mrs. Osla checked it out and Michael can get the same treatment there. They are also developing some new treatment that won't be available in the States for years."

"Max, how safe is it to move my son?" Michael looks like he is about ready to blow a gasket. I can't have him getting upset, it would only upset Junior.

"Michael, the safest thing for Junior is to move him. Staying here puts us all at a very high risk. In the last twenty-four hours, there have been a lot of developments. We need to remain calm, not only for Junior's benefit, but for everyone's safety. You need to continue to trust me."

Bella grabs me by my shirt collar. "You get us out of here in one piece—all of us—Max, or so help me; there will be hell to pay."

" That's my Bella. I'm going to talk to the doctor and let him know that Junior is being moved."

I head out to meet with the doctor, my mind trying to figure out how I'm going to get everyone out of here and then safely out of the country.

Vincent

IT'S FIVE AM AND the guards are already outside my cell. They inform me that I'm being transported by U.S. Marshals from Colorado to New York City. I'll be damn, that broad actually pulled it off; she got the bail hearing. Now let's hope she can argue my release. The Marshals shuffle me along to a private airport. When we're finally off the ground, I'm offered breakfast. Airline food has to be a step up from the prison shit they've been feeding me. In my mind, I can think of a dozen ways to escape, but then that won't get me what I want, at least, not yet. I can wait for now, enjoy the perks of a real chair and hot coffee. I close my eyes remembering all my time spent with Gabriella. The anticipation of possibly seeing her again sends the blood surging to my cock. I don't know how much time has passed, but I'm pulled back into the present when I'm told we are landing. When we finally land, we are at the furthest most point of the airport and waiting for us is an armor tank, along with six other vehicles. They fear me, and that's what will cause them to make mistakes. When we finally get to the courthouse, I'm shackled to the floor and given a moment alone with my new attorney.

"Well, well, well, Ms. Jade, not only do you have a great rack, but also some pair of coglioni."

"I'll take that as a compliment, Mr. Giaconna. When we get inside, please keep your mouth shut and let me do the talking. If the judge should ask you anything, look to me first before answering. Please remember to address him as 'your honor.' Prosecutor Hage will be there along with Mr. Phillips' attorneys. Whatever you do, try not to look so cocky. I'll let the guards know we are ready."

Like I said, some pair of coglioni.

Hage

I SPENT ALL NIGHT looking for some way of having Ms. Jade removed as Vincent's lawyer—nothing. There is no conflict of interest, since Marco was never directly involved with Vincent. I can't prove her motives—nothing. The stars seem to be aligning in Ms. Jade's favor, as she drew Judge Jepson, the bleeding-heart liberal, to rule on this. That's not good for me. Jax has a team of attorneys here, which I'm sure the judge will be pissed about. He finally steps in and we all rise. *Let the show begin.*

"Why are there so many spectators in my court house?" I knew that was going to happen.

Jax's attorney stands up. "Your Honor, I'm Matthew Turner, I represent the victims in this case."

"This is only a bail hearing Mr. Turner; no case has been presented. That is for another court at another time. I will give you a little leeway today. You can sit and observe, but only you." Matthew's colleagues get up and leave.

"Before we begin, there are a few rules to discuss. This is my court. This is not a trial." He eyes us all then turns his attention to the defendant's side. "Ms. Jade, tell me why you think your client should be granted bail."

"Your Honor, Mr. Giaconna was presented a deal while he was still recuperating from a gun shot wound to the head. He was not fully cognitive of what was being presented to him. My client still has the bullet lodged in his brain and must have access to better medical care than he is receiving now. His original council was also arrested, so he had no time to prepare with his new one. In question, is whether or not key evidence in the case was legally obtained and if the proper chain of command was followed. Basic *fruit of the poisonous tree,* your Honor."

"The issue of the evidence, Ms. Jade, is not for this court to decide." He peers over the rim of his glasses at her, slides them back up his nose with his finger, and then turns to me. "Mr. Hage, you're up."

"Your Honor, Mr. Giaconna was cognitive when he was arrested for his crimes. He was presented with a plea or the death penalty. He was advised by his counsel to accept the deal. He had ample time to secure new council, had he chosen to do so. He is a major flight risk and a risk to the community around him. He was not the only one who went to prison on the deal he agreed to. All of those cases would be in question if bail were granted. This would cause a major upheaval in the justice system, your Honor."

"The court will take a thirty minute recess while I review everything." He slams down the gavel. Now . . . we wait.

Every minute feels like an hour. If he grants bail, every case will be reopened. It will be a nightmare for everyone. I look over to Amelia and she is keeping herself busy, never once speaking to Vincent. It's past thirty now. I turn around to Matthew. "What do you think?"

"Well, Hage, I think you just got fucked. It's past thirty; she argued a good case. As far as judges go, you drew every defense attorney's dream judge. He is the most liberal judge in the circuit. Plus he couldn't take his eyes off of Jade's tits. Yep you're fucked, and I'm not looking forward to calling my client." Before I can answer him, the judge returns.

"Will the defendant please rise? I have reviewed all the information before me. Mr. Giaconna, I am granting bail in the amount of twenty-million dollars. You are to be under house arrest and will be required to wear an ankle monitor. You may only leave your residence for religious expectations, medical appointments, and court appearances. Since the federal government has seized all of your residences in this country and abroad, you will be put up in a safe house at the expense of our federal government. Mr. Giaconna's passport needs to be turned over to this court until any other action is taken."

He slams his gavel and Matthew is already racing out the door, I'm sure to deliver the bad news. All of Vincent's assets were seized; maybe it won't be so easy for him to come up with the bond. That is until Amelia tells Vincent the bond is being wired as we speak. He turns toward me with that Cheshire cat look and I want to rip his fucking eyes out.

"Don't get too comfortable, Mr. Giaconna, I'm like a dog with a bone and this is far from over." I head out the door to start damage control; it's gonna be a long day. RICO, Patriot Act, Treason—basically any and everything I can throw at this fucker, I will.

Jaxson

MAX IS BUSY WITH Sammy, making arrangements to secure our living arrangements for the time being and then get us all out of here. The meeting with Dr. Dave went great. He was already aware of the work being done at the clinic and he doesn't see any reason Junior's treatments can't continue on schedule, once the initial thirty day treatment is done. That means we have to stay put for another three weeks. Jackie is sitting with Junior and his new friend, Josiah, going over the blueprints. She brings such happiness to everything she does. Max told me about the shoes and it makes sense. She silently does so much, like this room. I know that she helped Mrs. Osla and her secret will always be safe with me. The alert on my phone goes off. It's a text from Matthew:

Get some place quiet. Make sure Max is with you. Call me NOW!

This doesn't sound good. "Raven, I need to make a call; have everyone stay put."

I pull Mick aside. "Hey, no one leaves this room; Max and I need to make a call."

I step outside the room and find Max finishing up a call. "Hey, we have to call Matthew now. There is a supply closet across the hall." Max seems apprehensive about neither of us having Jackie in sight. "Don't worry, Mick is with them and they've been instructed not to leave the room." We step into the closet and I ring up Matthew. "We're here and you're on speaker, what's going on?"

"Vincent made bail. The judge set bail at twenty-million, house arrest, and an ankle bracelet. He can only leave his residence for religious expectations, medical appointments, and court appearances. The money has already been wired and he will be released within the hour. Hage is having the feds keep detail on him. I would suggest you do the same." He then goes on to give us the breakdown of what happened. "Hage has a lot of ways he could go with this, all of which will take time, but will ultimately get him his conviction. Unfortunately, time is not your friend. Ms. Jade is going to push for a trial and she is going to subpoena Raven and probably Max. She wants her day in court. You never heard this from me, but get out of the country, sooner rather than later."

"If you find out anything more, let me know." I hang up and I can feel my heart pounding.

"Max, have you figured out how we are getting out of here?"

"I'm working on some different ideas. I need to get with Sammy on some of it. We need to let everyone know what is going on. They need to understand the extreme danger."

We step out and head back to Junior's room. My mum and Mrs. Osla are playing with Antonia. Jackie and Michael are playing with Junior and Josiah. Raven is in a heated conversation with her mum. "Where the *fuck* is Bella?!" Everyone turns to me as the bathroom door opens and she steps out.

"Oh thank God." I pull her into my arms.

"Jax, I can't breathe." I loosen my grip and try to calm down.

"What happened, bro, you're more than your typical crazy self."

"Come on, I need to tell everyone what is going on." The nurse comes in to take Josiah for his treatment; her timing is perfect.

Amelia Jade

THE BAIL HEARING WENT better than I expected. I need to play nice now with Hage. I leave the feds to sort out Vincent, and try to catch up to Hage. I find him right before he steps into his building. "Mr. Hage, do you think I can have a few minutes of your time?"

His glare is very intense. "Ms. Jade, how much more do you want to fuck me and the good people of this country? You just aided in putting a ruthless killer back on the street."

"Don't you think you're being a bit over dramatic?"

"Over dramatic! Do you even know who your client really is? If revenge is your game, Ms. Jade, or . . . is it Ms. Greene?—you are sadly mistaken. Did you think I wouldn't find out? I've already filed to have you removed as council. The emergency Special Grand Jury hearing is scheduled for tomorrow at one, so I suggest you get to work. The sooner I get that animal off the street, the better," he growls. Bingo—*just what I wanted!*

"You can try to have me removed as council, but I have no conflict. Mr. Giaconna did not shoot my brother in the head. That was Duke; a man, whom *you* gave full immunity to. I will see you in court, Mr. Hage."

He turns on his heels in haste, leaving me to line up all the pieces of my plan. Next up, I need to contact my investigator to see if the lady in the baseball cap really is Gabriella Giaconna. I call Johnston Investigators. Apparently, they lost their man on the inside. Still nothing, but I can string Vincent along until they find out something. Right now I need to prepare for the hearing tomorrow. The quicker this goes to trial, the sooner I can have my revenge.

Hage

WHAT THE HELL IS wrong with that woman? She can't possibly think I would just lie down and let her walk all over me. I'm sure Matthew already called Jax, however, I still have to make the call. He answers on the first ring.

"Jax, by now you must know Vincent made bail. I got an emergency Special Grand Jury hearing for tomorrow at one."

"Hage, just so we are clear, my wife and my brother will not be there." I knew this was going to happen; the man is over the top protective, and personally, I don't blame him.

"Look, Jax, I don't want to put either of them through that, but if the evidence gets thrown out, then we might not have a choice."

"There's always a choice, Hage." The bastard just hung up on me. Someone has to reason with him and I know it won't be me. Maybe his attorney can talk some sense into him. I'm about to call Matthew when my assistant steps in.

"Sir, I'm leaving for the night and Matthew Turner is on line one for you. Do you need anything else?"

"No, thanks for staying."

"Matthew, I just hung up with Jax or should I say he hung up on me? You need to try and talk some sense into him."

"Look, I know he is intense, but the risk to his family is very high right now."

"If he pushes me, I'm going to order a Material Witness Warrant for the both of them. I can detain Mrs. Phillips from her husband for quite some time."

"Hage, do you really think you're going to get anywhere with me by threatening my clients? You can prove that the chain of evidence was not tampered with. When that video was obtained, the letter of the law was followed. As far as the deal with Duke, that is also iron clad. Look, Ms. Jade is throwing up shit to get my clients out into the open. You're playing right into her hands. They will not, under any circumstances, be anywhere near that courthouse. Enraging my client is the worst possible thing you could have done. If you have any questions, feel free to contact me, but under no circumstances are you ever to contact my clients again. Goodnight, Hage."

Matthew is right; I need to keep in mind Ms. Jade is out for revenge. I can't play into her hands. I can prove my case. I look up at the clock, it's gonna be an all-nighter.

Jaxson

I NEED SOMEPLACE TO work and the storage closet is getting old. Unfortunately, I really have no choice; it's that or the washroom. I pull Max aside. "We need to talk to Matthew now. Hage called and had the fucking gall to threaten me. He told me he might not have a choice; you and Raven might have to testify."

"Get Matthew on the line." He shuffles his hand at my cell.

I hit Mathew's number. "Matthew, you're on speaker with us. What's the status?"

"Hage is at a loss as to what to do. Honestly, how the fuck this guy got where he is, is beyond me." He quickly catches us up on his conversation with Hage. "The special grand jury must first say there is enough for a trial. They are meeting tomorrow at one. This is the fastest I've ever seen anyone pull this off. If they say there is enough for a trial, then they have to do a jury selection before it begins. We are talking months. What is the status with Junior?"

"We have to stay here for a month for his initial treatment before we can head to the clinic."

"Maybe that will work to our favor. Let me tell Hage that you are not leaving the country. You need to stay here for Junior's treatments. He doesn't need to know that as soon as the kid can travel, you will be leaving. I will tell him that Raven and Max will be available to testify, this way he doesn't order the warrants."

Max grabs the phone, "Matthew, there is a big problem with your plan. After everything happened the last time, and I enlisted help from the Queen's grandson; I was made active in MI6. I can't, and won't testify; I have immunity. I wouldn't be surprised if Ms. Jade tries to file civil charges against me for shooting the fucker. I will refuse to answer."

"Can I ask why I'm just finding this out now?"

"With everything going on, I forgot all about it until now. While we are full disclosure, Jackie and I are married, and she will not be going anywhere near the court house."

"Okay, well, congratulations on the marriage and I don't think that will be a problem. Like I said, I think the less we say the better we are. I will let Hage know that you're not leaving the country. That should keep him calm. Max, keep your mouth shut about your status. I will keep everyone updated."

"Matthew, you're sure Raven and Max shouldn't leave tonight?"

"Yes, Jax, please don't poke the bear. I'll keep you posted."

He hangs up and all I can think about is Hage trying to separate me from Raven.

"Max, I need my wife now."

I walk out of the closet and head right into Junior's room. Everyone is sitting around watching television like nothing has happened. If only . . .

Chapter Twenty-One

Amelia Jade

SO HAGE FIGURED OUT who I am a lot quicker than I thought he would. I wonder if it really was him that figured it out. Doesn't matter—he can't stop me—no one can. I will get my revenge. She will suffer a loss greater than she can ever imagine. *You took from me, now I will do the same . . . an eye for an eye Raven.* I've combed through the all the boxes that Hage sent over, looking for mistakes. He is very thorough, but I might be able to convince the Grand Jury that the tape was compromised. If they agree, I get my trial. I can then subpoena Raven to tell what she saw. After all, she is the only living witness to the events that day. That will put her in the same room with me. I can argue that when Maxwell Fleming and Jaxson Phillips rescued Raven from the villa in Italy, they planted that thumb drive for Duke to find. Thanks to Hage, Duke's not here to say otherwise. The puzzle piece I can't figure out is the lady in the hat. Still no word back from my investigator. Hopefully, he will have something for me before court tomorrow. In the meantime I need to check on Vincent to make sure he doesn't do anything crazy. I'll bring him dinner and prep him for court tomorrow. I also need to make sure he has the proper clothing, I can't have him looking like the animal he really is. I'm reduced to a glorified babysitter. But if that's what it takes, then I will do it. I head out and notice that I'm being followed. Chances are it's the feds, they are not very subtle. I pick up everything I need to bring to Vincent and head over to the safe house. He ratted so many people out, I'd be surprised if he lives to even see the inside of a courtroom.

Maxwell

I STEP OUT OF the closet and find Sammy waiting for me. "Max, what's the problem?"

I bring him up to speed on what I know. "Have you come up with any options for housing while we're here for the month?"

"Well, we could stay at the hotel downtown, which means a car ride everyday. We could fly by helicopter, but everyone can't go at one time. The helipad is not big enough for anything very large. I think we should stay where we are. We can board up some of the windows so it's not like a fish bowl." He rubs the scruff on his chin then his eyes widen as if he's thought of something. "The chief contacted me. Apparently Gerhard is applying pressure, which I suspected he would. More men will be arriving within the hour." I hear what he is saying but something is bothering me.

"Max, are you even listening to me?"

"Yeah, something is bothering me and I'm not sure what—tingle sense."

"Oh hell, talk it out. When did it start?"

"It's like a giant chess board; the pieces are floating around in my head." I close my eyes and rub my temples like Jackie usually does for me. The fog starts clearing. I need to talk to Jax *now*.

"Sammy, can you quietly get Jax for me. If I go in there, they will know something is wrong."

He goes and it gives me a little bit more time to clear my head. Jax steps out of the room. I'm just now noticing how pale his face is and I wonder when the last time he slept was. This is going to put him over the edge, but I have to tell him.

"Hey, what's the problem?"

"Well, something has been bugging me. In order for Jade to get Vincent to go along with her twisted plan, she needed to offer him Jackie. Now, I'm not saying that Jackie is no longer a target, I just think she was never the original target. The target has always been Raven. Raven's brother killed Jade's brother. But since Duke is no longer in the equation, she needs someone else. She doesn't know about Rose, otherwise, she would not only be in Vincent's crosshairs but Jade's too. That leaves you and Antonia. Losing a child cuts to your soul, it's a loss that not everyone can come back from. Think about it; when will Antonia be the most vulnerable? I know she has guards around her twenty-four seven, however, a mother's worst fear is that something will happen to her child when she is not there to protect her. Jax, I need to stop thinking like a normal person and think like the sociopath Jade is. Once she has Raven in that courthouse, she will taunt her and make her believe she can and has gotten to Antonia. It's a chess game of sorts. Personally, I don't think Vincent realizes what he's gotten himself into, or maybe he just doesn't care. I'm sure she will do something to make sure in the end, Vincent rots in hell. After all, his son did murder her brother."

Jax is quiet and that's bad for everyone. Sammy finally breaks the silence.

"I have an idea. You may not like it, but hear me out. You've seen Gerhard's compound. You know it's locked up tighter than your *Fort Knox*. I say you take

Rose, your mum, and Antonia out of the equation, move them to the compound tonight. Gerhard's plane is like *Air force One* and I can have it ready within the hour. Once they are in that compound, they are locked up tight."

He's still not saying a word, his jaw is tight and his eyes are closed. "Jax, talk to me, mate. What are you thinking?"

"When I think with my head and leave my heart out of the equation, what you're saying makes sense. It's sick and twisted, but that's what Jade is. I need to talk to Raven and Rose. I'm sure I can get Raven to go along with the plan, but Rose . . . I'm not so sure about. We will need to let everyone know what's going on. What are we going to tell Junior?"

"The truth. He can handle it. He would never believe that his grams just left for no apparent reason. Come on, Jax, let's go talk to everyone while Sammy makes the arrangements." We head back into the room and everyone is still sitting around watching television.

The best thing right now is honesty. I don't think sugarcoating the situation will help anyone.

$\mathcal{J}axson$

WE ENTER THE ROOM and everyone is still engrossed in a movie. I pull Raven close to me and whisper in her ear, "I love you." She pulls back and searches my eyes, she can read so much.

"What's wrong, Jax?"

Before I can answer, Max flips the television off and announces a family meeting.

"There has been a change of plans. Junior, your doctor said we have to stay here for a month, so you can finish your initial chemo treatment. Unfortunately, not everyone can stay here for a month and remain safe. There is some danger and I need to move some of us to Jackie's parents' house ahead of schedule. Rose, An, and Mrs. Osla will take Antonia to Switzerland tonight, along with Jackie."

Jackie leaps up, "Max, you said I wouldn't be without you!"

He begins to explain the plan and I can feel Raven tense up. Rose is showing no emotion whatsoever and I just can't get a read on her.

"I know I did, but the more I take my heart out of the equation, the more it makes sense. You and Antonia are the triggers for a whole lot of pain for all of us. Knowing that the both of you are safe will help us do what we need to make sure everyone survives this nightmare."

Raven has a death grip on my arm. "Jax, you're asking me to be separated from my baby for three weeks?!" She can barely get the words out.

"Yes, sweetheart, I am. Ms. Jade wants you to pay the ultimate price and hurting our daughter would do it. Vincent wants Max to pay, and what better way than to hurt Jackie? I'm sorry it's come to this, but there is no choice for any of us." I hope Rose understands that includes her, too.

"When will they have to 1-leave?" I pull her tightly against me, bracing for what's coming. "Within the hour." She begins to tremble and cry and my heart is breaking.

"Why can't I leave with my daughter and not come back? There is nothing legally keeping me here."

"Matthew is trying to pacify Hage by guaranteeing him you will not leave the country. He threatened to serve you with a Material Witness Warrant, which means he could detain you and keep us separated indefinitely."

"Max, can't you have a passport made for me under another name?"

"Oh, Raven, I wish I could, but this is not the movies and things like that don't happen overnight. You are the only living witness. You and everyone around you are in a world of danger. You're going to have to do this to protect your daughter . . . *I'm sorry.*"

Sammy's phone rings. Max and I get a text all at the same time. I look down and then to Max, will this madness ever end? A text from Matthew:

Vincent escaped and took Ms. Jade hostage. Your men and the two feds are dead. Get the hell out of the country, be safe. I will keep in touch.

I grab Max by the arm, "What do we do?"

Sammy hangs up and stuffs his phone back in his pocket. "Vincent's escaped! We need to get the hell out of here. Some of you will be taken to the roof where a helicopter will take you to the plane. We can't all go together, but Michael Jr. needs to go first," He starts barking orders. "I've had a medical team on stand-by in anticipation of any type of emergency. They have informed me that we must secure that he has minimal exposure to anything that might cause an infection. I have a Huey helicopter on the roof next door with some of my men on standby. They will shadow the transport helicopter to and from the airport. The first set to go: Michael, Bella, Junior, Antonia, Mick, and An. The next set will be: Rose, Jackie, Raven, Jax, Max and me. We need to move now," he finishes out his commands, none of us getting a word in otherwise.

He hands Max an ear bud. "Put this in so you can hear everything that is going on."

Raven grabs Antonia and holds her tightly in her arms. "Jax, please, I can't leave my baby."

"I don't like it any more than you do, but we have to protect her no matter what. Mick, so help me God, this is my family . . ."

"Jax, I promise you; I would lay down my life for any one of them—you know that. They are like my family and all I have."

Bella secures a mask on Junior as we head to the rooftop heliport. Once again, we are running for our lives. It's like being in a time warp over and over again. We reach the roof, and the first group is loaded. Raven and I are kissing the baby, trying desperately to let her go. Finally, Mick takes her and secures her in her seat. Raven gives Bo the sign to go with Antonia and protect her. Sammy closes the doors, and they take off. My wife collapses in my arms, hysterical. My heart is in my throat as I watch them fly away, not knowing if I will ever see my daughter again. I don't know how much time passes, but I realize alarms are blaring and lights are flashing.

"Max, what's going on?" He's got Jackie tightly in his arms.

"There has been a breach in security. They are reporting that a man with a gun has entered the hospital. They are evacuating the patients that can be moved now." He holds the ear bud in tighter, and then looks to Sammy. "Sammy, how much longer before the chopper is back with the guards?"

"At best—fifteen minutes. We were limited to space and we wanted the heaviest protection on Antonia."

"We are on our own up here. I want everyone to do exactly as I tell you," Max takes his turn at barking out orders. "Head to the far west corner of the building. There are stairs there leading to the landing below, take them *now!*" Before any of us can move, the door opens and Vincent steps through with Ms. Jade at gun point. Sammy turns and puts himself between Vincent and Jackie. Sammy gets a shot off, but his focus is on shielding Jackie. His shot is wide, but Vincent's is not, and he hits Sammy in the chest. He collapses to the floor. Jackie is screaming as Max tries to hold her back, shielding her with his body. I'm trying to hold Raven back as Rose steps out from behind me. She drops to her knees and tries to stop the bleeding. The rage that takes over Vincent is like nothing I've ever seen before.

"Gabriella, it's true; you're alive, you cold-hearted bitch. You fucking gave my son away! I never had a chance with him. Was it because of Joseph? Were you in love with him and he didn't want your bastard son? Is that why you gave away that bitch daughter of yours, too? Where have you been hiding?" He's waving his gun around with one hand and has the other fisted in

Ms. Jades hair. "Answer me, God damn it. Where the fuck have you been for the last twenty years?"

Rose lifts her hands from Sammy's chest and, at the same time, takes the gun from his hand. I see it, but I don't know if Vincent does. "He's dead. Another kind man; dead by your hands. You want to know where I've been? I've been in a clinic—silent—for twenty years, all because of *you*. I had to give my daughter up to protect her from *you*. I gave up your bastard son because I couldn't look at him without being reminded of *you* raping and torturing me on a daily basis. You always looked for someone else to blame for who *you* are. You blamed Antonio because *you* couldn't measure up to him. I could have saved your father if you would have come to me sooner, but you purposely waited until it was too late. Did you think I didn't know? It was so obvious, but he told me right before he went under that *you* withheld his treatment. It was all about money and power for you. You think fear brings you power? You have taken so much from me, but so help me God, with all that I have, you will never take another person from me ever again." Before any of us can react, she lifts the gun and shoots him in the chest. He lets go of Ms. Jade and drops to his knees.

"I loved you, Gabriella."

"The only one you ever loved, Vincent, was yourself. I hope you rot in hell for an eternity." She drops the gun and we are stunned as we watch the life fade out of him.

Ms. Jade reaches behind her back and pulls out a gun, aiming it at my wife! "Well, that's one less person I have to deal with. Did you really think I would have let him live or even rot in a tiny cell for the rest of his life? He was just a means to an end; a dead man the day I met him. Raven, my brother dedicated his life to you. He took you in and made sure you were safe. He loved you, and how did you repay him? You skewed his way of thinking. You got him mixed up in things that he never would have. You should have tried to get him to go home, to make amends with his family."

Raven has a grip on my arm and I can feel her trembling. I try to pull her behind me but Ms. Jade points her gun at Raven's chest, making me freeze. Raven tries to calm her down. "Don't you think I tried? I loved Marco like a brother. I even offered to go home with him, but he said his parents disowned him. If he was such a loving brother then why did he never mention you? You have some twisted idea in your head that I'm somehow responsible for Marco's death. You have no clue what he did to me. He lied to and betrayed me, pretending to be my friend. He used me, had me kidnapped twice. He hit me, and then claimed to love me. He knew I had a brother and withheld that information from me. He kept your existence hidden away because he knew how twisted he really was. You have these dreams of the type of brother you wanted. They are the same dreams I had about the friend I wanted. Those where just that—dreams. Dreams that Marco could never live up to. Don't become like him. Put the gun down. Please think of what you're doing."

I see Max in the corner of my eye inching his way toward her, but she sees it too. "Take another step, Mr. Fleming, and I will shoot her." He freezes as she's waving the fucking gun around like a mad woman.

"Raven, you may have gotten your daughter out of here safely, but I can guarantee you that your husband will not make it out of here alive. You will know what it feels like to suffer great loss."

As she lifts the gun toward me, police storm the roof, but she doesn't flinch. I look at her eyes; they take upon a darkness that is unexplainable. Just as I pull Raven behind me, Max tries to go for her gun . . . she pulls the trigger. It's at that moment that Rose steps in front of me, taking the bullet that is meant for me. The police shoot and Ms. Jade is dead.

Raven drops to her knees and is screaming over and over again. "Mommy, please, please don't leave me again. Please don't die. I only just got you back. Help! Please, someone help her! God, no please . . . no."

I drop to my knees and apply pressure to her wound to try to stop the bleeding. "Rose, why? Why did you do this?"

"I've known great love, my daughter and granddaughter need to know that, too. I know you will love them with all that you've got." She takes Raven's hand. "I love you. I'm so proud of who you've become, my *Cara*."

The hospital staff finally gets to us. They are trying to start her heart again as they are rushing her down to emergency. Raven is screaming she wants to go with her, but the police are trying to ask her fucking questions now. I grab her hand and we run toward the exit, trying to keep up with the doctors.

The police try to stop us. "Get the fuck out of our way, so help me if you don't—." They get the hell out of the way. We make it to the emergency room and they are still trying to restart her heart. I stare at my hands covered in blood . . . blood that was shed to save me. I watch the seconds on the clock tick away. The wait seems like an eternity. I finally see the doctor coming and the look on his face is grim. I pull Raven into my arms; she needs me to be her rock right now. I only hope I can.

"I'm sorry, we did all we could. The nurse will come and get you so you can have a few minutes alone with her before we have to move her."

I hold her tight and we fall apart. I don't think I will ever be the same again. Someone gave up their life for mine. How can I live with that?

Maxwell

I TRY TO EXPLAIN to the police as best as I can the events that unfolded here tonight. Jackie is sitting on the floor next to Sammy's body, crying. He always said that he would protect her at all cost. He paid so dearly, giving his life to protect my wife.

"Jackie, you need to let the police do their job. Please come with me." She's shaking and crying uncontrollable.

"I can't leave him, Max. Please, I need to stay with him."

"You can't and right now, Raven really needs you. Rose is fighting for her life.

Jackie, please, we need to find Raven." I finally get through to her. We head downstairs to find out Rose's status.

Jax is very quiet, probably still in shock, as we all are. Knowing that someone took a bullet for you and might not survive is overwhelming. We find Raven sitting in Jax's lap, crying and rocking back and forth. I don't need to ask the question, I already know the answer. An answer I'm dreading.

Jax looks up at me. "She didn't make it," he whispers.

Time stands still for all of us.

A nurse comes out and escorts us back to say our goodbyes. If only it were that easy. How do you say goodbye to someone who, in such a short time, has done so much for you? How was that even possible? We thought we were saving her, yet she saved each one of us when no one else could. Hell, Junior wouldn't be getting the early treatment if it wasn't for her insistence. She helped Jackie get over her fear of having a child. She saved An when she had a heart attack. She helped me through the realization that my father, quite possibly, had a hand in killing his grandson and daughter in-law. She saved my brother by taking a bullet meant for him. I can only hope if there is a God, he has reunited her with Antonio. I reach down and brush my fingers along her cheek. "Fly with the angels, Rose."

Jackie bows her head, reciting some sort of prayer in Japanese. I have no clue what she is saying, but it sounds almost musical. She buries her face in my chest and sobs.

"Raven, Jackie and I are going to step out and give you some privacy." I don't even know if she heard me. I look back and Raven crawls into the bed, curls into Rose, and loses it. I know none of us will ever be the same again.

My phone buzzes, it's Mick. I need to get him updated on everything. "Hey, Max, what's going on? The pilot radioed and said something big went down. The heliport is full of police."

"Vincent made it to the roof with Ms. Jade. He shot Sammy. Rose tried to help him but he didn't make it."

"Oh, I'm sorry—."

"There's more. Ms. Jade was not a hostage as first thought; she pulled a gun on Raven." I hear him gasp. "There was a heated confrontation. She had every intention of shooting Jax. I tried to get to the gun before she could shoot him, but Rose jumped in front of him. Rose didn't make it, Mick. She's *gone.*"

"R-rose, is gone? Oh my God, no, she was so much to so many. Never asking for anything in return and now she's g-gone."

"Mick, I need you more now than ever before. You need to get the family to Gerhard's compound and whatever you do, don't let them watch the news. Tell them that we have some stuff to follow up with and then we will be there in a couple of days. I don't want Mum to hear any of this right now. I know the stress is taking a toll on her. Junior can't find out either, he needs to focus on his treatment."

"Max, you can't keep everyone in the dark for too long. Within a couple of hours this is going to hit the press. You know Raven and Jackie are not leaving there without Rose and Sammy. Shit that can take weeks and tons of red tape. I have an idea, let me call Gerhard and have him arrange to have a doctor at the house, just in case. You know An and I are pretty close, I promise I will be with her and support her through all of this."

"Mick, thank you, I'm proud and honored to call you my friend."

"Let everyone know that they are in my prayers and if they need me to do anything else, let me know."

"I will. Check in when you get to the compound."

I hang up just as Hage comes rushing in. I don't think I can deal with another thing right now. I know if Jax sees him, he will unload on him.

"Hage, why are you here?"

"Why wouldn't I be here? What the fuck went down?"

"I'm sure by now you know, so again, why the fuck are you here?"

"You know, Max, I'm not the bad guy here. I'm sorry for your loss, but you should have told me that Gabriella was alive. I might have been able to protect her."

"Don't go there, Hage. You really need to shut the fuck up right now."

Every man has a breaking point. We always think we can take just a tad more, but then it happens, that point when your mind snaps. I try everything I know to get myself past that point. I slowly count down from ten, trying to block out his irritating voice.

"Maybe if I knew she would still be—."

Oh bloody hell no. I snap. I'm done. One swift move and he's down on all fours. "I fucking told you not to go there, now shut the fuck up! If you have any questions contact my attorney. Now, I suggest you get out of here before Jax and Raven get back."

"You just assaulted a federal prosecutor. You can't order me around. I can have you arrested. I'll leave when I have all the answers and, if need be, I will detain you."

"Good luck with that." I take Jackie's hand and we head in search of Jax and Raven.

Chapter Twenty-Two

Jaxson

MY WIFE IS CURLED up next to her mum, begging her to come back to life. I can't stop staring at my hands that are covered in blood . . . Rose's blood. How do I go through this life and not feel her blood on my hands every day? I close my eyes and all I see is Rose, leaping out in front of me. Everything happened so fast, yet it seems like slow motion. I stand over the sink and try to wash the blood off; it will never truly be gone. *Nothing ever is.* I need to snap out of this and tend to my wife. "Raven, we need to let the staff take care of your mum now." I don't even know if she hears me. I try to lift her up in my arms, but she is fighting me.

"No, I'm not going without my mom . . . *please.*" Her arms are clutched around her mum and she is begging me to help her.

"Sweetheart, the sooner we let them do their job, the sooner we can bring her home. Our daughter needs you, too, Raven." Finally, she puts her arms around me and lets me carry her out of the room. Max and Jackie are waiting for us, and I notice Hage is down the hall barking at someone.

"Give me an update, Max. Where is the family? How soon can we get out of here?"

I put Raven down and Jackie pulls her into her arms. "Come on, Raven, let's go wash up."

I watch them leave and realize they both have blood all over them.

"I called Mick and told him everything. I had them leave without us. I'm not sure how long this is going to take, and I know Raven and Jackie will not leave here without Rose and Sammy. Mick is going to have a doctor at Gerhard's when he tells mum. I think we should be the ones to tell Junior." I'm looking down at my hands and I keep wringing them, hoping to will the image of all that blood out of my head. I focus my attention back to the problems at hand.

"I agree. What the fuck is Hage doing here?"

"I lost it on him. He really said the wrong thing. I reached my breaking point and knocked him out, so he threatened to detain me. I already put a call into Matthew."

"Don't worry; you did what I've been wanting to do." He is mindlessly rubbing his knuckles, no doubt sore from punching Hage.

"What happened to the other helicopter?"

"By the time they got back, everything was over. The pilots dropped off the few remaining guards to take care of us until we get to Switzerland."

"How long do you think this is going to take? I think getting Raven back with Antonia, would be best for everyone."

"Matthew is working on it now. We have to wait for the coroner to finish an autopsy and issue a cause of death."

"Oh bloody hell, we know they were both shot." I'm about ready to punch the wall but he grabs my arm, stopping me.

"Standard procedure they have to follow. Rose really loved the estate in Scotland and I was thinking, if it's okay with Raven, we could have something built there in her honor."

"Do we even know what her wishes were?"

"Actually, I do. When I had myself removed as her guardian, she came to me and asked me to be the executor of her estate. She wanted all of her assets dissolved and given to certain charities. She made all her own arrangements. She told me when her parents died, she had no one to turn to. She had to make all the arrangements herself and she never wanted Raven to go through that. She kept it simple, requesting to be cremated and have her ashes scattered in the ocean. She named a beach in North Carolina, where Antonio asked her to marry him, called Topsail Island." I'm feeling anxious without Raven, and I begin to pace.

"Okay, let me know if you need me to help you with any of it. I'm not surprised that she made all her arrangements. She never wanted to burden anyone. Thank you for handling everything so quickly. I know it must be hard on you too." I stop pacing and pat his back. Acknowledging that I'm grateful for all he has done.

"Do we have someplace to stay for the next few days?"

The girls come back looking a little bit better. "Yeah, come on, I got us a couple of rooms downtown while we wait."

We go out the back, taking the few remaining guards with us. Unfortunately, the press has gotten wind of what happened. Max and I take off our jackets and use them to shield Raven and Jackie. I get it, better than anyone, that everything that went down here is newsworthy but for Christ's sake, give people a chance to grieve.

When we pull up to the hotel, there is a crowd waiting out front. We try the back entrance and it's just as bad. "Max, get us to the nearest helipad. We can easily fly to the rooftop of our New York penthouses. We will hold up there until we can make arrangements to leave the country."

Within minutes, he has everything lined up for us.

Mick

I HANG UP THE phone and the realization that she's gone begins to sink in. How could this possibly have happened? I was able to get everyone safely from the heliport to the plane, but I can't stop now to grieve. I need to get everyone safely to Switzerland and keep them from seeing the news. I step out of the onboard office and find An waiting for me. "Hey, is everything okay?"

"You tell me, and don't say 'nothing.' I'm strong, Mick, please tell me my children are okay." I take her hand and squeeze it up to my lips.

"They are fine, we, however, need to get to Switzerland, so please get into your seat and buckle up. I'm going to meet with the captain." She cocks her head and glares at me. Before she can say anything more, I guide her back to one of the chairs. I head into the flight deck and give the captain the go ahead to take off. I also have him disable the Wi-Fi and television. I strap into the additional jump seat in the flight deck. I know that the crew is more than capable to do their job, but it gives me some sense of peace being in there. It's the one place I can totally relax, letting the world go by. The captain, informing me that Mr. Gerhard is on the line, interrupts my few moments of bliss. I know I need to bring him up to speed and I've been dreading it. I've never even met the man and now I have to greet him with this type of news. "I will take it in the office, and thanks again for letting me in here for takeoff." I head to the office, avoiding An's stare.

"Hello, sir, I'm not sure how much you know but I will start by telling you your daughter is safe."

"Who the hell are you?! Where *is* my daughter and Max? Why is Sammy not taking any of my calls?"

"Sir, my name is Mick and I'm one of the guards. I'm sorry, sir, Sammy was shot while protecting Jackie . . . he didn't make it . . . neither did Rose, Raven's mom. We are on our way to you, however, Jackie, Max, Raven, and Jax are still in the States. They are waiting for the bodies to be released and then they will be on their way. I have not told anyone yet what happened. I was hoping to hold out until we got to you. Is it possible to have a doctor on hand when I do tell them? I'm afraid An's health is frail and the shock might be to much for her, not to mention Michael Jr."

"Of course. How is my daughter and Raven? When can I speak to them?"

"The only thing I know is that they are safe. I've only spoken to Max, but I'm sure you will hear from them today. We should be to you in about seven hours. I will keep you posted, if I hear anything else."

"Thank you. I will have everything ready for your arrival," he states before ending the call. I hang up and pray that I can make it through the next seven hours. I hear the tap on the door and I know it's An. My hopes of avoiding telling her anything have just been squashed. I open the door expecting An but it's Mrs. Osla.

"Mrs. Osla, is everything okay?"

"Yes, Mick, everyone is asleep so I figured now would be a good time for you to tell me what you're trying to hide. This family has been through so much, I don't know if they could take anything else. I know you care deeply for An; she is my best friend. If there is a problem, I want to be there for her . . . to help in any way possible."

"Please, ma'am, have a seat. I really don't know where to start? So much has happened."

"Did something happen to Maxwell? Is that what you're afraid to tell u-us?"

For the first time since I met this woman, I see a look of dread and fear come over her. "Oh no, Maxwell is safe. There was a confrontation on the roof of the hospital after we evacuated. Sammy and Rose were shot, neither of them made it."

She gasps, "Oh God, no." I rush to give her a glass of water but she pushes it away.

"I spoke with Mr. Gerhard and he will have a doctor at the house. I would rather wait to tell An until we get there, if that's possible."

She gets up, walks to the bar, and, pours herself a whisky. "You might not have that luxury. This is a long flight, and you can only hide out in here for so long. She is sleeping right now, so you have some time. When she wakes, I think we should tell her together. If you try to wait, her mind will run rampant, which could be even worse for her health."

I close my eyes, trying so hard to keep the fear at bay—sometimes, it's a losing battle. I get up and pour myself a whisky, feeling the burn as it goes down. My grip on the glass is so tight, I'm afraid it might shatter in my hand. I feel her hand on my shoulder and I nearly jump out of my skin. She squeezes my shoulder even tighter. I know she can help, but it's not easy for me to share my fear with anyone but *An*.

"I know what you've been through; let me handle some of this. Please, Mick, it's what I do best. What are you not telling me?"

"I haven't heard from Max since they left the hospital, no one has. He had a reservation at a hotel downtown but he never checked in. They are probably lying low due to the press, but I just wish he would check in."

She takes out her phone and sends a text. "Ma'am, he hasn't answered my texts, believe me I've tried."

Just then, her phone begins to ring. "Maxwell, where are you and is everyone safe? I know about Sammy and Rose." She listens and then hangs up without even a goodbye.

"They are at their New York flats. He said they are resting as best they can and he will call you later."

I feel the tension release from my body and wipe the sweat from my brow. "I have to ask you how on earth did you get him to respond to you so quickly when no one else can?"

She takes another sip of her whisky. "Maxwell's first wife, Samantha, was my niece. We were always very close and, after her death, we remained very close. He gave me a word and told me whenever I need him right away, no matter what time of day or night, all I had to do was get that word to him. Page, text, voice mail, email—anyway possible, and he would always find me."

"Wow, and to think, we all thought he was afraid of you."

She chuckles, "Oh he is, and you might keep that in mind. I'm going to get some rest before An wakes up. Unless you need me for something else?"

"No, ma'am, and thank you."

I feel a little bit better that I know where everyone is and I won't have to tell An by myself. I only hope that everyone doesn't have to stay in New York too long.

Maxwell

WE LAND IN NEW York and head right down to my place. I'm not sure Raven will want to go next door; there is so much of Rose everywhere. Jax lifts her up and carries her to their flat anyhow. My phone beeps with a text from Mrs. Osla; one word—Piglet. My heart stops. That's our word for immediate contact. I should have contacted her so she wouldn't worry. I quickly call her to make sure she is okay, and assure her I will call her later. Right now, I need to take care of my wife. I gently lift her and carry her to our bedroom. I need to get her clothes off; they still have blood on them. I quickly set up the tub for a soak and begin undressing her. I want to burn these clothes so she never has to look at them again. The huge tub is finally full, and I hold her in my arms as we slowly sink in. The hot water warms her and she slowly stops shivering but she is vigorously wiping her hands. I take them in mine and kiss them. "Babe, there is no blood, I promise. It's gone."

I hold her close so she can feel safe and she begins to sob. My heart is breaking for her—hell—for all of us. Neither of us say a word, we don't have to. I'm not sure how much time has passed, but the water is getting cold and her fingers are pruned. "Babe, let's try and get some sleep. We have some long, emotional days ahead of us."

"When can we leave? There are so many arrangements that have to be made and Sammy's partner, Ian, needs to be told," Her voice trails off and she's crying again.

"I will talk to your father and see how he would like to handle it. This is not something one should hear over the phone. Besides, Sammy was active MI6 and there are certain protocols that need to be followed. Right now, let's try to get some sleep."

When we get into bed, I tuck the blanket tightly around us, just like she does every night. We lie there in silence. Finally, she begins to drift off to sleep. I can only pray it will be a restful one for her.

Jaxson

RAVEN IS IN SHOCK and I'm numb from everything that went down. I need to get her out of these clothes; they are stained with blood—her mother's blood. She sits on the edge of the bed and allows me to take care of her. It's what I do best, what I've always done. I need to do this and she needs me to do this for her. I put her in one of my shirts, knowing that she will find comfort from it. I climb into bed and wrap my arms and legs around her. As I gently stroke her back, I keep reminding her that I love her and need her . . . our daughter needs her. She finally falls asleep. It's only then that it really hits me; Rose will never see Antonia grow up. My daughter may not remember her, but I will make sure she knows how much she loved her. The sacrifice that she made so Antonia would have a mum and a dad. I can't fall apart, my family needs me, and they need my strength. I close my eyes and drift off, praying I can be strong.

The constant rattling awakens me and I realize it's my phone, bouncing on the night stand. I grab it, trying not to wake Raven.

"Hello."

"Hey, Jax, sorry to wake you so early."

My brain is not really functioning. "Matthew?"

"Yeah, like I said, sorry to wake you, but I pulled some strings. The bodies are being released today. They will be delivered to the hanger at Teeterborough by noon today. All the arrangements have been made. Make sure you inform your pilots."

"Thank you, man. How the hell did you get this pulled off so quickly?"

"Well, Sammy was MI6, so I went to them and they want this wrapped up just a quickly as you do. They were able to pull some strings with The State Department."

"Thank you. The sooner we get out of here, the happier I will be. Will we have to come back here for anything?"

"I don't think so. I have everything I need to execute Rose's will, and Hage should be able to wrap everything up without you."

"Okay, I will let Max know what's going on, thanks."

I'm about to call Max when Raven begins to whimper in her sleep. All I can do is hold her tighter to me. "Shh, I've got you, sweetheart, and I always will." She finally falls back to sleep. I wiggle out from under her, being careful not to wake her. We've got two hours before we need to head to the airport and I've got calls to make.

I walk into the living room and take a minute to watch the sun rising over the city. Reflecting can be like a piece of wood. Run your finger with the grain and it's silky, almost soft. Run your fingers against the grain and it can be rough and painful. So much like life, itself. Time moves on whether we want it to or not. I have to put all of that aside and concentrate on my family and what they need now. I grab my phone and call Mick.

He answers on the first ring. I'm sure the added stress is taking a toll on him, too. "Hey, Mick, how is everyone?"

"I'm glad you checked in, Jax. I'm sorry about Rose and Sammy."

"Thanks, what's your status?" I need to keep my mind focused on business.

"I told Mrs. Osla, she really didn't give me a choice. I was going to wait till we got to Mr. Gerhard's house to tell your mom, but I don't think she will wait. Antonia is fine, she only woke up once and Bella took care of her."

"Mick, get my mum, Skype me, and I will tell her. She will take this better coming from me."

"Okay, give me ten minutes and then call me back."

While he takes care of that, I put a call into my pilots and inform them of our plans. I want to have wheels up as soon as possible. I would like to have Max with me when I tell Mum but I'm not leaving Raven, and I don't expect him to leave Jackie. I take a few deep breaths and dial, the screen comes to life and it's Bella.

"Hey, sis, how's Junior doing?" I have not seen my sister look this bad since that day at the hospital in Vegas.

"Mrs. Osla went to get Mum. Mick told me everything; He wanted to make sure I try to keep it together for Mum when you tell her. I'm so sorry. She was a great friend to all of us. Hell, she probably saved my son's life. Raven must be destroyed, she just got her back in her life and now she has to mourn her all over again." Before I can answer, Mrs. Osla arrives with Mum.

"Hey, Mum, how are you feeling?" Oh no, I'm getting the look. Damn, I'm so busted.

"Jaxson, please stop worrying about my health and tell me what everyone is trying to hide from me."

"Mum, there was a confrontation with Vincent and Ms. Jade. Vincent tried to shoot Jackie but Sammy was shot. Rose tried to help him, but he didn't make it. She picked up Sammy's gun and she killed Vincent. We thought it was over, but Ms. Jade pulled a gun. Raven tried to talk her down—to explain—but she was hell bent on making Raven pay. Her plan was to go after Antonia, but since that failed, she was going to shoot me. Rose stepped in front of me and she was shot. Mum . . . Rose didn't make it."

"Oh, son, I'm so very sorry. She was such a wonderful lady. She saved my family and I will forever be grateful for that. How are the girls holding up?"

"They're destroyed, Mum. The feeling that someone sacrificed their life so you could live is overwhelming."

"What about Maxwell? I know him and he is probably blaming himself." I didn't even think that.

"Why would he blame himself? He did all he could possibly do, Mum."

"*Why?* Because that's Maxwell; he thinks he can save the world and that he's invincible. He will always think he should have done more." She shakes her head and pushes away a few whispers of hair that have fallen out of place. "When are you coming home?"

"We will be leaving in a few hours. How is Junior? I don't think we should tell him just yet."

"He's fine, but tired. I think when we land we should get him to the clinic right away. There will be plenty of time to tell him what happened. Let him concentrate on getting better."

"Okay, I need to get going. I love you, Mum."

"I love you too. Safe travels."

I hang up and take a moment for myself. "*I will love them and protect them with all that I am, Rose,*" I say softly as if she could hear me.

"She knows, Jax." I nearly leap out of my own skin.

"I'm sorry, sweetheart, I didn't even hear you."

"I know. What's the plan?"

"I need to call Max, and then we have to be at the airport in two hours. Matthew worked his magic and got them to release your mum and Sammy. I spoke to Mum, and Antonia is fine. Everyone knows, except Junior. I think it's best to wait and tell him later. Max is the executor of your mum's will and Matthew said we don't need to be there to execute it. If I'm overstepping the line, please tell me. I just want to help." I've never had to deal with anything like this; all I can do is take my cues from her.

"You are fine, Jax, it's what I need right now. Besides, I don't even know what her wishes were. I did know she wanted Max as the executor. I was one of her witnesses when it was notarized. She said she didn't want to burden me. I never wanted to think about it. I always thought we would have more time." That thought hits home. Time is a precious commodity that we fight so hard for, but always seems to slide through our fingers like grains of sand.

"Max told me her wishes, and we will make sure they are followed. She was an amazing woman, and I'm lucky to have known her." I hug her, not sure if I'm trying to comfort her or myself.

"While you call Max, I'm going to have a long, hot shower. Join me when you're done."

I call Max and it goes to voicemail, so I leave him an update. I head off to the shower to join my wife.

Anwan

"I WOULD LIKE TO get some rest before we land," I announce before I get up and head into one of the cabins to be alone. It's only then, in the privacy of my cabin, that I let myself feel. I know everyone is worried about my health, but I don't need to be sheltered. The thought that I will never see my friend again is overwhelming. "Oh, Rose, we will meet again, my friend. I could never repay you for saving my family, but I promise you, I will find a way. Your death will not be in vain. This world will know what a beautiful and wonderful person you were." I curl in a ball and, in the privacy of my own world, let my tears fall.

Chapter Twenty-Three
Maxwell

I WATCH JACKIE SLEEP and it's very restless. When I look at my phone to check the time, I notice I have a voicemail from Jax. I hit the message and put it up to my ear to listen as I turn away from Jackie. *Thank God . . .* Matthew was able to pull some strings. The further we are away from all of this, the happier I will be. As many enemies as Vincent had, he had just as many friends. I never want to come near the States again, but we will have to come back one more time to execute Rose's will. After that, I'm done here. I slowly stroke Jackie's cheek, trying to gently wake her. Her eye's flutter open and she pulls me tightly against her.

"Max? Oh thank God you're safe! Please don't leave m-me."

"Shh, babe, I'm here. I'll always be here. Matthew was able to get Sammy and Rose released. We're leaving for the airport soon; we need to get ready. I never had the flat packed up, so I'm sure you have some clothes here. I want to check in with Mick before we leave." Her arms are tightly around me and she's not letting go.

"The sooner we get to the airport, the sooner we can get home. I promise you, I'm not leaving your side."

"I'm s-sorry, Max, it's just so much . . ."

"Hey, don't be sorry. You've been through a lot. It's okay to be scared. I would worry more if you weren't. Come on, I'll get ready with you, and then I can call Mick."

"Thank you." She tenderly kisses me and I feel the tightness in her body relax.

We silently go about getting ready which doesn't take too long. I wish I knew what to do for her . . . to help her.

"Would you like some tea while I call Mick?"

"If only tea could solve everything, Max. Make your call; I'm fine."

I kiss her and head out to make my call.

Jackie

I SIT AT THE vanity and begin side-braiding my hair. I know Max likes it this way. My thoughts are all over the place. I can't believe Sammy is dead because of me. I know Max would say otherwise, but he died protecting *me*. How do I live with that? How do I face Ian and try to explain what happened? My thoughts stray to Rose and I feel my heart in my throat. She was like a mom to me, giving me hope and the strength to face my fears. I know Raven will go on; she's the strongest person I've ever met, but it will be hard. "Ah!" I gasp, remembering how much Michael loves to explore with Rose. "I promise you, Rose, I will never let him forget you." I look in the mirror and find Max in the doorway. "How long have you been there?"

He doesn't say a word, only opening his arms for me. I get up and head right into them, my home, my sanctuary. "I love you."

"I love you and I know we will get through this. We will be strong for each other."

"Did you get in touch with Mick?"

"Yes, no worries, everyone is fine. Jax told An via Skype. They opted not to tell Junior right away. Let him get settled in at the clinic and continue his treatment. When we are all together, then we will tell him. I also put a call into your dad to let him know you are safe. Mick had already contacted him and made all the arrangements. I called the chief and requested that they let your dad and I tell Ian."

"I would like to be there when you do."

She looks down, averting her eyes away from mine. "I figured you would. Jackie, look at me please." I lift her chin, so I can see her face. "None of this was your fault. I know you and you're acting like you are to blame. Sammy's job was to protect you. That's what he was trained to do. It's sad—very sad—that he lost his life at the hands of a madman, but he knew what he was signing up for when he took the job."

"That sounds so cold and harsh."

"Yes, to you, it does. But to someone like me, it's the only way to survive. When I did protection detail, I had to leave my heart out of it. If not, I would have made mistakes. That's why I agreed to have Sammy come on board."

"Can I ask you a hard question?"

"Of course, you can ask me anything."

"After everything that went down, doesn't it make you question our decision to have children? After all the loss you have suffered, and the continued craziness that always seems to surround us, do you really feel that bringing a child into this world is such a great idea?" His jaw ticks with tension.

"If every good person in the world thought like that, there would never be a balance. Am I scared? Oh bloody hell, yeah. Will I let that fear rule me? Never again, Jackie, never. That fear almost cost me you. You're the one who taught me to fight to live life and not live to die. If we give up, then evil will win. I know it's not that simple. And I know we will have hard times, but I know together, we can make a difference. I will fight for us until my last breath."

I wrap my hands around his collar, pulling him closer to me. "I'm going to tell you this only one time. You will *never*, in my lifetime, do any of this cloak and dagger type of work again. So help me, Maxwell Fleming, if I have to tie you to a chair to stop you, I will!"

"Oh, now that could be very interesting, babe. Maybe when we get home I can teach you some rope tricks."

"Ah, Max, you are such a sex feign. Let's go get Jax and Raven. I want to go home."

We head out into the living room where Jax and Raven are already waiting. As lost and hurt as I feel, I realize that Raven must feel ten times worse. She has to mourn her mom all over again. "Max, why don't you and Jax give us a few minutes, please."

"Come on, Jax, I want to hear what happened when you told Mum."

They leave and I wrap my arms around Raven. "Let it go. I know you're trying to be strong." We drop to the floor and I rock her in my arms, letting her cry. Holding her and taking care of her like she did for me when Max was shot.

"Jackie, I just found her and now she's gone. How can this be happening to me again, why? I'm not a bad person; at least, I don't think I am. I try to do the right thing even when it's not always easy. Why?"

"It's not you, it was never you. There are evil people in this world. You can't give up. If you do, then evil wins. I think we need to honor her by doing good things in her memory. Don't make her death in vain." I stop rocking her and rest my forehead upon hers. I take both her hands and hold on tight.

"We are married to two of the wealthiest and most powerful men in the world. They want nothing more than to make us happy. Let's take this world by storm and kick some ass. Rose didn't die; she lives on in all of us. In such a short time, she made a huge difference. Let's show her what we've got."

She looks at me, and finally, I see a smile. "Does Max know yet that he's married to the most stubborn, strong, obstinate woman I've ever met?"

"Shh, some things are best left alone. He's liking the discovery as much as I am."

"Oh, Jackie, thank you. I love you so much, please never change. Come on, let's go get the guys; I'm ready to go home."

Jaxson

MAX AND I HEAD into the office. It seems like a lifetime ago that we were last in here. What happened when you told mum? I wished you would have called me, mate, you know how she worries."

"She handled it better than I thought she would. Mrs. Osla, Bella, and Mick were with her. Of course she was worried about Raven and Jackie. We are going to wait to tell Junior, he needs to concentrate on his treatments."

"That's all well and good but you know he's going to want to see her. He's too smart to put off for too long."

"I know. I honestly don't know how he's going to handle this. I didn't realize how close they were until that day he hid in the tunnels." I slump down into one of the chairs, feeling overwhelmed by all of this.

"I know you reviewed the research on the clinic, are you sure it's going to be okay for him?"

"Yeah, it's cutting edge research that's not available in the States. I feel comfortable sending him there. Junior's doctor and Rose looked over everything and they thought it was a good fit."

He closes his eyes and begins to rub his temples. This usually helps him, but I notice his jaw is clenched and I know there's more he's not telling me. "Max, what is it? Please just tell me and I'll deal with it."

"The clinic's research is done with stem cells early on in the treatment. The hospital in Philly doesn't bring that in until the end of treatment and only if they feel that it is warranted. Bella is only a seventy percent match. You know that Michael is not a match. I thought about cord blood, but that takes time—"

"—Stop. I know where you're going with this. If we need him, I promise you, I will be the one to go. I would never put you in that position, Max—ever." We sit quietly for a bit and it's these times with him that are the best for me. "You know what Jackie gave me the night of our wedding? Her birth control pills. She stopped them before the wedding."

I begin to laugh so hard, tears are falling.

"Jax, you want to tell me what's so funny?"

"Oh, yeah, Raven is subscribing to the let-the-chips-fall-where-they-may method." I lean back and prop my feet up on the desk right next to his.

"Well, Jax, you just might get your wish for ten babies."

"One at a time, Max. Let's grab the girls and go home." I get up. Max follows suit and we head out to the living room only to find the girls waiting for us by the elevators. "Hey, I guess everyone is ready to go."

Jackie puts her hand out to Raven. "Are you ready to go live that life we talked about?"

"Ready as I'll ever be." She puts the key in the elevator.

"Well, I believe the helicopter is waiting on the roof to take us to the airport. Are you guys coming?" Jackie raises her brows at us. Raven is giggling and it's such a beautiful sound and so rare.

"Max, who is this woman you married?" I cock my head toward him and ask out of the side of my mouth.

"Every day is a new experience with her." The elevator doors open, we step in and head up to the roof.

The guards are waiting and escort us to the helicopter. Within minutes, we are on our way.

Isabella

EVERYONE IS FINALLY ASLEEP, so I pull out the file on the clinic to see what it's all about. It seems they are pretty advanced in their research. Oh my God, the words are staring me in the face: *stem cells*—used in the early stages of treatment. What the hell am I going to do? I'm not prepared to tell my son. Jax said he would go to Dad if we need them. I know he thought we might be able to use cord blood but that was down the road. He's my son and if I have to, I would make a deal with the devil himself to save him. Why couldn't one of us be a better match? Why is God doing this to my son, to our family? I lie down and curl into Michael.

"Bella, what's troubling you now?" he whispers.

"Nothing, Michael, go back to sleep."

"I read the file. I will find a way. He's my son in every way that matters. Please never doubt that."

"I love you, Michael."

"Per il cielo e amore indietro. Now try and get some sleep."

Mick

WE ARE ABOUT TWO hours out and I still haven't seen An. I know she wanted some time to be alone and rest, but I need to know she's okay. I'm about to knock on her door when she opens it.

"I'm sorry, I need to know that you're okay, and then I will leave you alone. I'm sorry I can't help it—"

Before I can finish, she pulls me inside her cabin.

"I'm sorry; I should have told you I was okay. I needed some time to rest and think." She reaches up and brushes her lips across mine. "Mick, I made some tea, have a seat."

Tea? What the hell?!

"I think we need to talk."

Talk? Tea? She kissed me!

"You seem surprised, Mick. Can I ask why?"

"Surprised? Yeah, you could say surprised. We're friends, An. I feel comfortable talking to you. I don't want to lose that." My whole body becomes tight and I feel like any movement might make it snap.

"You would never lose my friendship, that's a given. I know I'm a little older than you, is that a problem?" Her voice has a quiver to it, and I realize she's worried about what I think.

"Honestly, I've never thought about it. Whether you were eighteen or eighty it wouldn't matter. It's about trust with me, you know that. I care about you a lot. You are the one person I can be myself with and not worry. I don't always have to be perfect; you accept me for who I am, scars and all."

"Then, why were you so shocked that I kissed you?" She sits down next to me and takes my hand. Rubbing her fingers over one of the scars on my hand. "I already know the answer, Mick. I need you to say it out loud . . . to own up to it. You'll never get past your fear if you don't."

I close my eyes tight, I can't look at her. "My body is very marred up, An, I can barely look in a mirror. How can I expect you to look at me without disgust? This family is all I have. I can't lose any of you; I won't survive it."

"Do you think so little of me that you feel a few scars would push me away? Look at the shame I've lived with for all these years. The mistakes I've made. Mick, no one is perfect. My point is, we all have scars; some are just more visible than others. Those scars make up who you are and all you've been through. But, they shouldn't decide where you're going. They shouldn't define you as a man. You need to let yourself feel again. Look what happened to Rose; that should be a wake-up call for all of us. Life is too short, Mick, and I don't want to spend the rest of my life alone."

She reaches up and rests her hand on my cheek. The fear makes me want to run, but she makes me want to stay. I pull her hand away and gently brush my lips across her knuckles, as I tightly squeeze my eyes shut. "Give me time to wrap my head around this. Time to deal with the fear, please."

"Open your eyes, Mick, and look at me." My eyes immediately open and look into hers, and all I see is kindness.

"One day at a time, one step at a time. Never be afraid to talk it out with me. First and foremost, we will always be friends. Now, I think we need to get ready, we should be landing soon."

I get up and pull her to her feet, "Yes, let's get seated and ready for landing."

"Thank you," It's just a whisper but her beautiful smile lets me know she heard me.

We head out to the main cabin and everyone is already seated. I feel like all eyes are on me. I hurry over to the inflight phone and check with the captain that everything is still on schedule. He assures me it is and that Mr. Gerhard is personally at the airport awaiting our arrival. I know I will feel a little bit calmer once we are all safely tucked away at the Gerhard compound. The captain asks if I would like to come into the flight deck for landing. I quickly take him up on his offer; it's the one place I find peace.

Maxwell

THE FLIGHT FROM THE Tower to Teeterborough is quick. I was hoping the caskets would have been loaded before our arrival, but no such luck. As we are approach, Raven and Jackie stop, frozen in place. I feel Jackie sway in my arms. *Fuck,* we're almost there; please hang on.

"I can't do this, Max." She closes her eyes and her tears are falling. She is shaking in my arms.

"Yes you can. You're a lot stronger than you think. That's not them in there anymore, you know that. Your faith tells you they are already with the angels. Be strong, babe, I know you can. Raven needs you to be . . . we all do." I finally get through to her and she steps forward, taking Raven's hand.

"Come on, Raven, we will do this together. Their death will not be in vain, let's prove it to the world." They walk up to the caskets, kiss each one, then walk up the steps, and enter the plane arm in arm. With a bond this strong, I know nothing will break it.

"Come on, Jax, we need to go." I watch my brother trying to be strong, but I know this hit him hard. Watching someone die for you is not something he will ever get over. I know . . . it stays with you for life. We head up the steps and give the customs agent our documents. When we are all cleared, we buckle up and head out. I, for one, am happy to be getting out of the States. Raven and Jackie are curled up together, each gaining comfort from the other.

I grab a bottle of water and nudge Jax to get his attention, "Let's go in the office, we have lots to discuss." I need to get him out of his head for his own good.

" Have a seat; I need to talk and you need to listen." He sits down and I pour him a scotch.

"I know what you're going through; I've been down this road before." He looks at me wide-eyed and shocked.

"Yeah, my partner took a bullet that was meant for me. It almost broke me, made me second guess myself. I felt doubt all the time. Was it my fault? Did I provoke the shooter? Maybe I didn't do my job properly? It was eating me up alive, and making me a danger to everyone around me. No one wanted to partner with me. My mind wasn't in the game." I pour myself a drink, my mind instantly flashing back to that day.

"So what did you do? I mean, how do you live with it, knowing that person's life is over, but you get to live on?"

"You just said it, Jax. You live. You do your best to be the best you can be. Don't make that person's death be for nothing. Don't waste your life doing nothing or wallowing in self-pity. Do something to honor that person. Make a difference in the world. Jackie asked me why I wanted to bring a child into this world that is so full of evil. I told her there has to be a balance or evil wins. I have hope, even after all I've been through."

I hold my glass up toward him, "Here's to grabbing life by the bullocks, mate."

We toast and finish our drinks. "Now, on to business, we need to check in with Mick. They should have arrived there by now."

"Raven spoke to Bella right before we left. She said everyone was doing okay. I know Bella is eager to get Junior checked into the clinic. Did you get a chance to read the file from the clinic?"

"Yeah, Jax, do you have a plan?" I know him and he thinks he has this all figured out.

"As a matter of fact, I do. After everyone is safely tucked away, I will be heading to Capri—alone. I told you I would handle it. I won't put you in that position."

"Cold day in hell, mate. Never gonna happen, so get that shit out of your head. We go together and we cover each other's arse. That's what brothers do."

"What if you can't control yourself, have you thought of that?!"

"Have you thought about what you would do if you can't control yourself?"

"You're. Not. Going. With. Me. Max!"

"You're. Not. Going. Without. Me. Jax!"

We are just about to come to blows when the door flies open. Jackie and Raven are both standing there, hands on hips, glaring at us. We let go of each other and sit back down. Raven steps forward and I swear she's about ready to explode.

"What the hell is going on in here? You are fighting like kids on a playground! You're grown adults, what the hell is the problem?"

"Um, sweetheart, we had a difference of opinion, nothing more." I'm trying not to laugh as Raven is tearing into him, that is, until she turns her attention to me.

"Max, why do you push his buttons? You know how crazy he can be, but you're like a dog with a bone. What is the problem? And don't tell me nothing!"

I look to Jackie for help, but my wife is not budging. "Don't even think that I'm going to help you out of this one, Max. Nope, you are on your own. Now, what the hell is going on back here?"

"Jackie, It's all Max's fault."

"Oh, bloody hell—no! Don't you dare throw me under the fucking bus!"

Jackie leans on the desk, her face only inches from Jax's. "Spill, Jax, all of it and *I mean* all of it."

"Okay, all I did was tell Max that I would go see Dad as soon as Junior is settled in and get the test for the stem cells. He is insisting that he has to go with me. I don't think it is necessary. That's all, just a little difference of opinion."

"Ah!" Raven gasps. "What happened that Michael is getting stem cells now? Why didn't you tell us sooner? Jackie, did you know any of this?"

"No, this is all new to me. Why now?"

"This clinic does things differently; they treat early on with the stem cells."

"Well, isn't Bella or Michael Sr. a close match?" Jax and I look at each other and I realize I need to tell Jackie everything. It's always been so hard for Jax and me to talk about.

"Jackie, Bella had every intention of disclosing this to you, she just never had a chance. Michael is not Michael Jr's biological father. Bella was drugged and raped at a convention in Las Vegas. She didn't think she would ever have to deal with this again, but then everything happened. She is only a seventy percent match. I mentioned to her about the cord blood you told me about. I really couldn't remember much, only that the baby needs to be born in a hospital. We figured we had three years, that one of us would have a baby by then."

"Well, Bella and Michael are the best parents—biology has nothing to do with that. Now, as far as going to see James, we either all go, or no one goes. No more fighting, no more yelling, and no more secrets—ever. We have a long flight ahead of us and I'm tired. Is everyone good here now?" she asks, hand on her hip.

"All good, babe, I'm going to come with you."

I rush out the door after her, hoping to finally have some alone time with my beautiful wife.

Raven

"HEY, YOU OKAY?" I know he needs me just as much as I need him. He seems a little distant. Usually, he is all over me. I wonder if there's something more with Michael that he hasn't told me?

"Yeah, I'll be okay. With everything going on, I didn't get a chance to talk to you about the clinic. I looked at the research and I think it will be a good fit for him. Raven, I'd go to hell and back if it meant he would get better. I just worry about Max going with me."

"One thing at a time; let's get through today first."

I get up and lock the door. "Jax, I need you, more than you will ever realize. I need to lose myself in you. I need you to take away the pain and the hurt. I miss my mom and I miss our daughter. I miss you and all your crazy intense ways. I need you . . . please."

"Are you sure?"

"Yes." I remember the day in the washroom and how much he loved to watch me. I lift off my shirt and shimmy out of my jeans. His eyes follow my every move.

He leans back and props his feet on the desk. "Carry on, sweetheart."

I turn around so my back is toward him as I reach behind and unhook my bra, letting it fall to the floor. I'm left in nothing but a thong. I take my hair down and let it tumble down my back. I turn around and he hasn't moved. He's letting me take the lead. I run my fingers up and down my neck and chest. My breasts are still producing milk but I haven't pumped today, so I need to tread lightly here. I glide my fingers down my ribs and pull at the thong. I know he loves to snap them. I let go and continue running my fingers down into my thong until I reach, what he calls, cock heaven. I throw my head back and let out a long, low moan. "Oh, Jax." My fingers are moving faster. I look at him and his eyes are wide as he takes his feet off the desk. He's almost ready to pounce. "Oh, Jax, please now."

That's all it takes, he leaps out of his chair and in one quick move he snaps my thong. He drops to his knees and his lips and tongue are all over me. "I can't hold it, Jax." He's not stopping. He reaches his hands up and rolls my nipples between his fingers. I'm screaming and I don't care if the world hears me. All of my emotions are flooding to the surface; every nerve ending is on fire. "Jax, I need more—now!"

He gets up and his jeans are around his knees. I don't give him a chance to even get them off. I jump into his arms and wrap my legs around his waist. In one swift move, he's inside me. He's pounding into me, it's—hard and fast, love and lust—a release beyond compare. He tilts his head back, and I know that he's close. The most beautiful sight in the world—his unraveling within me. "Yes, Jax!"

"Show me. Oh God, Raven. Violet to blue . . . yes!"

He falls to his knees and lays me down, slowly working us down. I finally catch my breath, but he's not stopping. "Jax?"

"Never enough, sweetheart."

He's taking is time, kissing my neck and moving his hips in and out. I'm clenching and he begins to do that swivel thing I love. I'm there and I want him to feel my release, like I can feel his. I drag my nails over his nipples and that's his undoing. That's my tipping point. I reach up and kiss him and then everything I've kept bottled up inside me rises to the surface. I start to shake and cry. I can't seem to catch my breath. He wipes away my tears and gently kisses me.

"You're okay, sweetheart. I've got you, I always will."

Jackie

"MAX, DID YOU REALLY think either one of you would go to see James without us?" I ask him as I undress. He opens his mouth about to answer but I hold up my hand. "Wait. Don't even answer that, because in some strange part of your brain, I really think you believed you would go it alone. Maybe I should just chalk it up to the after effects of being shot in the head. You know, the more I think about it, the more pissed off I'm getting. Let me tell you something, Maxwell Fleming, we are part of a large family. We work together or not at all. Your days of going off half-cocked, on your own, are over! We all have a say in what goes on. That's what a family does, so you better learn to start playing by the rules."

He's leaning against the wall with his arms crossed and his feet crossed at the ankles. He's got a smirk on his face and damn I feel my heart flutter. "Well, are you going to say anything?"

"I was waiting until you were done, babe. First, I have to say right now, while you're getting all pissed off, I'm getting turn-on—it's hot. Second, I don't want anyone in danger and, no matter what happens, I will always be over-the-top protective with everyone. Lastly, you standing there, in nothing but your knickers, is driving me crazy. Come here *now,* but leave the braid. Fucking sexy as hell."

I step up to him and begin to slowly undress him, starting with his shirt. When I trail my fingers over his nipples, he takes a few deep steadying breaths. His eyes are watching my every move, but he's not touching me. I undo his jeans and slowly slide them down, taking his hipsters with them. He steps out of them and I remain on my knees. I keep my eyes cast downward, knowing how much he loves it. I don't want to look up; if I do, it will be over before we start. My fingertips are gliding up and down his legs. I reach for his cock and rub my thumb over the tip. I can hear his breathing become rapid. The heat coming off of his body is unreal. I slowly trail my tongue up his cock and then take him in my mouth. At first, I give a little tease with my tongue swirling gently around the head. I glance up and notice his eyes have darkened. I quickly look back down.

"Take me deeper, Jackie . . . *please.*" I relax my muscles and give him what he wants. I might be on my knees right now, but I hold all the power. It's heady to realize that I can do this to him. I know he's close. I don't want this to end. I stop and stand up, his eyes on me. "Make love to me, Max."

He lifts me up and carries me to the bed, kissing me the entire time. His lips are so soft, yet the heat they leave in their wake is so intense. I feel the heat rising in my body; all my nerve endings feel electrified. He lays me down, his mouth slowly working its way down to my legs. Every inch—covered . . . up one side and down the other. I listen to the sound of him groaning and mumbling as he pulls my panties off. Positioning himself on his knees, he slowly enters me. He then stops and leans down, resting his forehead on mine. Our eyes gaze intensely into each other.

"Babe, are you okay?" He's always worried about me, making sure that he's pleasing me.

"Yes, love me, Max." He begins to move, slowly at first, but then I can feel the build-up in me, rising to the top. I dig my heels into his ass, trying to push him, but he's fighting me . . . holding back. Then, he tilts his hips and with each thrust I swear he gets harder. Every emotion rushes to the surface, a rush that is so intense, I feel lightheaded. I let go and let the rush wash over me.

"Oh, babe, yeah." His voice is deep and raspy and his release seems endless. His eyes never leave mine. He gently presses his lips to mine. I wrap myself tightly around him and close my eyes.

As I drift off to sleep I hear him whisper, "I love you."

Chapter Twenty-Four
Maxwell

I COULD SPEND MY whole life with Jackie tucked safely in my arms, and I know I would be happy. It's so different with her; she feels what I feel. She knows my fears and she accepts me just the same. We fit each other's needs, yet we challenge each other. She's finally asleep, so I tuck her in tightly and check in with Mick.

He answers on the first ring and sounds a little off. "Hey, you okay?"

"Yeah, everything is fine. Mr. Gerhard was waiting for us when we landed. We went directly to the clinic and got Junior settled in. Heads up—he's upset that he doesn't have his *Doctor Who* room. Let Raven know that Mrs. Gerhard is in love with Antonia and refusing to let anyone hold her."

"What about An? How is she doing?"

"She is fine, all settled in and she is getting along wonderfully with Mrs. Gerhard. When can we expect you to get here?"

"We should be landing in a few hours. I'm sure we will go straight to the house. Where are Bella and Michael?"

"They stayed at the clinic with Junior. Mr. Gerhard has arranged for transport when you land. Do you need me to do anything else?"

"No, get some rest. Thanks for everything."

I crawl back into bed, trying not to disturb Jackie but no such luck. "Hey, we have time yet, go back to sleep."

I stroke her back and twirl her braid around, as she drifts off to sleep. There are going to be many more emotional days ahead for all of us. All we can do is rely on each other for strength and support.

Jaxson

I HOLD RAVEN IN my arms and somehow manage to get us into bed without breaking my neck. Lately, everything has been so intense. Even making love to her feels like it's laced with a fear of great loss at an extreme intensity.

I mindlessly twirl her hair around my fingers and she seems to be calming down.

"Sweetheart, when we land, I want to check on the baby and then head to the clinic to check on Junior. Are you okay with that?"

"Of course, do you want me with you when you tell him?"

"Actually, I'm going to talk to his doctors first and see what they think is best for him. I know Bella wanted to shield him from any hurt, that's what mums do. But Junior is like me, he wants everything upfront and honest from the get go."

"You go; I'll be fine. Besides, I really need to spend some quiet time with our daughter. Make sure you let Michael know that we will all be there in the morning."

"There's something else I need to talk to you about." Even though I'm trying to hide it, I can hear the dread in my own voice. "Jackie will probably want to be there when Sammy's family is told. She is going to need you for support. I know that you're grieving also, but you're her best friend. I don't know what to do for her." We are both silent for a bit, her fingers tracing hearts on my chest while I twirl her hair mindlessly around my finger.

"You're right, she is my best friend and I will do whatever she needs me to do. She is a lot stronger than you think."

"Oh trust me, sweetheart, I learned that one today. I do believe my brother is going to have his hands full with her."

She giggles again and it's music to my soul. "We need to get ready; we should be landing in thirty minutes."

We get up and move about the room, getting ready for the next hurdle. I watch her doing all the simple things: brushing her teeth, pulling her hair up, and I know she's the total package—the real deal. As crazy and fucked up as things have been, I'm still the luckiest man in the world. I've grabbed that brass ring and I'm holding on tight with both hands. I'm never letting go . . . ever.

Isabella

MY SON IS AMAZING; so resilient and strong. Through everything, he always remains so positive. I admire his strength and wish I had more of it. I know the next few months will be difficult to deal with. I thank God that I have my family's unwavering support. I know, in that sense, I am very blessed. After speaking with my mum and my son's doctors, Michael and I think it's best to wait and tell him about Rose later. I can't wait till the rest of the family gets here; I offer Michael a smile as he finally comes back in with coffee.

"Where is Junior?"

"The nurses took him for his treatment. I know he wasn't too happy about giving up that room, but this is like a small apartment for us. It will be better in the long run, don't you think?" He doesn't answer me. Hell, I don't even know if he heard a word I said.

"Michael, what's wrong?"

"I've come to a decision. I am going to see your father and ask him to be tested."

"What?! Have you lost your mind? Jax said—."

"—He's *my* son, Bella, in every way that counts. I know what Jax said and, believe me, I do appreciate that he wants to spare all of us, but when it comes to my son, I will move heaven and earth for him." He puts his cup on the table, sits down, and squeezes my hand.

"Everyone at the winery has volunteered to be tested. I've also contacted my family. They have agreed to be tested." I'm totally floored.

"Michael, your family? The same family that wanted nothing to do with us once you told them everything? Why would they agree to this? Michael, what did you do?"

He closes his eyes, looking beyond stressed. "I agreed to let them meet him, and I agreed to be a part of the family again."

"What?! What if they aren't even a match? They wanted nothing to do with us, Michael! Hell, they called my son a bastard! How could you want to have anything to do with them?"

"For the same reason I will go to your father and beg him to try and save my son's life. That's what a parent would do to save their child. He's my world; the sun rises and sets with him. We have no idea who or what he will become, but I know that he is destined to do great things. I will make sure that he is around to do them."

I put my arms around his waist and hold on tight. He's right—no matter what happens—we will do all that we can possibly do for him. "I love you so much. You're the best dad any child could ever dream of having."

"Well, don't praise me, yet. I haven't found a match and I still have to figure out how to explain to Junior why he never met his grandparents or any of my family."

"We will tell him that not all family is as crazy close as ours. Sometimes, there is a difference of opinion and families separate. What matters is that all of that is in the past. If he chooses, he can get to know them now. We keep it simple, and show him it's not a big deal."

"Okay, I can do that. Have you heard from your brothers?"

"No, but they should be landing soon. I, for one, will feel better when everyone is all in one place. Just because Vincent and that crazy lawyer are dead, doesn't guarantee that everyone is safe. There will always be someone out there trying to take the easy way out to get money."

"I would love it if we could live at the vineyard in Italy. Even though it would be very safe, I know it would be a lonely life for Junior. In a lot of ways, he's like Jax—always wanting lots of family around."

"Well, if my brothers get their wish, Jackie and Raven will both be pregnant soon." Before I can say anything more, the nurse wheels Michael in the room. He is finally back from his treatment.

He gets up and sits on the couch between Michael and me. "Mum, when is everyone getting here?" His voice is tired and raspy.

I need to keep it light for him. "They should be here soon, do you need something?"

"Take a look around this place—it's boring; not even a *Doctor Who* DVD. I hope Uncle Jax remembered to take them."

"Don't worry about it. If he didn't, then Dad will replace them."

He pulls out his cell phone. "Michael, who are you calling?"

"Miss Rose, I want to make sure she comes here as soon as possible. I found a tunnel in the blueprints that Uncle Max gave me and I want to show it to her."

His words twist like a knot in my stomach. I'm about to answer, when the door opens and Jax walks in . . . alone.

"Uncle Jax!" He jumps up and runs into his arms. "Where is everyone? Did you remember the DVDs? They have no clue who the *Doctor* is. How long do I have to stay here?"

"Slow down, buddy, it was a long flight and everyone was very tired, so when we landed, they went directly to Mr. Gerhard's house. I will order everything and have it sent here tomorrow. You know me, Junior, I always tell you the truth. Your health is not worse. You know bad people were trying to hurt us." Jax puts his hand on the back of Michael's shoulder and guides him over to the couch to sit.

I know my son needs to be told. Michael and I sit next to them. "Jax, please, let me." I take a deep breath and take a hold of his hand.

"Michael, I need to tell you something, and I need you to be really brave for me. The bad people that were after us were trying really hard to hurt Aunt

Raven and Antonia, and even Aunt Jackie. They were finally stopped, but not before they hurt Miss Rose and Sammy."

His eyes fill with tears and my heart is breaking for him, for all of us. "Mum, they d-died?"

"Yes, I'm so sorry." I hold him close to me, rocking him in my arms as he cries. Michael wraps his arms around both of us, trying to comfort us.

Junior finally pulls away from us and looks to Jax. "You promised me we would all be together. You said you would be right behind us. How could you let that happen? How could you let her die? I trusted you!" he yells at him and I think I can safely say that we are all shocked. Jax sits there and doesn't say a word, taking everything that Michael is throwing at him. I see a tear escape Jax's eye and he quickly wipes it away. I can see that he's holding back; there must be more. He tries to wipe away Michael's tears but he pushes him away.

"Answer me, Uncle Jax, how could you let this happen?!"

"I tried to stop it. I was pulling your Aunt Raven behind me when Rose stepped in front of me, taking the bullet that was meant for me. She gave her life for *me.*" He opens his arms and Michael leaps into them. The two of them are rocking and crying. My brother keeps saying he's sorry over and over again. They have a bond like nothing I've ever seen before. It's being tested and rocked to the core, but it will never break. I sit here stunned by what Jax has said. Mick said Sammy and Rose were shot and didn't make it, he never went into detail. Then it hits me, the guilt is what Jax has been hiding. He feels responsible for Rose's death. I can tell him till I'm blue in the face that he wasn't, but he will never believe me. From when he was a young boy, he always felt responsible for us. He thought he had to be the man of the family. My rape almost destroyed him, but we survived. This, however, is something that he needs to come to terms with on his own.

"Let's give them some time alone," my husband whispers near my ear. Even though I don't want to, I know he's right. "I'm going to give Raven a call and check in." We get up to leave but I don't think either of them notices.

Jaxson

JUNIOR FINALLY SEEMS TO be calming down. I look around and realize Bella and Michael left. I need Junior to stay focused on his treatment and getting better.

"Hey, I know you and Rose were close but the one thing she wouldn't want is for you to get sick over all of this. She fought for you to get tested, and it's because of her that we knew very early about your cancer. You need to fight harder than you've ever fought for anything before. Do it for Rose; become a man she would be proud to always call her friend."

"I will, Uncle Jax, I promise. How is Aunt Raven?"

"She is doing the best she can. She will be by here in the morning to see you. Try and be strong for her, too, okay?"

"Yeah, I will. Now . . . about this place . . ." he trails off, eyeing the room.

I begin to laugh and it feels so good. "How about we start with a quick tour and then we can talk about what we are going to change."

Raven

JEFF MADE SURE THAT my mom's and Sammy's caskets were already removed by the time we got off the plane. Jackie held it together until she saw her dad. I know we have so much more stress coming our way, I just don't know how any of us are going to deal with it. The pain I feel can overtake me, if I let it. My daughter is my salvation, my lifeline. As long as I keep my focus on her, I can and will survive. We finally pull up to the house and I can't get out of this car fast enough. Everyone is here, offering their condolences, but all I want right now is my daughter.

Mrs. Osla embraces me, "Up the steps, second door on the left. Good luck getting her away from Emi; go."

I don't think I will ever understand why anyone is afraid of her. "Thank you." I race up the stairs to be with my daughter. I need her to comfort me. I open the door and freeze in my spot. Jeff and Emi had a complete nursery set up for Antonia. They even took the cranes from the wedding and hung them from the ceiling. It's like being under a giant mobile. Emi is holding her and singing, the site makes me realize all over again how much my mom will miss. My daughter will never know her, the price she paid for Antonia's happiness. Emi puts her in my arms and the emotions are overwhelming.

"Raven, your mother's spirit will live on forever. She is within your heart and around you always. It is never goodbye forever."

"Thank you, Emi. And thank you for all you have done for her."

I lean down to kiss her little hands and breathe in her scent. It's sweet and all her. "Oh, my beautiful baby girl. So much has happened and, through it all, you still go on, we all do. Your grandmother gave her life so you could be happy. Live it to the fullest, and be all that you can be—the best of the best."

I watch Emi leave as I take a seat with my daughter securely in my arms. I let myself feel all the emotions and the fears that I've been keeping bottled up deep inside of me. I rock my daughter and let my tears wash over every thought.

I don't know how much time has passed. Antonia is fast asleep and everyone has kept their distance. I'm grateful for that. I needed the stillness that comes with the quite.

Jackie and Max were going to see Ian today. I know I should go with them, but a part of me feels like I'm to blame. I know I'm not responsible for Sammy's death, but I can't stop what I'm feeling, I don't know how. I keep running through the events on that roof over and over again. My mom new that Vincent withheld my grandfather's medicine until there was no hope. She understood, better than anyone, the depths of his hatred and jealousy for his whole family. So many lives lost at the hands of a madman.

By tomorrow night, I'm sure we will be off to Capri; another huge emotional hurdle to deal with. I wish we could have found a donor and avoided the entire thing, but no luck, so far. We might go through all of this for nothing; James might not even be a match. As a parent, I understand why we must go. But it doesn't make it any easier.

I get up and put Antonia in her crib. She needs to rest and I need to put away my fears and emotions; my family needs me now. I lean down and kiss her little cheeks. "Watch over her Mom and Dad, be her angels. I love you."

Jackie

MAX AND PAPA ARE waiting for me, but I needed a few minutes alone. Time to gather up my courage to see Ian. How do I face him? How can I make him understand when I don't understand myself? I have to be strong. Sammy would want me to be strong for Ian. I wipe away my tears and open the door, only to find Max sitting on the floor.

"What are you doing on the floor?"

"I didn't want to bother you, but I wanted to be here for you."

I reach down, take his hand, and pull him up off the floor. "I know that you are my strength when I need it; always there for me, no matter what. I will always be here for you, too, Max. Now, let's go find Papa; we need to get going."

"We will be okay; one day at a time."

We head into the drawing room and find my father and Dylan in a heated discussion.

I feel Max's grip around my waist tighten. "Max, please let me go. I'm asking you to remain calm and let me handle my brother."

He lets me go of me but remains at my side. "Dylan, why are you here? What are you two arguing about?"

"Why the hell wouldn't I be here? You're not that naive to think that none of this is your fault."

"How is it my fault, Dylan? Sammy was doing his job—the same job he has done for the last *ten years*."

"It's your fault because you put yourself in danger. You brought all this on yourself by hooking up with him. I warned you, but you were too blinded by lust to think about anyone but you."

I snap. I smack Dylan so hard across the face, that I've left a handprint. In my whole life, I have never hit another person—*ever*. "Don't you *ever* talk about my husband *ever* again. You are being judgmental about me and my decisions. You're upset because I've decided to live my life and not sit on the sidelines. Sammy was doing his job, a job he was proud to do. I will not have you taint it. Get out of my life, stay away from me and my family." I feel myself beginning to shake uncontrollably and then I hear Raven behind me yell at Dylan.

"Leave her alone, Dylan!"

"You can't make me stay away from my sister. I'm entitled to my opinion. This nightmare began with you. Maybe you need to step up to the plate and take some responsibility for the bloodshed," he barks back at Raven.

Raven turns pale as Papa steps between them. "I think you've said enough, son. You gave your opinion, now put it to bed. We need to move forward. We have guests and they will be remaining here with us until young Michael's treatment is done. Now, we need to get going."

"We won't be staying here." All of us turn to find Jax in the doorway.

"Dylan, out of respect for your parents and your sister, I have put up with your bullshit, but you just crossed the line. You've done nothing but talk out of your arse the entire time I've known you. Jeff, we will be moving out tomorrow. I appreciate your help and your hospitality, but my family's safety and well-being is my top priority. You and Emi are always welcome to my home. Now, if you'll excuse me, my wife and I have a lot to discuss."

"This isn't over, Jax, you can't just dismiss me like some servant. If I want to see my sister, I will. You can't stop me—no one can."

Jax stops and looks back over his shoulder towards Dylan. "Watch me!"

I'm holding onto Max, trying to keep him calm. Jax totally ignores anything else Dylan is saying.

"Max, while you and Jackie go talk to Ian, Raven and I will be getting everything firmed up on this end." Their eyes lock and then he excuses himself, taking Raven's hand and walking out.

"Papa, are you coming?" I ask.

He looks at Dylan and then back to me. "Tell Ian that Mom and I will be by tomorrow." I feel like a little child again, being dismissed. I hated it then, and I hate it even more now.

We head out to the car and Max is very quiet . . . too quiet. We get in the car and I tell the driver where to take us. "Are you going to tell me what the hell is going on?"

"Honestly, I have no idea. One minute your brother is flipping out on us. The next minute, Jax is cueing me to shut up and get out."

Before I can ask any more questions, he gets a text. He allows me to lean over and read it with him.

Jax: Pay your condolences and then get back here. Say nothing. I'm making other arrangements now.

Max: Call Tony; he can handle it all.

Jax: Done.

"Now are you going to tell me what is going on?" I slap his knee.

"I really don't know anything."

I'm not going to fight with him over this. I need to mentally prepare myself on what I'm going to tell Ian. We pull up to Ian's and I can tell from the surprised look on Max's face, it's not what he was expecting. "Ian's parents left it to him. Sammy enjoyed doing all the renovations himself. Ian, on the other hand, wouldn't know which end of the hammer did what."

"The grounds are impeccable, who takes care of them?"

"Ian does all that. He finds it very relaxing. When I first moved to the States, Ian came over with Sammy and helped decorate my flat. The week after he left, I killed the plant. He never lets me forget it."

Before he can ask me anything else, Ian comes flying out the door. He grabs me, hugs me, and then pulls away, his eyes on mine. He begins to cry, I don't need to say a word.

"Let's go inside, please. Jackie, I need to hear it all."

We head in the door and Ian leads us right into the kitchen. That's his comfort zone. "Ian, this is my husband, Maxwell."

Max places a hand on his shoulder try to offer him comfort. "Sorry to meet you under these circumstances. I'm sorry for your loss; Sammy was a good guy."

Ian grabs onto the counter for support, and I wipe away his tears. "Were you with him when it happened? Oh what a stupid question, of course you were, tell me what happened? I need to hear it all."

"He jumped in front of someone that tried to shoot me. Raven's mom tried to save him but she couldn't. In the end she was also shot and killed."

He begins to sway on his feet and Max tries to steady him. "Please, why don't we sit down?" He guides him to a chair.

"How is Raven? Is she going to be okay?"

"It's going to be very hard on her; she just got her mom back into her life only to lose her again."

"Did my Sam suffer? Was it quick?" He puts his head in his hands and cries. Max grabs some tissues off the counter, clearly not knowing what to do to help Ian.

"It was very quick. I held him, Ian. He wasn't alone."

He stops crying and lifts his head. He offers me a tissue. "I hope you're not blaming yourself for any this. Just like the last time, Jackie, it wasn't your fault."

Max sits down next to me and squeezes my hand, "Last time?"

"When Sammy first became my guard, he didn't know how to ride. I was jumping and competing, I was being very stubborn at the time and I refused to change my routine. He thought it was no big deal; just get on the horse and go. Needless to say, he fell off and broke his leg. In the end, I changed my routine so I could stay here to look after him."

"You should have seen him giving her a hard time and ordering her around. But she got even with him. As soon as the doctor said he was okay, she put him right back on that horse."

Ian takes my hand, "Oh, Jackie, I always knew this day would come. I worried every time he stepped out that door. He would tease me, always saying he would outlive me. I don't even know where to begin. I want to see him, Jackie. Please, I need to."

I get up, go to the fridge, and grab a couple of bottles of water. I don't know how to answer him. Max takes one of the bottles and hands it to Ian. "My attorney has already contacted MI6 on your behalf, letting them know that he will be handling everything so you won't have to. I can set up a viewing and I will go with you."

"Thank you. You're very kind."

We get up to leave and Max stops. "Ian, I would like to do something to honor him, if it would be okay with you. Think about what you would feel comfortable with and let me know."

We make our goodbyes and head out, promising to keep in touch. We head toward home; both of us are very quiet.

"Max, we need to create a project for Ian. He is going to be very lost without Sammy. I can't leave him all alone in that huge home. We need to come up with something."

"Well, we are not going to be leaving the area for the next three years, so how about some sort of garden sanctuary. It could be set up like a memorial garden for Sammy."

"That might work. I'll talk to him when we get back from Capri. Don't even think of telling me we're not going."

The quiet that envelops us is extremely deafening.

Chapter Twenty-Five

Jaxson

RAVEN AND I HEAD upstairs and into Antonia's room. While Raven is tending to the baby, I send a quick text to Max letting him know to keep his mouth shut. Next, I shoot one off to Tony.

> **Jax: Are my text messages secure?**

> **Tony: Yes, they are encrypted to the outside world. Is there a problem?**

> **Jax: Maybe. We are at the Gerhard compound. I'm uncomfortable with the situation here. That wanker, Dylan Gerhard, is here and causing trouble. I need a safe place near the clinic for the family. We need to head out to Capri, can't leave until I know the family is safe.**

> **Tony: Stay calm and don't use your tablets. If you have to, use the new iPhones I gave you. They have enhanced security in place. I will take care of everything on my end.**

Now we wait, something I've never been good at. I don't trust Dylan and knowing that he would have unfettered access to my child—never gonna happen. I watch Raven playing with Antonia and I wish all our days could be like this very moment. "Sweetheart, I want the baby to sleep in our room tonight." She doesn't question me. She knows I need to feel like my family is safe. My phone vibrates with a group text to Max and me.

> **Tony: I have secured a place near the clinic. The information will only be sent to your phone. I have a friend in Geneva who is headed to the new place now. He will have everything wired up before morning. I ordered all the stuff you requested and had it sent overnight to the clinic. I also threw**

in some new stuff that just came out. I'm sure he will be very excited. All new electronics will be waiting at the new place. Have the old ones shipped to me; don't leave them behind.

Jax: Thank you. Have you informed Mrs. Osla?

Tony: No, I'm not telling her. You or Max can tell her.

Max: Jax can tell her. :)

Jax: Max, where are you?

Max: Just pulling up now. I'll meet you upstairs.

I hand my phone to Raven, so she can read what is going on while I lie on the floor and play with the baby.

"Jax, do you really feel this way?" Before I can answer, Jackie comes storming in.

"Jax, do you seriously think my brother would hurt us? I get he's an ass, but he would never lay a hand on any of us."

"Jackie, you are probably right, however, I just can't take a chance. I can't leave for Capri and not feel like my family is safe. If your parents want to come over and visit with you and the baby, I would never stop them. Your brother, well, that's another story."

My phone beeps with an urgent message from Tony.

Tony: Not sure if this will matter to you or not, but Dylan is in financial trouble. He has closed up his shop in Japan. He is in debt to some nasty men. Mr. Gerhard is giving his son money. You know desperate men do desperate things. Stay safe.

I hand Jackie my phone. "Maybe you should read this."

"How could this be? Can I confront Dylan and Papa?"

"I would rather you wait until we are back from Capri."

She hands me back my phone and I know this has hit her hard. She always sees the good in people. "I'm sorry, Jackie, I don't know what to believe anymore."

"My head is spinning. I need some food and sleep. I promise I won't confront them."

"Well, I, for one, am going to take my daughter downstairs and make myself something to eat." All heads turn toward my wife and I start laughing. Maybe it's the stress, but the thought of her in the kitchen makes me lose it. Jackie is trying not to laugh and Max is laughing so hard, he's crying.

"Oh come on. People! I'm not that hopeless in the kitchen."

As I guide her out the door, I can hear Max tell Jackie it would be a bloody cold day in hell before he eats a peanut butter and jelly sandwich. I would pay big bucks to see that, but right now I have to talk to Mrs. Osla, since everyone is afraid of her.

"I will meet everyone in the kitchen. I want to talk to Mrs. Osla before she turns in for the night."

I find Mrs. Osla in the sitting room, by the fire. She is working on her needlepoint; bless her and her patience. "Mrs. Osla, I need to speak to you about some things."

"Pull up a seat and tell me what's troubling you."

I show her the text messages and when she reads the one about Dylan's financial situation, she takes a deep breath and her eyes are wide.

"Lad, let me work with Tony. I promise not to scare him too much."

She takes my phone, pulls up notes, and then proceeds to type away. I lean over, watching as she does so.

Don't speak about any of this in this house, it could be wired. If Mr. Gerhard is as security conscious as he seems, then it wouldn't surprise me. Tomorrow we leave to go see young Michael, and we don't come back. Anything we need, I can make arrangements for.

I nod. "So how is my mum feeling? She took Rose's death very hard."

"We all did. But she seems to be gaining her strength back a little bit every day. Have you decided what type of arrangements you are going to make? I could handle them for you, if you would like."

"Max is the executor of her will but she had everything already planned out. She never wanted to burden Raven with anything. Matthew will handle it all."

"What about you? How are you dealing with everything?"

"I'm dealing. It's not like I have a choice. I have a family that is counting on me. I have to be the strong one. I still need to get to Capri and deal with that whole nightmare."

"So, you are going? What about Maxwell?" She is mindlessly playing with the strings of her needlepoint.

"I tried to go it alone, but we almost came to blows over it. Raven and Jackie stepped in and now the four of us are going. We don't even know if he's going to be a match. I wish they would let me go alone, but they are all so stubborn."

"Ha, yeah look who's calling the kettle black. Do you want me to try and talk to Maxwell?"

"No, he won't listen and then he will get mad at me for having you talk to him. I'm in a no-win situation here."

"I would offer to handle James for you, but I fear I would be worse than Maxwell, if put in that situation. What if he refuses to be tested, have you thought about that? Not everyone is willing to do this, and—let's face it—we already know he has no conscience."

"Sometimes in life, Mrs. Osla, we don't have a choice."

"So be it. What time would you like us all ready tomorrow?"

"Right after breakfast. Now I need to find my wife, she was headed to the kitchen acting as if she could cook us something."

She makes the sign of the cross, "Lord, have mercy. You better go rescue everyone."

I laugh as I head out the door in search of my wife.

Raven

I HAVE NO IDEA why everyone thinks I will poison them. I take Jackie's hand, "Come on, we can do this."

"Have you lost your mind? I can make coffee and a salad."

"I know, but Max is such a good cook, surely you learned something being in the kitchen with him all the time."

She turns fifty shades of red. "Okay, never mind; I don't think I want to know what you've learned in the kitchen."

Max hands me Antonia, "How about you and Jackie play with my beautiful niece while Jax and I make dinner?"

Jax comes in just at the right time. "Okay, hit me, mate, what are we cooking?"

We let them get started while we play with the baby. Jackie takes Antonia while I set the table. "Raven, are you ready for Capri? I want all of this to be over with, so we can get on with our lives. I want Michael to get better, so we can get back to Scotland. I love it there. I don't think I ever want to leave the castle. What about you, are you ready?"

"Oh, Jackie, I want to be done with this, too. I had an idea that I talked to Jax about before we left Scotland and he was all for it. Maybe you and Max might want to be a part of it, too?"

Max comes over and puts the plates down. I don't know what it is, but it smells wonderful. "It's a potatoes and eggs frittata on Cuban bread and a salad; simple, comfort food."

"Amazing what you two can do in the kitchen. Alright, Jackie, I'll admit it, we are very lucky."

Max pours everyone craft beer, which goes perfect with the sandwich. "So, Raven, what is this idea that you came up with?" he asks.

"I would like to set up some sort of foster child program. Young kids get adopted a lot quicker than the older ones. I think if we can give them a safe place to learn, and have Jackie introduce them to working with the horses, they might excel. The money that the government pays us to take care of the kids can go into a fund that we could match, if they keep their grades up. When they turn eighteen, they can use that money for a start in life. It would be a way of giving back. I haven't worked out all the kinks yet, but it's a starting point."

"Scotland's foster care program is complex, but I'm sure we can figure out some way around it. What do you think, babe?"

"Well, I would love to teach more kids on the horses. It really is good therapy for them." She can barely keep her eyes open as she tries to stifle a yawn.

"Jackie, get some rest. Jax and I can clean up here. We have a long day tomorrow."

They leave and we begin clearing the table. I know the housekeepers will do this for us, but I've never been comfortable with that. Just then, Antonia starts to fuss. "Jax, why don't you change her while I get her bottle ready? I'll be up in a few." I smile as I throw the rag I was using in the sink. They leave and I go about getting Antonia's bottle ready so Jax can feed her. Mick comes in, announcing the need for a snack.

"Hey, Mick, how are you feeling?"

"Shouldn't I be asking you that? I'm so sorry about your mom. She was a very brave, kind woman. Very easy to talk, too. I will miss her."

I'm trying not to cry but isn't easy. "In such a short time, she touched so many people."

"What do you need me to do for you?"

"Just keep my family safe. We are leaving for Capri and I need you to be with Antonia twenty-four seven. I trust you with her."

"I promise I will protect her, you don't have to ever worry about that."

I hug him and he no longer pulls back from it. "Thank you. There are some leftover potatoes and eggs, if you want it. Don't worry, I didn't cook it. I need to go feed Antonia before she wakes up the entire house."

I head up the stairs, but then I stop when I hear Dylan and Jeff arguing in the drawing room. Normally, I wouldn't eavesdrop, but after the last few days, I realize, lives are at stake. The argument is confirming what Tony said about Dylan being in financial trouble. I feel so sorry for Jackie. On top of everything we've been through, now she has to deal with this. I head up the stairs reminding myself, *only one more night here.* The sad part is, I used to love coming here. Now, I just want to get as far away as possible.

Maxwell

WE HEAD UPSTAIRS AND she can barely keep her eyes open. She slept a lot today; I hope she's not getting sick. The stress we've been under has taken a toll on all of us. I scoop her up and carry her the rest of the way.

"I can walk; you don't have to carry me."

"Nonsense, it gives me great pleasure to take care of you." She snuggles into me, seemingly too tired to argue.

When we get into our room, I begin to undress her. "You know, I can do this myself."

"I know you can, but I want to feel like I'm doing something, besides it calms me down." I get undressed and climb into bed with her.

"Max, I can't have sex with you in this room . . . it's creepy." I spoon up against her and tuck the covers tight, just the way she likes them.

"I wouldn't dream of it, babe. Besides, you're exhausted and tomorrow is another busy day."

"My body is so tired, but my mind keeps racing. I can't seem to shut it off."

I run my fingertips gently up and down her side, singing Beyoncé's "Halo" softly to help her relax.

"You're everything I need and more." I look down and she is fast asleep.

I could watch her sleep all night long; her golden hair, shimmering in the moonlight.

Yeah, I definitely have my angel now. Oh how true. We just need to get through Capri. I wish Jax wasn't going. I know he's reached his limit, and I fear what he might do if James declines to be tested. We need to be strong and support each other. I haven't seen An and I'm sure she doesn't know we are going. I'm not looking forward to that conversation. At least Bella isn't going, so we might have a shot of getting out of there quickly. Jackie's tossing around in her sleep. Usually, she barely moves. I sing a little more, and she falls back to sleep. I just realized that I gave her the pendant for her birthday but I never gave her the wedding present I got her. I will give it to her first thing, so she can tell Junior all about it.

I close my eyes and try to fall asleep. *Fuck*—tingle. Why? What the hell did I miss? I'm going through all the events in my mind and then, it hits me.

Sometimes something is right in front of you, but you never see it. I shoot a quick text off to Tony with my question. I need to see Jax right now. I text him one word: tingle. Slowly, I wiggle out of bed, not wanting to disturb her sleep. I grab my sweats and race out the door. I find Jax and drag him into the kitchen.

"What the fuck is going on? Can't we have one night of uninterrupted sleep?"

"Trust me, I would love nothing more, but that damn tingle sense kicked in. Look at Tony's last message; it was staring me in the face the whole time."

He pulls out his phone and scrolls through his messages. His eyes look from the screen to mine a couple of times and then it hits him, just like it hit me. "Max, Who?"

I pull up the notes on my phone, not sure if it's safe to talk here. I feverishly begin to type my answer, however, my mind is moving faster than my fingers can.

Yeah, that's my question. Tony is looking to see if there is a connection. Remember what Hage said, Vincent's reach was all over the world. The drug business usually is like that. What if he was in business with Vincent?

Raven said that Dylan and Jeff were arguing about money when she came up to bed.

Seconds seem like hours as we wait for Tony to get back with us. "Jax, I don't feel comfortable not having one of us stay at the hospital tomorrow."

"Then maybe you should listen to me and stop arguing all the fucking time. Let me handle this. I promise you, I will not kill him . . . only because we might need him."

Tony's message finally comes through.

Tony: I went as far back as I could find, which was early into Gerhard's career. There is no connection between them. Dylan dealt with Yakuza only. Jeff Gerhard has never had any connection to the Giaconna family. The Yakuza make Vincent look like a pussycat. It looks like Gerhard made a payment, but they want more. I don't see this ending well for them. I suggest you tighten security around Jackie.

"Well, that settles it, you are staying here. I'm going alone. Don't argue with me on this, please."

"Okay, Jax, I agree with you; one of us needs to stay here. You must stay in touch with me the entire time. Better yet, I'm going to have you wear a wire."

"I'm not wearing a fucking wire. Go to bed, tomorrow is going to be a long day and I'm not looking forward to telling Mum what is going on."

"Either way, you know we will both get in trouble with her. Try and get some rest, I'll see you in a few hours."

I quickly head back to Jackie's old room. I need to be with her, even if it's just to hold her. She comforts me without even trying. Hopefully she didn't wake up while I was gone.

Jackie

THE SUNSHINE IS PEAKING through the curtains and Max has a grip around my waist. I tilt my head up and he's smiling at me. I should have known; *this man never sleeps.* "Good morning, how long have you been up?"

"Not that long. I've been waiting for you to wake up. I have a present for you."

"For me, why?"

"Well, I got it for our wedding, but in all the confusion, I forgot to give it to you."

He pulls an envelope off of the side table and hands it to me. He has the most joyful smile on his face and I know this must mean a lot to him. I open it up and inside is an official certificate from Lamborghini stating that a purple Lamborghini Huracán GT3 is being custom made for me! "Oh my God! No way. Oh my God! Really? You really did this? A real car and not the golf cart?"

"Yes, I really did this, and yes, a real car, not the golf cart. You have to promise me you will be careful."

"Oh my God! I'm speechless; a real purple car!" I guess now might be a good time to make a huge confession.

"Max, I have to tell you something and you have to promise me that you will not blow a gasket. You have to swear, Max."

"Okay, what's the problem?"

"I don't have a driver's license."

"What do you mean, you don't have one? You mean a current one or one for Scotland?"

"Like . . . I never had one in my life."

"Wait, how can that be? I've never met anyone who didn't have their license. Do you even know how to drive?"

"Of course I know how! Sammy showed me in case there was ever an emergency and I needed to drive to safety. I never had the need for a license, since I was driven everywhere by security. Then, when I moved to New York, I took trains and cabs. Will you teach me the right way to drive?"

"Well, I guess so, since you're getting a purple car and I have no intention of driving it."

I leap out of bed, clutching my certificate. I can't wait to show everyone. "Oh, Max, my very first car and it's purple!"

"Come on, babe, we need to get ready. I can't believe you don't have a license." He shakes his head.

We go about getting ready and I can't think of anything else but my gift. I watch him shave as I finish side braiding my hair. "You are very handsome."

"You're just telling me that because I bought you a purple Lamborghini."

I whip his towel off from around his waist and smack his beautifully sculptured ass. "Oh, trust me, it's a lot more than the car. Hurry up and finish. I can't wait to tell everyone."

We finish up and quickly head downstairs. I can barely contain my excitement. Everyone is gathered in the dining room for breakfast. I notice my brother is absent, which is good. I don't think I can deal with him today. Everyone is lost in their conversations and I just want to shout from the rooftops. "Excuse me, everyone, I have a very important announcement to make." The room falls silent.

"Max ordered me my very own purple Lamborghini!" Why is no one saying anything? I'm so excited and they are acting like it's no big deal. "Excuse me, did everyone hear me? My very own car and it's purple!"

Raven starts laughing, "You know you need a license, right?"

"Yes, and Max is going to teach me."

Jax finally stops laughing, "Jackie, I only ask one thing of you, please take a picture of Max driving a purple Lamborghini for me."

The two of them start bickering back and forth until An pulls Max's ear. "Ouch, what was that for?"

"Jackie, am I to understand that you've never had a license?"

"I never had the need for one until now."

"Well, it's settled then. I will be the one to teach you how to drive."

Jax drops his fork and Max almost chokes on his coffee.

"Why do you get to teach her? Jax and I are both capable."

"Jax has no patience, and you taught Bella how to drive; need I say anything more?"

"She has a point, mate."

"It's not my fault that she has no coordination."

They continue bickering throughout breakfast; I'm too excited and hungry to care. Besides, we need to get to the clinic. We finish up and head out to the waiting cars.

Jaxson

WE PULL UP TO the clinic and the security that Tony arranged is waiting for us. "Before we go inside, let's head into the garden area to talk." I point in the general direction.

Mick checks the area to make sure it's clear, and we all have a seat. "I can't get into details, but we will be moving into a private location this afternoon. Everything is already arranged and I need everyone to give your tablets to Mick. He will ship them to Tony. There are new ones at the house waiting for you. It's just a precaution; everything is fine. Junior's set up here is like a two bedroom apartment, so Bella and Michael have decided to live here. When Junior is not having treatments, he will be at the house with us. I will be leaving in a few hours for Capri—alone. Max will be staying here with everyone. I will not be gone very long; for all we know, he might not even be a match. Junior knows about Rose, I told him last night. As you can imagine, he took it very hard. We need to stay upbeat and positive for him."

Jackie's upset, apparently Max never told her about the change of plans. "Jax, why are we staying behind?"

"Jackie, I need to know that Antonia is safe. I also need to make the arrangements for Junior. I trust my brother; I know that my family will be safe."

My mum is not saying a word but she is giving me that look; it's never a good thing. "Come on, everyone, we need to see Junior before his next chemo treatment." I don't give them time for any more questions. I hurry up and head into the clinic.

When we get into Junior's room, it looks like a toy store explosion. He is so happy to see everyone. He is going on and on about all the stuff that showed up in the middle of the night. I take Bella by the hand and go outside.

"What's wrong, bro?"

I give her the quick rundown on the move and then tell her I'm leaving.

"By yourself? Why?"

"Safety reasons' I need Max here with everyone. It's quick and easy if I go alone. Don't worry, I will be safe. I promise to touch base when I get there and when I leave. Now, I need to talk to Raven before I leave."

"Be safe. I love you."

"I love you too, sis." We head back in the room and Jackie is telling Junior all about her purple car. Poor Max, he is going to have his hands full with her. I lean down and whisper in Raven's ear. "Step outside."

"You're leaving, aren't you? Will you reconsider and let me go with you?"

"No. I love you; please don't make this harder on me. I promise I will come back to you. Take care of Antonia and watch over Junior." I close my eyes and try to keep it together. If I see a single tear from her, I'll lose it. I kiss her, turn around, and run out before I change my mind.

Chapter Twenty-Six

I HEAD TO THE airport with my heart breaking. Having to leave my wife and daughter behind is killing me, but I have no choice. If there is a possible threat to my family, then the only person I would ever trust is Max. I need to do this for Junior. No matter what, I am determined to get this done and over with. The crew is getting ready to close up the cabin, but there is a commotion just outside the door. I hear her threatening everyone from the pilot to the guards . . . my mother.

"Jaxson James Phillips, you might as well let me on here. You will not be leaving here without me."

She barrels her way past the guard and onto the plane. "How did you even know where I was?"

"Your sister can't lie her way out of a wet paper bag. There is no way you are doing this alone. Now, let's get going; the sooner we get there, the sooner we get back."

Mick comes racing in the door, his hands tied together with ropes. "Jax, do you see what she did? An, you can't tie me up and run away. I'm here for your safety, this is not a game! How did you even learn to make these knots?"

"My father worked on the docks, you would be surprised what he taught me. I'm sorry, but my son needed me."

"Mum, get him out of those knots and then both of you buckle up; we need to leave. Oh and how the hell did you get away from Max?"

"You know when I put my mind to something, there is no stopping me. I assure you, the only thing that's hurt is probably his pride."

She makes quick work of the ropes, and they both buckle up. "Jax, I swear she just doesn't listen. She is going to be the death of me."

"Yeah, Mick, welcome to my world. It's a quick flight, so we shouldn't be too long. Any sign of trouble, you are to get her out of there. I don't care if you have to throw her over your shoulder—you protect her, no matter what." I close my eyes and reel in my temper. God only knows what she did to Max.

James

Present Time

NO MATTER HOW MUCH I try to wipe the images from my mind, I never can. This is my daily cross to bear. I open my eyes and Reynolds is still standing there, waiting for me to make a decision.

"So if we are not running, sir, then, what exactly are we going to do?"

"I am going to wait right here and face the music. You are free to go."

"Sir, we have been together all these years. Besides, I have no place to go."

The doorbell rings. Reynolds leaves, closing the door behind him. Old habits die hard. I get up and look out the window. The view from here always takes my breath away. There is a light tap on the door.

"Come in, Reynolds."

"Sir, your guests have arrived."

I turn around and in walks An with Jaxson and a man I've never seen before. He appears to be a bodyguard. "An, you look beautiful. I wasn't expecting to ever see you again."

"Who were you expecting to see, James?"

"The rest of my children; you must be Jaxson." I extend my hand out but he doesn't take it. "Where are Maxwell and Isabella?"

"This is not a social visit. My grandson is undergoing cancer treatment. He needs stem cells and we haven't found a match. You need to be tested to see if you are a close enough match."

"Always the bossy one, An. Would you like a drink?"

"A drink? James, please, for once in your life, please, do the right thing. He's your grandson; you already let one boy die, are you going to let another one?"

"Have a seat, everyone. Please, I have some questions." I'm watching Jax and he is wound up real tight, to the point, he could be dangerous.

"Tell me about the boy."

"My grandson is nine years old, very smart with a heart of gold. What else do you want to know? What do I need to tell you to make you have some compassion?"

"So he is Isabella's son from when she was raped." Her eyes grow wide, shocked that I know.

"I have followed all my children's lives; some of them I'm a part of and some of them I chose to stay away." I'm watching Jax's eyes as I tell my story and, there it is—I hit a nerve with him. He leaps out of the chair so fast, I don't have a chance to defend myself. His hands are around my throat, and the body guard steps forward, trying to pull him back.

"You *chose* to stay away? Did you choose to let your grandson and daughter-in-law be slaughtered in the street? Do you care that Cindy killed herself because of you? You've left nothing but destruction and mayhem in your path, and for what, money? Is money that fucking important to you? If it's money that you want, I will give you one million dollars in cash to be tested. If you're a match and you donate, I will give you an additional fifty million in cash. Does that make you happy?"

He finally lets go of my throat and I'm able to talk. "Maybe you should let me explain before you go off half-cocked, son."

"Son? Don't even think you can call me that. You are nothing but a sperm donor. My mum wore both hats; she carried the load for both parents. You are nothing to me."

"An, if you want me to explain, I will . . . but you need to calm him down."

"Jax, please let him explain, and then we can leave."

I'll say one thing, no matter how much of a hot head he is, he listens to her.

"Do you really want him here when I explain everything?"

He sits back down next to her. "I'm not leaving, so deal with it." She doesn't seem to mind if he knows all the details, so why should I?

"Have it your way. An, you were so young when I met you and I never expected to fall in love. I had a great set up with Cindy; she let me have my space. I'm sure, by now, you've figured out that the trinkets I gave you were stolen. You remember that day we took the train and met up with my friends?"

"How could I forget, I was very pregnant with Jax. I wanted to stay home, but you insisted that I had to go with you. That was the day I took that picture."

"That picture was like the start of a bad dominos game. Miguel was very upset over that picture. It's one of the few pictures of him in existence. He was also upset that I left you with those trinkets."

"You pulled him into that picture. It was very clear he didn't want any part of it."

"He is the reason I was in that hospital the day we met. He was a violent, vicious man."

"If you knew this then why did you hang out with him?"

"He was family, my cousin through marriage. We went into business together; I was the thief and he was the fence. Women flocked to me, making it easy for me to steal from them. They were always married, so they never wanted to press charges. Then you came along and I got caught up in a whirlwind romance. When you told me you were pregnant, I panicked. I was already married, but your father's friends really didn't give me a way out. I figured I could somehow juggle you and Cindy, but then you became pregnant again. I realized I was in too deep, so I walked away. I felt it was best for everyone. You were young and pretty; you would find someone. I told Cindy everything in hopes that she would forgive me. Honestly, I would have stayed with her and continued doing what I was doing, but she finally stood up to me and said she had enough. She said her son deserved better. I don't believe she killed herself. I think her overdose was accidental. Then again, maybe that is wishful thinking."

"Let me get this straight," Jax speaks up. "You thought it would be okay to stay with Cindy and continue to steal from other women, pretending to love and want to be with them? You thought it was fine to toss *my* mum and *your* children aside for money? What kind of sick monster are you?"

"If you are done criticizing my choices, I will continue."

He waves his hand, "Oh, please go on, the sooner you finish, the sooner we are out of here."

"After Cindy died, I went to Miguel and told him I wanted out. I thought I could take Maxwell and beg you to forgive me. Miguel had other plans for me. It was always one more job. He was always threatening me with one thing or another. He threatened to hurt Isabella if I didn't get that picture back from you. I convinced him I destroyed everything before I left you. Going back to you would have put you in even more danger. The best thing you did was move to the States. Maxwell was living with his grams. I continued to work with Miguel, but then he got into drug dealing. That's when his business took off. He couldn't get the drugs cut and sent out fast enough. Money was coming in so quickly and he needed to turn it as fast as possible. At one point, he had storage units filled with cash, waiting to get back into circulation. At that point, I wasn't sleeping with women and stealing their jewels, I was laundering drug money." I pour myself a scotch, feeling the knot in my stomach. I know this is the part they want to know, the hardest part for me to relive.

"More time passed and then Maxwell joined the police force. Of all the things he could have become, he chose the worst possible thing. Miguel flipped out; he wanted me to do something. He wanted me to turn him, but I knew there was no way that would ever happen. The threats went back and forth until I got wind of what he was planning to do. I raced to the park that day, but I was too late—they were dead. I was there when Maxwell showed up. I saw my son fall apart that day; watched silently as his world crumbled around him. At that moment, I knew there was no redemption for me. Miguel went into hiding, and surrounded himself with layers upon layers of very bad men. It took years, but I finally found Miguel; he paid for what he did. However, the damage was already done. I will live with their blood on my hands for the rest of my life."

"Was Miguel responsible for my daughter's rape?" She was always too smart for her own good.

"I could never prove it, but I had my suspicions. "

"I've listened to your story, now will you be tested?"

"Will you let me see the boy?"

"Will you be tested?"

I go to the desk and get out the test results. "I've already been tested and the information has been sent to his doctors. I don't want your money, Jax. I want to see the boy, will you let me?"

Jax leaps up but An takes his arm. "Jax, please let me handle this."

"James, I have to do what is best for my grandson. Learning about you and what you've done will not be in his best interest. He needs to stay focused and positive on his recovery. He just lost someone very close to him. I don't think he can take anymore."

I know I won't get anywhere with her. Once her mind is made up, there is no changing it. Maybe I can get through to Jax.

"Jax, as you know, you also have three brothers that you've had some business dealings with. I contacted them and they have all been tested. The results have been sent to the doctors. I'm not the bad guy here. I want to help."

"If you're a match, will you donate?"

"Of course I will. All I want is to meet the boy."

"My work here is done. Come on, Mum, let's go."

He gets up to leave. "That's it? Not even a thank you?"

"You want me to thank you?! Have you lost your fucking mind? I hate you! I'm not here for your approval or to make friends with you. You have no fucking clue what you've done; all in the name of the almighty buck. I was a little boy when you left. I had no one. I had a mum and sister to protect. I never had a normal childhood. I was too busy doing your job so you could go out and fuck the world. Well, I hope it was worth it. Oh and while were on the subject, if you come anywhere near my family, I will fucking kill you. Stay away from all of us; you've done more than enough. Come on, Mum, we are leaving *now!*"

I watch them leave and Reynolds comes back in. "Sir, did you tell them you're a match?"

"No, let them digest everything I told them. I'm sure they will be back again when they find out."

Jaxson

WHAT THE FUCK IS this man thinking? Like I would ever let him see Junior. I've got the papers clutched in my hand but I don't need to look at them, I already know what they will say. It's like a chess board that I'm looking down on. Of course he knew we were coming; he was expecting it. He's been watching all of us for a long time. How much did he know? Did he know about Raven, her kidnapping? Did he know where she was for three months, while I was going out of my mind searching for her? The more I think about all the pieces to this game, the more pissed off I get. He's a match and he will use it for leverage to see Junior. Bella will let him if it means her son will survive; what parent wouldn't? The problem is, once he gets his foot in the door, there's no turning back. He'll be like a cancer, leaving death and destruction in his wake.

We board the jet and everyone is very quiet. I'm glad Mick is here to take care of Mum. I can't even begin to understand what she is feeling right now.

"Jax, is he a match?"

"Of course he is. Why do you think he made it so easy to see him? He wants Junior for his redemption. What he doesn't get is that there is no redemption for him. He will go to hell with Cindy, Samantha, Elliott, and God knows how many others' blood on his hands. All those lives destroyed for what—money? How is that worth anything?"

"So, what do we do?"

"What we always do, Mum; we survive."

I turn my phone on and there is a message from Max.

Max: So help me God, when she gets back here, there will be hell to pay. Is everything okay?

Jax: Everything is fine, he was already tested and he's a match. I will give you all the details when I see you. Should be back in an hour. How is everyone?

Max: Everyone is good. Safe travels.

"Mum, what did you do to Max?" She's picking imaginary lint off of her pants, it must be bad.

"He's a stubborn man and when I told him where I was going, he was yelling. You know I don't like when he gets upset. I went to the ladies room and climbed out the window." I know I must have a shocked look on my face. Part of me wants to yell and the other part can't help but laugh.

"Oh please, Mum, don't stop there. Go on, I really need to hear the rest of this."

"I got outside and the Gardner was there. He was very gracious and offered to drive me to the airport. I saw that Mick was following us, so I asked the man for some of his rope. When I got to the airport, I thanked the man and got out. Mick pulled up and was demanding I get in the car. Rather than make a scene I did."

"So when did the ropes come into play?"

"I held Mick's hands and pretended I was crying. I leaned against his chest and tied his hands to the shift stick. I jumped out of the car and ran. There, now you know the whole story. I'm not proud of it, but I had to do this. I needed to understand why."

"And do you? Was it worth it?"

"As a matter of fact, yes, it was worth it. It confirmed what I knew all along, I was a fool. He made me believe I was the great love of his life. I know now that he is a con artist and I was a pawn in his games. I also learned that I'm so much better off without him. I learned that while I was pining away for an unrealistic love, he was using people. I learned that no matter how much I despise the man, he still gave me the greatest gift of all, my children. For that, I will always be thankful to the man."

"I like to believe we are who we are because of the person who raised us and not who donated their sperm; nature versus nurture." I put my seat back and rub my temples, trying to squash the raging headache. "You will have to deal with Max when we get back. Good luck with that."

I close my eyes for the rest of the flight. I don't think I can handle anything more without saying something I might end up regretting later. I need to mentally prepare myself for the next hurdle, dealing with Bella.

Maxwell

I'M PACING AND I swear, if Jax doesn't get back soon, I will wear a hole in the floor. What the hell was she thinking?! Climbing out the bloody window like some sort of teenager! Why the hell did Mick let her get on that plane? I love her, I respect her, and hell, at times, I even fear her but right now, I want to tear into her.

Jackie takes my hand and squeezes it, pulling me toward her. She kisses me. "Max, I know you're upset but you might want to try and relax a little before you see her. She did what she felt she had to do, granted, it was a little extreme, however, it's done and she's safe. If you flip out on her, you will hate yourself for it later."

"I know you're right, but why does she continue to do things that will upset me?"

"No one is perfect and neither is the world we live in. Free will doesn't always mean people will make the right choices."

I rest my forehead on hers and close my eyes. She calms me like no one else can. "You're smart *and* beautiful; I'm so lucky."

"I'm also hungry . . . very hungry, actually. I ordered lunch for everyone, it should be here shortly. You need to eat something, and try to calm down before they get here."

"No such luck, babe, they're here," I announce as I watch them walk through the entrance. I'm holding her so tight, I'm afraid I might break her.

Before I can say a word, Mum walks up to me and wraps her arms around Jackie and me, damn it!

"I'm sorry, Maxwell, I know what I did was wrong. I should have told you my intentions, however, in my defense, you never would have gone along with it. I know it was foolish and reckless, but I needed to do it."

"I really want to yell at you right now, but I know it won't change anything. It's over, but never again, in my lifetime, will you ever pull such a crazy arse stunt."

She yanks my ear. "Language, please. I promise I will try not to."

"Mick, you have a lot of explaining to do, like how the hell did you let her get that far?"

He's about to explain when Jax stops him. "In Mick's defense, Mum tied him to the stick shift in his car. You've seen her when she is determined, Mate, there is no stopping her."

Jackie starts laughing so hard, she can barely catch her breath. "Oh my God, I can't believe she tied you up!" She says as she watches the food being wheeled in. "The lunch I ordered is here. Come on and tell me all about it. After lunch, Michael has a treatment; you can tell us what happened with James."

Everyone heads into Junior's room but Jax and I stay back. "Okay, what the hell went down?" Before he can answer, Mick comes out of the room.

"Here's my cell phone; I recorded everything for you. I knew you would be overwhelmed."

"Thank you. Mick, Can you make some excuse for us while we go listen to this, please?"

"Sure, Max, I'll take care of it."

"Come on Jax, let's grab a cup of coffee."

We head into the lounge and I don't think I've seen Jax this bad since Raven was kidnapped. I'm almost afraid to listen to the recording.

"Max, are you sure you want to hear this? He talks about everything, even your mum."

"Yeah, I don't see that I have a choice." He gets up and walks over to the window while I hit play. I have to stop it a few times to catch my breath. To hear him talk about my mum, so cavalier like, makes me sick. When I get to the part about my family, I know I won't be able to be in the same room with him; I'll kill him with my bare hands. He was there; he knew what was going to happen. He never called the police, hell—he could have called me. I was five fucking minutes from that park. I close my eyes and try to gain some composure to finish listening. Being a match, I know he wants to come swooping in at the end, like a white knight, saving the day. This isn't a fucking fairytale, he doesn't get to ride into the sunset and all is forgiven. I don't even hear Jax come back to the table.

"Max, what are we going to do? I have the paperwork; he's a ninety-seven percent match. I think the only way he's going to donate is if we let him meet Junior. Our other three brothers aren't a match. I can run with this if you want, but I need to know what you want to do. Max, are you listening to me?"

"He was there, Jax . . . in the park. He knew and he could have stopped it. He's the reason I never found Miguel. Was my mum's death really an accident? I can't see him. I'm barely hanging on as it is. I think if I do, I will snap."

"Well, ultimately, it has to be Bella's decision. But, if it were Elliot that needed to be saved, you would do whatever you had to. How do you think she is going to react when she finds out about the rape?"

"He said Miguel was a cousin by marriage but there is no record of that. If I were Bella, it would make me sick to think that the rape could have been some sort of warning for James. No matter what happens, Jax, we need the stem cells. I will not have Jackie or Mrs. Olsa anywhere near him. He breeds death and destruction."

"Bella needs to listen to this recording. I will be with her when she does. I don't expect you to listen to it again. I won't have my family anywhere near him, either."

"She's my sister too, and I need to be there for her. I'll be okay . . . I have to be."

"Come on, let's get back before they send out a search party for us. I still can't believe Mum ditched you and climbed out the bathroom window."

"Not funny, Jax, and what's up with her and Mick?"

"I'm choosing to not go there. Sometimes, in life, ignorance really is bliss."

We head into Junior's room, ready as I'll ever be, to face what I know are going to be some very difficult times ahead.

Chapter Twenty-Seven

Jaxson

WE HEAD INTO JUNIOR'S room and seeing him laughing and playing puts everything into perspective. I know I have to do this for him. Antonia is sitting in her baby recliner, laughing and kicking her feet, not a care in the world; as life should be. I feel her arms wrap around my waist and it's a comfort, it's home.

"I'm glad you made it back safe, I was worried."

"I was never in danger, sweetheart, only James was. We got what we needed. He's a perfect match and will be donating stem cells."

"At what price, Jax?"

I turn around so I can see her eyes, they ground me. "What makes you ask that?"

"Any man, who could do the things he has done, would never do a kind act without wanting something. So what price are we going to have to pay?"

"He wants to meet Junior." I can barely get the words out, my stomach in knots at the sheer thought of it.

"Oh."

"Yeah, oh. Mick recorded everything, which I'm glad he thought to do. Max already listened to it, but Bella still has to. In the end, she will have to go along with it. Sometimes, in life, there really is no choice. When the day comes that they have to meet, I don't want you or Antonia anywhere near here. Please don't fight me on this, allow me a little peace of mind . . . please."

"Okay, I can do that. Why don't you go spend some time with Michael? Tony sent him something very special that he's been bursting to tell you about."

I make my way further into the room and Junior sees me. He comes running and leaps into my arms. "Hey, guess you're excited to see me."

"Oh, you are not going to believe what Tony sent! Hurry up, I have to show you. He designed a gaming system and he wants me to test it out for him. And guess what, Uncle Jax, the very first game he made is a *Doctor Who* game. It's so cool! I know it's going to be a big hit." I put him down and he's still going on and on about the wonders of the game. It doesn't matter who Junior's real father is, it's the love and nurturing that's made him the fantastic kid he is.

"Uncle Jax, are you okay?"

"Yeah, now let's see what this bad boy can do."

Isabella

JAX MADE IT BACK okay but he looks really bad, I'm worried. What if Dad isn't a match or what if he won't agree to be tested, what will I do? Playing with Michael always seems to bring him back to life.

Max puts his arm around my waist and kisses may forehead. "Bella, let's go get a cup of tea." He says low enough so only I can hear.

"Are you going to be delivering bad news?" He doesn't say anything as we head to the cafe.

"First, I will tell you the good news is our father is a perfect match. He has agreed to the donation. The paperwork is being processed now."

"And the bad news? He cocks his head, lifts his eyebrows, and tightens his grip around my waist. "Don't look at me like that, Max, we both know he's got to want something."

"Mick recorded the entire conversation. I know that—no matter what—you will do what you have to in order to save Junior. If you don't want to listen to it, you don't have to. The choice is yours," he offers.

"I want to listen to it, but will you stay with me?"

He hands me a headset. "I will, if you put these on. I don't know that I can listen to it ever again."

Max gets tea and I know it's that act not the tea that is comforting. I press play. His voice is deep and raspy . . . not what I was expecting. My poor mum having to listen to him, reminding her of her naivety. I understand why Max can't listen to this again. He could have saved them. "Ah" I gasp and drop my cup, my whole body begins to shake. Max races over and pulls the headset off.

"Shh, I've got you."

"M-max, could it be I was raped because of him? He wants to meet my son. That's the price I have to pay? He's a sick and twisted person." He lifts me up and carries me out of the cafe. I can't stop shaking. What kind of person would ever let their child go through what I did? If he knew Miguel was that crazy, why didn't he protect his family? Instead, it's like he threw us to the wolves. Oh dear God, how can I do this?

I finally stop shaking. I open my eyes, but it's dark and I have no clue where I am. I only know that I'm in Max's arms and he's rocking me like a child.

"Were are we?"

"A quiet room off the solarium; you're safe."

"How am I going to do this? I have no choice, I know that, but . . . how can I look at him? Why does it have to be him who can save my son?"

"Bella, look at me. Jax and I will be with you the entire time. We will explain to Junior what is going on. We will get through this, and then, we never have to see him again. Meeting Junior is not going to give him redemption. In his eyes, he's doing something good. But, one good act doesn't erase all the bad. When you do something good for someone, you do it because you want to, with no ulterior motives. He will always be damned to hell and nothing he does will ever change that."

"What about you? Are you going to be able to do this without killing him?"

"I will do whatever I have to for my nephew and if it means I have to deal with him, then so be it. We need to get back before we are missed. Are you ready?"

I get up and wipe my face as best I can. "I am a very lucky girl to have two of the best brothers in the world."

"Jax and I want to tell him in the morning, if that's okay with you."

"That's fine. So what happened that everyone moved out of Mr. Gerhard's home very quickly?"

"Can't get nothing past you, can I?"

"Nope, eventually I find out everything. I'm worse than Mum."

"Dylan came back and was causing a scene. The whole thing didn't feel right. Then we found out that he is in financial trouble and dealing with some shady characters. Best to be in our own place. Besides, that was just a place to regroup after fleeing the States."

We step back into the room and find Jax and Michael asleep with the remotes in their hands. Raven comes up and gives me a hug. "Are you okay, Bella?"

"Yeah, I will be. I see they are out cold. I can't tell you how many nights I've found them like that. If you take the remote out of Jax's hand, he will wake right up." I walk over, take the remote, and just like always . . ."Bella, I'm playing."

"Jax, go home; everyone is tired. I promise you can come back tomorrow and play again."

Everyone makes their goodbyes. Now I have to explain everything to my husband. I'm not looking forward to this conversation. Once again, I have no choice.

I crawl onto Michael's lap and begin to tell him everything. He surprises me by remaining calm and agreeing to everything. "What happened? Why are you so calm?"

"I told you, I would do whatever I had to do to save my son."

"What about your parents? Are you still going to have them meet Michael?"

"Yes, it's time, Bella. I am willing to let them try. In the end, it's my son's decision if he wants a relationship with them."

I snuggle into him, "You are such a kind man. I love you."

"Ti amo più della vita stessa e amerò sempre."

"It sounds beautiful, whatever it means."

"Oh, Bella, someday you will learn my language. I said, I love you more than life itself, and I always will."

Raven

WE FINALLY GET TO the estate and it's extremely secluded, even more so than the Gerhard compound. Electric fence and armed guards; God only knows what the house is like. Jax has his head on my shoulder and he is asleep. He hasn't given me any details of what happened today only that James is a match. I can't believe that An climbed out the bathroom window. She is always surprising me, but she probably knew that was the only way she would get to go.

"Jax, wake up; were here." He opens his eyes and throws his arms around me.

"Hey, we're safe. I'm here." My heart is breaking for him. God only knows what went down today. It's eating him up inside.

He grabs Antonia's carrier and we all head inside. The place is huge and fully staffed, something I'm never comfortable with. Max is already going over all the details with the head of security. Mrs. Osla must be able to tell that I'm at a loss here. She takes out a chart and begins assigning rooms.

"Thank you, Mrs. Osla, we would be very lost without you." She doesn't take compliments well and shoos me away.

"Jax, I'm going to get Antonia ready for bed, and then I'm going to soak in the tub. When you're done here, please join me."

"Of course, I'll be up in a minute. I want to go over some stuff with Max before we turn in."

Jaxson

MRS. OSLA DIRECTS EVERYONE to their rooms while I drag Max into the den. "Okay, what happened with Bella? I wanted to be there when she heard the recording."

"You can't be everywhere, Jax. You were gone for a good portion of the day and Junior really wanted to spend some time with you. I stayed with Bella the whole time. She was destroyed to find out about the rape. In the end, she knows she has to let him meet Junior. She wants it to be very quick and she was going to explain everything to Michael tonight. She also wants you and me there when she tells Junior about James."

"I'm not sure the kid can take much more. Rose's death hit him really hard. Michael's family will be coming sometime soon. Not only will he be meeting them for the first time but also James. You know how important state of mind is; I'm worried."

"I understand what you're saying, but we don't have a choice. James attached a condition on giving the stem cells. Granted he didn't say he would withhold them, but after listening to that recording, there is no doubt in my mind that is his intention."

"Maybe we can get him in and out very quickly. Do we know how long the procedure is?"

"I spoke to the doctor and he said they do two different procedures. The one like Jackie had where then remove the stem cells from the bone marrow in the hip. The other is a procedure called peripheral blood stem cell donation. The donor is given injections of Filgrastim to aid in cell reproduction. He said he uses both, especially after chemo. From the sound of it, I don't think it's a quick thing. Look, whatever it is, we will have to deal with it."

"How the hell are we going to do this without losing it? You don't know how hard it was."

"Mick told me you had him around the throat. You're a better man than me; I would have snapped his neck."

"That's my point, Max. How the fuck are we going to do this? I think I've spent what little control I had. You're talking about being around him for days. I don't want my family around him at all. I think his meeting with Junior should be hi and goodbye."

"That's not realistic. What will you do if Junior says he wants to get to know him, have you thought about that?"

"Get to know him?! Have you lost your bloody mind?"

"He's a nine-year-old boy who knows nothing about James or anything that he's done. All he knows is what he's been told; keep that in mind."

"I'll negotiate with Junior, he will listen to me."

"Look, it's been a long, emotional day, let's get some sleep and we can deal with this in the morning."

"Okay, except I have no clue where my room is, so lead the way." He's right, it's been a long day and the only thing I'm looking forward to right now is getting lost within my beautiful wife.

Raven

I HOPE JAX WON'T be too long. When he's with Max, they tend to lose track of time. I like this house. Tony did a good job of finding it and getting everything set up so quickly. We have access to Antonia's room right through ours, which is perfect. Hopefully, this will be our last move for quiet some time. I peak in her crib; I could watch her sleep all night long but I want to get the tub set up for Jax. He's had two emotional days back to back and he needs to unwind. I go about setting everything up when I hear him come in. My God, he looks like a beaten man. My heart is breaking for him.

"Jax, let me take care of you tonight, please. We will have a nice soak in this beautiful tub, and you can just close out the world for awhile."

"That sounds good to me. I really need to be alone with you."

I pour him a glass of wine, and then help him get undressed. "Climb in and I will sit behind you so I can massage your shoulders."

"Wow, take-charge-Raven is here tonight. It's okay; I need her to help me forget my horrific day."

"Is that your way of telling me you don't want to talk about it?"

"Part of me wants to yell and punch something and the other part of me wants to close my eyes and forget this whole week has ever happened," he groans. I keep massaging his neck and shoulders. I know if I wait long enough, he will tell me everything.

"When Bella came back with Max, she was very upset. You were sleeping, but do you know what happened?"

"Yeah, she listened to the recording."

"What recording?"

He takes in a deep breath, and then tells me about Mick recording the whole confrontation with his father. Both Max and Bella have listened to it. "How bad was it?"

"Bad, sweetheart, really bad." He leans his head back and continues to tell me what happened. He admitted a lot of stuff that made it seem like he just used my mum and Cindy. He thought Cindy's death was accidental. Then he wanted to take Max and hook back up with my mum but she was already in the States. Apparently that photograph with the four men was a bone of contention for Miguel who by the way is James's cousin."

"Ah, no Max is related to the man that killed his family?"

"He's a cousin through marriage. When Max became a cop, Miguel wanted our father to turn him. When he couldn't, he killed Samantha and Elliot. Our father was in the park that day and knew what was going to happen. He could have stopped it and he didn't."

"Oh, how sick is that?"

"Wait, there's more. He believes that Miguel was behind Bella's rape."

"That's why she was so upset. Bella knows this now. Oh, how sad. All these years she blamed herself, like she did something wrong, but, in essence, it was all planed."

"You want to know what the kicker is? He is a perfect match for Junior. I offered him fifty-million dollars in cash for his donation, but the only thing he wants is to meet Junior. Bella has no choice; she's going to have to do it. I'm telling you now, Raven, I don't want you or Antonia anywhere near my father."

I pull him tightly up against my chest. "I have no desire to ever meet James and he will never get near our daughter. I'm worried about Michael Jr., though. I don't know how much more that boy can take. Bella told me that Michael's parents are also being tested and want to finally meet their grandson. This is an awful lot for a nine-year-old to deal with."

"Max told me tonight about Michael's parents. I give Michael a lot of credit. I don't know that I could be as strong as he is. When he told his parents what happened to Bella and that he was marrying her, they said some pretty harsh stuff. They weren't dating very long and I admire him for his choices. I was prepared to take care of her and Junior for the rest of my life. I told you that Max was part owner of Raiders, but what I didn't tell you is that Junior owned a higher percentage than Max. It's all in a trust for him. He has no clue, but if he never wanted to work a day in his life, he wouldn't have to. The only person who knows about it is Max and now, you. Not even Bella knows. I never wanted money to get in the way of their lives."

"Why didn't you tell Bella?"

"Can you imagine the creeps that would have come out of the woodwork if they knew that a single mum has a son who's worth a fortune? Michael came to me when Bella was about seven months pregnant and asked for her hand in marriage. I told him no and sent him away. The next day, Bella came to me crying and begged me for my blessing. Again, I said no. So, she said she would get married without it. The fight was huge and finally, my mum sat the three of us in a room to hash it out. I offered to pay Michael to go away."

"Wow, I know you can be tough, but that was very harsh."

"Maybe, but there was a lot at stake and I'm not talking about money. Whomever she chose would be around Junior and that was my sticking point. I didn't doubt that he loved her, he showed her in so many ways. I had blinders on when it came to the baby. Finally, I agreed to the wedding, but there were certain things that had to happen. A prenup had to be in place. He had to agree that the baby would be brought up Catholic. He had to agree that if they split up, he would have no legal rights to the child. He had to agree to it all before I would say yes. His parents said if he married her, they would disown him. They said Bella was using him for his name and for money. He walked away from his family, and they got married. Then Bella had major complications with her pregnancy. It was so bad that, at one point, we called in a priest. She's tough and pulled through, but she can't have any more children. Michael stood beside her the entire time, even though he knew he would never have a child of his own. I admire him for that more than I could ever explain."

"I didn't know that she went through all of that, she never really talked about her pregnancy. I wonder why Michael is forgiving his parents now."

"Max and I tease Michael all the time, telling him that he is up for sainthood being married to Bella. In reality, he is a very kind man and maybe after all of this, he realizes, like the rest of us, that life is short, and it can change on a dime."

"Do you feel like you got the answers from James that you were looking for?"

"Actually, yeah, I did. It had nothing to do with me or Bella. He never wanted us; we were his mistake. His attitude made me sick—we had his wonderful DNA and everything we accomplished was because of it. You can imagine how well that went over with me."

"I'm sorry you had to go through all of that, but maybe it's put everything into prospective for you. Now you can believe what I keep telling you, that none of it was your fault. You are a good son and brother." I kiss his neck before tapping his shoulder. "Now I think we need to get out of here."

"Thank you. I know life with me can get a little crazy, but I promise I will always love you as fiercely as I did from the first day you doused me with your coffee."

We get out and we wrap each other in the warm towels. "Make love to me, Jax, softly, all night long."

He lifts me up and carries me into the bedroom, climbing into bed while he kisses me. He slowly enters me and stops. He takes my hand and places it on his heart. "I will love you, with all that I am, for the rest of my life. Nothing will ever change that." He kisses me and begins to move slowly at first, but then he flips over so I'm on top, our lips never breaking their connection. His hands on my hips, guiding his every move, I can feel him so deep, with each upward thrust. He's holding back, I know he's there. "Don't hold back, I want it all."

He slows me down and then holds me tightly so I can't move. He begins to tilt his hips back and forth without pulling out. The sensation as he hits my clitoris is so intense, that my whole body begins to tremble. A tingling wave rushes through me like hot lava. As he flips me over, I clench; it's his undoing. His release is so powerful. He tells me he loves me over and over again. When I finally find my wits, I open my eyes and he's smiling. "That was different and intense, are you okay?" He's twirling my hair and still smiling.

"I'm fantastic, sweetheart, I'm in cock heaven." He tilts his hips up and he's ready again.

I can't help but giggle and his smile gets brighter. "Aimez-moi à nouveau avec tout ce que vous avez."

"Oh, dirty talk—French. More . . . *please.*"

"Nothing dirty, Jax, only love. Je espère que nous faisons un bébé ce soir. Je te aime."

I clench his cock and begin to move faster, driving him crazy. Over and over again, he's begging for more. He reaches up and rolls my nipples between his fingertips. My body flushes, my release is so strong and so powerful, my heart skips a beat as I call out his name. I collapse onto his chest and try to come back to earth. He's stroking my back, soothing me. "I hope so, too," he whispers.

Jackie

MAX HAS FINALLY FALLEN asleep but it's not a peaceful one. An told me a little of what happened, but I need to hear it from Max. I wrap my self around him and gently rub his temple, it always seems to help. "I love you so much, and I'm so sorry you have to relive this nightmare. Whatever I have to do to help you, I will."

Whenever he's restless he pulls me tightly against him. His fear comes through more when he's asleep. His eyes open and he pulls me even tighter. "Jackie, oh thank God! I dreamt you were gone."

"I'm safe, Max, but ease up a little, please."

"I'm sorry, did I hurt you?"

"No, tell me what happened yesterday. Bella looked destroyed last night. An said James is a match and he wants to meet Michael. Does this mean that James will be around us?"

"The way the doctor explained it, he does it two different ways. I'm not sure how much time that will take."

"Max, hold on; let me put your mind at ease here. While you were talking with Bella last night, Mrs. Osla and I did some research. James needs to get injections of Filgrastim to aid in cell reproduction. They are usually given over the course of a few days, but he doesn't have to get them here, he just has to get them. The actual procedure is anywhere from two to four hours. It's not a big deal; he's playing upon everyone's emotions. He wants to be the white knight coming in to save the day. Well, guess what?—never going to happen. If he insists he wants to meet Michael, then he gets five minutes and that's it. We are not about to bow down to him."

"Wow, you never cease to amaze me. So, he doesn't need to be here until he has to donate."

"Even the donation can be done elsewhere. Have you thought about what you're going to do? I would rather you weren't around him. I know Mrs. Osla said she can't be anywhere near him."

He's quiet for a bit, playing with my braid. He then tells me about the recording.

"Are you sure he knew?"

"Miguel was his cousin. He wanted my dad to turn me into a bad cop. He knew that he wouldn't be able to, so Miguel was teaching him a lesson." I'm trying to be strong for him, but I can't stop my tears.

"How will everyone be able to face him? Michael needs him, but can our family survive this?"

"What choice do we have? I don't want you, or Mrs. Osla, anywhere near him. I need to know that you're both safe . . . *please.*"

"What about me? I don't want you anywhere near James! But I know you; you'll do whatever you have to do for Michael. How are you going to be in the same room with him? How the hell is Bella going to do it? Why can't we all stand strong together?"

"What are you saying?"

"What I'm suggesting is, when Michael has to meet that bastard, we stand together and make a united front. James needs to see that he can't break us. I hate bullies and we will not be bullied into doing what James wants. We are a strong, loving family and all the DNA means nothing. We did it with love and respect. I'm not running and hiding, none of us are. I'm not letting Michael meet him without all the love and support that child deserves. James might think he has us by the balls, but he doesn't. We have options." I grab my bag off the floor and dig around till I find the box I had in there for him.

"I was waiting to give you this for your birthday, but—here—happy birthday."

He takes the top off and stares into the box. His eyes grow wide and a tear slides down his cheek. I kiss it away. "We always have options, and we always have faith. I love you and we're in this journey together. I never thought it would happen this quickly, but you know that saying: *we make plans and God just laughs,* well I think right about now he's hysterical."

"This is real? You're really pregnant?"

"Oh, it's real all right." He's on me in a second, kissing me so deeply. He pulls away and now he's staring at me.

"How pregnant are you?"

"I was using an app on my phone to track my cycle. I'm only one day late, but you can test up to five days early before a missed period with most home pregnancy tests. I wanted to wait until I was further along before I said anything but, because of everything with Michael, maybe we should discuss it with his doctor. I want to get a blood test done today." I realize he hasn't said a word. "Max, are you okay?" Now he has me worried.

"Okay? I'm in shock, Jackie. You're giving me the gift of life. I'm speechless, and you're like some kind of warrior princess. You're amazing."

"When I took that test, I cried. It's because of Sammy that I was here to even take the test."

"I will always be in debt to him. How do you feel? Are you ill at all?"

"Other than tired and my breast are a little sore, I feel fine."

He gets up and begins pacing. "All right, I can do this. I need to be calm and form a plan. I will talk to Junior's doctor today. I need to find the top OBGYN. I need to make sure she is getting the proper nutrition. I have to triple up security. I need an armor car. Oh. My. God. Jackie you're not driving that Lamborghini!"

"Remember what I told you, I'm not a child or a porcelain doll. Pregnant women drive cars all the time. I will be able to make my own doctor appointments and even feed myself—imagine that."

"Babe, we need to talk. I'm going to be calm here. No bloody way in hell I'm putting you behind the wheel of a powerhouse Lamborghini while you're pregnant, and you don't even have a fucking driver's license! I'll give you the doctor and the food, but you have got to give me the car."

"Do I get the car after the baby comes?"

"Ugh, you are the most stubborn woman I have ever met. You realize this whole car thing happened because you had your knickers around your knees! Fine, after the baby comes, you can have your car."

I leap out of bed and jump into his arms.

"Oh, for the love of all that's holy, no leaping and no jumping about."

"It's going to be a long pregnancy if you keep acting like this. Now, I think you need to feed me." I squish his cheeks with my hands, making his lips pucker. I lay a good one on him, making him chuckle.

"What would you like to eat?" he asks when I pull away.

"While I jump . . . I mean, *walk* into the shower, you can make me a three egg omelet with cheese, tomato, and toast. Please and thank you."

He smacks my ass and I giggle. It reminds me of that day with the car. "Oh, and don't tell anyone without me and, by anyone—I mean Jax. I know you two are joined at the hip, and I want to see the look on his face." I kiss him and race into the bathroom.

The shower is wonderful; four shower heads from every direction. I blast that hot water and climb in. I'm going to be someone's mom, how exciting?! I wish Rose was here; she made me realize that I'm strong and I can do this. I turn around and find Max behind me, totally naked and leaning against the wall. The sight of him takes my breath away. "I thought you were making me breakfast?"

"It won't take me too long. I got as far as the kitchen and then I realized you knew the car wasn't going to be delivered until May. You knew by then you wouldn't be driving, but you love to get me riled up. Look at you . . . biting that lip . . . trying not to laugh. One smack on that beautiful arse and your face lit up." I am so busted. I might as well have a little fun.

"Oh, Max, I've been a bad girl; whatever will you do about it?"

"Get out, dry off, and meet me in the bedroom." I watch him leave and I can barely contain my excitement. I grab a towel and head into the bedroom. He's sitting in the chair, looking unbelievably sexy. His jaw is tight, complimenting the serious look on his face.

"So, you said you've been a bad girl. How bad?" His voice is deep and my skin begins to prickle.

"Pretty bad; you might have to discipline me."

"Drop the towel."

I follow his command, trying to contain my excitement. I'm standing before him, totally naked. He's waiting and watching me. He knows what he's doing to me. His eyes never leaving mine—intense. "Over my knee—*now!*" I know how much he likes it when I seem submissive to him. I hesitate and bite my lip. He cocks his head to the side, eyes still locked on mine. "Jackie, don't make this harder on yourself. I won't ask you again."

Holy hell, I'm so turned on right now, I think I might combust before he even starts. I slowly drape myself over his knee. He moans as our bodies make contact, the sound vibrates to my core. He begins gently stroking each of my butt cheeks with only his fingertips. The gentleness and the anticipation is driving me crazy and he knows it. Finally, he gives quick alternating smacks, first right and then left. When he reaches six, he stops and kisses each cheek. I can feel his lips on my skin and it sends chills through me. I want more, so I begin to wiggle. I can feel his cock pulse against me and I know he wants more, too. He trails his fingers across the top of my legs, and then, spreads them slightly. I take a deep breath and wait, I know what he's going to do, what I want him to do, but the anticipation is the build up. "Ah!" He quickly swipes my clitoris and then begins spanking me again. I lose it. The buildup is so intense. I want to feel him deep inside of me, but my body has other intentions. I'm coming and it's not a gentle wave, it's a heart-stopping explosion. In one quick move he's out of the chair, bringing me with him to a standing position.

"Bend over and hold onto the bedpost—don't let go!" I obey. He enters me from behind, one hand wrapped around my braid, gently pulling me back to meet his trust. I want it to last, but then I hear him grunting and I know he's there. "My angel, I love you," he groans as he takes his final step to the edge. The minute I feel him explode, that feeling of warmth is my tipping point and I scream out my release. He's still moving, slowing it down but never stopping. He lets go of my braid and pulls out of me. Before I can protest, he spins me around and lifts me up. "Wrap those glorious legs around me . . . now!" He carries me back into the shower and the hot water hits us from every direction.

"Max, now will you feed me?" I ask after several minutes of collecting my wits about me.

He's laughing and I love the sound. He slowly puts me down. "I think I need a little attention first." He takes my hand and kisses my palm before guiding it over his cock. He's hard as stone and my touch brings a huge smile to his face.

"What would you like, Max." I'm playing with him and he knows it.

"Babe, I'm thinking you should tie me to a chair and have your way with me."

"Ah!" I gasp. You would let me do that?"

"I would let you do whatever you want. . . . . . within reason." He's smirking and I feel like a kid in a candy store. I shut the water off and quickly push him out of the shower. "Oh, Max, breakfast will definitely have to wait." I toss him a towel and pull him into the bedroom. I can't believe he is going to let me tie him up! I sit him in the chair and quickly hunt around the room for something to tie him up with. I hurry into the closet and find one of his belts. I also go into his valet and pull out the nipple clamps he used on me. When I come out, he's still sitting in the chair smiling.

"Put your hands behind your back." I try to sound dominant like he does. He smiles and complies. I make sure I secure the belt tightly around his wrists, and then I take a step back to admire my handy work. I know exactly what I'm going to do. I stand in front of him, bend down, and take one of his nipples in my mouth, gently pulling it between my teeth. He moans and I slip on the clamp. His eyes grow wide and he smiles. "Babe, you need to do both if this is going to work."

"Patience, Max." I reach down and do the other one. His jaw is tight as I kiss my way down his chest. I get on my knees and kiss his thighs. I start at his knee and work my way up. When I get to his cock I stop and go to the other one. He begins to growl and tries to use his feet to push me forward.

"My speed; not yours, Max." I reach my hands up and tighten the clamps. His groans are louder. I take his cock in my hand and rub my thumb over the top, followed by my tongue.

"Oh, babe, take me deep—please."

I swirl my tongue around as I go deeper and he is lifting his hips to meet me. I don't want this to end, so I stop.

"Oh bloody hell, don't stop."

I straddle his lap and lower myself on to his rock-hard cock. "Max, oh yeah." I slowly work my way up and down. His hips are following my lead. I tighten the clamps again and he grits his teeth. I'm trying to hold back, but he tilts his hips as he rises up, hitting my clitoris over and over again.

"Max, are you ready?" I don't give him a chance to answer, I release both nipple clamps at the same time. He throws his head back and lets out a long low groan, just as I find my own release. He is slowly coming back to earth as his rapid breathing begins to taper down.

"Untie my hands, please."

I reach around and loosen the belt and it falls away. He throws his arms around me and holds me close. I rest my forehead on his, "I love you. I think we need to try that shower again, and then you need to feed me."

I climb off of him and offer him my hand. Even though I would love to spend the day in bed with him, I know we can't. We head into the bathroom and quickly get cleaned up.

Max finishes up first and goes downstairs to start breakfast while I finish getting ready, basking in the knowledge that I got to reverse roles with him this morning.

Chapter Twenty-Eight

Jaxson

I DON'T KNOW WHAT the hell is taking Max so long this morning, but he better get his arse down here soon. I want to talk to him before everyone else wakes up. Raven is busy with Antonia, so now would be the perfect time to tell him my plan . . . if he ever gets down here. I head into the kitchen to make coffee and find it already done. I've never had staff around twenty-four seven, only guards, and I'm not sure I like it. Max finally comes down and grabs a cup. "Took you long enough, you're usually up at dawn."

He laughs and I get it. "Okay, don't need the details. I was thinking that you and I should talk to Junior alone."

"Hold up, Jax, Mrs. Osla and Jackie did some research on the procedure the doctor was talking about. Our father can get the shots in Capri. He doesn't have to show up here until the day of the procedure, and technically, he doesn't even have to be here for that. I get that will never happen, but we need to dictate how this is going to work, not the other way around. Oh, and my wife is pretty adamant about not staying away from the hospital. She said we are family and we must form a united front, we won't be bullied by the likes of him. I swear she's going to put me in an early grave."

"I told Raven everything that went down, and knowing my wife, she won't let him bully us either. We need to have a solid plan in place before we contact him again. I won't be caught off guard again." I go fill up my coffee again. I offer Max more but he is staring into space.

"Hey, what the hell is wrong with you this morning? Get your head in the game and concentrate."

Jackie walks in with Antonia in her arms and Raven right behind her. "Cut him some slack, it's not everyday a man finds out he's going to be a father."

Raven is laughing and crying and Max is sitting here with a faraway look on his face.

"Well, that's the best news I've heard in a while. When is the baby due?"

She hands me Antonia, who is laughing and drooling. "I wanted to wait and tell Max on his birthday and then, when I was through with the first trimester, tell everyone else, but . . . with everything going on, I thought we should talk to Michael's doctor. Maybe there are other options. If I calculated it correctly, then I'm due in June. Do you think we can hold off telling the whole family?"

I begin to laugh and I can't stop. I know all eyes are on me. "Oh, Jackie, look at your husband, do you really think no one will notice? It only took me five minutes to notice his head is in his arse. How long do you think it will take Mum?"

Max gets up and begins cooking, avoiding our gawking. I know there is going to be no living with him from now until June, and I can only hope Jackie doesn't kill him before that. One of the staff members comes in and lets us know that breakfast is already set up in the dining room. Max stops cooking. I don't think we will every get used to having staff.

"Jackie, you grew up with staff around all the time, how did you deal with it?"

"Since I don't cook, for me, it was easy. You need to sit them down and tell them what you would like them to handle and what you would rather do on your own. Would you like me to take care of it?"

"You're the best, thank you." I raise my coffee mug to her. Suddenly, I hear the clickety-clack of my mother's heels, coming down the hall. "I hear mum, are you ready to face the music?"

"As ready as I'll ever be."

I put my arm around her, "You'll be fine, I will keep the family in check."

"That's great, Jax, but who will keep you in check?"

We head into the dinning room, trying to act nonchalant. Everyone is busy eating and chatting. We just, kind of, slide into conversation. I'm trying not to look at Max or it's game over. My daughter is loving the toys, hanging from the bar above and across on her baby recliner. Then I hear Mum clear her throat obnoxiously, and I can't look up. "Jaxson, what are you trying to hide from me? The same goes for you, Maxwell."

I'm trying so hard not to laugh (a dead giveaway for me) but then I make the mistake of glancing over to Max. Now we are both laughing uncontrollably.

"An, I'm pregnant. I only let them know this morning: no one is keeping anything from you," Jackie announces, putting us out of our misery.

Everyone is congratulating them; everyone—*but* Mrs. Osla. I see her wipe away a tear and quietly excuse herself. I slip out after her.

"Mrs. Osla, what's wrong? You know that no one will ever replace Samantha and Elliot. Max has so much love to give."

"Oh, Jax, I know that and I am very happy for them both. I'm happy that Max has finally let himself be loved again. Most days, I'm okay. But times like this, I'm reminded of how much was lost."

I hug her, which is rare for us. "One day at a time is all we can do. We are always here to support each other, through the good and the bad." Just then, Max comes out to look for us. "I'll give you a moment with him." I smile and give her upper arms a little squeeze before letting go.

Max puts his arms around her, and she begins to cry. I back away, giving them their privacy.

I'm not in the room for two seconds and my mum is all over me. "Jaxson what is the plan for dealing with James?"

"Max and I were going to talk to Junior today. Then we will talk to the doctors. I'm not making any decisions until after that. Right now, I just want to bask in the glory that I'm going to be an uncle again."

"I want to be with my grandson when you talk to him about James."

I'm not going to get anywhere with her. I look to Raven for help but she's busy with Jackie.

"Mum, it's what's best for Junior. I think coming from Max and me will make it easier for him. I don't even want Bella there; Junior will pick up on everyone's emotions. Right now, it has to be all about him. Please don't fight me on this."

"Of course, you're right. I just want my grandson to know that I'm always there for him." I get up and hug her.

"He knows, Mum."

Max and Mrs. Osla are back and she seems to be okay. "All right, everyone, we need to get going. We will speak to Junior's doctor first and see what he thinks we should do. Jackie, before I forget, I called your dad and told him where we are. I didn't want him to think that we weren't grateful for his hospitality. I just told him that with such a big family, we wanted to have our own place. He said he understood and knew that it was only temporary. I let him know he can come and visit whenever he wants."

"Thank you. I know things are weird with my brother, but I don't think he would ever intentionally harm any of us."

I don't say anything. I'd rather keep my reservations about Dylan to myself. I wonder how he is going to react to the pregnancy. Between Max and me, we will keep him in line.

The drive to the clinic is quick and I can't wait to see Junior, but we need to tell Bella what's going on, and then talk to the doctor.

"Max, you and Jackie can tell Bella about the baby; we won't steal your thunder."

We head into Junior's room and find him playing the new gaming system that Tony built. Michael is on the phone, yelling in Italian, and Bella is reading. Everything seems totally normal for a change. I stand here enjoying it. Michael finally hangs up and I grab Junior away from the game.

Bella looks at Max and after everything that's gone on, I'm sure, is expecting the worse. "Max, what's wrong?"

I nudge him. I swear he better get his head out of his arse or it's going to be a long pregnancy for all of us. "I'm pregnant. This is causing Max to be a little speechless right now," Jackie saves the day again.

Bella leaps out of the chair, almost knocking him over. "Oh my God, I'm so happy for you! When are you due?"

"I just found out; probably mid-June or early July."

"Aunt Jackie, can I have a boy cousin since I already have Antonia?"

"It's not up to me, Michael; we will have to wait and see."

"Michael, Tony gave me a list of questions for you to answer about this new gaming system, so I suggest we get started." Mrs. Osla offers up a distraction for Junior, knowing that we need to speak to his doctor. She's the best and I'd be so lost without her. She pulls out her pad and starts peppering him with questions.

"Bella, we have a meeting with Junior's doctor to discuss all of our options. Max and Jackie wanted to make sure you knew about the baby before time. If we don't get going, we will be late."

THIS IS THE FIRST time I'm actually getting to meet Dr. Campbell. He seems like nice guy and is very accommodating to the fact that we are a large family with no secrets. We explain everything to him about James and about the pregnancy. We also give him details as to everything Junior has gone through. I feel he needs to understand that Junior is a smart kid, not one you can hide stuff from. He's quiet, taking lots of notes.

"First, thank you for your honesty about everything. He has been through quite a bit in such a short time. I looked at the test results and James is an ideal candidate. I would like for him to have the shots we spoke about. They can be done locally, so he doesn't need to be here. I would much rather have him here when it comes time for the final procedure. As far as the cord blood from your pregnancy, we won't know if it's a match until after the baby is born. If you were in your last trimester I would wait, but you're only in the early stages of your pregnancy. However, it is a good backup plan, if needed. At this point, you've only done a home test I would recommend a blood test. If your hcg levels are higher than they should be for a singleton, I would suggest an ultra sound, since there's a family history of multiples. We have a great OBGYN here and I can get you the number to set up an appointment." He turns his attention back to Bella and Michael. "I think before you tell Michael about James, I should contact him and discuss the injections. The injections for peripheral blood stem cell donation, or PBSC, only take four days. So next week, at this time, it can all be over. If this was my child, I wouldn't tell him about James until the day before the procedure. What if he changes his mind about donating? There is no reason for Michael to go through any additional stress."

We all agree and I give him the contact information for James. He turns back to Jackie. "I'll have my nurse give you the number for Dr. Patel. They may just send you for blood work first." He closes his folder and gives his nurse a nod. She nods back and leaves the room. "Are there any other questions I can answer for you?" he asks.

"No, thank you, Dr. Campbell," Bella says. Just then, the nurse comes back in and hands Jackie a business card. My guess—Dr. Patel's.

"Bella, can you take care of Antonia? Raven and I are going with Jackie and Max." I don't give anyone a chance to protest, something is off with Max. He wanted this badly, so I know that's not it.

Raven pulls my hands out of my hair, and then she reaches up to kiss my cheek, "Follow my lead," she whispers.

"We will be back in a minute. I need to use the ladies room." She takes Jackie's arm and they duck into the ladies room.

"Okay, what the hell is going on? Don't tell me nothing, you've had your head up your arse all morning. I know you wanted the baby, so what the hell is it?"

"I'm scared to death that something will happen to her, the baby, or both. How am I going to make it to the end of this pregnancy without losing my mind? I want to lock her in a cage, and then a big huge bubble. What happens after the baby comes? I'm working myself into a full blown panic attack!"

"Were you this bad when Samantha was pregnant?"

"No, but now I'm wiser to the danger. And now that bastard father of ours is in the picture. Jackie is so stubborn; she won't back down from him.

You know she was so quiet when we first got together, and I really thought she was more submissive."

"You need to calm down. This is not good for anyone, including Jackie. You know that I will always have your back. Together, we will get through this. You need to let me handle some of the load and just enjoy the pregnancy."

The girls are back and he seems to be a little bit better. We head toward Dr. Patel's office. Jackie is offered some paperwork to fill out; they just so happened to have a cancellation this morning. I sit here and all I can think about is how much I want another baby. I don't even realize it, but the nurse already called them back.

"Jax, I would love to know what is going through that beautiful mind of yours right now."

"Honestly, all I can think about is how much I want more babies."

She hands me a magazine, "It will happen on God's time, not yours."

Maxwell

THE NURSE TAKES US back, takes Jackie's vitals, and draws some blood. She then has her head into the bathroom to give a urine sample. So far I'm doing okay. I need to keep my head in the game. I know she's scared and I know why, but the last thing she needs is to be worrying about me. Jax is right; it's time I got my head out of my arse. Jackie comes back in followed by Dr. Patel who quickly introduces herself. She seems nice enough. I'll have Tony run a check on her, just to be safe.

"I've gone over all your paperwork and I spoke to Dr. Campbell. He informed me about your nephew and your wanting to donate your cord blood, if need be. I see from your family history that multiples run in your family. If your hcg levels are suspiciously high when we get the blood work back, we'll schedule an ultrasound to see if there is more than one. For now, we're just going to touch upon your intake and go over what you can expect during your pregnancy; answer any and all questions for you." She smiles in a reassuringly manner. I'm standing next to Jackie and I know I have her hand in a death grip. My eyes are locked on to Jackie's, I can't look anywhere else.

"Why don't you have a seat? Mr. Fleming, are you okay?" I assure her that I'm fine and she continues. It all sounds simple enough. When she's done, she tells us to relax and enjoy the pregnancy. Easy for her to say. We head out to find Raven and Jax.

"Let's go get something to eat; we have a baby to feed."

"Max, I'm warning you now, if you know what's good for you, you will behave during this pregnancy."

We head down the hall and I pray that I'm able to survive this. "Why don't we go to Junior's room and I'll have lunch brought to us. I'm not locking you away I just figured everyone can pepper you with questions in one shot."

"You're probably right. Was Mrs. Osla okay this morning?"

"Yeah, sometimes it hits her hard. Trust me she is over the moon about the pregnancy, it's just every now and again something reminds her of her loss. She will be fine."

Jax hangs up the phone and he looks at me and says nothing. "Why don't you go inside and put your feet up. I'll order the food and be right in."

"If you need alone time with Jax, you only have to ask."

I pull her into a hug and whisper in her ear. "Remember what happened the last time you were naughty."

"Yeah, well remember, the road goes both ways."

They step inside the room and I know I've turned red. "Jax, what's the problem?"

"The fucker is insisting on getting the shots done here. He wants to spend some time with Junior before the treatment."

"And if we say no?"

"What do you think? Are you prepared to take that chance?"

"I think we load up security around Junior, and then we put those new found negotiating skills of yours to work."

"I can hear them going crazy from out here, poor Jackie."

"Yeah, I better get in there and rescue her; you order lunch."

I head in the room and they have Jackie surrounded. "Okay, everyone, how about we let my beautiful wife get some air."

Raven steps out of the room, leaving me to deal with all the craziness.

I GO LOOK FOR Jax. I know something is bothering him. Sure enough, he's on the phone and pulling his hair. He hangs up and kicks the chair. He finally turns around and sees me. He opens his arms and I can't get to him fast enough.

"What's going on?"

"I ordered lunch."

"You don't kick the chair over your lunch order."

"*He* is insisting he get his shots and the treatment done here. He wants to be around Junior for more than five minutes. I told him he's not welcome here."

"So, he's not going to do anything unless he gets to spend some time with Michael?"

"Exactly. On top of that, I'm worried about Max. He's trying to be strong, but he's scared to death. I know once Dylan finds out, he will cause some sort of trouble. Why can't everyone just behave, do what they are supposed to do. You know, follow the fucking rules."

"It's not realistic to think that everyone will follow the rules, or should I say *your* rules? Max will survive as long as Jackie doesn't kill him. As far as Dylan is concerned, he's an annoyance and nothing more. If he shows up here, I will deal with him. Now, as far as James is concerned, I think the best thing to do is talk to Michael. You have always been very upfront and honest with him. Why change now? Tell him who James is. Let him know that not everyone in this world is good. Then go and make the deal with the devil. If it means that Michael will survive, then we have to do it. You're driving this bus, Jax, not James."

"I have no idea what I would ever do without you. I love you."

"Well, you will never have to find out. Lunch is here and I'm hungry. I love you. Come on, let's have lunch and then we will talk to Michael."

James

HE'S GOT THE NERVE to try and dictate to me how this is going to go down. Who the hell does he think he is? I'm the one who can save the kid, not him. I throw my glass against the wall. It shatters, sending shards everywhere. I'll let him sweat it out until it works on my time. I can't clear my calendar for at least a month, so that should make him stew.

"Sir, is everything okay?" Reynolds asks as he knocks on the other side of the door.

He opens it and sees the glass. "I'm fine. I need you to clear my schedule next month. I will be gone for a week."

"Will I be going with you, sir?"

"No, this is one trip I must make alone. He thinks he can dictate to me what I can and can't do. He has no idea who he's up against."

"Maybe, you've met your match, sir."

"Or . . . maybe he's met his."

Reynolds leaves and I'm left to figure out how I can pull this off. I'm not asking for a lot, but Jax is over the top. He doesn't want me to have any contact with any of the family members. All contact is to go through him. He is out of his mind if he thinks that's going to fly. I want back in, and this is my one shot. I'll be damned if I'm going to let him stop me.

Maxwell

One month later

JUNIOR HAS BEEN OVER the top, about the baby, since we gave him the news. I can't help but laugh when he tells Jackie that if this one is a girl, then we need to have another. so the odds will be in his favor of getting a boy out of the deal. Some days he's just like Jax. Lunch arrives and Jax ordered enough for an army. He seems off. I know something is bothering him. He puts on a brave face, but I know better. He's barely eating and he keeps checking his phone, and then he quietly slips out of the room.

"Jackie, I have some stuff to check on. Stay here, please, and keep Mum entertained."

I don't give her a chance to fight me on it, I hurry out the door and smack right into a wall of guards. He's pulling his hair and pacing. What the hell is going on now?

"Jax, what the hell is going on and why so many guards?"

At the sound of my voice, he spins around and he has a look of panic on his face.

"Nothing is going on, get back in the room . . . *now!*"

"I'm not going back in the room, and call these guards off right now, Jax!"

Suddenly, the hair on the back of my neck stands up and a tingle runs down my spine.

"Listen to me, Max, please. I need you to trust me. Go back in the room, and lock the door. For Christ sake, just trust me."

"He's here, isn't he?"

He doesn't have to answer me, I feel it. My heart and my mind collide with a one big bang. I want to kill him, break every bone in his body. Make him suffer like my family suffered. My head is telling me to listen to Jax. Junior needs this bastard to stay alive. My family needs me to keep it together. My heart is telling me something else.

"Junior needs him, Jax, remember that." I step back into the room, close and lock the door.

Jaxson

WITH MAX BACK IN the room, I inform the guards that—under no circumstances—is anyone allowed to leave the room. I head down the hall, trying to intercept him, but when I turn the corner, the elevator doors open and the fucker steps out, accompanied by only one guard. I block his path, ready to snap his neck with my bare hands, but I remind myself that Junior needs this bastard to survive.

"What are you doing here? I told you that you will not be allowed to see him until the day of the procedure."

He's got a smug look on his face; I'm trying so hard not to knock it off of him.

"You don't dictate to me what I can and cannot do. You need me, so I think I should be the one calling the shots right now."

"Don't be so sure of that. I've placed an ad for a donor, offering ten-million in cash for a match. I'm sure someone will step forward."

"What if no one does, have you thought about that? Is your hatred of me that great that you would let your nephew die?"

"I could say the same to you. You're holding a little boy's life over my head, and for what? What's your end game, *James?* What do you really want?"

"I want to make amends with everyone. I'm trying to make things right."

"Yeah, and I fell out of the turnip truck yesterday. What do we have that you want? Just tell me and I'll give it to you."

He takes a few steps forward and I can't hold back, God knows I've tried. I take one perfect swing and connect with his jaw. He goes down in a heap, his guard goes to help him up, but he shoos him away.

"Be a man, James; get up and tell me what you want."

He gets up and wipes the blood from the corner of his mouth. "I want to talk to Maxwell and An—alone. "

"Never gonna happen. You nearly destroyed Max. I will never let you anywhere near him again. What could you possibly want with my mother? You've already made her feel like a fool."

"An and I have unfinished business. I assure you that I won't hurt her."

"You have no business with her. Dr. Campbell is aware that you are on the premises and is preparing your shot. You can stay in town for the next four days. When the Doctor says you're ready for the procedure, you will meet Junior. That's what I'm offering—take it or leave it."

"I'm not doing anything until my needs are met, so you take it or leave it."

I take out my phone and call Mrs. Osla. "I need you to change the ad you did for me. Change the amount from ten-million to fifty-million cash. I also want commercials run on every network and cable channel. Call Matthew to make sure everything can be set up legally outside of the US."

I hang up and grab him around the neck. His bodyguard attempts to pull me off, except Mick has stepped up next to me and put a gun to the back of the guard's head. "Listen up, *James,* my terms—*not* yours—so you can take it or leave it."

"You won't let your guard shoot him."

Before I can answer, Mick laughs. "I had orders to shoot Max and he's my friend, I could care less about this garbage."

I let go and turn to Mick, "Let him go, for now. Come on, I'm sure everyone is wondering where we are."

"This isn't over, Jax! I will get to them and you can't stop me!" James yells, following after me.

We turn the corner and there is a wall of fifteen guards with guns drawn. Max knew and told them to step up. I turn around and James is stunned into silence.

"I told you, James, don't fuck with me or my family ever again. Let me know what you decide."

Mick and I walk away, leaving James there with the guards, who are ready to take action, if needed.

I head into Junior's room, ready to do some damage control. Everyone is very quiet. Junior is playing a game with his headset on. My mum finally breaks the silence. "What did he want?"

"I can't believe anything he said, so I have no idea. He claims he wants to make amends. He wanted to talk to you and Max. He said he had unfinished business. There's nothing he could say that would make up for all the destruction he has left in his wake."

"What about my grandson? If James doesn't donate, then what?"

"I'm looking at other options, trying to offer a large cash payment for a match."

"Is that even legal?"

"As of 2011, it is legal in the US. Even though we are in Switzerland, there are always ways around it. I've already put Matthew on it."

"Don't you think this is ridiculous? I can have a conversation with him as long as Max is left out of it. You can negotiate that, can't you?"

"Why would I subject you to that?"

There's a knock on the door that makes everyone jump. Mick checks and it's Dr. Campbell.

"Sorry about the all the guards, Dr. Campbell, I needed to up security."

"I understand, however, could you have them be a little bit more discreet. Some of the other patients are nervous. I also wanted to let you know that I just administered James's first shot. He requested to stay in the hospital for the four days. I put him in our facility for plastic surgery. It's the furthest building from Michael's room. Here are the details."

I take the paper and hand it to Mick; I don't need Max seeing it. "Thank you for all of your understanding."

"Trust me, I have some family members I could do without. I would casually start bringing up to Michael who this man is and his purpose here. If you would like, I can be there to explain the procedure."

"Thank you. If I need you to explain anything, I will let you know."

He leaves and my head is pounding. I just have to keep reminding myself the end is in sight. I grab a bottle of water and decide to go for walk; I need to clear my head. Max stops me before I can make it out the door.

"We need to talk, Jax. Let's go for that walk."

"Do you promise to behave?"

He rolls his eyes and we head out the door.

"Jax, come with me. There's a quiet solarium just off of the cafe that Bella and I went to yesterday; we can talk there."

I motion Mick to come with us. "What is it that you want to know?"

"What went down, give me details."

"You heard what I told Mum, that's it." He wants details and I'm not ready to share that with him.

"Jax, you are by far the worst liar I have ever met in my life. What don't you want me to know? Look if you don't tell me I'll get it out of Mick."

"Hey, don't bring me into this. Just tell him, Jax."

"He said he had unfinished business with Mum."

"What the hell does that mean?"

"I don't know, and I don't know how to ask her."

"I think I might have an idea."

Max and I both turn to Mick at the same time, "You do?"

"Remember, I'm not emotionally invested like you both are. I was thinking back to the meeting in Capri and then I played the recording over and over again. James said that Miguel was upset that James left An the picture and the trinkets. He mentioned them twice. Max, where is everything?"

"The jewels are locked up in a safe deposit box at The Royal Bank of Scotland and the picture is in a drop box on my computer."

"When you aged the picture, I know you focused in on James and Miguel. What about the other two men, did you find out who they were?"

"Mick, you saw me that day. The only thing I could focus on was Miguel, the man whose gang killed my family."

Max closes his eyes, trying to remember the faces, I'm sure. "That's my leverage. I knew if I dug deep enough, something would come to the surface. I think the jewelry is just gravy for him, it's the picture. Remember he said that he convinced Miguel that he destroyed the picture. Why go through all of that, if the picture was no big deal? He has unfinished business with Mum; he wants that picture. Saying that he wanted to talk to you is just smoke in mirrors. A distraction for Mum; play on her heart strings. Come on, I've got a plan."

We race back to Junior's room so I can get to the computer. "Max, I need you to pull up that picture. Print out the original and the aged one. Mick, you and I are going to see James. We will take two extra guards with us and leave the rest here."

I look over at Raven and I know she's worried. I need to reassure her that everything will be fine. I walk up to her, her eyes locked on mine the whole time.

"Raven, I assure you that I will be fine. I'm going to have a conversation with James, that's all. I promise, I will be back shortly." I kiss her trembling lips and then whisper, "Please keep it together for the rest of the family. I need you, sweetheart."

"More, Jax."

I grab the picture as Mick and I race out the door. "Okay, Mick, let's get this over with. Just follow my lead."

We get to his room and there are two guards stationed outside his door. "They are ours; I had them keep a watch on him."

I push open the door and James is on the phone. He sees it's me and quickly hangs up.

"I stayed and got the shot, Jax. Now, when can I see everyone?"

I take out the pictures and throw them in front of him. "Is this what you want, these and those trinkets, as you call them?"

"Where's the original?"

"Why is this picture so important to you? Who are the other two men? I'm sure if I put the picture in all the newspapers and all over social media, I could find out rather quickly."

"You can't do that . . . not if you value your mother's life."

I freeze and Mick takes a step forward, I put my hand out, stopping him. "What does this picture have to do with my mother?"

"The man at the end of the picture is Valad Yager, the head of a major Russian Cartel. Many governments want him dead. He has information that could destroy many secret government operations. He worked both sides of the fence for years. That picture is the only known picture of him in existence. Having that picture puts An in a world of danger. I always operated very clean; flying just under the radar. But then Max started digging up the past. The guy next to me in the picture, Oliver Davis, became Miguel's right hand man. When Miguel died, he told the Valad about the picture. He knew An took the picture that day, but like Miguel, he thought it was destroyed. I loved your mother; I just wasn't in love with her. I never wanted any harm to come to her. Even now, I'm only trying to protect her."

"Were you ever in love with anyone other than yourself?"

"Yes, I was in love with Cindy. When I found out what happened to her, I realized the best thing for everyone was to walk away and never look back."

"Here's what's going to happen. You will stay in this room for the next four days. You will get the shots and then you will donate your stem cells. You will never meet Junior. You will never get to talk to Max or my mum. When the donation is complete, you will get the original photo. You will make it known to all interested parties that you are in possession of the picture, and that you always were. If anything were to happen to anyone in my family, the copies that I have will go public, along with all the details of your life."

"And if I don't go along with your plan?"

"Oh, I always have an alternate plan, James. You don't become one of the richest, most powerful men in the world by resting on one's laurels. I have the ability to keep my family tucked away someplace very safe and very quiet, while I release the photo and the details. If all else fails, I will have Mick shoot you in the balls, that is . . . if he can even find them."

"You have a deal. Just one thing, Jax. You might be more like me than you're willing to admit."

I don't even dignify that with an answer. Mick and I leave and head back to Junior's room.

We walk in the room and everyone stops what they are doing, all eyes on us. "It's done. Junior gets what he needs and no one has to see James ever again."

Bella throws her arms around me, and cries hysterically. "Shh, come on, sis, it's no big deal. Please let it go, for everyone's sake."

I look up and see Raven wipe away a tear and then I hear the most beautiful sound in the world; Antonia cooing.

I can't catch my breath; she's on the floor with Junior, playing with her toy. It almost sounds like she is singing to her toy.

"Oh, Raven, I'm telling you, she's a genius. Three months old and she's already singing."

"You're probably right. How about we go home and continue that little project we started, especially since this one turned out so well."

"I'm more than ready, sweetheart."

Chapter Twenty-Nine

Jaxson

I THOUGHT TODAY WOULD never get here. It's been a long time coming. Junior finally gets the stem cells from James and then he is out of our lives. Raven and I took a little day trip yesterday to the castle in Scotland. I wanted to make sure I had that picture in hand. I put it in the pouch with the trinkets. After talking with Max and Matthew, we decided it was best to give James everything. Keeping the jewels, or even turning them in, would open up a whole new can of worms. I need to keep my mum permanently out of this mess and although it slays me to give that bastard anything, this is the safest way to do that. It was good to go back home for the day and I can't wait till the day we can stay forever.

"Raven, will you please hurry up! I swear, I don't know what you do in the morning that takes so long."

She comes strolling in the bedroom wearing a pair of tight jeans, her bra, with Antonia in her arms. "Umm, sweetheart, I think you forgot your shirt."

"I didn't forget my shirt. I just couldn't dodge your daughter's spit up fast enough. You should try it sometime, dear."

"Why don't I take her while you finish getting ready?"

"We will meet you downstairs."

I take Antonia and go in search of Max. I know today will be another hard day for him. I thank Jackie for keeping him together.

I find Max in the kitchen, getting a cup of coffee, "Hey, I'll take one of those, too."

He passes me my coffee and takes Antonia. "Uncle Max is the best in the world. Let's practice that, my beautiful niece," Max replies to my daughter's cooing.

"Quit filling her head, mate. How's Jackie feeling?"

"Amazing, no sickness at all, but she does get tired rather quickly."

"I'm so ready for today to be over. I hope we never have to deal with him again."

"Secrets always seem to have a way of coming out. I only hope that these can stay buried forever."

"I'm happy that we never had to tell Junior any of it."

"I'm glad that Michael decided to put off the meeting with his parents until after this treatment. The less stress, the better."

"Did you run a check on Dr. Patel? Will you and Jackie keep her?"

"I had Tony run the check. Her credentials are top notch and Jackie is comfortable with her. We have an appointment later today to find out the results of the blood work."

Antonia takes my spoon and keeps banging on the table. "I think my daughter is very musically talented."

I hear that giggle that I love so much and I know Raven is behind me. "Everyone is ready to go. You left your phone upstairs. Michael called, he's nervous about today. I told him we will be there shortly."

"I don't know what to say to him. I mean, I'm probably more nervous than he is."

"Come on, guys, Jackie is going to talk to Michael about her experience with donating. That should ease some of his fears."

As we head out to the clinic, I can only focus on one thing: today is my last confrontation with James.

Junior

I TRY PLAYING MY new game, but I can't concentrate on anything. Dr. Campbell explained what will happen and I know he was trying to make it seem like no big deal. It's not him getting the needles, so what does he care? Aunt Raven said they would have been here sooner but Antonia got her good with spit up. Even though she's a girl, she makes me laugh. I wanted to go exploring, but it's kind of hard to do with so many guards watching my every move. I asked Dr. Campbell about the person that is donating their stem cells for me, but he gave me some story about confidentiality. That's okay, I know how to get around that; I have a plan. I have to go for an X-ray this morning, that's when I will put my plan in motion. The nurse is here to take me with her stupid wheelchair. Rules, yeah, we'll see about that.

"Good morning, Michael, today's a big day for you. My name is Sophia and I'm going to take you to X-ray and then we will come back here."

I hop in the chair and away we go, with my guards behind us. The guards can't go in the X-ray room, they have to wait outside. That's when I will have my chance. "Sophia, can I ask you a question?"

"Sure, what's up?"

"Dr. Campbell told me what room my donor is in, but I got lost trying to find it. I thought it was close to my room. I wanted to thank him again Do you know where it is?"

She pulls out my chart, "No he's in the plastic surgery wing, not sure why, but it's room 306. That building is two away from this one. We can take the bridgeway, do you want me to show you?"

Crap, that would ruin my plan. I'll never get the guards to go along with that. "No, that's okay. I'm sure I can find it. Thanks."

"Okay, well, you know the routine, wait here while I get the doctor to look at these."

Game on. She leaves and I sneak out the back way. I've been here enough times that I know every exit out of here. I find the bridgeway and head over to the plastic surgery wing. This was not as hard as I thought, until I get to the room and see two guards by the door. Geez, who the heck is this guy that there are guards everywhere? *I need a distraction.* I pull the fire alarm. I'm going to get in so much trouble for this one. Everyone begins racing around, trying to get the patients out. The guards go into room 306, so I run into the room next door. The room is empty and dark, I can wait it out. I look at the clock on the wall, and now I know I'm in trouble. Everyone is probably here and with the alarms going off, my uncles will freak out. I can't wait any longer. I have to just go in there. I peak out and the guards are at the nurse's station. I take my only shot and slip into room 306, locking the door behind me. I need to know who is in here and what the big secret is.

Jaxson

WE PULL UP TO the clinic and alarms are going off. Patients are being brought out of all the exits. My heart is in my throat as I see Bella frantically yelling for Junior. I yell at Mick to keep everyone in the car as Max and I race toward Bella.

"Where's Junior? What's going on?"

"He went for an X-ray, and then the alarms went off. I can't find him. Please find him."

"Get in the car with Mum and don't leave. Michael, come with us."

"I tried back searching from X-ray, but it's sheer chaos."

"Max, maybe you should wait in Junior's room in case he comes back there." I have a good idea what happened here and I need to keep Max away. He's not even listening to me, he's in his zone and running toward the bridgeway. God help us all if Max gets his hands on James. He's picking up speed;

Michael and I can barely keep up with him. We get to the room and the guards are banging on the door. Max begins kicking the door—nothing. I'm yelling for Junior to unlock the door. I hear a loud crash. When I turn around, I see Max has thrown a chair at the window and is climbing outside onto the ledge! "Michael, get the key from the nurses station, I need to follow him!"

I look out and it's a three story drop. Max has a grip on a drain pipe as he's kicking in the window. I've never seen him like this—ever! He jumps into the room and I'm right behind him. The door swings open and Michael comes racing in. Max grabs Junior and pulls him into his arms.

"What the hell were you thinking?"

"Uncle Max, I'm sorry. I needed to know why everyone was keeping secrets from me. I wanted to know what the big deal was about this guy. I wanted to thank him."

"Did he touch you? Did he hurt you? What did he tell you?"

"Uncle Max, he said he's a family friend, that's it. What's going on?"

"Nothing. Everything is fine. Go with your father back to your room, your mum is worried sick."

"That's it? You came racing in here, like something out of movie, and all you can tell me is go back to my room? Why is his last name the same as Uncle Jax and Grams?"

Max looks at me and then closes his eyes. "Uncle Jax, you never lie to me. Are you going to tell me what's going on?"

"You're right, Junior, I never lie to you. Just because you are related to someone, doesn't mean that they should be a part of your life. This man is our father, your grandfather. He is not a parent, he never was. A father . . . he's the man that raises and loves you. He's there for you every day through the good times and the bad. This man has done nothing but cause problems."

"If he's such a bad person, then why do you want me to get his stem cells?"

"Because I love you more than life itself and if it means that I have to make a deal with him, I will."

Junior has tears in his eyes, trying to be brave. He walks up to James and extends his hand, and I have to hold Max back. "Mr. Phillips, thank you for your donation. You might not be a good person, but you gave me the best family."

Michael bends down and Junior climbs on his back. "We need to go; you have a lot of explaining and apologizing to do."

"Come on, Max, let's go." He's not moving, frozen in place, his eyes tightly shut.

When Junior is out of the room, James turns to me. "At least my grandson has manners."

Why can't he just *shut the fuck up?* Max finally opens his eyes and they are very dark. I know I don't have a shot at talking him down.

"What the *fuck* do you know about manners? You're a pathetic excuse for a man. You could have stopped my family from being killed that day and you didn't. How do you live with yourself?"

"I tried to get there in time, but I couldn't."

"All you had to do was make one phone call—that's it—and they never would have been in the park that day! You knew how to get a hold of me, yet you chose to do *nothing!* Don't think that you will get any redemption for what you're doing here today. You're still going to rot in hell."

"I understand that you've found another family to move on with, how does that feel, son?"

The words are barely out of his mouth and Max has him up against the wall with his hands around his throat. Does this guy have a death wish?

"Max, let him go." He doesn't hear me, or . . . he just doesn't care.

"You come anywhere near my family and you will never live to see the light of day again. You will learn what hell on earth is all about." He lets go and James falls to the floor.

"I'm done here, Jax, let's go."

I lift James off the floor, reach back, and punch him in the face. Damn, that felt good. He's lucky that's all he's getting.

"When you are finished here, there will be an envelope waiting for you with the picture and the stolen jewels. I never want to see or hear from you again."

I instruct the guards to make sure he doesn't leave this room until the nurse comes to take him. Max and I head back to Junior's room.

"I can't believe you broke the window and climbed right out there." He's not saying anything. "I can't believe you hung on a drain pipe and kicked in the other window." Still nothing. "Max, it's over, we never have to see or hear from him again. No more secrets, all the lies he told have been shattered like that broken glass. Which, by the way, you're paying for, not me."

"Thanks, Jax."

"For what?"

"For covering my arse, and knowing how to pull me back to the present."

"That's what brothers do."

"Jax, one more thing . . . you can't run for shit."

I laugh, knowing Max is back and we will be okay. We get into the room and Dr. Campbell is there with some of the nursing staff. Junior is offering up his heartfelt apology. The kid is good, by the time he's done, the nurses are in tears.

I lean into Max and whisper, "That kid is going to go far in life."

"Yeah, mate, he's a mini version of you; wouldn't expect anything less."

Everyone is very quiet as the nurses prep Junior for the procedure. That is, until, my daughter begins banging her spoon singing; music to my ears.

THE PROCEDURE DIDN'T TAKE as long as expected and Dr. Campbell thought it went well. If there is no fever, he can go home in a few days. The majority of his treatments can be done on an outpatient basis. James has been released and Mick personally put him on the plane bound for Capri.

I look around the room and I feel relief. Everyone is doing mundane normal stuff and it feels wonderful. My daughter is fast asleep, clutching her spoon. I don't think I will be getting that away from her anytime soon. Raven is curled into my side and I'm twirling her hair.

She looks up at me with those beautiful violets. "Penny for your thoughts, Jax."

"I'm happy that everything turned out okay. I'm sad that so many lives were lost to get us to this point. I'm hopeful for the future of this family. I've decided I want to do that foster care program we talked about. Even if we don't have any more children of our own, I will always be helping children; they are the future. I don't want to work, making millions anymore. I want to only do philanthropist work. We will always have more than enough and, if I learned anything this past year, it's that there really is no luggage rack on the hearse. I want to watch our family grow and see what they will achieve. I want to spend the rest of my days, loving you, like the line in our favorite Snow Patrol song, "Chasing Cars," 'Would you lie with me and just forget the world?'"

"Always, Jax. There's just one thing I have to ask you. How do you feel about even numbers?"

She has a huge smile as I pull her hand from her ear and kiss the inside of her wrist, just like I did so long ago, and I feel that familiar shiver run through her. "Sweetheart, are you?"

She giggles, "I am."

Epilogue

Twelve years Later

Jaxson

I AM SO NERVOUS and yet very excited. Today is Junior's college graduation. There was a time, for a quick second, I thought we would never see this day. I could never be more proud of him than I am today. Even after all the interruptions in his education, he still managed to graduate top of his class. He has decided to go to The University of Liverpool for his Master's Degree in Geotechnical Engineering. I'm happy that he found his niche, doing something that makes a difference. He asked to speak with me alone today, before the ceremony. He probably wants me to run interference for him with his mum. Lord knows Bella can be a handful.

Junior had so much fun showing his cousins all the different tunnels he found. He studied the blueprints Max gave him and explored each one of them. Every new tunnel, he etched Rose's name on the wall with the date. It's because of her that he's here today, and he never forgets it. Since Junior has been away at school, Antonia thinks she can run circles around everyone else. The triplets have other ideas.

They found out she was having triplets a few months after Junior's treatment. You could have heard Jackie yelling at Max three countries over. Something about titanium sperm and a monster cock. Max barely survived the delivery but God only knows how he's going to survive the teenage years. The last part of Jackie's pregnancy, she was on complete bed rest. Raven was at the start of her last trimester and decided she would be a great best friend and stay in bed with her. I think it was their plan all along to have Max and me take care of them and their crazy cravings. Max had it worse than me. Raven craved bubble gum and oranges. Jackie had to have dark chocolate covered graham crackers from a little shop in Cary, North Carolina, called: Chocolate Smiles. The girls found this shop when we went to scatter Rose's ashes. It was such a somber day, but Rose left very detailed instructions. Raven picked a beautiful song by Beyoncé called "I Was Here" to play, while we scattered her ashes. She talked about the chocolates that Antonio had gotten her on the day he proposed. After that, Max arranged for Lissah, the sales lady, to FedEx chocolates every week.

Jackie didn't make the full nine months. She tried and fought to keep them safely inside of her for as long as possible. When there was no more room for them to grow, Dr. Patel had to do a c-section. Samuel, Jeffery, and then little Grace. It's Grace that gives Max the most trouble. She is forever pushing him to his limit. She will either keep him young or put him in an early grave. Hell, she's even got Mrs. Osla wrapped around her finger.

Raven, on the other hand, went full term. We even made it to the hospital, well, almost. We, at least, made it to the parking lot. My beautiful daughter, Gabriella Rose, made her appearance in the back seat of Mick's brand new Rover. He only had the car for three days—quite the christening.

Raven's idea to revamp the foster care program has taken off. She's even gotten some top companies around the world to donate. Jackie maintains her riding academy with the help of the foster children. A few of the kids even ended up in veterinarian school. All in all, it's been a huge success.

The knocking on my office door pulls me out of my thoughts. It's Junior, and he's not alone. He's only been home a few times this past year, and the beautiful, young lady with him explains a lot.

"Uncle Jax, I wanted to introduce you to my girlfriend, Heather Davis."

"Hello, please, have a seat. Why so formal, Junior?"

"This is important and I don't want to mess it up. Heather and I want to get married. I'm afraid when I tell Mum, she will go through the roof."

"You want me to negotiate for you?"

"Oh God, no, Uncle Jax—I've seen how you negotiate. I just need you to keep her calm, and Grams, too."

"Why the rush to get married? You're not even finished with your studies." I don't like the direction this conversation is headed.

"I'm not pregnant, sir, if that's what you're thinking."

"I'm not sure what to think, and please don't call me sir. Jax is fine. So, why the rush?"

"We're not rushing. We know this is the next step we want to take in life. I love Heather and she is willing to transfer to Liverpool to finish her Master's Degree in Education."

What is it with this family and teachers? "I'll make you a deal. Can you please give me twenty-four hours to digest all of this?"

He reaches into his pocket and hands me some papers. "I know this is why you want twenty-four hours."

I look down and see that it is the background check on Heather Davis.

"Sir, I mean . . . Jax, I'm willing to sign a prenup, and so is Michael."

Before I can say another word, Raven comes barreling through the door. "Jax, you better get downstairs and do something about your daughter. Oh, Michael, you're early, and you brought your friend, Heather. So nice to finally meet you."

"What has Antonia done now?"

"She and Grace found the keys to Michael's golf cart and they are racing around in it."

"Where the hell is Max?"

"Trying to catch them, now go!"

I get halfway down the hall when it hits me—she knew.

Raven

"MICHAEL, ANY MINUTE NOW, it will hit him that I knew about Heather. Did you give him the papers?"

"Yeah, and we told him about prenups."

"Give him time to digest it, and in the meantime, I can work on him."

"I hope you're right about this. I still have to get this past Heather's father. I'm hoping with everyone on board, it will make it a little easier."

Jax comes back into the room but before he can say one word, I hug Michael and Heather. "All your uncle ever wanted was for you to be happy. I'm sure when he sees how much you love each other, he will be reminded of what love can do."

I glance up at Jax and he's leaning against the door frame with that crooked smirk I love so much. Even after all these years, it always feels like the first time with him.

"Oh, look whose back."

"Uncle Jax, I'm going to introduce Heather to the rest of the family. I'll meet you downstairs." Poor Michael, he can't get away fast enough.

"So, sweetheart, how long have you known about Heather?"

"For a little bit. Lighten up, Jax, he came to you first. He didn't have to; he's twenty-one, he could have just gotten married. They are trying to be responsible and do the right thing."

"I need to know more about her and her family before I make any kind of decision."

"Her father owns the oldest and largest pharmaceutical company in

Switzerland. She is an only child; her mother died from breast cancer when she was eleven. Her father never remarried. She is studying to be a special education teacher. I've been married to you long enough, Jax, I knew to have her checked out. Now, did you get a handle on your daughter?"

"Why is it when she's doing something wrong, she's my daughter?"

"Because that's when the Jaxson in her comes out."

"Come on, we have to go, the graduation ceremony will be starting soon."

WE ALL PILE INTO the auditorium, ready for the next milestone in this family. Jackie and I have to separate Antonia and Grace. "You know they are a younger version of us."

"Yeah, except I don't think this world is ready for them. What happened when Michael told Jax?"

"Let's just say he took it about the same way he did when Mick and An told him they went to the justice of the peace."

"Oh, well, did Michael give him the background report?"

"Yes, and it helped. I told him all about Heather's family. He agreed to at least look into them before he said no. I made sure I reminded Jax about how powerful love can be. That might work in Michael's favor."

"Did you talk to Jax about that school that Gabriella wants to go to?"

"Not yet. I can only hit him with one thing at a time. You know anything more and he'll go crazy. He already told Antonia she can't date until she's eighteen. Can you imagine what he will do when I tell him Gabriella wants to go to boarding school?"

"Grace wanted to go to a sleepover and after running a check on the family, Max said no. Apparently, the father has outstanding parking tickets."

The ceremony starts and of course, with a last name like Vizzano, Michael is always toward the end. When the Chancellor calls him to accept his diploma, he is also given a special humanitarian award for his dedication and service to others. The Chancellor talks about how Michael goes to the children's hospital once a week to cheer up the kids. He talks to the children about courage and about his journey. Knowing how far this boy has come and all that he's been through, everyone stands and cheers him on. There is not a dry eye in the house. I'm so proud of the man he has grown to be and knowing that I might have helped in that process is very humbling.

Through all my tears and all the heartache I have survived, some things have always remained constant: true love, respect, and honesty. Without that, no relationship could ever survive. I will love Jax with all that I am and all that I will ever be. He is my end all.

Violet to Blues
The end . . .

Acknowledgements

Rick, thank you for always having my back. You're unwavering love and support is priceless. No matter what the course may be, I know you're always by my side. My end all. I love you.

My mom, Jean, my sister, Fran, and all my family and friends, you have all been so supportive through all of this, making sure I never give up. Your constant love and support has taught me to be a better person. I can only hope I've passed this on to others in my lifetime.

My street team, Theresa's Sinfully Sexy Angels—you girls rock!

Thank you to the little boy who agreed to let me use his published poem as long as I kept him anonymous. Your secret is safe with me.

Finally, my son, Leif. I learn from you everyday. You really are everyone's wingman. I have the pleasure of watching the world through your eyes. Your loyalty and courage are beyond reason. You're more than I ever dreamed possible, and I thank God every day for the gift of you.

A Little More

Thank you to the wonderful readers who came and fell in love with The Unraveled Trilogy. I know it has been a crazy ride for all of us. I laughed, cried, and yelled right along with you. Is it the end? Just like in life, sweetheart, never say never. May your days be filled with Nutella, espresso, and a love so intense, it rocks you to your core.

About the Author

Theresa Sederholt was born and raised in Brooklyn New York. She is a graduate of Campbell University in North Carolina, with a degree in Criminal Justice. Theresa now calls North Carolina home, with her husband, a professional chef, and her two dogs.

Experiencing life first hand is what she does best. Believing she can do anything has put her in many crazy situations. Whether it's babysitting a pig farm or cutting the top off of a mini truck; nothing is ever out of reach. Her list is endless, A to Z.

As a flight attendant (there's that list again), she would make up stories about all of her passengers as they came and went. It seemed only natural to put pen to paper and see where these characters led her. What started out as a single woman, having a cup of coffee—trying to make it through life—grew into a complex story of romance, mystery, and murder. *The Unraveled Trilogy* was born.

Theresa's beliefs are pretty simple. There isn't a luggage rack on the hearse, and give a girl Nutella and espresso and she can change the world.

Theresa enjoys connecting with her fans. She can always be reached through her website at:

www.theresasederholt.com

9 780099 766 9251